Mario Puzo

THE SICILIAN
OMERTÀ

WILLIAM HEINEMANN : LONDON

Published in the United Kingdom in 2004 by
William Heinemann

Copyright © Mario Puzo, 2004

The Sicilian first published in the United Kingdom in 1984 by
Bantam Press, a division of Transworld Publishers Ltd,
in association with Simon & Schuster Inc.

Omertà first published in the United Kingdom in 2004 by
William Heinemann

William Heinemann
The Random House Group Limited
20 Vauxhall Bridge Road, London SW1V 2SA

Random House Australia (Pty) Limited
20 Alfred Street, Milsons Point, Sydney,
New South Wales 2061, Australia

Random House New Zealand Limited
18 Poland Road, Glenfield,
Auckland 10, New Zealand

Random House (Pty) Limited
Enduini, 5a Juliee Road, Parktown 2193, South Africa

The Random House Group Limited Reg. No. 954009

www.randomhouse.co.uk

A CIP catalogue record for this book
is available from the British Library

Papers used by Random House are natural, recyclable
products made from wood grown in sustainable forests.
The manufacturing processes conform to the
environmental regulations of the country of origin.

ISBN 0 09 190409 9

Printed and bound in Great Britain by
CPI Bath

THE SICILIAN

For Carol

CHAPTER

1

MICHAEL CORLEONE stood on a long wooden dock in Palermo and watched the great ocean liner set sail for America. He was to have sailed on that ship, but new instructions had come from his father.

He waved goodbye to the men on the little fishing boat who had brought him to this dock, men who had guarded him these past years. The fishing boat rode the white wake of the ocean liner, a brave little duckling after its mother. The men on it waved back; he would see them no more.

The dock itself was alive with scurrying laborers in caps and baggy clothes unloading other ships, loading trucks that had come to the long dock. They were small wiry men who looked more Arabic than Italian, wearing billed caps that obscured their faces. Amongst them would be new bodyguards making sure he came to no harm before he met with Don Croce Malo, *Capo di Capi* of the "Friends of the Friends," as they were called here in Sicily. Newspapers and the outside world called them the Mafia, but in Sicily the word Mafia never passed the lips of the ordinary citizen. As they would never call Don Croce Malo the *Capo di Capi* but only "The Good Soul."

In his two years of exile in Sicily, Michael had heard many tales about Don Croce, some so fantastic that he almost did not believe in the existence of such a man. But the instructions relayed from his father were explicit: he was ordered to have lunch with Don Croce this very day. And the two of them were to arrange for the escape from Sicily of the country's greatest bandit, Salvatore Guiliano. Michael Corleone could not leave Sicily without Guiliano.

Down at the end of the pier, no more than fifty yards away, a huge dark car was parked in the narrow street. Standing before it were three men, dark rectangles cut out of the glaring sheet of light that fell like a wall of gold from the sun. Michael walked toward them. He paused for a moment to light a cigarette and survey the city.

Palermo rested in the bottom of a bowl created by an extinct volcano, overwhelmed by mountains on three sides, and escaping into the dazzling blue of the Mediterranean Sea on the fourth side. The city shimmered in the golden rays of the Sicilian noontime sun. Veins of red light struck the earth, as if reflecting the blood shed on the soil of Sicily for countless centuries. The gold rays bathed stately marble columns of Greek temples, spidery Moslem turrets, the fiercely intricate façades of Spanish cathedrals; on a far hillside frowned the battlements of an ancient Norman castle. All left by diverse and cruel armies that had ruled Sicily since before Christ was born. Beyond the castle walls, cone-shaped mountains held the slightly effeminate city of Palermo in a strangler's embrace, as if both were sinking gracefully to their knees, a cord pulling tightly around the city's neck. Far above, countless tiny red hawks darted across the brilliant blue sky.

Michael walked toward the three men waiting for him at the end of the pier. Features and bodies formed out of their black rectangles. With each step he could see them more clearly and they seemed to loosen, to spread away from each other as if to envelop him in their greeting.

All three of these men knew Michael's history. That he was the youngest son of the great Don Corleone in America, the Godfather, whose power extended even into Sicily. That he had

murdered a high police official of New York City while execut-
ing an enemy of the Corleone Empire. That he had been in
hiding and exile here in Sicily because of those murders and that
now finally, matters having been "arranged," he was on his way
back to his homeland to resume his place as crown prince to the
Corleone Family. They studied Michael, the way he moved so
quickly and effortlessly, his watchful wariness, the caved-in side
of his face which gave him the look of a man who had endured
suffering and danger. He was obviously a man of "respect."

As Michael stepped off the pier the first man to greet him was
a priest, body plump in cassock, his head crowned by a greasy
batlike hat. The white clerical collar was sprinkled with red Sicilian dust, the face above was worldly with flesh.

This was Father Benjamino Malo, brother to the great Don
Croce. He had a shy and pious manner, but he was devoted to
his renowned relative and never flinched at having the devil so
close to his bosom. The malicious even whispered that he
handed over the secrets of the confessional to Don Croce.

Father Benjamino smiled nervously as he shook Michael's
hand and seemed surprised and relieved by Michael's friendly,
lopsided grin, so unlike that of a famous murderer.

The second man was not so cordial, though polite enough.
This was Inspector Frederico Velardi, head of the Security Police of all Sicily. He was the only one of the three who did not
have a welcoming smile on his face. Thin and far too beautifully
tailored for a man who received a government salary, his cold
blue eyes shot two genetic bullets from long-ago Norman con-
querors. Inspector Velardi could have no love for an American
who killed high-ranking police officials. He might try his luck in
Sicily. Velardi's handshake was like the touching of swords.

The third man was taller and bulkier; he seemed huge beside
the other two. He imprisoned Michael's hand, then pulled him
forward into an affectionate embrace. "Cousin Michael," he
said. "Welcome to Palermo." He drew back and regarded Michael with a fond but wary eye. "I am Stefan Andolini, your

father and I grew up together in Corleone. I saw you in America, when you were a child. Do you remember me?"

Oddly enough Michael did remember. For Stefan Andolini was that rarest of all Sicilians, a redhead. Which was his cross, for Sicilians believe that Judas was a redheaded man. His face too was unforgettable. The mouth was huge and irregular, the thick lips like bloody hacked meat; above were hairy nostrils, and eyes cavernous in deep sockets. Though he was smiling, it was a face that made you dream of murder.

With the priest, Michael understood the connection at once. But Inspector Velardi was a surprise. Andolini, carrying out the responsibility of a relative, carefully explained to Michael the Inspector's official capacity. Michael was wary. What was the man doing here? Velardi was reputed to be one of Salvatore Guiliano's most implacable pursuers. And it was obvious that the Inspector and Stefan Andolini disliked each other; they behaved with the exquisite courtesy of two men readying themselves for a duel to the death.

The chauffeur had the car door open for them. Father Benjamino and Stefan Andolini ushered Michael into the back seat with deferential pats. Father Benjamino insisted with Christian humility that Michael sit by the window while he sat in the middle, for Michael must see the beauties of Palermo. Andolini took the other back seat. The Inspector had already jumped in beside the chauffeur. Michael noticed that Inspector Velardi held the door handle so that he could twist it open quickly. The thought passed through Michael's mind that perhaps Father Benjamino had scurried into the middle seat to make himself less of a target.

Like a great black dragon, the car moved slowly through the streets of Palermo. On this avenue rose graceful Moorish-looking houses. massive Greek-columned public buildings, Spanish cathedrals. Private houses painted blue, painted white, painted yellow, all had balconies festooned with flowers that formed another highway above their heads. It would have been a pretty sight except for squads of *carabinieri,* the Italian National Police, who patrolled every corner, rifles at the ready. And more of them on the balconies above.

Their car dwarfed the other vehicles surrounding it, especially the mule-drawn peasant carts which carried in most of the fresh produce from the countryside. These carts were painted in gay, vivid colors, every inch of them down to the spokes of the wheels, the shafts that held the mules. On the sides of many carts were murals showing helmeted knights and crowned kings in dramatic scenes from the legends of Charlemagne and Roland, those ancient heroes of Sicilian folklore. But on some carts Michael saw scrawled, beneath the figure of a handsome youth in moleskin trousers and sleeveless white shirt, guns in his belt, guns slung over his shoulder, a legend of two lines which always ended with great red letters that spelled out the name GUILIANO.

During his exile in Sicily, Michael had heard a good deal about Salvatore Guiliano. His name had always been in the newspapers. People everywhere talked about him. Michael's bride, Apollonia, had confessed that every night she said prayers for the safety of Guiliano, as did nearly all the children and young people of Sicily. They adored him, he was one of them, he was the man they all dreamed of becoming. Young, in his twenties, he was acclaimed a great general because he outfought the *carabinieri* armies sent against him. He was handsome and he was generous, he gave most of his criminal earnings to the poor. He was virtuous and his bandits were never permitted to molest women or priests. When he executed an informer or a traitor, he always gave the victim time to say his prayers and cleanse his soul in order to be on the best of terms with the rulers of the next world. All this Michael knew without being briefed.

They turned off the avenue and a huge black-lettered poster on a house wall caught Michael's eye. He just had time to see the word GUILIANO on the top line. Father Benjamino had been leaning toward the window and said, "It is one of Guiliano's proclamations. Despite everything he still controls Palermo at night."

"And what does it say?" Michael asked.

"He permits the people of Palermo to ride the streetcars again," Father Benjamino said.

"He permits?" Michael asked with a smile. "An outlaw permits?"

On the other side of the car Stefan Andolini laughed. "The *carabinieri* ride the trams so Guiliano blows them up. But first he warned the public not to use them. Now he is promising not to blow them up anymore."

Michael said dryly, "And why did Guiliano blow up trams full of police?"

Inspector Velardi turned his head, blue eyes glaring at Michael. "Because Rome in its stupidity arrested his father and mother for consorting with a known criminal, their own son. A Fascist law never repealed by the republic."

Father Benjamino said with quiet pride. "My brother, Don Croce, arranged for their release. Oh, my brother was very angry with Rome."

Christ, Michael thought. Don Croce was angry with Rome? Who the hell was this Don Croce besides being *pezzonovante* in the Mafia?

The car stopped in front of a block-long, rose-colored building. Blue minarets crowned each separate corner. Before the entrance an extraordinary, wide green-striped canopy lettered HOTEL UMBERTO was guarded by two doormen stuffed into dazzling gold-buttoned uniforms. But Michael was not distracted by this splendor.

His practiced eye photographed the street in front of the hotel. He spotted at least ten bodyguards walking in couples, leaning against the iron railings. These men were not disguising their function. Unbuttoned jackets revealed weapons strapped to their bodies. Two of them smoking thin cigars blocked Michael's path for a moment when he came out of the car scrutinizing him closely—measuring him for a grave. They ignored Inspector Velardi and the others.

As the group entered the hotel, the guards sealed off the entrance behind them. In the lobby four more guards materialized and escorted them down a long corridor. These men had the proud looks of palace servants to an emperor.

The end of the corridor was barred by two massive oaken doors. A man seated in a high, thronelike chair stood up and unlocked the doors with a bronze key. He bowed, giving Father Benjamino a conspiratorial smile as he did so.

The doors opened into a magnificent suite of rooms; open French windows revealed a luxuriously deep garden beyond, which blew in the smell of lemon trees. As they entered Michael could see two men posted on the inside of the suite. Michael wondered why Don Croce was so heavily guarded. He was Guiliano's friend, he was the confidant of the Minister of Justice in Rome and therefore safe from the *carabinieri* who filled the town of Palermo. Then who, and what, did the great Don fear? Who was his enemy?

The furniture in the living room of the suite had been originally designed for an Italian palace—gargantuan armchairs, sofas as long and deep as small ships, massive marble tables that looked as if they had been stolen from museums. They suitably framed the man who now came in from the garden to greet them.

His arms were held out to embrace Michael Corleone. Standing, Don Croce was almost as wide as he was tall. Thick gray hair, crinkly as a Negro's, carefully barbered, crowned a head massively leonine. His eyes were lizardly dark, two raisins embedded on top of heavily fleshed cheeks. These cheeks were two great slabs of mahogany, the left side planed smooth, the other creased with overgrown flesh. The mouth was surprisingly delicate, and above it was a thin mustache. The thick imperial spike of a nose nailed his face together.

But beneath that emperor's head he was all peasant. Huge ill-fitting trousers encircled his enormous middle, and these were held up by wide off-white suspenders. His voluminous shirt was white and freshly laundered but not ironed. He wore no tie or coat and his feet were bare on the marble floor.

He did not look like a man who "wet his beak" from every business enterprise in Palermo down to the lowly market stalls in the square. It was hard to believe that he was responsible for a thousand deaths. That he ruled Western Sicily far more than did the government in Rome. And that he was richer than the dukes and barons who owned great Sicilian estates.

The embrace he gave Michael was swift and light as he said, "I knew your father when we were children. It is a joy to me that he has such a fine son." Then he inquired as to the comfort of his guest's journey and his present necessities. Michael smiled and said he would enjoy a morsel of bread and a drop of wine. Don Croce immediately led him into the garden, for like all Sicilians he ate his meals out of doors when he could.

A table had been set up by a lemon tree. It sparkled with polished glass and fine white linen. Wide bamboo chairs were pulled back by servants. Don Croce supervised the seating with a vivacious courtesy, younger than his age; he was now in his sixties. He sat Michael on his right and his brother, the priest, on his left. He placed Inspector Velardi and Stefan Andolini across from him and regarded them both with a certain coolness.

All Sicilians are good eaters, when there is food to be had, and one of the few jokes people dared to make about Don Croce was that he would rather eat well than kill an enemy. Now he sat with a smile of benign pleasure on his face, knife and fork in hand as the servants brought out the food. Michael glanced around the garden. It was enclosed by a high stone wall and there were at least ten guards scattered around at their own small luncheon tables, but no more than two at each table and well away to give Don Croce and his companions privacy. The garden was filled with the fragrance of lemon trees and olive oil.

Don Croce served Michael personally, ladling roasted chicken and potatoes onto his plate, supervising the tossing of grated cheese on his little side dish of spaghetti, filling his wineglass with cloudy local white wine. He did this with an intense interest, a genuine concern that it was a matter of importance for his new friend to eat and drink well. Michael was hungry, he had not tasted food since dawn, and the Don was kept busy replenishing his plate. He also kept a sharp eye on the plates of the other guests, and when necessary he made a gesture for a servant to fill a glass or cover an empty dish with food.

Finally they were done, and sipping his cup of espresso, the Don was ready for business.

He said to Michael, "So you're going to help our friend Guiliano run off to America."

"Those are my instructions," Michael said. "I must make certain he enters America without misfortune."

Don Croce nodded; his massive mahogany face wore the sleepy amiable look of the obese. His vibrant tenor voice was surprising from that face and body. "It was all arranged between me and your father, I was to deliver Salvatore Guiliano to you. But nothing runs smooth in life, there is always the unexpected. It is now difficult to keep my part of the bargain." He held up his hand to keep Michael from interrupting. "Through no fault of my own. I have not changed. But Guiliano no longer trusts anyone, not even me. For years, almost from the first day he became an outlaw, I helped him survive; we were partners. With my help he became the greatest man in Sicily though even now he is a mere boy of twenty-seven. But his time is over. Five thousand Italian soldiers and field police are searching the mountains. Still he refuses to put himself in my hands."

"Then there is nothing I can do for him," Michael said. "My orders are to wait no more than seven days, then I must leave for America."

And even as he said this he wondered why it was so important for his father to have Guiliano escape. Michael desperately wanted to get home after so many years of exile. He worried about his father's health. When Michael had fled America his father had been lying, critically wounded, in the hospital. Since his flight his older brother Sonny had been murdered. The Corleone Family had been engaged in a desperate battle for survival against the Five Families of New York. A battle that had reached from America into the heart of Sicily to kill Michael's young bride. It was true that messengers from his father had brought news that the old Don had recovered from his wounds, that he had made peace with the Five Families, that he had arranged for all charges against Michael to be dropped. But Michael knew that his father was waiting for him to come to be his right-hand man. That everyone in his family would be anxious to see him—his sister, Connie, his brother Freddie, his foster brother, Tom Hagen, and his poor mother, who would certainly still be grieving over the death of Sonny. Michael thought fleetingly of Kay—would she still be thinking of him after his vanishing for two years? But the crucial thing was: Why was his father delaying his return? It could only be for something of the utmost importance connected with Guiliano.

Suddenly he was aware of Inspector Velardi's cold blue eyes studying him. The thin aristocratic face was scornful, as if Michael had shown cowardice.

"Be patient," Don Croce said. "Our friend Andolini still serves as contact between me and Guiliano and his family. We will all reason together. When you leave here, you will visit Guiliano's father and mother in Montelepre, it is on your way to Trapani." He paused for a moment and smiled, a smile that did not break the massiveness of his cheeks. "I have been told of your plans. All of them." He said this with peculiar emphasis, but, Michael thought, he could not possibly know all the plans. The Godfather never told anyone all of anything.

Don Croce went on smoothly. "All of us who love Guiliano agree on two things. He can no longer stay in Sicily and he must emigrate to America. Inspector Velardi is in accord."

"That is strange even for Sicily," Michael said with a smile. "The Inspector is head of the Security Police sworn to capture Guiliano."

Don Croce laughed, a short mechanical laugh. "Who can understand Sicily? But this is simple. Rome prefers Guiliano happy in America, not screaming accusations from the witness cage in a Palermo court. It's all politics."

Michael was bewildered. He felt an acute discomfort. This was not going according to plan. "Why is it in Inspector Velardi's interest to have him escape? Guiliano dead is no danger."

Inspector Velardi answered in a contemptuous voice. "That would be my choice," he said. "But Don Croce loves him like a son."

Stefan Andolini stared at the Inspector malevolently. Father Benjamino ducked his head as he drank from his glass. But Don Croce said sternly to the Inspector, "We are all friends here, we must speak the truth to Michael. Guiliano holds a trump card. He has a diary he calls his Testament. In it he gives proofs that the government in Rome, certain officials, have helped him during his years of banditry, for purposes of their own, political purposes. If that document becomes public the Christian Democratic government would fall and we would have the Socialists and Communists ruling Italy. Inspector Velardi agrees with me that anything must be done to prevent that. So he is willing to help Guiliano escape with the Testament with the understanding that it will not be made public."

"Have you seen this Testament?" Michael asked. He wondered if his father knew about it. His instructions had never mentioned such a document.

"I know of its contents," Don Croce said.

Inspector Velardi said sharply, "If I could make the decision I would say kill Guiliano and be damned to his Testament."

Stefan Andolini glared at the Inspector with a look of hatred so naked and intense that for the first time Michael realized that here was a man almost as dangerous as Don Croce himself. Andolini said, "Guiliano will never surrender and you are not a good enough man to put him in his grave. You would be much wiser to look after yourself."

Don Croce raised his hand slowly and there was silence at the table. He spoke slowly to Michael, ignoring the others. "It may be I cannot keep my promise to your father to deliver Guiliano to you. Why Don Corleone concerns himself in this affair, I can't tell you. Be assured he has his reasons and that those reasons are good. But what can I do? This afternoon you go to Guiliano's parents, convince them their son must trust me and remind those dear people that it was I who had them released from prison." He paused for a moment. "Then perhaps we can help their son."

In his years of exile and hiding, Michael had developed an animal instinct for danger. He disliked Inspector Velardi, he feared the murderous Stefan Andolini, Father Benjamino gave him the creeps. But most of all Don Croce sent alarm signals clanging through his brain.

All the men at the table hushed their voices when they spoke to Don Croce, even his own brother, Father Benjamino. They leaned toward him with bowed heads waiting for his speech, they even stopped chewing their food. The servants circled around him as if he were a sun, the bodyguards scattered around the garden constantly kept their eyes on him, ready to spring forward at his command and tear everyone to pieces.

Michael said carefully, "Don Croce, I am here to follow your every wish."

The Don nodded his huge head in benediction, folded his well-shaped hands over his stomach and said in his powerful tenor voice, "We must be absolutely frank with each other. Tell me, what are your plans for Guiliano's escape? Speak to me as a son to his father."

Michael glanced quickly at Inspector Velardi. He would never speak frankly before the head of the Security Police of Sicily. Don Croce understood immediately. "Inspector Velardi is completely guided by my advice," he said. "You may trust him as you do me."

Michael raised his glass of wine to drink. Over it he could see the guards watching them, spectators at a play. He could see

Inspector Velardi grimace, not liking even the diplomacy of the Don's speech, the message being clear that Don Croce ruled him and his office. He saw the frown on the murderous huge-lipped face of Stefan Andolini. Only Father Benjamino refused to meet his gaze and bowed his head. Michael drank the glass of cloudy white wine and a servant immediately refilled it. Suddenly the garden seemed a dangerous place.

He knew in his bones that what Don Croce had said could not be true. Why should any of them at this table trust the head of the Security Police of Sicily? Would Guiliano? The history of Sicily was larded with treachery. Michael thought sourly; he remembered his dead wife. So why was Don Croce being so trustful? And why the massive security around him? Don Croce was the top man of the Mafia. He had the most powerful connections in Rome and indeed served as their unofficial deputy here in Sicily. Then what did Don Croce fear? It could only be Guiliano.

But the Don was watching. Michael tried to speak with the utmost sincerity. "My plans are simple. I am to wait in Trapani until Salvatore Guiliano is delivered to me. By you and your people. A fast ship will take us to Africa. We will of course have the necessary papers of identity. From Africa we fly to America where it has been arranged for us to enter without the usual formalities. I hope it will be as easy as they have made it sound." He paused for a moment. "Unless you have another counsel."

The Don sighed and drank from his glass. Then he fixed his eyes on Michael. He started to speak slowly and impressively "Sicily is a tragic land," he said. "There is no trust. There is no order. Only violence and treachery in abundance. You look wary, my young friend, and you have every right. And so, too, our Guiliano. Let me tell you this: Turi Guiliano could not have survived without my protection; he and I have been two fingers on one hand. And now he thinks me his enemy. Ah, you can't know what sorrow this brings me. My only dream is that one day Turi Guiliano can return to his family and be acclaimed the champion of Sicily. He is a true Christian and a brave man. And with a heart so tender that he has won the love of every Sicilian." Don Croce paused and drank off a glass of wine. "But the tide has turned against him. He is alone in the mountains with barely a handful of men to face the army that Italy sends against him. And he has been betrayed at every turn. So he trusts no one, not even himself."

The Don looked at Michael for a moment very coldly. "If I were completely honest," he said, "if I did not love Guiliano so much, perhaps I would give advice I do not owe you. Perhaps I should say, in all fairness, go home to America without him. We are coming to the end of a tragedy which in no way concerns you." The Don paused for a moment and sighed again. "But of course, you are our only hope and I must beg you to stay and help our cause. I will assist in every way, I will never desert Guiliano." Don Croce raised his wineglass. "May he live a thousand years."

They all drank and Michael calculated. Did the Don want him to stay or to desert Guiliano? Stefan Andolini spoke. "Remember we have promised the parents of Guiliano that Michael will visit them in Montelepre."

"By all means," Don Croce said gently. "We must give his parents some hope."

Father Benjamino said with a too humble insistence, "And perhaps they will know something about the Testament."

Don Croce sighed. "Yes, Guiliano's Testament. He thinks it will save his life or at least avenge his death." He spoke directly to Michael. "Remember this. Rome fears the Testament, but I do not. And tell his parents what is written on paper affects history. But not life. Life is a different history."

■ ■ ■

THE ROAD from Palermo to Montelepre was no more than a one-hour drive. But in that hour Michael and Andolini went from the

civilization of a city to the primitive culture of the Sicilian countryside. Stefan Andolini drove the tiny Fiat, and in the afternoon
sun his close-shaved cheeks and chin blazed with countless
grains of scarlet hair roots. He drove carefully and slowly, as
men do who have learned to drive motor vehicles late in life.
The Fiat panted as if short of breath as it wound uphill
through the enormous range of mountains.

At five different points they were stopped by roadblocks of
the National Police, platoons of at least twelve men backed by
an armored car bristling with machine guns. Andolini's papers
got them through.

It was strange to Michael that the country could become so
wild and primitive such a short distance from the great city of
Palermo. They passed tiny villages of stone houses that were
precariously balanced on steep slopes. These slopes were carefully gardened into terraced narrow fields growing neat rows of
spiky green plants. Small hills were studded with countless huge
white boulders half-buried in moss and bamboo stalks; in the
distance they looked like vast unsculptured cemeteries.

At intervals along the road were holy shrines, padlocked
wooden boxes that held statues of the Virgin Mary or some
particular favored saint. At one of these shrines, Michael saw
a woman on her knees praying, her husband sitting in their
donkey-drawn cart guzzling a bottle of wine. The donkey's head
drooped like a martyr's.

Stefan Andolini reached over to caress Michael's shoulder
and said, "It does my heart good to see you, my dear cousin.
Did you know that the Guilianos are related to us?"

Michael was sure this was a lie; there was something in that
foxily red smile. "No," he said. "I only knew the parents
worked for my father in America."

"As I did," Andolini said. "We helped build your father's
house on Long Island. Old Guiliano was a fine bricklayer, and
though your father offered him a place in the olive oil business,
he stuck to his trade. He worked like a Negro for eighteen years

and saved like a Jew. Then he came back to Sicily to live like an Englishman. But the war and Mussolini made their lire worthless and now he owns only his house and a small piece of land to farm. He curses the day he left America. They thought their little boy would grow up a prince and now he is a bandit."

The Fiat had stirred up a cloud of dust; alongside the road growths of prickly pears and bamboo had a ghostly appearance, the pears in their clusters seeming to form human hands. In the valleys they could see the olive groves and grapevines. Suddenly Andolini said, "Turi was conceived in America."

He saw Michael's questioning glance. "Yes, he was conceived in America but born in Sicily. A few months' wait and Turi would be an American citizen." He paused for a moment. "Turi always talks about that. Do you really think you can help him escape?"

"I don't know," Michael said. "After lunch with the Inspector and Don Croce, I don't know what anything means. Do they want me to help? My father said Don Croce would do so. He never mentioned the Inspector."

Andolini brushed back his thinning hair. Unconsciously his foot pressed down on the gas pedal and the Fiat scooted forward. "Guiliano and Don Croce are enemies now," he said. "But we have made plans without Don Croce. Turi and his parents count on you. They know your father has never been false to a friend."

Michael said, "And whose side are you on?"

Andolini sighed. "I fight for Guiliano," he said. "We have been comrades for the last five years and before that he spared my life. But I live in Sicily and so cannot defy Don Croce to his face. I walk a tightrope between the two, but I will never betray Guiliano."

Michael thought, What the hell was the man saying? Why couldn't he get a straight answer from any of them? Because this was Sicily, he thought. Sicilians had a horror of truth. Tyrants and Inquisitors had tortured them for the truth over thousands of years. The government in Rome with its legal forms demanded the truth. The priest in the confessional box commanded the truth under pain of everlasting hell. But truth was a source of power, a lever of control, why should anyone give it away?

He would have to find his own way, Michael thought, or perhaps abandon the mission and hurry home. He was on dangerous ground here, there was obviously some sort of vendetta between Guiliano and Don Croce and to be caught in the vortex of a Sicilian vendetta was suicidal. For the Sicilian believes that vengeance is the only true justice, and that it is always merciless. On this Catholic island, statues of a weeping Jesus in every home, Christian forgiveness was a contemptible refuge of the coward.

"Why did Guiliano and Don Croce become enemies?" Michael asked.

"Because of the tragedy at the Portella della Ginestra," Andolini said. "Two years ago. After that it was never the same. Guiliano blamed Don Croce."

Suddenly the car seemed to drop almost vertically, the road was descending out of the mountains into a valley. They passed the ruins of a Norman castle, built to terrorize the countryside nine hundred years ago and now crawling with harmless lizards and a few stray goats. Down below, Michael could see the town of Montelepre.

It was buried deep in the closely surrounding mountains as if it were a bucket hanging in the bottom of a well. It formed a perfect circle, there were no outlying houses, and the late afternoon sun bathed the stones of its walls with dark red fire. Now the Fiat was coasting down a narrow twisting street and Andolini braked it to a stop where a roadblock manned by a platoon of *carabinieri* barred their way. One motioned with his rifle for them to get out of the car.

Michael watched Andolini show his documents to the police. He saw the special red-bordered pass that he knew could only be issued by the Minister of Justice in Rome. Michael had one himself which he had been instructed to show only as a last resort. How did a man like Andolini get such a powerful document?

Then they were back in the car and rolling through the narrow streets of Montelepre, so narrow that if a car came from the opposite direction they could not pass each other. The houses all had elegant balconies and were painted different colors. Many were blue, a few less were white and there were some painted pink. A very few were yellow. At this time of the day the women were inside cooking dinner for their husbands. But no children were in the streets. Instead, each corner was patrolled by a pair of *carabinieri*. Montelepre looked like an occupied town under martial law. Only a few old men looked down from their balconies with faces of stone.

The Fiat stopped in front of a row of attached houses, one of which was painted a bright blue and had a gate in which the grillwork formed the letter "G." The gate was opened by a small wiry man of about sixty who wore an American suit, dark and striped, a white shirt and a black tie. This was Guiliano's father. He gave Andolini a quick but affectionate embrace. He patted Michael on the shoulder almost gratefully as he ushered them into the house.

Guiliano's father had the face of a man suffering the awaited death of a loved one terminally ill. It was obvious he was controlling his emotions very strictly, but his hand went up to his face as if to force his features to keep their shape. His body was rigid, moving stiffly, yet wavering slightly.

They entered a large sitting room, luxurious for a Sicilian home in this small town. Dominating the room was a huge enlargement of a photograph, too fuzzy to be recognizable, framed in oval cream-colored wood. Michael knew immediately this must be Salvatore Guiliano. Beneath, on a small round black table, was a votive light. On another table was a framed picture defined more clearly. Father, mother and son stood against a red curtain, the son with his arm possessively around his mother. Salvatore Guiliano looked directly into the camera, as if challenging it. The face was extraordinarily handsome, like that of a Grecian statue, the features a little heavy as though wrought in marble, the lips full and sensual, the eyes oval with half-closed lids set wide apart. It was the face of a man without self-doubt, determined to impose himself upon the world. But what no one had prepared Michael for was the good-humored sweetness of that handsome face.

There were other pictures of him with his sisters and their husbands, but these were almost hidden on shadowy corner tables.

Guiliano's father led them into the kitchen. Guiliano's mother turned from the cooking stove to greet them. Maria Lombardo Guiliano looked much older than the photograph of her in the other room, indeed looked like some other woman. Her polite smile was like a rictus on the bone-set exhaustion of her face, her skin chapped and rough. Her hair was long and full over her shoulders but streaked with heavy ropes of gray. What was startling was her eyes. They were almost black with an impersonal hatred of this world that was crushing her and her son.

She ignored her husband and Stefan Andolini, she spoke directly to Michael. "Have you come to help my son or not?" The other two men looked embarrassed at the rudeness of her question, but Michael smiled at her gravely.

"Yes, I am with you."

Some of the tension went out of her, and she bowed her head into her hands as if she had expected a blow. Andolini said to her in a soothing voice, "Father Benjamino asked to come, I told him you did not wish it."

Maria Lombardo raised her head and Michael marveled at how her face showed every emotion she felt. The scorn, the hatred, the fear, the irony of her words matching the flinty smile, the grimaces she could not repress. "Oh, Father Benjamino has a good heart, without a doubt," she said. "And with that good heart of his he is like the plague, he brings death to an entire village. He is like the sisal plant—brush against him and you will bleed. And he brings the secrets of the confessional to his brother, he sells the souls in his keeping to the devil.''

Guiliano's father said with quiet reasonableness, as if he were trying to quiet a madman, "Don Croce is our friend. He had us released from prison.''

Guiliano's mother burst out furiously, "Ah, Don Croce, 'The Good Soul,' how kind he is always. But let me tell you, Don Croce is a serpent. He aims a gun forward and slaughters his friend by his side. He and our son were going to rule Sicily together, and now Turi is hiding alone in the mountains and 'The Good Soul' is free as air in Palermo with his whores. Don Croce has only to whistle and Rome licks his feet. And yet he has committed more crimes than our Turi. He is evil and our son is good. Ah, if I were a man like you I would kill Don Croce. I would put 'The Good Soul' to rest.'' She made a gesture of disgust. "You men understand nothing.''

Guiliano's father said impatiently, "I understand our guest must be on the road in a few hours and that he must eat something before we can talk.''

Guiliano's mother suddenly became quite different. She was solicitous. "Poor man, you've traveled all day to see us, you had to listen to Don Croce's lies and my ravings. Where do you go?''

"I must be in Trapani by morning," Michael said. "I stay with friends of my father until your son comes to me.''

There was a stillness in the room. He sensed they all knew his history. They saw the wound he had lived with for two years, the caved-in side of his face. Guiliano's mother came to him and gave him a quick embrace.

"Have a glass of wine," she said. "Then you go for a walk through the town. Food will be waiting on the table within the hour. And by that time Turi's friends will have arrived and we can talk sensibly.''

Andolini and Guiliano's father put Michael between them and

strolled down the narrow, cobbled streets of Montelepre, the stones gleaming black now that the sun had fallen out of the sky. In the hazy blue air before twilight, only the figures of the National Police, the *carabinieri,* moved around them. At every intersection, thin snakelike alleyways ran like venom off the Via Bella. The town seemed deserted.

"This was once a lively town," Guiliano's father said. "Always, always very poor, like all of Sicily, a lot of misery, but it was alive. Now more than seven hundred of our citizens are in jail, arrested for conspiracy with my son. They are innocent, most of them, but the government arrests them to frighten the others, to make them inform against my Turi. There are over two thousand National Police around this town and other thousands hunt Turi in the mountains. And so people no longer eat their dinner out of doors, their children can no longer play in the street. The police are such cowards they fire their guns if a rabbit runs across the road. There is a curfew after dark, and if a woman of the town wants to visit a neighbor and is caught they offer her indignities and insults. The men they cart off to torture in their Palermo dungeons." He sighed. "Such things could never happen in America. I curse the day I left."

Stefan Andolini made them pause as he lit a small cigar. Puffing, he said with a smile, "Tell the truth, all Sicilians prefer smelling the shit of their villages to the best perfumes in Paris. What am I doing here? I could have escaped to Brazil like some others. Ah, we love where we are born, we Sicilians, but Sicily does not love us."

Guiliano's father shrugged. "I was a fool to come back. If I had only waited a few more months my Turi would have been an American by law. But the air of that country must have seeped into his mother's womb." He shook his head in bewilderment. "Why did my son always concern himself with the troubles of other people, even those not related by blood? He always had such grand ideas, he always talked of justice. A true Sicilian talks of bread."

As they walked down the Via Bella, Michael saw that the

town was built ideally for ambush and guerrilla warfare. The streets were so narrow that only one motor vehicle could pass through, and many were only wide enough for the small carts and donkeys Sicilians still used for the transport of goods. A few men could hold back any invading force and then escape to the white limestone mountains that encircled the town.

They descended into the central square. Andolini pointed to the small church that dominated it and said, "It was in this church that Turi hid when the National Police tried to capture him that very first time. Since then, he has been a ghost." The three men watched the church door as if Salvatore Guiliano might appear before them.

The sun dropped behind the mountains, and they returned to the house just before curfew. Two strange men were waiting inside for them, strangers only to Michael, for they embraced Guiliano's father and shook Stefan Andolini's hand.

One was a slim young man with extremely sallow skin and huge dark feverish eyes. He had a dandyish mustache and an almost feminine prettiness, but he was in no way effeminate looking. He had the air of proud cruelty that comes to a man with a will to command at any cost.

When he was introduced as Gaspare Pisciotta, Michael was astonished. Pisciotta was Turi Guiliano's second in command, his cousin and his dearest friend. Next to Guiliano, he was the most wanted man in Sicily, with a price of five million lire on his head. From the legends Michael had heard, the name Gaspare Pisciotta conjured up a more dangerous and evil-looking man. And yet here he stood, so slender and with the feverish flush of the consumptive on his face. Here in Montelepre surrounded by two thousand of Rome's military police.

The other man was equally surprising but for a different reason. At first glance, Michael flinched. The man was so small that he could be taken for a dwarf but had such dignified bearing that Michael sensed immediately that his flinching might give mortal offense. He was dressed in an exquisitely tailored gray pin-

striped suit, and a wide, rich-looking silver-toned tie rode down
his creamy white shirt. His hair was thick and almost white; he
could be no more than fifty years of age. He was elegant. Or as
elegant as a very short man could be. He had a craggy, handsome face with a generous but sensitively curved mouth.

He recognized Michael's discomfort and greeted him with an
ironic but kindly smile. He was introduced as Professor Hector
Adonis.

Maria Lombardo Guiliano had dinner set out on the table in
the kitchen. They ate by a window near the balcony where they
could see the red-streaked sky, the darkness of night snuffing
out the surrounding mountains. Michael ate slowly, aware they
were all watching him, judging him. The food was very plain but
good, spaghetti with the black inky sauce of squid and rabbit
stew, hot with red pepper tomato sauce. Finally Gaspare Pisciotta spoke in the local Sicilian dialect. "So, you are the son of
Vito Corleone who is greater even than our own Don Croce,
they tell me. And it is you who will save our Turi."

His voice had a cool mocking tone, a tone that invited you to
take offense if you dared. His smile seemed to question the
motive behind every action, as if to say, "Yes, it's true you are
doing a good deed, but for what purpose of your own?" Yet it
was not at all disrespectful, he knew Michael's history, they
were fellow murderers.

Michael said, "I follow my father's orders. I am to wait in
Trapani until Guiliano comes to me. Then I will take him to
America."

Pisciotta said more seriously, "And once Turi is in your
hands, you guarantee his safety? You can protect him against
Rome?"

Michael was aware of Guiliano's mother watching him intently, her face strained with anxiety. He said carefully, "As
much as a man can guarantee anything against fate. Yes, I'm
confident."

He saw the mother's face relax, but Pisciotta said harshly, "I am not. You put your trust in Don Croce this afternoon. You told him your plan of escape.''

"Why should I not?" Michael fired back. How the hell did Pisciotta know the details of his lunch with Don Croce so quickly? "My father's briefing said that Don Croce would arrange Guiliano's delivery to me. In any case I told him only one escape plan.''

"And the others?" Pisciotta asked. He saw Michael hesitate. "Speak freely. If the people in this room cannot be trusted then there is no hope for Turi.''

The little man, Hector Adonis, spoke for the first time. He had an extraordinarily rich voice, the voice of a born orator, a natural persuader of men. "My dear Michael, you must understand that Don Croce is Turi Guiliano's enemy. Your father's information is behind the times. Obviously we can't deliver Turi to you without taking precautions.'' He spoke the elegant Italian of Rome, not the Sicilian dialect.

Guiliano's father broke in. "I trust Don Corleone's promise to help my son. Of that there can be no question.''

Hector Adonis said, "I insist, we must know your plans.''

"I can tell you what I told Don Croce," Michael said. "But why should I tell anyone my other plans? If I asked you where Turi Guiliano was hiding now, would you tell me?''

Michael saw Pisciotta smile with genuine approval of his answer. But Hector Adonis said, "It's not the same thing. You have no reason for knowing where Turi hides. We must know your plans to help.''

Michael said quietly, "I know nothing about you.''

A brilliant smile broke across the handsome face of Hector Adonis. Then the little man stood up and bowed. "Forgive me," he said with the utmost sincerity. "I was Turi's schoolteacher when he was a little boy and his parents honored me by making me his godfather. I am now a Professor of History and Literature at the University of Palermo. However, my best credentials can be vouched for by everyone at this table. I am now, and have always been, a member of Guiliano's band.''

Stefan Andolini said quietly, "I too am a member of the band.
You know my name and that I am your cousin. But I am also
called *Fra Diavalo*."

This too was a legendary name in Sicily that Michael had
heard many times. He has earned that murderer's face, Michael
thought. And he too was a fugitive with a price on his head. Yet
that afternoon he had sat down to lunch next to Inspector Velardi.

They were all waiting for him to answer. Michael had no intention of telling them his final plans, but he knew he must tell
them something. Guiliano's mother was staring at him intently.
He spoke directly to her. "It's very simple," Michael said.
"First I must warn you I can wait no longer than seven days. I
have been away from home too long and my father needs my
help in troubles of his own. Of course you understand how anxious I am to return to my family. But it is my father's wish that
I help your son. My last instructions from the courier were that
I visit Don Croce here, then proceed to Trapani. There I stay at
the villa of the local Don. Waiting there will be men from America whom I can trust absolutely. Qualified men." He paused for
a moment. The word "qualified" had a special meaning in Sicily, usually applied to high-ranking Mafia executioners. He went
on. "Once Turi comes to me he will be safe. The villa is a
fortress. And within a few hours we will board a fast ship to a
city in Africa. There a special plane waits to take us immediately
to America and there he will be under my father's protection
and you need fear for him no more."

Hector Adonis said, "When will you be ready to accept Turi
Guiliano?"

Michael said, "I will be in Trapani by early morning. Give me
twenty-four hours from then."

Suddenly Guiliano's mother burst into tears. "My poor Turi
trusts no one any longer. He will not go to Trapani."

"Then I can't help him," Michael said coldly.

Guiliano's mother seemed to fold up with despair. It was Pisciotta unexpectedly who went to comfort her. He kissed her and

held her in his arms. "Maria Lombardo, don't worry," he said. "Turi still listens to me. I will tell him we all believe in this man from America, isn't that true?" He looked at the other men inquiringly and they nodded. "I will bring Turi to Trapani myself."

Everyone seemed content. Michael realized that his cold reply was what had convinced them to trust him. Sicilians all, they were suspicious of a too warm and human generosity. On his part, he was impatient with their carefulness and the disarray of his father's plans. Don Croce was now an enemy, Guiliano might not come to him quickly, indeed might not come at all. After all, what was Turi Guiliano to him? For that matter, he wondered again, what was Guiliano to his father?

They were ushering him into the small living room where the mother served coffee and anisette, apologizing that there was no sweet. The anisette would warm Michael for his long night journey to Trapani, they said. Hector Adonis took a gold cigarette case out of his elegantly tailored jacket and offered it around, then put a cigarette into his own delicately cut mouth and so far forgot himself that he leaned back in his chair so that his feet no longer touched the floor. For a moment he looked like a puppet dangling from a cord.

Maria Lombardo pointed to the huge portrait on the wall. "Isn't he handsome?" she said. "And he is as good as he is beautiful. My heart broke when he became an outlaw. Do you remember that terrible day, Signor Adonis? And all the lies they tell about the Portella della Ginestra? My son would never have done such a thing."

The other men were embarrassed. Michael wondered for the second time that day what had happened at the Portella della Ginestra but did not want to ask.

Hector Adonis said, "When I was Turi's teacher, he was a great reader, he knew the legends of Charlemagne and Roland by heart and now he is one of the myths himself. My heart broke, too, when he became an outlaw."

Guiliano's mother said bitterly, "He will be lucky if he remains alive. Oh, why did we want our son born here? Oh, yes, we wanted him to be a true Sicilian." She gave a wild and bitter laugh. "And so he is. He goes in fear of his life and with a price on his head." She paused and then said with fierce conviction, "And my son is a saint."

Michael noticed that Pisciotta smiled in a peculiar way, as people do when listening to fond parents who speak too sentimentally about their children's virtues. Even Guiliano's father made a gesture of impatience. Stefan Andolini smiled in a crafty way and Pisciotta said affectionately but coolly, "My dear Maria Lombardo, don't make out your son to be so helpless. He gave better than he received and his enemies fear him still."

Guiliano's mother said more calmly, "I know he's killed many times, but he never committed an injustice. And he always gave them time to cleanse their souls and say their last prayers to God." Suddenly she took Michael by the hand and led him into the kitchen and out onto the balcony. "None of those others really know my son," she said to Michael. "They don't know how kind and gentle he is. Maybe he has to be one way with other men, but he was his true self with me. He obeyed my every word, he never said a harsh word to me. He was a loving dutiful son. In his first days as an outlaw he looked down from the mountains but could not see. And I looked up and could not see. But we felt each other's presence, each other's love. And I feel him now tonight. And I think of him alone in those mountains with thousands of soldiers hunting him down and my heart breaks. And you may be the only one who can save him. Promise me you will wait." She held his hands tightly in her own and tears streamed down her cheeks.

Michael looked out on the dark night, the town of Montelepre nestled in the belly of the great mountains, only the central square showing a pinpoint of light. The sky was stitched with stars. In the streets below there came the occasional clank of small arms and the hoarse voices of patrolling *carabinieri*. The town seemed full of ghosts. They came on the soft, summer night air laden with the smell of lemon trees, the small whirring of countless insects, the sudden shout of a roving police patrol.

"I'll wait as long as I can," Michael said gently. "But my father needs me at home. You must make your son come to me."

She nodded and then led him back to the others. Pisciotta was pacing up and down the room. He seemed nervous. "We have decided that we must all wait here until daybreak and curfew is over," he said. "There are too many trigger-happy soldiers out there in the dark and there could be an accident. Do you object?" he asked Michael.

"No," Michael said. "As long as it's not too much of an imposition on our hosts."

They dismissed this as irrelevant. They had stayed up through the night many times when Turi Guiliano had sneaked into town to visit his parents. And besides they had many things to talk about, many details to settle. They got comfortable for the long night ahead. Hector Adonis shed his jacket and tie but still looked elegant. The mother brewed fresh coffee.

Michael asked them to tell him everything they could about Turi Guiliano. He felt he had to understand. His parents again told him what a wonderful son Turi had been always. Stefan Andolini told about the day Turi Guiliano had spared his life. Pisciotta told funny stories about Turi's daring and sense of fun and lack of cruelty. Though he could be merciless with traitors and enemies, he never offered an insult to their manhood with torture and humiliation. And then he told the story of the tragedy at the Portella della Ginestra. "He wept that day," Pisciotta said. "In front of all the members of his band."

Maria Lombardo said, "He could not have killed those people at Ginestra."

Hector Adonis soothed her. "We all know that. He was born gentle." He turned to Michael and said, "He loved books, I thought he would become a poet or a scholar. He had a temper,

but he was never cruel. Because his was an innocent rage. He
hated injustice. He hated the brutality of the *carabinieri* toward
the poor and their obsequiousness toward the rich. Even as a
boy he was outraged when he heard of a farmer who could not
keep the corn he grew, drink the wine he pressed, eat the pigs
he slaughtered. And yet he was a gentle boy."

Pisciotta laughed. "He is not so gentle now. And you, Hector,
don't play the little schoolteacher now. On horseback you were
as big a man as any of us."

Hector Adonis looked at him sternly. "Aspanu," he said,
"this is not the time for your wit."

Pisciotta said to him excitedly, "Little man, do you think I
can ever be afraid of you?"

Michael noted that Pisciotta's nickname was Aspanu, and that
there was ingrained dislike between the two men. Pisciotta's
constant reference to the other man's size, the stern tone in
which Adonis always spoke to Pisciotta. There was, in fact, a
distrust in the air amongst all of them; the others seemed to hold
Stefan Andolini at arm's length, Guiliano's mother seemed to
trust no one completely. And yet as the night wore on it was
clear that they all loved Turi.

Michael said cautiously, "There is a Testament written by
Turi Guiliano. Where is it now?"

There was a long silence, all of them watching him intently.
And suddenly their distrust included him.

Finally Hector Adonis spoke. "He started writing it on my
advice and I helped him with it. Every page is signed by Turi.
All the secret alliances with Don Croce, with the government in
Rome and the final truth about the Portella della Ginestra. If it
were made public the government must surely fall. It is Guiliano's last card to play if things come to the worst."

"I hope then you have it in a safe place," Michael said.

Pisciotta said, "Yes, Don Croce would like to get his hands
on the Testament."

Guiliano's mother said, "At the proper time we will arrange

to have the Testament delivered to you. Perhaps you can send it to America with the girl."

Michael looked at them all with surprise. "What girl?" They all looked away, as if with embarrassment or apprehension. They knew this was an unpleasant surprise and were afraid of his reaction.

Guiliano's mother said, "My son's fiancée. She is pregnant." She turned to the others. "She won't vanish into thin air. Will he take her or not? Let him say so now." Though she tried to maintain her composure it was obvious she was worried about Michael's reaction. "She will come to you in Trapani. Turi wants you to send her ahead of him to America. When she sends word back that she is safe, then Turi will come to you."

Michael said cautiously, "I have no instructions. I would have to consult my people in Trapani about the time element. I know that you and your husband are to follow once your son gets to America. Can't the girl wait and go with you?"

Pisciotta said harshly, "The girl is your test. She will send back a code word and then Guiliano will know he is dealing not only with an honest man but an intelligent one. Only then can he believe you can get him safely out of Sicily."

Guiliano's father said angrily, "Aspanu, I have already told you and my son. Don Corleone has given his word to help us."

Pisciotta said smoothly, "Those are Turi's orders."

Michael thought quickly. Finally he said, "I think it's very clever. We can test the escape route and see if it is compromised." He had no intention of using the same escape route for Guiliano. He said to Guiliano's mother. "I can send you and your husband with the girl." He looked at them questioningly. but both the parents shook their heads.

Hector Adonis said to them gently, "It's not a bad idea."

Guiliano's mother said, "We will not leave Sicily while our son is still here." Guiliano's father folded his arms and nodded in agreement. And Michael understood what they were thinking. If Turi Guiliano died in Sicily, they had no wish to be in America. They must stay to mourn him, to bury him, bring flowers to his grave. The final tragedy belonged to them. The girl could go, she was bound only by love, not by blood.

Sometime during the night Maria Lombardo Guiliano showed Michael a scrapbook filled with newspaper stories, posters showing the different prices placed on Guiliano's head by the government in Rome. She showed a picture story published in America by *Life* magazine in 1948. The story stated that Guiliano was the greatest bandit of modern times, an Italian Robin Hood who robbed the rich to help the poor. It also printed one of the famous letters that Guiliano had sent to the newspapers.

It read: "For five years I have fought to make Sicily free. I have given to the poor what I have taken from the rich. Let the people of Sicily speak out whether I am an outlaw or a fighter for freedom. If they speak against me, I will deliver myself into your hands for judgment. As long as they speak for me I will continue to wage total war."

It sure as hell didn't sound like a bandit on the run, Michael thought, as Maria Lombardo's proud face beamed at him. He felt an identification with her, she looked very much like his own mother. Her face was seamed with past sorrows, but her eyes blazed with a natural love for even more combat against her fate.

Finally it was dawn and Michael rose and said his goodbyes. He was surprised when Guiliano's mother gave him a warm embrace.

"You remind me of my son," she said. "I trust you." She went to the mantel and took down a wooden statue of the Virgin Mary. It was black. The features were Negroid. "Take this as a gift. It is the only thing I own worthy to give you." Michael tried to refuse, but she pressed it on him.

Hector Adonis said, "There are only a few of those statues left in Sicily. Curious, but we are very close to Africa."

Guiliano's mother said, "It doesn't matter what she looks like, you can pray to her."

"Yes," Pisciotta said. "She can do as much good as the other." There was contempt in his voice.

Michael watched Pisciotta take his leave of Guiliano's mother. He could see the real affection between them. Pisciotta kissed her on both cheeks and patted her reassuringly. But she put her head on his shoulder for a brief moment and said, "Aspanu, Aspanu, I love you as I love my son. Don't let them kill Turi." She was weeping.

Pisciotta lost all his coldness, his body seemed to crumple, his dark bony face softened. "You will all grow old in America," he said.

Then he turned to Michael. "I will bring Turi to you within the week," he said.

He went out the door quickly and silently. He had his own special red-bordered pass and he could melt again into the mountains. Hector Adonis would remain with the Guilianos, though he owned a house in town.

Michael and Stefan Andolini got into the Fiat and drove through the central square and onto the road that led to Castelvetrano and the coastal city of Trapani. With Andolini's slow tentative driving and the numerous military roadblocks, it was noon before they came to the town of Trapani.

Book
II

TURI GUILIANO

1943

CHAPTER

2

IN SEPTEMBER of 1943 Hector Adonis was a Professor of History and Literature at the University of Palermo. His extremely short stature caused his colleagues to treat him with less respect than his talents deserved. But this was foreordained in the Sicilian culture, which commonly and brutally based nicknames on physical shortcomings. The one person who knew his true value was the President of the University.

In this September of 1943, Hector Adonis' life was about to change. For southern Italy, the war was over. The American Army had already conquered Sicily and gone on to the mainland. Fascism was dead, Italy was reborn; for the first time in fourteen centuries, the island of Sicily had no real master. But Hector Adonis, knowing the ironies of history, had no great hopes. The Mafia had already begun to usurp the rule of law in Sicily. Their cancerous power would be as deadly as that of any corporate state. From his office window he looked down on the grounds of the University, at the few buildings that could be called a campus.

There was no need for dormitories, there was no college life as known in England and America. Here most students studied at home and consulted with their professors at stated intervals. The professors gave lectures which students could ignore with impunity. They needed only to take their exams. It was a system

47

that Hector Adonis thought disgraceful in general and stupid in particular as it affected Sicilians, who, he thought, required a pedagogical discipline even more severe than students in other countries.

Watching from his cathedral-like window he could see the seasonal influx of Mafia chiefs from all the provinces of Sicily, come to make their lobbying calls on the professors of the University. Under Fascist rule, these Mafia chiefs had been more circumspect, more humble, but now under the beneficent rule of American-restored democracy, they had risen like worms struggling through rain-broken earth and resumed their old ways. They were no longer humble.

The Mafia chiefs, the Friends of the Friends, heads of small local clans in the many villages of Sicily, came in holiday finery to plead the cause of students who were relatives or sons of wealthy landowners, or sons of friends, who were failing in their courses at the University, who would not get degrees unless some firm action was taken. And these degrees were of the utmost importance. How else would families get rid of sons who had no ambition, no talent, no intelligence? Parents would have to support sons the rest of their lives. But with degrees, slips of parchment from the University, these same rascals could become teachers, doctors, members of Parliament, or if worse came to worst, minor administrative functionaries of the state.

Hector Adonis shrugged; history consoled him. His beloved British, in their greatest days of Empire, had entrusted their armies to equally incompetent sons of the rich, whose parents bought them commissions in the army and the commands of great ships. Still the Empire had prospered. True these commanders had led their men to unnecessary slaughters, yet it must be said that the commanders had died with their men, bravery had been an imperative of their class. And that dying had at least solved the problem of incompetent and feckless men becoming a burden to the state. Italians were not so chivalrous or so coldly practical. They loved their children, saved them from personal disasters and let the state look after itself.

From his window, Hector Adonis could spot at least three local Mafia chiefs wandering around looking for their victims. They wore cloth caps and leather boots and carried over their arms heavy velvet jackets, for the weather was still warm. They carried baskets of fruit, bamboo-jacketed bottles of home-grown wine to give as gifts. Not bribes but courteous antidotes for the terror that would rise in the breasts of the professors at the sight of them. For most of the professors were natives of Sicily and understood that the requests could never be refused.

One of the Mafia chiefs, in dress so countrified he could have stepped onto the stage of *Cavalleria Rusticana*, was entering the building and ascending the stairs. Hector Adonis prepared, with sardonic pleasure, to play the familiar comedy to come.

Adonis knew the man. His name was Buccilla and he owned a farm and sheep in a town called Partinico, not far from Montelepre. They shook hands and Buccilla handed him the basket he was carrying.

"We have so much fruit dropping to the ground and rotting that I thought, I'll carry some to the Professor," Buccilla said. He was a short but broad man, his body powerful from a lifetime of hard work. Adonis knew he had a reputation for honesty, that he was a modest man though he could have turned his power into riches. He was a throwback to the old Mafia chiefs who fought not for riches but for respect and honor.

Adonis smiled as he accepted the fruit. What peasant in Sicily ever let anything go to waste? There were a hundred children for each olive that fell to the ground, and these children were like locusts.

Buccilla sighed. He was affable, but Adonis knew this affability could turn to menace in the fraction of a second. So he flashed a sympathetic smile as Buccilla said, "What a nuisance life is. I have work to do on my land and yet when my neighbor asked me to do this little favor, how could I refuse? My father knew his father, my grandfather his grandfather. And it is my nature, perhaps my misfortune that I will do anything a friend asks me to do. After all, are we not Christians together?"

Hector Adonis said smoothly, "We Sicilians are all the same. We are too generous. That is why the northerners in Rome take such a shameful advantage of us."

Buccilla stared at him shrewdly. There would be no trouble here. And hadn't he heard somewhere that this professor was one of the Friends? Certainly he did not seem frightened. And if he was a Friend of the Friends, why had not he, Buccilla, known this fact? But there were many different levels in the Friends. In any event, here was a man who understood the world he lived in.

"I have come to ask you a favor," Buccilla said. "As one Sicilian to another. My neighbor's son failed at the University this year. You failed him. So my neighbor claims. But when I heard your name I said to him, 'What! Signor Adonis? Why, that man has the best heart in the world. He could never do such an unkindness if he knew all the facts. Never.' And so they begged me with tears to tell you the whole story. And to ask with the utmost humbleness to change his grade so that he can go into the world to earn his bread."

Hector Adonis was not deceived by this exquisite politeness. Again it was like the English he so much admired, those people who could be so subtly rude that you basked in their insults for days before you realized they had mortally wounded you. A figure of speech in regard to the English, but with Signor Buccilla, his request, if denied, would be followed by the blast of a *lupara* on some dark night. Hector Adonis politely nibbled on the olives and berries in the basket. "Ah, we can't let a young man starve in this terrible world," he said. "What is the fellow's name?" And when Buccilla told him, he took up a ledger from the bottom of his desk. He leafed through it, though of course he knew the name well.

The failed student was a lout, an oaf, a lummox; more a brute than the sheep on Buccilla's farm. He was a lazy womanizer, a shiftless braggart, a hopeless illiterate who did not know the difference between the *Iliad* and Verga. Despite all this, Hector

Adonis smiled sweetly at Buccilla and in a tone of the utmost surprise said, "Ah, he had a little trouble with one of his examinations. But it is easily put to order. Have him come see me and I will prepare him in these very rooms and then give him an extra examination. He will not fail again."

They shook hands, and the man left. Another friend made, Hector thought. What did it signify that all these young good-for-nothings got University degrees they did not earn or deserve? In the Italy of 1943 they could use them to wipe their pampered asses and decline into positions of mediocrity.

The ringing phone broke his train of thought and brought a different irritation. There was a short ring, then a pause before three curter rings. The woman at the switchboard was gossiping with someone and flipped her tab between the pauses in her own conversation. This exasperated him so that he shouted, *"Pronto"* into the phone more rudely than was seemly.

And unfortunately it was the President of the University calling. But the President, a notorious stickler for professional courtesy, obviously had more important things on his mind than rudeness. His voice was quivering with fear, almost tearful in its supplication. "My dear Professor Adonis," he said, "could I trouble you to come to my office? The University has a grave problem that only you may be able to resolve. It is of the utmost importance. Believe me, my dear Professor, you will have my gratitude."

This obsequiousness made Hector Adonis nervous. What did the idiot expect of him? To jump over the Cathedral of Palermo? The President would be better qualified, Adonis thought bitterly, he was at least six feet. Let him jump and not ask a subordinate with the shortest legs in Sicily to do his job for him. This image put Adonis into a good humor again. So he asked mildly, "Perhaps you could give me a hint. Then on my way I might prepare myself."

The President's voice sank to a whisper. "The estimable Don Croce has honored us with a visit. His nephew is a medical

student, and his professor suggested he retire gracefully from
the program. Don Croce has come to beg us in the most courteous way possible to reconsider. However, the professor in the
Medical College insists that the young man resign.''

''Who is the fool?'' Hector Adonis asked.

''Young Doctor Nattore,'' the President said. ''An estimable
member of the faculty but as yet a little unworldly.''

''I shall be in your office within five minutes,'' Hector Adonis
said.

As he hurried across the open ground to the main building,
Hector Adonis pondered what course of action to take. The
difficulty lay not with the President; he had always summoned
Adonis on matters such as these. The difficulty lay with Doctor
Nattore. He knew the Doctor well. A brilliant medical man, a
teacher whose death would definitely be a loss to Sicily, his
resignation a loss to the University. Also that most pompous of
bores, a man of inflexible principles and true honor. But even he
must have heard of the great Don Croce, even he must have a
grain of common sense embedded in his genius brain. There
must be something else.

In front of the main building was a long black car and leaning
against it were two men dressed in business suits which failed to
make them look respectable. They must be the Don's bodyguards and chauffeur left down here out of respect for the aca-
demics Don Croce was visiting. Adonis saw their looks of
astonishment and then amusement at his small stature, his perfect tailoring, the briefcase under his arm. He flashed a cold
stare which startled them. Could such a small man be a Friend
of the Friends?

The office of the President looked more like a library than a
business center; he was a scholar more than an administrator.
Books lined all the walls, the furniture was massive but comfortable. Don Croce sat in a huge chair sipping his espresso. His
face reminded Hector Adonis of the prow of a ship in the *Iliad*,
warped by years of battle and hostile seas. The Don pretended

they had never met, and Adonis allowed himself to be introduced. The President of course knew this was a farce, but young
Doctor Nattore was taken in.

The President was the tallest man at the University; Hector
Adonis was the shortest. Immediately, out of courtesy, the President sat down and slumped in his chair before he spoke.

"We have a small disagreement," the President said. At this
Doctor Nattore snorted with exasperation, but Don Croce in-
clined his head slightly in accord. The President went on. "Don
Croce has a nephew who yearns to be a doctor. Professor Nattore says he does not have the necessary grades to be certified.
A tragedy. Don Croce has been so kind as to come and present
his nephew's case, and since Don Croce has done so much for
our University, I thought we should try our best to grant him
some accommodation."

Don Croce said amiably without a hint of sarcasm, "I'm illiterate myself, yet no one can say I have been unsuccessful in the
world of business." Certainly, Hector Adonis thought, a man
who could bribe ministers, order murders, terrify shopkeepers
and factory owners did not have to read and write. Don Croce
continued, "I found my path by experience. Why could not my
nephew do the same? My poor sister will be heartbroken if her
son does not have the word 'Doctor' in front of his name. She is
a true believer in Christ, she wants to help the world."

Doctor Nattore, with that insensitivity so common to one who
is in the right, said, "I cannot change my position."

Don Croce sighed. He said cajolingly, "What harm can my
nephew do? I will arrange a government post with the army, or
with a Catholic hospital for the aged. He will hold their hands
and listen to their troubles. He is extremely amiable, he will
charm the old wrecks. What do I ask? A little shuffling of the
papers you shuffle here." He glanced around the room, contemptuous of the books that formed its walls.

Hector Adonis, extremely disturbed by this meekness of Don
Croce, a danger signal in such a man, thought angrily that it was

53

easy for the Don to take such a position. His men immediately shipped him to Switzerland at the slightest indisposition of his liver. But Adonis knew it was up to him to solve this impasse. "My dear Doctor Nattore," he said, "surely we can do something. A little private tutoring, extra training at a charity hospital?"

Despite his birth in Palermo, Doctor Nattore did not look Sicilian. He was fair and balding and he showed his anger, something no true Sicilian would ever do in this delicate situation. Doubtless it was the defective genes inherited from some long-ago Norman conqueror. "You don't understand, my dear Professor Adonis. The young fool wants to be a surgeon."

Jesus, Joseph, our Virgin Mary and all her Saints, Hector Adonis thought. This is real trouble.

Taking advantage of the stunned silence on his colleague's face, Doctor Nattore went on. "Your nephew knows nothing about anatomy. He hacked a cadaver to pieces as if he were carving a sheep for the spit. He misses most of his classes, he does not prepare for his test papers, he enters the operating room as if he were going to a dance. I admit he is amiable, you couldn't find a nicer chap. But, after all, we are talking about a man who will someday have to enter a human body with a sharp knife."

Hector Adonis knew exactly what Don Croce was thinking. Who cared how bad a surgeon the boy would make? It was a matter of family prestige, the loss of respect if the boy failed. No matter how bad a surgeon, he would never kill as many as Don Croce's more busy employees. Also, this young Doctor Nattore had not bent to his will, not taken the hint, that Don Croce was willing to let the surgeon business go by, that he was willing for his nephew to be a medical doctor.

So now it was time for Hector Adonis to settle the issue. "My dear Don Croce," he said, "I am sure that Doctor Nattore will accede to your wishes if we continue to persuade him. But why this romantic idea of your nephew to be a surgeon? As you say,

Doctor Nattore muttered that no compromise was possible. For the first time the lizardlike eyes of Don Croce flashed fire. Doctor Nattore fell silent and Hector Adonis rushed on. "Your nephew will receive passing marks to become a doctor, not a surgeon. We will say he has too kind a heart to cut."

Don Croce spread wide his arms, his lips parted in a cold smile. "You have defeated me with your good sense and your reasonableness," he said to Adonis. "So be it. My nephew will be a doctor, not a surgeon. And my sister must be content." He made haste to leave them, his real purpose achieved; he had not hoped for more. The President of the University escorted him down to the car. But everyone in that room noted the last glance Don Croce gave Doctor Nattore before he left. It was a glance of the closest scrutiny as if he were memorizing the features, to make sure that he did not forget the face of this man who had tried to thwart his will.

When they had left, Hector Adonis turned to Doctor Nattore and said, "You, my dear colleague, must resign from the University and go practice your trade in Rome."

Doctor Nattore said angrily, "Are you mad?"

Hector Adonis said, "Not as mad as you. I insist you have dinner with me tonight and I will explain to you why our Sicily is no Garden of Eden."

"But why should I leave?" Doctor Nattore protested.

"You have said the word 'no' to Don Croce Malo. Sicily is not big enough for both of you."

"But he's gotten his way," Doctor Nattore cried out in despair. "The nephew will become a doctor. You and the President have approved it."

"But you did not," Hector Adonis said. "We approved it to save your life. But still, you are now a marked man."

That evening Hector Adonis was host to six professors, including Doctor Nattore, at one of Palermo's best restaurants. Each of these professors had received a visit from a "man of honor" that day and each had agreed to change the marks of a failing pupil. Doctor Nattore listened to their stories with horror and then finally said, "But that cannot be in a medical school, not a doctor," until finally they lost their temper with him. A Professor of Philosophy demanded to know why the practice of medicine was more important to the human race than the intricate thought processes of the human mind and the immortal sanctity of one's soul. When they were finished Doctor Nattore agreed to leave the University of Palermo and emigrate to Brazil, where, he was assured by his colleagues, a good surgeon could make his fortune in gall bladders.

That night Hector Adonis slept the sleep of the just. But the next morning he received an urgent phone call from Montelepre. His godson, Turi Guiliano, whose intelligence he had nurtured, whose gentleness he had prized, whose future he had planned, had murdered a policeman.

3

MONTELEPRE WAS a town of seven thousand people, sunk as deeply in the valley of the Cammarata Mountains as it was in poverty.

On the day of September 2, 1943, the citizens were preparing for their Festa, to start the next day and continue for the following three days.

The Festa was the greatest event of the year in each town, greater than Easter or Christmas or New Year's, greater than the days celebrating the end of the great war or the birthday of a great national hero. The Festa was dedicated to the town's own particular favorite saint. It was one of the few customs the Fascist government of Mussolini had dared not meddle with or try to forbid.

To organize the Festa, a Committee of Three was formed each year, composed of the most respected men of the town. These three men then appointed deputies to collect money and offerings of goods. Every family contributed according to their means. In addition deputies were sent out into the streets to beg.

Then as the great day approached, the Committee of Three started to spend the special fund accumulated over the past year. They hired a band, and they hired a clown. They set up generous money prizes for horse races to be held over the three days. They hired specialists to decorate the church and the streets so that the grim poverty-stricken town of Montelepre suddenly looked like some medieval citadel in the midst of the Fields of the Cloths of Gold. A puppet theater was hired. Food peddlers set up their booths.

The families of Montelepre used the Festa to show their marriageable daughters; new clothes were bought, chaperones detailed. A bevy of prostitutes from Palermo set up a huge tent just outside of town, their licenses and medical certificates adorning the red-, white-, and green-striped canvas sides. A famous holy friar, who years ago had grown stigmata, was hired to preach the formal sermon. And finally, on the third day, the saint's bier was carried through the streets followed by all the townspeople, with their livestock of mules, horses, pigs and donkeys. On top of the bier rode the effigy of the saint, crusted with money, flowers, varicolored sweets and great bamboo-sheathed bottles of wine.

These few days were their days of glory. It did not matter that for the rest of the year they starved and that in the same village square where they honored the saint, they sold the sweat of their bodies to the land barons for a hundred lire a day.

On the first day of the Montelepre Festa, Turi Guiliano was designated to take part in the opening ritual, the mating of the Miracle Mule of Montelepre with the town's largest and strongest donkey. It is rare that a female mule can conceive; they are classified as a sterile animal, product of the union between a mare and donkey. But there was such a mule in Montelepre; it had borne a donkey two years before, and its owner had agreed, as his family's duty share to the town Festa, to donate the mule's services and, if the miracle should occur, its offspring to the next year's Festa. There was in this particular ceremony a sardonic mockery.

But the ritualistic mating was only partly a mockery. The Sicilian peasant has an affinity with his mule and donkey. They are hard-working beasts, and like the peasant himself have flinty, dour natures. Like the peasant they can work steadily for very long hours without breaking down, unlike the higher-nobility horse, who must be pampered. Also, they are sure-footed and can pick their way along the mountain terraces without falling and breaking a leg, unlike the fiery stallions or the high-blooded, flighty mares. Also, peasant and donkey and mule subsist and thrive on food that kills other men and animals. But the greatest affinity was this: Peasant, donkey and mule had to be treated with affection and respect, otherwise they turned murderous and stubborn.

The Catholic religious festivals had sprung from ancient pagan rituals to beg miracles from the gods. On this fateful day in September 1943, during the Festa of the town of Montelepre, a miracle would occur that would change the fate of its seven thousand inhabitants.

At twenty years of age Turi Guiliano was considered the bravest, the most honorable, the strongest, the young man who inspired the most respect. He was a man of honor. That is to say, a man who treated his fellow man with scrupulous fairness and one who could not be insulted with impunity.

He had distinguished himself at the last harvest by refusing to be hired out as a laborer at the insulting wages decreed by the overseer of the local estates. He then gave a speech to the other men urging them not to work, to let the harvest rot. The *carabinieri* arrested him on charges made by the Baron. The other men went back to work. Guiliano had not shown any hard feelings toward these men or even the *carabinieri*. When he was released from prison through the intervention of Hector Adonis, he developed no rancor of any kind. He had stood up for his principles and that was enough for him.

On another occasion, he had broken up a knife fight between Aspanu Pisciotta and another youth simply by interposing his unarmed body between them and with good-humored reasoning disarming their anger.

What was unusual about this was that in any other person these actions would have been taken as signs of cowardice masquerading as humanity, but something in Guiliano forbade this interpretation.

On this second day of September, Salvatore Guiliano, called Turi by his friends and family, was brooding over what was to him a devastating blow to his masculine pride.

It was only a little thing. The town of Montelepre had no movie theater, no community hall, but there was one little café with a billiard table. The night before, Turi Guiliano, his cousin Gaspare "Aspanu" Pisciotta and a few other youths had been playing billiards. Some of the older men of the town had been watching them while drinking glasses of wine. One of the men, by the name of Guido Quintana, was slightly drunk. He was a man of reputation. He had been imprisoned by Mussolini for being a suspected member of the Mafia. The American conquest of the island had resulted in his being released as a victim of fascism, and it was rumored that he was going to be named as Mayor of Montelepre.

As well as any Sicilian, Turi Guiliano knew the legendary power of the Mafia. In these past few months of freedom, its snakelike head had begun weaving over the land, as if fertilized by the fresh loam of a new democratic government. It was already whispered in town that shopkeepers were paying "insurance" to certain "men of respect." And of course Turi knew the history, the countless murders of peasants who tried to collect their wages from powerful nobles and landlords, how tightly the Mafia had controlled the island before Mussolini had decimated them with his own disregard for the lawful process, like a deadlier snake biting a less powerful reptile with its poisoned fangs. So Turi Guiliano sensed the terror that lay ahead.

Quintana now regarded Guiliano and his companions with a slightly contemptuous eye. Perhaps their high spirits irritated him. He was, after all, a serious man, about to embark on a pivotal part of his life: Exiled by Mussolini's government to a desert island, he was now back in the town of his birth. His aim in the next few months was to establish respect in the eyes of the townspeople.

Or perhaps it was the handsomeness of Guiliano that irritated him, for Guido Quintana was an extremely ugly man. His appearance was intimidating not from any single feature but from a lifelong habit of presenting a formidable front to the outside world. Or perhaps it was the natural antagonism of a born villain toward a born hero.

In any case he got up suddenly just in time to jostle Guiliano as he went by to the other side of the billiard table. Turi, naturally courteous to a much older man, made an apology that was gentle and sincere. Guido Quintana looked him up and down with contempt. "Why aren't you home sleeping and resting to earn your bread tomorrow?" he said. "My friends have been waiting to play billiards for an hour." He reached out and took the billiard cue from Guiliano's hand and, smiling slightly, waved him away from the table.

Everybody was watching. The insult was not mortal. If the man were younger or the insult more pointed, Guiliano would have been forced to fight and keep his reputation for manhood. Aspanu Pisciotta always carried a knife, and now he positioned himself to intercept Quintana's friends if they decided to interfere. Pisciotta had no respect for older people, and he expected his friend and cousin to finish the quarrel.

But at that moment Guiliano felt a strange uneasiness. The man looked so intimidating and ready for the most serious consequences of any dispute. The companions in the background, also older men, were smiling in an amused way as if they had no doubt of the outcome. One of them wore hunting attire and carried a rifle. Guiliano himself was unarmed. And then for one shameful moment, he felt fear. He was not afraid of being hurt, of being struck, of finding this man was the stronger of the two. It was the fear that these men knew what they were doing, that they had the situation under control. He did not. That they could gun him down in the dark streets of Montelepre as he walked home. That he would appear a dead fool the next day. It was the inborn tactical sense of the born guerrilla soldier that made him retreat.

So Turi Guiliano took his friend by the arm and led him out of the café. Pisciotta came without a struggle, amazed that his friend had yielded so easily but never suspecting the fear. He knew Turi was good-hearted and assumed he did not wish to quarrel and injure another man over so small a thing. As they started up the Via Bella to their homes they could hear the click of billiard balls behind them.

All that night Turi Guiliano had not been able to sleep. Had he really been afraid of that man with the evil face and threatening body? Had he shivered like a girl? Were they all laughing at him? What did his best friend, his cousin, Aspanu, think of him now? That he was a coward? That he, Turi Guiliano, the leader of the youth of Montelepre, the most respected, the one acknowledged as the strongest and most fearless, had buckled at the first threat of a true man? And yet, he told himself, why risk a vendetta that could lead to death over the small matter of a billiard game, an older man's irascible rudeness? It would not have been like a quarrel with another youth. He had known that this quarrel could be serious. He had known that these men were with the Friends of the Friends, and it had made him afraid.

Guiliano slept badly and woke in that sullen mood so dangerous in adolescent males. He seemed to himself ridiculous. He had always wanted to be a hero, like most young men. If he had lived in any other part of Italy he would have become a soldier long before, but as a true Sicilian he had not volunteered, and his godfather, Hector Adonis, had made certain arrangements so that he wouldn't be called. After all, though Italy governed Sicily, no true Sicilian felt he was an Italian. And then, if the truth be told, the Italian government itself was not so anxious to draft Sicilians, especially in the last year of the war. Sicilians had too many relatives in America, Sicilians were born criminals and renegades, Sicilians were too stupid to be trained in modern warfare and they caused trouble wherever they went.

In the street Turi Guiliano felt his moodiness fade with the sheer beauty of the day. The golden sun was glorious, the smell of lemon and olive trees filled the air. He loved the town of Montelepre, its crooked streets, the stone houses with their balconies filled with those gaudy flowers that grew in Sicily without the slightest encouragement. He loved the red-tiled roofs that stretched away to the end of the small town, buried in this deep valley on which the sun poured like liquid gold.

The elaborate decorations of the Festa—the streets overhung with an aerial maze of colorful papier-mâché saints, the houses decorated with great bamboo-strutted flowers—disguised the essential poverty of what was a typical Sicilian town. Perched high, yet shyly hidden in the creases of the surrounding mountains, its garlanded houses were mostly filled with men, women, children and animals occupying three or four rooms. Many houses had no sanitation, and even the thousands of flowers and the cold mountain air could not overcome the smell of offal that rose with the sun.

In good weather the people lived outside their houses. The women sat in wooden chairs on their cobbled terraces preparing food for their tables, also set outside the door. Young children filled the streets chasing chickens, turkeys, young goats; older children wove bamboo baskets. At the end of the Via Bella, before it emptied into the square, was a huge demon-faced fountain, built by the Greeks two thousand years before, water pouring from its rock-toothed mouth. Alongside the surrounding mountains green gardens grew precariously, built on terraces. On the plains below were the visible towns of Partinico and Castellammare; the bloody dark stone town of Corleone lurked murderously beyond the horizon.

From the far end of the Via Bella, the end of the street that led into the road of the Castellammare plain, Turi could see Aspanu Pisciotta leading a small donkey. For a moment he was worried about how Aspanu would treat him after his humiliation of the night before. His friend was noted for his sharp wit. Would he make some contemptuous remark? Guiliano felt again the rush of futile rage and swore he would not be so unready again. There would be no regard for any consequences, he would show them all he was no coward. Yet in a corner of his mind he saw the whole scene sharp and clear. Quintana's friends waiting behind him, one of them with a hunting rifle. They were Friends of the Friends and would avenge themselves. He did not fear them, he feared only his defeat by them, which seemed so sure because though they were not so strong, they were more cruel.

Aspanu Pisciotta wore his wickedly cheery grin as he said, "Turi, this little donkey can't do it all by himself. We'll have to help."

Guiliano didn't bother to answer; he was relieved that his friend had forgotten about last night. It always touched his heart that Aspanu, who was so caustic and penetrating with the faults of others, never treated him with anything but the utmost affection and respect. They walked together toward the town square, the donkey behind. Children scurried around and before them like pilot fish. The children knew what was going to happen with the donkey and were wild with excitement. For them it would be a great treat, an exciting event in the usually dull summer day.

A small platform four feet high stood in the town square. It was formed by heavy blocks of stone carved from the mountains around them. Turi Guiliano and Aspanu Pisciotta pushed the donkey up the dirt ramp of the platform. They used a rope to tie the donkey's head to a short vertical iron bar. The donkey sat down. There was a patch of white skin over his eyes and muzzle that gave him a clownish look. The children gathered around the platform, laughed and jeered. One of the little boys called out, "Which one is the donkey?" and all the children laughed.

Turi Guiliano, not knowing this was the last day of his life as an unknown village boy, looked down on the scene with the sweet possessive contentment of a man placed exactly as he should be. He was in the small spot of earth in which he had been born and spent his life. The outside world could never harm him. Even the humiliation of the night before had disappeared. He knew those looming limestone mountains as intimately as a little child knew his sandbox. Those mountains grew slabs of stone as easily as they grew grass, and formed caves and hiding places that could shelter an army. Turi Guiliano knew every house, every farm, every laborer, and all the ruined castles left by the Normans and Moors, the skeletons of beautifully decayed temples left by the Greeks.

From another entrance to the square appeared a farmer leading the Miracle Mule. This was the man who had employed them for this morning's work. His name was Papera, and he was held in much respect by the citizens of Montelepre for having waged a successful vendetta against a neighbor. They had quarreled over an adjoining piece of land which held an olive grove. The quarrel went on for ten years, had in fact lasted longer than all of the wars Mussolini had foisted on Italy. Then one night shortly after the Allied Armies had liberated Sicily and installed a democratic government, the neighbor had been found almost cut in two by the blast of a *lupara,* the sawed-off shotgun so popular in Sicily for such matters. Suspicion immediately fell on Papera, but he had conveniently allowed himself to be arrested in a quarrel with the *carabinieri* and had spent the night of the murder safely in the prison cell of the Bellampo Barracks. It was rumored that this was the first sign of the old Mafia coming to life, that Papera—related by marriage to Guido Quintana—had enlisted the Friends of the Friends to help settle the quarrel.

As Papera led the mule to the front of the platform, the children swarmed around it so that Papera had to scatter them with mild curses and casual waves of the whip he held in his hand. The children escaped the whip easily as Papera snapped it over their heads with a good-humored smile.

Smelling the female mule below, the white-faced donkey reared against the rope that held him to the platform. Turi and Aspanu lifted him up as the children cheered. Meanwhile Papera was maneuvering the mule to present its hindquarters to the edge of the platform.

At this point Frisella, the barber, came out of his shop to join in the fun. Behind him was the Maresciallo, pompous and important, rubbing his smooth red face. He was the only man in Montelepre who had himself shaved every day. Even on the platform Guiliano could smell the strong cologne with which the barber had showered him.

Maresciallo Roccofino cast a professional eye over the crowd that had accumulated in the square. As the Commander of the local National Police detachment twelve men strong he was responsible for law and order in the town. The Festa was always a troublesome time, and he had already ordered a four-man patrol for the town square, but they had not yet arrived. He also watched the town benefactor, Papera, with his Miracle Mule. He was certain that Papera had ordered the murder of his neighbor. These Sicilian savages were quick to take advantage of their sacred liberties. They would all regret the loss of Mussolini, the Maresciallo thought grimly. Compared with the Friends of the Friends, the dictator would be remembered as another gentle Saint Francis of Assisi.

Frisella the barber was the buffoon of Montelepre. Idle men who could not find work clustered in his shop to hear his jokes and listen to his gossip. He was one of those barbers who serviced himself better than his customers. His mustache was exquisitely trimmed, his hair pomaded and strictly combed, but he had the face of a clown in the puppet shows. Bulbous nose; a wide mouth that hung open like a gate and a lower jaw without a chin.

Now he shouted, "Turi, bring your beasts into my shop and I'll anoint them with perfume. Your donkey will think he's making love to a duchess."

Turi ignored him. Frisella had cut his hair when he was a little boy, and so badly that his mother had taken over the task. But his father still went to Frisella to share in the town gossip and tell his own tales about America to awestruck listeners. Turi Guiliano did not like the barber because Frisella had been a strong Fascist and was reputed to be a confidant of the Friends of the Friends.

The Maresciallo lit a cigarette and strutted up the Via Bella not even noticing Guiliano—an oversight he was to regret in the weeks to come.

The donkey was now trying to jump off the platform. Guiliano let the rope slacken so that Pisciotta could lead the animal to the edge and position it above where the Miracle Mule was standing. The mare's hindquarters were just above the edge of the platform. Guiliano let the rope slacken a little more. The mare gave a great snort and pushed her rump back at the same moment the donkey plunged downward. The donkey grasped the hindquarters of the mare with his forelegs, gave a few convulsive jumps and hung in midair with a comical look of bliss on his white-patched face. Papera and Pisciotta were laughing as Guiliano pulled savagely on the rope and brought the limp donkey back to its iron bar. The crowd cheered and shouted blessings. The children were already scattering through the streets in search of other amusements.

Papera, still laughing, said, "If we could all live like donkeys, eh, what a life."

Pisciotta said disrespectfully, "Signor Papera, let me load your back with bamboo and olive baskets and beat you up the mountain roads for eight hours every day. That's a donkey's life."

The farmer scowled at him. He caught the sly reproach, that he was paying them too little for this job. He had never liked Pisciotta and had in fact given Guiliano the job. Everybody in the town of Montelepre was fond of Turi. But Pisciotta was another matter. His tongue was too sharp and his manner too languid. Lazy. The fact that he had a weak chest was no excuse. He could still smoke cigarettes, court the loose girls of Palermo and dress like a dandy. And that clever little mustache in the French style. He could cough himself to death and go to the devil with his weak chest, Papera thought. He gave them their two hundred lire, for which Guiliano thanked him courteously, and then took himself and his mare back on the road to his farm. The two young men untied the donkey and led it back to Guiliano's house. The donkey's work had just begun; he had a much less pleasant task before him.

Guiliano's mother had an early lunch waiting for the two boys. Turi's two sisters, Mariannina and Giuseppina, were helping their mother make pasta for the evening meal. Eggs and flour were mixed into a huge mountain on a shellacked square wooden board, kneaded solid. Then a knife was used to cut the sign of the cross into the dough to sanctify it. Next Mariannina and Giuseppina cut off strips they rolled around a blade of sisal grass, and then pulled out the grass to leave a hole in the tube of dough. Huge bowls of olives and grapes decorated the room.

Turi's father was working in the fields, a short working day so he could join the Festa in the afternoon. On the next day Mariannina was to become engaged and there was to be a special party at the Guiliano house.

Turi had always been Maria Lombardo Guiliano's most beloved child. The sisters remembered him as a baby being bathed every day by the mother. The tin basin carefully warmed by the stove, the mother testing the temperature of the water with her elbow, the special soap fetched from Palermo. The sisters had been jealous at first, then fascinated by the mother's tender washing of the naked male infant. He never cried as a baby, was always gurgling with laughter as his mother crooned over him and declared his body perfect. He was the youngest in the family but grew to be the most forceful. And he was to them always a little strange. He read books and talked about politics, and of course it was always remarked that his height and formidable physique came from his time in the womb in America. But they loved him too because of his gentleness and his selflessness.

On this morning, the women were worried about Turi and watched him with a loving fretfulness as he ate his bread and goat cheese, his plate of olives, drank his coffee made of chicory. As soon as he finished his lunch he and Aspanu would take the donkey all the way to Corleone and smuggle back a huge wheel of cheese and some hams and sausage. He would miss a day of the Festa to do this just to please his mother and make his sister's engagement party a success. Part of the goods they would sell for cash on the black market for the family coffers.

These three women loved to see the two young men together. They had been friends since they were little children, closer than brothers in spite of being such opposites. Aspanu Pisciotta, with his dark coloring, his thin movie star mustache, the extraordinary mobility of his face, the brilliant dark eyes and jet black hair on his small skull, his wit, always enchanted the women. And yet in some curious way all this flamboyance was overwhelmed by Turi Guiliano's quiet Grecian beauty. He was massively built like the ancient Greek statues scattered all over Sicily. And his coloring was all light brown—his hair, his tawny skin. He was always very still, and yet when he moved it was with a startling quickness. But his most dominating feature was his eyes. They were a dreamy golden brown, and when they were averted they seemed ordinary. But when he looked at you directly the lids came halfway down like the lids carved in statues and the whole face took on a quiet masklike serenity.

While Pisciotta kept Maria Lombardo amused, Turi Guiliano went upstairs to his bedroom to prepare himself for the journey he was about to make. Specifically to get the pistol he kept hidden there. Remembering the humiliation of the previous night, he was determined to go armed on the job he had ahead this day. He knew how to shoot, for his father took him hunting often.

In the kitchen, his mother was waiting alone for him to say goodbye. She embraced him and felt the pistol he had in his waistband.

"Turi, be careful," she said, alarmed. "Don't quarrel with the *carabinieri*. If they stop you, give up what you have."

Guiliano reassured her. "They can take the goods," he said. "But I won't let them beat me or take me to prison."

She understood this. And in her own fierce Sicilian pride was proud of him. Many years ago her own pride, her anger at her

69

poverty, had led her to persuade her husband to try a new life in America. She had been a dreamer, she had believed in justice and her own rightful place in the world. She had saved a fortune in America, and that same pride had made her decide to return to Sicily to live like a queen. And then everything had turned to ashes. The lira became worthless in wartime, and she was poor again. She was resigned to her fate but hoped for her children. And she was happy when Turi showed the same spirit that had possessed her. But she dreaded the day when he must come into conflict with the stone-hard realities of life in Sicily.

She watched him go out into the cobbled street of the Via Bella to greet Aspanu Pisciotta. Her son, Turi, walked like a huge cat, his chest so broad, his arms and legs so muscular he made Aspanu seem no more than a stalk of sisal grass. Aspanu had the hard cunning that her son lacked, the cruelty in his courage. Aspanu would guard Turi against the treacherous world they all had to live in. And she had a weakness for Aspanu's olive-skinned prettiness, though she believed her son more handsome.

She watched them go up the Via Bella to where it led out of town toward the Castellammare plain. Her son, Turi Guiliano, and her sister's son, Gaspare Pisciotta. Two young men just barely twenty years old, and seeming younger than their years. She loved them both and she feared for them both.

Finally the two men and their donkey vanished over a rise in the street, but she kept watching and finally they appeared again, high above the town of Montelepre, entering the range of mountains that surrounded the town. Maria Lombardo Guiliano kept watching, as if she would never see them again, until they disappeared in the late morning mist around the mountaintop. They were vanishing into the beginning of their myth.

CHAPTER

4

IN SICILY this September of 1943, people could only exist by trading in the black market. Strict rationing of foodstuffs still carried over from the war, and farmers had to turn in their produce to central government storehouses at fixed prices and for paper money that was almost worthless. In turn the government was supposed to sell and distribute these foodstuffs at low prices to the people. Under this system everybody would get enough to remain alive. In reality, the farmers hid what they could because what they turned in to the government storehouses was appropriated by Don Croce Malo and his mayors to be sold on the black market. The people themselves then had to buy on the black market and break smuggling laws merely to exist. If they were caught doing this they were prosecuted and sent to jail. What good was it that a democratic government had been established in Rome? They would be able to vote as they starved.

Turi Guiliano and Aspanu Pisciotta, with the lightest of hearts, were in the process of breaking these laws. It was Pisciotta who had all the black market contacts and who had arranged this affair. He had contracted with a farmer to smuggle a great wheel of cheese from the countryside to a black market dealer in Montelepre. Their pay for this would be four smoked hams and a basket of sausage which would make his sister's

71

engagement party a great celebration. They were breaking two laws, one forbidding dealing in the black market, the other smuggling from one province of Italy to another. There was not much the authorities could do to enforce the black market laws; they would have had to jail everyone in Sicily. But smuggling was another matter. Patrols of National Police, the *carabinieri*, roamed the countryside, set up roadblocks, paid informers. They could not of course interfere with the caravans of Don Croce Malo who used American Army trucks and special military government passes. But they could net many of the small farmers and starving villagers.

It took them four hours to get to the farm. Guiliano and Pisciotta picked up the huge grainy white cheese and the other goods and strapped them onto the donkey. They formed a camouflage of sisal grass and bamboo stalks over the goods so that it would appear they were merely bringing in fodder for the livestock kept in the households of many villagers. They had the carelessness and confidence of youth, of children really, who hide treasures from their parents, as if the intention to deceive were enough. Their confidence came too from the knowledge that they could find hidden paths through the mountains.

As they set out for the long journey home, Guiliano sent Pisciotta ahead to scout for the *carabinieri*. They had arranged a set of whistling signals to warn of danger. The donkey carried the cheeses easily and behaved amiably—he had had his reward before setting out. They journeyed for two hours, slowly ascending, before there was any sign of danger. Then Guiliano saw behind them, perhaps three miles away, following their path, a caravan of six mules and a man on horseback. If the path was known to others in the black market, it could have been marked by the field police for a roadblock. As a caution, he sent Pisciotta scouting far ahead.

After an hour he caught up with Aspanu, who was sitting on a huge stone smoking a cigarette and coughing. Aspanu looked pale; he should not have been smoking. Turi Guiliano sat down beside him to rest. One of their strongest bonds since childhood was that they never tried to command each other in any way, so Turi said nothing. Finally Aspanu stubbed out the cigarette and put the blackened butt into his pocket. They started walking again, Guiliano holding the donkey's bridle, Aspanu walking behind.

They were traveling a mountain path that bypassed the roads and little villages but sometimes they saw an ancient Greek water cistern that spouted water through a crumpled statue's mouth, or the remains of a Norman castle that many centuries ago had barred this way to invaders. Again Turi Guiliano dreamed of Sicily's past and his future. He thought of his godfather, Hector Adonis, who had promised to come after the Festa and prepare his application to the University of Palermo. And when he thought of his godfather he felt momentary sadness. Hector Adonis never came to the Festas; the drunken men would make fun of his short stature, the children, some of them taller than he, would offer him some insult. Turi wondered about God stunting the growth of a man's body and bursting his brain with knowledge. For Turi thought Hector Adonis the most brilliant man in the world and loved him for the kindness he had showed him and his parents.

He thought of his father working so hard on their small piece of land, and of his sisters with their threadbare clothes. It was lucky that Mariannina was so beautiful that she had caught a husband despite her poverty and the unsettled times. But most of all he anguished over his mother, Maria Lombardo. Even as a child he had recognized her bitterness, her unhappiness. She had tasted the rich fruits of America and could no longer be happy in the poverty-stricken towns of Sicily. His father would tell the tales of those glorious days and his mother would burst into tears.

But he would change his family's fortune, Turi Guiliano thought. He would work hard and study hard and he would become as great a man as his godfather.

Suddenly they were passing through a stand of trees, a small forest, one of the few left in this part of Sicily, which now seemed to grow only the great white stones and marble quarries. On the other side of the mountain they would begin the descent into Montelepre and would have to be careful of the roving patrols of National Police, the *carabinieri*. But now they were coming to the Quattro Moline, the Four Crossroads, and it would pay to be a little careful here too. Guiliano pulled on the donkey's bridle and motioned Aspanu to halt. They stood there quietly. No strange sound could be heard, only the steady hum of the countless insects that swarmed over the ground, their whirring wings and legs buzzing like a far distant saw. They moved forward over the crossroads and then safely out of sight into another small forest. Turi Guiliano started to daydream again.

The trees widened out suddenly, as if they had been pushed back, and they were picking their way across a small clearing with a rough floor of tiny stones, cropped bamboo stalks, thin balding grass. The late afternoon sun was falling far away from them and looked pale and cold above the granite-studded mountains. Past this clearing the path would begin to drop in a long winding spiral to the town of Montelepre. Suddenly Guiliano came out of his dreams. A flash of light like the striking of a match lanced his left eye. He jerked the donkey to a halt and held up his hand to Aspanu.

Only thirty yards away, strange men stepped out from behind a thicket. There were three of them, and Turi Guiliano saw their stiff black military caps, the black uniforms with white piping. He felt a sick foolish feeling of despair, of shame, that he had been caught. The three men fanned out as they advanced, weapons at the ready. Two were quite young with ruddy shining faces and crusted military caps tilted almost comically to the backs of their heads. They seemed earnest yet gleeful as they pointed their machine pistols.

The *carabiniere* in the center was older and held a rifle. His face was pockmarked and scarred and his cap was pulled firmly over his eyes. He had sergeant's stripes on his sleeve. The flash of light Guiliano had seen was a sunbeam drawn by the steel rifle barrel. This man was smiling grimly, his rifle pointed unwaveringly at Guiliano's chest. Guiliano's despair turned to anger at that smile.

The Sergeant with the rifle stepped closer, his two fellow guards closing in from either side. Now Turi Guiliano was alert. The two young *carabinieri* with their machine pistols were not so much to be feared; they were carelessly approaching the donkey, not taking their prisoners seriously. They motioned Guiliano and Pisciotta away from the donkey and one of them let his pistol sway back on its sling as he stripped the camouflage bamboo from the donkey's back. When he saw the goods he let out a whistle of greedy delight. He didn't notice Aspanu edging closer to him but the Sergeant with the rifle did. He shouted, "You, with the mustache, move away," and Aspanu stepped back closer to Turi Guiliano.

The Sergeant moved a little closer. Guiliano watched him intently. The pockmarked face seemed to be fatigued; but the man's eyes gleamed when he said, "Well, young fellows, that's a nice bit of cheese. We could use it in our barracks to go with our macaroni. So just tell us the name of the farmer you got it from and we'll let you ride your donkey back home."

They did not answer him. He waited. Still they did not answer.

Finally, Guiliano said quietly, "I have a thousand lire as a gift, if you can let us go."

"You can wipe your ass with lire," the Sergeant said. "Now, your identity papers. If they're not in order I'll make you shit and wipe your ass with them too."

The insolence of the words, the insolence of those black-and-white piped uniforms, aroused an icy fury in Guiliano. At that moment he knew he would never allow himself to be arrested, never allow these men to rob him of his family's food.

Turi Guiliano took out his identity card and started to approach the Sergeant. He was hoping to get under the arc of the pointed rifle. He knew his physical coordination was faster than that of most men and he was willing to gamble on it. But the rifle motioned him back. The man said, "Throw it on the ground." Guiliano did so.

Pisciotta, five paces on Guiliano's left, and knowing what was in his friend's mind, knowing he carried the pistol under his shirt, tried to distract the Sergeant's attention. He said with studied insolence, his body thrust forward, hand on hip touching the knife he carried in a sheath strapped to his back, "Sergeant, if we give you the farmer's name, why do you need our identity cards? A bargain's a bargain." He paused for a moment and said sarcastically, "We know a *carabiniere* always keeps his word." He spat out the word *"carabiniere"* with hatred.

The rifleman sauntered a few steps toward Pisciotta. He stopped. He smiled and leveled his gun. He said, "And you, my little dandy, your card. Or do you have no papers, like your donkey, who has a better mustache than you?"

The two younger policemen laughed. Pisciotta's eyes glittered. He took a step toward the Sergeant. "No, I have no papers. And I know no farmer. We found these goods lying in the road."

The very foolhardiness of this defiance defeated its purpose. Pisciotta had wanted the rifleman to move closer within striking distance, but now the Sergeant took a few steps backward and smiled again. He said, "The *bastinado* will knock out some of your Sicilian insolence." He paused for a moment and then said, "Both of you, lie on the ground."

The *bastinado* was a term loosely used for a physical beating with whips and clubs. Guiliano knew some citizens of Montelepre who had been punished in the Bellampo Barracks. They had returned to their homes with broken knees, heads swollen as big as melons, their insides injured so that they could never work again. The *carabinieri* would never do that to him. Guiliano went to one knee as if he were going to lie down, put one hand on the ground and the other on his belt so that he could draw the pistol from beneath his shirt. The clearing was now bathed with the soft hazy light of beginning twilight, the sun far over the trees had dipped below the last mountain. He saw Pisciotta standing proudly, refusing the command. Surely they would not shoot him down over a piece of smuggled cheese. He could see the pistols trembling in the hands of the young guards.

At that moment there was the braying of mules and the clatter of hooves from behind and bursting into the clearing came the caravan of mules that Guiliano had spotted on the road behind him that afternoon. The man on horseback leading it carried a *lupara* slung over his shoulder and looked huge in a heavy leather jacket. He jumped down off his horse and took a great wad of lire notes from one of his pockets and said to the *carabiniere* with the rifle, "So, you've scooped up a few little sardines this time." They obviously knew each other. For the first time the rifleman relaxed his vigilance to accept the money offered to him. The two men were grinning at each other. The prisoners seemed to have been forgotten by everyone.

Turi Guiliano moved slowly toward the nearest guard. Pisciotta was edging toward the nearest bamboo thicket. The guards didn't notice. Guiliano hit the nearest guard with his forearm, knocking him to the ground. He shouted to Pisciotta, "Run." Pisciotta dove into the bamboo thicket and Guiliano ran to the trees. The remaining guard was too stunned or too inept to bring his pistol around in time. Guiliano, about to plunge into the shelter of the forest, felt a quick sense of exultation. He launched his body into midair to dive between two sturdy trees that would shield him. As he did so he drew the pistol free from beneath his shirt.

But he had been right about the rifleman being the most dangerous. The Sergeant dropped the wad of money to the ground, swung his rifle up and very coolly shot. There was no mistaking the hit; Guiliano's body dropped like a dead bird.

77

Guiliano heard the shot at the same time he felt his body wracked with pain, as if he had been hit with a giant club. He landed on the ground between the two trees and tried to get up, but could not. His legs were numb; he could not make them move. Pistol in hand he twisted his body and saw the Sergeant shake his rifle in the air in triumph. And then Guiliano felt his trousers filling with blood, the liquid warm and sticky.

In the fraction of a second before he pulled the trigger of his pistol, Turi Guiliano felt only astonishment. That they had shot him over a piece of cheese. That they had smashed the fabric of his family with such a cruel carelessness just because he was running away from such a small breaking of the law that everyone broke. His mother would weep to the end of her days. And now his body was awash in blood, he who had never done anyone any harm.

He pulled the trigger and saw the rifle fall, saw the Sergeant's black cap with its white piping seem to fly in the air as the body with its mortal head wound crumpled and floated to the rock-filled earth. It was an impossible shot with a pistol at that range but it seemed to Guiliano that his own hand had traveled with the bullet and smashed it like a dagger through the Sergeant's eye.

A machine pistol began to pop but the bullets flew upward in harmless arcs, chattering like small birds. And then it was deadly still. Even the insects had stopped their incessant whirring.

Turi Guiliano rolled into the bushes. He had seen the enemy's face shatter into a mask of blood and that gave him hope. He was not powerless. He tried to get up again and this time his legs obeyed him. He began to run but only one leg sprang forward, the other dragged along the ground, which surprised him. His crotch was warm and sticky, his trousers soaked, his vision cloudy. When he ran through a sudden patch of light, he was afraid he had circled back into the clearing again and tried to turn back. His body started to fall—not to the ground, but into an endless red-tinted black void, and then he knew he was falling forever.

■ ■ ■

IN THE clearing the young guard took his hand off the trigger of his machine pistol and the chattering stopped. The smuggler rose from the ground with the huge wad of money in his hand and offered it to the other guard. The guard pointed his machine pistol at him and said, "You're under arrest."

The smuggler said, "You only have to split it two ways now. Let me go on."

The guards looked down at the fallen Sergeant. There was no doubt he was dead. The bullet had smashed eye and socket to pieces, and the wound was bubbling with a yellow liquid into which a gecko was already dipping its feelers.

The smuggler said, "I'll go into the bushes after him, he's hurt. I'll bring back his carcass and you two will be heroes. Just let me go."

The other guard picked up the identity card Turi had thrown down on the ground at the Sergeant's command. He read it aloud, "Salvatore Guiliano, the town of Montelepre."

"No need to look for him now," the other said. "We'll report back to headquarters, that's more important."

"Cowards," the smuggler said. He thought for a moment of unslinging his *lupara* but saw that they were looking at him with hatred. He had insulted them. For that insult they made him load the Sergeant's body onto his horse and made him walk back to their barracks. Before that they relieved him of his weapon. They were very skittish and he hoped they would not shoot him by mistake out of sheer nervousness. Aside from that he was not too concerned. He knew Maresciallo Roccofino of Montelepre very well. They had done business before and they would do business again.

In all that time not one of them had given a thought to Pisciotta. But he had heard everything they had said. He was lying

79

in a deep grassy hollow, knife drawn. He was waiting for them to try hunting down Turi Guiliano, and he planned to ambush one of them and get his gun after he had cut his throat. There was a ferocity in his soul that banished all fear of death, and when he heard the smuggler offer to bring back Turi's carcass, he burned that man's face forever in his brain. He was almost sorry they retreated to leave him alone on the mountainside. He felt a pang when they tied his donkey to the end of the mule train.

But he knew that Turi was badly wounded and would need help. He circled around the clearing, running through the woods to get to the side where his comrade had disappeared. There was no sign of a body in the underbrush and he started to run down the path from which they had come.

There were still no signs until he climbed over a huge granite boulder whose top shallowed out into a small basin. In that basin of rock was a small pool of almost black blood and the other side of the rock was smeared with long ropy gouts of blood that were bright red. He kept running and was caught by surprise when he saw Guiliano's body sprawled across his path, the deadly pistol still clutched in his hand.

He knelt and took the pistol and thrust it into his belt. At that moment Turi Guiliano's eyes opened. The eyes were alive with an awesome hatred, but they were staring past Aspanu Pisciotta. Pisciotta almost wept with relief and tried to get him to his feet, but he was not strong enough. "Turi, try to get up, I'll help you," Pisciotta said. Guiliano pushed his hands against the earth and raised his body. Pisciotta put an arm around his waist and his hand became warm and wet. He jerked his hand away and pulled aside Guiliano's shirt, and with horror he saw the huge gaping hole in Guiliano's side. He propped Guiliano up against a tree, ripped off his own shirt and shoved it into the hole to staunch the blood, tying the sleeves together around the waist. He put one arm around his friend's middle and then with his free hand took Guiliano's left hand and raised it high in the air. This balanced them both as he guided Guiliano down the path with careful, mincing steps. From a distance it looked as if they were dancing together down the mountain.

■ ■ ■

AND SO Turi Guiliano missed the Festa of Saint Rosalie, which the citizens of Montelepre hoped would bring a miracle to their town.

He missed the shooting contest which he surely would have won. He missed the horse races in which the jockeys hit opposing riders over the head with clubs and whips. He missed the purple, yellow and green rockets that exploded and tattooed the star-filled sky.

He never tasted the magical sweets made of almond paste molded into the form of carrots, bamboo stalks and red tomatoes, all so sweet they numbed your entire body; or the spun sugar figures of the puppet knights of mythical romance, of Roland, Oliver and Charlemagne, their sugar swords studded with peppermints of ruby, emeralds of tiny fruit bits that the children brought home to bed to dream over before they went to sleep. At home his sister's engagement party went on without him.

The mating of the donkey and the Miracle Mule failed. There was no offspring. The citizens of Montelepre were disappointed. They did not know until years later that the Festa had produced its miracle in the person of the young man who had held the donkey.

CHAPTER

5

THE ABBOT made his evening tour of the Franciscan monastery, spurring his lazy, good-for-nothing monks to earn their daily bread. He checked the bins in the holy relic workshop and visited the bakery turning out huge crusty loaves for nearby towns. He inspected the produce garden and the bamboo baskets filled to the brim with olives, tomatoes and grapes, looking for bruises on their satiny skins. His monks were all as busy as elves—though not so merry. In fact they were a sullen crew, with none of the joy necessary to serve God. The Abbot took a long black cheroot from beneath his cassock and strolled around the monastery grounds to sharpen his appetite for the evening meal.

It was then that he saw Aspanu Pisciotta drag Turi Guiliano through the monastery gates. The gatekeeper tried to keep them out, but Pisciotta put a pistol to his tonsured head and he fell to his knees to say his last prayers. Pisciotta deposited Guiliano's bloody, almost lifeless, body at the Abbot's feet.

The Abbot was a tall, emaciated man with an elegant monkey-like face, all tiny bones, a nub of a nose and querying little brown buttons for eyes. Though seventy years of age, he was vigorous, his mind as sharp and cunning as in the old days before Mussolini, when he had written elegant ransom notes for Mafia kidnappers who employed him.

Now though it was known to all, peasants and authorities alike, that his monastery was the headquarters of black market operators and smugglers, he was never interfered with in his illegal activities. This out of respect for his holy calling, and a feeling that he deserved some material reward for his spiritual guidance to the community.

So the Abbot Manfredi was not dismayed to find two peasant scoundrels covered with blood breaking into the sacred domain of Saint Francis. In fact, he knew Pisciotta well. He had used the young man in a few smuggling and black market operations. They had in common a sly cunning that delighted them both—one surprised to find it in a man so old and holy, the other to find it in one so young and unworldly.

The Abbot reassured the gatekeeper monk, then said to Pisciotta, "Well, my dear Aspanu, what mischief are you into now?" Pisciotta was tightening the shirt around Guiliano's wound. The Abbot was surprised to see that his face was grief-stricken; he did not think the lad was capable of such emotion.

Pisciotta, seeing again that huge wound, was sure his friend was going to die. And how could he tell the news to Turi's mother and father? He dreaded Maria Lombardo's grief. But for now, a more important scene would have to be played. He must convince the Abbot to give Guiliano sanctuary in the monastery.

He looked the Abbot straight in the eye. He wanted to convey a message that would not be a direct threat but would make the priest understand that if he refused he would make a mortal enemy. "This is my cousin and dearest friend, Salvatore Guiliano," Pisciotta said. "As you can see, he has been unfortunate, and in a short time the National Police will be all over the mountains looking for him. And for me. You are our only hope. I beg you to hide us, and send for a doctor. Do this for me and you have a friend forever." He emphasized the word "friend."

None of this escaped the Abbot. He understood perfectly. He had heard of this young Guiliano, a brave boy well respected in Montelepre, a great shooter and hunter, manlier than his years.

Even the Friends of the Friends had their eyes on him as a possible recruit. The great Don Croce himself, on a social and business visit to the monastery, had mentioned his name to the Abbot as someone it might be profitable to cultivate.

But studying the unconscious Guiliano, he was almost sure that this man would need a grave rather than sanctuary, a priest to administer the last rites rather than a doctor. There was very little risk in granting Pisciotta's request, giving sanctuary to a corpse was not a crime even in Sicily. But he did not want to let this young man know that the favor he was about to do had such little value. He said, "And why are they searching for you?"

Pisciotta hesitated. If the Abbott knew that a policeman was dead he might refuse them sanctuary. But if he were unprepared for the search that was sure to come, he might be surprised into betraying them. He decided to tell the truth. He did so very quickly.

The Abbot lowered his eyes in sorrow for another soul lost to hell and to study closely Guiliano's unconscious form. Blood was leaking through the shirt tied around his body. Perhaps the poor lad would die as they talked, and solve the whole problem.

As a Franciscan monk, the Abbot was filled with Christian charity, but in these terrible times he had to consider the practical and material consequences of his merciful deeds. If he gave sanctuary and the boy died, he could only come out with a profit. The authorities would be satisfied with the corpse, the family would be forever in his debt. If Guiliano recovered, his gratitude might be even more valuable. A man who could, while grievously wounded, still fire his pistol and kill a policeman was a man worth having in your debt.

He could of course deliver both of these rascals to the National Police, who would then make short work of them. But what would be the profit? The authorities could do no more for him than they were doing now. The area in which they held power was already secure to him. It was on the other side of the fence he needed friends. Betraying these youngsters would only earn him enemies among the peasants and the undying hatred of two families. The Abbot was not so foolish as to think his cassock could protect him from the vendetta that would surely follow, and also he had read Pisciotta's mind; this was a young fellow who would go far before he trod the road to hell. No, the hatred of the peasant Sicilian could never be taken lightly. True Christians, they would never shame a statue of the Virgin Mary, but in the hot blood of vendetta they would shotgun the Pope himself for breaking *omerta*, the ancient code of silence to any authority. In this land with its countless statues of Jesus, there was no belief in the doctrine of turning the other cheek. In this benighted land "forgiveness" was the refuge of the coward. The Sicilian peasant did not know the meaning of mercy.

Of one thing he was sure. Pisciotta would never betray him. In one of their little smuggling deals, the Abbot had arranged for Pisciotta to be arrested and interrogated. The interrogator, a member of the Palermo Security Police, not one of the *carabinieri* blockheads, had been subtle and then blunt. But neither cunning nor cruelty had moved Pisciotta. He had remained silent. The interrogator released him and assured the Abbot that this was a lad who could be trusted with more important errands. Since then the Abbot had always held a special place in his heart for Aspanu Pisciotta and often said a prayer for his soul.

The Abbot put two fingers in his bony shrunken mouth and whistled. Monks came running and the Abbot instructed them to carry Guiliano into a far wing of the monastery, the Abbot's own special quarters where he had hidden deserters, sons of rich farmers, from the Italian Army during the war. Then he sent one of his monks for the doctor in the village of San Giuseppe Jato, only five miles away.

Pisciotta sat on the bed and held his friend's hand. The wound was no longer bleeding, and Turi Guiliano's eyes were open, but there was a glaze over them. Pisciotta, almost in tears, did not dare to speak. He wiped Guiliano's forehead, which was running with perspiration. There was a blue tinge to the skin.

It was an hour before the doctor arrived and, having observed a horde of *carabinieri* scouring the mountainside, was not surprised that his friend, the Abbot, was concealing a wounded man. This did not concern him; who cared about the police and government? The Abbot was a fellow Sicilian who needed help. And who always sent him a basket of eggs on Sunday, a barrel of wine for Christmas and a young lamb for Holy Easter.

The doctor examined Guiliano and dressed the wound. The bullet had gone through the belly and probably torn up some vital organs, certainly hit the liver. A great deal of blood had been lost, the young lad had a ghostly pallor, the skin all over his body was bluish white. Around the mouth was that circle of white the doctor knew so well as one of the first signals of death.

He sighed and said to the Abbot, "I've done all I can. The bleeding has stopped, but he's already lost more than a third of his blood, and that's usually fatal. Keep him warm, feed him a little milk and I'll leave you some morphine." He looked down at Guiliano's powerful body with regret.

Pisciotta whispered, "What can I tell his father and mother? Is there a chance for him?"

The doctor sighed. "Tell them what you like. But the wound is mortal. He's a strong-looking lad so he may live a few days more, but it's wise not to hope." He saw the look of despair in Pisciotta's eyes and the fleeting look of relief on the Abbot's face and said with ironic humor, "Of course in this holy place there could always be a miracle."

The Abbot and the doctor went out. Pisciotta leaned over his friend to wipe the sweat from his brow and was astonished that in Guiliano's eyes was a hint of mockery. The eyes were dark brown but edged with a circle of silver. Pisciotta leaned closer. Turi Guiliano was whispering; it was a struggle for him to speak.

"Tell my mother I will come home," Turi said. And then he did something Pisciotta would never forget in the years to follow. His hands came up suddenly and grabbed Pisciotta by the hair of his head. The hands were powerful; they could never be the hands of a dying man. They yanked Pisciotta's head down close. "Obey me," Guiliano said.

■ ■ ■

THE MORNING after Guiliano's parents called him, Hector Adonis arrived in Montelepre. He rarely used his house in Montelepre. He hated the place of his birth in his young manhood. He especially avoided the Festa. The decorations always distressed him, their brightness seemed to him some evil disguise for the poverty of the town. And he had always endured humiliations during the Festa—drunken men jeering at his short stature, women giving him amused contemptuous smiles.

It did not help that he knew so much more than they did. They were so proud, for instance, that every family painted its house the same color their fathers had. They didn't know that the color of the houses gave away their origins, the blood they had inherited from their ancestors along with their houses. That centuries ago the Normans had painted their houses white, the Greeks always used blue, the Arabs various pinks and red. And the Jews used yellow. Now they all considered themselves Italian and Sicilian. The blood had become so intermingled in a thousand years that you could not identify the owner of a house by his features, and if you told the owner of a yellow house that he had Jewish ancestors you could get a knife in your belly.

Aspanu Pisciotta lived in a white house though he looked more like an Arab. The Guilianos' was predominantly Grecian blue, and Turi Guiliano's face was truly Greek, though he had the body of the lusty large-boned Normans. But apparently all that blood had boiled together into something strange and dangerous to make the true Sicilian, and that was what had brought Adonis to Montelepre today.

The Via Bella was straddled at each corner by a pair of *carabinieri*, grim faced, holding rifles and machine pistols at the ready. The second day of the Festa was beginning but this part of town was curiously deserted and there were no children on the street. Hector Adonis parked his car in front of the Guiliano house, up on the strip of sidewalk. A pair of *carabinieri* watched him suspiciously until he got out of the car, then smiled with amusement at his short stature.

It was Pisciotta who opened the door and led him inside. Guiliano's mother and father were in the kitchen waiting, a breakfast of cold sausage, bread and coffee on the table. Maria Lombardo was calm, reassured by her beloved Aspanu that her son would recover. She was more angry than fearful. Guiliano's father looked more proud than sad. His son had proved himself a man; he was alive and his enemy was dead.

Again Pisciotta told his story, this time with comforting humor. He made light of Guiliano's wound and very little of his own heroism in carrying Guiliano down to the monastery. But Hector Adonis knew that helping an injured man over three miles of rough terrain must have been grueling for the slightly built Pisciotta. Also, he thought Pisciotta skipped over the description of the wound too glibly. Adonis feared the worst.

"How did the *carabinieri* know enough to come here?" he asked. Pisciotta told him about Guiliano giving up his identity card.

Guiliano's mother broke out in lamentation. "Why didn't Turi let them have the cheese? Why did he fight?"

Guiliano's father said harshly to his wife, "What would you have him do? Inform on that poor farmer? He would have disgraced the family name forever."

Hector Adonis was struck by the contradiction in these remarks. He knew the mother was much stronger and more fiery than the father. Yet the mother had uttered the words of resignation, the father the words of defiance. And Pisciotta, this boy Aspanu—who would have thought he would be so brave, to rescue his comrade and bring him to safety? And now lying so coolly to the parents about the hurt their son had suffered.

Guiliano's father said, "If only he had not given up his iden-

tity card. Our friends would have sworn he was in the streets
here.''

Guiliano's mother said, ''They would have arrested him anyway.'' She began to weep. ''Now he will have to live in the
mountains.''

Hector Adonis said, ''We must make certain the Abbot does
not deliver him to the police.''

Pisciotta said impatiently, ''He will not dare. He knows I'll
hang him in his cassock.''

Adonis gave Pisciotta a long look. There was a deadly menace
in this young boy. It was not intelligent to damage the ego of a
young man, Adonis thought. The police never understood that
you can, with some impunity, insult an older man who has already been humiliated by life itself and will not take to heart the
small slights of another human being. But a young man thinks
these offenses mortal.

They were looking for help to Hector Adonis, who had helped
their son in the past. Hector said, ''If the police learn his whereabouts, the Abbot will have no choice. He is not above suspicion
himself in certain matters. I think it best, with your permission,
to ask my friend, Don Croce Malo, to intercede with the
Abbot.''

They were surprised that he knew the great Don, except for
Pisciotta, who gave him a knowing smile. Adonis said to him
sharply, ''And what are you doing here? You'll be recognized
and arrested. They have your description.''

Pisciotta said contemptuously, ''The two guards were scared
shitless. They wouldn't recognize their mothers. And I have a
dozen witnesses who will swear I was in Montelepre yesterday.''

Hector Adonis adopted his most imposing professional manner. He said to the parents, ''You must not attempt to visit your
son or tell anyone, even your dearest friends, where he is. The
police have informers and spies everywhere. Aspanu will visit
Turi at night. As soon as he can move I'll make arrangements

for him to live in another town until this all quiets down. Then, with some money, things can be arranged, and Turi can come home. Don't worry about him, Maria, guard your health. And you, Aspanu, keep me informed."

He embraced the mother and father. Maria Lombardo was still weeping when he left.

He had many things to do—most importantly to get word to Don Croce and make sure that Turi's sanctuary remained safe. Thank God the government in Rome did not offer rewards for information on the murder of a policeman, or the Abbot would have sold Turi as quickly as he sold one of his holy relics.

■ ■ ■

TURI GUILIANO lay on the bed without moving. He had heard the doctor pronounce his wound mortal, but he could not believe he was dying. His body seemed suspended in air, free of pain and fear. He could never die. He did not know that great loss of blood produces euphoria.

During the days, one of the monks tended him, fed him milk. Evenings, the Abbot came with the doctor. Pisciotta visited him in the night and held his hand and nursed him through the long evil hours of darkness. At the end of two weeks, the doctor proclaimed a miracle.

Turi Guiliano had willed his body to heal, to materialize the lost blood, to meld together the vital organs that had been torn by the steel-jacketed bullet. And in the euphoria inspired by the draining of the blood from his body he dreamed of future glory. He felt a new freedom, that he could no longer be held accountable for anything he did from this time on. That the laws of society, the stricter Sicilian laws of family, could no longer bind him. That he was free to commit any act; that his bloody wound made him innocent. And all this because a foolish *carabiniere* had shot him over a piece of cheese.

For the weeks of his convalescence, he played over and over in his mind the days he and his fellow villagers had congregated

in the town square waiting for the *gabellotti,* the overseers of
the large land estates, to pick them out for a day's work, offering
starvation wages with the contemptuous take-it-or-leave-it sneer
of men who had all the power. The unfair sharing of crops that
left everyone impoverished after a year's hard work. The overbearing hand of the law which punished the poor and let the rich
go free.

If he recovered from his wound, he swore he would see justice
done. He would never again be a powerless boy at the mercy of
fate. He would arm himself, physically and mentally. Of one
thing he was sure: He would never again stand helpless before
the world, as he had before Guido Quintana, and the policeman
who had shot him down. The young man who had been Turi
Guiliano no longer existed.

■ ■ ■

AT THE end of a month, the doctor advised another four weeks
of rest with some exercise, and so Guiliano donned a monk's
habit and strolled around the grounds of the monastery. The
Abbot had become fond of the young man, and often accompanied him, telling stories about his youthful travels to far-off
lands. The Abbot's affection was not lessened when Hector
Adonis sent him a sum of money for his prayers for the poor
and Don Croce himself advised the Abbot that he had an interest
in the young man.

As for Guiliano, he was astonished at how these monks lived.
In a countryside where people were almost starving, where laborers had to sell their sweat for fifty cents a day, the monks of
Saint Francis lived like kings. The monastery was really a huge
and rich estate.

They had a lemon orchard, a scattering of stout olive trees as
old as Christ. They had a small bamboo plantation and a butcher
shop into which they fed their flock of sheep, their pen of piglets.
Chickens and turkeys roamed at will, crowds of them. The
monks ate meat every day with their spaghetti, drank homemade

wine from their own huge cellar, and traded on the black market for tobacco, which they smoked like fiends.

But they worked hard. During the day they labored barefoot in cassocks tucked up to their knees, sweat pouring down their brows. On their tonsured heads, to protect them from the sun, they wore oddly shaped American fedoras, black and brown, which the Abbot had acquired from some military government supply officer for a cask of wine. The monks wore the fedoras in many different styles, some with the brims snapped down, gangster style, others with the brims flapped upward all around to form gutters in which they kept their cigarettes. The Abbot had come to hate these hats and had forbidden their use except when actually working in the fields.

For the second four weeks, Guiliano was a fellow monk. To the Abbot's astonishment he worked hard in the fields and helped the older monks carry the heavy baskets of fruit and olives back to the storage shed. As he grew well, Guiliano enjoyed the work, enjoyed showing off his strength. They piled his baskets high and he never let his knees buckle. The Abbot was proud of him and told him he could stay as long as he liked, that he had the makings of a true man of God.

Turi Guiliano was happy that four weeks. He had after all returned from the dead in body and in his head he was weaving daydreams and miracles. And he enjoyed the old Abbot, who treated him with absolute trust and revealed the secrets of the monastery to him. The old man boasted that all the products of the monastery were sold directly on the black market, not turned over to the government warehouses. Except for the wine, which was swilled down by the monks themselves. At night there was a great deal of gambling and drunkenness, and even women were smuggled in, but to all this the Abbot closed his eyes. "These are hard times," he said to Guiliano. "The promised reward of heaven is too far away, men must have some pleasure now. God will forgive them."

One rainy afternoon, the Abbot showed Turi another wing of

the monastery which was used as a warehouse. This was over-
flowing with holy relics manufactured by a skilled team of old
monks. The Abbot, like any shopkeeper, bewailed hard times.
"Before the war, we had a very good business," he sighed.
"This warehouse was never more than half full. And just look
what sacred treasures we have here. A bone from the fish multiplied by Christ. The staff carried by Moses on his way to the
Promised Land." He paused to watch Guiliano's astonished
face with amused satisfaction. Then his bony face contorted into
a wicked grin. Kicking a huge pile of wooden sticks, he said
almost gleefully, "This used to be our best item. Hundreds of
pieces of the cross on which our Lord was crucified. And in this
bin are fragments of any saint you can name. There isn't a
household in Sicily that doesn't have the bone of a saint. And
locked away in a special storeroom we have thirteen arms of
Saint Andrew, three heads of John the Baptist and seven suits
of armor worn by Joan of Arc. In the winter, our monks travel
far and wide to sell these treasures."

Turi Guiliano was laughing now and the Abbot smiled at him.
But Guiliano was thinking how the poor were always deceived,
even by those who pointed the road to salvation. It was another
important fact to remember.

The Abbot showed him a huge tub full of medallions blessed
by the Cardinal of Palermo, thirty shrouds that Jesus wore when
he died, and two black Virgin Marys. That stopped Turi Guiliano's laughter. He told the Abbot about the black Virgin statue
owned by his mother and so treasured by her since she was a
little girl; that it had been in her family for generations. Could it
possibly be a forgery? The Abbot patted him kindly on the
shoulder and told him the monastery had been making replicas
for over a hundred years carved from good olive wood. But he
assured Guiliano that even the replicas had value, since only a
few were made.

The Abbot saw no harm confiding in a murderer such venial
sins of holy men. Still Guiliano's disapproving silence disturbed

the Abbot. Defensively, he said, "Remember that we men who
devote our lives to God must also live in the material world of
men who do not believe in waiting for their rewards in heaven.
We too have families and must aid and protect them. Many of
our monks are poor and come from the poor, who we know are
the salt of the earth. We cannot permit our sisters and brothers,
our nephews and cousins to starve in these hard times. The Holy
Church itself needs our help, must defend itself against powerful
enemies. The Communists and Socialists, those misguided liberals, must be fought against, and that takes money. What a
comfort to Mother Church are the faithful! Their need for our
holy relics supplies the money to crush the infidels and fills a
need in their own souls. If we did not supply them they would
waste their money on gambling and wine and shameful women.
Don't you agree?"

Guiliano nodded, but he was smiling. It was dazzling for one
so young to meet such a master of hypocrisy. The Abbot was
irritated by that smile; he had expected a more gracious response from a murderer to whom he had given sanctuary and
nursed back from the gate of death. Grateful respect dictated a
properly hypocritical response of the utmost sincerity. This
smuggler, this murderer, this *peasant*, Master Turi Guiliano,
should show himself more understanding, more a Christian. The
Abbot said sternly, "Remember our true faith rests on our belief
in miracles."

"Yes," Guiliano said. "And I know with all my heart that it
is your duty to help us find them." He said it without malice, in
a spirit of fun, with a sincere good will to please his benefactor.
But it was all he could do to keep from laughing outright.

The Abbot was pleased and all his affection returned. This
was a fine fellow, he had enjoyed his company the past few
months, and it was comforting to know that the man was deeply
in his debt. And he would not be ungrateful; he had already
shown a noble heart. He expressed in word and deed, every
day, his respect and gratitude to the Abbot. He did not have the

hard heart of an outlaw. What would happen to such a man in this present-day Sicily, full of informers, poverty, bandits, and sundry sinners? Ah, well, the Abbot thought, a man who has murdered once can do it again, in a pinch. The Abbot decided that Don Croce should counsel Turi Guiliano on the right path to life.

One day, while resting on his bed, Turi Guiliano had a strange visitor. The Abbot presented him as Father Benjamino Malo, a very dear friend, then left them alone together.

Father Benjamino said solicitously, "My dear young man, I hope you have recovered from your wound. The Holy Abbot tells me it was truly a miracle."

Guiliano said politely, "God's mercy." And Father Benjamino bowed his head as if he himself had received that benediction.

Guiliano studied him. This was a priest who had never labored in the fields. His cassock was too clean at the hem, his face too puffily white, his hands too soft. But the countenance was holy enough; it was meek and had a Christlike resignation, a Christian humility.

The voice too was soft and gentle when Father Benjamino said, "My son, I will hear your confession and give you Holy Communion. Shriven of sin, you can go out into the world with a pure heart."

Turi Guiliano studied this priest who wielded such sublime power. "Forgive me, Father," he said. "I am not yet in a state of contrition and it would be false of me to make a confession at this time. But thank you for your blessing."

The priest nodded and said, "Yes, that would compound your sins. But I have another offer that is perhaps more practical in this world. My brother, Don Croce, has sent me to ask if you would like to take refuge with him in Villaba. You would be paid a good wage, and of course, as you must know, the authorities would never dare molest you while you are under his protection."

Guiliano was astonished that word of his deed had reached such a man as Don Croce. He knew he had to be careful. He detested the Mafia, and did not wish to be caught in their web.

"This is a very great honor," he said. "I thank you and your brother. But I must consult with my family, I must honor the wishes of my parents. So for now permit me to refuse your kind offer."

He saw the priest was surprised. Who in Sicily would refuse the protection of the great Don? So he added, "Perhaps in a few weeks, I will think differently and come to see you in Villaba."

Father Benjamino had recovered. He raised his hands in benediction. "Go with God, my son," he said. "You will always be welcome in my brother's house." He made the sign of the cross and left.

■ ■ ■

TURI GUILIANO knew it was time to leave. When Aspanu Pisciotta came to visit that evening Guiliano instructed him on what preparations to make for his return to the outside world. He saw that as he had changed, so had his friend. Pisciotta did not flinch or make any protest at receiving orders that he knew would profoundly alter his life. Finally Guiliano told him, "Aspanu, you can come with me or you can remain with your family. Do what you feel you must do."

Pisciotta smiled. "Do you think I'm going to let you have all the fun and glory? Let you play in the mountains while I bring donkeys out to work and pick olives? And what about our friendship? Am I to let you live in the mountains alone when we have played and worked together since we were children? Only when you return to Montelepre in freedom will I return there too. So no more foolish talk. I'll come to get you in four days. It will take a little time to do all you want me to do."

■ ■ ■

PISCIOTTA WAS busy those four days. He had already tracked down the smuggler on horseback who had offered to go after the wounded Guiliano. His name was Marcuzzi, and he was a feared man and a large-scale smuggler operating under the protection of Don Croce and Guido Quintana. He had an uncle of the same name who was a great Mafia chief.

Pisciotta discovered that Marcuzzi made regular trips from Montelepre to Castellammare. Pisciotta knew the farmer who kept the smuggler's mules, and when he saw the animals taken out of the fields and brought to a barn near the town, he gambled that Marcuzzi was making a trip the next day. At dawn Pisciotta stationed himself along the road that he knew Marcuzzi had to take, and waited for him. He had a *lupara*, which many Sicilian families owned as part of their household equipment. Indeed, the deadly Sicilian shotgun was so common and so often used for assassination that when Mussolini cleaned out the Mafia, he had ordered all stone walls to be knocked down to at most three feet in height so that murderers could not use the walls as ambush points.

He had decided to kill Marcuzzi not only because the smuggler had offered to help the police kill the wounded Guiliano, but because he had also boasted of it to his friends. By killing the smuggler he would give warning to any others who might betray Guiliano. Also he needed the weapons he knew Marcuzzi carried.

He did not have to wait long. Because Marcuzzi was leading empty mules to pick up black market goods in Castellammare, he was careless. He rode his lead mule down a mountain trail with his rifle slung over his shoulder, instead of at the ready. When he saw Pisciotta standing in the trail in front of him, he was not alarmed. All he saw was a short slender boy with a thin dandyish mustache who was smiling in a way that irritated him. It was only when Pisciotta swung the *lupara* out from beneath his jacket that Marcuzzi paid full attention.

He said gruffly, "You've got me going the wrong way. I haven't picked up my goods yet. And these mules are under the protection of the Friends of the Friends. Be clever and find yourself another customer."

Pisciotta said softly, "I only want your life." He smiled cruelly. "There was a day you wanted to be a hero for the police. Just a few months ago, do you remember?"

Marcuzzi remembered. He turned the mule sideways, as if by accident, to shield his hand from Pisciotta's gaze. He slid his hand into his belt and drew his pistol. At the same time he yanked on the mule's bridle to bring himself around in a shooting position. The last thing he saw was Pisciotta's smile as the *lupara* blasted his body out of the saddle and flung it into the dust.

With grim satisfaction Pisciotta stood over the body and fired another blast into the head, then took the pistol still in Marcuzzi's hand and the rifle wrapped on the body by its sling. He emptied the man's jacket pocket of rifle bullets and put them into his own. Then quickly and methodically he shot each of the four mules, a warning to anyone who might help the enemies of Guiliano, even indirectly. He stood on the road, his *lupara* in his arms, the dead man's rifle slung over his shoulder, the pistol in his waistband. He felt no sense of pity and his ferocity pleased him. For despite his love for his friend they had always striven against each other in many ways. And though he acknowledged Turi as his chief, he always felt he had to prove his claim to their friendship by being as courageous and as clever. Now he too had stepped out of the magic circle of boyhood, of society, and joined Turi on the outside of that circle. With this act he had bound himself forever to Turi Guiliano.

■ ■ ■

TWO DAYS later, just before the evening meal, Guiliano left the monastery. He embraced all of the monks as they gathered in the eating hall and thanked them for their kindnesses. The monks were sorry to see him go. True, he had never attended their religious rites, and had not made a confession and act of contrition for the murder he had committed, but some of these monks had started their manhood with similar crimes and were not judgmental.

The Abbot escorted Guiliano to the gate of the monastery where Pisciotta was waiting. He presented him with a going-away gift. It was a statue of the black Virgin Mary, a duplicate of the one owned by Maria Lombardo, Guiliano's mother. Pisciotta had an American green duffel bag and Guiliano put the black Virgin statuette into it.

Pisciotta watched with a sardonic eye as the Abbot and Guiliano said their goodbyes. He knew the Abbot to be a smuggler, a secret member of the Friends of the Friends, and a slave-driving taskmaster with his poor monks. So he could not understand the sentimentality of the Abbot's farewell. It did not occur to Pisciotta that the love and affection and respect that Guiliano inspired in him he could also inspire in as powerful and as old a man as the Abbot.

Though the Abbot's affection was genuine, it was tinged with self-interest. He knew this boy might one day become a force to reckon with in Sicily. It was like spotting the trace of godliness. As for Turi Guiliano, he was genuinely grateful. The Abbot had saved his life, but more than that, had instructed him in many things and had been a delightful companion. The Abbot had even let him have the use of his library. Curiously, Guiliano had affection for the Abbot's chicanery; it seemed to him a nice balance to strike in life, the doing of good without doing great visible harm, the balancing of power to make life go smoothly.

The Abbot and Turi Guiliano embraced each other. Turi said, "I am in your debt. Remember me when you need help of any kind. Whatever you ask, I must do."

The Abbot patted his shoulder. "Christian charity does not require repayment," he said. "Return to the ways of God, my son, and pay his tribute." But he was speaking by rote. He knew well this kind of innocence in the young. Out of it a devil could rise in flames to do his bidding. He would remember Guiliano's promise.

Guiliano shouldered the duffel bag despite Pisciotta's protest, and they walked through the monastery gate together. They never looked back.

CHAPTER

6

FROM A jutting cliff edge near the top of Monte d'Ora, Guiliano and Pisciotta could look down on the town of Montelepre. Only a few miles below them, the house lights were coming on to fight the falling darkness. Guiliano even imagined he could hear the music coming from the loudspeakers in the square, which always played Rome radio station broadcasts to serenade the town's strollers before their evening meal.

But the mountain air was deceiving. It would take two hours to make his way down to the town and four hours to get back up. Guiliano and Pisciotta had played here as children; they knew every rock on this mountain and every cave and every tunnel. Further back on this cliff was the Grotta Bianca, the favorite cave of their childhood, bigger than any house in Montelepre.

Aspanu had followed his orders well, Turi Guiliano thought. The cave was stocked with sleeping bags, cooking pans, boxes of ammunition and sacks of food and bread. There was a wooden box holding flashlights, lanterns and knives, and there were also some cans of kerosene. He laughed. "Aspanu, we can live up here forever."

"For a few days," Aspanu said. "This is the first place the *carabinieri* came when they went looking for you."

"The cowards only look in daylight," Turi answered. "We are safe at night."

A great cloak of darkness had fallen over the mountains, but the sky was so full of stars that they could see each other clearly. Pisciotta opened the duffel bag and started pulling out weapons and clothes. Slowly and ceremonially, Turi Guiliano armed himself. Taking off his monk's cassock, he donned the moleskin trousers, then the huge sheepskin jacket with its many pockets. He put two pistols in his waistband and strapped the machine pistol inside the jacket so it could be covered and yet swung into action immediately. He buckled an ammunition belt around his waist and put extra boxes of bullets in the jacket pockets. Pisciotta handed him a knife, which he put in the army boots he had drawn on. Then another small pistol, which fit into a string holster tied into the inside of the collar flap of the sheepskin jacket. He checked all the guns and ammunition carefully.

The rifle he carried openly, its sling over his shoulder. Finally he was ready. He smiled at Pisciotta, who carried only a *lupara* out in the open and his knife in a holster at his back. Pisciotta said, "I feel naked. Can you walk with all that iron on your body? If you fall down I'll never be able to lift you up."

Guiliano was still smiling, the secret smile of a child who believes he has the world at bay. The huge scar on his body ached with the weight of the weapons and ammunition, but he welcomed that ache. It gave him absolution. "I'm ready to see my family or meet my enemies," he said to Pisciotta. The two young men started down the long winding path from the top of Monte d'Ora to the town of Montelepre below.

They walked below a vault of stars. Armed against death and his fellow man, drinking in the smell of far-off lemon orchards and wild flowers, Turi Guiliano felt a serenity he had never known. He was no longer helpless against some random foe. He no longer had to entertain the enemy within himself that doubted his courage. If he had willed himself not to die, had willed his torn body to knit together, he now believed that he could make his body do this over and over again. He no longer doubted that he had some magnificent destiny before him. He shared the magic of those medieval heroes who could not die until they came to the end of their long story, until they had achieved their great victories.

He would never leave these mountains, these olive trees, this Sicily. He had only a vague idea of what his future glory would be, but he never doubted that glory. He would never again be a poor peasant youth going in fear of the *carabinieri*, the judges, the pulverizing corruption of law.

They were coming down out of the mountains now and onto the roads that lead to Montelepre. They passed a padlocked roadside shrine of the Virgin Mary and child, the blue plaster robes shining like the sea in moonlight. The smell of the orchards filled the air with a sweetness that made Guiliano almost dizzy. He saw Pisciotta stoop and pick a prickly pear made sweet by the night air, and he felt a love for this friend who had saved his life, a love with its root in their childhood spent together. He wanted to share his immortality with him. It was never their fate to die two nameless peasants on a mountainside in Sicily. In a great exuberance of spirit Guiliano called out, "Aspanu, Aspanu, I believe, I believe," and started running down the final slope of the mountain, out of the ghostly white rocks, past the holy shrines of Christ and martyred saints standing in padlocked boxes. Pisciotta ran beside him, laughing, and they raced together into the arc of moonlight that showered the road to Montelepre.

■ ■ ■

THE MOUNTAINS ended in a hundred yards of green pasture that led to the back walls formed by the houses on the Via Bella. Behind these walls, each house had its garden of tomatoes, and some, a lonely olive or lemon tree. The gate to the Guiliano garden fence was unlocked, and the two young men slipped through quietly and found Guiliano's mother waiting for them. She rushed into Turi Guiliano's arms, the tears streaming down her face. She kissed him fiercely and whispered, "My beloved son, my beloved son," and Turi Guiliano found himself standing in the moonlight not responding to her love for the first time in his life.

It was now nearly midnight, the moon still bright, and they hurried into the house to escape observation by spies. The windows were shuttered, and relatives of the Guiliano and Pisciotta families had been posted along all the streets to warn of police patrols. In the house Guiliano's friends and family waited to celebrate his homecoming. A feast worthy of Holy Easter had been laid out. They had this one night with him before Turi went to live in the mountains.

Guiliano's father embraced him and slapped him on the back to show his approval. His two sisters were there, and Hector Adonis. Also there was a neighbor, a woman called La Venera. She was a widow of about thirty-five. Her husband had been a famous bandit named Candeleria, who had been betrayed, then ambushed by the police, only a year ago. She had become a close friend of Guiliano's mother, but Turi was surprised that she was present at this reunion. Only his mother could have invited her. For a moment he wondered why.

They ate and drank and treated Turi Guiliano as if he had returned from a long holiday in foreign countries. But then his father wanted to see his wound. Guiliano lifted his shirt out of his trousers and revealed the great flaming scar, the tissue around it still blue-black from the trauma of the gunshot. His mother broke into lamentations. Guiliano said to her with a smile, "Would you rather have seen me in prison with the marks of the *bastinado?*"

Though the familiar scene duplicated the happiest days of his childhood, he felt a great distance from them all. There were all his favorite dishes, the inky squid, the fat macaroni with its herbed sauce of tomato, the roasted lamb, the great bowl of olives, green and red salad doused with the pure first pressing of olive oil, bamboo-covered bottles of Sicilian wine. Everything from the earth of Sicily. His mother and father told their fairy tales about life in America. And Hector Adonis regaled them on the glories of the history of Sicily. Of Garibaldi and his famous Redshirts. Of the day of the Sicilian Vespers, when the people of Sicily had risen to slaughter the French occupying army so many hundreds of years ago. All the tales of Sicily oppressed starting with Rome, followed by the Moors and Normans and the French and the Germans and the Spanish. Woe was Sicily! Never free, its people always hungry, their labor sold so cheap, their blood spilled so easily.

And so now there was not a Sicilian who believed in government, in law, in the structured order of society which had always been used to turn them into beasts of burden. Guiliano had listened to these stories through the years, imprinting them on his brain. But only now did Guiliano realize that he could change this.

He watched Aspanu smoking a cigarette over his coffee. Even at this joyful reunion, Aspanu had an ironic smile on his lips. Guiliano could tell what he was thinking and what he would say later: All you have to do is to be stupid enough to get shot by a policeman, commit murder, become an outlaw, and then your loved ones will show their affection and treat you like a saint from heaven. And yet Aspanu was the only one he did not feel cut off from.

And then there was the woman, La Venera. Why had his mother invited her, and why did she come? He saw that her face was still handsome, bold and strong with jet-black eyebrows and lips so dark and red that they seemed almost purple in this smoky curtained light. There was no way to tell what her figure was like, for she wore the Sicilian widow's shapeless black dress.

Turi Guiliano had to tell them the whole story of the shooting at the Four Crossroads. His father, a little drunk with wine, emitted growls of approval at the death of the policeman. His mother was silent. His father told the story of how the farmer had come looking for his donkey and his own remark to the farmer: "Stay content you have lost a donkey. I have lost a son."

Aspanu said, "A donkey looking for a donkey."

They all laughed. Guiliano's father went on: "When the farmer heard that a policeman was killed he was too afraid to make his claim, that he might be *bastinado*ed."

Turi said, "He will be repaid."

Finally Hector Adonis outlined his plans to save Turi. The family of the dead man would be paid an indemnity. Guiliano's parents would have to mortgage their little piece of land to raise the money. Adonis himself would contribute a sum. But this tactic would have to wait until feelings of anger had died down. The influence of the great Don Croce would be brought to bear on government officials and the family of the slain man. After all, it had been more or less an accident. There had been no real ill will on either side. A farce could be played out as long as the victim's family and key government officials cooperated. The only drawback was the identity card at the scene of the killing. But in a year's time Don Croce could cause that to vanish from the prosecutor's files. Most important, Turi Guiliano must remain out of trouble for that year. He must disappear into the mountains.

Turi Guiliano listened to them all patiently, smiling, nodding his head, not showing his irritation. They still thought of him as he had been at Festa time over two months ago. He had taken off his sheepskin jacket and stripped himself of arms; his guns lay at his feet beneath the table. But that had not impressed them, nor the ugly huge scar. They could not imagine how his mind had been torn apart by that great blow to his body, or that he would never again be the young man they had known.

In this house, he was for this moment safe. Trusted people patrolled the streets and watched the *carabinieri* barracks to give him warning of any attack. The house itself, built many hundreds of years ago, was made of stone; its windows had heavy wooden shutters locked and a foot thick. The wooden door was strong and iron barred. Not a chink of light could escape this house, no enemy could force his way in quickly in a surprise attack. And yet Turi Guiliano felt himself in danger.

These loved ones would trap him into his former life, persuade him to become a peasant farmer, to lay down his arms against his fellow men and leave him helpless to their laws. At that moment he knew that he would have to be cruel to those he loved most. It had always been the young man's dream to acquire love rather than power. But that was all changed. He now saw clearly that power came first.

He spoke gently to Hector Adonis and to the others. "Dear godfather, I know you speak out of affection and concern. But I can't let my mother and father lose their little bit of land to help me out of my trouble. And all of you here, don't worry so much about me. I'm a grown man who must pay for his carelessness. And I won't have anyone paying an indemnity for that *carabinieri* I shot. Remember, he tried to kill me just because I was smuggling a bit of cheese. I would never have fired at him except that I thought I was dying and wanted to even the score. But all that's past. I won't be so easy to shoot the next time."

Pisciotta said with a grin, "It's more fun in the mountains anyway."

But Guiliano's mother was not to be distracted. They could all see her panic, the fear in her burning eyes. She said desperately, "Don't become a bandit, don't rob poor people who have enough misery in their lives. Don't become an outlaw. Let La Venera tell you what kind of life her husband lived."

La Venera raised her head and looked directly at Guiliano. He was struck by the sensuality in her face, as if she were trying to attract his passion toward her. Her eyes were bold and stared at him almost in invitation. Before he had thought of her only as an older woman; now he felt her sexually.

When she spoke her voice was husky with emotion. She said, "In those same mountains you wish to go to my husband had to live like an animal. Always in fear. Always. He could not eat. He could not sleep. When we were in bed together every little noise would make him jump. We slept with guns on the floor beside the bed. But that didn't help him. When our daughter was ill, he tried to visit her, and they were waiting for him. They knew he was softhearted. He was shot down like a dog in the streets. They stood over him and laughed in my face."

Guiliano could see the grin on Pisciotta's face. The great bandit, Candeleria, softhearted? He had massacred six men as suspected informers, preyed on wealthy farmers, extorted money from poor peasants, struck terror into a whole countryside. But his wife saw him differently.

La Venera did not notice Pisciotta's smile. She went on: "I buried him and then buried my child a week later. They said it was pneumonia. But I know her heart was broken. What I remember most was when I visited him in the mountains. He was always cold and hungry, and sometimes ill. He would have given anything to return to the life of an honest peasant. But worst of all, his heart became as hard as an olive pit. He was no longer human, may he rest in peace. So, dear Turi, don't be so proud, We will help you in your misfortune, don't become what my husband was before he died."

Everyone was silent. Pisciotta was no longer smiling. Guiliano's father murmured that he would be glad to be rid of the farm; he could sleep late mornings. Hector Adonis was staring down at the tablecloth, frowning. None of them spoke.

The silence was broken by a quick tapping on the door, a signal from one of the watchers. Pisciotta went to speak to the man. When he came back he made a signal for Guiliano to arm himself. "The *carabinieri* barracks are blazing with light," he said. "And there is a police van blocking the end of the Via Bella where it enters the town square. They are getting ready to raid this house." He paused for a moment. "We must be quick with our goodbyes."

What struck everyone was the calmness with which Turi Guiliano prepared his escape. His mother rushed into his arms and as he embraced her he already had his sheepskin jacket in his hands. He said his goodbyes to the others and in the next instant seemed to be fully armed, his jacket on, his rifle slung. And yet he had not moved quickly or hurriedly. He stood there for a moment smiling at them and then said to Pisciotta, "You can stay and meet me in the mountains later, or you can come with me now." Wordlessly Pisciotta moved to the back door and opened it.

Guiliano gave his mother a final embrace, and she kissed him fiercely and said, "Hide, don't do anything rash. Let us help you." But he was already out of her arms.

Pisciotta was leading the way, across the fields to the beginning slopes of the mountains. Guiliano whistled sharply and Pisciotta stopped and let Turi catch up to him. The way was clear to the mountains, and his watchers had told him there were no police patrols in that direction. They would be safe in the Grotta Bianca after a four-hour climb. If the *carabinieri* chased them through the darkness, it would be an extraordinary act of bravery and foolishness.

Guiliano said, "Aspanu, how many men do the *carabinieri* have in their garrison?"

"Twelve," Pisciotta said. "And the Maresciallo."

Guiliano laughed. "Thirteen is an unlucky number. And why are we running away from so few?" He paused for a moment and then said, "Follow me."

He led the way back through the fields so that they entered the town of Montelepre further down the street. Then across the Via Bella so that they could watch the Guiliano house from the safety of a dark narrow alley. They crouched in the shadows waiting.

Five minutes later they could hear a jeep rattling down the Via Bella. Six *carabinieri* were crammed into it including the Maresciallo himself. Two of the men immediately went through the side street to block the back entrance. The Maresciallo and three of his men went up to the door and hammered on it. At the same time a small covered truck pulled up behind the jeep and two more *carabinieri*, rifles ready, jumped out to command the street.

Turi Guiliano watched all this with interest. The police raid was based on the assumption that the targets would never be in a position to launch a counterattack; that their only alternative would be to run from a superior force. Turi Guiliano at that moment made it a basic principle always to be in a position to counterattack when he was being hunted, no matter how great the odds, or perhaps the greater the odds the better.

This was Guiliano's first tactical operation and he was astonished at how easily he could command the situation if he chose to shed blood. True, he could not shoot at the Maresciallo and the three men at the door since the bullets might go into the house and hit his family. But he could easily slaughter the two men commanding the street and the two drivers in their vehicles. If he wished, he could do this as soon as the Maresciallo and his men were in the Guiliano house. They would not dare come out, and he and Pisciotta could make their way through the fields at their leisure. As for the police blocking the end of the street with their van, they would be too far out of the way to be a factor. They would not have the initiative to come up the street without receiving orders.

But at this point he had no desire to shed blood. It was still an intellectual maneuver. And he particularly wanted to see the Maresciallo in action, since this was the man who would be his principal opponent in the future.

At that moment the door of the house was being opened by Guiliano's father, and the Maresciallo took the old man roughly by the arm and thrust him out into the street with a shouted order to wait there.

A Maresciallo of the Italian *carabinieri* is the highest ranking noncommissioned officer of the National Police force and usually is the commander of a small town detachment. As such he is an important member of the local community and treated with the same respect as the local Mayor and priest of the parish. So he was not expecting the greeting from Guiliano's mother when she barred his way and spit on the ground in front of him to show her contempt.

He and his three men had to force their way into the house

and search it while being scathingly abused and cursed by Guiliano's mother. Everyone was taken out into the street to be questioned; the neighboring houses emptied of their women and men who also verbally abused the police.

When the search of the house proved fruitless, the Maresciallo attempted to question the inhabitants. Guiliano's father was astonished. "Do you think I would inform on my own son?" he asked the Maresciallo, and a great roar of approval came from the crowd in the streets. The Maresciallo ordered the Guiliano family back into their house.

In the shadow of their alley, Pisciotta said to Guiliano, "Lucky for them your mother doesn't have our weapons." But Turi didn't answer. The blood had rushed to his head. It took an enormous effort to control himself. The Maresciallo lashed out with his club and hit a man in the crowd who dared to protest the rough treatment of Guiliano's parents. Two other *carabinieri* began grabbing citizens of Montelepre at random and throwing them into the waiting truck, kicking and clubbing them on their way, ignoring their cries of fear and protest.

Suddenly there was one man standing alone on the street facing the *carabinieri*. He lunged at the Maresciallo. A shot rang out, and the man fell to the cobblestones. From one of the houses a woman began to scream and then she ran out and threw her body over her fallen husband. Turi Guiliano recognized her; she was an old friend of his family who always brought his mother freshly baked Easter cake.

Turi tapped Pisciotta on the shoulder and whispered, "Follow me," and started running down the narrow crooked streets toward the central square of the town, at the other end of the Via Bella.

Pisciotta yelled fiercely, "What the hell are you doing?" but then fell silent. For he suddenly knew exactly what Turi had in mind. The truck full of prisoners would have to go down the Via Bella to turn around and make its run back to the Bellampo Barracks.

As he ran down the dark parallel street, Turi Guiliano felt invisible, godlike. He knew the enemy would never dream, could never even imagine, what he was doing, that they thought he was running for safety in the mountains. He felt a wild elation. They would learn they could not raid his mother's home with impunity, they would think twice before doing it again. They could not again shoot a man in cold blood. He would make them show respect for his neighbors and his family.

He reached the far side of the square, and in the light of its single streetlamp he could see the police van blocking the entrance into the Via Bella. As if he could have been caught in such a trap. What could they have been thinking of? Was that a sample of official cleverness? He switched to another side street to bring him to the back entrance of the church that dominated the square, Pisciotta following him. Inside, they both vaulted the altar rail and then both stopped for a fraction of a second on the holy stage where long ago they had performed as altar boys and served their priest while he was giving the people of Montelepre Sunday Mass and Communion. Holding their guns at the ready they genuflected and crossed themselves clumsily; for a moment the power of the wax statues of Christ crowned with thorns, the gilded chalky blue-robed Virgin Marys, the batteries of saints blunted their lust for battle. Then they were running up the short aisle to the great oaken door that gave a field of fire to the square. And there they knelt again to prepare their weapons.

The van blocking the Via Bella backed off to let the truck with the arrested men enter the square to make its circle and go back up the street. At that moment Turi Guiliano pushed open the church door and said to Pisciotta, "Fire over their heads." At the same moment he fired his machine pistol into the blocking van, aiming at the tires and the engine. Suddenly the square flamed with light as the engine blew up and the van caught fire. The two *carabinieri* in the front seat tumbled out like loose-jointed puppets, their surprise not giving their bodies time to tighten against the shock. Beside him Pisciotta was firing his rifle at the cab of the truck holding the prisoners. Turi Guiliano saw the driver leap out and fall still. The other armed *carabinieri* jumped out and Pisciotta fired again. The second policeman went down. Turi turned to Pisciotta to reproach him but suddenly the stained glass windows of the church shattered with machine gun fire and the colored bits scattered on the church floor like rubies. Turi realized that there was no longer any possibility of mercy. That Aspanu was right. They must kill or be killed.

Guiliano pulled Pisciotta's arm and ran back through the church and out the back door and through the dark crooked streets of Montelepre. He knew that tonight there was no hope of helping the prisoners to escape. They slipped through the final wall of the town over the open fields and kept running until they were safely into the rising slopes covered with huge white stones. Dawn was breaking when they reached the top of Monte d'Ora in the Cammarata Mountains.

Over a thousand years ago Spartacus had hidden his slave army here and led them out to fight the Roman legions. Standing on the top of this Monte d'Ora watching the sun come radiantly alive, Turi Guiliano was filled with youthful glee that he had escaped his enemies. He would never obey a fellow human being again. He would choose who should live and who should die, and there was no doubt in his mind that all he would do would be for the glory and freedom of Sicily, for good and not for evil. That he would only strike for the cause of justice, to help the poor. That he would win every battle, that he would win the love of the oppressed.

He was twenty years old.

CHAPTER

7

DON CROCE MALO was born in the village of Villaba, a little mudhole he was to make prosperous and famous all through Sicily. It was not ironic, to Sicilians, that he sprang from a religious family who groomed him for priesthood in the Holy Catholic Church, that his first name had originally been Crocefisso, a religious name given only by the most pious parents. Indeed, as a slender youth he was forced to play the part of Christ in those religious plays put on in celebration of Holy Easter and was acclaimed for his marvelous air of piety.

But when he grew to manhood at the turn of the century, it was clear that Croce Malo had difficulty accepting any authority other than himself. He smuggled, he extorted, he stole, and finally, worst of all, he impregnated a young girl of the village, an innocent Magdalene in the plays. He then refused to marry her, claiming they had both been carried away with the religious fervor of the play, and therefore he should be forgiven.

The girl's family found this explanation too subtle to accept and demanded matrimony or death. Croce Malo was too proud to marry a girl so dishonored and fled to the mountains. After a year as a bandit, he had the good fortune to make contact with the Mafia.

"Mafia," in Arabic, means a place of sanctuary, and the word took its place in the Sicilian language when the Saracens ruled

the country in the tenth century. Throughout history, the people
of Sicily were oppressed mercilessly by the Romans, the Papacy, the Normans, the French, the Germans, and the Spanish.
Their governments enslaved the poor working class, exploiting
their labor, raping their women, murdering their leaders. Even
the rich did not escape. The Spanish Inquisition of the Holy
Catholic Church stripped them of their wealth for being heretics.
And so the "Mafia" sprang up as a secret society of avengers.
When the royal courts refused to take action against a Norman
noble who raped a farmer's wife, a band of peasants assassinated him. When a police chief tortured some petty thief with
the dreaded *cassetta,* that police chief was killed. Gradually the
strongest-willed of the peasants and the poor formed themselves
into an organized society which had the support of the people
and in effect became a second and more powerful government.
When there was a wrong to be redressed, no one ever went to
the official police, they went to the leader of the local Mafia,
who mediated the problem.

The greatest crime a Sicilian could commit was to give any
information of any kind to the authorities about anything done
by the Mafia. They kept silent. And this silence came to be
called *omerta.* Over the centuries the practice enlarged to never
giving the police information about a crime committed even
against oneself. All communications broke down between the
people and the law enforcement agencies of reigning governments so that even a small child was taught not to give a stranger
the simplest directions to a village or a person's house.

Through the centuries the Mafia governed Sicily, a presence
so shadowy and indistinct that the authorities could never quite
grasp the extent of its power. Up until World War II, the word
"Mafia" was never uttered on the island of Sicily.

■ ■ ■

FIVE YEARS after Don Croce's flight into the mountains, he was
well known as a "Qualified Man." That is, someone who could

be entrusted with the elimination of a human being without causing more than a minimal amount of trouble. He was a "Man of Respect," and after making certain arrangements, he returned to live in his native town of Villaba, some forty miles south of Palermo. These arrangements included paying an indemnity to the family of the girl he had dishonored. This was later heralded as the measure of his generosity, but it was rather the proof of his wisdom. The pregnant girl had already been shipped to relatives in America with the label of a young widow to hide her shame, but her family still remembered. They were, after all, Sicilian. Don Croce, a skilled murderer, a brutal extorter, a member of the dreaded Friends of the Friends, could not comfortably count on all this to protect him from the family that had been disgraced. It was a matter of honor, and if not for the indemnity, they would have had to kill him no matter what the consequences.

By combining generosity with prudence, Croce Malo acquired the respectful title of "Don." By the time he was forty years old he was acknowledged as the foremost of the Friends of the Friends and was called upon to adjudicate the most desperate disputes between rival *cosce* of the Mafia, to settle the most savage vendettas. He was reasonable, he was clever, he was a born diplomat, but most important of all, he did not turn faint at the sight of blood. He became known as the "Don of Peace" throughout the Sicilian Mafia, and everyone prospered; the stubborn were eliminated with judicious murders and Don Croce was a rich man. Even his brother, Benjamino, had become a secretary to the Cardinal of Palermo, but blood was thicker than holy water and he owed his first allegiance to Don Croce.

He married and became father to a little boy he adored. Don Croce, not so prudent as he was later to become, not so humble as he later learned to be under the whip of adversity, engineered a coup that made him famous all through Sicily, and an object of wonder to the highest circle of Roman society. This coup sprang from a bit of marital discord which even the greatest men in history have had to endure.

Don Croce, because of his position in the Friends of the Friends, had married into a proud family who had recently bought patents of nobility for such a huge sum that the blood in their veins turned blue. After a few years of marriage, his wife treated him with a lack of respect he knew he had to correct, though of course not in his usual fashion. His wife's blue blood had made her disenchanted with Don Croce's no-nonsense, earthy peasant ways, his practice of saying nothing if he had nothing to the point to say, his casual attire, his habit of rough command in all things. There was also the remembrance of how all her other suitors melted away when Don Croce announced his candidacy for her hand.

She did not of course show her disrespect in any obvious fashion. This was, after all, Sicily, not England or America. But the Don was an extraordinarily sensitive soul. He soon observed that his wife did not worship the ground upon which he walked, and that was proof enough of her disrespect. He became determined to win her devotion in such a way that it would last a lifetime and he could then devote his full attention to business. His supple mind wrestled with the problem and came up with a plan worthy of Machiavelli himself.

The King of Italy was coming to Sicily to visit his devoted subjects, and devoted they were. All Sicilians hated the Roman government and feared the Mafia. But they loved the monarchy because it extended their family, which consisted of blood relations, the Virgin Mary and God himself. Great festivals were prepared for the King's visit.

On his first Sunday in Sicily the King went to Mass at the great Cathedral of Palermo. He was to stand godfather to the son of one of the ancient nobles of Sicily, the Prince Ollorto. The King was already godfather to at least a hundred children, sons of field marshals, dukes and the most powerful men of the Fascist party. These were political acts to cement relationships between the crown and the executives of the government. Royal godchildren automatically became Cavaliers of the Crown and were sent the documents and sash to prove the honor given them. Also a small silver cup.

Don Croce was ready. He had three hundred people in the festival throng. His brother, Benjamino, was one of the priests officiating at the ceremony. The baby of Prince Ollorto was baptized, and his proud father came out of the cathedral holding the baby aloft in triumph. The crowd roared its approval. Prince Ollorto was one of the less hated of the gentry, a slim handsome man; looks always counted for something in Sicily.

At that moment a crowd of Don Croce's people surged into the cathedral and effectively blocked the King's exit. The King was a little man with a mustache thicker than the hair on his head. He was in the full gaudy uniform of the Cavaliers, which made him look like a toy soldier. But despite his pompous appearance he was extremely kindhearted, so when Father Benjamino thrust another swaddled infant into his arms he was bewildered but did not protest. The surging crowd had, on Don Croce's instructions, cut him off from his retinue and the officiating Cardinal of Palermo so they could not interfere. Father Benjamino hastily sprinkled holy water from a nearby font and then snatched the baby out of the King's arms and handed it to Don Croce. Don Croce's wife wept tears of happiness as she knelt before the King. He was now the godfather of their only child. She could ask no more.

■ ■ ■

DON CROCE grew fat and the bony face grew cheeks that were huge slabs of mahogany; his nose became a great beak that served as an antenna for power. His crinkly hair grew into a barbed-wire gray. His body ballooned majestically; his eyes became lidded with flesh that grew like a heavy moss over his face. His power increased with each pound until he seemed to become an impenetrable obelisk. He seemed to have no weaknesses as a man; he never showed anger, never showed greed. He was affectionate in an impersonal way but never showed love. He was conscious of his grave responsibilities and so never voiced his fears in his wife's bed or on her breast. He was the true King of Sicily. But his son—the heir apparent—was struck with the strange disease of religious social reform and had emigrated to Brazil to educate and uplift savage Indians along the Amazon. The Don was so shamed he never uttered his son's name again.

At the beginning of Mussolini's rise to power, Don Croce was not impressed. He had observed him carefully and had come to the conclusion that the man had neither cunning nor courage. And if such a one could rule Italy then it followed that he, Don Croce, could rule Sicily.

But then calamity fell. After a few years in power Mussolini turned his baleful eye on Sicily and the Mafia. He recognized that this was not a raggedy set of criminals but a true inner government that controlled a part of his empire. And he recognized that all through history the Mafia had conspired against whatever government ruled in Rome. Rulers of Sicily for the last thousand years had tried and failed. Now the Dictator vowed to strike them down forever. The Fascists did not believe in democracy, the legal rule of society. They did what they pleased for what they regarded as the good of the state. In short, they used the methods of Don Croce Malo.

Mussolini sent his most trusted Minister, Cesare Mori, to Sicily as a Prefect with unlimited powers. Mori started by suspending the rule of all judicial courts in Sicily and bypassing all legal safeguards of Sicilians. He flooded Sicily with troops who were ordered to shoot and ask questions later. He arrested and deported entire villages.

Before the dictatorship, Italy had had no capital punishment, which left it at a disadvantage against the Mafia, which used death as its chief enforcing tool. All this changed under the Prefect Mori. Proud Mafiosi, who adhered to the law of *omerta*, resisting even the dreaded *cassetta*, were shot. So-called conspirators were exiled to small isolated islands in the Mediterranean. In a year the island of Sicily was decimated, the Mafia destroyed as a governing force. It was of no consequence to Rome that thousands of innocent people were caught up in this wide net and suffered with the guilty.

■ ■ ■

DON CROCE loved the fair rules of democracy and was outraged by the actions of the *Fascisti*. Friends and colleagues were jailed on trumped-up charges, since they were far too clever to leave evidence of their crimes. Many were imprisoned on hearsay, secret information from scoundrels who could not be tracked down and reasoned with, because they did not have to appear in open court and testify. Where was judicial fair play? The Fascists had gone back to the days of the Inquisition, of the divine right of kings. Don Croce had never believed in the divine right of kings, indeed he asserted that no reasonable human being had ever believed in it except when the alternative was being torn apart by four wild horses.

Even worse, the Fascists had brought back the *cassetta,* that medieval instrument of torture—a terrible box three feet long, two feet wide, which worked wonders on stubborn bodies. Even the most determined Mafioso found his tongue as loose as the morals of an Englishwoman when subject to the *cassetta.* Don Croce indignantly boasted that he had never used torture of any kind. Simple murder sufficed.

Like a stately whale, Don Croce submerged himself in the murky waters of the Sicilian underground. He entered a monastery as a pseudo Franciscan monk, under Abbot Manfredi's protection. They had had a long and pleasurable association. The Don, though proud of his illiteracy, had been obliged to employ the Abbot to write necessary ransom letters when early in his career he had followed the trade of kidnapping. They had always been honest with each other. They found they had common tastes—loose women, good wine and complex thievery. The

Don had often taken the Abbot on trips to Switzerland to visit his doctors and sample the placid luxuries of that country. A restful and pleasant change from the more dangerous pleasures of Sicily.

When World War II started, Mussolini could no longer give Sicily his closest attention. Don Croce immediately took this opportunity to very quietly build up lines of communication with the remaining Friends of the Friends, sending messages of hope to the old Mafia stalwarts who had been exiled on the tiny islands of Pantelleria and Stromboli. He befriended the families of those Mafia leaders who had been imprisoned by the Prefect Mori.

Don Croce knew his only hope, ultimately, was an Allied victory, and that he must exert all his efforts to that end. He made contact with underground partisan groups and gave orders to his men to aid any Allied pilots who survived being shot down. And so, at the crucial hour, Don Croce was prepared.

When the American Army invaded Sicily in July of 1943, Don Croce extended his helping hand. Were there not many fellow Sicilians in this invading army, the sons of immigrants? Should Sicilian fight against Sicilian for the sake of the Germans? Don Croce's men persuaded thousands of Italian soldiers to desert and retire to a hiding place prepared for them by the Mafia. Don Croce personally made contact with secret agents of the American Army and led the attacking forces through mountain passages so that they could outflank the entrenched German heavy guns. And so while the British invading force on the other side of the island met with huge casualties and could only advance slowly, the American Army accomplished its mission far ahead of schedule and with very little loss of life.

Don Croce himself, though now almost sixty-five years of age and enormously heavy, led a band of Mafioso partisans into the city of Palermo and kidnapped the German general commanding its defense. He hid with his prisoner in the city until the front was broken and the American Army marched in. The American

Supreme Commander of southern Italy referred to Don Croce in his dispatches to Washington as "General Mafia." And so he was known by American staff officers in the months that followed.

■ ■ ■

THE AMERICAN Military Governor of Sicily was a Colonel Alfonso La Ponto. As a high-ranking politician in the state of New Jersey, he had received a direct commission and had been trained for this particular job. His greatest assets were his affability and knowing how to put together a political deal. His staff officers in military government had been chosen for similar qualifications. The headquarters of AMGOT consisted of twenty officers and fifty enlisted men. Many of them were of Italian extraction. Don Croce took all of them to his bosom with the sincere love of a blood brother, showing them every mark of devotion and affection. This despite the fact that with his friends he often referred to them as our "Lambs in Christ."

But Don Croce had "delivered the goods," as the Americans often said. Colonel La Ponto made Don Croce his chief adviser and boon companion. The Colonel came often to dine at his house and groaned with pleasure eating the familiar cooking.

The first problem to be solved was appointing new mayors for all the small towns in Sicily. The former mayors had been Fascists, of course, and had been thrown into American prisons.

Don Croce recommended Mafia leaders who had been imprisoned. Since their records clearly showed that they had been tortured and jailed by the Fascist government for resistance to the aims and welfare of the state, it was assumed that the crimes of which they were accused were trumped-up charges. Don Croce, over his wife's superb fish and spaghetti dishes, told beautiful stories about how his friends, murderers and thieves all, had refused to surrender their beliefs in the democratic principles of justice and freedom. The Colonel was delighted at finding so quickly the ideal people to run the civilian population under his direction. Within a month most of the towns in Western Sicily had as their mayors a set of the most diehard Mafiosi to be found in Fascist prisons.

And they functioned superbly for the American Army. Only a minimum of Occupation troops had to be left behind to preserve order over the conquered people. As the war continued on the mainland, there was no sabotage behind American lines, no spies roamed. Black-marketing by the common people was held to a minimum. The Colonel received a special medal and promotion to Brigadier General.

Don Croce's Mafia mayors enforced the smuggling laws with the utmost severity and the *carabinieri* patrolled the roads and mountain bypasses ceaselessly. It was like old times. Don Croce gave orders to both. Government inspectors made sure that stubborn farmers turned in their grain and olives and grapes to government warehouses at officially set prices—these, of course, to be rationed out to the people of Sicily. To ensure this, Don Croce requested and received the loan of American Army trucks to transport these foodstuffs to the starving cities of Palermo, Monreale, and Trapani, to Syracuse and Catania, and even to Naples on the mainland. The Americans marveled at Don Croce's efficiency and awarded him written commendations for his services to the armed forces of the United States.

But Don Croce could not eat these commendations, he could not even read them for his pleasure, as he was illiterate. The backslappings of Colonel La Ponto did not fill his enormous belly. Don Croce, not trusting to the gratitude of the Americans or the blessings given by God for virtue, was determined that his many good works in the service of humanity and democracy be rewarded. So these cram-filled American trucks, their drivers armed with official road passes signed by the Colonel, rolled to quite different destinations designated by Don Croce. They unloaded at the Don's own personal warehouses located in small towns like Montelepre, Villaba and Partinico. Then Don Croce and his colleagues sold them for fifty times their official prices on the flourishing black market. So he cemented his relationships with the most powerful leaders of the resurgent Mafia. For Don Croce believed that greediness was the greatest of all human failings, and he shared his profits freely.

He was more than generous. Colonel La Ponto received magnificent presents of antique statues, paintings and ancient jewelry. It was the Don's pleasure. The officers and men of the American Military Government detachment were like sons to him, and like any doting father he showered them with gifts. These men, specially chosen for their understanding of Italian character and culture, since many of them were of Sicilian origin, returned his love. They signed special travel passes, they maintained the trucks assigned to Don Croce with particular care. They went to his parties where they met good Sicilian girls and became entwined in the loving warmth which is the other side of the Sicilian character. Taken into these Sicilian families, fed the familiar food of their emigrant mothers, many of them wooed Mafioso daughters.

Don Croce Malo had everything in position to resume his former power. Mafia chiefs all over Sicily were in his debt. He controlled the artesian wells that sold water to the population of the island at prices that would give him a good profit. He created the monopolies on foodstuffs; he levied a tax on every market stall that sold fruit, every butcher shop that sold meat, the cafés with their coffee bars, and even the strolling bands of musicians. Since the only source of gasoline was the American Army, he controlled that also. He furnished overseers to the huge estates of the nobility, and in time planned to buy their lands at cheap prices. He was on the road to establishing the kind of power he wielded before Mussolini took over Italy. He was determined to become rich again. In the coming years he would, as the saying goes, put Sicily through his olive press.

Only one thing truly troubled Don Croce. His only son had gone mad with the eccentric desire to do good deeds. His brother, Father Benjamino, could have no family. The Don had no one of his blood to whom to bequeath his empire. He had no trusted warrior chieftain, young and tied by blood, to be a mailed fist when his velvet glove proved unpersuasive.

The Don's people had already marked young Salvatore Guiliano, and the Abbot Manfredi had confirmed his potential. Now more legends of this young boy's exploits were sweeping Sicily. The Don smelled an answer to his only problem.

CHAPTER

8

THE MORNING after their escape from Montelepre, Turi Guiliano and Aspanu Pisciotta bathed in a swift-running stream behind their cave on Monte d'Ora. They took their guns to the edge of the cliff and spread out a blanket to enjoy the pink-streaked dawn.

The Grotta Bianca was a long cave that ended in a mass of boulders that reached to the ceiling, or almost. When they were little boys Turi and Aspanu had managed to squeeze over those boulders and discover a passage that ran right through to the other side of the mountain. It had existed before Christ, dug by the army of Spartacus, hiding from Roman legions.

Far below, tiny as a toy village, lay Montelepre. The many paths that led to their cliff were thin chalky worms which clung to the sides of the mountains. One by one the gray stone houses of Montelepre were turned to gold by the rising sun.

The morning air was clear, the prickly pears on the ground were cool and sweet and Turi picked one up and bit into it carefully to freshen his mouth. In a few hours the heat of the sun would turn them into juiceless cottony balls. Gecko lizards, with huge balloonlike heads on tiny insect legs, crawled over his hand, but they were harmless despite their obscenely frightening appearance. He flicked them aside.

While Aspanu cleaned the guns, Turi watched the town

below. His naked eye picked out tiny black dots, people going into the countryside to work their little pieces of land. He tried to locate his own house. Long ago he and Aspanu had flown the flags of Sicily and America from that roof. Gleefully cunning children, they had accepted praise as patriots, but the real reason was to keep the house under observation while they roamed the tops of the nearby mountains—a reassuring link to the adult world.

Suddenly he remembered something that had happened ten years ago. The Fascist officials of the village had ordered them to take down the American flag from the Guiliano roof. The two boys had been so enraged that they had taken down both flags, the American and the Sicilian. Then they had taken the flags to their secret hideout, the Grotta Bianca, and buried the flags near the wall of boulders.

Guiliano said to Pisciotta, "Keep an eye on those trails," and went into the cave. Even after ten years, Guiliano remembered exactly where they had buried the flags, in the right-hand corner where the boulders met the earth. They had dug in the dirt underneath the boulder, then packed the earth back over it.

A mat of thin, slimy, green-black moss had grown over the spot. Guiliano dug into it with his boot and then used a small stone as a pick. In a matter of minutes the flags were uncovered. The American flag was a slimy mess of rags, but they had wrapped the Sicilian flag inside the American one, and the shielded one had survived. Guiliano flipped it open, the scarlet and gold colors as bold as when he was a child. There was not even a hole in it. He brought it outside and said to Pisciotta, laughing, "Do you remember this, Aspanu?"

Pisciotta stared at the flag. Then he too laughed, but in a more excited way. "It's fate," he shouted and jumped up and snatched the flag from Guiliano's hand. He went to the cliff's edge and waved it at the town below. They did not even have to speak to each other. Guiliano tore off a sapling that grew on the cliff face. They dug a hole and propped the sapling up with stones, then attached the flag to the sapling so that it flew free for all the world to see. Finally, they sat on the cliff edge to wait.

■ ■ ■

IT WAS midday before they saw anything and then it was just a lone man riding a donkey on the dusty path that led to their cliff.

They watched for another hour and then as the donkey entered the mountain range and took the upward path, Pisciotta said, "Damn, that rider is smaller than his donkey. It must be your godfather, Adonis."

Guiliano recognized the contempt in Pisciotta's voice. Pisciotta—so slender, so dapper, so well formed—had a horror of physical deformity. His tubercular lungs, which sometimes bloodied his mouth, disgusted him, not because of the danger to his life, but because it marred what he thought of as his beauty. Sicilians have a fondness for giving people nicknames related to their physical failings or abnormalities, and once a friend had called Pisciotta "Paper Lungs." Pisciotta had tried to stab him with his pocketknife. Only Guiliano's strength had prevented murder.

Guiliano ran down the mountainside for a few miles and hid behind a huge granite rock. It was one of his childhood games with Aspanu. He waited for Adonis to pass him on the trail, then he stepped out from his sheltering rock and called, "Stand where you are." He pointed his *lupara*.

Again it was the childhood game. Adonis turned slowly in such a way that he shielded the drawing of his pistol. But Guiliano, laughing, had stepped behind the sheltering rock; only the barrel of his *lupara* gleamed in the sunlight.

Guiliano called, "Godfather, it's Turi," and waited until Adonis put his gun back into his waistband and shrugged out of his knapsack. Then Guiliano lowered his *lupara* and stepped into the open. Guiliano knew that Hector Adonis always had trouble dismounting because of his short legs and he wanted to help him. But when he appeared on the path the Professor slid down quickly, and they embraced. They walked up to the cliff, Guiliano leading the donkey.

"Well, young man, you've burned your bridges," Hector Adonis said in his professional voice. "Two more dead policemen after last night. It's no longer a joke."

When they arrived on the cliff face and Pisciotta greeted him, Adonis said, "As soon as I saw the Sicilian flag I knew you were up here."

Pisciotta grinned and said good-humoredly, "Turi and myself and this mountain have seceded from Italy."

Hector Adonis gave him a sharp look. That self-centeredness of youth, stating its own supreme importance.

"The whole town has seen your flag," Adonis said. "Including the Maresciallo of the *carabinieri*. They will be coming up to take it down."

Pisciotta said impudently, "Always the schoolmaster giving knowledge. They're welcome to our flag, but that is all they'll find here. We're safe at night. It would be a miracle for the *carabinieri* to come out of their barracks after dark."

Adonis ignored him and unpacked the sack on his donkey. He gave Guiliano a pair of powerful binoculars and a first-aid kit, a clean shirt, some underwear, a knitted sweater, a shaving kit with his father's straight-edge razor and six bars of soap. "You will need these up here," he said.

Guiliano was delighted with the field glasses. They headed the list of things he needed to acquire in the next few weeks. He knew his mother had hoarded the soap over the last year.

In a separate package were a huge hunk of grainy cheese speckled with pepper, a loaf of bread, and two large round cakes that were really bread stuffed with prosciutto ham and mozzarella cheese and crowned with hard-boiled eggs.

Adonis said, "La Venera sent you the cakes. She says she always baked them for her husband when he was in the mountains. You can live on one for a week."

Pisciotta smiled slyly and said, "The older they get the better the taste."

The two young men sat in the grass and tore off pieces of the bread. Pisciotta used his knife to cut off hunks of the cheese. The grass around them was alive with insects, so they put the food sack on top of a granite boulder. They drank water from a clear stream that ran only a hundred feet below them. Then they rested where they could see over the cliff.

Hector Adonis sighed. "You two are very pleased with yourselves, but it is no joke. If they catch you, they'll shoot you."

Guiliano said calmly, "And if I catch them, I'll shoot them."

Hector Adonis was shocked at this. There would never be hope of a pardon. "Don't be rash," he said. "You're still only a boy."

Guiliano looked at him for a long moment. "I was old enough for them to shoot me over a piece of cheese. Do you expect me to run? To let my family starve? To let you bring me packages of food while I take a vacation in the mountains? They come to kill me, and so I'll kill them. And you, my dear godfather. When I was a child, didn't you lecture me on the miserable life of the Sicilian peasant? How oppressed they are, by Rome and its tax collectors, by the nobility, by rich landowners who pay for our labor with lire that can barely keep us alive? I went to the marketplace with two hundred other men of Montelepre and they bid for us as if we were cattle. A hundred lire for a morning's work they said, take it or leave it. And most of the men had to take it. Who then will be the champion of Sicily, if not Salvatore Guiliano?"

Hector Adonis was truly dismayed. It was bad enough to be an outlaw, but to be a revolutionary was more dangerous. "That's all very well in literature," he said. "But in real life you can go to an early grave." He paused for a moment. "What good did your heroics the other night do? Your neighbors are still in jail."

"I'll free them." Guiliano said quietly. He could see the astonishment on his godfather's face. He wanted his approval, his help, his understanding. He could see that Adonis still thought of him as the good-hearted village youth. "You must understand how I am now." He paused for a moment. Could he say exactly what he thought? Would his godfather think him insanely proud? But he went on. "I am not afraid of dying." He smiled at Hector Adonis, the boyish smile Adonis knew so well and loved. "Really, I'm astonished by it myself. But I'm not afraid of being killed. It doesn't seem possible to me." He laughed aloud. "Their field police, their armored cars, their machine guns, all of Rome. I'm not afraid of them. I can beat them. The mountains of Sicily are full of bandits. Passatempo and his band. Terranova. They defy Rome. What they can do, I can do."

Hector Adonis felt a mixture of amusement and anxiety. Had the wound affected Guiliano's brain? Or was what he saw now the same as the beginning of history's heroes, the Alexanders, the Caesars, the Rolands? When did the dreams of heroes begin, if not when sitting in a lonely glen, talking to dear friends. But he said casually, "Forget about Terranova and Passatempo. They have been captured and are sitting in the jail at the Bellampo Barracks. They will be transported to Palermo in a few days."

Guiliano said, "I'll rescue them, and then I'll expect their gratitude."

The grimness with which he said this astonished Hector Adonis and delighted Pisciotta. It was startling to them to see the change in their Guiliano. They had always loved and respected him. He had always had great dignity and poise for such a young man. But now for the first time they sensed his drive for power.

Hector Adonis said, "Gratitude? Passatempo killed the uncle who gave him his first donkey."

"Then I must teach him the meaning of gratitude," Guiliano said. He paused for a moment. "And now I have a favor to ask of you. Think it over carefully, and if you refuse, I will still be your devoted godson. Forget that you're the dear friend of my parents and forget your affection for me. I ask this favor for the Sicily you taught me to love. Be my eyes and ears in Palermo."

Hector Adonis said to him, "What you're asking me, as Professor at the University of Palermo, is to become a member of your band of outlaws."

Pisciotta said impatiently, "That's not so strange in Sicily, where everyone is hooked to the Friends of the Friends. And where else but in Sicily does a Professor of History and Literature carry a pistol?"

Hector Adonis studied both of the young men as he pondered his answer. He could easily promise to help and forget his promise. He could just as easily refuse and promise only to give the aid a friend would give from time to time, as he was doing today. After all, the comedy might be short. Guiliano might be killed fighting or betrayed. He might emigrate to America. And the problem would be solved, he thought sadly.

Hector Adonis remembered a long-ago summer day, a day very like this one, when Turi and Aspanu were no more than eight years old. They had been sitting in the pasture lying between the Guiliano house and the mountains, waiting for supper. Hector Adonis had brought a bag of books for Turi. One of them was the *Song of Roland*, and he had read it to them.

Adonis knew the poem almost by heart. It was dear to every literate Sicilian, and its story was beloved by the illiterate. It was the mainstay of the puppet theater that played every town and village, and its legendary characters were painted on the side of every wagon that rolled along the Sicilian hills. Emperor Charlemagne's two great knights, Roland and Oliver, slaughtered the Saracens, protecting their Emperor's retreat into France. Adonis told how they had died together in the great battle of Roncevalles—how Oliver begged three times for Roland to blow his horn to bring back Charlemagne's army and how Roland refused out of pride. And then when the Saracens overwhelmed them, Roland blew his great horn, but it was too late. When Charlemagne returned to rescue his knights, he found their bodies among the thousands of dead Saracens and rent his beard. Adonis remembered the tears in Turi Guiliano's eyes and, oddly enough, the look of scorn on the face of Aspanu Pisciotta. To one it was the greatest moment a man could live, to the other child it was a humiliating death at the hands of the infidel.

The two young boys had gotten up from the grass to run into the house for supper. Turi threw his arms across Aspanu's shoulder, and Hector had smiled at the gesture. It was Roland holding Oliver erect so that they could both die on their feet before the charging Saracens. Roland, dying, had reached out his gauntlet to the azure sky, and an angel had plucked it from his hand. Or so the poem and legend said.

That was a thousand years ago, but Sicily still suffered in the same brutal landscape of olive groves and scorching plains, of roadside shrines built by the first followers of Christ, the countless crosses holding the crucified rebellious slaves led by Spartacus. And his godson would be another of these heroes, not understanding that for Sicily to change, there would have to be a moral volcano that would incinerate the land.

As Adonis watched them now, Pisciotta lounging on his back in the grass, Guiliano staring at him with dark brown eyes and with a smile that seemed to say he knew exactly what his godfather was thinking, a curious transformation of the scene took place. Adonis saw them as statues carved in marble, their bodies wrenched out of ordinary life. Pisciotta became a figure on a vase, the gecko in his hand an adder, all finely etched in the morning sunlight of the mountains. Pisciotta looked dangerous, a man who filled the world with poison and daggers.

Salvatore Guiliano, his godson Turi, was the other side of the vase. His had the beauty of some Greek Apollo, the features fully molded flesh, the eyes with whites so clear they gave almost the impression of blindness. His face was open and frank with the innocence of a legendary hero. Or rather, thought Adonis, rejecting his sentimentality, the resolution of a young man determined to be heroic. His body had the muscular fleshiness of those Mediterranean statues, the heavy thighs, the muscular back. His body was American, taller and broader than most Sicilians'.

Even when they were boys Pisciotta had showed a practical cunning. Guiliano had been the generous believer in the goodness of man, and proud of his own truthfulness. In those days Hector Adonis had often thought that Pisciotta would be the leader when they were men, Guiliano the follower. But he should have known better. A belief in one's own virtue is far more dangerous than a belief in one's cunning.

Pisciotta's mocking voice broke into these daydreams of Hector Adonis. "Please say yes, Professor. I am the second in command of Guiliano's band, but I have no one under me to give orders." He was grinning. "I am willing to start small."

Though Adonis was not provoked, Guiliano's eyes flashed with anger. But he said quietly, "What is your answer?"

Hector Adonis said, "Yes." What else could a godfather say?

Then Guiliano told him what he had to do when he returned to Montelepre and outlined his plans for the next day. Adonis was again appalled at the boldness and ferocity of this young man's schemes. But when Guiliano lifted him onto his donkey he leaned over and kissed his godson.

Pisciotta and Guiliano watched Adonis riding down the trail toward Montelepre. "He's such a little man," Pisciotta said. "He would have fitted in much better when we were playing bandits as children."

Guiliano turned to him and said gently, "And your jokes would have been better then. Be serious when we talk of serious things." But that night before they went to sleep, they embraced each other. "You are my brother," Guiliano said. "Remember that." Then they wrapped themselves in their blankets and slept away the last night of their obscurity.

CHAPTER

9

TURI GUILIANO and Aspanu Pisciotta were up before the dawn, before the first light, for though it was unlikely, the *carabinieri* might start in darkness to surprise them with the morning sun. They had seen the armored car from Palermo arrive in the Bellampo Barracks late the evening before with two jeeploads of reinforcements. During the night Guiliano made scouting patrols down the side of the mountain and listened for any sounds that would be made by anyone approaching their cliff—a precaution Pisciotta ridiculed. "When we were children we would have been such daredevils," he told Guiliano, "but do you think those lazy *carabinieri* will risk their lives in darkness, or even miss a good night's sleep in soft beds?"

"We have to train ourselves into good habits," Turi Guiliano said. He knew that someday there would be better enemies.

Turi and Aspanu worked hard laying out guns on a blanket and checking them in every detail. Then they ate some of La Venera's bread cake, washed down with a flask of wine Hector Adonis had left them. The cake, with its heat and spices, lay glowingly in their stomachs. It gave them the energy to construct a screen of saplings and boulders on the edge of the cliff. Behind this screen, they watched the town and the mountain paths with their binoculars. Guiliano loaded the guns and put boxes of ammunition into the pockets of his sheepskin jacket while Pisciotta kept watch. Guiliano did his job carefully and slowly. He even buried all the supplies and covered the ground with huge rocks himself. He was never to trust anyone to check these details. So it was Pisciotta who spotted the armored car leaving the Bellampo Barracks.

"You're right," Pisciotta said. "The car is going down the Castellammare plain away from us."

They grinned at each other. Guiliano felt a quiet elation. Fighting the police would not be so difficult after all. It was a child's game with a child's cunning. The armored car would disappear around a curve of the road and then circle back and come into the mountains to the rear of their cliff. The authorities must know about the tunnel and expect them to use it to escape and run right into the armored car. And its machine guns.

In an hour the *carabinieri* would send a detachment up the sides to Monte d'Ora in a frontal attack to flush them out. It helped that the police thought of them as wild youths, simple outlaws. The scarlet and gold flag of Sicily that they flew from the cliff edge confirmed their careless impudence, or so the police would think.

An hour later, a troop van and a jeep carrying the Maresciallo Roccofino left through the gates of the Bellampo Barracks. The two vehicles traveled leisurely to the foot of Monte d'Ora and stopped to unload. Twelve *carabinieri* armed with rifles deployed on the tiny paths that led up the slope. Maresciallo Roccofino took off his braided cap and pointed it toward the scarlet and gold flag flying over the cliff above them.

Turi Guiliano was watching through the binoculars from behind the screen of saplings. For a moment he worried about the armored car on the other side of the mountain. Would they have sent some men up the opposite slope? But those men would take hours to climb, they could not be close. He put them out of his mind and said to Pisciotta, "Aspanu, if we're not as clever as we think, we won't be going home to our mothers and a plate of spaghetti this night, as we used to do when we were children."

Pisciotta laughed. "We always hated going home, remember? But I have to admit, this is more fun. Shall we kill a few of them?"

"No," Guiliano said. "Fire over their heads." He thought about how Pisciotta disobeyed him two nights before. He said, "Aspanu, obey me. There's no point in killing them. It can't serve any purpose this time."

They waited patiently for an hour. Then Guiliano pushed his shotgun through the screen of saplings and fired twice. It was amazing how that straight confident line of men scattered so quickly, like darting ants disappearing into the grass. Pisciotta fired his rifle four times. Smoke puffs appeared in different parts of the slope as the *carabinieri* fired back.

Guiliano put down his shotgun and took up the binoculars. He could see the Maresciallo and his Sergeant working a radio communications set. They would be contacting the armored car on the other side of the mountain, warning them that the outlaws would be on their way. He picked up his shotgun again and fired twice, then said to Pisciotta, "It's time to leave."

The two of them crawled to the far side of the cliff out of view of the advancing *carabinieri,* then slid down the boulder-strewn slope, rolling for fifty yards before they came to their feet, weapons ready. Crouched low, they ran down the hill stopping only for Guiliano to observe the attackers through his binoculars.

The *carabinieri* were still firing up at the cliff, not realizing the two outlaws were now on their flanks. Guiliano led the way down a tiny, hidden path through massive boulders and entered a little forest. They rested for a few minutes and then they both started running down the path swiftly and silently. In less than an hour they emerged onto the plain that separated the mountains from the town of Montelepre, but they had circled around to the far side of the town; it lay between them and the troop-carrying van. They hid their weapons under their jackets and walked across the plain, looking like two peasants on their way to work in the fields. They entered Montelepre at the top of the Via Bella, only a hundred yards from the Bellampo Barracks.

At that same moment the Maresciallo Roccofino ordered his men to continue climbing the slopes toward the flag on the edge of the cliff. There had been no answering fire for the last hour and he was sure the two outlaws had fled through their tunnel and were now going down the other side of the mountain toward the armored car. He wanted to close the trap. It took his men another hour to reach the cliff edge and tear down the flag. Maresciallo Roccofino went into the cave and had the boulders pushed aside to open up the tunnel. He sent his men down that stone corridor and down the other side of the mountain to rendezvous with the armored car. He was astounded when he found that his quarry had escaped him. He broke up his men into searching and scouting parties, sure they would flush the fugitives from their holes.

■ ■ ■

HECTOR ADONIS had followed Guiliano's instructions perfectly. At the top of the Via Bella was a painted cart, the ancient legends covering every inch, inside and out. Even the spokes of the wheels and the rims were painted with tiny armored figures so that when the wheels rolled they cleverly gave the illusion of men whirling in combat. The shafts too were colored in bright red curlicues with silver dots.

The cart looked like a man with tattoos that covered every inch of his body. Between the shafts stood a sleepy white mule. Guiliano jumped into the empty driver's seat and looked into the cart. It was packed with huge jugs of wine cradled into bamboo baskets. There were at least twenty of them. Guiliano slipped his shotgun behind a row of jugs. He gave a quick look toward the mountains; there was nothing to be seen, except the flag still flying. He grinned down at Pisciotta. "Everything is in place," he said. "Go and do your little dance."

Pisciotta gave a little salute, serious yet mocking, buttoned his jacket over his pistol, and started walking toward the gates of the Bellampo Barracks. As he walked he glanced down the road that led to Castellammare, just to make sure there was no armored car on its way back from the mountains.

High up on the cart seat, Turi Guiliano watched Pisciotta walk slowly across the open field and onto the stone path that led to the gate. Then he looked down the Via Bella. He could see his house, but there was nobody standing in front of it. He had hoped he might catch a glimpse of his mother. Some men were sitting in front of one of the houses, their table and wine bottles shaded by an overhanging balcony. Suddenly he remembered the binoculars around his neck and he unclipped the strap and threw them into the back of the cart.

A young *carabiniere* stood guard at the gate, a boy no more than eighteen. His rosy cheeks and hairless face proclaimed his birth in the northern provinces of Italy; his black uniform with white piping, baggy and untailored, and his braided fiercely military cap gave him the look of some puppet or clown. Against regulations he had a cigarette in his adolescent, cupid's bow mouth. Approaching on foot, Pisciotta felt a surge of amused contempt. Even after what had happened in the last few days the man did not have his rifle ready.

The guard only saw a scruffy peasant who dared to grow a mustache more elegant than he deserved. He said roughly, "You there, you lump, where do you think you're going?" He did not unsling his rifle. Pisciotta could have cut his throat in a second.

Instead he tried to look obsequious, tried to suppress his mirth at this child's arrogance. He said, "If you please, I wish to see the Maresciallo. I have some valuable information."

"You can give it to me," the guard said.

Pisciotta could not help himself. He said scornfully, "And can you pay me too?"

The guard was astounded by this impudence. Then he said contemptuously but a little warily, "I wouldn't pay you a lira if you told me Jesus had come again."

Pisciotta grinned. "Better than that. I know where Turi Guiliano has come again, the man who bloodied your noses."

The guard said suspiciously, "Since when does a Sicilian help
the law in this damned country?"

Pisciotta moved a little closer. "But I have ambitions," he
said. "I've put in an application to become a *carabiniere*. Next
month I go to Palermo for my examination. Who knows, both
of us might soon be wearing the same uniform."

The guard looked at Pisciotta with a more friendly interest. It
was true that many Sicilians became policemen. It was a road
out of poverty, it was a small piece of power. It was a well-
known national joke that Sicilians became either criminals or
policemen and that they did equal damage on both sides. Meanwhile Pisciotta was laughing inwardly at the thought that he
would ever become a *carabiniere*. Pisciotta was a dandy; he
owned a silk shirt made in Palermo. Only a fool would preen in
that white-piped black uniform and that ridiculous braided stiff
billed cap.

"You'd better think twice," the guard said, not wanting
everybody to be in on a good thing. "The pay is small and we'd
all starve if we didn't take bribes from smugglers. And just this
week two of the men of our barracks, good friends of mine,
were killed by that damned Guiliano. And every day the insolence of your peasants who won't even give you directions to
the barber in town."

Pisciotta said gaily, "We'll teach them some manners with the
bastinado." Then, with a confidential air, as if they were already
brothers in arms, he said, "Have you a cigarette for me?"

To Pisciotta's delight, the moment of good will fled. The guard
was outraged. "A cigarette for you?" he said incredulously.
"Why in Christ's name should I give a piece of Sicilian dung a
cigarette?" And now finally the guard unslung his rifle.

For a moment Pisciotta felt the savage urge to throw himself
forward and slit the guard's throat. "Because I can tell you
where to find Guiliano," Pisciotta said. "Your comrades searching the mountains are too stupid to find even a gecko."

The guard looked bewildered. The insolence had him confused; the information offered made him realize he had better consult his superior. He had a feeling that this man was too slippery and could get him into trouble of some kind. He opened the gate and motioned Pisciotta with his rifle to enter the grounds of the Bellampo Barracks. His back was to the street. At that moment, Guiliano, a hundred yards away, kicked the mule awake and started his cart onto the stone pathway to the gate.

The grounds of the Bellampo Barracks consisted of four acres. On the land was the large administration building with an L-shaped wing that held the jail cells. Behind it was the living barracks for the *carabinieri* themselves, large enough to hold a hundred men with a specially partitioned section that served as a private apartment for the Maresciallo. Off to the right side was a garage for vehicles that was really a barn and still served partially as such since the detachment supported a troop of mules and donkeys for mountain travel where mechanical vehicles were useless.

Far in the rear were a munitions shed and a supply shed, both made of corrugated steel. Surrounding the whole area was a seven-foot barbed wire fence with two high towers for sentries, but these had not been used for many months. The barracks had been built by the Mussolini regime and then enlarged during the war on the Mafia.

When Pisciotta went through the gate he checked for danger signals. The towers were empty, there were no roaming armed guards. It looked like some peaceful deserted farm. There were no vehicles in the garage; in fact there were no vehicles in sight anywhere, which surprised him, and made him worry that one would be returning soon. He could not conceive of the Maresciallo being so stupid as to leave his garrison without a vehicle. He would have to warn Turi that they might get unexpected visitors.

Shepherded by the young guard, Pisciotta entered the wide

doors of the administration building. This was a huge room with ceiling fans which did little to dispel the heat. There was a large raised desk dominating the room, and on the sides were railings which enclosed smaller desks for clerks; around the room were wooden benches. These were all empty except for the raised desk. Seated at this was a *carabinieri* corporal who was an altogether different proposition from the young guard. An ornate gold nameplate on the desk read CORPORAL CANIO SILVESTRO. The upper part of his body was massive—great shoulders and thick columnar neck crowned by a huge boulder of a head. A pink scar, a slab of shiny dead tissue, seemed pasted from his ear down to the end of his rocklike jaw. A long bushy handlebar mustache flew out like two black wings over his mouth.

He wore the stripes of a corporal on his sleeve, a huge pistol at his belt and worst of all he regarded Pisciotta with the utmost suspicion and distrust as the guard recited his story. When Corporal Silvestro spoke his accent revealed him to be a Sicilian. "You are a lying piece of shit," he said to Pisciotta. But before he could go any further, Guiliano's voice could be heard shouting inside the gate.

"Hey there, *carabiniere*, do you want your wine or not? Yes or no?"

Pisciotta admired the style of Guiliano's voice; the tone coarse, the dialect so thick it was almost unintelligible except to natives of this province, the choice of words arrogantly typical of the well-to-do peasant.

The Corporal growled with exasperation, "What in Christ's name is that fellow bellowing about?" and with great strides was out the door. The guard and Pisciotta followed him.

The painted cart and its white mule were outside the gate. Bare to the waist, his broad chest streaming with sweat, Turi Guiliano was swinging a jug of wine. There was a huge idiotic grin on his face; his whole body seemed oafishly askew. His appearance disarmed suspicion. There could be no weapon concealed on his person, he was drunk and the accent was that of the most loutish dialect in all of Sicily. The Corporal's hand dropped from his pistol, the guard lowered his rifle. Pisciotta took a step backward ready to draw his own gun from beneath his jacket.

"I have a wagonload of wine for you," Guiliano bawled out again. He blew his nose with his fingers and snapped the mucus off into the gate.

"Who ordered this wine?" the Corporal asked. But he was walking down to the gate and Guiliano knew he would open it wide to let the wagon through.

"My father told me to bring it for the Maresciallo," Guiliano said with a wink.

The Corporal was staring at Guiliano. The wine was undoubtedly a gift for letting some farmer do a bit of smuggling. The Corporal thought uneasily that as a true Sicilian the father would have brought the wine himself to be more closely associated with the gift. But then he shrugged. "Unload the goods and bring them into the barracks."

Guiliano said, "Not by myself, I don't."

Again the Corporal felt a twinge of doubt. Some instinct warned him. Realizing this, Guiliano climbed down from the wagon in such a way that he could easily snatch the *lupara* from its hiding place. But first he lifted up a jug of wine in its bamboo case and said, "I have twenty of these beauties for you."

The Corporal roared out a command toward the quarters barracks and two young *carabinieri* came running out; their jackets were unbuttoned and they wore no caps. Neither did they bear weapons. Guiliano standing on top of his cart thrust jugs of wine into their arms. He gave a jug to the guard with the rifle, who tried to refuse. Guiliano said with rough good humor, "You'll certainly help drink it, so work."

Now with the three guards immobilized, their arms full of jugs, Guiliano surveyed the scene. It was exactly as he had wished. Pisciotta was directly behind the Corporal, the only soldier with his arms free. Guiliano scanned the slopes; there was no sign of any of the searching party returning. He checked the road to Castellammare; there was no sign of the armored car. Down the Via Bella the children were still playing. He reached into the wagon and pulled out the *lupara* and pointed it at the astonished Corporal. At the same time Pisciotta pulled the pistol from beneath his shirt. He pressed it against the Corporal's back. "Don't move an inch," Pisciotta said, "or I'll barber that great mustache of yours with lead."

Guiliano kept the *lupara* on the other three frightened guards. He said, "Keep those jugs in your arms and everybody go into the building." The armed guard hugging the jug let his rifle drop to the ground. Pisciotta picked it up as they moved inside. In the office, Guiliano picked up the name plaque and admired it. "Corporal Canio Silvestro. Your keys, please. All of them."

The Corporal's hand rested on his pistol and he glared at Guiliano. Pisciotta knocked his hand forward and plucked out his weapon. The Corporal turned and gave him a cold examining stare that was deadly. Pisciotta smiled and said, "Excuse me."

The Corporal turned to Guiliano and said, "My boy, run away and become an actor, you're very fine. Don't go on with this, you'll never escape. The Maresciallo and his men will be back before nightfall and will hunt you to the ends of the earth. Think it over, my young fellow, what it is to be an outlaw with a price on your head. I'll be hunting for you myself and I never forget a face. I'll find out your name and dig you out if you hide yourself in hell."

Guiliano smiled at him. For some reason he liked the man. He said, "But if you want to know my name, why don't you ask?"

The Corporal looked at him scornfully. "And you'll tell me, like an idiot?"

Guiliano said, "I never lie. My name is Guiliano."

The Corporal put his hand to his side for the pistol Pisciotta had already removed. Guiliano liked the man more for that instinctive reaction. He had courage and a sense of duty. The other guards were terrified. This was the Salvatore Guiliano who had already killed three of their comrades. There was no reason to think that he would leave them alive.

The Corporal studied Guiliano's face, memorizing it, then, moving slowly and carefully, took a huge ring of keys from a desk drawer. He did so because Guiliano had the shotgun pressed tightly against his back. Guiliano took the keys from him and tossed them to Pisciotta.

"Release those prisoners," he said.

In the prison wing of the administration building, in a large caged area, were ten citizens of Montelepre who had been arrested the night of Guiliano's escape. In one of the separate small cells were the two locally famous bandits, Passatempo and Terranova. Pisciotta unlocked their cell doors and they gleefully followed him into the other room.

The arrested citizens of Montelepre, all neighbors of Guiliano, flooded into the office and crowded around Guiliano to embrace him with gratitude. Guiliano permitted this but was always alert, his eyes on the captive *carabinieri*. His neighbors were in a delighted good humor at Guiliano's exploit; he had humiliated the hated police, he was their champion. They told him that the Maresciallo had ordered them to be *bastinado*ed but the Corporal had effectively stopped this punishment from being carried out by the sheer force of his character and his argument that such an action would create so much ill will that it would affect the safety of the barracks. Instead, the next morning they were to have been transported to Palermo to appear before a magistrate for interrogation.

Guiliano held his *lupara* muzzle down to the floor, afraid that an accidental shot would go into the crowd around him. These men were all older, neighbors he had known as a child. He was careful to speak to them as he had always spoken to them. "You are welcome to come with me to the mountains," he said. "Or you can go visit relatives in other parts of Sicily until the authorities come to their senses." He waited but there was only silence. The two bandits, Passatempo and Terranova, stood aside from the others. They were extremely alert, as if poised to spring. Passatempo was a short, squat ugly man with a gross face marked by childhood smallpox, his mouth thick and unshaped. The peasants in the countryside called him "The Brute." Terranova was small and built like a ferret. Yet his small features were pleasant, his lips molded into a natural smile. Passatempo had been the typical greedy Sicilian bandit who simply stole livestock and killed for money. Terranova had been a hard-working farmer and had started his career as an outlaw when two tax collectors came to confiscate his prize pig. He had killed both of them, slaughtered his pig for his family and relatives to eat and then fled to the mountains. The two men had joined forces but had been betrayed and captured when they were hiding in a deserted warehouse in the grain fields of Corleone.

Guiliano said to them, "You two have no choice. We will go to the mountains together and then if you like you can stay under my command or go off on your own. But for today I need your help and you do owe me a small service." He smiled at them, trying to soften the demand that they submit to his orders.

Before the two bandits could answer, the Corporal of the *carabinieri* committed an insane act of defiance. Perhaps it was out of some injured Sicilian pride, perhaps out of some inborn animal ferocity, or simply that the fact that the noted bandits in his custody were about to escape enraged him. He was standing only a few paces from Guiliano and with a surprising quickness he took a long step forward.

At the same time he drew a small pistol concealed inside his shirt. Guiliano swung the *lupara* up to fire but he was too late. The Corporal thrust the pistol to within two feet of Guiliano's head. The bullet would smash directly into Guiliano's face.

Everyone was frozen with shock. Guiliano saw the pistol pointed at his head. Behind it the red raging face of the Corporal was contorting its muscles like the body of a snake. But the pistol seemed to be coming very slowly. It was like falling in a nightmare, falling forever and yet knowing it was only a dream and that he would never hit the bottom. In the fraction of a second before the Corporal pulled the trigger, Guiliano felt an enormous serenity and no fear. His eyes did not blink when the Corporal pulled the trigger, indeed he took a step forward. There was a loud metallic click as the hammer hit the defective ammunition in the barrel. A fraction of a second afterward, he was swarmed over by Pisciotta, Terranova and Passatempo, and the Corporal was falling under the weight of bodies. Terranova had grasped the pistol and was twisting it away, Passatempo had the Corporal by the hair of his head and was trying to gouge out his eyes, Pisciotta had his knife out and ready to plunge it into the Corporal's throat. Guiliano caught it just in time.

Guiliano said quietly, "Don't kill him." And pulled them off the Corporal's now prone and defenseless body. He looked down and was dismayed to see the damage that had been done in that flashing moment of mob fury. The Corporal's ear was half-ripped off his skull and was bleeding great gouts of blood. His right arm hung grotesquely twisted at his side. One of his eyes was spouting blood, a great flap of skin hung over it.

The man was still not afraid. He lay there awaiting death, and Guiliano felt an overwhelming wave of tenderness for him. This was the man who had put him to the test, and who had confirmed his own immortality; this was the man who had certified the impotence of death. Guiliano pulled him to his feet and to the astonishment of all the others gave him a quick embrace. Then he pretended that he was merely helping the Corporal to stand erect.

Terranova was examining the pistol. "You are a very fortunate man," he said to Guiliano. "Only one bullet is defective."

Guiliano held out his hand for the gun. Terranova hesitated for a moment, then gave it to him. Guiliano turned to the Corporal. "Behave yourself," he said in a friendly tone, "and nothing will happen to you or your men. I guarantee it."

The Corporal, still too dazed and weak from his injuries to reply, did not even seem to understand what was being said.

Passatempo whispered to Pisciotta, "Hand me your knife and I'll finish him off."

Pisciotta said, "Guiliano gives the orders here and everybody obeys." Pisciotta said it matter-of-factly so as not to alert Passatempo that he was ready to kill him in an instant.

The Montelepre citizens who had been prisoners left hastily. They did not want to be witnesses to a massacre of *carabinieri*. Guiliano shepherded the Corporal and his fellow guards to the prison wing and locked them in the communal cell together. Then he led Pisciotta, Terranova and Passatempo on a search through the other buildings of the Bellampo Barracks. In the weapons shed they found rifles, pistols and machine pistols, with boxes of ammunition. They draped the weapons over their bodies and loaded the boxes of ammunition into the cart. From the living quarters they took some blankets and sleeping bags and Pisciotta threw two *carabinieri* uniforms into the cart just for good luck. Then, with Guiliano in the driver's seat, the cart brimming over the top with looted goods, the other three men, walking with weapons ready, spread out to protect against any attack. They moved quickly down the road toward Castellammare. It took them over an hour to make their way to the house of the farmer who had loaned Hector Adonis the cart and to bury their loot in his pigpen. Then they helped the farmer cover his cart with olive green paint stolen from an American Army supply depot.

Maresciallo Roccofino returned with his search party in time for dinner; the sun was falling out of the sky and it had never burned so brightly that day as the Maresciallo's rage burned at the sight of his men imprisoned in their own cages. The Maresciallo sent his armored car screaming down all the roads for a trace of the outlaws, but by that time Guiliano was deep in the sanctuary of his mountains.

■ ■ ■

NEWSPAPERS ALL over Italy gave the story great prominence. Just three days before, the killing of the two other *carabinieri* had also been front-page news, but then Guiliano had just been another desperate Sicilian bandit whose only claim to fame was ferocity. This exploit was another matter. He had won a battle of wits and tactics against the National Police. He had freed his friends and neighbors from what was obviously an unjust imprisonment. Journalists from Palermo, Naples, Rome and Milan descended on the town of Montelepre, interviewing Turi Guiliano's family and friends. His mother was photographed holding up Turi's guitar which she claimed he played like an angel. (This was not true; he was only beginning to play well enough to make his tune recognizable.) His former schoolmates confessed that Turi was such a great reader of books that he had been nicknamed "The Professor." The newspapers seized upon this with delight. A Sicilian bandit who could actually read. They mentioned his cousin Aspanu Pisciotta, who had joined him in his outlawry out of sheer friendship, and wondered at a man who could inspire such loyalty.

That an old photograph taken of him when he was seventeen showed him to be incredibly handsome in a Mediterranean manly fashion made the whole story irresistible. But perhaps what appealed to the Italian people most of all was Guiliano's act of mercy in sparing the Corporal who had tried to kill him. It was better than opera—it was more like the puppet shows so popular in Sicily, where the wooden figures never lost blood or had their flesh torn and mangled by bullets.

The newspapers only deplored the fact that Guiliano had chosen to free two such villains as Terranova and Passatempo, implying that two such evil companions might tarnish the image of this knight in shining armor.

Only the Milan newspaper pointed out that Salvatore "Turi" Guiliano had already killed three members of the National Police, and suggested that special measures should be taken for his apprehension, that a murderer should not be excused his crimes merely because he was handsome, well-read and could play the guitar.

CHAPTER

10

DON CROCE was now fully aware of Turi Guiliano and full of admiration for him. What a true Mafioso youth. He meant the usage, of course, in the old traditional form: a Mafioso face, a Mafioso tree, a Mafioso woman, that is, a thing foremost in beauty in its particular form.

What a mailed fist this young man would be for Don Croce. What a warrior chief in the field. Don Croce forgave the fact that Guiliano was at present a thorn in his side. The two bandits imprisoned in Montelepre, the feared Passatempo and the clever Terranova, had been captured with the Don's approval and complicity. But all this could be forgiven, bygones were bygones: the Don never held a grudge that impaired his future profits. He would now track Turi Guiliano very carefully.

■ ■ ■

DEEP IN the mountains, Guiliano had no knowledge of his growing fame. He was too busy making plans to build his power. His first problem was the two bandit chiefs, Terranova and Passatempo. He questioned them closely about their capture and came to the conclusion they had been betrayed, informed upon. They swore their men had been faithful and many had been killed in the trap. Guiliano pondered all this and came to the conclusion that the Mafia, which had acted as fences and go-

149

betweens for the band, had betrayed them. When he mentioned
this to the two bandits they refused to believe it. The Friends of
the Friends would never break the sacred code of *omerta* which
was so central to their own survival. Guiliano did not insist.
Instead he made them a formal offer to join his band.

He explained that his purpose was not only to survive but to
become a political force. He emphasized that they would not
rob the poor. Indeed half of the profit the band earned would be
distributed to the needy in the provinces around the town of
Montelepre reaching to the suburbs of Palermo. Terranova and
Passatempo would rule their own subordinate bands but would
be under Guiliano's overall command. These subordinate bands
would not launch any money-making expedition without Guiliano's approval. Together they would have absolute rule over
the provinces that held the great city of Palermo, the city of
Monreale, and the towns of Montelepre, Partinico and Corleone. He impressed upon them that they would take the offensive against the *carabinieri*. That it would be the field police who
would go in fear of their lives, not the bandits. They were astonished by this bravado.

Passatempo, an old-fashioned bandit who believed in rape,
small-time extortion and the murder of shepherds, immediately
began pondering how he could profit by this association and then
murder Guiliano and take his share of the loot. Terranova, who
liked Guiliano and was more grateful for his rescue, wondered
how he could tactfully steer this talented young bandit on a more
prudent path. Guiliano was now looking at them with a little
smile, as if he could read their minds and was amused by what
they thought.

Pisciotta was used to the grand ideas of his lifelong friend. He
believed. If Turi Guiliano said he could do something, Aspanu
Pisciotta believed he could do it. So now he listened.

In the bright morning sunlight that lit their mountains with
gold they all three listened to Guiliano, spellbound as he told
how they would lead the fight to make Sicilians a free people,

uplift the poor and destroy the power of the Mafia, the nobility and Rome. They would have laughed at anyone else, but they remembered what everyone who saw it would always remember: the Corporal of the *carabinieri* raising the pistol to Guiliano's head. The quiet stare of Guiliano, his absolute confidence that he would not die, as he waited for the Corporal to pull the trigger. The mercy he had shown to the Corporal after the pistol misfired. These were all acts of a man who believed in his own immortality and forced others to share that belief. And so now they stared at the handsome young man, and they were impressed by his beauty, his courage and his innocence.

■ ■ ■

THE NEXT morning Guiliano led his three men, Aspanu Pisciotta, Passatempo and Terranova, down out of the mountains on a path that would let them out on the plains near the town of Castelvetrano. He came down very early to scout the ground. He and his men were dressed as laborers.

He knew that truck convoys of foodstuffs passed by here on the way to bringing their wares to the markets of Palermo. The problem was how to get the trucks to stop. They would be going at high speed to foil hijackers and the drivers might be armed.

Guiliano made his men hide in the underbrush of the road just outside Castelvetrano, then sat himself on a large white boulder in plain view. Men going out to work in the fields stared at him with stony faces. They saw the *lupara* he was carrying and hurried on. Guiliano wondered if any of them had recognized him. Then he saw a legend-painted large cart coming down the road, drawn by a single mule. The old man driving was known by sight to Guiliano. He was one of the line of professional carters so plentiful in rural Sicily. He hired out his rig to haul bamboo from the outlying villages back to the factory in town. Long ago he had been to Montelepre and had done some hauling of produce for Guiliano's father. Guiliano stepped into the middle of the road. The *lupara* dangled from his right hand. The driver recognized him though there was no expression on his face, just a momentary flicker of the eyes.

Guiliano greeted him with the familiar style he had used as a child, calling him Uncle. "Zu Peppino," he said. "This is a lucky day for both of us. I am here to make your fortune and you are here to help me lighten the load of the poor." He was genuinely delighted to see the old man and burst into laughter.

The old man didn't answer. He stared at Guiliano, his stony face waiting. Guiliano climbed up on the cart and sat beside him. He put the *lupara* out of sight in the wagon and then he laughed again with excitement. Because of Zu Peppino he was sure this would be a lucky day.

Guiliano relished the freshness of the late autumn, the beauty of the mountains on the horizon, the knowledge that his three men in the underbrush commanded the road with their guns. He explained his plan to Zu Peppino, who listened to him without a word or change of expression. That is, not until Guiliano told him what his reward would be: his cart full of food from the trucks. Then Zu Peppino grunted and said, "Turi Guiliano, you were always a fine, brave, young lad. Good-hearted, sensible, generous and sympathetic. You have not changed since you became a man." Guiliano remembered now that Zu Peppino was one of those old school Sicilians given to flowery speech. "Count on my help in this and all other things. Give my regards to your father who should be proud to have such a son."

■ ■ ■

THE CONVOY of three trucks laden with foodstuffs appeared on the road at noontime. When they turned the curve that led straight out on the Partinico plain they had to stop. A cluster of carts and mules blocked the road completely. This had been contrived by Zu Peppino, to whom all the carters of the area owed favors and obedience.

The lead truck driver blew his horn and inched his truck so that it nudged the nearest cart. The man on the cart turned and gave him such a look of malevolence that he immediately halted his truck and waited patiently. He knew that these carters, despite their humble profession, were proud fierce men who, in a matter of honor, their right to the road over motorized vehicles, would stab him to death and go on their way with a song on their lips.

The other two trucks ground to a halt. The drivers got out. One of them was from the eastern end of Sicily and one was a foreigner; that is, he came from Rome. The Roman driver approached the carters unzipping his jacket, shouting angrily for them to get their damn mules and shitboxes out of the way. And leaving one hand inside his jacket.

Guiliano jumped off the cart. He didn't bother to get his *lupara* out of the wagon nor did he bother to draw the pistol in his belt. He gave a signal to his men waiting in the underbrush and they ran onto the road holding their weapons. Terranova split off to walk to the rearmost truck so that it could not be moved. Pisciotta slid down the embankment and confronted the raging Roman truck driver.

Meanwhile Passatempo, more excitable than the others, yanked the first trucker out of his vehicle and threw him on the road at Guiliano's feet. Guiliano extended a hand and lifted him up. By that time, Pisciotta had herded the driver of the rear truck up to join the other two. The Roman had withdrawn his empty hand from his jacket and erased the anger from his face. Guiliano smiled with genuine good will and said, "This is a fortunate day for the three of you. You won't have to make the long trip to Palermo. My carters will unload the trucks and distribute the food to the needy of this district, under my supervision of course. Allow me to introduce myself. I am Guiliano."

The three drivers immediately became apologetic and affable. They were in no hurry, they said. They had all the time in the world. In fact, it was time for their lunch. Their trucks were comfortable. The weather was not too warm. Indeed, it was a happy chance, a stroke of fortune.

Guiliano saw their fear. "Don't worry," he said. "I don't kill men who earn bread by the sweat of their brow. You will join me for lunch while my people do their work, and then you will go home to your wives and children and tell them of your good fortune. When the police question you, help them as little as possible and you will earn my gratitude."

Guiliano paused. It was important to him that these men should feel no shame or hatred. It was important that they should report their good treatment. For there would be others.

They let themselves be herded to the shade of a giant boulder by the side of the road. They voluntarily offered Guiliano their pistols without being searched. And they sat like angels as the carters unloaded their trucks. When the carters were finished, there was still one fully loaded truck whose contents could not fit into their wagons. Guiliano put Pisciotta and Passatempo into this vehicle with a driver and told Pisciotta to deliver food to the farm laborers of Montelepre. Guiliano himself and Terranova would supervise the distribution of the food in the district of Castelvetrano and the town of Partinico. Later they would rendezvous at the cave on top of Monte d'Ora.

With this one deed Guiliano was on the road to winning the support of the whole countryside. What other bandit had given his spoils to the poor? The next day the newspapers all over Sicily had stories about the Robin Hood bandit. Only Passatempo grumbled that they had done a day's work for nothing. Pisciotta and Terranova understood that their band had gained a thousand supporters against Rome.

What they did not know was that the goods had been destined for the warehouse of Don Croce.

■ ■ ■

IN ONLY a month Guiliano had informers everywhere—telling him what rich merchants traveled with black market money, the habits of certain noble persons and those few wicked people who gossiped with highly placed police officials. And so the rumor came to Guiliano of the jewels that the Duchess of Alcamo sometimes flaunted. It was said that for most of the year they were kept in a bank vault in Palermo but that she took them out on some occasions to wear to parties. To learn more about what he sensed might be a rich prize, Guiliano dispatched Aspanu Pisciotta to the Alcamo estate.

Twenty miles southwest of Montelepre, the estate of the Duke and Duchess of Alcamo was walled, its gates manned by armed guards. The Duke also paid "rent" to the Friends of the Friends, which guaranteed that his livestock would not be stolen, his house burglarized or any member of his family kidnapped. In ordinary times and with ordinary criminals this would have made him safer than the Pope in the Vatican.

In early November the great estates of Sicily harvest their grapes, and to do so hire laborers from the nearby villages. Pisciotta reported to the town square and let himself be recruited for work on the Duke of Alcamo's estate. He spent the first day in backbreaking labor, filling baskets with clusters of black purple fruit. There were more than a hundred people in the vineyard —men, women and small children who sang together as they worked. At midday, a huge lunch was served outdoors.

Pisciotta sat alone, watching the others. He noticed one young woman who brought a tray of bread from the castle. She was pretty but pale; obviously she rarely worked in the sun. Also she was better dressed than the other women. But what struck Pisciotta was the disdainful pout on her face, and the way she avoided all contact with the other workers. He learned that this girl was the personal maid of the Duchess.

Pisciotta knew immediately that she would serve his purposes better than anyone else. Guiliano, who knew Pisciotta's ways, had ordered him strictly not to shame any of the local girls in the process of getting information; but Pisciotta considered Turi too much a romantic and too innocent in the ways of the world. The prize was too rich, the girl too pretty.

When she came out with another huge tray of bread, ne lifted it out of her hands and carried it for her. She was startled, and when he asked her name, she refused to answer.

Pisciotta put down the tray and grasped her by the arm. He gave her a ferocious smile. "When I ask you a question, answer me. If you don't, I'll bury you in that mountain of grapes." And then he laughed to show he was joking. He gave her his most charming smile, spoke in his gentlest voice. "You're the most beautiful girl I've seen in Sicily," he said. "I had to speak to you."

The maid was both terrified and enticed by him. She noted the dangerous cutting knife dangling from his waist, the way he carried himself, as if he too were a duke. Now she was interested. She told him her name was Graziella.

When the workday was finished Pisciotta boldly knocked at the back kitchen of the castle and asked for Graziella. The old woman who opened the door listened to him, then said curtly, "The servants are not allowed to receive visitors." She slammed the door in his face.

The next day Pisciotta took the tray Graziella was carrying and whispered to her that he wanted to see her after work. He slipped a little gold bracelet over her wrist as he caressed her arm. She promised she would slip out after dark and meet him in the empty vineyard.

That night Aspanu Pisciotta wore the special silk shirt tailored for him in Palermo. He waited for her in a valley formed by mountains of cut grapes on every side. When Graziella came to him he embraced her, and when she lifted her mouth to be kissed he brushed her lips with his and put his hand between her legs at the same time. She tried to twist away but he gripped her firmly. They kissed more deeply and he lifted her woolen skirt, surprised to find that she was wearing silken undergarments. She must have borrowed them from the Duchess, Pisciotta thought. She was a bold little piece, and a bit of a thief.

He pulled her down to the blanket he had spread on the ground. They lay there together. She was kissing him passionately and he could feel her response through the silk underpants.

With a quick movement he pulled them down and the warm wet flesh was in his hands. She was unbuckling his belt and as they continued to kiss he pushed his trousers down to his ankles. He rolled over on top of her, took his hand away, and then thrust inside her. Graziella gave a little moan and bucked upward with astonishing strength and Aspanu Pisciotta felt himself rising and falling, rising and falling, and then suddenly Graziella gave a little shriek and lay still. Damn, Pisciotta thought, she was too quick. But it was just as well. His main purpose was information, his own satisfaction could wait.

They wrapped themselves in the blanket and hugged each other. He told her that he was working to earn some money to enter the University of Palermo, that his family wanted him to be a lawyer. He wanted her to think he was a good catch. Then he asked her about herself, how she liked her work, what kind of people were her fellow servants? Gradually he directed the conversation to her mistress, the Duchess.

Graziella put Aspanu's hand back between her legs and then told him how beautiful the Duchess looked dressed in her fine clothes and jewelry, and how she, Graziella, was a favorite and was allowed to wear the out-of-fashion frocks the Duchess discarded.

"I would like to see you in your mistress's finery. Does she let you try on her jewels, too?"

"Well, on Christmas Eve she always lets me wear a necklace for the evening." So as Guiliano had guessed, the jewels would be in the house for the holiday season. He needed to find out one more thing, but suddenly she was straddling him, trying to keep the blanket over her shoulders. Aspanu was fully aroused, the blanket fell away, the skirt flew over Graziella's head and the force of their thrusts carried them into the wall of grapes. When they were done, their exhausted bodies were covered with the sticky juice of the fruit and of their own bodies.

Aspanu said, "Fresh air is all very well, but when can I come into the house and make love to you properly?"

"Not while the Duke is here. When he goes on his trips to

Palermo, the household is more lax. Next month, he will go away for several weeks, just before Christmas."

Aspánu smiled. And now that he had all the information he needed, he paid full attention to the job at hand. He pounced on Graziella's body and pinned her again to the blanket, making love with a ferocity that made the girl helpless with pleasure, and frightened her a little. Just enough that she would want more of him in the month ahead.

■ ■ ■

FIVE DAYS before Christmas, Guiliano, Passatempo, Pisciotta, and Terranova pulled up before the gates of the Alcamo Estate in a wagon drawn by mules. They were dressed in the hunting garb of well-to-do peasant landowners, bought in Palermo with the spoils of their truck raid: corduroy trousers, red woolen shirts, heavy shooting jackets that held boxes of bullets. Two security guards barred their way. Since it was broad daylight they were not alert and kept their weapons on their shoulders.

Guiliano strode toward them briskly. He was unarmed except for the pistol hidden beneath his rough carter's coat. He smiled at them broadly. "Gentlemen," he said. "My name is Guiliano and I've come to wish your charming Duchess a good Christmas and beg for alms to help the poor."

The guards were frozen with astonishment when they heard the name Guiliano. Then they started to swing their guns loose. But by that time Passatempo and Terranova had them covered with machine pistols. Pisciotta relieved the guards of their guns and threw the weapons into the wagon. Passatempo and Terranova were left to stroll with the guards in front of the gates.

The approach to the mansion consisted of an enormous stone courtyard. In one corner a group of chickens fluttered around an old woman servant scattering grain. Beyond the manor house, the four children of the Duchess were playing in a garden, supervised by governesses in black cotton dresses. Guiliano walked up the path to the house, Pisciotta beside him. His information was correct, there were no other guards. Beyond the garden was a far larger piece of land, which served to grow vegetables and held a grove of olive trees. In this field six laborers toiled. He rang the bell and then pushed the door just as the maid was opening it. Graziella was startled by Pisciotta's appearance at the front door and stepped aside.

Guiliano said gently, "Don't be alarmed. Tell your mistress we are sent here by the Duke on business. I must speak to her."

Still puzzled, Graziella led them into the drawing room where the Duchess was reading. The Duchess waved the maid from the room, annoyed by the unannounced intrusion and said sharply, "My husband is away. Can I help you?"

Guiliano could not answer her. He was stunned by the beauty of the room. It was the largest he had ever seen and, more amazingly, it was round rather than square. Golden drapes guarded the huge French windows, the ceiling above was hollowed to a dome and decorated with frescoes of cherubim. Books were everywhere—on the sofa, the coffee tables and in special cases along the walls. Great massive paintings in rich oils hung on the walls and huge vases of flowers were every place. Silver and gold boxes were scattered on tables that kneeled before massive stuffed chairs and sofas. The room could hold a hundred people easily and the only person using it was this solitary woman dressed in white silk. Sunlight and air and the shouts of the children playing in the garden came through the open windows. For the first time Guiliano understood the seductiveness of wealth, that money could create such beauty, and he was reluctant to mar that beauty by any crassness or cruelty. He would do what he must do and not leave a scar on this lovely scene.

The Duchess, waiting patiently for an answer, was struck by this young man's handsome virility. She saw he was impressed by the beauty of the room, and she was a little annoyed that he did not notice her own beauty. She thought it was too bad he was so obviously a peasant and did not move in her circles, where a little innocent flirtatiousness would not have been inappropriate. All this made her say more charmingly than she ordinarily would, "Young man, I'm so sorry, but if it's business about the estate you will have to come back another time. My husband is not at home."

Guiliano looked at her. He felt that flush of antagonism a poor man feels for a rich woman who is in some way asserting her superiority to him because of her wealth and social position. He bowed politely, noticing the spectacular ring on her finger, and said with an ironic submissiveness, "My business is with you. My name is Guiliano."

But the irony of his submissiveness was wasted on the Duchess, who was too accustomed to the slavishness of her servants. She took it as a matter of course. She was a cultured woman, interested in books and music, and took no interest in the daily affairs of Sicily. She rarely read the local newspapers; she considered them barbarous. So she only said courteously, "I am pleased to make your acquaintance. Have we met in Palermo? At the opera perhaps?"

Aspanu Pisciotta, who had been observing the scene with amusement, laughed openly and strolled over to the French windows so as to intercept any servant who might come from that direction.

Guiliano, a little angered by Pisciotta's laughter but charmed by the Duchess's ignorance, said firmly, "My dear Duchess, we have never met. I am a bandit. My full name is Salvatore Guiliano. I think of myself as the Champion of Sicily, and my purpose in coming to see you today is to ask you to donate your jewelry to the poor so that they may enjoy and celebrate the birth of Christ on Christmas day."

The Duchess smiled unbelievingly. This young boy whose face and body aroused an unfamiliar hunger in her could not possibly mean her harm. And now with the hint of danger she was positively intrigued. She would tell this story at the parties in Palermo. So she said with an innocent smile, "My jewels are in the bank vaults in Palermo. Whatever cash is in the house you may have. With my blessing." No one had ever doubted her word in her whole life. Even as a little girl she had never lied. This was the first time.

Guiliano looked at the diamond pendant around her throat. He knew she was lying, but he was reluctant to do what he must do. Then he nodded to Pisciotta, who put his fingers between his teeth and whistled three times. In just a few minutes Passatempo appeared at the French windows. His short, squat ugly figure, his evil scarred face could have come out of the puppet shows. His face was broad with hardly any forehead, and his thick bushy black hair and bulging eyebrows made him look like a gorilla. He smiled at the Duchess and showed huge discolored teeth.

The appearance of the third bandit finally frightened the Duchess. She undid her necklace and handed it over to Guiliano. "Will that satisfy you?" she said.

"No," Guiliano said. "My dear Duchess, I'm a soft-hearted man. But my colleagues are different propositions altogether. My friend Aspanu, though handsome, is as cruel as that little mustache he wears that breaks so many hearts. And the man at the window, though he is my subordinate, gives me nightmares. Don't make me unleash them. They will sweep into your garden like hawks and carry your children away into the mountains. Now bring me the rest of your diamonds."

The Duchess fled into her bedroom and returned in a few minutes with a box of jewelry. She had been quick-witted enough to hide a few valuable pieces before she brought it out. She gave the box to Guiliano. He thanked her graciously. Then he turned to Pisciotta. "Aspanu," he said, "the Duchess may have forgotten a few things. Go take a look in the bedroom just to be certain." Pisciotta found the hidden jewels almost immediately and brought them to Guiliano.

Guiliano meanwhile had opened the jewelry box and his heart jumped with elation at the sight of the precious gems. He knew the contents of this box would feed the entire city of Montelepre for months. And it was a greater source of joy that they had been bought by the Duke with the money sweated from the hides of his laborers. Then as the Duchess was wringing her hands he noticed again the huge emerald on her finger.

"My dear Duchess," he said, "how could you be so foolish as to try to cheat me by hiding those other pieces? I would have expected that from some miserly peasant who slaved for his treasure. But how could you risk your life and those of your children for two pieces of jewelry that you would no more miss than your husband the Duke would miss the hat on his head? Now without any fuss, give me that ring you wear on your finger."

The Duchess was in tears. "My dear young man," she said, "please let me keep this ring. I will send you its value in money. But my husband gave it to me as an engagement gift. I could not bear to be without it. It would break my heart."

Again Pisciotta laughed. He did so deliberately. He was afraid that Turi would let her keep the ring out of the sentimentality of his own heart. And the emerald was obviously of the highest value.

But Guiliano had no such sentimentality. Pisciotta would always remember the look in his eye when Turi took the Duchess's arm roughly and pulled the emerald ring off her trembling hand. He stepped back quickly and then he put the ring on the little finger of his left hand.

Turi saw the Duchess was blushing and there were tears in her eyes. His manner was once again courtly when he said, "In honor of your memories I will never sell this ring—I will wear it myself." The Duchess searched his face for a look of irony, but there was none.

But it was a magic moment for Turi Guiliano. For when he slipped it on his finger, he felt the transference of power. With this ring he wedded himself to his destiny. It was the symbol of the power he would win from the world of the rich. In that pool of dark green, bounded by its circle of gold, still smelling of the perfume of a beautiful woman who had worn it without ceasing for many years, he had captured a tiny essence of life that could never be his.

■ ■ ■

DON CROCE listened without saying a word.

The Duke of Alcamo was making his complaint to Don Croce in person. Had he not paid his "rent" to the Friends of the Friends? Had they not guaranteed his immunity against all forms of theft? What were things coming to? In the old days nobody would have dared. And what would Don Croce do now to recover the jewelry? The Duke had reported the theft to the authorities, though this was futile he knew and might displease Don Croce. But there was some insurance to be collected; perhaps the government in Rome would take this bandit Guiliano seriously.

Don Croce reflected that it was time to take him very seriously indeed. He said to the Duke, "If I recovered your jewelry would you pay a quarter of their value?"

The Duke was furious. "First I pay you the rent to keep me and my possessions safe. Then, when you fail in your duty, you ask me to pay ransom. How can you hope to keep the respect of your clients if you do business in this way?"

Don Croce nodded. "I must admit you speak with reason. But think of Salvatore Guiliano as a force of nature, as a scourge of God. Surely you cannot expect the Friends of the Friends to guard you against earthquakes, volcanoes, floods? In time Guiliano will be controlled, I guarantee. But think: You pay the ransom I will arrange. You will have your protection without paying my usual rent for the next five years, and under the agreement Guiliano will not strike again. And why should he, since I and he presume you will have the good sense to keep these valuables in the bank vaults of Palermo? Women are too innocent—they do not know the lust and greed with which men

163

pursue the material goods of this world." He paused for a moment to allow the slight smile that had appeared on the Duke's face to disappear. Then he said, "If you calculate the rent to pay for the protection of your whole estate for five years in the troubled times ahead, you will see that you have lost very little by this misfortune."

The Duke did think it over. Don Croce was quite right about the hard times that lay ahead. He would lose more than a little by ransoming the jewels, despite the remission of five years' "rent"; who was to say that Don Croce would be alive for another five years or that he could contain Guiliano? But still it was the best bargain to be made. It would prevent the Duchess from wheedling more jewelry out of him in the years to come and that would be an enormous savings. He would have to sell another piece of land, but his ancestors had been doing that for generations to pay for their follies, and he still had thousands of acres left. The Duke agreed.

■ ■ ■

DON CROCE summoned Hector Adonis. The next day Adonis made a trip to visit his godson. He explained his mission. He was absolutely straightforward. "You won't get a better price even if you sell the jewelry to thieves in Palermo," he said. "And even then it will take time and you certainly won't get the money before Christmas, which I know is your wish. And beyond that you will earn the good will of Don Croce which it is important for you to have. You have, after all, caused him a loss of respect, which he will forgive if you do him this favor."

Guiliano smiled at his godfather. He cared nothing for Don Croce's good will; after all, one of his dreams was to slay the dragon of the Mafia in Sicily. But he had already sent emissaries to Palermo to find buyers for the stolen jewelry, and it was clear that it would be a long and torturous process. So he agreed to the bargain. But he refused to give up the emerald ring.

Before Adonis left he abandoned finally his role as a teacher of romances to Guiliano. For the first time he spoke to him of the realities of Sicilian life. "My dear godson," he said, "no one admires your qualities more than I do. I love your high-mindedness, which I hope I helped instill in you. But now we must speak of survival. You can never hope to win against the Friends of the Friends. For the last thousand years, like a million spiders, they have spun a gigantic web over all of life in Sicily. Don Croce now stands in the center of that web. He admires you, he wants your friendship, he wants you to grow rich with him. But you must bend sometimes to his will. You can have your empire, but it must exist within his web. One thing is certain—you cannot directly oppose him. If you do so, history itself will help Don Croce destroy you."

■ ■ ■

AND so the jewelry was returned to the Duke. Guiliano kept half the money from the jewelry to be distributed among Pisciotta, Passatempo and Terranova. They eyed the emerald ring on Guiliano's finger but said nothing, for Guiliano refused to take any of the money from the sale of the jewels.

The other half of the money Guiliano was determined to distribute among the poor shepherds who guarded the flocks of sheep and cattle that belonged to the rich, the old widows and orphan children, all the poor around him.

He gave out most of the money through intermediaries, but one fine day he filled the pockets of his sheepskin jacket with packets of lire notes. He also filled a canvas sack with money and decided to walk through the villages between Montelepre and Piani dei Greci with Terranova at his side.

In one village there were three old women who were almost starving. He gave each of them a packet of lire. They wept and kissed his hands. In another village was a man who was about to lose his farm and land because he could not make the mortgage payments. Guiliano left him enough to pay off the mortgage in full.

In another village he took over the local bakery and grocery store, paying the owner for the goods, and distributed bread and cheese and pasta to all the village people.

In the next town he gave money to the parents of a sick child so they could take him to the hospital in Palermo and pay for the visits of the local doctor. He also attended the wedding of a young couple and gave them a generous dowry.

But what he loved most was to give money to the ragged young children who thronged the streets of all the little towns in Sicily. Many of them knew Guiliano. They gathered around him as he distributed the packets of money telling them to bring it to their parents. Guiliano watched them as they joyfully ran to their homes.

He only had a few packets of money left when he decided to visit his mother before nightfall. Crossing a field behind his home he encountered a little boy and a little girl who were crying. They had lost money entrusted to them by their parents and said the *carabinieri* had taken it from them. Guiliano was amused by this little tragedy and gave them one of the two packets of money he had left. And then, because the little girl was so pretty and he couldn't bear to think of her being punished, he gave her a note for her parents.

The little girl's parents were not the only ones who were grateful. The people in the towns of Borgetto, Corleone, Partinico, Monreale, and Piani dei Greci began to call him the "King of Montelepre" to show their loyalty.

■ ■ ■

DON CROCE was happy despite the loss of the five years' "rent" from the Duke. For though Don Croce had told Adonis that the Duke would pay only twenty percent of the value of the jewels, he had collected twenty-five percent from the Duke, and put five percent in his pocket.

What delighted him even more was his satisfaction that he had spotted Guiliano so early and judged him so accurately. What a fine upstanding lad. Who could believe that one so young could see so clearly, act so wisely, listen so temperately to older and wiser heads? And yet all this with a cool intelligence that guarded his own interests, which of course the Don admired, for who would wish to associate himself with a fool? Yes, the Don thought Turi Guiliano would be his strong right arm. And with time, a beloved titular son.

■ ■ ■

TURI GUILIANO saw clearly through all these machinations around him. He knew his godfather was sincerely concerned about his welfare. But that did not mean he trusted the older man's judgment. Guiliano knew he was not yet strong enough to fight the Friends of the Friends; indeed he needed their help. But he was under no illusions about the long run. Eventually, if he listened to his godfather, he would have to become a vassal to Don Croce. This he was determined he would never do. For now, he must bide his time.

CHAPTER

11

GUILIANO'S BAND now numbered thirty men. Some of these were former members of the Passatempo and Terranova bands. Some were citizens of Montelepre who had been freed from prison by Guiliano's raid. They had found there was to be no forgiveness by the authorities despite their innocence; they were still being hunted. They decided to be hunted with Guiliano rather than be tracked down alone and friendless.

One fine April morning Guiliano's informants in Montelepre sent word that a dangerous-looking man, perhaps a police spy, was making inquiries about joining the band. He was waiting in the central square. Guiliano sent Terranova and four men into Montelepre to investigate. If the man was a spy they would kill him; if he was someone of use, they would recruit him.

Early in the afternoon, Terranova returned and told Guiliano, "We have the fellow and before we shoot him, we thought you might like to make his acquaintance."

Guiliano laughed when he saw the burly figure dressed in the traditional peasant Sicilian working garb. "Well, old friend, did you think I could ever forget your face. Have you come with better bullets this time?"

It was the Corporal of the *carabinieri*, Canio Silvestro, who had fired his pistol at Guiliano's head during the famous jail-break.

Silvestro's strong scarred face was intent. The face appealed to Guiliano for some reason. He had a soft spot in his heart for this man who had helped him prove his immortality.

Silvestro said, "I've come to join up. I can be invaluable to you." He said this proudly as one who is about to make a gift. This also pleased Guiliano. He let Silvestro tell his story.

After the raid on the jail, Corporal Silvestro had been sent to Palermo to face a court-martial for dereliction of duty. His Maresciallo had been furious with him and had interrogated him closely before recommending prosecution. Oddly enough the one circumstance that inflamed the Maresciallo's suspicions was the Corporal's attempted shooting of Guiliano. The cause of the misfire had been found to be defective ammunition. The Maresciallo claimed that the Corporal had loaded his gun with that one harmless bullet knowing it was defective. That the whole attempted resistance had been a charade and that Corporal Silvestro had helped Guiliano plan the jailbreak and stationed his guards to help the raid succeed.

Guiliano interrupted. "How did they think you could have known the bullets were defective?"

Silvestro looked sheepish. "I should have known. I was the armorer in the infantry, an expert." His face became grim and he shrugged. "I had a lapse, true. They made me a desk man and I didn't pay too much attention to my real business. But I can be valuable to you. I can be your armorer. I can check all your weapons and repair them. I can make sure your ammunition is properly handled so that your supply dumps don't blow up. I can modify your weapons so that they will suit the use you put them to, here in the mountains."

"Tell me the rest of your story," Guiliano said. He was studying the man closely. This could be a plan to infiltrate his band with an informer. He could see that Pisciotta, Passatempo and Terranova were full of distrust.

Silvestro went on. "They were all fools and they were all frightened women. The Maresciallo knew that it was stupid of him to take most of the men into the mountains when we had a barracks full of prisoners. The *carabinieri* regard Sicily as some foreign occupied country. I used to protest against that attitude, and that got me into their bad books. And the authorities in Palermo wanted to protect their Maresciallo—they were responsible for him after all. It would look better if the Bellampo Barracks had been betrayed from within instead of taken over by men who were braver and more clever. They didn't court-martial me. They told me to resign. They said it would be without prejudice, but I know them better than that. I'll never get a government job again. I'm fitted for nothing else and I'm a Sicilian patriot. So I thought to myself—what can I do with my life? And I said to myself—I will go to Guiliano."

Guiliano sent to the cooking site for food and drink and then conferred with his chiefs.

Passatempo was gruff and positive. "What kind of fools do they think we are? Shoot him and throw his body off the cliff. We don't need *carabinieri* in our band."

Pisciotta saw that Guiliano was once again taken by the Corporal. He knew his friend's impulsive emotions, so he said carefully, "It's most likely a trick. But even if it's not, why take the chance? We'll have to worry all the time. There will always be doubt. Why not just send him back?"

Terranova said, "He knows our camp. He's seen some of our men and he knows their number. That is valuable information."

Guiliano said, "He's a true Sicilian. He acts out of a sense of honor. I can't believe he would act the part of a spy." He saw that they all smiled at his innocence.

Pisciotta said, "Remember, he tried to kill you. He had a concealed weapon and he was a prisoner and he tried to kill you out of sheer temper and with no hope of escape."

Guiliano thought, And that's what makes him valuable to me. Aloud he said, "Doesn't that prove he is a man of honor? He was defeated but felt that he had to die avenging himself. And what harm can he do? He'll be a member of the common band

—we won't take him into our confidence. And we'll keep a close eye on him. I'll give him my personal attention. When the time is ripe we'll put him to a test that he must refuse if he is a spy for the *carabinieri*. Leave him to me."

Later that evening when he told Silvestro that he was now a member of the band, the man simply said, "You can count on me for anything." He understood that Guiliano had again saved him from death.

■ ■ ■

AT EASTERTIME Guiliano visited his family. Pisciotta had argued against this, saying the police might set a trap. Easter in Sicily had always been a traditional death day for bandits. The police counted on the deep ties of family to bring outlaws sneaking down from the mountains to visit their loved ones. But Guiliano's spies brought word that the Maresciallo himself would be visiting his family on the mainland and that half the garrison at the Bellampo Barracks had been given leave to celebrate the holiday in Palermo. Guiliano decided that he would bring enough men with him to make it safe. He slipped into Montelepre on Holy Saturday.

He had sent word of his visit a few days before and his mother had prepared a feast. That night he slept in his childhood bed, and the next day, when his mother went to morning Mass, Guiliano accompanied her to church. He had a bodyguard of six men who were also visiting their families in the town but had orders to accompany Guiliano wherever he went.

As he came out of the church with his mother, his six bodyguards were waiting for him with Pisciotta. Aspanu's face was white with fury as he said, "You have been betrayed Turi. The Maresciallo has returned from Palermo with twenty extra men to arrest you. They have your mother's house surrounded. They think you're inside."

Guiliano felt for one moment a kind of anger at his own rashness and stupidity and resolved he would never be so careless again. Not that the Maresciallo with his twenty men could have captured him even in his mother's house. His bodyguards would have ambushed them, and there would have been a bloody battle. But that would have spoiled the spirit of his Easter homecoming. The day Christ had risen was not the day to break the peace.

He kissed his mother goodbye and told her to return home and freely admit to the police that she had left him at the church. In that way she could not be charged with any conspiracy. He told her not to worry, that he and his men were heavily armed and would easily escape; there would not even be any fighting. The *carabinieri* would not dare to follow them into the mountains.

Guiliano and his men left without even being sighted by the police. That night in the mountain camp, Guiliano questioned Pisciotta. How could the Maresciallo have known about the visit? Who was the informer? Everything must be done to find out. "That will be your special task, Aspanu," he said. "And if there is one, there may be others. I don't care how long it takes or how much money we spend, you must find out."

■ ■ ■

EVEN AS a child, Pisciotta had never liked the buffoonish barber of Montelepre. Frisella was one of those barbers who cut hair to suit his mood of the day, one time modishly, another time puckishly, another time with the extreme conservativeness of a peasant farmer. By varying his style he put forward his claim to being an artist. He was also too familiar with his superiors and too patronizing to his equals. With children he was playful in that particularly spiteful Sicilian style which is one of the less pleasant sides of the island character; he would nip their ears with his scissors and sometimes cut their hair so short that their heads looked like billiard balls. So it was with grim satisfaction that Pisciotta reported to Guiliano that Frisella the barber was the police spy and had broken the sacred code of *omerta*. It was obvious that the Maresciallo was not making a random strike that Easter day. He must have received information that Turi would be there. And how could he have gotten that information since Turi had sent word to his family only twenty-four hours before?

Pisciotta used his own informers in the village to check on every step the Maresciallo had taken during that twenty-four hours. And since only Guiliano's mother and father had known about the visit, he questioned them casually to see if they might have accidentally given anything away.

Maria Lombardo soon smelled out his intention. She said to him, "I spoke to no one, not even my neighbors. I stayed in the house and cooked so that Turi would have an Easter feast."

But Guiliano's father had gone to the barber Frisella on the morning of his son's visit. The old man was a little vain, and he wanted to look his best on the rare occasions when his son Turi came to visit at the house in Montelepre. Frisella had shaved and barbered the old man and made his usual jokes. "Was Signor perhaps going into Palermo to visit certain young ladies there? Was he receiving important visitors from Rome?" He, Frisella, would make Signor Guiliano look handsome enough to receive a "king." And Pisciotta visualized the setting. Guiliano's father with a little secretive smile on his face as he grumbled that a man could look like a gentleman for no reason except his own satisfaction. And yet the swelling of importance at knowing his son was famous enough to be called the "King of Montelepre." Perhaps the old man had come in on other occasions and the barber had learned that Guiliano visited the same day and so put two and two together.

Maresciallo Roccofino dropped into the barbershop every morning for his daily shave. There did not seem to be any conversation that could convey information from the barber to the policeman. But Pisciotta was certain. He sent spies to the barbershop to lounge around all day and play cards with Frisella at the little table he kept out on the street. They drank wine, talked politics and shouted insults at friends who passed by.

Over the weeks Pisciotta's spies gathered more information.

Frisella always whistled the tune of one of his favorite opera arias when he shaved and cut hair; sometimes the large oval-shaped radio would play with recordings from Rome. This would always be the case when he attended the Maresciallo. And there would always be a time when he leaned over the police officer and whispered something. If you were not suspicious it was only a barber being deferential to the wishes of his customer's pleasure. But then one of Pisciotta's spies got a look at the lire note the Maresciallo used to pay for his service. They noticed it was folded, and the barber put it in a special watch fob pocket in his vest, underneath his white coat. When the spy and one of his helpers confronted Frisella and forced him to show the note, it was of ten thousand lire denomination. The barber swore it was for his services over the past few months, and the spies pretended to believe him.

Pisciotta gave his evidence to Guiliano in the presence of Terranova, Passatempo and Corporal Silvestro. They were in their camp in the mountains, and Guiliano went to the edge of one of the cliffs that overlooked Montelepre and stared down at the town.

Master Frisella, the barber, had been a part of that town ever since Guiliano could remember. As a little boy he had gone to Frisella to have his hair cut for Holy Confirmation, and Frisella had given him a small silver coin as a gift. He knew Frisella's wife and son. Frisella had shouted jokes to him in the street and always asked after his mother and father.

But now Frisella had broken the sacred law of *omerta*. He had sold secrets to the enemy; he was a paid informant of the police. How could he have been so foolish? And what was he, Guiliano, to do with him now? It was one thing to kill the field police in hot combat, it was another thing to execute, in cold blood, an avuncular older man. Turi Guiliano was only twenty-one years of age and this was the first time he had to use the cold cruelty so necessary in great endeavors.

He turned back to the others. "Frisella has known me all my

life. He gave me lemon ices when I was a child, do you remember, Aspanu? And maybe he just gossips with the Maresciallo, doesn't really give him information. It's not as if we told him I was coming to town and then he told the police. Maybe he just gives theories and accepts the money because it is offered. Who would refuse?"

Passatempo was looking at Guiliano with narrowed eyes, as a hyena would regard the body of a dying lion, wondering if the time was ripe and safe to dash in and tear off a piece of flesh. Terranova shook his head slightly, a smile on his lips as if he were listening to a child tell some foolish story. But only Pisciotta answered him.

"He's as guilty as a priest in a whorehouse," Pisciotta said.

"We could give him a warning," Guiliano said. "We could bring him over to our side and use him to give false information to the authorities when it suits our purpose." Even as he spoke, he knew he was wrong. He could no longer afford such gestures.

Pisciotta said wrathfully, "Why not give him a present, a sack of grain or a chicken while you're at it? Turi, our lives and the lives of all the men out there in the mountains depend on your courage, on your will, on your leadership. How can we follow if you forgive a traitor like Frisella? A man who breaks the law of *omerta*. The Friends of the Friends would have his liver and heart hanging from the barber pole by this time and on less evidence. If you let him go then every greedy traitor will know he can inform once without punishment. One of those 'onces' could be our death."

Terranova spoke judiciously. "Frisella is a stupid buffoon, a greedy and treacherous man. In ordinary times he would only be the village nuisance. Now he is dangerous. To let him off would be foolhardy—he is not intelligent enough to mend his ways. He would think we are not serious people. And so would many others. Turi, you have suppressed the activities of the Friends of the Friends in the town of Montelepre. Their man Quintana moves very cautiously, though he makes some imprudent statements. If you let Frisella off with anything less than death, the Friends would think you weak and test you further. The *carabinieri* would become bolder, less afraid, more dangerous. Even the citizens of Montelepre would think less of you. Frisella cannot live." He said this last almost with regret.

Guiliano listened to them thoughtfully. They were right. He was conscious of Passatempo's look and read to the man's heart. Passatempo could never be trusted if Frisella lived. There was no going back to being one of Charlemagne's knights, there was no going back to resolving differences in honorable combat on the Fields of the Cloths of Gold. Frisella would have to be executed and in such a way as to achieve maximum terror.

Guiliano had an idea. He turned to Corporal Silvestro and asked, "What do you think? Surely the Maresciallo would have told you his informants. Is the barber guilty?"

Silvestro shrugged, his face impassive. He did not speak. They all recognized that it was a point of honor for him not to speak, not to betray his former trust. That his not answering was his way of telling them that the barber certainly had some contact with the Maresciallo. Still Guiliano had to be sure. He smiled at the Corporal and said, "Now is the time to prove your loyalty to us. We will all go to Montelepre together and you will personally execute the barber in the public square."

Aspanu Pisciotta marveled at his friend's cunning. Guiliano had always surprised him. He had always acted nobly and yet he could plant a trap worthy of Iago. They had all come to know the Corporal as a truthful and honest man with a sense of fair play. He would never consent to perform the execution if he was not sure the barber was guilty, no matter what the cost to him. Pisciotta saw that Guiliano had a little smile on his face—that if the Corporal refused, the barber would be judged innocent and go free.

But the Corporal stroked his bushy mustache and looked them all in the eye. He said, "Frisella cuts hair so badly he deserves to die for that alone. I'll be ready in the morning."

At dawn Guiliano and Pisciotta and ex-Corporal Silvestro took the road down to Montelepre. An hour before them Passatempo had left with a squad of ten men to seal off all streets emptying into the central square of the town. Terranova was left in charge of the camp and prepared to lead a strong band into the town if they ran into serious trouble.

It was still early morning when Guiliano and Pisciotta entered the town square. The cobbled streets and narrow sidewalks had been flushed with water and some children were playing around the raised platform where the donkey and mare had been mated on that long-ago fateful day. Guiliano told Silvestro to chase the children out of the square so they could not witness what was about to happen. Silvestro did so with such temper that the children scattered like chickens.

When Guiliano and Pisciotta entered the barbershop with machine pistols at the ready, Frisella was cutting the hair of a wealthy landowner of the province. The barber assumed they had come to kidnap his customer and he whipped off the cloth with a cunning smile as if to present a prize. The landowner, an old Sicilian peasant who had grown rich during the war by selling livestock to the Italian Army, stood up proudly. But Pisciotta motioned him to one side and said with a grin, "You don't have enough money to pay our price and for us to take the trouble."

Guiliano was extremely alert and kept his eyes on Frisella. The barber was still holding his scissors. "Put them down," he said. "You won't need to cut hair where you're going. Now get outside."

Frisella dropped the scissors and turned his wide buffoon's face into a clown's grimace as he attempted to smile. "Turi," he said, "I have no money, I've just opened the shop. I'm a poor man."

Pisciotta grabbed him by his full bushy hair and dragged him out of the shop and into the cobblestoned street where Silvestro was waiting. Frisella fell on his knees and began to scream.

"Turi, Turi, I cut your hair when you were a child. Don't you remember. My wife will starve. My son is weak in the head."

Pisciotta could see Guiliano wavering. He kicked the barber and said, "You should have thought of those things when you informed."

Frisella began to weep. "I never informed on Turi. I told the Maresciallo about some sheep stealers. I swear on my wife and child."

Guiliano looked down at the man. At that moment he felt that his heart would break, that what he was about to do would destroy him forever. But he said gently, "You have a minute to make your peace with God."

Frisella looked up at the three men surrounding him and saw no mercy. He bowed his head and murmured a prayer. Then looked up and said to Guiliano, "Don't let my wife and child starve."

"I promise you they will have bread," Guiliano said. He turned to Silvestro. "Kill him," he said.

The Corporal had watched the scene in a daze. But at these words he triggered his machine pistol. The bullets lifted Frisella's body and sent it skittering across the wet cobblestones. Blood darkened the little pools of water between the cracks. Blood ran black over the cracks the water had not reached and flushed out little lizards. There was a long moment of hushed silence in the square. Then Pisciotta knelt over the body and pinned a white square of paper on the dead man's chest.

When the Maresciallo arrived that was all he found as evidence. The shopkeepers had seen nothing, they claimed. They had been working in the rear of the store. Or they had been studying the beautiful clouds over Monte d'Ora. Frisella's customer said that he was washing his face in the basin when he heard the shots, he had never seen the murderers. But despite all this it was clear who was guilty. The square paper on Frisella's body read, SO DIE ALL WHO BETRAY GUILIANO.

CHAPTER

12

THE WAR was now over but Guiliano's had just begun. In the course of two years, Salvatore Guiliano had become the most famous man in Sicily. He built up his domination of the northwest corner of the island. At the heart of his empire was the town of Montelepre. He controlled the towns of Piani dei Greci, Borgetto and Partinico. And the murderous town of Corleone, whose inhabitants were so ferocious they were notorious even in Sicily. He ranged just short of Trapani, and he threatened the town of Monreale and the capital of Sicily itself, Palermo. When the new democratic government in Rome put a price of ten million lire on his head, Guiliano laughed and continued to move confidently through many of the towns. He even dined occasionally in the restaurants of Palermo. At the end of the meal he would always leave a note under the plate which read, "This is to show that Turi Guiliano can go wherever he likes."

Guiliano's impregnable fortress was the vast galleries of the Cammarata Mountains. He knew all the caves and all the secret paths. He felt invincible here. He loved the view of Montelepre below him, the Partinico plain that stretched away to Trapani and the Mediterranean Sea. As twilight became blue, reflecting the faraway sea, he could see the ruined Greek temples, the orange groves, the olive orchards and the grain-filled fields that were Western Sicily. With his binoculars he could see the padlocked roadside shrines holding their dusty saints inside.

From these mountains he sallied forth with his men onto the white dusty roads to rob government convoys, stick up railway trains, and relieve rich women of their jewels. The peasants riding on their painted carts in holy festivals saluted him and his men at first with fear and then with respect and affection. There was not one of them, not a shepherd or laborer who had not benefited from his distribution of loot.

The whole countryside became his spies. At night when children said their prayers they included a plea to the Virgin Mary "to save Guiliano from the *carabinieri*."

It was a countryside that fed Guiliano and his men. There were the olive and orange groves, the vineyards of grapes. There were the flocks of sheep whose shepherds looked the other way when the bandits came for a few lambs. Through this landscape Guiliano moved like a ghost, lost in the hazy blue light of Sicily which is the cerulean Mediterranean Sea reflected from the sky.

The winter months were long in the mountains, cold. And yet Guiliano's band grew. At night scores of campfires freckled the slopes and valleys of the Cammarata range. The men used the firelight to clean their guns, repair their clothing, do their laundry in the nearby mountain stream. Preparing the communal evening meal sometimes caused arguments. Every village in Sicily had a different recipe for squid and eels, disagreed on what herbs should be disbarred from the tomato sauce. And whether sausages should ever be baked. Men partial to the knife for murder liked to do laundry; the kidnappers preferred the cooking and sewing chores. The raiders of banks and trains stuck to cleaning their guns.

Guiliano made them all dig defense trenches and establish far-flung listening posts so they could not be surprised by government forces. One day when the men were digging they came upon the skeleton of a giant animal, bigger than they could imagine. Hector Adonis arrived that day bringing books for Guiliano to study, for Guiliano was curious now to know everything in the world. He studied books of science, of medicine, of politics, philosophy and military techniques. Hector Adonis brought him sackfuls every few weeks. Guiliano took him to where the men had dug up the skeleton. Adonis smiled at their puzzlement. "Haven't I given you enough books on history?" he said to Guiliano. "A man who does not know the history of mankind for the last two thousand years is a man living in the dark." He paused for a few moments. The mellow voice of Adonis was the lecturing voice of a professor.

"This is a skeleton of a war machine employed by Hannibal of Carthage who two thousand years ago traveled over these mountains to destroy imperial Rome. It is the skeleton of one of his war elephants, trained to combat and never before then seen on this continent. How frightening they must have been to those Roman soldiers. Yet they availed Hannibal nothing; Rome vanquished him and destroyed Carthage. These mountains have so many ghosts, and you have found one of them. Think, Turi, one day you will be one of the ghosts."

And Guiliano did think all that night. The idea pleased him that he would someday be one of the ghosts of history. If he were killed he hoped it would be in the mountains; he had the fantasy that, wounded, he would crawl into one of the thousands of caves and never be found until some accident discovered him, as had happened with Hannibal's elephant.

They changed encampments many times during the winter. And for weeks at a time the band dispersed altogether and slept in the houses of relatives, friendly shepherds, or the great empty granaries that belonged to the nobility. Guiliano spent most of the winter studying his books and making his plans. He had long talks with Hector Adonis.

In early spring he went with Pisciotta down the road that led to Trapani. On that road they saw a cart with new painted legends on its sides. For the first time they saw a panel showing the legend of Guiliano. It was a scene painted in gaudy reds, Guiliano taking the emerald ring from the finger of the Duchess as he bowed before her. In the background was Pisciotta holding a machine gun and threatening a group of cowering armed men.

It was on that day too that they first wore the belt buckles with an eagle and a lion rampant etched on a rectangular block of gold. The buckles had been made by Silvestro, who now served as their armorer. He had given them to Guiliano and Pisciotta. It became an emblem of their leadership of the band. Guiliano always wore it; Pisciotta only when he was with Guiliano. For Pisciotta often went into the towns and villages disguised, even into the city of Palermo.

At night in the mountains Guiliano, when he took off the belt, studied the rectangular buckle of gold. On the left side, there was an eagle that looked like a man in feathers. On the right side was a lion rampant, its paws—like the eagle's winged arms—supporting a filigree circle between them. It looked as if together they were spinning a wheel of the world. The lion especially fascinated him with its human body below the leonine head. The king of the air, the king of the ground, etched into soft yellow gold. Guiliano thought of himself as the eagle, Pisciotta the lion, and that circle, Sicily.

■ ■ ■

FOR CENTURIES, kidnapping of the rich had been one of the cottage industries of Sicily. Usually the kidnappers were the most fearsome of the Mafiosi, who had merely to send a letter before the kidnapping. This would be in the polite form, to the effect that to avoid troublesome details the ransom be paid in advance. Like a wholesaler's discount for immediate cash payment, the ransom would be considerably less because all the irritating details, such as the actual kidnapping, did not have to be performed. For in all truth, such a thing as kidnapping a famous personage was not as easy as people thought it was. It was not a business for greedy amateurs or scatterbrained lazy good-for-nothings who refused to work for a living. Nor was it ever the harebrained, suicidal event that it was in America, where its practitioners had given kidnapping a bad name. Even the word "kidnapping" was not used in Sicily, since children were not held for ransom unless they were accompanied by an adult. For say what you would of a Sicilian: that they were born criminals, that they murdered as easily as a woman picks flowers, that they were as cunningly treacherous as Turks, that they were socially three hundred years behind the times; yet no one could dispute that Sicilians loved, no, they idolized children. So there was no such thing called kidnapping in Sicily. They would "invite" a rich person to be their guest, and he could not be released until he had paid room and board, as in a fine hotel.

This cottage industry had developed certain rules over hundreds of years. The price was always negotiable through intermediaries such as the Mafia. There was never any violence offered to the "guest," if he cooperated. The "guest" was treated with the utmost respect, always addressed by his rank, such as Prince or Duke or Don or even Archbishop, if some bandit chose to endanger his soul by seizing a member of the cloth. Even a Member of Parliament was called Honorable to his face though everyone knew these rascals were greater thieves than anyone.

This was done out of prudence. History showed it was a policy that paid off. Once the prisoner was released he did not show any desire for vengeance as long as his dignity had been preserved. There was the classic case of a great Duke, who, after being released, and then leading the *carabinieri* to where he knew the bandits were hiding, had then paid for their defense lawyers. When despite this they were convicted, the Duke interceded to cut their long prison term in half. This was because they had treated him with such exquisite tact and politeness that the Duke declared he had never encountered such fine manners even in the highest society of Palermo.

Conversely a prisoner who had been ill-treated would, upon his release, spend a fortune having his captors hunted down, sometimes offering a reward larger than the ransom paid.

But in the ordinary course of things, if both parties behaved in a civilized manner, the price was haggled over and the prisoner released. The rich of Sicily had come to think of this as a sort of unofficial tax for their living in the land they loved, and since they paid so little taxes to the official government, they bore this cross with Christian resignation.

Stubborn refusal or extended haggling was remedied by mild coercion. Then perhaps an ear was cut off, a finger amputated. Usually these were sufficient to bring everybody to his senses. Except for those extremely sad, rare cases when the body had to be delivered, ritually mutilated and riddled with bullets, or, in the olden days, stabbed numerous times in the pattern of the cross.

But "Inviting a Guest" was always a painstaking endeavor. The victim had to be observed for a period of time so that he could be snatched with minimum violence. Even before that, five or six hiding places had to be prepared and stocked with supplies and guards, for it was understood that the negotiations would be drawn out and the authorities would search for the victims. It was a complicated business not for amateurs.

When Guiliano decided to enter the kidnapping business, he was determined to entertain only the richest clients in Sicily. In fact his first victim was the island's wealthiest and most powerful noble. This was Prince Ollorto, who not only had vast estates in Sicily but also a virtual empire in Brazil. He was the landlord for most of the citizens of Montelepre—their farms and their houses. Politically he was the most powerful man behind the scenes; the Minister of Justice in Rome was a close personal friend, and the former King of Italy himself had stood godfather to the Prince's child. In Sicily the overseer for all his estates was Don Croce himself. It went without saying that the magnificent salary Don Croce was paid also included insurance payments to preserve Prince Ollorto's person from kidnappers and murderers and his jewels and cattle and sheep from thieves.

■ ■ ■

SAFE IN his castle, the walls guarded by Don Croce's retainers, the gatesmen, and his own personal guards, Prince Ollorto prepared for a peaceful and enjoyable evening of watching the stars in the heavens through the huge telescope which he loved more dearly than anything on earth. Suddenly there was the sound of heavy footsteps on the winding stairs that led to his observatory tower. The door crashed in and four roughly clad men holding guns filled the tiny room. The Prince covered his telescope protectively with his arm and turned away from the innocent stars to face them. When the Prince saw Terranova's ferretlike face, he offered up his prayers to God.

But Terranova said to him courteously, "Your Lordship, I am ordered to bring you to the mountains for a holiday with Turi Guiliano. You will be charged room and board for your visit, that is our custom. But you will be looked after like a newborn babe."

The Prince tried to hide his fear. He bowed and asked gravely, "May I take some medicines and a few clothes?"

Terranova said, "We will send for them. Speed now is of the essence. The *carabinieri* will arrive shortly and they are not invited to our little party. Now please go before me down the steps. And don't try to make a run for it. Our men are everywhere and even a Prince can't outrun bullets."

At the side gate far down the wall an Alfa Romeo and a jeep were waiting. Prince Ollorto was thrust into the Alfa Romeo with Terranova, the others jumped into the jeep, and the two vehicles sped up the mountain road. When they were a half-hour from Palermo and a short distance from Montelepre, the cars stopped and all the men got out. There was a roadside shrine with the figure of the Madonna, and Terranova knelt briefly before it and crossed himself. The Prince, who was a religious man, suppressed the impulse to do likewise, fearing it would be taken as a sign of weakness or of supplication to these men not to harm him. The five men spread out into a wide star formation, the Prince in its center. Then they started walking down a steep slope until they came upon a narrow path that led into the vast wilderness of the Cammarata Mountains.

They walked for hours, and often the Prince had to ask for a rest, which the men accompanying him granted courteously. They sat beneath a huge granite rock and ate supper. There was bread, a coarse loaf, a huge hunk of cheese and a bottle of wine. Terranova shared this equally among the men, including the Prince, and even with an apology. "I'm sorry to offer you nothing better," he said. "When we get to our camp Guiliano will give you a hot meal, perhaps some good rabbit stew. We have a cook who worked for restaurants in Palermo."

The Prince thanked him courteously and ate with good appetite. Indeed with better appetite than for the grand dinners he was used to. The exercise had made him ravenous, he had not felt such hunger for many years. Taking a packet of English cigarettes from his pocket, he offered them around. Terranova and each of his men took one gratefully and smoked avidly. The Prince mentally noted the fact that they did not appropriate the packet for their own use. So he was emboldened to say, "I have to take certain medicines. I am diabetic and must have insulin every day."

He was surprised at Terranova's concern. "But why didn't you say so?" he asked. "We could have waited a minute. But in any case don't worry. Guiliano will send for it and you will have it in the morning. I give you my promise."

"Thank you," the Prince said. Terranova's thin, whippetlike body seemed always to crouch with courteous and intense attention. His ferret face was always smiling and receptive. But he was like a razor: of use for service but also able to turn into something deadly. And then they resumed their march, Terranova at the point of the star formation. Often Terranova would drop back to chat with the Prince and reassure him he would come to no harm.

They had been ascending and finally they reached the flat top plain of a mountain. Three fires were going and picnic tables with bamboo chairs rested near the cliff edge. At one table Guiliano was reading a book by the light of an American Army battery lamp. There was a canvas bag filled with other books resting at his feet. The bag was covered with geckos and indeed there was a loud steady hum that filled the mountain air which the Prince recognized as the sound of millions of insects. It did not seem to bother Guiliano.

Guiliano rose from the table and greeted the Prince with courtesy. There was no air about him of captor to prisoner. But there was a curious smile on his face, for Guiliano was thinking how far he had come. Two years before he had been a poor peasant; now he held at his mercy the man with the bluest blood and richest purse in all of Sicily.

"Have you eaten?" Guiliano asked. "Is there anything you need to make your visit with us more pleasant? You will be with us for some time."

The Prince admitted to hunger and explained his need for insulin and other medicines. Guiliano called down over the side of the cliff and soon one of his men came rushing up the path with a pot of hot stew. Guiliano had the Prince write in great detail exactly what medicines he needed. "We have a chemist friend in Monreale who will open his shop for us no matter what the hour," Guiliano said. "You will have your medicine by noon tomorrow."

When the Prince had finished eating Guiliano led him down a slope and into a small cave where there was a straw bed with a mattress on it. Two of the bandits following them had blankets, and the Prince was amazed to see they even had white sheets and a huge lumpy pillow. Guiliano noticed his amazement and said, "You are an honored guest and I will do everything so that you may enjoy your little vacation. If any of my men offer you any disrespect, please inform me. They have received strict instructions to treat you with all regard for your rank, and your reputation as a patriot of Sicily. Now sleep well, you will need all your strength, for we make a long march tomorrow. A ransom note has been delivered and the *carabinieri* will be out in force searching so we must be a long way from here."

The Prince thanked him for his courtesy and then asked what the ransom would be.

Guiliano laughed and the Prince was charmed by that youthful laugh, the boyish handsomeness of his face. But with Guiliano's answer the charm vanished. "Your government has set a price of ten million lire on my head. It would be an insult to Your Lordship if the ransom were not ten times as high."

The Prince was stunned then said ironically, "I hope my family thinks as highly of me as you do."

"It will be open to negotiation," Guiliano said. When he left the two bandits prepared the bed and then sat outside the cave. Despite the absolute roar of the insects, Prince Ollorto slept better than he had in years.

■ ■ ■

GUILIANO HAD been busy throughout the night. He had sent men to Montelepre for the medicine; he had lied to the Prince when he said Monreale. Then he had sent Terranova to the Abbot Manfredi at his monastery. He wanted the Abbot to handle the ransom negotiations, though he knew that the Abbot would have to work through Don Croce. But the Abbot would be a perfect buffer, and Don Croce would get his commission.

The negotiations would be long, and it was understood that the full sum of one hundred million lire could not be paid. Prince Ollorto was very rich, but, historically, the first demand was not the real price.

The second day of Prince Ollorto's kidnapping was a very pleasant one for him. There was a long but not arduous march to a deserted farmhouse deep in the mountains. Guiliano was very much the lord of the comfortable manor, as if he were a wealthy countryman honored by a surprise visit from his king. With his sharp eye Guiliano saw that Prince Ollorto was distressed by the condition of his clothes. That he looked regretfully at the carefully tailored English suit he had paid so much for being frayed by wear.

Guiliano asked him without contempt but only with real curiosity, "Do you really care so much for what you wear on the outside of your skin?"

The Prince had always had a pedagogical turn of mind. And certainly in these circumstances they both had time on their hands. So he gave Guiliano a speech on how correct clothing, beautifully tailored and of the finest materials, could enrich a man such as himself. He described the tailors in London, so snobbish that they made Italian Dukes seem like Communists in comparison. He told of all the different kinds of fabrics, the great skills, the time spent in getting innumerable fittings. "My dear Guiliano," Prince Ollorto said, "it's not the money, though Saint Rosalie knows that what I paid for this suit would keep a Sicilian family for a year, and pay for their daughter's dowry too. But I have to go to London. I have to spend days with tailors who push me back and forth. It is a miserable experience. So I regret that this suit is ruined. It can never be replaced."

Guiliano was studying the Prince with sympathy and he asked, "Why is it so important to you and your class that you must dress so extravagantly, or forgive me, so correctly? Even now you still wear your tie though we are in the mountains. When we entered this house I noticed you buttoned your jacket as if some Duchess were waiting to greet you."

Now Prince Ollorto, though he was an extreme reactionary politically, and like most of the Sicilian nobility had no sense of economic justice, had always a sense of identity with the lower classes. He felt that they were human beings like himself and no man who worked for him and minded his manners and knew his place would be left in want. The servants in his castle adored him. He treated them like members of the family. There were always gifts for their birthdays and little treats for them on the holidays. During family meals when no outside guests were present, the servants waiting on the table would join in the family discussion and give their opinions on the noble family's problems. And this was not uncommon in Italy. The lower classes were treated cruelly only when they fought for their economic rights.

And now the Prince took the same attitude toward Guiliano. As if his captor were only his servant who wanted to share his life, the enviable life of a very rich and powerful man. The Prince was suddenly aware that he could turn his period of captivity into an advantage that might even make paying his ransom worthwhile. But he knew he had to be very careful. That he had to exert his charm to the utmost without any condescension. That he had to be frank and sincere and as truthful as he could be. And that he could not try to make too much capital of the situation. For Guiliano could spring from weakness to strength.

So now he answered Guiliano's question seriously and with great genuineness. He said with a smile, "Why do you wear that emerald ring, that gold buckle?" He waited for an answer, but Guiliano only smiled. The Prince went on. "I married an even richer woman than myself. I have power and political duties. I have estates here in Sicily and an even larger estate in Brazil through my wife. People in Sicily kiss my hands as soon as I take them out of my pockets, and even in Rome I am held in great esteem. For in that city, money commands. Everyone's eyes are upon me. I feel ridiculous—I have done nothing to earn all this. But it is mine to keep and I must keep it, I cannot disgrace that public person. Even when I go out hunting in what seems to be a rough garb of the countryman, I must look the part perfectly. That of a rich and great man going hunting. How I envy men like you and Don Croce sometimes, who hold your power in your head and your heart. Who have won your power by your courage and your cunning. Isn't it laughable that I do almost the same thing by going to the best tailor in London?"

He delivered this speech so prettily that Guiliano laughed aloud. In fact Guiliano was so amused that the two of them ate dinner together and talked long of the miseries of Sicily and the poltrooneries of Rome.

The Prince knew of Don Croce's hope to enlist Guiliano and tried to further that aim. "My dear Guiliano," he said, "how is it that you and Don Croce do not join together to rule Sicily? He has the wisdom of age, you have the idealism of youth. There is no question that both of you love Sicily. Why can you not join forces in the times ahead which are dangerous for all of us? Now that the war is over, things are changing. The Communists and Socialists hope to degrade the Church, destroy blood ties. They dare to say that duty to a political party is more important than the love for your mother, the devotion you owe your brothers and sisters. What if they were to win the elections and set these policies in motion?"

"They can never win," Guiliano said. "Sicilians will never vote Communist."

"Don't be so sure," the Prince said. "You remember Silvio Ferra, he was your boyhood friend. Good boys like Silvio went to the war and came back infected with radical notions. Their agitators promise free bread, free land. The innocent peasant is like a donkey following a carrot. They may very well vote Socialist."

"I have no love for the Christian Democrats, but I would do everything to prevent a Socialist government," Guiliano said.

"Only you and Don Croce can ensure the freedom of Sicily," the Prince said. "You must join together. Don Croce speaks always as if you were his son—he has a positive affection for you. And only he can avert a great war between you and the Friends of the Friends. He understands that you do what you must do; I understand it too. But even now the three of us can work together and preserve our destinies. If not we can all go down to destruction."

Turi Guiliano could not contain his anger. What insolence the rich had. He said with lethal calm, "Your own ransom has not yet been settled and yet you propose an alliance. You may be dead."

The Prince slept badly that night. But Guiliano showed no further ill will, and the Prince spent his next two weeks in a very profitable fashion. His health improved and his body toned up with the daily exercise and fresh air. Though he had always been slim, he had acquired deposits of fat around his middle and these now disappeared. Physically he had never felt better.

And mentally too he was exhilarated. Sometimes when he was moved from place to place, Guiliano was not with the party guarding him, and he had to make conversation with men who were illiterate and ignorant of any culture. But he was surprised at their character. Most of these bandits were naturally courteous, had a native dignity, and were by no means unintelligent. They always addressed him by his rank and tried to grant his every request. He had never come so close to his fellow Sicilians before, and he was surprised to feel a renewed affection for his land and his people. The ransom, finally settled at sixty million lire in gold, was paid through Don Croce and the Abbot Manfredi. The night before his release, Prince Ollorto was given a banquet by Guiliano and his chiefs and twenty of the most important members of the band. Champagne was brought from Palermo to celebrate the occasion and they all toasted his imminent freedom, for they had grown fond of him. The Prince gave the final toast. "I have been a guest at the most noble family houses in Sicily," he said. "But I have never received such good treatment, such hospitality, or men with such exquisite manners as I have here in these mountains. I have never slept so soundly or eaten so well." He paused for a moment and said with a smile, "The bill was a little high, but good things always come dear." This brought a roar of laughter, Guiliano laughing loudest of all. But the Prince noticed that Pisciotta did not even smile.

They all drank to his health and gave him a cheer. It was a night the Prince would remember for the rest of his life, and with pleasure.

The next morning, a Sunday, the Prince was deposited in front of the Cathedral of Palermo. He went into the church for early

Mass and said a prayer of Thanksgiving. He was dressed exactly as on the day he was kidnapped. Guiliano, as a surprise and a token of his esteem, had had his English suit repaired and cleaned by the finest tailor in Rome.

CHAPTER

13

THE MAFIA chiefs of Sicily demanded a meeting with Don Croce. Though Don Croce was acknowledged as the chief among the chiefs, he did not rule them directly. They had their own empires. The Mafia was like one of those medieval kingdoms where powerful barons banded together to support the wars of their most powerful member, whom they acknowledged as their nominal ruler. But like those ancient barons they had to be wooed by their king, they had to be rewarded with the spoils of war. Don Croce ruled them not by force but by the power of his intelligence, his charisma, his lifelong acquisition of "respect." He ruled by combining their divergent interests into one general interest, by which they all benefited.

Don Croce had to be careful with them. They all had their private armies, their secret assassins, stranglers, poisoners, honorable wielders of straightforward death by the dreaded *lupara*. In that area their strength was equal to his; that was why the Don had wanted to enlist Turi Guiliano as his own personal warrior chief. These men were clever, too, in their own right, some of them the most cunning men living in Sicily. They did not begrudge the Don the building of his power; they trusted and believed in him. But even the most intelligent man in the world can be wrong sometimes. And they believed that the Don's infatuation with Guiliano was the only failure that had emerged from the labyrinth of his mind.

Don Croce arranged a sumptuous lunch for the six chiefs in the garden of the Hotel Umberto in Palermo where secrecy and security were assured.

The most fearful of these chiefs and the most outspoken was Don Siano, who ruled the town of Bisacquino. He had agreed to speak for the others and he did so with the harsh courtesy that was the rule of the Friends of the Friends at their highest level.

"My dear Don Croce," Don Siano said, "you know the respect we all have for you. It was you who resurrected us and our families. We owe you a great deal. So it is only to do you a service that we speak out now. This bandit Turi Guiliano has become too strong. We have treated him with too much deference. He is a mere boy and yet he defies your authority and ours. He robs the jewels from our most illustrious clients. He abducts the olives, the grapes, the corn of our richest landowners. And now he shows us a final disrespect we cannot ignore. He kidnaps Prince Ollorto whom he knows to be under our protection. And yet you continue to treat with him, you continue to extend your hand in friendship. I know he is strong, but are we not stronger? And if we let him go his way, will he not grow stronger still? We all of us agree that now is the time to resolve this question. We must take all the measures possible to negate his strength. If we ignore his kidnapping of Prince Ollorto we will be the laughingstock of all Sicily."

Don Croce nodded his head as if in agreement with all that had been said. But he did not speak. Guido Quintana, the least of the men present, said almost plaintively, "I am the Mayor of Montelepre and everybody knows I am one of the Friends. But nobody comes to me for judgment or redress or gifts. Guiliano rules the town and permits me to live there on his sufferance so as not to provoke a quarrel with you gentlemen. But I cannot make a living, I have no authority. I am a mere figurehead. While Guiliano lives, the Friends do not exist in Montelepre. I am not afraid of this lad. I faced him down once. Before he became a bandit. I do not think him a man to be feared. If this council agrees I will attempt to eliminate him. I have made plans and I only await your approval to execute them."

Don Piddu of Caltanissetta and Don Arzana of Piani dei Greci nodded. Don Piddu said, "Where would be the difficulty? With our resources we can deliver his corpse to the Cathedral of Palermo and go to his funeral as we would to a wedding."

The other chiefs, Don Marcuzzi of Villamura, Don Buccilla of Partinico, and Don Arzana voiced their approval. Then they waited.

Don Croce lifted his massive head. His spike of a nose impaled them each in turn as he spoke. "My dear friends, I agree with everything you feel," he said. "But I think you underrate this young man. He is cunning beyond his years and perhaps as brave as any of us here. He will not be so easy to kill. Also I see a use for him in the future, not just for myself but for all of us. The Communist agitators are whipping the people of Sicily into a madness that makes them expect another Garibaldi, and we must make sure that Guiliano is not flattered into being their savior. I do not have to tell you the consequences to us if those savages ever come to rule Sicily. We must persuade him to fight on our side. Our position is not yet so secure that we can afford to throw away his strength by assassinating him." The Don sighed, washed down a morsel of bread with a glass of wine and mopped his mouth daintily with his napkin. "Do me this one favor. Let me make a last effort to persuade him. If he refuses, then do what you feel you must do. I will give you your answer within three days' time. Just let me make one last effort to come to a reasonable agreement."

It was Don Siano who first bowed his head in agreement. After all, what reasonable man would be so impatient to commit murder that he could not wait three days? When they left, Don Croce summoned Hector Adonis to his home in Villaba.

■ ■ ■

THE DON was peremptory with Adonis. "I have come to the end of my patience with your godson," he said to the little man.

"He must now be with us or against us. The kidnapping of Prince Ollorto was a direct insult to my person, but I am willing to forgive and forget. After all he is young, and I remember when I was his age I had his high spirits. As I have said always, I admire him for it. And believe me, I value his abilities. I would be overjoyed if he agreed to be my right hand. But he must recognize his place in the scheme of things. I have other chiefs who are not so admiring, not so understanding. I will not be able to hold them back. So go to your godson and tell him what I have told you. And bring me back his answer tomorrow at the latest. I can wait no longer."

Hector Adonis was frightened. "Don Croce, I recognize your generosity in spirit and deed. But Turi is willful and like all young men too sure of his power. And it is true he is not altogether helpless. If he wars on the Friends, I know he cannot win, but the damage could be frightful. Is there some reward I can promise him?"

The Don said, "Promise him this. He will have a high place in the Friends, and he will have my personal loyalty and my love. And after all he cannot live in the mountains forever. There will come a time when he will wish to take his place in society, to live within the law in the bosom of his family. When that day comes, I am the only man in Sicily who can assure him his pardon. And it will be my greatest happiness to do so. I mean this sincerely." And indeed when the Don spoke in this fashion he could not be disbelieved, he could not be resisted.

■ ■ ■

WHEN HECTOR ADONIS went up into the mountains to meet with Guiliano he was very troubled and frightened for his godson and he resolved to speak frankly. He wanted Guiliano to understand that their love for each other came first, even above his allegiance to Don Croce. When he arrived, chairs and folding tables were set up at the edge of the cliff. Turi and Aspanu sat alone.

He said to Guiliano, "I must talk to you privately."

Pisciotta said angrily, "Little man, Turi has no secrets from me."

Adonis ignored the insult. He said calmly, "Turi can tell you what I will tell him, if he likes. That is his affair. But I cannot tell you. I cannot take that responsibility."

Guiliano patted Pisciotta's shoulder. "Aspanu, leave us alone. If it's something you should know, I'll tell you." Pisciotta rose abruptly, gave Adonis a hard stare and walked away.

Hector Adonis waited for a long time. Then he began to speak. "Turi, you are my godson. I have loved you since you were an infant. I taught you, gave you books to read, helped you when you became an outlaw. You are one of the few people in the world who makes living worthwhile for me. And yet your cousin Aspanu insults me without a word of reproach from you."

Guiliano said sadly, "I trust you more than I trust anyone except for my mother and father."

"And Aspanu," Hector Adonis said reproachfully. "Has he not grown too bloodthirsty for any man to trust?"

Guiliano looked him in the eyes and Adonis had to admire the serene honesty of his face. "Yes, I must confess, I trust Aspanu more than I do you. But I have loved you since I was a little boy. You freed my mind with your books and wit. I know you've helped my mother and father with your money. And you have been a true friend in my troubles. But I see you entangled with the Friends of the Friends, and something tells me that is what brings you here today."

Once again, Adonis marveled at his godson's instincts. He presented the case to Turi. "You must come to an accommodation with Don Croce," he said. "Not the King of France, not the King of the Two Sicilies, not Garibaldi, not even Mussolini himself could ever completely crush the Friends of the Friends. You cannot hope to win a war against them. I beg of you to come to an accommodation. You must bend your knee to Don Croce at the beginning, but who knows what your position will be in the future. I tell you this on my honor and on the head of your mother whom we both adore: Don Croce believes in your genius and bears the seed of a true love for your person. You will be his heir, the favored son. But for this time you must bow to his rule."

He could see that Turi was moved by this and took him very seriously. Hector Adonis said passionately, "Turi, think of your mother. You cannot live in the mountains forever, risking your life to see her a few days every year. With Don Croce you can hope for a pardon."

The young man took some time to collect his thoughts and then spoke to his godfather in a slow serious tone. "First of all I wish to thank you for your honesty," he said. "The offer is very tempting. But I am now committed to free the poor in Sicily, and I do not believe the Friends have that same aim. They are servitors of the rich and the politicians in Rome and these are my sworn enemies. Let us wait and see. Certainly I kidnapped Prince Ollorto and stepped on their toes but I continue to permit Quintana to live and he is a man I despise. I forbear out of respect for Don Croce. Tell him that. Tell him that and tell him that I pray for the day when we can become equal partners. When our interests will not conflict. As for his chiefs, let them do what they will. I have no fear of them."

It was with a heavy heart that Hector Adonis brought this answer back to Don Croce, who nodded his leonine head as if he had expected nothing else.

■ ■ ■

IN THE following month three separate attempts were made on Guiliano's life. Guido Quintana was allowed the first pass. He planned with an elaborateness that was worthy of the Borgias. There was a road that Guiliano frequently used when he made a sortie out of the mountains. Alongside the road were lush fields which Quintana filled with a great flock of sheep. Guarding these sheep were three harmless-looking shepherds, natives of the town of Corleone and old friends of Quintana.

For almost a week, when Guiliano was sighted coming down the road, the shepherds would greet him respectfully and in the old tradition ask for his hand to kiss. Guiliano engaged them in friendly conversation; shepherds were often part-time members of his band and he was always looking for new recruits. He did not feel himself in any danger since he nearly always traveled with bodyguards and often with Pisciotta, who was worth at least two men. The shepherds were unarmed and wore light clothing that could not conceal weapons.

But the shepherds had *lupare* and ammunition belts strapped to the bellies of some sheep in the middle of the flock. They waited for an opportunity when Guiliano would be alone or not so heavily guarded. But Pisciotta had wondered about the friendliness of these shepherds, the sudden appearance of this flock of sheep, and he made inquiries through his network of informants. The shepherds were identified as assassins employed by Quintana.

Pisciotta wasted no time. He took ten members of his own private band and rounded up the three shepherds. He questioned them closely about who owned the sheep, how long they had been shepherds, where they had been born, the names of their mothers and fathers, their wives and children. The shepherds answered with seeming frankness, but Pisciotta had the proof they were lying.

A search uncovered the weapons hidden in the fleece of the animals. Pisciotta would have executed the imposters, but Guiliano vetoed this. After all, no harm had been done and the real villain was Quintana.

So the shepherds were made to drive the flock of sheep into the town of Montelepre. And there in the main square they were made to sing out, "Come claim your gift from Turi Guiliano. A lamb for every household, a blessing from Turi Guiliano." And then the shepherds would do the slaughtering and skinning for any who requested such services.

"Remember," Pisciotta told the shepherds, "I want you to be as obliging as the sweetest shopgirl in Palermo, as if you were getting a commission. And give my regards and thanks to Guido Quintana."

Don Siano was not so elaborate. He sent two men as emissaries to bribe Passatempo and Terranova to act against Guiliano. But Don Siano could not comprehend the loyalty Guiliano inspired even in such a brute as Passatempo. Again Guiliano vetoed death, but Passatempo himself sent the two emissaries back with the mark of the *bastinado*.

The third attempt was made by Quintana again. And it was this attempt that made Guiliano lose his patience.

A new priest came to Montelepre, a traveling friar bearing various religious stigmata on his body. He said Mass at the local church one Sunday morning and showed his holy wounds.

His name was Father Dodana, and he was a tall athletic man who walked so briskly that his black cassock swirled in the air above his cracked leather shoes. His hair was a whitish blond, his face wrinkled and brown as a nut though he was still a young man. Within a month he was a legend in the town of Montelepre, for he was not afraid of hard work; he helped the local farmers gather their crops, he chastised mischievous children in the streets, he called on sick old women in their homes to confess their sins. And so one Sunday when he was standing outside the church after saying Mass, Maria Lombardo Guiliano was not surprised that he stopped her and asked if he could do something for her son.

"Surely you worry about his immortal soul," Father Dodana said. "The next time he comes to visit you send for me and I will hear his confession."

Maria Lombardo had no love for priests though she was religious. But this man impressed her. She knew Turi would never make a confession, but perhaps he would have use for a holy man sympathetic to his cause. She told the priest that her son would be informed of his offer.

Father Dodana said, "I would even go into the mountains to

help him. Tell him that. My only business is to save souls in danger of hell. What a man does is his own business."

Turi Guiliano came to visit his mother a week later. She urged him to see the priest and make a confession. Perhaps Father Dodana would give him Holy Communion. She would be easier in mind if he were shriven of his sins.

Turi Guiliano was very interested, which surprised his mother. He agreed to see the priest and he sent Aspanu Pisciotta to the church to escort him back to the Guiliano home. As Guiliano had suspected, when Father Dodana appeared, he moved too much like a man of action; he was too vigorous and he was too sympathetic to Guiliano's cause.

Father Dodana said, "My son, I will listen to your confession in the privacy of your bedroom. And then I will give you Communion. I have all my things here." He patted the wooden case under his arm. "Your soul will be as pure as your mother's, and if some evil befalls you, you will go straight to heaven."

Maria Lombardo said, "I'll make coffee and some food for you and the holy father." She went into the kitchen.

"You can confess me here," Turi Guiliano said with a smile.

Father Dodana glanced at Aspanu Pisciotta. "Your friend will have to leave the room," he said.

Turi laughed. "My sins are public. They appear in every newspaper. My soul is pure otherwise, except for one thing. I must confess to a suspicious nature. So I would like to see what is in that box you carry under your arm."

"The wafers of Holy Communion," Father Dodana said. "I will show you." He started to open the box but at that moment Pisciotta pressed a pistol against the back of his neck. Guiliano took the box away from the priest. At that moment they looked into each other's eyes. Guiliano opened the box. A dark blue automatic nestled in a bed of holy velvet glinted up at him.

Pisciotta saw Guiliano's face go pale, his eyes with their silver circles go black with a subdued fury.

Guiliano closed the box and looked up at the priest. "I think we should go to the church and pray together," he said. "We will say a prayer for you and we will say a prayer for Quintana. We will pray to the good Lord to take the evil out of Quintana's heart and the greediness out of yours. How much did he promise to pay you?"

Father Dodana was not worried. The other would-be assassins had been let off so lightly. He shrugged and then smiled. "The government reward and five million lire extra."

"A good price," Guiliano said. "I don't blame you for trying to make your fortune. But you deceived my mother and that I can't forgive. Are you a real priest?"

"Me?" Father Dodana said contemptuously. "Never. But I thought no one would suspect me."

The three of them walked down the street together, Guiliano carrying the wooden box, Pisciotta trailing behind. They entered the church. Guiliano made Father Dodana kneel at the altar, then took the automatic out of the wooden box. "You have a minute to say your prayers," Guiliano said.

■ ■ ■

THE NEXT morning Guido Quintana rose to go down to the café for his morning coffee. When he opened the door of his house, he was startled by a massive shadow blocking off the usual early morning sunlight. In the next instant a huge roughly made wooden cross tumbled inside, almost knocking him down. Nailed to that cross was the bullet-ridden body of Father Dodana.

■ ■ ■

DON CROCE pondered these failures. Quintana had been warned. He must devote himself to his duties as Mayor or the city of Montelepre would be forced to govern itself. It was clear Guiliano had lost patience and might launch an all-out war against the Friends. Don Croce recognized the sureness of a master in Guiliano's retribution. Only one more strike could be made and it must not fail. Don Croce knew that he must, finally, take a stand. And against his judgment and his true will, he sent for his most reliable assassin, a certain Stefan Andolini, also known as *Fra Diavalo*.

CHAPTER

14

THE GARRISON of Montelepre had been increased to more than a hundred *carabinieri*, and on the rare times Guiliano crept into town to spend an evening with his family, he was in constant fear that the *carabinieri* would swoop down upon them.

One such evening, listening to his father talk of the old days in America, the idea had come to him. Salvatore Senior was drinking wine and swapping tales with an old and trusted friend who had been in America also and had returned to Sicily with him, and they good-naturedly reproached each other for being so stupid. The other man, a carpenter named Alfio Dorio, reminded Guiliano's father of their first few years in America before they had worked for the Godfather, Don Corleone. They had been hired to help build a huge tunnel under a river, either to New Jersey or to Long Island, they quarreled about that. They reminisced about how eerie it was to work beneath a flowing river, their dread that the tubes holding out the water would collapse and they would drown like rats. And suddenly it came to Guiliano. These two men with some trusted helpers could build a tunnel from his parents' house to the base of the mountains only a hundred yards away. The exit could be hidden by the huge granite rocks and the source of the tunnel in the house could be hidden in one of the closets or beneath the stove in the kitchen. If that could be done Guiliano might come and go as he pleased.

The two older men told him that it was impossible, but his mother was wild with pleasure at the idea that her son could secretly come and sleep in his bed on cold winter nights. Alfio Dorio said that given the necessity for secrecy, the limited amount of men who could be used, and since the work could only be done at night, it would take too long to complete such a tunnel. And then there were problems. How would they get rid of the dirt excavated without being observed? And the soil here was full of stones. What if they came up against a strain of granite underground? And then what if the tunnel were betrayed by some of the men recruited to work on it? But the persistent objection of the two older men was that it would take at least a year. And Guiliano realized that they harped on this because they believed in their heart of hearts that he would not be alive so long. His mother realized the same thing.

She said to the two older men: "My son asks you to do something that may help save his life. If you are too lazy to do so, then I will. We can try at least. What do we have to lose except our labor? And what can the authorities do even if they discover the tunnel? We have a perfect right to dig on our land. We'll say we're making a cellar for vegetables and wine. Just think. This tunnel may someday save Turi's life. Isn't that worth some sweat?"

Hector Adonis was also present. Adonis said he would get some books on excavation and the necessary equipment. He also came up with a variation that pleased them all: that they build a little offshoot tunnel that would lead into another house on the Via Bella, an escape hatch in case the exit of the tunnel was compromised or betrayed by an informer. This offshoot tunnel would be dug first, and only by the two old men and Maria Lombardo. Nobody else would know about it. And it would not take so long to dig.

They had a long discussion on which house was trustworthy. Guiliano's father suggested the home of Aspanu Pisciotta's parents, but this was immediately vetoed by Guiliano. The house was too suspect, would be closely watched. And there were too many relatives living in that house. Too many people would know. Besides, Aspanu was not on good terms with his family. His natural father had died, and when his mother remarried he had never forgiven her.

Hector Adonis volunteered his house but it was too far away, and Guiliano did not want to endanger his godfather. For if the tunnel was discovered the owner of the house would surely be arrested. Other relatives and friends were considered and rejected, and then finally Guiliano's mother said, "There is only one person. She lives alone, just four houses down the street. Her husband was killed by the *carabinieri,* she hates them. She is my best friend and she is fond of Turi, she has watched him grow from a boy to a man. Didn't she send him food all the winter he spent in the mountains? She is my true friend and I have complete trust in her."

She paused for a moment and then said, "La Venera." And of course since the discussion had begun, they had been waiting for her to say that name. From the first, La Venera had been the only logical choice in all their minds. But they were Sicilian males and could not make such a suggestion. If La Venera agreed and the story came out, her reputation would be ruined forever. She was a young widow. She would be granting her privacy and her person to a young male. Who could ever doubt that she would lose her virtue? No man in that part of Sicily could marry or even respect such a woman. It was true that La Venera was at least fifteen years older than Turi Guiliano. But she was not yet forty. And though her face was not beautiful, it was attractive enough, and there was a certain fire in her eyes. In any case she was female and he was male and with the tunnel they would be alone together. There could not therefore be any doubt that they would become lovers, for no Sicilian believed that any male and female alone together, no matter what difference in age, could refrain. And so the tunnel into her house that perhaps might one day save Turi Guiliano's life would also mark her as a woman of ill repute.

What they all understood except for Turi Guiliano himself was that Guiliano's sexual chastity worried them. It was not natural in a Sicilian male. He was almost prudish. His band of men went to Palermo to visit whores; Aspanu Pisciotta had scandalous love affairs. His bandit chiefs Terranova and Passatempo were known to be the lovers of poor widows to whom they gave gifts. Passatempo even had a reputation as a man who used persuasion more typical of rapist than suitor, though he trod carefully now that he was under Guiliano's orders. Guiliano had decreed execution for any of his men who raped.

For all these reasons they had to wait for Guiliano's mother to put forth the name of her friend, and they were a little surprised when she did so. Maria Lombardo Guiliano was a religious, old-fashioned woman who did not hesitate to call the young girls of the town whores if they so much as took a stroll in the village square without a chaperone. They did not know what Maria Lombardo knew. That La Venera, because of the sufferings of childbirth, the lack of proper medical care, could no longer become pregnant. They could not know that Maria Lombardo had already decided that La Venera could best comfort her son in the safest possible way. Her son was an outlaw with a price on his head and could easily be betrayed by a woman. He was young and virile and needed a woman—who better than an older woman who could not bear children, and who could not make any claims for marriage? And indeed would not want to marry a bandit. She had had her fill of that misery. A husband shot down before her eyes. It was a perfect arrangement. Only La Venera's reputation would suffer, and so she would have to make the decision herself. It would be on her head if she agreed.

When Guiliano's mother made that request a few days later she was surprised when La Venera gave a proud and joyful yes. It confirmed a suspicion that her friend had a weakness for Turi. So be it, Maria Lombardo thought as she took La Venera into her arms with grateful tears.

The offshoot tunnel was completed in four months; the main

tunnel would not be completed for another year. Periodically Guiliano would sneak into town at night and visit his family and sleep in a warm bed, after his mother's hot meals; there would always be a feast. But it was nearly spring before he found it necessary to use the offshoot tunnel. A *carabinieri* patrol in strength came down the Via Bella and passed by. They were armed to the teeth. Guiliano's bodyguard of four men hidden in nearby houses was ready to do battle. But they passed on. Still there was the fear that on their return they might decide to raid the Guiliano home. So Turi Guiliano went through the trapdoor in his parents' bedroom and into the tunnel.

The offshoot was disguised by a wooden panel covered with a foot of dirt so that workers on the main tunnel would not know it existed. Guiliano had to dig away the dirt and remove the wooden disc. It took him another fifteen minutes to crawl through the narrow space that led under La Venera's house. The trapdoor there led to the kitchen and was covered by a huge iron stove. Guiliano tapped on the trapdoor with the prearranged signal and waited. He tapped again. He never feared bullets, but he feared this darkness. Finally there was a faint noise above him and then the trapdoor was raised. It could not rise all the way because the stove above it broke the plane of the lid. Guiliano had to squeeze through the opening and wound up on his belly on La Venera's kitchen floor.

Though it was the middle of the night, La Venera was still in her usual ill-fitting black dress, the mourning for her husband though he was three years dead. Her feet were bare. She wore no stockings, and as Guiliano rose from the floor he could see the skin on her legs was a startling white, so very much in contrast to the brown skin of her sunburned face and the jet black, coarse and heavily woven hair. For the first time he noticed that her face was not as broad as that of most of the older women in his town, that it was triangular, and though her eyes were dark brown, they had little black flecks in them he had never seen before. In her hand she held a scuttle full of live coals as if ready to throw them at the open trapdoor. Now she calmly slid the coals back into the stove and replaced the lid. She looked a little frightened.

Guiliano reassured her. "It's just a patrol roaming around. When they return to their barracks, I'll leave. But don't worry, I have friends out in the street."

They waited. La Venera made him coffee and they chatted. She noted that he did not have any of the nervous movements of her husband. He did not peer out the windows, his body did not tense at sudden noises in the street. He seemed completely relaxed. She did not know he had trained himself to act this way because of her stories about her husband and because he did not want to alarm his parents, especially his mother. He projected such an air of confidence that she soon forgot the danger he was in and they gossiped about the little happenings of the town.

She asked him if he had received the food she had sent him in the mountains from time to time. He thanked her and said how he and his companions had fallen on her food packets as if they were gifts from the Magi. How his men had complimented her cooking. He did not tell her of the coarse jokes some of his companions had made, that if her lovemaking equaled her cooking she would be a prize indeed. Meanwhile he was watching her closely. She was not being as friendly to him as usual; she did not show that fond tenderness she had always shown in public. He wondered if he had offended her in some way. When the danger was past and it was time for him to leave, they were formal with each other.

Two weeks later, Guiliano came to her again. The winter was near its end, but the mountains were filled with storm gales and the padlocked shrines of saints along the roads were dripping with rain. Guiliano in his cave dreamed of his mother's cooking, a hot bath, his soft bed in his childhood room. And mixed with these longings, much to his surprise, was the memory of the white skin of La Venera's legs. Night had fallen when he whistled up to his bodyguards and took the road down to Montelepre.

His family greeted him with joy. His mother started to cook his favorite dishes and as they were cooking she prepared a hot bath. His father had poured him a glass of anisette when one of the network of spies came to the house and told him that *carabinieri* patrols were surrounding the town and the Maresciallo himself was about to lead a flying squadron out of the Bellampo Barracks to raid the Guiliano household.

Guiliano went through the closet trapdoor and into the tunnel. It was muddy with rain and the earth clung to him and made the trip long and laborious. When he crawled into La Venera's kitchen his clothes were covered with slime, his face black.

When La Venera saw him, she laughed and it was the first time Guiliano could ever remember her laughing. "You look like a Moor," she said. And for a moment he felt a child's hurt, perhaps because the Moors were always the villains in the puppet shows of Sicily, and instead of being a hero in danger of his life, he could be seen as a villain. Or perhaps because her laugh made her seem inaccessible to his inner desire. She saw that in some way she had injured his vanity. "I'll fill the bath tin and you can get clean," she said. "And I have some of my husband's clothes you can wear while I clean yours."

She had expected him to object, that he would be too nervous to bathe in such a moment of danger. Her husband had been so jumpy when he visited her that he would never undress, never leave his guns out of reach of his hands. But Guiliano smiled at her and took off his heavy jacket and his guns and put them over the wooden box that held her firewood.

It took time to heat pots of water and fill the tin tub. She gave him coffee while they waited and studied him. He was handsome as an angel, she thought, but she was not deceived. Her husband had been as handsome and murdered men. And the bullets that killed him had made him ugly enough, she thought with misery; it was not clever to love a man's face, not in Sicily. How she had wept, but secretly there was the tremendous surge of relief. His death had been certain, once he had turned bandit, and every day she had waited, hoping he would die in the mountains or some far-off town. But he had been shot down before her eyes. And ever since she had been unable to escape the shame, not of his being a bandit, but of his dying an inglorious and not a brave death. He had surrendered and begged for mercy and the *carabinieri* had massacred him before her eyes. Thank God her daughter had not seen her father slain. A small mercy from Christ.

She saw that Turi Guiliano was watching her with that special light on his face that signaled desire in all men. She knew it well. Her husband's followers often had such a look. But she knew Turi would not try to seduce her, out of respect for his mother, out of respect for her sacrifice in allowing the tunnel to be built.

She left the kitchen and went into the small living room so that he could bathe in privacy. When she left, Guiliano stripped and stepped into the bath. The act of being naked with a woman nearby was erotic to him. He washed with scrupulous care and then put on her husband's clothes. The trousers were a little short and the shirt was tight around his chest so that he had to leave the top buttons undone. The towels she had warmed near the stove were little more than rags, his body still felt damp, and for the first time he realized how poor she was and resolved to supply her with money through his mother.

He called out to La Venera that he was dressed and she came back into the kitchen. She looked him over and said, "But you haven't washed your hair, you have a nest of geckos hiding there." She said this roughly but with a warm affection so that he did not take offense. Like some old grandmother she ran her hands over his matted hair, then took him by the arm and led him to the sink.

Guiliano felt a warm glow where her hand had touched his skull. He quickly put his head under the faucet and she ran water over him and shampooed his hair with the yellow kitchen soap; she had no other. When she did so her body and legs brushed against him and he felt the sudden urge to pass his hands over her breast, her soft belly.

When she finished washing his hair, La Venera made him sit on one of her black enameled kitchen chairs and vigorously dried his hair with a rough, raggedy brown towel. His hair was so long that it covered the collar of his shirt.

"You look like one of those ruffian English lords in the movies," she said. "I must cut your hair, but not in the kitchen. It will blow into my pots and spoil your dinner. Come into the other room."

Guiliano was amused by her sternness. She was assuming the role of an aunt or mother as if to prevent any show of a more tender feeling. He was aware of the sexuality behind it, but he was wary. In this area he was inexperienced and he did not want to look foolish. It was like the guerrilla warfare he waged in the mountains; he would not commit himself until all the odds were on his side. This was not scouted terrain. But the last year of commanding and killing men made his natural boyish fear seem more like a joke, the rejection by a woman not so paralyzing to his ego. And despite his reputation for chastity, he had gone to Palermo with his friends to visit prostitutes. But that was before he had become an outlaw and acquired the dignity of a bandit chief, and of course a romantic hero who would never do such a thing.

La Venera led him into the small living room cluttered with stuffed furniture, small tables topped with black varnished wood. On these tables were photographs of her dead husband and dead child, singly and together. Some were of La Venera with her family. The photos were framed in black oval wood, the prints tinged with sepia brown. Guiliano was surprised by the beauty of La Venera in these younger, happier days, especially when she was dressed in pretty, youthful clothes. There was a formal portrait of her alone, dressed in a dark red dress, that struck him to the heart. And for a moment he thought of her husband and how many crimes he must have committed to bring her such finery.

"Don't look at those pictures," La Venera said with a sad

smile. "That was in a time when I thought the world could make me happy." He realized that one of the reasons she had brought him into this room was to make him see these pictures.

She kicked the small stool from a corner of the room and Guiliano sat on it. From a leather box, beautifully made and stitched with gold, she took scissors, razor and comb—a prize the bandit Candeleria had brought home one Christmas from one of his crimes. Then she went into the bedroom and brought a white cloth which she hung over Guiliano's shoulders. She also brought a wooden bowl which she placed on the table beside her. A jeep went by the house.

She said, "Should I bring your guns from the kitchen? Would you be more comfortable?"

Guiliano looked at her calmly. He seemed absolutely serene. He did not want to alarm her. They both knew the jeep going by was full of *carabinieri* on their way to raid the Guiliano home. But he knew two things: If the *carabinieri* came here and tried to enter the barred door, Pisciotta and his men would massacre them all; and before he had left the kitchen he had moved the stove so that no one could raise the trapdoor.

He touched her gently on the arm. "No," he said. "I don't need my guns unless you plan to cut my throat with that razor." They both laughed.

And then she began to cut Turi Guiliano's hair. She did so carefully and slowly, grasping strands to snip, then depositing the hair into the wooden bowl. Guiliano sat very quietly. Mesmerized by the tiny snipping noises, he stared at the walls of the room. On them were huge portraits of La Venera's husband, the great bandit Candeleria. But great only in this little province of Sicily, Guiliano thought, his youthful pride already in competition with the dead husband.

Rutillo Candeleria had been a handsome man. He had a high forehead surmounted by wavy chestnut hair carefully cut, and Guiliano wondered if his wife had cut it for him. His face was adorned with full cavalry mustaches which made him seem older, though he had only been thirty-five when the *carabinieri* shot him. Now his face looked down from the oval portrait almost kindly, in a benediction. Only the eyes and mouth betrayed his ferocity. And yet at the same time there was a resignation in that face, as if he knew what his fate must be. Like all who raised their hands against the world and tore from it what they wished by violence and murder, like others who made personal law and tried to rule society with it, he must come finally to sudden death.

The wooden bowl was filling with glossy brown hair, clumped like the nests of small birds. Guiliano felt La Venera's legs pressed against his back; her heat came through the rough cotton of her dress. When she moved in front of him to cut around his forehead she kept well away from his leg, but when she had to lean forward, the swelling of her bust almost brushed against his lips and the clean heavy scent of her body made his face as warm as if he were standing before a fire. The portraits on the wall were blotted out.

She swiveled her rounded hips to deposit another clump of hair in the wooden bowl. For one moment her thigh rested against his arm and he could feel the silky skin even through the heavy black dress. He made his body steady as a rock. She leaned against him harder. To keep himself from pulling up her skirt and clasping those thighs, he said jokingly, "Are we Samson and Delilah?"

She stepped away from him suddenly. And he was surprised by the tears running down her face. Without thinking he put his hands on her body and pulled her closer. Slowly she reached out and lay the silver scissors across the mound of brown hair that filled the wooden bowl.

And then his hands were under her black mourning dress and clutching her warm thighs. She bent down and covered his mouth with hers as if she would swallow it. Their initial tenderness was a second's spark that roared into an animal passion fed by her three years of chaste widowhood, his springing from the sweet lust of a young man who had never tasted the love of a woman but only the bought exercise of whores.

For that first moment, Guiliano lost all sense of himself and his world. La Venera's body was so lush, and it burned with a tropical heat that went to his very bones. Her breasts were fuller than he could ever have imagined; the black widow's dress had cleverly disguised and protected them. At the sight of those oval globes of flesh he felt the blood pounding in his head. And then they were on the floor making love and taking off their clothing at the same time. She kept whispering, "Turi, Turi," in an agonized voice, but he said nothing. He was lost in the smell, the heat and fleshiness of her body. When they finished, she led him into the bedroom and they made love again. He could not believe the pleasure he found in her body, and even felt some dismay at his own surrender and was only comforted that she succumbed even more completely.

When he fell asleep she stared down into his face for a long time. She imprinted it on her memory in fear she would never see him alive again. For she remembered the last night she had slept with her husband before he died, when she had turned her back after making love and fallen asleep and ever since could not remember the sweet mask that comes over every lover's face. She had turned her back because she could not bear the fearful nervousness of her husband when he was in the house, his terror of being trapped so that he could never fall asleep, the way he started up if she rose from the bed to cook or do some chore. She marveled now at Guiliano's calm; she loved him for it. She loved him because, unlike her husband, he did not bring his guns to bed, he did not interrupt his lovemaking to listen for the sound of lurking enemies, he did not smoke or drink and tell his fears. He was gentle in his speech, but took his pleasure with fearless and concentrated passion. She rose noiselessly from the bed and still he did not stir. She waited a moment and then went out and into the kitchen to cook him her best dish.

When he left her house in the morning he went through the

front door, stepping out carelessly but with guns hidden beneath his jacket. He had told her he would not stop to say goodbye to his mother and asked her to do so for him, to let her know he was safe. She was frightened at his boldness, not knowing he had a small army in the town, not noticing that he had held her door open a few minutes before he went out so that Pisciotta would be warned and would eliminate any *carabinieri* going by.

She kissed him goodbye with a shyness that moved him and then she whispered, "When will you come to see me again?"

"Whenever I come to see my mother, I'll come to you afterward," he said. "In the mountains I'll dream about you every night." And at these words she felt an overwhelming joy that she had made him happy.

She waited until noon before she went down the street to see Guiliano's mother. Maria Lombardo had only to see her face to know what had happened. La Venera looked ten years younger. Her dark brown eyes had black flecks dancing in them, her cheeks were rosy with color, and for the first time in almost four years she wore a dress that was not black. It was the frilly dress beribboned with velvet that a girl wears to show the mother of her lover. Maria Lombardo felt a rush of gratitude for her friend, for her loyalty and her courage and also a certain satisfaction that her plans had come out so well. This would be a wonderful arrangement for her son, a woman who would never be a traitor, a woman who could never make a permanent claim upon him. Though she loved her son fiercely she felt no jealousy. Except when La Venera told how she had cooked her best dish, a pie stuffed with rabbit meat and chunks of strong cheese riddled with fat grains of pepper, and how Turi had devoured enough for five men and sworn he had never eaten anything better in his life.

CHAPTER

15

EVEN IN SICILY, a land where men killed each other with the same ferocious enthusiasm with which the Spaniards slaughtered bulls, the murderous madness of the citizens of Corleone inspired a universal dread. Rival families exterminated each other in a quarrel over a single olive tree, neighbors might kill each other over the amount of water one took from a communal stream, a man could die from love—that is, if he looked too disrespectfully at a wife or daughter. Even the cool-headed Friends of the Friends succumbed to this madness and their different branches warred to death in Corleone until Don Croce brought them to peace.

In such a town, Stefan Andolini had earned the nickname of *Fra Diavalo*, Brother Devil.

Don Croce had summoned him from Corleone and instructed him. He was to join Guiliano's band and win their confidence. He was to stay with them until Don Croce gave orders as to his future course of action. Meanwhile he was to send back information as to Guiliano's real strength, the loyalty of Passatempo and Terranova. Since Pisciotta's loyalty was unquestioned there remained only to evaluate that young man's weaknesses. And if the opportunity arose, Andolini was to kill Guiliano.

Andolini had no fear of the great Guiliano. Also, since he was redheaded, and redheads were so rare in Italy, Stefan Andolini secretly believed he had been excused from the rules of virtue. As a gambler believes his system can never lose, so Stefan Andolini believed himself so cunning he could never be outwitted.

He picked two young *picciotti* to go with him, that is, apprentice killers, who had not yet been admitted to the Mafia but hoped for that honor. They journeyed into the mountain haunts of Guiliano carrying knapsacks and *lupare* and sure enough were picked up by a roving patrol headed by Pisciotta.

Pisciotta listened to Stefan Andolini's story with an impassive face. Andolini told him that the *carabinieri* and Security Police were looking for him because of the murder of a Socialist agitator in Corleone. This was quite true. What Andolini did not say was that the police and *carabinieri* had no proof and were merely seeking him for questioning. A questioning that would be more kindly than exhaustive due to the influence of Don Croce. Andolini also told Pisciotta that the two *picciotti* with him were men who were also being sought by the police as co-conspirators in the killing. This was also true. But as he was telling this story Stefan Andolini felt a mounting uneasiness. Pisciotta was listening with the expression of a man who has met someone he has known before or of whom he has heard a great deal.

Andolini said that he had come into the mountains in the hope of joining Guiliano's band. And then he played his trump card. He had the stamp of approval from Guiliano's father himself. He, Stefan Andolini, was a cousin of the great Don Vito Corleone, in America. Pisciotta nodded. Andolini went on. Don Vito Corleone had been born an Andolini in the village of Corleone. His father killed, himself hunted as a boy, he had escaped to America where he had become the great Godfather. When he had returned to Sicily to wreak vengeance on his father's murderers, Stefan Andolini had been one of his *picciotti*. Thereafter he had visited the Don in America to receive his reward. While there he had met Guiliano's father who worked as a bricklayer on the Don's new mansion on Long Island. They had become friends, and Andolini, before he came into the mountains, had stopped in Montelepre to receive the blessing of Salvatore Guiliano Senior.

Pisciotta's face became thoughtful as he listened to this story. He distrusted this man, his red hair, his face of a murderer. And Pisciotta didn't like the look of the two *picciotti* with *Malpelo*, for so he called him in the Sicilian style.

Pisciotta said to him, "I'll take you to Guiliano, but keep your *lupare* strapped to your shoulders until he's spoken to you. Don't unsling them without permission."

Stefan Andolini grinned widely and said with the utmost affability, "But I recognized you, Aspanu, I trust you. Take my *lupara* off my shoulder and your men can do the same with my *picciotti* here. After we speak with Guiliano I'm sure he'll return our guns."

Pisciotta said, "We're not pack animals to carry your weapons for you. Carry them yourselves." And he led the way through the mountains to Guiliano's hideout on the edge of the cliff overlooking Montelepre.

More than fifty of the band were scattered around the cliff cleaning guns and repairing equipment. Guiliano was seated at the table, watching through his binoculars.

Pisciotta talked to Guiliano before he had the new recruits brought forward. He told all the circumstances and then he said, "Turi, he seems a little 'moldy' to me." "Moldy," the Sicilian idiom for a man who informs.

"And you think you've seen him before?" Guiliano asked.

"Or heard of him," Pisciotta said. "He is familiar to me somehow, but redheaded men are rare. I should remember him."

Guiliano said quietly, "You heard about him from La Venera. She called him *Malpelo*—she didn't know his name was Andolini. She told me about him too. He joined her husband's band. A month later her husband was ambushed and killed by the *carabinieri*. La Venera didn't trust him either. He was full of little tricks, she said."

Silvestro came over to them. "Don't trust that redhead. I've seen him at Palermo headquarters for private visits with the Commandant of *Carabinieri.*"

Guiliano said, "Go down to Montelepre and bring my father here. Meanwhile keep them under guard."

Pisciotta sent Terranova to fetch Guiliano's father and then he went to the three men, who were sitting on the ground. He bent down and picked up Stefan Andolini's weapon. Members of the band encircled the three men like wolves surrounding a fallen prey. "You don't mind if I relieve you of the task of caring for this weapon now?" Pisciotta asked with a grin. Stefan Andolini looked startled for a moment, his face twisting into a grimace. Then he shrugged. Pisciotta tossed the *lupara* to one of his men.

He waited for a few moments, making sure his men were ready. Then he reached down to take the *lupare* from Andolini's two *picciotti*. One of them, more from fear than malice, pushed Pisciotta away and put his hand on his shotgun. In the next moment, quickly as a snake baring its tongue, a knife appeared in Pisciotta's hand. His body darted forward and the knife cut the *picciotto*'s throat. A fountain of pink blood burst into the clear mountain air and the *picciotto* slumped over on his side. Pisciotta was straddling his body, leaning down, and another quick stroke finished the job. Then, with a series of quick kicks, he rolled the body into a gully.

The other men of Guiliano's band had sprung to their feet leveling their guns. Andolini, sitting on the ground, raised his hands in the air and looked around him beseechingly. But the other *picciotto* lunged for his weapon and tried to bring it around. Passatempo, standing behind him and grinning with enjoyment, emptied his pistol into the man's head. The shots echoed through the mountains. They all remained frozen, Andolini pale and shaking with fear, Passatempo holding his pistol. And then Guiliano's voice from the edge of the cliff said quietly, "Get rid of the bodies and tie that *Malpelo* to a tree until my father comes."

The bodies were wrapped in bamboo nets and carried to a

deep crevice. They were thrown in with stones tumbled down after them to keep the stench from rising, according to old superstition. This was a task for Passatempo, who robbed the bodies before he buried them. Guiliano constantly fought against his distaste for Passatempo. No amount of rationalization could turn that animal into a knight.

It was after dusk, almost seven hours later, that Guiliano's father was finally brought into the camp. Stefan Andolini was released from his tree and brought over to the cave lit with kerosene lamps. Guiliano's father was angry when he saw Andolini's condition.

"But this man is my friend," he said to his son. "We both worked for the Godfather in America. I told him he could come and join your band, that he would be well treated."

He shook hands with Andolini and said, "I apologize. My son must have misunderstood or heard some gossip about you." He paused for a moment, troubled. It distressed him to see his old friend so full of fear. For Andolini could barely stand.

Andolini was sure he would be killed. That this was all a charade. The back of his neck ached as the muscles tensed to receive the bullets. He almost wept at his own brashness that had made him underestimate Guiliano. The quick killings of his two *picciotti* had sent him into shock.

Signor Guiliano sensed that his friend was in mortal danger from his son. He said to him, "Turi, how often do I ask you to do something for me? If you have anything against this man forgive him and let him go. He was kind to me in America and he sent you a gift when you were christened. I trust him and hold his friendship dear."

Guiliano said, "Now that you have identified him, he will be treated as an honored guest. If he wishes to remain as a member of my band he is welcome."

Guiliano's father was taken back to Montelepre by horse so that he could sleep in his own bed. And after he was gone Guiliano spoke to Stefan Andolini alone.

"I know about you and Candeleria, ' he said. "You were a spy for Don Croce when you joined Candeleria's band. A month later Candeleria was dead. His widow remembers you. From what she told me it wasn't hard for me to figure out what happened. We Sicilians are good at putting together puzzles of treacheries. Bands of outlaws are disappearing. The authorities have become amazingly clever. I sit on my mountain and think all day. I think of the authorities in Palermo—they have never been so clever before. And then I learn that the Minister of Justice in Rome and Don Croce are hand in glove. And we know, you and I, that Don Croce is clever enough for both of them. So then it is Don Croce who is clearing away these bandits for Rome. And then I think soon it will be my turn to be visited by the spies of Don Croce. And I wait and I wait and I wonder why the Don is taking so long. For, with all modesty, I am the biggest prize of all. And then today I see the three of you in my binoculars. And I think, 'Ha, it's *Malpelo* again. I will be glad to see him.' But I must kill you all the same. I won't distress my father so your body will disappear."

Stefan Andolini lost his fear for a moment in his outrage. "You would deceive your own father?" he shouted. "You call yourself a Sicilian son?" He spat on the ground. "Then kill me and go straight down to hell."

Pisciotta, Terranova and Passatempo were also astonished. But they had been astonished many times in the past. Guiliano who was so honorable, who prided himself on keeping his word, who spoke always of justice for everyone, would suddenly turn and do something that seemed to them villainous. It was not that they objected to him killing Andolini—he could kill a hundred Andolinis, a thousand. But that he should break his word to his father and deceive him seemed to them unforgivable. Only Corporal Silvestro seemed to understand and said, "He can't endanger all our lives because his father is soft-hearted."

Guiliano said to Andolini in a quiet voice, "Make your peace with God." He motioned to Passatempo. "You will have five minutes."

Andolini's red hair seemed to bristle all over his head. He said frantically, "Before you kill me speak to the Abbot Manfredi."

Guiliano stared at him with amazement and the redheaded man spoke in an outpouring of words. "You once said to the Abbot that you owed him a service. That he could ask you for anything." Guiliano remembered his promise well. How did the man know about it?

Andolini continued, "Let us go to him and he will beg for my life."

Pisciotta said contemptuously, "Turi, it will take another day to send a messenger and get his answer back. And does the Abbot have more influence with you than your own father?"

Guiliano astonished them again. "Bind his arms and put a halter on his feet so that he can walk but not run. Give me a guard of ten men. I'll bring him to the monastery myself, and if the Abbot does not ask for his life, he can make his last confession. I'll execute him and give his body to the monks for burial."

■ ■ ■

GUILIANO AND his band arrived at the monastery gates as the sun was rising and the monks were going out to work the fields. Turi Guiliano watched them, a smile on his lips. Was it only two years ago that he had gone into the fields with these priests, wearing his brown cloak and the crumpled black American fedora on his head? He remembered how this amused him. Who would have dreamed then of his future ferocity? A nostalgia came for those old days of peace working in the fields.

The Abbot himself was coming toward the gate to greet them. The tall black-robed figure hesitated when the prisoner stepped forward, then opened his arms. Stefan Andolini rushed to embrace the old man, kissed him on both cheeks and said, "*Father*, these men are going to kill me, only you can save me."

The Abbot nodded. He held out his arms to Guiliano, who

came forward to embrace him. Guiliano understood everything now. The peculiar accent on the word "Father" was not how a man addressed his priest but as a son addressed his parent.

The Abbot said, "I ask you for this man's life, as a boon to me."

Guiliano took the ropes off Andolini's arms and feet. "He is yours," Turi Guiliano said.

Andolini was sagging to the ground; the fear rushing out of his body made him weak. The Abbot supported him with his own frail frame. He said to Guiliano, "Come into my dining room. I will have your men fed and the three of us can talk about what we must do." He turned to Andolini and said, "My dear son, you are not yet out of danger. What will Don Croce think when he learns of all this? We must take counsel together or you are lost."

■ ■ ■

THE ABBOT had his own small coffee room and the three men sat comfortably. Cheese and bread were brought for the two younger men.

The Abbot turned and smiled sadly at Guiliano. "One of my many sins. I fathered this man when I was young. Ah, nobody knows the temptations of a parish priest in Sicily. I did not resist them. The scandal was covered up and his mother was married to an Andolini. A great deal of money passed and I was able to rise in the Church. But the irony of heaven no man can foretell. My son grew up to be a murderer. And that is a cross I have to bear though I have so many of my own sins to answer for."

The Abbot's tone changed when he turned to Andolini. He said, "Listen to me carefully, my son. For a second time you owe your life to me. Understand your first loyalty. It is now to Guiliano.

"You cannot go back to the Don. He will ask himself, Why did Turi spare your life and kill the other two? He will suspect treachery and that will be your death. What you must do is confess everything to the Don and ask to remain with Guiliano's band. That you will give him information and serve as a link between the Friends of the Friends and Guiliano's army. I will go to the Don myself and tell him the advantages of this. I will also tell him that you will remain faithful to Guiliano but that will not be to his disadvantage. He will think you will betray this man here who spared your life. But I tell you that if you do not remain faithful to Guiliano I will damn you to hell forever. You will bear your father's curse to the grave."

He addressed himself again to Guiliano. "So now I ask you a second favor, my dear Turi Guiliano. Take my son into your band. He will fight for you and do your bidding and I swear he will be faithful to you."

Guiliano thought about this carefully. He was sure he could, with time, secure Andolini's affection, and he knew the man's devotion to his father, the Abbot. The chances of betrayal were therefore small and could be guarded against. Stefan Andolini would be a valuable subchief in the operations of his band but even more valuable as a source of information about the empire of Don Croce.

Guiliano asked, "And what will you tell Don Croce?"

The Abbot paused for a moment. "I will speak to the Don. I have influence there. And then we shall see. Now will you take my son into your band?"

"Yes, by my sworn word to you," Guiliano said. "But if he betrays me your prayers will not be swift enough to catch him on his way to hell."

◻ ◼ ◼

STEFAN ANDOLINI had lived in a world of little trust which perhaps was why over the years his face had become formed in such a murderer's mask. He knew that in the coming years he would be like a trapeze artist, constantly teetering on the wire of death. There was no safe choice. It comforted him that the spirit of mercy that radiated from Guiliano's person had saved him. But he had no illusions. Turi Guiliano was the only man who had ever made him afraid.

From that day Stefan Andolini was a member of Guiliano's band. And in the years to come he became so known for ferociousness and religious piety that his nickname, *Fra Diavalo*, became famous all over Sicily. The piety came from the fact that every Sunday he went to Mass. He usually went in the town of Villaba, where Father Benjamino was the priest. And in the confessional he told the secrets of Guiliano's band to his confessor to be relayed to Don Croce. But not the secrets Guiliano ordered him not to tell.

Book
III

MICHAEL CORLEONE

1950

CHAPTER

16

THE FIAT skirted the town of Trapani and took a road along the beach. Michael Corleone and Stefan Andolini came to a villa, larger than most, with three outlying houses. There was a wall around the villa with only a gap left on the beach side. The gate to the villa was guarded by two men, and just inside Michael could see a wide fat man dressed in clothes that looked alien in this landscape: a sport jacket and slacks with an open, knit polo shirt. As they waited for the gate to open Michael saw the grin on the man's broad face and was astonished to see it was Peter Clemenza.

Clemenza was the chief underling of Michael Corleone's father back in America. What was he doing here? Michael had last seen him that fatal night when Clemenza had planted the gun he had used to assassinate the police captain and the Turk, Sollozzo. He had remembered the look of pity and sadness on Clemenza's face at that moment over two years ago. Now Clemenza was genuinely overjoyed to see Michael. He pulled him out of the tiny Fiat and almost crushed him in a bear hug.

"Michael, it's great to see you. I've been waiting for years to tell you how proud I am of you. What a great job you did. And now all your troubles are over. In a week you'll be with the family, there'll be a great feast. Everybody's waiting for you, Mikey." He stared into Michael's face fondly while holding him within his two massive arms, and as he did so he made an assessment. This was no longer just the young war hero. During his time in Sicily the boy had grown into a man. That is to say, Michael's face was no longer open; it had the proud closed look of the born Sicilian. Michael was ready to take his rightful place in the family.

Michael was happy to see Clemenza's huge, bulky form, his broad heavily featured face. He asked for news of his family. His father had recovered from the assassination attempt, but his health was not good. Clemenza shook his head mournfully. "It never does anybody any good when they get holes punched in their body, no matter how good they recover. But it's not the first time your father was shot. He's like an ox. He'll be okay. Sonny getting killed, that's what did the damage to him and your mother. It was brutal, Mikey—they cut him to pieces with machine guns. That wasn't right, they didn't have to do that. That was spite work. But we're making plans. Your father will tell you when we get you home. Everybody is happy you're coming back."

Stefan Andolini nodded to Clemenza; they obviously had met before. He shook hands with Michael and said he had to leave —there were things he had to do back in Montelepre. "Remember this, whatever you may hear," he said, "that I always remained faithful to Turi Guiliano and that he trusted me to the end. If he is betrayed it is not I who will have betrayed him." He stuttered with sincerity. "And I will not betray you."

Michael believed him. "Won't you come and rest and have something to eat and drink?" he asked.

Stefan Andolini shook his head. He got into the Fiat and drove back out the gates which immediately clanged shut behind him.

Clemenza led Michael across the open grounds to the main villa. There were armed men patrolling the walls and on the beach where the estate was open to the sea. A small dock stretched toward the faraway coast of Africa, and tethered to the dock was a large sleek motorboat flying the flag of Italy.

Inside the villa were two old crones dressed in black without one color of light on their persons, their skin dark with the sun, black shawls over their heads. Clemenza asked them to bring a bowl of fruit to Michael's bedroom.

The terrace of the bedroom looked over the blue Mediterranean Sea which seemed to part in the middle when hit by a shaft of morning sunlight. Fishing boats with bright blue and red sails bobbed on the horizon like balls skipping over the water. There was a small table on the terrace covered with a heavy dark brown cloth, and the two men sat on the chairs around it. There was a pot of espresso and a jug of red wine.

"You look tired," Clemenza said. "Get some sleep and then I'll spell everything out for you in detail."

"I could use it," Michael said. "But first, tell me, is my mother all right?"

"She's fine," Clemenza said. "She's waiting for you to get home. We can't disappoint her, it would be too much for her after Sonny."

Michael asked again, "And my father, he's completely recovered?"

Clemenza laughed; it was an ugly laugh. "He sure is. The Five Families will find out. Your father is just waiting for you to get home, Mike. He's got big plans for you. We can't let him down. So don't worry too much for Guiliano—if he shows up we'll take him with us. If he keeps screwing off we leave him here."

"Are those my father's orders?" Michael asked.

Clemenza said, "A courier comes by air every day to Tunis and I go over by boat to talk to him. Those were my orders yesterday. At first Don Croce was supposed to help us, or so your father told me before I left the States. But you know what happened in Palermo after you left yesterday? Somebody tried to knock off Croce. They came over the wall of the garden and killed four of his bodyguards. But Croce got away. So what the hell is going on?"

Michael said, "Jesus." He remembered the precautions Don Croce had taken around the hotel. "I think that was our friend Guiliano. I hope you and my father know what you're doing. I'm so tired I can't think."

Clemenza rose and patted him on the shoulder. "Mikey, get some sleep. When you wake up you'll meet my brother. A great man, just like your father, just as smart, just as tough, and he's the boss in this part of the country, never mind Croce."

Michael undressed and got into bed. He had not slept for over thirty hours and yet his mind jumped and would not let his body rest. He could feel the heat of the morning sun though he had closed the heavy wooden shutters. There was a heavy fragrance of flowers and lemon trees. His mind worked over the events of the past few days. How did Pisciotta and Andolini move around so freely? Why did Guiliano seem to have decided Don Croce was his enemy at this most inappropriate of times? Such an error was not Sicilian. After all, the man had lived seven years in the mountains as an outlaw. Enough was enough. He must want to live a better life—not possible here, but certainly in America. And he definitely had such plans or he would not be sending his fiancée, pregnant, to America before him. The clarifying thought struck him that the answer to all this mystery was that Guiliano was bent on fighting one last battle. That he did not fear to die here on his native ground. There were plans and conspiracies spinning out to their final conclusions that he, Michael, could not be aware of, and so he must be wary. For Michael Corleone did not want to die in Sicily. He was not part of this particular myth.

■ ■ ■

MICHAEL AWOKE in the huge bedroom and opened the shutters, which swung outward to a white stone balcony glittering in the morning sun. Below the balcony, the Mediterranean Sea rolled like a deep blue carpet out to the horizon. Streaks of crimson laced the water, and on these boats fishermen sailed out of sight. Michael watched them for a few minutes, utterly bewitched by the beauty of the sea and the majestic cliffs of Erice up the coast to the north.

The room was full of huge rustic furniture. There was a table on which stood a blue enameled basin and a jug of water. Over a chair there was a rough brown towel. On the walls were paintings of saints and the Virgin Mary, with the infant Jesus in her arms. Michael washed his face and then left the room. At the bottom of the stairs Peter Clemenza was waiting for him.

"Ah, now you look better, Mikey," Clemenza said. "A good meal to give you back your strength and then we can talk business." He led Michael into a kitchen that held a long wooden table. They sat down and an old woman in black appeared magically at the stove and poured two cups of espresso and served them. Then just as magically she produced a platter of eggs and sausage which she put on the table. From the oven came a great sun-shaped brown-crusted loaf of bread. Then she disappeared into a room beyond the kitchen. She did not acknowledge Michael's thanks. At that moment a man entered the room. He was older than Clemenza but looked so much like him that Michael knew immediately that this was Don Domenic Clemenza, Peter Clemenza's brother. Don Domenic was attired much differently. He was in black velvet trousers that tucked into sturdy brown boots. He wore a white silk shirt with ruffled sleeves and a long black vest. On his head was a short billed cap. In his right hand he carried a whip which he threw into a corner. Michael rose to greet him and Don Domenic Clemenza took him into his arms with a friendly embrace.

They sat at the table together. Don Domenic had a natural dignity and air of command that reminded Michael of his own father. He also had the same old-fashioned courtliness. Peter Clemenza obviously was in awe of his older brother who treated him with the indulgent affection an older brother shows a flighty sibling. This astonished Michael and amused him too. Peter Clemenza was his father's most trusted and deadly *caporegime* back in America.

Don Domenic said gravely but with a twinkle in his eye, "Michael, it is such a great pleasure and honor to me that your father, Don Corleone, has put you in my care. Now you can solve my curiosity. My good-for-nothing brother here, is his success in America as great as he claims? Has he climbed so high, this younger brother of mine I could never trust to slaughter a pig properly? Does Don Corleone really set him on his right hand? And he says he commands over a hundred men. How can I believe all this?" But as he said this he patted his younger brother's shoulder fondly.

"It's all true," Michael said. "My father always says he would be selling olive oil if not for your brother."

They all laughed. Peter Clemenza said, "I would have spent most of my life in jails. He taught me how to think instead of just using a gun."

Don Domenic sighed. "I'm only a poor country farmer. It's true my neighbors come to me for counsel and here in Trapani they say I'm an important man. They call me 'The Unfaithful' because I won't do Don Croce's bidding. Perhaps that's not very clever, perhaps the Godfather would find ways to get along better with Don Croce. But I find it impossible. 'Unfaithful' I may be, but only to those who have no honor. Don Croce sells information to the government and to me that is an *infamita*. No matter how subtle the reasons. The old ways are still the best, Michael, as you will see after you have been here the next few days."

"I'm sure I will," Michael said politely. "And I must thank you for the help you are giving me now."

"I have work to do," Don Domenic said. "If you need anything, send for me." He picked up his whip and went out the door.

Peter Clemenza said, "Michael, your father agreed to help Turi Guiliano get out of this country out of his friendship and respect for Guiliano's father. But your safety comes first. Your father still has enemies here. Guiliano has a week to make a rendezvous with you. But if he doesn't appear you must go back to the United States alone. Those are my orders. We have a special plane waiting in Africa and we can leave anytime. You just give the word."

Michael said, "Pisciotta said he'd bring Guiliano to me very soon."

Clemenza whistled. "You saw Pisciotta? Hell, they're looking for him as hard as they are for Guiliano. How did he get out of the mountains?"

Michael shrugged. "He had one of the special red-bordered passes signed by the Minister of Justice. And that worries me too."

Peter Clemenza shook his head.

Michael continued. "That guy who brought me here, Andolini, do you know him, Pete?"

"Yeah," Peter Clemenza said. "He worked for us in New York, a couple of button jobs, but Guiliano's father was straight and a great artist with brick. They were both stupid to come back. But a lot of Sicilians are like that. They can't forget their shitty little houses in Sicily. I brought two men over with me this time, to help out. They haven't been back in twenty years. So we take a walk in the country up near Erice, a beautiful town, Mikey, and we were out in the fields with all those sheep they have and drinking wine and we all had to take a leak. So there we were pissing and when we finished, these two guys jump about ten feet in the air and yell, 'Long live Sicily.' What are you gonna do? That's how they are, Sicilians till they die."

Michael said, "Yeah, but what about Andolini?"

Clemenza shrugged. "He's your father's cousin. He's been one of Guiliano's right-hand men for the last five years. But before that he was close with Don Croce. Who knows? He's dangerous."

Michael said, "Andolini is bringing Guiliano's fianceé here. She's pregnant. We have to ship her to the States and she sends back a code word to Guiliano saying that the route works and then Guiliano comes to us. I promised we'd do it. Is that okay?"

Clemenza whistled. "I never heard Guiliano had a girl. Sure we can do it."

They went outside to a huge garden. Michael could see guards at the gate and down at the beach at least six armed men strolling up and down. There was a large motorboat docked against a short pier. In the garden itself was a group of men obviously waiting for an audience with Peter Clemenza. There were about twenty of them, all typical Sicilians with their dusty clothes and brimmed caps, like poorer versions of Don Domenic.

In a corner of the garden, beneath a lemon tree, was an oval wooden table with rustic wooden chairs around it. Clemenza and Michael sat in two of the chairs and then Clemenza called out to the group of men. One of them came over and sat down. Clemenza asked questions about the man's personal life. Was he married? Did he have children? How long had he worked for Don Domenic? Who were his relatives in Trapani? Did he ever think of going to America to make his fortune? The answer to this last question was invariably a Yes.

An old woman in black brought out a huge jug of wine mixed with fresh lemons, then brought out a tray with many glasses. Clemenza offered each man he interviewed a drink and a cigarette. When he had finished and the last one was gone and the group had left the garden, Clemenza said to Michael, "Any of them hit you wrong?"

Michael shrugged and said, "They all seemed the same to me. They all want to go to America."

Clemenza said, "We need fresh blood back home. We lost a lot of men and we might lose a lot more. Every five years or so I come back and bring about twelve guys back with me. I train them myself. Little jobs first—collections, strong-arm, guard duty. I test their loyalty. When I feel the time is right and the opportunity comes along, I give them a chance to make their bones. But I'm very careful about that. Once they get that far they know they have a good living for the rest of their lives as long as they remain loyal. Everybody here knows I'm the recruiter for the Corleone Family and every man in the province wants to see me. But my brother picks them out. Nobody gets to see me without his okay.''

Michael looked around the beautiful garden with its many colored flowers, fragrant lemon trees, the old statues of the gods dug from ancient ruins, other newer ones of holy saints, the rose-colored walls around the villa. It was a lovely setting for the examination of twelve murderous apostles.

■ ■ ■

IN THE late afternoon the small Fiat reappeared at the villa gates and was waved through by the guards. Andolini was driving, and beside him there was a girl with long jet-black hair and the exquisite oval features of a painter's Madonna. When she got out of the car Michael could see she was pregnant; though she wore the modest loose dress of the Sicilian woman it was not black, rather a hideous floral rose and white. But her face was so pretty the dress didn't matter.

Michael Corleone was surprised to see the small figure of Hector Adonis get out of the back seat. It was Adonis who made the introductions. The girl's name was Justina. She had none of the shyness of the young; and at only seventeen years of age, her face had the strength of an older woman, as if she had already tasted the same tragedies of life. She studied Michael closely before she bowed her head to acknowledge his introduction. As if she were studying him to find any hint of treachery in his face.

One of the old women took her away to her room and Andolini took her luggage out of the car. It consisted of only a small suitcase. Michael carried it into the house himself.

That night they all had dinner together except for Andolini, who had left in the Fiat. Hector Adonis remained. At the dinner table they made plans to get Justina to America. Don Domenic said the boat to Tunis was ready; it always would be since they did not know when Guiliano would arrive and they would have to move quickly when he did. "Who knows what evil companions he will bring after him," Don Domenic said with a little smile.

Peter Clemenza said he would accompany Justina to Tunis and make sure she was put on a special plane with special documents that would enable her to enter the United States without trouble. Then he would return to the villa.

When Justina arrived in America she would send her code word back and the final operation to save Guiliano would begin.

Justina said very little during the meal. Don Domenic asked her if she was up to making the journey this very night after she had traveled so much of the day.

When she answered Michael could see the attraction she must have had for Guiliano. She had the same flashing black eyes, the determined jaw and mouth of the strongest Sicilian women and spoke as imperiously.

"Traveling is easier than working and less dangerous than hiding," she said. "I've slept in the mountains and in the fields with sheep, so why can't I sleep in a ship or on an airplane? Surely it won't be as cold?" She said this with all the pride of the young, but her hands trembled as she lifted her glass of wine. "I worry only that Turi be able to escape. Why couldn't he come with me?"

Hector Adonis said gently, "Justina, he didn't want to endanger you with his presence. It is more difficult for him to travel; more precautions must be taken."

Peter Clemenza said, "The boat takes you to Africa just before dawn, Justina. Perhaps you'd better get some rest."

Justina said, "No, I'm not tired and I'm too excited to sleep. Could I have another glass of wine?"

Don Domenic poured her glass full. "Drink, it's good for your baby and it will help you sleep later. Did Guiliano give you any messages for us?"

Justina smiled at him sadly. "I haven't seen him for months. Aspanu Pisciotta is the only one he trusts. Not that he thinks I would betray him but that I am his weakness through which they might snare him. It's from his reading all those romances where the love of women brings about the downfall of heroes. He thinks his love for me his most terrible weakness, and of course he never tells me his plans.''

Michael was curious to find out more about Guiliano, the man he might have been if his father had remained in Sicily, the man Sonny might have been. "How did you meet Turi?" he asked Justina.

She laughed. "I fell in love with him when I was eleven years old," she said. "That was almost seven years ago and the first year that Turi was an outlaw, but he was already famous in our little village in Sicily. My younger brother and I were working in the fields with my father and Papa gave me a packet of lire notes to bring back to my mother. My brother and I were silly children and we flaunted the notes, we were so excited at having that much money in our hands. Two *carabinieri* saw us on the road and took away our money and laughed at us when we cried. We didn't know what to do, we were afraid to go home and we were afraid to go back to our father. Then this young man came out of the bushes. He was taller than most men in Sicily and much broader in the shoulders. He looked like the American soldiers we had seen during the war. He carried a machine gun under his arm yet he had such gentle brown eyes. He was very handsome. He asked us, 'Children, why are you crying on such a wonderful day? And you, young lady, you're ruining your beautiful looks, who will want to marry you?' But he was laughing and you could see that the sight of us delighted him for some reason. We told him what had happened and he laughed again and said we must always beware of the *carabinieri* and that this was a good lesson for us to learn so early in life. Then he gave my brother a huge wad of lire to bring home to our mother and to me he gave a note for my father. I can still remember it word for word. It said, 'Don't reproach your two beautiful children who will be the pleasure and comfort of your old age. The money I have given them is far greater than you have lost. And know this: From today on, you and your children are under the protection of GUILIANO.' I thought that name was so wonderful and he had written it in large letters. I saw that name in my dreams for months. Just those letters. GUILIANO.

"But what made me love him was the pleasure he received in doing a good deed. He was really delighted to help someone else. That never changed. I always saw the same pleasure, as if he gained more from the giving than they did from the taking. That is why the people of Sicily love him."

Hector Adonis said quietly, "Until the Portella della Ginestra."

Justina lowered her eyes and said fiercely, "They love him still."

Michael said quickly, "But how did you meet him again?"

Justina said, "My older brother was a friend of his. And maybe my father was a member of the band. I don't know. Only my family and Turi's chiefs know we were married. Turi swore everybody to secrecy, afraid the authorities would arrest me."

Everybody at the table was stunned at this news. Justina reached inside her dress and drew out a small purse. From it she took out a cream-colored stiff-papered document with a heavy seal and offered it to Michael, but Hector Adonis took it and read it. Then he smiled at her. "You will be in America tomorrow. Can I tell Turi's parents the good news?"

Justina blushed. "They always thought I was pregnant without being married," she said. "They thought less of me for it. Yes, you can tell them."

Michael said, "Have you ever seen or read the Testament that Turi has hidden?"

Justina shook her head. "No," she said. "Turi never spoke of it to me."

Don Domenic's face had gone wintry, but he also looked curious. He had heard about the Testament, Michael thought, but didn't approve of it. How many people did know? Certainly not the people of Sicily. Only members of the government in Rome, Don Croce and Guiliano's family and his inner circle of outlaws.

Hector Adonis said, "Don Domenic, may I ask to be your guest until word arrives from America that Justina is safely there? Then I can arrange for Guiliano to receive the news. It should be for no more than an extra night."

Don Domenic said with blunt forcefulness, "You will do me an honor, my dear Professor. Stay as long as you like. But now it's time for us all to go to bed. Our young *Signora* must get some sleep for her long journey and I am too old to stay up so late. *Avanti.*" And he made a shooing gesture like a great affectionate bird, to send them on their way. He personally took Hector Adonis by the arm to lead him to a bedroom, shouting orders to the women servants to take care of the rest of his guests.

When Michael rose the next morning Justina was gone.

■ ■ ■

HECTOR ADONIS had to sleep over for two nights before the courier letter came from Justina that she was safely in America. Somewhere in the letter was the code word that satisfied Adonis, and the morning he was to leave he asked Michael for a private conference.

Michael had spent the two days tense with anticipation, anxious to get home to America himself. Peter Clemenza's description of Sonny's murder had filled Michael with a sense of foreboding about Turi Guiliano. In his mind the two men were growing intertwined. They looked somewhat alike and they both had the same sense of physical vitality and power. Guiliano was only Michael's age, and Michael was intrigued by the man's fame; he was anxious at the thought that they would finally meet face to face. He wondered what use his father could put Guiliano to in America. For he had no doubt that was his father's purpose. Otherwise the assignment of bringing Guiliano home with him did not make sense.

Michael walked with Adonis down to the beach. The armed guards saluted them both: *"Vossia,"* Your Lordship. Not one of them showed any sign of derision at the sight of the tiny elegantly dressed Hector Adonis. The motorboat had come back, and now closer to it Michael could see it was almost as big as a small yacht. The men aboard it were armed with *lupare* and machine guns.

The July sun was very hot and the sea so blue and so still that the sun reflected off of it as if it were metal. Michael and Hector Adonis sat on two chairs on the pier.

"Before I leave this morning, I have a final instruction for you," Hector Adonis said quietly. "It is the most important thing that you can do for Guiliano."

"With all my heart," Michael said.

"You must send Guiliano's Testament to America immediately, to your father," Adonis said. "He will know how to use it. He will make sure that Don Croce and the government in Rome will know it is safely in America and then they will not dare harm Guiliano. They will let him emigrate safely."

"Do you have it with you?" Michael asked.

The little man smiled at him slyly and then laughed, "You have it," he said.

Michael was astonished. "You've been misinformed," he said. "No one has given it to me."

"Yes they have," Hector Adonis said. He put a friendly hand on Michael's arm and Michael noticed how small and dainty his fingers were, like a child's. "Maria Lombardo, Guiliano's mother, gave it to you. Only she and myself know where it is, not even Pisciotta knows."

He saw Michael's uncomprehending look. "It's in the black Madonna," Hector Adonis said. "It's true the Madonna has been in the family for generations and is valuable. Everybody knows about it. But Guiliano was given a replica. It is hollow. The Testament is written on very thin paper and each sheet has Guiliano's signature. I helped him compose it over the last few years. There are also some incriminating documents. Turi always knew what the end might be and wanted to be prepared. For a young man he has a great sense of strategy."

Michael laughed. "And his mother is a great actress."

"All Sicilians are," Hector Adonis said. "We trust no one and dissemble before everyone. Guiliano's father is certainly trustworthy, but he might be indiscreet. Pisciotta has been Guiliano's truest friend since their childhood, Stefan Andolini has saved Guiliano's life in battle with the *carabinieri,* but men change with time or under torture. So it's best they do not know."

"But he trusted you," Michael said.

"I am blessed," Hector Adonis said simply. "But you see how clever Guiliano can be? He trusts only me with the Testament and he trusts only Pisciotta with his life. Both of us must betray him if he is to fail."

CHAPTER

17

MICHAEL CORLEONE and Hector Adonis walked back to the villa and sat under a lemon tree with Peter Clemenza. Michael was eager to read the Testament, but Hector Adonis said that Andolini was due to pick him up for the trip back to Montelepre and Michael waited to see if Andolini had any messages for him.

An hour passed. Hector Adonis looked at his watch, his face worried.

Michael said, "His car probably broke down. That Fiat is on its last legs."

Hector Adonis shook his head. "Stefan Andolini has the heart of a murderer, but he is the soul of punctuality. And dependable. I'm afraid that since he is already an hour late, something has gone wrong. And I must be in Montelepre before dark when curfew begins."

Peter Clemenza said, "My brother will give you a car and driver."

Adonis thought about this for a moment. "No," he said, "I will wait. It's important that I see him."

Michael said, "Do you mind if we go on and read the Testament without you? How do you open the statue?"

Hector Adonis said, "Of course—read it. As for opening it there's no trick. It is carved out of solid wood. The head was soldered on after Turi put the papers inside. You simply chop off the head. If you have trouble reading it, I will be glad to assist you. Send one of the servants for me."

Michael and Peter Clemenza went up to Michael's bedroom. The statue was still in Michael's jacket; he had completely forgotten it. When he took it out, both men stared at the black Virgin Mary. The features were definitely African yet the expression was exactly that of the white Madonnas that decorated almost every poor household in Sicily. Michael turned it over in his hands. It was very heavy—you could not guess that it was hollow.

Peter Clemenza went to the door and shouted an order down to one of the woman servants. The woman appeared carrying the kitchen cleaver. She stared into the room for a moment and handed the cleaver to Clemenza. He shut the door to close out her curious eyes.

Michael held the black Madonna on the heavy wooden dresser table. He grasped the disc carved into the bottom with one hand and used his other to clasp the top of the statue's head. Clemenza carefully put the cleaver to the neck of the Madonna, raised his burly arm, and with one quick powerful stroke, chopped off the head and sent it flying across the room. A sheaf of papers bound with a piece of soft gray leather sprouted out of the hollow neck.

Clemenza had hit exactly on the seam where it had been soldered; the cleaver could never have cut through the hard olive wood. He put the cleaver on the table and pulled the papers out of the headless statue. He loosened the leather thong and spread the papers out on the table. They consisted of one sheaf of about fifteen onionskin pages covered with close handwriting in black ink. The bottom of each page was signed by Guiliano in the careless scrawl of kings. There were also documents with official government seals, letters with government letterheads and statements bearing notary seals. The papers were curling up to resume the shape of their confinement and Michael used the two pieces of the statue and the cleaver to hold them flat on the table. Then he ceremoniously poured two glasses of wine from the jug on the night table and handed one to Clemenza. They drank and then started to read the Testament.

It took them almost two hours to finish.

Michael marveled that Turi Guiliano, so young, so idealistic, had lived through these treacheries. Michael knew enough of the world to imagine that Guiliano harbored his own cunning, his own scheme of power, in order to remain dedicated to his mission. Michael was filled with an enormous sense of identification and commitment to the cause of Guiliano's escape.

It was not so much Guiliano's diary which recounted his history for the past seven years but the documents supporting it that could surely topple the Christian Democratic government in Rome. How could these powerful men have been so foolish, Michael wondered: a note signed by the Cardinal, a letter sent by the Minister of Justice to Don Croce asking what could be done to crush the demonstration at Ginestra, all coyly worded to be sure, but damning in the light of the events that followed. Each thing by itself was innocent enough, brought together they built a mountain of evidence as imposing as the Pyramids.

There was a letter from Prince Ollorto full of flowery compliments to Guiliano and assuring him that all the men in high places of the Christian Democratic government in Rome had assured the Prince that they would do everything in their power to have Guiliano pardoned, providing he did what they had asked of him. In his letter Prince Ollorto claimed he had a complete understanding with the Minister of Justice in Rome.

There were also copies of operational plans prepared by high officials of the *carabinieri* to capture Guiliano—plans that had been turned over to Guiliano in exchange for services rendered.

"No wonder they don't want to catch Guiliano," Michael said. "He can blow them all up with these papers."

Peter Clemenza said, "I'm taking this stuff to Tunis right away. By tomorrow night they'll be in your father's safe."

He picked up the headless Madonna and stuffed the papers

back inside. He put the statue in his pocket and said to Michael, "Let's get going. If I start now I can be back here tomorrow morning."

They went out of the villa, Clemenza depositing the cleaver with the old crone in the kitchen, who examined it suspiciously as if for some sign of blood. They started down toward the beach when they were surprised by the sight of Hector Adonis still waiting. Stefan Andolini had not appeared.

The little man had unloosened his tie and taken off his jacket; his shiny white shirt was dulled with sweat though he was in the shade of a lemon tree. He was also a bit drunk—the big wine jug on the wooden garden table was empty.

He greeted Michael and Peter Clemenza despairingly. "The final treacheries are beginning. Andolini is three hours late. I must get to Montelepre and Palermo. I must send word to Guiliano."

Peter Clemenza said with rough good humor, "Professor, his car might have broken down, or he might have been detained by some other more urgent business, any number of things. He knows you're here in safety and will wait. Spend another night with us if he doesn't come today."

But Hector Adonis kept muttering, "It will all go badly, it will all go badly," and begged them for transportation. Clemenza ordered two men to use one of the Alfa Romeos and drive Hector Adonis as far as Palermo. He told the men to be sure to have the car back at the villa before nightfall.

They helped Hector Adonis get into the car and told him not to worry. The Testament would be in America within twenty-four hours and Guiliano would be safe. After the car rolled through the gates, Michael walked down to the beach with Clemenza and watched him get on the motor launch, and continued watching as the boat started its journey to Africa. "I'll be back in the morning," Peter Clemenza called out. And Michael wondered what would happen if this was the night Guiliano chose to appear.

Later he had dinner, the two old women serving him. Afterward he walked along the beach until turned back by the guards at the perimeter of the villa's estate. It was the few minutes before darkness, and the Mediterranean Sea was the deepest and most velvety blue and from beyond the horizon he could smell the continent of Africa, a perfume of wild flowers and wild animals.

Here by the water there was not the whirring of insects; those creatures needed the lush vegetation, the smoky heated air of the interior. It was almost as if a machine had stopped running. He stood on the beach feeling the peace and beauty of a Sicilian night and he pitied all the others voyaging fearfully in the darkness; Guiliano in his mountains, Pisciotta with the fragile shield of his special red-bordered pass going through enemy lines, Professor Adonis and Stefan Andolini searching for each other on the dusty roads of Sicily, Peter Clemenza riding the blue-black sea to Tunis; and where had Don Domenic Clemenza gone that he had not appeared for dinner? They were all shadows in the Sicilian night, and when they reappeared the stage would be set for the life or death of Turi Guiliano.

BOOK
IV

DON CROCE

1947

18

THE HOUSE of Savoy's King Umberto II was a humble sweet-natured man much beloved by the people, and he had approved the referendum on whether or not Italy should remain a nominal monarchy. He did not wish to remain a king if his people did not want him. And in this he was like his predecessors. The Savoy kings had always been unambitious rulers; their monarchies had been really democracies ruled by Parliament. The political experts were sure the referendum would be in favor of the monarchy.

The island of Sicily was counted on to give heavy majorities to retain the status quo. At this time the two most powerful forces on the island were Turi Guiliano, whose band controlled the northwest corner of Sicily, and Don Croce Malo, who with his Friends of the Friends controlled the rest of Sicily. Guiliano took no part in the election strategies of any political party. Don Croce and the Mafia exerted every effort to ensure the re-election of the Christian Democrats and the retention of the monarchy.

But to the surprise of everyone, the voters of Italy swept away the monarchy; Italy became a republic: And the Socialists and Communists made such a strong showing that the Christian Democrats tottered and almost fell. The next elections might see a godless, Socialist government ruling from Rome. The Christian Democratic party began marshaling all its resources to win the next election.

The biggest surprise had been Sicily. They elected many deputies to Parliament who belonged to the Socialist and Communist parties. In Sicily a trade union was still considered the work of the devil, and many industries and landowners refused to deal with them. What had happened?

Don Croce was enraged. His people had done their job. They had made threats that frightened the villagers in all the rural areas, but obviously the threats had failed in the end. The Catholic Church had priests preaching against the Communists, and the nuns gave their charity baskets of spaghetti and olive oil only to those who promised to vote the Christian Democratic ticket. The church hierarchy in Sicily was stunned. It had distributed millions of lire in food, but the sly Sicilian peasant had swallowed the charitable bread and spit on the Christian Democratic party.

Minister of Justice Franco Trezza was angry with his fellow Sicilians too—a treacherous lot, cunning even when it brought them no profit, proud of their personal honor when they did not have a pot to piss in. He despaired of them. How could they have voted for the Socialists and Communists who would eventually destroy their family structure and banish their Christian God from all the magnificent cathedrals of Italy? There was only one person who could give him the answer to that question and the solution to the elections coming up that would decide the future political life of Italy. He sent for Don Croce Malo.

■ ■ ■

THE PEASANTS of Sicily who had voted for the left-wing parties and elected to abolish their beloved king would have been astonished to learn of the anger of all these high personages. They would have been amazed that the powerful nations of the United States, France and Great Britain were concerned that Italy was going to become an ally of Russia. Many of them had never even heard of Russia.

The poor people of Sicily, presented with the gift of a democratic vote for the first time in twenty years, had simply voted for the candidates and political parties that promised them the opportunity to purchase their own little bit of land for a minimal sum.

But they would have been horrified to know that their vote for the left-wing parties was a vote against their family structure, a vote against the Virgin Mary and the Holy Catholic Church whose holy images lit by red candles adorned every kitchen and bedroom in Sicily; horrified to know that they had voted to turn their cathedrals into museums and banish their beloved Pope from the shores of Italy.

No. The Sicilians had voted to be given a piece of land for themselves and their families, not for a political party. They could not conceive of any greater joy in life; to work their own land, to keep what they produced by the sweat of their brow, for themselves and their children. Their dream of heaven was a few acres of grain, a vegetable garden terraced on a mountainside, a tiny vineyard of grapes, a lemon tree and an olive tree.

■ ■ ■

MINISTER OF Justice Franco Trezza was a native of Sicily and a genuine anti-Fascist who had spent time in Mussolini's jails before escaping to England. He was a tall aristocratic-looking man with hair still jet black, though his full beard was peppered with gray. Though a true hero, he was also a thoroughgoing bureaucrat and politician, a formidable combination.

The Minister's office in Rome was huge, with massive antique furniture. On the walls were pictures of President Roosevelt and Winston Churchill. The windows were of stained glass and outside them was a little balcony. The Minister poured wine for his honored guest, Don Croce Malo.

They sat sipping wine and talking over the political picture in Sicily and the coming regional elections. Minister Trezza voiced his fears. If Sicily continued its leftist trend at the ballot boxes, the Christian Democratic party might well lose its control of the government. The Catholic Church might well lose its legal position as the official state religion of Italy.

Don Croce did not respond to any of this. He ate steadily, and had to admit to himself that the food in Rome was far better than the food in his native Sicily. The Don bent his huge emperor's head close over his dish of spaghetti filled with truffles; the great jaws chewed steadily and inexorably. Occasionally he wiped his thin mustache with his napkin. The imperial beak of a nose stood sentinel over each new dish brought in by the servants as if scenting them for some poison. The eyes darted back and forth over the lavishly burdened table. He never said a word as the Minister droned on about momentous affairs of state.

They finished up with a huge platter of fruits and cheeses. Then over the ceremonial cup of coffee and a balloon glass of brandy, the Don made himself ready to speak. He shifted his huge bulk in the inadequate chair, and the Minister hastily led him into a drawing room with overstuffed armchairs. He ordered a servant to bring in the coffee and brandy and then dismissed him. The Minister himself poured the Don's espresso, offered a cigar which was refused, then prepared himself to hear the Don's wisdom which he knew would be to the point.

Don Croce regarded the Minister steadily. He was not impressed with the aristocratic profile, blunt thick features, the forcefulness. And he despised the Minister's beard which he thought an affectation. This was a man who could impress in Rome but never in Sicily. Yet this was the man who could consolidate the Mafia's power in Sicily. It had been a mistake in the old days to sneer at Rome; the result had been Mussolini and the Fascists. Don Croce had no illusions. A left-wing government could be serious about reforms, about the sweeping out of the subterranean government of the Friends of the Friends. Only a Christian Democratic government would maintain the legal processes that made Don Croce invulnerable, and he agreed to come to Rome with the satisfaction of a faith healer visiting a horde of crippled supplicants who suffered mostly from hysteria. He knew he could effect a cure.

"I can deliver Sicily to you in the next election," he said to Minister Trezza. "But we have need of armed men. You must assure me that you will not move against Turi Guiliano."

"That is the one promise I cannot make," said Minister Trezza.

"That is the one promise you must make," answered Don Croce.

The Minister stroked his small beard. "What kind of man is this Guiliano?" he asked reluctantly. "He is far too young to be so ferocious. Even for a Sicilian."

"Ah, no, he's a gentle lad," said Don Croce, ignoring the Minister's sardonic smile and failing to mention that he had never met Guiliano.

Minister Trezza shook his head. "I don't think that possible," he said. "A man who has killed so many *carabinieri* cannot be called a gentle lad."

It was true. Don Croce thought that Guiliano had been particularly reckless during the past year. Since the time he had executed "Father" Dodana, Guiliano had unleashed his fury against all his enemies, Mafia and Rome alike.

He had begun sending letters to the newspapers proclaiming he was the ruler of Western Sicily, let Rome do what it may. He also sent letters forbidding the *carabinieri* of the towns of Montelepre, Corleone and Monreale to go out on patrol in the streets after midnight. His explanation for this was that his men had to get to certain points to visit friends or family, and he did not want them arrested in their beds or shot when they came out of their houses or when he himself wished to visit his family in Montelepre.

The newspapers printed these letters with gleeful sidebars. Salvatore Guiliano forbade the *cassetta*? This bandit forbids the police from performing their lawful patrols in the towns of Sicily? What impudence. What colossal effrontery. Did this young man think he was the King of Italy? There were cartoons showing *carabinieri* hiding in an alley of Montelepre as the huge figure of Guiliano stepped majestically into the square.

Of course there was only one thing the Maresciallo of Montelepre could do. Every night he sent patrols into the streets.
Every night his garrison, beefed up to one hundred men, were
at alert, guarding the entries into the town from the mountains
so that Guiliano could not mount an attack.

But on the one occasion he sent his *carabinieri* into the mountains, Guiliano and his five chiefs—Pisciotta, Terranova, Passatempo, Silvestro and Andolini—each leading a band of fifty
men, ambushed them. Guiliano showed no mercy, and six *carabinieri* were killed. Other detachments fled from a devastating
fire of machine guns and rifles.

Rome was up in arms, but it was this very recklessness of
Guiliano that could serve them all now if only Don Croce could
convince this eggplant of a Minister of Justice.

"Trust me," Don Croce said to Minister Trezza. "Guiliano
can serve our purposes. I will persuade him to declare war on
the Socialist and Communist parties in Sicily. He will attack
their headquarters, he will suppress their organizers. He will be
my military arm on a broad scale. Then of course my friends
and myself will do the necessary work that cannot be done in
public."

Minister Trezza did not seem shocked by this suggestion, but
he said in a supercilious voice, "Guiliano is already a national
scandal. An international scandal. I have on my desk a plan from
the Chief of Staff of the army to move in troops to suppress him.
There is a price of ten million lire on his head. A thousand
carabinieri have been alerted to move to Sicily to reinforce the
ones already there. And you ask me to protect him? My dear
Don Croce, I expected you to help deliver him to us as you
helped with the other bandits. Guiliano is the shame of Italy.
Everyone thinks he must be eliminated."

Don Croce sipped his espresso and wiped his mustache with
his fingers. He was a little impatient with this Roman hypocrisy.
He shook his head slowly. "Turi Guiliano is far more valuable
to us alive and doing heroic deeds in his mountains. The people

of Sicily worship him; they say prayers for his soul and his safety. There is not a man on my island who will betray him. And he is far more cunning than all those other bandits. I have spies in his camp, but such is his personality that I don't know how loyal they are to me. That is the kind of man you talk about. He inspires affection from everyone. If you send your thousand *carabinieri* and your army and they fail—and they have failed before—what then? I tell you this: If Guiliano decides to help the leftist parties in the next election, you will lose Sicily and therefore, as you must surely know, your party loses Italy." He paused for a long moment and fastened his gaze on the Minister. "You must come to an accommodation with Guiliano."

"And how would all this be arranged?" Minister Trezza asked with the polite, superior smile that Don Croce despised. It was a Roman smile and the man was Sicilian born. The Minister went on. "I have it on good authority that Guiliano has no love for you."

Don Croce shrugged. "He has not endured for the last three years without being clever enough to forget a grudge. And I have a connection with him. Doctor Hector Adonis is one of my people, and he is also Guiliano's godfather and most trusted friend. He will be my intermediary and make my peace with Guiliano. But I must have the necessary assurances from you in some concrete form."

The Minister said sarcastically, "Would you like a signed letter saying I love the bandit I'm trying to catch?"

It was the Don's greatest strength that he never took notice of an insulting tone, a lack of respect, though he stored it away in his heart. He answered quite simply, his face an inscrutable mask. "No," he said. "Simply give me a copy of your Army Chief of Staff plans to mount a campaign against Guiliano. Also a copy of your order to send a thousand *carabinieri* reinforcements to the island. I will show them to Guiliano and promise him you will not implement the orders if he helps us to educate the Sicilian voters. That will not incriminate you later on—you can always claim that a copy was stolen. Also I will promise Guiliano that if the Christian Democrats win the next election, he will receive a pardon."

"Ah, that no," Minister Trezza said. "A pardon is beyond my powers."

"A *promise* is not beyond your powers," Don Croce said. "And then if it can be done, very well. If you find it impossible, I will tell him the bad news."

The Minister saw the light. He saw, as Don Croce intended him to see, that in the end Don Croce must be rid of Guiliano, that the two of them could not exist together in Sicily. And that Don Croce would take all the responsibility for this, that the Minister need not concern himself in solving the problem. Certainly promises could be made. He had only to give Don Croce copies of the two military plans.

The Minister pondered his decision. Don Croce lowered his massive head and said softly, "If the pardon is at all possible I would urge it."

The Minister was striding up and down the room thinking out all the complications that could arise. Don Croce never moved his head or body to follow his movements. The Minister said, "Promise him the pardon in my name, but you must know now it will be difficult. The scandal may be too much. Why, if the newspapers even knew that the two of us met they would flay me alive and I would have to retire to my farm in Sicily and shovel shit and shear sheep. Now is it truly necessary for you to have copies of those plans and my order?"

"Nothing can be done without them," Don Croce said. His tenor voice was as powerful and convincing as that of a great singer. "Guiliano needs some proof that we two are friends and some prior reward from us for his services. We accomplish both when I show him the plans and promise that they will not be implemented. He can operate as freely as before without having to fight an army and extra police. My possession of the plans verifies my connection with you, and when the plans do not go into effect, it will establish my influence with Rome."

Minister Trezza poured Don Croce another cup of espresso. "I agree," he said. "I trust in our friendship. Discretion is all. But I worry about your safety. When Guiliano performs his task and is not pardoned, surely he will hold you responsible."

The Don nodded his head but did not speak. He sipped his espresso. The Minister was watching him intently and then said, "The two of you cannot exist together on such a small island."

The Don smiled. "I will make room for him," he said. "There is plenty of time."

"Good, good," Minister Trezza said. "And remember this. If I can promise my party the votes of Sicily in the next election, and if then I can solve the problem of Guiliano with glory to the government, there is no telling how high my rise will be in the rule of Italy. But no matter how high, I will never forget you, my dear friend. You will always have my ear."

Don Croce shifted his huge bulk in the chair and mused whether it would really be worthwhile making this olive-head of a Sicilian the Premier of Italy. But his very stupidity would be an asset to the Friends of the Friends, and if he turned treacherous he would be an easy man to destroy. Don Croce said in the sincere tone for which he was famous, "I thank you for your friendship and will do everything in my power to help you in your fortunes. We are agreed. I leave for Palermo tomorrow afternoon and would be grateful if you had the plans and other papers delivered to my hotel in the morning. As for Guiliano, if you cannot manage a pardon for him after he has done his work, I will arrange for him to vanish. To America, perhaps, or some other place where he cannot cause you any further trouble."

And so the two men parted. Trezza the Sicilian, who had chosen to uphold society, and Don Croce, who regarded the structure and law of Rome as the devil put on earth to enslave him. For Don Croce believed in freedom, a freedom belonging personally to himself, which owed nothing to any other force, won only by the respect he earned from his fellow Sicilians. It was unfortunate, Don Croce thought, that fate opposed him to Turi Guiliano, a man after his own heart, and not this hypocritical scoundrel of a Minister.

■ ■ ■

BACK IN Palermo, Don Croce summoned Hector Adonis. He told him about his meeting with Trezza and the agreement to which they had come. Then he showed him the copies of the plans made by the government for their war against Guiliano. The little man was distressed, which was the effect the Don had hoped for.

"The Minister has promised me that these plans will be disapproved by him and never implemented," Don Croce said. "But your godson must use all his power to influence the next election. He must be firm and strong and not worry about the poor so much. He must think of his own skin. He must understand that an alliance with Rome and the Minister of Justice is an opportunity. Trezza commands all the *carabinieri,* all the police, all the judges. He may someday be the Premier of Italy. If that happens Turi Guiliano can return to the bosom of his family and perhaps even have a great career himself in politics. The people of Sicily love him. But for now he must forgive and forget. I count on you to influence him."

Hector Adonis said, "But how can he believe the promises of Rome? Turi has always fought for the poor. He would not do anything against their interests."

Don Croce said sharply, "He's not a Communist, surely. Arrange for me to meet with Guiliano. I will convince him. We are the two most powerful men in Sicily. Why should we not work together? He refused before, but times change. Now this will be his salvation as well as ours. The Communists will crush us both with equal pleasure. A Communist state cannot afford a hero like Guiliano or a villain like myself. I will come to meet him wherever he wishes. And tell him that I guarantee the promises of Rome. If the Christian Democrats win the next election I will be responsible for his pardon. I pledge my life and honor."

Hector Adonis understood. That Don Croce would risk Guiliano's wrath against him if the promises of Minister Trezza were broken.

"May I take these plans with me to show Guiliano?" he asked.

Don Croce considered for a moment. He knew he would never get the plans back and that in turning them over he would be giving Guiliano a powerful weapon for the future. He smiled at Hector Adonis. "My dear Professor," he said, "of course you may take them with you."

■ ■ ■

WAITING FOR Hector Adonis, Turi Guiliano pondered what his course of action should be. He had understood that the elections and the victories of the left-wing parties would bring Don Croce to him for help.

For nearly four years Guiliano had distributed hundreds of millions of lire and food to the poor in his corner of Sicily, but he could only really help them by seizing some sort of power.

The books on economics and politics that Adonis brought him to read troubled him. The course of history showed that the left-wing parties were the only hope for the poor in every country except for America. Still, he could not side with them. He hated their preaching against the Church and their scoffing at the medieval family ties of Sicilians. And he knew that a Socialist government would make a greater effort to dislodge him from his mountains than the Christian Democrats.

It was nighttime, and Guiliano watched the fires of his men spread out down the mountain. From the cliff looking down on Montelepre, he could occasionally hear snatches of music played over the loudspeakers in the village square, music from Palermo. He could see the town as a geometric pattern of lights that formed an almost perfect circle. He thought for a moment that when Adonis came and they had done their business he would accompany his godfather back down the mountain and then visit his parents and La Venera. He had no fear of doing so. After three years he completely controlled movement in the province. The *carabinieri* detachment in the town was fully covered, and besides he would bring enough members of his band to massacre them if they dared venture near his mother's house. He now had armed supporters living on the Via Bella itself.

When Adonis arrived, Turi Guiliano took him into the large cave that held a table and chairs and was lit with American Army battery lamps. Hector Adonis embraced him and gave him a small bag of books which Turi accepted gratefully. Adonis also gave Turi an attaché case filled with papers. "I think you will find this interesting. You should read it immediately."

Guiliano spread the papers out on the wooden table. They were the orders signed by Minister Trezza authorizing another thousand *carabinieri* to be sent from the mainland to Sicily to fight against Guiliano's bandits. There were also the plans drawn up by the Army Chief of Staff. Guiliano studied them with interest. He was not afraid; he would simply have to move deeper into the mountains, but the advance warning was timely.

"Who gave you these?" he asked Adonis.

"Don Croce," Adonis said. "He received them from Minister Trezza himself." Turi did not seem as surprised as he should have been by the news. In fact he was smiling slightly.

"Is this supposed to frighten me?" Guiliano asked. "The mountains are deep. All the men they send can be swallowed up and I'll be whistling myself to sleep under a tree."

"Don Croce wants to meet with you. He will come to you at any place you name," Adonis said. "These plans are a token of his good will. He has a proposition to make."

Turi said, "And you, my godfather, do you advise me to meet with Don Croce?" He was watching Hector intently.

"Yes," Adonis said simply.

Turi Guiliano nodded. "Then we will meet in your home, in Montelepre. Are you sure Don Croce will risk that?"

Adonis said gravely, "Why should he not? He will have my word that he will be safe. And I will have your word which I trust more than anything else in the world."

Guiliano took Hector's hands in his. "As I do yours," he said. "Thank you for these plans and thank you for these books you have brought me. Will you help me with one of them tonight before you leave?"

"Of course," Hector Adonis said. And for the rest of the night in his magnificent professorial voice, he explained difficult passages in the books he had brought. Guiliano listened intently and asked questions. It was as if they were schoolmaster and child together as they had been so many years ago.

It was on that night that Hector Adonis suggested Guiliano keep a Testament. A document that would be a record of everything that happened to the band, that would detail any secret deal Guiliano made with Don Croce and Minister Trezza. It could become a great protection.

Guiliano was immediately enthusiastic. Even if it had no power, even if it were lost, he dreamed that perhaps in a hundred years some other rebel might discover it. As he and Pisciotta had discovered the bones of Hannibal's elephant.

CHAPTER
19

THE HISTORIC meeting took place two days later. And in that short space of time the town of Montelepre was bursting with rumors that the great Don Croce Malo was coming, hat in hand, to meet with their own glorious hero, Turi Guiliano. How the secret got out was not known. Perhaps it was because Guiliano took extraordinary precautions for the meeting. His patrols moved into position to seal off the Palermo road, and almost fifty of his men who were related by blood to people living in Montelepre went to visit their relatives and stay in their houses overnight.

Passatempo was sent with his men to seal off the Bellampo Barracks and immobilize the *carabinieri* if they ventured out on patrol. Terranova's men controlled the road from Castellammare and Trapani. Corporal Canio Silvestro was on a rooftop with his five best riflemen and a heavy machine gun camouflaged by the bamboo frames used to dry tomatoes into paste that many families used in the town of Montelepre.

Don Croce came at twilight in a large Alfa Romeo touring car which parked in front of the house of Hector Adonis. He came with his brother, Father Benjamino, and two armed guards who remained in the car with the chauffeur. Hector Adonis was waiting for them at the door attired even more elegantly than usual in his specially London-tailored gray suit and a red and black striped tie on his dazzling white shirt. He made a startling contrast to the Don, who seemed to be attired even more carelessly than usual, his huge girth girdled by a pair of trousers that made him look like a huge goose waddling, his shirt, collarless and unbuttoned at the neck, and a heavy black jacket that did not even come together at the front, so that you could see the simple white suspenders, an inch wide, that held up the trousers. His shoes were thin slippers.

Father Benjamino was in his clerical garb and wore his usual dusty black hat shaped like a round pan. He blessed the house before he entered, making the sign of the cross and murmuring a benediction.

Hector Adonis owned the finest house in Montelepre and was proud of it. The furniture was from France and the paintings had been bought carefully from minor living artists of Italy. His dinnerplate was from Germany and his house servant was a middle-aged Italian woman who had been trained in England before the war. She served them coffee as the three men sat in the drawing room waiting for Guiliano.

Don Croce felt absolutely secure. He knew that Guiliano would not dishonor his godfather by betraying his word. The Don was filled with a pleasurable anticipation. He would now meet and judge for himself the true greatness of this rising star. And yet even he was a little startled at how quietly Guiliano slipped into the house. There was no sound out in the cobbled street, no sound of a door opening or being shut. But suddenly Guiliano was standing in the archway that led to the dining room. Don Croce was struck by his handsomeness.

Life in the mountains had broadened his chest and slimmed down his face. It was still oval and yet the cheeks were lean, the chin pointed. There were the statuelike eyes, golden brown with their curious circle of silver that seemed to embed the eyeballs into their sockets. His clothes too set him off to advantage—the moleskin trousers snug, a white shirt freshly washed and ironed. He wore a hunting jacket of russet velvet, loose, underneath which was slung a machine pistol he always carried. Above all he looked incredibly young, no more than a boy, though his age was twenty-four.

Could such a boy have defied Rome, outwitted the Friends of the Friends, inspired devotion in the murderous Andolini, kept in check the brutishness of Passatempo, conquered a quarter of Sicily and the love of the people of the whole island? Don Croce knew that Guiliano was incredibly brave, but Sicily was full of brave men who had gone to early graves, easy prey to treacheries.

And then even as Don Croce doubted him, Turi Guiliano did something that gladdened the Don's heart and reassured him that he was right to make this boy his ally. He came into the room and advanced directly to Don Croce and said, *"Bacio tua mano."*

It was the traditional Sicilian peasant greeting to a man of higher rank—a priest, a landowner or a noble. "I kiss your hand." And Guiliano had a cheerful grin on his face. But Don Croce knew exactly why he had said it. It was not to show his subservience to the Don or even in respect for his age. It was said because the Don had put himself in Guiliano's power and Guiliano was showing respect for the trust. Don Croce rose slowly, his heavy cheeks becoming darker with the effort of rising. He took Guiliano in his arms. This was a noble young man and he wanted to show his affection. As he did so he could see the face of Hector Adonis beaming proudly—his godson had shown himself a gentleman.

Pisciotta came through the archway and watched this with a small smile on his saturnine face. His handsomeness too was remarkable but in direct contrast to Guiliano. The illness of his lungs had thinned his body and his features. The bones of his face seemed to press outward against his olive skin. His hair was carefully combed and sleekly black whereas Guiliano wore his tawny hair closely cropped as if it were a helmet.

As for Turi Guiliano, he had expected to take the Don by

surprise with his greeting and had been surprised in his turn by the Don's complete understanding and graceful affectionate acceptance. He studied the huge hulk of Don Croce and became even more alert. This was a dangerous man. Not only by reputation but by the aura of power around him. The bulk of his body, which should have been grotesque, seemed to give off a heated energy; it filled the room. And when the Don spoke, the voice coming from that massive head had almost the magic of choral music. There was an extraordinary fascination about him when he set out to convince that was a combination of sincerity, forcefulness and exquisite courtesy which was strange in a man who seemed so uncouth in everything else he did.

"I've watched you for years and waited long for this day. Now that it has arrived, you fulfill every expectation."

Guiliano said, "I am flattered." He measured his next words, knowing what was expected of him. "I have always hoped we would be friends."

Don Croce nodded and proceeded to explain the agreement that he had come to with Minister Trezza. That if Guiliano helped "educate" the populace of Sicily to vote properly in the next elections, then a way would be found for a pardon. Guiliano could return to his family as an ordinary citizen and no longer be a bandit. As evidence of the reality of this agreement, Minister Trezza had given the plans for the fight against Guiliano to the Don. The Don raised a hand in the air to emphasize his next point. "If you agree, these plans will be vetoed by the Minister. There would be no army expedition or extra thousand *carabinieri* sent to Sicily."

Don Croce saw that Guiliano was listening attentively but did not seem surprised by all this. He went on. "Everyone in Sicily knows your concern for the poor. One might think that you would support the leftist parties. But I know of your belief in God, you are after all a Sicilian. And who does not know of your devotion to your mother? Do you really want Communists running Italy? What would happen to the Church? What would happen to the family? The young men of Italy and Sicily who fought in the war are infected by foreign beliefs, political doctrines that have no place in Sicily. Sicilians can find their own way to a better fate. And do you really want an all-powerful state that would brook no rebelliousness from its citizens? A left-wing government would surely mount a major campaign against both of us, for are we not the true rulers of Sicily? If the leftist parties win the next election, the day might come when there are Russians in the villages of Sicily deciding who might go to church. Our children would be made to go to schools that would teach them that the state comes before the sacred mother and father. What is worth that? No. Now is the time for every true Sicilian to defend his family and his honor against the state."

There was an unexpected interruption. Pisciotta was still leaning against the wall of the archway. He said sardonically, "Maybe the Russians will give us our pardon."

A cold wind blew through the Don's mind. But he in no way showed the anger he felt at this insolent mustachioed little dandy. He studied the man. Why had he called attention to himself at this moment? Why had he wanted the Don to notice him? Don Croce wondered if this man might be put to some use. With his unerring instinct he smelled a rottenness in this most trusted lieutenant of Guiliano. Perhaps it was the lung disease, perhaps the cynicism of mind. Pisciotta was a man who could never trust anyone completely and was therefore a man who by definition could not be trusted by anyone completely. Don Croce turned all this over before he spoke to answer.

"When has a foreign nation ever helped Sicily?" he said. "When has a foreigner ever given justice to a Sicilian? Young men like yourself," he said directly to Pisciotta, "are our only hope. Cunning and brave and a pride in honor. For a thousand years such men have joined the Friends of the Friends to fight against oppressors, to seek the justice that Turi Guiliano fights for now. This is the time for us to stand together and preserve Sicily."

Guiliano seemed impervious to the power of the Don's voice. He said with deliberate bluntness, "But we have always fought against Rome and the men sent to govern us. They have always been our enemies. And now you ask us to help them, to trust them?"

Don Croce said gravely, "There are times when it is proper to make common cause with an enemy. The Christian Democrats are the least dangerous to us if they win Italy. It is to our purpose therefore that they rule. What could be simpler?" He paused for a moment. "The leftists will never give you a pardon. Rest assured of that. They are too hypocritical, too unforgiving, they do not understand the Sicilian character. Certainly the poor will get their land, but will they be able to keep what they grow? Can you picture our people working in a cooperative? God in heaven, they kill each other now in a quarrel over whether the Virgin Mary will wear a white robe or a red robe in our religious processions."

All this was delivered with the ironical wit of a man who wanted his audience to know he was exaggerating and yet know the exaggeration held a good deal of truth.

Guiliano listened with a slight smile. He knew that someday it might be necessary to kill this man and such was the respect Don Croce inspired by his presence and the power of his personality that Guiliano flinched from the thought. As if by even thinking such a thing he went against his own father, some deep feeling of family. He had to make a decision and it would be the most important since he had become an outlaw.

Guiliano said softly, "I agree with you on the Communists. They are not for Sicilians." Guiliano paused. He felt that now was the moment to make Don Croce bend to his will. "But if I do Rome's dirty work, I have to promise my men some reward. What can Rome do for us?"

Don Croce had finished his cup of coffee. Hector Adonis sprang to replenish it, but Don Croce waved him away. Then he said to Guiliano, "We have not done too badly for you. Andolini brings you information on the movements of the *carabinieri* so that you can always keep your eye on them. They have not taken extraordinary measures to root you out of your mountains. But I know that is not enough. Allow me to do you a service that will gladden my heart and bring joy to your mother and father. Before your godfather here at our table, before your true friend, Aspanu Pisciotta, I will tell you this: I will move heaven and earth to secure your pardon and of course for your men."

Guiliano had already made up his mind, but he wanted to nail down such guarantees as he could. He said, "I agree with almost everything you say. I love Sicily and its people and though I live as a bandit, I believe in justice. I would do almost anything to return to my home and my parents. But how do you make Rome keep their promises to me? That is the key. The service you ask is dangerous. I must have my reward."

The Don considered. Then he said slowly and carefully, "You are right to be cautious. But you have those plans I requested Professor Adonis to show you. Keep them as evidence of your relationship to Minister Trezza. I will try to secure other documents for you that you may be able to use and that Rome must fear you may make public in one of your famous letters to the newspapers. And then finally I guarantee the pardon personally if you complete your task and the Christian Democrats win the election. Minister Trezza has the greatest respect for me and would never break his promise."

Hector Adonis had an excited, pleased look on his face. He was already envisioning Maria Lombardo's happiness when her son returned home no longer a fugitive. He knew Guiliano was acting out of necessity, but he thought that this alliance of Guiliano and Don Croce against the Communists might be the first link in a chain that could bind the two men together in true friendship.

That the great Don Croce guaranteed the government's pardon impressed even Pisciotta. But Guiliano saw the essential flaw in the Don's presentation. How could he know that this was not merely all an invention by the Don? That the plans had not been stolen? That they had not already been vetoed by the Minister? He needed a direct meeting with Trezza.

"That reassures me," Guiliano said. "Your personal guarantee. shows the kindness of your heart and why people in Sicily call you 'The Good Soul.' But the treachery of Rome is notorious, and politicians—we know what they are. I would like someone I trust to hear Trezza's promise from his own lips and a document from him that gives some assurances."

The Don was astounded. All during the interview he had had feelings of fondness for Turi Guiliano. He had thoughts of what it would have been if this youth had been his son. Oh, how they could have ruled Sicily together. And with what grace he had said, "I kiss your hand." The Don for one of the few times in his life had been charmed. But now he realized that Guiliano was not accepting his assurances, and his feeling of affection dimmed. He was conscious of those curiously half-closed eyes resting on him with a peculiar stare awaiting further proofs, further assurances. The guarantees of Don Croce Malo were not enough.

There was a long silence, the Don considering what he should say, the rest waiting. Hector Adonis tried to cover his dismay at Guiliano's persistence and his fear of the Don's reaction. Father Benjamino's white pudgy face had the look of an insulted bulldog. But finally the Don spoke and reassured them all. He had reasoned out what was in Guiliano's mind and what he would need.

"It is to my interest that you agree," he said to Guiliano, "and so perhaps I was carried away with my own arguments. But let me help you decide in this fashion. Let me say first of all that Minister Trezza will never give you any document—that is too dangerous. But he will speak to you and speak the promises he spoke to me. I can secure letters from Prince Ollorto and other powerful members of the nobility who are committed to our cause. Perhaps better than that, I have a friend who may

273

convince you more—the Catholic Church will support your pardon. I have the word of the Cardinal of Palermo. After you hear Minister Trezza I will arrange an audience with the Cardinal. He too will make the promise directly to you. And there you have it, the promise of the Minister of Justice for all of Italy, the sacred word of a Cardinal of the Holy Catholic Church who might someday be our Pope, and myself."

It was impossible to describe the manner in which the Don spoke the last two words. His tenor voice sank humbly as if he almost did not dare to include his name with the others, and there was an extra charge of energy in the words "and myself" that left no doubt as to the importance of his promise.

Guiliano laughed. "I can't go to Rome."

Don Croce said, "Then send someone you trust absolutely. I will bring him to Minister Trezza personally. And then I will bring him to the Cardinal. Surely you can trust the word of a prince of the Holy Church?"

Guiliano watched Don Croce intently. Warning signals were going off in his brain. Why was the Don so anxious to help him? Certainly he knew that he, Guiliano, could not go to Rome, that he would never take that risk, even if a thousand cardinals and ministers gave their word. So whom did the Don expect him to name as his emissary?

"There is no person I trust more than my second in command," he said to the Don. "Bring Aspanu Pisciotta with you to Rome, and to Palermo. He likes the big cities, and maybe if the Cardinal hears his confession, even his sins will be forgiven."

Don Croce leaned back and motioned to Hector Adonis to fill his coffee cup. It was an old trick of his, to mask his satisfaction and sense of triumph. As if the matter at hand was so uninteresting that an external desire could take its place. But Guiliano, who had proved such a brilliant guerrilla fighter once he became a bandit, had an intuitive insight into the reading of men's motions and patterns of thought. He immediately sensed the feeling of satisfaction. Don Croce had won a very important goal. He could not guess that Don Croce wanted more than anything else time to be alone with Aspanu Pisciotta.

■ ■ ■

TWO DAYS later Pisciotta accompanied Don Croce to Palermo and Rome. Don Croce treated him as if he were royalty. And indeed Pisciotta had the face of the Borgia general, Cesare. The sharp planes, the tiny mustache, the Asiatic sallow darkness of the skin, the cruel and insolent eyes, so alive with charm and an impudent suspicion of everything in the world.

In Palermo they stayed in the Hotel Umberto, owned by Don Croce, and Pisciotta was shown every courtesy. He was taken out to buy new clothes for his meeting in Rome with the Minister of Justice. He dined with Don Croce at the finest restaurants. And then Pisciotta and Don Croce were received by the Cardinal of Palermo.

It was extraordinary that Pisciotta, a young man from a small town in Sicily, brought up in the Catholic faith, was not awed by this audience, by the great halls of the Cardinal's palace, the dignified obsequiousness to the holy power shown by all. When Don Croce kissed the Cardinal's ring, Pisciotta looked at the Cardinal with a proud stare.

The Cardinal was a tall man. He wore a red beret and a scarlet sashed cloak. His features were coarse and marked with small-pox. He was not a man who would ever receive a single vote for the papacy, despite Don Croce's rhetoric, but he was a seasoned intriguer, a Sicilian born.

There were the usual politenesses. The Cardinal gravely inquired after Pisciotta's spiritual health. He reminded him that whatever sins were committed here on earth, no man must forget that eternal forgiveness awaited him if he were a proper Christian.

After thus assuring Pisciotta of his spiritual amnesty, the Cardinal got down to the pit of the olive. He told Pisciotta that the

Holy Church was in mortal danger here in Sicily. If the Communists won the national elections, who could know what would happen? The great cathedrals would be burned and gutted and turned into machine tool plants. The statues of the Virgin Mary, the crosses of Jesus, the effigies of all the saints would be thrown into the Mediterranean. The priests would be murdered, nuns raped.

At this last, Pisciotta smiled. What Sicilian, no matter how mad dog a Communist, would ever dream of raping a nun? The Cardinal saw that smile. If Guiliano would help suppress the Communist propaganda before the next election, he, the Cardinal himself, would preach a sermon on Easter Sunday exhorting the virtues of Guiliano and asking the clemency of the government in Rome. And Don Croce could tell the same thing to the Minister when they met in Rome.

With this the Cardinal concluded the interview and blessed Aspanu Pisciotta. Before he left, Aspanu Pisciotta asked the Cardinal for a little note he could give to Guiliano to show the interview had taken place. The Cardinal complied. The Don was astonished by this idiocy on the part of a Prince of the Holy Church but said nothing.

■ ■ ■

THE MEETING in Rome was more Pisciotta's style. Minister Trezza did not pretend to the spiritual qualities of the Cardinal. After all he was a Minister of Justice and this Pisciotta merely a bandit's courier. He explained to Pisciotta that if the Christian Democratic party lost the election, the Communists would take extraordinary measures to wipe out the last bandits remaining in Sicily. It was true that the *carabinieri* still mounted expeditions against Guiliano, but that could not be helped. Appearances must be preserved or the radical newspapers would scream to the high heavens.

Pisciotta interrupted him. "Is Your Excellency telling me that your party can never give Guiliano amnesty?"

"It will be difficult," Minister Trezza said, "but not impossible. If Guiliano helps us win the election. If he then remains quiet for a time without committing any kidnappings or robberies. If he lets his name be not so notorious. Perhaps he could even emigrate to America for a time and return forgiven by everyone. But one thing I can guarantee, if we win the election. We will not mount serious efforts to capture him. And if he wishes to emigrate to America we will not prevent him or persuade the American authorities to deport him." He paused for a moment. "Personally I will do everything in my power to persuade the President of Italy to pardon him."

Pisciotta said again with his slight smile, "But if we become model citizens, how do we eat, Guiliano and his men and their families? Is there perhaps a way of the government paying us? After all, we're doing their dirty work."

Don Croce who had been listening with his eyes shut, like a sleeping reptile, spoke quickly to stop the angry reply of the Minister of Justice who was bursting with fury that this bandit dared to ask the government for money.

"A joke, Your Excellency," Don Croce said. "He's a young lad his first time out of Sicily. He doesn't understand the strict moralities of the outside world. The question of support does not concern you in the least. I will arrange that with Guiliano myself." He gave Pisciotta a warning glance to keep still.

But the Minister suddenly had a smile on his face and said to Pisciotta, "Well, I'm glad to see the youth of Sicily have not changed. I was like that once. We're not afraid to ask what's due us. Maybe you would like something more concrete than promises." He reached into his desk and pulled out a red-bordered laminated card. Tossing it to Pisciotta, he said, "This is a special pass signed by me personally. You can move anyplace in Italy or Sicily without the police bothering you. It's worth its weight in gold."

Pisciotta bowed his thanks and put the pass in his jacket pocket, inside next to his breast. On their journey to Rome he had seen Don Croce use such a pass; he knew he had received something of value. But then the thought struck him: What if he were captured with it? There would be a scandal that would shake the country. The second in command of Guiliano's band carrying a security pass issued by the Minister of Justice? How could that be? His mind raced to solve the puzzle, but he could come up with no answer.

The gift of such an important document showed an act of faith and good will on the Minister's part. The magnificence of Don Croce's hospitality on the trip was gratifying. But all this did not convince Pisciotta. Before he left he asked Trezza to write a note to Guiliano verifying that the meeting had taken place. Trezza refused.

■ ■ ■

WHEN PISCIOTTA returned to the mountains Guiliano questioned him closely, making him repeat every word he could remember. As Pisciotta showed him the red-bordered pass and voiced his puzzlement as to why it had been given him and the dangers the Minister ran in signing such a pass, Guiliano patted him on the shoulder. "You're a true brother," he said. "You're so much more suspicious than I am, and yet your loyalty to me has blinded you to the obvious. Don Croce must have told him to give you the pass. They hope you will make a special trip to Rome and become their informer."

"That whore's goat," Pisciotta said with terrible anger. "I'll use this pass to go back and slit his throat."

"No," Guiliano said. "Keep the pass. It will be useful to us. And another thing. That may look like Trezza's signature, but of course it's not. It's a forgery. If it suits their purpose they can deny the pass is legitimate. Or if it suits their purpose they can say certainly it's in order and produce records that the pass was authorized by Trezza. If they claim it's a forgery they just destroy the records."

Pisciotta recognized the truth of this. With each day he felt a growing amazement that Guiliano who was so open and honest in his feelings could fathom the twisted schemes of his enemies. He realized that at the root of Guiliano's romanticism was the brilliant penetration of paranoia.

"Then how can we believe they will keep their promises to us?" Pisciotta said. "Why should we help them? Our business isn't politics."

Guiliano considered this. Aspanu had always been cynical, and a little greedy too. They had quarreled a few times about the spoils of some robberies, Pisciotta urging a larger share for members of the band.

"We have no choice," Guiliano said. "The Communists will never give me amnesty if they win control of the government. Right now the Christian Democrats and Minister Trezza and the Cardinal of Palermo and of course Don Croce must be our friends and comrades in arms. We must neutralize the Communists, that's the most important thing. We'll meet with Don Croce and settle the matter." He paused and patted Pisciotta's shoulder. "You did well to get the Cardinal's note. And the pass will be useful."

But Pisciotta was not convinced. "We'll do their dirty work for them," he said. "And then we'll hang around like beggars waiting for their pardon. I don't believe any of them—they talk to us as if we were foolish girls, promising us the world if we get into bed with them. I say we fight for ourselves, keep the money we make with our work instead of distributing it to the poor. We could be rich and live like kings in America or Brazil. That's our solution and then we won't have to count on those *pezzonovanti*."

Guiliano decided to explain exactly how he felt. "Aspanu," he said, "we must gamble on the Christian Democrats and Don Croce. If we win and gain our pardon, the people of Sicily will elect us to lead them. We'll win everything." Guiliano paused for a moment and smiled at Pisciotta. "If they play us false, neither you nor I will faint with surprise. But how much will we have lost? We must fight the Communists in any case; they are more our enemies than the Fascists. And so their doom is certain. Now, listen to me carefully. You and I think alike. The final battle will be after we defeat the Communists and must take arms against the Friends of the Friends and Don Croce."

Pisciotta shrugged. "We are making a mistake," he said.

Guiliano, though he smiled, was thoughtful. He knew Pisciotta liked the life of an outlaw. It fitted his character, and though he was quick-witted and cunning, he did not have imagination. He could not make a jump into the future and see the inescapable fate that awaited them as outlaws.

■ ■ ■

LATER THAT night, Aspanu Pisciotta sat on the edge of the cliff and tried to smoke a cigarette. But a sharp pain in his chest made him stub it out and put the butt in his pocket. He knew his tuberculosis was getting worse, but he also knew that if he rested in the mountains for a few weeks, he would feel better. What worried him was something he had not told Guiliano.

All during the voyage to see Minister Trezza and the Cardinal, Don Croce had been his constant companion. They had eaten dinner together every night, and the Don had discoursed on the future of Sicily, the troublesome times to come. It had taken some time for Pisciotta to realize that the Don was courting him, trying to win him over to some sympathy for the Friends of the Friends, and in a very subtle way attempting to convince Pisciotta that perhaps, like Sicily, his own future might be rosier with the Don than with Guiliano. Pisciotta had given him no sign that he understood these messages. But it made him more worried about the Don's good faith. He had never before been in fear of any man, except perhaps Turi Guiliano. But Don Croce, who had spent his whole life acquiring that "respect" which is the badge of a great Mafia chief, inspired in him a sense of dread. What he realized now was that he feared the Don would outwit and betray them and that someday they would lie with their faces in the dust.

CHAPTER

20

THE 1948 April elections of the Sicilian legislature were a disaster for the Christian Democratic party in Rome. The "People's Bloc," the combination of Communist Socialist left-wing parties, polled 600,000 votes, to the Christian Democratic 330,000. Another 500,000 votes were split between the Monarchist and two other splinter parties. Panic reigned in Rome. Something drastic had to be done before the national election or Sicily, the most backward region of the country, would be decisive in turning all of Italy into a Socialist country.

Over the previous months Guiliano had lived up to his agreement with Rome. He had torn down all the posters of rival parties, had raided the headquarters of left-wing groups and broken up their meetings in Corleone, Montelepre, Castellammare, Partinico, Piani dei Greci, San Giuseppe Jato and the great city of Monreale. His bandits had put posters in all these cities that proclaimed in great black letters, DEATH TO THE COMMUNISTS, and he had burned some of the community houses established by the Socialist Workers groups. But his campaign had started too late to affect the regional elections, and he had been reluctant to use the ultimate terror of assassination. Messages flew between Don Croce, Minister Trezza, the Cardinal of Palermo and Turi Guiliano. Reproaches were made. Guiliano was urged to step up his campaign so that the situation could be reversed for the national elections. Guiliano saved all these messages for his Testament.

A great stroke was needed, and it was the fertile brain of Don Croce that conceived it. He sent a message to Guiliano through Stefan Andolini.

The two most left-wing and generally rebellious towns in Sicily were Piani dei Greci and San Giuseppe Jato. For many years, even under Mussolini, they had celebrated the first of May as the day of revolution. Since May first was also the name day of Saint Rosalie, their celebration would be disguised as a religious festival not forbidden by the Fascist authorities. But now their May Day parades were bold with red flags and inflammatory speeches. The coming May Day in a week's time was to be the greatest in history. As was the custom, the two towns would combine to celebrate and envoys from all over Sicily would bring their families to rejoice over their recent victory. The Communist Senator, Lo Causi, a renowned and fiery orator, would give the main speech. It was to be the official celebration of the Left of their recent stunning victory in the elections.

Don Croce's plan was that this celebration was to be attacked by Guiliano's band and broken up. They would mount machine guns and fire over the heads of the crowd to disperse them. It was to be the first step in a campaign of intimidation, a paternal warning, a soft advisory hand of admonishment. The Communist Senator, Lo Causi, would learn that his election to Parliament did not give him license in Sicily or make sacred his person. Guiliano agreed to the plan and ordered his chiefs, Pisciotta, Terranova, Passatempo, Silvestro and Stefan Andolini to stand by to carry it out.

For the last three years the celebration had always been held on a mountain plain between Piani dei Greci and San Giuseppe Jato, sheltered by the twin peaks of Monte Pizzuta and Monte Cumeta. The people of the towns would climb up to the plain on wildly curving roads that joined near the top, so that the populations of the two towns would meet and become a single procession. They would enter the plain through a narrow pass, and then spread out to celebrate their holiday. This pass was called the Portella della Ginestra.

■ ■ ■

THE VILLAGES of Piani dei Greci and San Giuseppe Jato were poor, their houses ancient, their agriculture archaic. They believed in the ancient codes of honor; the women sitting outside their houses had to sit in profile to keep their good reputations. But the two villages were home to the most rebellious people on the island of Sicily.

The villages were so old that most of the houses were built of stone, and some had no windows but only small apertures covered with iron discs. Many families housed their animals in the rooms in which they lived. The town bakeries kept goats and young lambs huddled by their ovens, and if a freshly baked loaf dropped to the floor it would usually hit a pile of dung.

The village men hired themselves out as laborers to wealthy landowners for a dollar a day and sometimes even less, not enough to feed their families. So when the nuns and priests, "Black Crows," came with their packets of macaroni and charity clothes, the villagers swore the necessary oaths: to vote for the Christian Democrats.

But in the regional election of April 1948 they had treacherously voted overwhelmingly for the Communist or Socialist parties. This had enraged Don Croce who thought that the local Mafia chief controlled the area. But the Don declared that it was the disrespect to the Catholic Church that saddened him. How could devout Sicilians have so deceived the holy sisters who with Christian charity put bread into the mouths of their children?

The Cardinal of Palermo also was vexed. He had made a special trip to say a Mass in the two villages and had warned them not to vote for the Communists. He had blessed their children and even baptized them, and still they had turned on

their Church. He summoned the village priests to Palermo and
warned them that they must increase their efforts for the national elections. Not only in the political interests of the Church
but to save ignorant souls from hell.

Minister Trezza was not so surprised. He was Sicilian and
knew the island's history. The people of the two villages had
always been proud and ferocious fighters against the rich in
Sicily and the tyranny of Rome. They had been the first to join
Garibaldi, and before that they had fought the French and Moor-
ish rulers of the island. In Piani dei Greci the villagers descended
from Greeks who had fled to Sicily to escape Turkish invaders.
These villagers still retained their Greek customs, spoke the
language and observed the Greek holidays by wearing ancient
costumes. But it had been a stronghold of the Mafia which had
always fostered rebellion. So Minister Trezza was disappointed
by Don Croce's performance, his inability to educate them. But
he also knew that the vote in the villages and the whole surrounding countryside had been engineered by one man, a Socialist party organizer named Silvio Ferra.

Silvio Ferra was a highly decorated soldier in the Italian Army
of World War II. He had won his medals in the African campaign and then had been captured by the American Army. He
had been an inmate of a prisoner of war camp in the United
States where he had attended educational courses designed to
make prisoners understand the democratic process. He had not
quite believed them until he had been given permission to work
outside the camp for a baker in the local town. He had been
amazed at the freedom of American life, the ease with which
hard work could be turned into a lasting prosperity, the upward
mobility of the lower classes. In Sicily the hardest-working peasant could only hope to provide food and shelter for his children;
there could be no provision for the future.

When he was returned to his native Sicily, Silvio Ferra became an ardent advocate of America. But he soon saw that the
Christian Democratic party was a tool of the rich and so joined

a Socialist Workers' study group in Palermo. He had a thirst for education and a passion for books. Soon he had gobbled up all the theories of Marx and Engels and then joined the Socialist party. He was given the assignment of organizing the party club in San Giuseppe Jato.

In four years he had done what the agitators from the north of Italy could not do. He had translated the Red Revolution and Socialist doctrine into Sicilian terms. He convinced them that a vote for the Socialist party meant getting a piece of land. He preached that the great estates of the nobles should be broken up since the nobles left them uncultivated. Land that could grow wheat for their children. He convinced them that under a Socialist government the corruption of Sicilian society could be wiped out. There would be no bribing of officials for preference, no one would have to give a priest a pair of eggs to read a letter from America, the village postman would not have to be given a token lira to ensure delivery of mail, men would not have to auction off the labor of their bodies at a pittance to work the fields of dukes and barons. There would be an end to starvation wages, and the officials of the government would be servants of the people, as it was in America. Silvio Ferra quoted chapter and verse to show that the official Catholic Church propped up the debased capitalistic system, yet he never attacked the Virgin Mary, the diversified useful saints, or a belief in Jesus. On Easter mornings he greeted his neighbors with the traditional, "Christ is risen." On Sundays he went to Mass. His wife and children were strictly supervised in true Sicilian style for he was a believer in all the old values, the son's absolute devotion for his mother, respect for his father, the sense of obligation for his most obscure cousins.

When the Mafia *cosce* in San Giuseppe Jato warned him that he was going too far, he smiled and intimated that in the future he would welcome their friendship, though in his heart he knew that the last and greatest battle would be against the Mafia. When Don Croce sent special messengers to try to make an accommodation, he put them off. Such was his reputation for bravery in the war, the respect in which he was held in the village and his indication that he would be judicious with the Friends of the Friends that Don Croce decided to be patient, especially since he was sure the election was won anyway.

But most of all Silvio Ferra had a sympathy for his fellow man, a rare quality in the Sicilian peasant. If a neighbor became ill he brought food for his family, he did chores for ailing old widows who lived alone, he cheered all those men who eked out a bare living and were fearful of their futures. He proclaimed a new dawn of hope under the Socialist party. When he gave political speeches he used the southern rhetoric so dearly loved by Sicilians. He did not explain the economic theories of Marx but spoke with fire of the vengeance owed to those who had oppressed the peasants for centuries. "As bread is sweet to us," he said, "so is the blood of the poor to the rich who drink it."

It was Silvio Ferra who organized a cooperative of laboring men who refused to submit to the labor auction where the lowest wage got the work. He established a set wage per day, and the nobility was forced to meet it at harvesting or watch their olives, grapes and grain rot. And so Silvio Ferra was a marked man.

What saved him was that he was under the protection of Turi Guiliano. That had been one of the considerations that had persuaded Don Croce to stay his hand. Silvio Ferra had been born in Montelepre. Even as a youth his qualities had been evident. Turi Guiliano had admired him extravagantly, though they had not been close friends because of the difference in their ages— Guiliano was four years younger—and because Silvio had gone off to war. Silvio had returned a much decorated hero. He met a girl from San Giuseppe Jato and moved there to marry her. And as the political fame of Ferra grew, Guiliano let it be known the man was his friend though their politics were different. Thus when Guiliano began his program to "educate" the voters of Sicily, he gave orders that no action was to be taken against the village of San Giuseppe Jato or the person of Silvio Ferra.

Ferra had heard of this and was clever enough to send a message to Guiliano thanking him and saying he would be of service to Guiliano at his command. The message was sent via Ferra's parents who still lived in Montelepre with their other children. One of the children was a young girl named Justina, only fifteen, who carried the note to the Guiliano home to deliver it to his mother. It so happened that Guiliano was visiting at the time and was there to receive the message personally. At fifteen most Sicilian girls are already women, and she fell in love with Turi Guiliano, as how could she not? His physical power, his feline grace fascinated her so that she stared at him almost rudely.

Turi Guiliano and his parents and La Venera were drinking coffee and asked the girl if she would like a cup. She refused. Only La Venera noticed how pretty the girl was and was aware of her fascination. Guiliano did not recognize her as the little girl whom he had once met crying in the road and given lire to. Guiliano said to her, "Give your brother my thanks for his offer and tell him not to worry about his mother and father, they will always be under my protection." Justina quickly left the house and dashed back to her parents. From that time on she dreamed of Turi Guiliano as her lover. And she was proud of the affection he had for her brother.

And so when Guiliano agreed to suppress the festival at the Portella della Ginestra, he sent a friendly warning to Silvio Ferra that he should not take part in the May Day meeting. He assured him that none of the villagers of San Giuseppe Jato would be harmed but that there might be some danger he could not protect him from if he persisted in his Socialist party activities. Not that he, Guiliano, would ever do anything to harm him, but the Friends of the Friends were determined to crush the Socialist party in Sicily and Ferra would certainly be one of their targets.

When Silvio Ferra received this note he assumed it was another attempt to frighten him off, instigated by Don Croce. It did not matter. The Socialist party was on the march to victory, and he would not miss one of its great celebrations of the victory they had already won.

■ ■ ■

ON MAY DAY of 1948 the populace of the two towns of Piani dei Greci and San Giuseppe Jato rose early to start on their long march up mountain trails to the plain beyond the Portella della Ginestra. They were led by bands of musicians from Palermo especially hired for the occasion. Silvio Ferra, flanked by his wife and two children, was in the vanguard of the San Giuseppe Jato procession, proudly carrying one of the huge red flags. Dazzlingly painted carts, with their horses in special red plumes and colorful tasseled blankets, were loaded with cooking pots, huge wooden boxes of spaghetti, enormous wooden bowls for salads. There was a special cart for the jugs of wine. Another cart fitted with blocks of ice carried wheels of cheese, great salami logs and the dough and ovens to bake fresh bread.

Children danced and kicked soccer balls along the column. Men on horseback tested their steeds for the sprint races that were to be a highlight of the afternoon games.

As Silvio Ferra led his townspeople toward the narrow mountain pass called the Portella della Ginestra, the people of Piani dei Greci converged from the other road, holding their red flags and Socialist party standards high. The two crowds mixed, exchanging exuberant greetings as they walked on, gossiping about the latest scandals in their villages and speculating on what their victory in the election would bring, what dangers lay ahead. Despite rumors that there would be trouble on this May Day they were by no means afraid. Rome they despised, the Mafia they feared, but not to submission. After all they had defied both in the last election and nothing had happened.

By noontime more than three thousand people had spread out over the plain. The women started the portable ovens to boil water for pasta, the children were flying kites over which flew the tiny red hawks of Sicily. The Communist Senator, Lo Causi, was going over his notes for the speech he was to deliver; a group of men led by Silvio Ferra was putting together the wooden platform which would hold him and prominent citizens of the two towns. The men helping him were also advising him to keep his introduction of the Senator short—the children were getting hungry.

At that moment there were light popping sounds in the mountain air. Some of the children must have brought firecrackers, Silvio Ferra thought. He turned to look.

■ ■ ■

ON THAT same morning but much earlier, indeed before the smokey Sicilian sun had risen, two squads of twelve men each had made the march from Guiliano's headquarters in the mountains above Montelepre down to the mountain range which held the Portella della Ginestra. One squad was commanded by Passatempo and the other by Terranova. Each squad carried a heavy machine gun. Passatempo led his men high up on the slopes of Monte Cumeta and carefully supervised the emplacement of his machine gun. Four men were detailed to service and fire it. The remaining men were spread out on the slope with their rifles and *lupare* to protect them from any attack.

Terranova and his men occupied the slopes of Monte Pizzuta on the other side of the Portella della Ginestra. From this vantage point, the arid plain and the villages below were under the barrels of his machine gun and the rifles of his men. This was to prevent any surprise by the *carabinieri* if they should venture out from their barracks.

From both mountain slopes men of the Guiliano band watched the townspeople from Piani dei Greci and San Giuseppe Jato make their long marches to the tabletop plain. A few of the men had relatives in these processions, but they felt no twinge of conscience. For Guiliano's instructions had been explicit. The machine guns were to be fired over the heads of crowds until they dispersed and fled back to their villages. Nobody was to be hurt.

■ ■ ■

GUILIANO HAD planned to go with this expedition and command it personally, but seven days before May Day, Aspanu Pisciotta's weak chest had finally succumbed to a hemorrhage. He had been running up the side of the mountain to the band's headquarters when blood spurted out of his mouth and he collapsed to the ground. His body started rolling downhill. Guiliano, climbing behind him, thought it was one of his cousin's pranks. He stopped the body with his foot and then saw the front of Pisciotta's shirt covered with blood. At first he thought Aspanu had been hit by a sniper and he had missed the sound of the shot. He took Pisciotta in his arms and carried him uphill. Pisciotta was still conscious and kept murmuring, "Put me down, put me down." And Guiliano knew it could not be a bullet. The voice betrayed the weariness of an inner breakage, not the savage trauma of a body violated by metal.

Pisciotta was put on a stretcher and Guiliano led a band of ten men to a doctor in Monreale. The doctor was often used by the band to treat gunshot wounds and could be counted on to keep secrets. But this doctor reported Pisciotta's illness to Don Croce as he had all the other transactions with Guiliano. For the doctor hoped to be appointed head of a Palermo hospital and he knew this would be impossible without Don Croce's blessing.

The doctor brought Pisciotta to the Monreale hospital for further tests and asked Guiliano to remain to wait for the results.

"I'll come back in the morning," Guiliano told the doctor. He detailed four of his men to guard Pisciotta in the hospital and with his other men he went to the home of one of his band to hide.

The next day the doctor told him that Pisciotta needed a drug called streptomycin that could only be obtained in the United States. Guiliano thought about this. He would ask his father and

Stefan Andolini to write Don Corleone in America and ask that some be sent. He told the doctor this and asked if Pisciotta could be released from the hospital. The doctor said yes, but only if he rested in bed for several weeks.

So it was that Guiliano was in Monreale taking care of Pisciotta, arranging a house for him to recuperate in, as the attack was made at the Portella della Ginestra.

■ ■ ■

WHEN SILVIO FERRA turned to the sound of the firecrackers, three things registered simultaneously on his mind. The first was the sight of a small boy holding up his arm in astonishment. At the end of it, instead of a hand holding a kite, was a bloody horrible stump, the kite sailing off to the sky above the slopes of Monte Cumeta. The second was his shock of recognition—the firecrackers were machine-gun fire. The third was a great black horse plunging wildly through the crowd, riderless, its flanks streaming blood. Then Silvio Ferra was running through the crowd, searching for his wife and children.

■ ■ ■

ON THE slopes of Monte Pizzuta, Terranova watched the scene through his field glasses. At first he thought people were falling to the ground out of terror, and then he saw motionless bodies sprawled with that peculiar abandon of death and he struck the machine gunner away from his weapon. But as his machine gun fell silent, he could still hear the gun on Monte Cumeta chattering. Terranova thought Passatempo had not yet seen that the gunfire had been aimed too low and people were being massacred. After a few minutes the other gun stopped and an awful stillness filled the Portella della Ginestra. Then floating up to the twin mountain peaks came the wails of the living, the shrieks of the wounded and the dying. Terranova signaled his men to gather close, had them dismantle the machine gun, and then led them away around the other side of the mountain to make their escape. As they did so he was pondering whether he should return to Guiliano to report this tragedy. He was afraid Guiliano might execute him and his men out of hand. Yet he was sure Guiliano would give him a fair hearing, and he and his men could truly swear that they had elevated their fire. He would return to headquarters and report. He wondered if Passatempo would do the same.

■ ■ ■

BY THE time Silvio Ferra found his wife and children, the machine guns had stopped. His family was unhurt and were starting to rise from the ground. He flung them down again and made them stay prone for another fifteen minutes. He saw a man on a horse galloping toward Piani dei Greci to get help from the *carabinieri* barracks, and when the man was not shot off his horse he knew the attack was over. He got up.

From the tabletop of the plain that crowned the Portella della Ginestra, thousands of people were streaming back to their villages at the bottom of the mountains. And on the ground were the dead and wounded, their families crouched over them weeping. The proud banners they had carried that morning were lying in the dust, their dark golds, brilliant greens and solitary reds startlingly bright in the noon sun. Silvio Ferra left his family to help the wounded. He stopped some of the fleeing men and made them serve as stretcher bearers. He saw with horror that some of the dead were children, and some were women. He felt the tears come to his eyes. All his teachers were wrong, those believers in political action. Voters would never change Sicily. It was all foolishness. They would have to murder to get their rights.

■ ■ ■

IT WAS Hector Adonis who brought the news to Guiliano at Pisciotta's bedside. Guiliano immediately went to his mountain headquarters, leaving Pisciotta to recover without his personal protection.

There on the cliffs above Montelepre, he summoned Passa-tempo and Terranova.

"Let me warn you before you speak," Guiliano began. "Whoever is responsible will be found out no matter how long it takes. And the longer it takes the more severe the punishment. If it was.an honest mistake, confess now and I promise you won't suffer death."

Passatempo and Terranova had never seen such fury in Gui-liano before. They stood rigid, not daring to move as Guiliano interrogated them. They swore their guns had been elevated to fire over the heads of the crowd, and when they had observed the people being hit, they had halted the guns.

Guiliano next questioned the men in the squads and the men on the machine guns. He pieced the scene together. Terranova's machine gun had fired about five minutes before being halted. Passatempo's about ten minutes. The gunners swore they had fired above the heads of the crowds. None of them would admit they had possibly made an error or depressed the angle of the guns in any way.

After he dismissed them, Guiliano sat alone. He felt, for the first time since he had become a bandit, a sense of intolerable shame. In more than four years as an outlaw he could boast that he had never harmed the poor. That boast was no longer true. He had massacred them. In his innermost heart he could no longer think of himself as a hero. Then he thought over the possibilities. It could have been a mistake: His band was fine with *lupare*, but the heavy machine guns were not too familiar to them. Firing downward, it was possible they had misjudged the angle. He could not believe that Terranova or Passatempo had played him false, but there was always the awful possibility that one or both had been bribed to commit the massacre. Also, it had occurred to him the moment he heard the news that there might have been a third ambush party.

But surely, if it had been deliberate, more people would have been shot. Surely it would have been a far more terrible slaugh-ter. Unless, Guiliano thought, the aim of the massacre had been to disgrace the name of Guiliano. And whose idea had it been, the attack on the Portella della Ginestra? The coincidence was too much for him to swallow.

The inevitable and humiliating truth was that he had been outwitted by Don Croce.

CHAPTER

21

THE MASSACRE at the Portella della Ginestra shocked all of Italy. Newspapers screamed in glaring headlines the slaughter of innocent men, women and children. There were fifteen dead and over fifty wounded. At first there was speculation that the Mafia had committed the massacre, and indeed Silvio Ferra gave speeches laying the deed at the feet of Don Croce. But the Don had been prepared for this. Secret members of the Friends of the Friends swore before magistrates that they had seen Passatempo and Terranova set their ambush. The people of Sicily wondered why Guiliano did not deny this outrageous charge in one of his famous letters to the newspapers. He was uncharacteristically silent.

■ ■ ■

TWO WEEKS before the national election, Silvio Ferra rode on his bicycle from San Giuseppe Jato to the town of Piani dei Greci. He cycled along the river Jato and skirted the base of the mountain. On the road he passed two men who shouted at him to stop, but he cycled on swiftly. Looking back he saw the two men trudging after patiently but he soon outdistanced them and left them far behind. By the time he entered the village of Piani dei Greci, they were no longer in sight.

Ferra spent the next three hours in the Socialist community

house with other party leaders from the surrounding area. When they were done it was twilight, and he was anxious to get home before dark. He walked his bicycle through the central square, greeting cheerily some of the villagers he knew. Suddenly four men surrounded him. Silvio Ferra recognized one of them as the Mafia chief of Montelepre, and he felt a sense of relief. He had known Quintana as a child, and Ferra also knew that the Mafia was very careful in this corner of Sicily not to irritate Guiliano or break his rules about "insults to the poor." And so he greeted Quintana with a smile and said, "You're a long way from home."

Quintana said, "Hello, my friend. We'll walk along with you for a bit. Don't make a fuss and you won't be hurt. We just want to reason with you."

"Reason with me here," Silvio Ferra said. He felt the first thrill of fear, the same fear that he felt on the battlegrounds of war, a fear he knew he could master. And so now he restrained himself from doing something foolish. Two of the men arranged themselves alongside him and gripped his arms. They propelled him gently across the square. The bicycle rolled free, then toppled over on its side.

Ferra saw the people of the village sitting outside their homes become aware of what was happening. Surely they would come to his aid. But the massacre at the Portella della Ginestra, the general reign of terror, had broken their spirits. Not one of them raised an outcry. Silvio Ferra dug his heels into the ground and tried to turn back to the community house. Even this far away he could see some of his fellow party workers framed in the doorway. Couldn't they see he was in trouble? But nobody left the frame of light. He called out, "Help me." There was no movement in the village and Silvio Ferra felt a deep sense of shame for them.

Quintana pushed him forward roughly. "Don't be a fool," he said. "We only want to talk. Now come with us without making an uproar. Don't get your friends hurt."

It was almost dark, the moon was already up. He felt a gun being jabbed into his back and he knew they would kill him in the square if they really meant to kill him. And then they would kill any friends who decided to help. He started walking with Quintana to the end of the village. There was a chance they did not mean to kill him; there were too many witnesses and some had surely recognized Quintana. If he struggled now they might panic and fire their guns. Better to wait and listen.

Quintana was speaking to him in a reasonable voice. "We want to persuade you to stop all your Communist foolishness. We have forgiven your attack on the Friends of the Friends when you accused them of the Ginestra affair. But our patience was not rewarded and it grows short. Do you think it's wise? If you continue you will force us to leave your children without a father."

By this time they were out of the village and starting up a rocky path that would lead finally to Monte Cumeta. Silvio Ferra looked back despairingly but saw no one following. He said to Quintana, "Would you kill the father of a family over a small thing like politics?"

Quintana laughed harshly, "I've killed men for spitting on my shoe," he said. The men holding his arms disengaged themselves and at that moment Silvio Ferra knew his fate. He whirled and started to run down the rocky moonlit path.

■ ■ ■

THE VILLAGERS heard the gunfire and one of the Socialist party leaders went to the *carabinieri*. The next morning Silvio Ferra's body was found thrown into a mountain crevice. When the police questioned villagers, nobody admitted to seeing what had happened. Nobody mentioned the four men, nobody admitted to having recognized Guido Quintana. Rebellious as they might be, they were Sicilians and would not break the law of *omerta*. But some told what they had seen to one of Guiliano's band.

■ ■ ■

MANY THINGS combined to win the elections for the Christian Democrats. Don Croce and the Friends of the Friends had done their work well. The massacre at the Portella della Ginestra had shocked all Italy, but it had done more than that to Sicilians—it had traumatized them. The Catholic Church, electioneering under the banner of Christ, had been more careful with its charity. The murder of Silvio Ferra was the finishing blow. The Christian Democratic party won an overwhelming victory in Sicily in 1948, and that helped carry all of Italy. It was clear that they were to rule long into the foreseeable future. Don Croce was the master of Sicily, the Catholic Church would be the national religion and the odds were good that Minister Trezza, not for some years but also not too late, would someday be the Premier of Italy.

■ ■ ■

IN THE end Pisciotta was proved right. Don Croce sent word through Hector Adonis that the Christian Democratic party could not get the amnesty for Guiliano and his men because of the massacre at the Portella della Ginestra. It would be too much of a scandal; the charges that it had been politically inspired would flare up again. The newspapers would go berserk and there would be violent strikes all over Italy. Don Croce said that naturally Minister Trezza's hands were tied, that the Cardinal of Palermo could no longer help a man who was thought to have massacred innocent women and children; but that he, Don Croce, would continue to work for amnesty. However, he advised Guiliano that it would be better to emigrate to Brazil or the United States, and in that endeavor, he, Don Croce, would help in any way.

Guiliano's men were astonished that he showed no emotion at this betrayal, that he seemed to accept it as a matter of course. He took his men further into the mountains and told his chiefs to make their camps near his own so he could assemble them all at a moment's notice. As the days passed, he seemed to retire more and more deeply into his own private world. Weeks went by as his chiefs waited impatiently for his orders.

One morning he wandered deep into the mountains by himself without bodyguards. He returned in darkness and stood in the light of the campfires.

"Aspanu," he said, "summon all the chiefs."

■ ■ ■

PRINCE OLLORTO had an estate of hundreds of thousands of acres on which he grew everything that had made Sicily the breadbasket of Italy for a thousand years—lemons and oranges, grains, bamboo, olive trees which provided wells of oil, grapes for wine, oceans of tomatoes, green peppers, eggplants of the most royal purple as big as a carter's head. Part of this land was leased to the peasants on a fifty-fifty basis, but Prince Ollorto like most landowners would first skim off the top—fees for machinery used, seed supplied and transportation provided, all with interest. The peasant was fortunate to keep twenty-five percent of the treasures he had grown with the sweat of his brow. And yet he was well off compared with those who had to hire themselves out on a daily basis and accept starvation wages.

The land was rich, but unfortunately the nobles kept a good portion of their estates uncultivated and going to waste. As long ago as 1860 the great Garibaldi had promised the peasants they would own their own land. Yet even now Prince Ollorto had a hundred thousand acres that lay fallow. So did the other nobles who used their land as a cash reserve, selling off pieces to indulge their follies.

In the last election all the parties, including the Christian Democratic party, had promised to strengthen and enforce the sharing-of-land laws. These laws stated that the uncultivated lands of large estates could be claimed by peasant farmers on payment of a nominal sum.

But these laws had always been thwarted by the nobility's

practice of hiring Mafia chiefs to intimidate would-be claimers of land. On the day for the claiming of the lands a Mafia chief had only to ride his horse up and down the borders of the estate and no peasant would dare to make a claim. The few who chose to do so would invariably be marked down for assassination and the male members of his family with him. This had gone on for a century, and every Sicilian knew the rule. If an estate had a Mafia chief as its protector, no lands would be claimed from it. Rome could pass a hundred laws, those laws had no significance. As Don Croce once put it to Minister Trezza in an unguarded moment, "What do your laws have to do with us?"

Shortly after the election, the day came when Prince Ollorto's lands could be claimed from those parts of his estate that had not been cultivated. All one hundred thousand acres had been designated by the government, tongue in cheek. Left-wing party leaders urged the people on to make their claims. When the day arrived almost five thousand peasants congregated outside the gate of Prince Ollorto's palace. Government officials waited in a huge tent on the property furnished with tables and chairs and other official apparatus to formally register their claims. Some of the peasants were from the town of Montelepre.

Prince Ollorto, following the advice of Don Croce, had hired six Mafia chiefs as his *gabelloti*. And so on that bright morning, the smoky Sicilian sun making them sweat, the six Mafia chiefs rode their horses up and down along the wall surrounding Prince Ollorto's estate. The assembled peasants, under olive trees older than Christ, watched these six men, famous all over Sicily for their ferocity. They waited as if hoping for some miracle, too fearful to move forward.

But that miracle would not be the forces of law. Minister Trezza had sent direct orders to the Maresciallo commanding them that *carabinieri* were to be confined to their barracks. On that day, there was not a uniformed member of the National Police to be seen in the whole province of Palermo.

■ ■ ■

THE MULTITUDE outside the wall of Prince Ollorto's estate
waited. The six Mafia chiefs rode their horses up and down as
consistent as metronomes, their faces impassive, their guns
sheathed in rifle holsters, *lupare* on shoulder straps, pistols
tucked in their belts hidden by jackets. They made no menacing
signs toward the crowd—indeed they ignored them; they simply
rode in silence back and forth. The peasants, as if hoping the
horses would tire or carry these guardian dragons away, opened
their food sacks and uncorked their wine bottles. They were
mostly men, only a few women, and among these was the girl
Justina with her mother and father. They had come to show their
defiance for the murderers of Silvio Ferra. And yet none of them
dared pass the line of slowly moving horses, dared to claim the
land that was theirs by right of law.

It was not only fear that restrained them; these riders were
"men of respect" who were in fact the lawgivers of the towns
they lived in. The Friends of the Friends had established their
own shadowy government that functioned more effectively than
the government in Rome. Was there a thief or cattle rustler
stealing a peasant's cattle and sheep? If the victim reported the
crime to the *carabinieri*, he would never recover his goods. But
if he went to see these Mafia chiefs and paid a twenty percent
fee, the lost stock would be found and he would receive a guarantee that it would not happen again. If a hot-tempered bully
murdered some innocent workman over a glass of wine, the
government could rarely convict because of perjured testimony
and the law of *omerta*. But if the victim's family went to one of
these six men of respect, then vengeance and justice could be
had.

Chronic petty thieves in poor neighborhoods would be executed, feuds settled with honor, a quarrel over land boundaries
resolved without the expense of lawyers. These six men were
judges whose opinions could not be appealed or ignored, whose

punishments were severe and could not be evaded except by emigration. These six men had power in Sicily that not even the Premier of Italy could exercise. And so the crowd remained outside Prince Ollorto's walls.

The six Mafia chiefs did not ride close together; that would have been a sign of weakness. They rode separately, like independent kings, each carrying his own particular brand of terror. The most feared, riding a mottled gray horse, was Don Siano from the town of Bisacquino. He was now over sixty years of age and his face was as gray and as mottled as the hide of his horse. He had become a legend at the age of twenty-six when he had assassinated the Mafia chief preceding him. The man had murdered Don Siano's father when the Don himself had been a child of twelve and Siano had waited fourteen years for his revenge. Then one day he had dropped from a tree onto the victim and his horse and, clasping the man from behind, had forced him to ride through the main street of the town. As they rode in front of the people, Siano had slashed his victim to pieces, cutting off his nose, his lips, his ears and his genitals, and then holding the bloody corpse in his arms had paraded the horse in front of the victim's house. Afterward he had ruled his province with a bloody and iron hand.

The second Mafia chief, riding a black horse with scarlet plumes above its ears, was Don Arzana of the town of Piani dei Greci. He was a calm, deliberate man who believed that there were always two sides in a quarrel and had refused to kill Silvio Ferra for political purposes, had indeed forestalled that man's fate for years. He was distressed by Ferra's murder but had been powerless to intervene, since Don Croce and the other Mafia chiefs insisted that the time had come to make an example in his area. His rule had been tempered with mercy and kindness, and he was the most loved of the six tyrants. But now as he rode his horse in front of the assembled multitude his face was stern, all his inner doubts erased.

The third man on horseback was Don Piddu of Caltanissetta

and his steed's bridle was garlanded with flowers. He was known to be susceptible to flattery and vain of his appearance, jealous of power and murderous to the aspirations of young men. At a village festival, a young peasant gallant had stricken the local women dumb with admiration because he wore bells on his ankles when he danced, wore a shirt and trousers made of green silk, tailored in Palermo, and sang as he played a guitar manufactured in Madrid. Don Piddu had been incensed with the adulation shown this rural Valentino, furious that the women did not admire a real man like himself rather than this simpering, effeminate youth. Who danced no more after that fateful day but was found on the road to his farm, his body riddled with bullets.

The fourth Mafia chief was Don Marcuzzi of the town of Villamura, who was known to be an ascetic and had his own chapel in his home like the old nobility. Don Marcuzzi, despite this one affectation, lived very simply, and was personally a poor man since he refused to profit by his power. But he enjoyed that power enormously; he was tireless in his endeavors to help his fellow Sicilians but he was also a true believer in the old ways of the Friends of the Friends. He had become a legend when he executed his favorite nephew for committing an *infamita*, the breaking of the law of *omerta*, giving information to the police against a rival Mafia faction.

The fifth man on horseback was Don Buccilla of Partinico, who had come to see Hector Adonis in behalf of his nephew on the long-ago, fateful day when Turi Guiliano became an outlaw. Now, five years later, he was heavier by forty pounds. He still wore his opera peasant clothes despite the fact that he had become enormously wealthy in those five years. His ferocity was benign, but he could not abide dishonesty and executed thieves with the same righteousness as those eighteenth-century English High Justices proclaiming the death penalty on child pickpockets.

The sixth man was Guido Quintana, who, though nominally of Montelepre, had made his reputation by taking over the bloody battleground of the town of Corleone. He had been forced to do this because Montelepre was directly under the protection of Guiliano. But in Corleone, Guido Quintana had found what his murderous heart yearned for. He had settled four family feuds by the simple expedient of wiping out opponents to his decisions. He had murdered Silvio Ferra and other union organizers. He was perhaps the only Mafia chief who was hated more than he was respected.

These were the six men who, by their reputations and the respect and enormous amount of fear they could generate, barred the lands of Prince Ollorto to the poor peasants of Sicily.

■ ■ ■

TWO JEEPS full of armed men sped down the Montelepre-Palermo road and turned off on the path that led to the estate wall. All but two of the men were masked with wool coverings that had slits cut open over the eyes. The two unmasked men were Turi Guiliano and Aspanu Pisciotta. The masked men included Corporal Canio Silvestro, Passatempo and Terranova. Andolini, also masked, covered the road from Palermo. As the jeeps pulled up about fifty feet from the Mafia horsemen, additional men pushed through the crowd of peasants. They too were masked. They had been picnicking in the grove of olive trees. When the two jeeps appeared they had opened food baskets and taken out their weapons and their masks. They spread out into a long half circle and covered the horsemen with their rifles. All told, there were about fifty of them. Turi Guiliano jumped out of his jeep and checked to see that everyone was in place. He watched the six riders going back and forth. He knew they had seen him, and he knew the crowd too had recognized him. The smoky Sicilian afternoon sun tinged the green landscape with red. Guiliano wondered how these thousands of tough peasants could be so intimidated that they let six men keep the bread out of the mouths of their children.

Aspanu Pisciotta was waiting like an impatient viper beside

him. Only Aspanu had refused to wear a mask; all the others
had feared a vendetta from the families of the six Mafia chiefs
and from the Friends of the Friends. Now Guiliano and Pisciotta
would bear the brunt of the vendetta.

They both wore the gold buckles engraved with the lion and
the eagle. Guiliano had only a heavy pistol in a holster hanging
from his belt. He also wore the emerald ring he had taken from
the Duchess years ago. Pisciotta carried a machine pistol cradled
in his arms. His face was pale from his lung disease and excitement; he was impatient with Guiliano for taking so long. But
Guiliano was carefully watching the scene to make sure his orders had been carried out. His men had formed the half circle to
leave an escape route for the Mafia chiefs should they decide
to ride away. If they ran they would lose "respect" and a
great deal of their influence; the peasants would no longer fear
them. But he saw Don Siano turn his mottled gray horse and the
others follow him to parade again before the wall. They would not
run.

■ ■ ■

FROM ONE of the towers of his ancient palace, Prince Ollorto
watched the scene through the telescope he used to chart the
stars. He could see Turi Guiliano's face clearly and in detail—
the oval eyes, the clean planes of his face, the generous mouth
now pressed tight; and he knew that the strength in his face was
the strength of virtue, and thought it was a pity that virtue
was not a more merciful asset. For it was terrible indeed when
it was pure, as the Prince knew this to be pure. He was ashamed
of his own role. He knew his fellow Sicilians so well, and now
he would be responsible for what was about to happen. The six
great men he had bound with money would fight for him, they
would not run. They had intimidated the great multitude who
were before his wall. But now Guiliano was standing before
them like an avenging angel. Already it seemed to the Prince
that the sun was darkening.

■ ■ ■

GUILIANO STRODE to the path the six men rode. They were squat heavy men on horseback and they kept their mounts to a slow steady walk. From time to time they would feed their horses off a huge pile of oats heaped against the jagged white stone wall. This was so the horses would defecate continuously and leave a constant insulting trail of manure; then they would continue their slow ride.

Turi Guiliano placed himself very close to their path, Pisciotta a step behind. The six men on horseback did not look his way or stop. Their faces were inscrutable. Though they all wore *lupare* over their shoulders, they did not attempt to unsling them. Guiliano waited. The men rode past him three more times. Guiliano stepped back. He said quietly to Pisciotta, "Bring them down from their horses and present them to me." Then he crossed the path and leaned against the white stone wall of the estate.

Leaning against the wall he knew that he had crossed a fatal line, that what he was doing this day would decide his fate. But he felt no hesitation, no uneasiness, only a cold rage against the world. He knew that behind these six men loomed the enormous figure of Don Croce, and that it was the Don who was his final enemy. And he felt anger against this very multitude of people he was helping. Why were they so docile, so fearful? If only he could arm and lead them he could forge a new Sicily. But then he felt a wave of pity for these poorly clad, nearly starved peasants, and he raised his arm in a salute to encourage them. The crowd remained silent. For a moment he thought of Silvio Ferra, who might have roused them.

Now Pisciotta took command of the stage. He was wearing his cream-colored sweater with the dragons rampant woven darkly in the woolen material. His sleek dark head, narrow as a knife edge, was etched in the blood-red Sicilian sunlight. He turned that head like a blade toward the six obelisks riding their horses and watched them for a long moment with his deadly viper's gaze. Don Siano's mount defecated at his feet as the six men rode past.

Pisciotta stepped back one pace. He nodded toward Terranova, Passatempo and Silvestro, who ran to the fifty armed masked men forming the covering arc. The men spread out further to close off the escape route that had been left open. The Mafia chiefs continued riding proudly as if they noticed nothing, though they had of course observed and understood everything. But they had won the first round of their battle. Now it was for Guiliano to decide whether to take the last and most dangerous step.

Pisciotta moved into the path of Don Siano's horse and raised his hand imperiously to that gray fearful face. But Don Siano did not stop. When the horse tried to shy away the rider pulled his head tight, and they would have ridden over Pisciotta had he not stepped aside and, with a savage grin, bowed low to the Don as he passed by. Then Pisciotta stepped directly behind the horse and rider, sighted his machine pistol on the gray hindquarters of the horse and pulled the trigger.

The fragrant, flowered air was filled with ropy entrails, a vast shower of blood and a thousand golden flecks of manure. The hail of bullets swept the horse's legs beneath him and he fell straight down. Don Siano's body was trapped by the fallen body until four of Guiliano's men pulled him out and bound his arms behind his back. The horse was still alive and Pisciotta stepped forward and mercifully fired a spray of bullets into the animal's head.

A low moan of terror and exultation rose from the crowd. Guiliano remained leaning against the wall, his heavy pistol still in its holster. He stood with his arms folded as if he too were wondering what Aspanu Pisciotta would do next.

The remaining five Mafia chiefs continued their parade. Their mounts had reared up at the sound of gunfire, but the riders quickly brought them under control. They rode as slowly as before. Again Pisciotta stepped onto the path. Again he raised his hand. The lead rider, Don Buccilla, stopped. The others behind him reined their horses still.

Pisciotta called to them, "Your families will need your horses in the days to come. I promise to send them. Now dismount and pay your respects to Guiliano." His voice rang loud and clear to the ears of the multitude.

There was a long silence and then the five men dismounted. They stood there proudly gazing at the crowd, their eyes fierce and insolent. The long arc of Guiliano's men broke as twenty of them came close, guns ready. Carefully and gently they bound the arms of the five men behind their backs. Then they led all six chiefs to Guiliano.

Guiliano regarded these six men without expression. Quintana had humiliated him once, had even tried to assassinate him, but now the situation was reversed. Quintana's face had not changed over these five years—it had the same wolfish look—but at this moment the eyes seemed vacant and wandering behind the Mafioso mask of defiance.

Don Siano stared at Guiliano with contempt on his gray face. Buccilla seemed a little astonished, as if he were surprised by so much ill feeling in an affair that did not really concern him. The other Dons looked him coldly in the eye as ultimate men of respect must do. Guiliano knew them all by reputation; as a child he had feared some of these men, especially Don Siano. Now he had humiliated them before all Sicily and they would never forgive him. They would be deadly enemies forever. He knew what he must do, but he knew also that they were beloved husbands and fathers, that their children would weep for them. They gazed past him proudly, giving no signs of fear. Their message was clear. Let Guiliano do what he had to do, if he had the belly for it. Don Siano spat at Guiliano's feet.

Guiliano looked at them in the face, each separately. "Kneel and make your peace with God," he said. None of the men moved.

Guiliano turned and walked away from them. The six Mafia chiefs stood outlined against the white stone wall. Guiliano reached his line of men, then turned. He said in a loud clear voice that could be heard by the crowd, "I execute you in the name of God and Sicily," then touched Pisciotta on the shoulder.

At that moment Don Marcuzzi started to kneel but Pisciotta had already opened fire. Passatempo and Terranova and the Corporal, still masked, also fired. The six bound bodies were flung up against the wall by the storm of machine-gun bullets. The jagged white stones were splattered with red-purple gouts of blood and pellets of flesh torn from the galvanized bodies. They seemed to be dancing from strings as they were flung back again and again by the continuing hail of bullets.

High in the tower of his palace, Prince Ollorto turned away from the telescope. So he did not see what happened next.

Guiliano stepped forward and advanced to the wall. He drew the heavy pistol from his belt and slowly and ceremoniously shot each of the fallen Mafia chiefs through the head.

There was a great hoarse roar from the watching crowd and, in seconds, thousands were streaming through the gates of Prince Ollorto's estate. Guiliano watched them. He noticed that none of the crowd came near him.

CHAPTER

22

THAT EASTER morning of 1949 was glorious. The whole island was carpeted with flowers, and Palermo balconies held huge tubs of wildly rioting colors; the cracks in the sidewalk grew red- and blue- and white-petaled flowers, and so, even, did the sides of old churches. The streets of Palermo were thronged with citizens going to the nine o'clock High Mass at Palermo's great cathedral where the Cardinal himself would serve Communion. Countrymen from the nearby villages had come in to attend, and in their black mourning suits, with their wives and children, they greeted everyone they passed with the traditional Easter morning salute of the peasant, "Christ is risen." Turi Guiliano responded with the equally traditional, "Blessed be His name."

Guiliano and his men had infiltrated Palermo the night before. They were dressed in the sober country black of the peasants, but their suit jackets were loose and bulky, for beneath they wore their machine pistols. Guiliano was familiar with the streets of Palermo; in his six years as a bandit he had often sneaked into the city to direct the kidnapping of a wealthy noble or to dine at a famous restaurant and to leave his challenging note under the plate.

Guiliano was never in danger on these visits. He always walked the streets with Corporal Canio Silvestro by his side.

Another two men would walk twenty paces ahead of him, four more would walk on the other side of the street, another two men would walk twenty paces behind. And another two-man team still further back. If Guiliano were stopped by the *carabinieri* to show his identification papers, they were an easy target for these men who were prepared to shoot without mercy. When he entered a restaurant, the dining rooms would be crowded with his bodyguards at other tables.

This morning, Guiliano had brought fifty men into the city. They included Aspanu Pisciotta, the Corporal, and Terranova; Passatempo and Stefan Andolini had been left behind. When Guiliano and Pisciotta entered the cathedral, forty of his men entered with them; the other ten men with the Corporal and Terranova were with the escape vehicles in the rear of the building.

The Cardinal was conducting the Mass, and in his white and golden vestments, the great crucifix hanging from his neck, and with his melodious voice, he created an awesome aura of inviolable sanctity. The cathedral was filled with great statues of Christ and the Virgin Mary. Guiliano dipped his fingers into the holy water basin decorated with reliefs of the Passion of Christ. When he knelt he saw the vast domed ceiling and along the walls the banks of rose-colored candles that served as votive lights to the statues of saints.

Guiliano's men dispersed themselves along the walls close to the altar. The seats were filled by the vast multitude of worshippers, the countrymen in black, the townspeople in vivid Easter finery. Guiliano found himself standing by the famous statue of the Virgin and the Apostles, and he was caught by its beauty for one brief moment.

The chanting of the priests and altar boys, the murmured responses to the multitude of worshippers, the perfume of exotic subtropical flowers on the altar, the devoutness of these supplicants had their effect on Guiliano. The last time he had attended Mass was the Easter morning five years before when Frisella, the barber, had betrayed him. On this Easter morning he felt a sense of loss and of dread. How many times had he said to doomed enemies, ''I execute you in the name of God and Sicily,'' and waited for them to murmur the prayers he heard now. For a moment he wished he could make them all rise, as Christ had risen, to lift them out of the eternal darkness he had hurled them into. And now on this Easter morning he might have to send a Cardinal of the Church to join them. This Cardinal had broken his promise, had lied to and betrayed him, and become his enemy. It did not matter how beautifully he chanted in this vast cathedral. Would it be impertinent to tell the Cardinal to make his peace with God? Would not a Cardinal always be in a state of grace? Would he be humble enough to confess his betrayal of Guiliano?

The Mass was coming to its conclusion; the worshippers were going to the altar rail to receive Holy Communion. Some of Guiliano's men along the walls were kneeling to receive. They had confessed to Abbot Manfredi at his monastery the day before and were pure, since they would not have to commit their crime until after this ceremony.

The multitude of worshippers, happy with the Easter rising of Christ, cheerful for the washing out of their sins, exited the cathedral and filled the piazza going on to the avenue. The Cardinal went behind the altar and his acolyte pressed upon his brow the conical mitre of an Archbishop. With this headdress the Cardinal seemed a foot taller, the elaborate gold scrolls on the front of the miter gleamed over his rugged Sicilian face; the impression was one of power rather than holiness. Accompanied by a flock of priests, he started on his traditional steps of prayer at each of the four chapels of the cathedral.

The first chapel held the tomb of King Roger I, the second chapel that of the Emperor Frederick II; the third held the tomb of Henry IV, the last chapel held the ashes of Constanzia, the wife of Frederick II. These tombs were of white marble inlaid with beautiful mosaics. There was another separate chapel, the silver shrine, holding a thousand-pound statue of Saint Rosalie, the patron saint of Palermo, which the citizens of the city carried through the streets on her holy day. In this shrine were the remains of all the archbishops of Palermo, and it would be here that the Cardinal himself would be buried when he died. It was his first stop, and when he knelt to pray, it was here that Guiliano and his men surrounded him and his retinue. Other of Guiliano's men sealed off all the exits to the shrine so no alarm could be given.

The Cardinal rose to his feet to confront them. But then he saw Pisciotta. He remembered that face. But not as it was now. Now it was the face of the devil come for his soul, to roast his flesh in hell. Guiliano said, "Your Eminence, you are my prisoner. If you do what I say you will not be harmed. You will spend Easter in the mountains as my guest and I promise that you will dine as well there as in your palace."

The Cardinal said angrily, "You dare to bring armed men into this house of God?"

Guiliano laughed; all his feeling of awe had vanished in the delight of what he was about to do. "I dare more," he said. "I dare to reproach you for breaking your holy word. You promised a pardon for me and my men and you did not keep that promise. Now you and the Church will pay."

The Cardinal shook his head. "I will not move from this holy place," he said. "Kill me if you dare and you will be infamous all over the world."

"I have that honor already," Guiliano said. "Now if you do not do what I command, I will have to be more forceful. I will slaughter all your priests here, then bind and gag you. If you come with me quietly, no harm will be done to anyone and you will be back in your cathedral within the week."

The Cardinal crossed himself and walked toward the door of the shrine indicated by Guiliano. This door led to the back of the cathedral where other members of Guiliano's band had already commandeered the Cardinal's official limousine and chauffeur. The huge black car was decorated with bouquets of Easter flowers and flew the pennants of the church at each side of the radiator grille. Guiliano's men had also commandeered the cars of other dignitaries. Guiliano guided the Cardinal into his limousine and sat beside him. Two of his men also seated themselves in the rear of the car, and Aspanu Pisciotta got into the front seat beside the chauffeur. Then the procession of cars wound its way through the city, through the patrols of *carabinieri* who saluted them. At Guiliano's orders, the Cardinal waved back in benediction. On a deserted stretch of road the Cardinal was made to leave the car. Another band of Guiliano's men were waiting for them with a litter to carry the Cardinal. Leaving the vehicles and chauffeurs behind them, they all disappeared into a sea of flowers and the mountains.

Guiliano was as good as his word; deep in the caves of the Cammarata Mountains the Cardinal ate as good a meal as could be had in the palace. The awed bandits, respectful of his spiritual authority, asked for his blessing as they served each dish.

■ ■ ■

THE NEWSPAPERS of Italy went wild with indignation, while the people of Sicily were filled with two emotions: horror at the sacrilege committed and unholy glee at the shaming of the *carabinieri*. Riding over this was their enormous pride in Guiliano, that a Sicilian had defeated Rome; Guiliano was now the ultimate "man of respect."

What, everyone wondered, did Guiliano want in return for the Cardinal? The answer was simple: an enormous ransom.

The Holy Church, which after all was charged with the safekeeping of souls, did not stoop to the niggardly bargaining of nobles and rich merchants. It paid the ransom of one hundred million lire immediately. But Guiliano had one more motive.

He said to the Cardinal, "I'm a peasant, not instructed in the ways of heaven. But I have never broken my word. And you, a Cardinal of the Catholic Church, with all your holy garments and crosses of Jesus, lied to me like a heathen Moor. Your sacred office alone will not save your life."

The Cardinal felt his knees weaken.

Guiiiano continued. "But you are fortunate. I have another purpose for you." He then made the Cardinal read his Testament.

Now that he knew his life was to be spared, the Cardinal, trained to expect the chastisement of God himself, was more interested in the documents of the Testament than in the reproaches of Guiliano. When he saw the letter he had written to Pisciotta, the Cardinal crossed himself with a holy fury.

Guiliano said, "My dear Cardinal. Take the knowledge of this document back to the Church and Minister Trezza. You have seen the proof of my ability to destroy the Christian Democratic government. My death will be your great misfortune. The Testament will be in a safe place that you cannot reach. If any of them doubts me, tell them to ask Don Croce how I deal with my enemies."

■ ■ ■

IT WAS a week after the Cardinal's kidnapping that La Venera left Guiliano.

For three years he had crept through the tunnel into her house. In her bed, he reveled in the comforts of her solid body, the warmth and shelter. She had never complained, never asked for more than his pleasure.

But tonight was different. After they made love, she told him she was moving away to relatives who lived in Florence. "My heart is too weak," she told him. "I can't bear the danger that is your life. I dream of you being shot down before my eyes. The *carabinieri* killed my husband as if he were some animal, in front of his house. They kept firing until his body was a bundle of bloody rags. I dream of it happening to you." She pulled his head down to her breast. "Listen," she said, "listen to my heart."

And he listened. And was moved to pity and love by the pounding erratic beat. The bare skin beneath her heavy breast was salty with the sweat of her inner terror. She was weeping, and he stroked her thick black hair.

"You've never been afraid before," Guiliano said. "Nothing is changed."

La Venera shook her head violently. "Turi, you've become too reckless. You have made enemies, powerful enemies. Your friends fear for you. Your mother goes pale with every knock on the door. You can't escape forever."

Guiliano said, "But I haven't changed."

La Venera began to weep again. "Ah, Turi, yes you have changed. You are so quick to kill now. I don't say you're cruel; you are careless with death."

Guiliano sighed. He saw how frightened she was and it filled him with a sorrow he could not quite understand. "Then you must go," he said. "I'll give you enough money so that you can live in Florence. Someday this all will be over. There will be no more killing. I have my plans. I will not be a bandit forever. My mother will sleep at night and we will all be together again."

He could see that she did not believe him.

In the morning before he left, they made love again, all hot passion, their bodies plunging against each other wildly for the last time.

CHAPTER

23

TURI GUILIANO had finally succeeded in doing what no other statesman or national politician had succeeded in doing. He had united all the political parties in Italy to pursue one course of action: the destruction of Guiliano and his band.

In July of 1949 Minister Trezza announced to the press the formation of a special *carabinieri* army of five thousand men to be called the Special Force to Repress Banditry, without any reference to Guiliano himself. The newspapers soon rectified this sly coyness on the part of the government, which did not wish to make Guiliano seem the main target. They gleefully approved and congratulated the ruling Christian Democratic party for taking such a vigorous step.

The national press was also struck with wonder at Minister Trezza's genius on the organization of the special five thousand–man army. The army would be made up of bachelors so there would be no widows, and so their families could not be subjected to threats. There would be commandos, paratroopers, armored cars, heavy weapons and even aircraft. How could any two-penny bandit withstand such a force? And it would be commanded by Colonel Ugo Luca, one of the great Italian war heroes of World War II, who had fought with the legendary German general Rommel. The "Italian Desert Fox" the newspapers called him, skilled in guerrilla warfare, whose tactics and strategies would bewilder the unsophisticated Sicilian country boy, Turi Guiliano.

The press perfunctorily noted in small paragraphs the appointment of Frederico Velardi as the head of all Sicilian Security Police. Hardly anything was known of Inspector Velardi except that he had been handpicked by Minister Trezza to assist Colonel Luca.

■ ■ ■

JUST A month before there had been a fateful meeting between Don Croce, Minister Trezza and the Cardinal of Palermo. The Cardinal told them of Guiliano's Testament with its damning documentation.

Minister Trezza was frightened. The Testament must be destroyed before the army accomplished its mission. He wished he could rescind the orders for the Special Force that was now being assembled, but his government was under too much pressure from left-wing parties who were clamoring that Guiliano was being protected by the government.

For Don Croce the Testament only added a complication but did not change his resolve. He had already decided to kill Guiliano: the murder of his six chiefs gave him no alternative. But Guiliano could not die at the hand of the Friends of the Friends or himself. He was too great a hero; his murder would be too great a crime for even the Friends to live down. It would focus the hatred of Sicily upon them.

In any case, Don Croce realized he had to accommodate himself to Trezza's needs. After all, this was the man he wanted to make the Premier of Italy. He said to the Minister, "Our course must be this. Certainly you have no choice, you must pursue Guiliano. But try to keep him alive until I can nullify the Testament, which I guarantee I can do."

The Minister nodded grimly. He clicked on the intercom and said commandingly, "Send in the Inspector." A few seconds later a tall man with frigid blue eyes entered the room. He was thin, beautifully dressed and had an aristocratic face.

"This is Inspector Frederico Velardi," the Minister said. "I am about to announce his appointment as the head of all Security Police in Sicily. He will be coordinating with the head of the army I am sending to Sicily." He introduced the men to each other and explained to Velardi their problem about the Testament and its threat to the Christian Democratic regime.

"My dear Inspector," the Minister said. "I ask you to consider Don Croce as my personal representative in Sicily. You will give him any information he requires as you would to me. Do you understand?"

The Inspector took a long time to digest this particular request. Then he understood. His task would be to advise Don Croce as to all the plans the invasion army made in their war against Guiliano. Don Croce, in turn, would pass on that information to Guiliano so that he could escape capture until the Don thought it safe to end his career.

Inspector Velardi said, "Am I to give all information to Don Croce? Colonel Luca is no fool—he will soon suspect there is a leak and perhaps cut me out of his planning sessions."

"If you have any trouble," the Minister said, "refer him to me. Your real mission is to secure the Testament, and to keep Guiliano alive and free until that is done."

The Inspector turned his cold blue eyes on Don Croce. "I will be happy to serve you," he said. "But I must understand one thing. If Guiliano is captured alive before the Testament is destroyed, what do I do then?"

The Don did not mince words; he was not a government official and could speak frankly. "That would be an unbearable misfortune."

■ ■ ■

COLONEL UGO LUCA, the designated Commander of the Special Force to Repress Banditry, was hailed by the newspapers as an inspired choice. They hashed over his military record, his medals for bravery, his tactical genius, his quiet and retiring nature, and his abhorrence of any kind of failure. He was a small bulldog, the newspapers said, and would be a match for the ferocity of Sicily.

Before doing anything else, Colonel Luca studied all the intelligence documents on Turi Guiliano. Minister Trezza found him tucked in his office surrounded by folders full of reports and old newspapers. When the Minister asked him when he was taking his army to Sicily, the Colonel said mildly that he was assembling a staff, and that certainly Guiliano would still be there no matter how long he took.

Colonel Luca studied the reports for a week and came to certain conclusions. That Guiliano was a genius in guerrilla warfare and had a unique method of operation. He kept only a cadre of twenty men about his person, and these included his chiefs: Aspanu Pisciotta as his second in command, Canio Silvestro as his personal bodyguard and Stefan Andolini as chief of intelligence and his contact messenger to Don Croce and Mafia networks. Terranova and Passatempo had their own bands and were allowed to operate independently of Guiliano's direct command unless there was a concerted action. Terranova carried out Guiliano's kidnappings and Passatempo the train and bank holdups that Guiliano planned.

It became clear to the Colonel that there were no more than three hundred men in the whole Guiliano band. Then how, the Colonel wondered, had he existed for six years, how had he outfought the *carabinieri* of an entire province and almost absolutely controlled the entire northwest of Sicily? How had he and his men escaped searches of the mountains by large government forces? It could only be that Guiliano summoned up extra men from among the peasants of Sicily whenever he needed them. And then when the government searched the mountains, these part-time bandits would escape into the towns and farms to live like ordinary peasants. It also followed that many of the citizens of the town of Montelepre had to be secret members of the band. But most important was Guiliano's popularity; there was little chance that he would ever be betrayed, and there was no doubt that if he made an open call to revolution, thousands would flock beneath his banner.

Finally, there was another puzzling thing: Guiliano's cloak of invisibility. He appeared at one place and then seemed to vanish into thin air. The more Colonel Luca read, the more he was impressed. Then he came to something he knew he could take immediate action against. It might look like nothing much, but it would be important in the long run.

Guiliano had often written letters to the press that always began, "If, as I have been led to believe, we are not enemies, you will publish this letter," and then went on to present his point of view on his latest acts of banditry. To Colonel Luca's mind that opening phrase was a threat, a coercion. And the body of the letter was enemy propaganda. There were explanations of kidnappings, of robberies and how the money went to the poor of Sicily. When Guiliano had a pitched battle with the *carabinieri* and killed some of them, a letter was always sent to explain that in war soldiers had to die. There was a direct plea to the *carabinieri* not to fight. And another letter came after the execution of the six Mafia chiefs, explaining that only by that deed could the peasants claim the land due to them by law and human morality.

Colonel Luca was astounded that the government had allowed these letters to be published. He made a note to ask Minister Trezza for the power of martial law in Sicily so that Guiliano could be cut off from his public.

Another thing he searched for was any information that Guiliano had a woman, but he could find nothing. Though there were reports that the bandits used the brothels in Palermo and that Pisciotta was a womanizer, Guiliano seemed to have lived a sexless life for the last six years. Colonel Luca, being an Italian, could not believe this possible. There must be a woman in Montelepre, and when they found her half the job would be done.

What he also found interesting was the record of Guiliano's

attachment to his mother and hers to him. Guiliano was a devoted son to both parents, but he treated his mother with a special veneration. Colonel Luca made a particular note of this too. If Guiliano really had no woman, the mother could be used to bait a trap.

When all this preparation was over, Colonel Luca organized his staff. The most important appointment was Captain Antonio Perenze as his aide-de-camp and personal bodyguard. Captain Perenze was a heavy, almost fat, man with genial features and an easy disposition, but Colonel Luca knew him to be extraordinarily brave. There might come a time when that bravery could save the Colonel's life.

It was September 1949 before Colonel Luca arrived in Sicily with the first increment of two thousand men. He hoped this would be enough; he did not wish to glorify Guiliano by bringing a five thousand–man army against him. This was, after all, only a bandit who should easily have been dealt with sooner.

His first move was to order the Sicilian newspapers to discontinue the publication of Guiliano's letters. His second move was to arrest Guiliano's mother and father on the charge of conspiracy with their son. The next was to arrest and detain for questioning over two hundred men in Montelepre on charges that they were secret members of Guiliano's band. All those arrested were transported to jails in Palermo that were heavily guarded by Colonel Luca's men. All these actions were taken under laws from the Fascist regime of Mussolini still on the books.

The Guiliano house was searched and the secret tunnels found. La Venera was arrested in Florence. But she was released almost immediately when she claimed she never knew that the tunnels existed. Not that she was believed, but Inspector Velardi wanted her free in the hope that Guiliano would visit her.

The press of Italy lauded Colonel Luca to the skies; here finally was a man who was "serious." Minister Trezza was delighted with his choice, especially when he received a warm

letter of congratulation from the Premier. Only Don Croce was
not impressed.

■ ■ ■

THE FIRST month, Turi Guiliano had studied Luca's actions, the
deployment of the *carabinieri* army. He admired the Colonel's
astuteness in forbidding the newspapers to print his letters, cutting off his vital communication to the people of Sicily. But
when Colonel Luca indiscriminately arrested the citizens of
Montelepre—guilty and innocent alike—the admiration turned
into hatred. And with the arrest of his parents, Guiliano went
into a cold murderous rage.

For two days Guiliano sat in his cave deep in the Cammarata
Mountains. He made his plans and reviewed what he knew
about Colonel Luca's army of two thousand *carabinieri*. At least
a thousand of them were stationed in and around Palermo, waiting for him to try to rescue his parents. The other thousand were
concentrated in the area around the towns of Montelepre, Piani
dei Greci, San Giuseppe Jato, Partinico and Corleone, many of
its citizens secret members of the band who could be recruited
for a battle.

Colonel Luca himself made his headquarters in Palermo and
was invulnerable there. He would have to be lured out.

Turi Guiliano channeled his rage into the making of tactical
plans. They had a clear arithmetical pattern to him, simple as
the game of a child. They nearly always worked, and if they did
not he could always disappear back into his mountains. But he
knew that everything depended upon faultless execution, every
little detail perfected.

He summoned Aspanu Pisciotta to the cave and told him the
plans. Later, the other chiefs—Passatempo, Terranova, Corporal Silvestro and Stefan Andolini—were told only what each had
to know for his particular job.

■ ■ ■

CARABINIERI HEADQUARTERS in Palermo was paymaster for all forces in Western Sicily. Once a month a heavily guarded money wagon was sent out to pay the garrisons in all the towns and province headquarters. The pay was in cash, and an envelope for each individual soldier was made up, lire notes and coins to the exact pay, stuffed inside. These envelopes were put into slotted wooden boxes which were locked onto a truck that had formerly been an American Army weapons carrier.

The driver was armed with a pistol, the soldier paymaster beside him with a rifle. When this truck stuffed with millions of lire left Palermo, it was preceded by three scout jeeps, each with mounted machine guns and four men, and a troop carrier holding twenty men heavily armed with machine pistols and rifles. Behind the money truck came two command cars, each with six men. All these vehicles had radio communication to call Palermo or the nearest *carabinieri* barracks for reinforcements. There was never any fear that bandits would make an attack on such a force. It would be suicidal.

The payroll caravan left Palermo early in the morning and made its first stop at the small town of Tommaso Natale. From there it swung onto the mountainous road to Montelepre. The paymaster and his guards knew it would be a long day and they drove quickly. They ate pieces of salami and chunks of bread and drank wine from bottles as they rode. They joked and laughed and the drivers of the lead jeeps put their weapons down on the floors of their vehicles. But when the caravan rode over the top of the last hill that led down into Montelepre, they were amazed to see the road ahead filled with a vast flock of sheep. The jeeps leading the column made their way into the flock, and the guards shouted at the roughly clothed shepherds. The soldiers were anxious to get inside the cool barracks and eat a hot meal, to strip to their underwear and loll in the beds or play cards for their noon hour break. There could be no danger; Montelepre, only a few miles away, had a garrison of five hundred men of Colonel Luca's army. Behind them, they could see the truck carrying the payroll enter the vast sea of sheep but did not see that it had become becalmed there, that no path opened up for it.

The shepherds were trying to clear the way for the vehicle. They were so busy they did not seem to notice that the troop carriers blasted their horns, the guards shouted and laughed and cursed. There was still no alarm.

But suddenly there were six shepherds pressed close to the paymaster truck. Two of them produced guns from beneath their jackets and kicked the driver and paymaster out of the truck. They disarmed the two *carabinieri*. The other four men threw out the boxes full of pay envelopes. Passatempo was the leader of this band, and his brutish face, the violence of his body, cowed the guards as much as the guns.

At the same moment the slopes around the road came alive with bandits holding rifles and machine pistols. The two command cars at the rear had their tires blown out by gunfire and then Pisciotta stood in front of the first car. He called out, "Descend slowly, without your weapons, and you'll eat your spaghetti tonight in Palermo. Don't be heroes, it's not your money we're taking."

Far up in front, the troop carrier and the three scout jeeps reached the bottom of the last hill and were about to enter Montelepre when the officer in charge realized there was nothing behind him. Now even more sheep were on the road cutting him off from the rest of the convoy. He picked up his radio and ordered one of the jeeps to go back. With a hand signal he directed the other vehicles to pull over to the side of the road and wait.

The scout jeep made its turn and started back up the hill it had just come down. Halfway up it met a hail of machine-gun and rifle fire. The four men in the jeep were riddled with bullets, and without a driver the jeep lost momentum and slowly rolled back down the hilly road toward the convoy.

The *carabinieri* commanding officer sprang out of his scout jeep and shouted at the men in the troop carrier to dismount and form a skirmishing line. The other two jeeps took off like frightened hares scuttling for cover. But this force was effectively neutralized. They could not rescue the paymaster truck since it was over on the other side of the hill; they could not even fire on Guiliano's men, who were stuffing the money-filled envelopes into their jackets. Guiliano's men held the high ground and obviously had the fire-power to slaughter any attackers. The best the army could do was set up a skirmish line under cover and fire away.

■ ■ ■

THE MARESCIALLO of Montelepre had been waiting for the paymaster. By the end of the month he was always short of money and, like his men, anticipated a night in Palermo dining at a good restaurant with charming women and friends. When he heard the gunfire he was bewildered. Guiliano would not dare attack one of his patrols in broad daylight, not with Colonel Luca's auxiliary force of five hundred soldiers in the area.

At that moment the Maresciallo heard a tremendous explosion at the gate of the Bellampo Barracks. One of the armored cars parked in the rear had blown up into an orange torch. Then the Maresciallo heard the clatter of heavy emplaced machine guns from the direction of the road that led to Castelvetrano and the coast city of Trapani, followed by a constant rattling hail of small arms' fire from the base of the mountain range outside the town. He could see his patrols in the town of Montelepre itself streaming back to the barracks, in jeeps and on foot, fleeing for their lives; and slowly it dawned upon him that Turi Guiliano had thrown all his forces at the five hundred–man garrison of Colonel Luca.

■ ■ ■

ON A high cliff above Montelepre, Turi Guiliano observed the robbing of the payroll through his binoculars. By turning ninety degrees he could also see the battle in the streets of the town, the direct attack on the Bellampo Barracks and the engagement of *carabinieri* patrols on the coastal roads. All his chiefs were functioning perfectly. Passatempo and his men had the money from the payroll, Pisciotta had the rear of the *carabinieri* column immobilized, Terranova and his band, supplemented by new recruits, had attacked the Bellampo Barracks and engaged their patrols. The men directly under Guiliano commanded the bases of the mountain. And Stefan Andolini, truly a *Fra Diavalo*, was preparing a surprise.

■ ■ ■

AT HIS headquarters in Palermo, Colonel Luca received the news of his lost payroll with what seemed to his subordinates an unusual calm. But inwardly he could only seethe at Guiliano's cleverness and wonder where and how he acquired his information on the disposition of the *carabinieri* troops. Four *carabinieri* had been killed in the robbery and another ten killed in the pitched battle with the other Guiliano forces.

Colonel Luca was still on the phone receiving casualty reports when Captain Perenze burst through the door, his heavy jowls quivering with excitement. He had just received the report that some bandits had been wounded and that one had been killed and left on the field of battle. The dead bandit had been identified by documents on his body and personal identification by two citizens of Montelepre. The dead body was none other than Turi Guiliano.

Against all caution, against all intelligence, Colonel Luca felt a surge of triumph in his breast. Military history was full of great victories, brilliant tactical maneuvers, which were negated by small personal accidents. A mindless bullet directed by fate had magically sought out and found the elusive ghost of the great bandit. But then caution returned. The fortune was too good; it might be a trap. But if it was, then he would walk into it and trap the trapper.

Colonel Luca made his preparations, and a flying column was readied that would be invincible to any attack. Armored cars went ahead, followed by the bulletproof car that carried Colonel Luca and Inspector Frederico Velardi, who had insisted on going to help identify the body but really to make sure the body did not carry the Testament. Behind Luca's car were troop carriers with men at the alert, weapons ready to fire. Scout jeeps to the number of twenty, filled with armed paratroopers, preceded the column. The garrison at Montelepre was ordered to guard the immediate roads to the town and establish spotting posts in the nearby mountains. Foot patrols heavy in strength, massively armed, controlled the sides of the entire length of the road.

It took Colonel Luca and his flying column less than an hour to reach Montelepre. There were no attacks; the show of strength had been too much for the bandits. But a disappointment awaited the Colonel.

Inspector Velardi said the corpse, now resting in an ambulance at the Bellampo Barracks, could not possibly be Guiliano. The bullet from which the man had died disfigured him but not enough for the Inspector to be mistaken. Other citizens were forced to view the body, and they too said it was not Guiliano. It had been a trap after all, Guiliano must have hoped that the Colonel would rush to the scene with a small escort and lay himself open to ambush. Colonel Luca ordered all precautions to be taken, but he was in a hurry to start on the road back to Palermo and get to his headquarters; he wanted to report personally to Rome what had happened that day and also make sure no one had released the false report of Guiliano's death. Checking first to make sure all his troop elements were in place so the road back would not be ambushed, he commandeered one of the swift scout jeeps at the head of the column. Inspector Velardi rode with him.

The Colonel's hastiness saved both their lives. As the flying column neared Palermo, with Luca's command car in the middle, there was a tremendous explosion. The command car flew up over ten feet in the air and came down in flaming pieces that scattered over the slopes of the mountain. The troop carrier following closely behind had eight men killed and fifteen wounded out of a total of thirty. The two officers in Luca's car were blown to bits.

When Colonel Luca called Minister Trezza with the bad news, he also asked that his three thousand extra men waiting on the mainland be shipped immediately to Sicily.

■ ■ ■

DON CROCE knew that these raids would continue as long as Guiliano's parents were held prisoner, and so he arranged for their release.

But he could not prevent the incursion of new forces, and two thousand soldiers now occupied the town of Montelepre and the surrounding area. Another three thousand were searching the mountains. Seven hundred citizens of Montelepre and in the province of Palermo had been thrown into jail for questioning by Colonel Luca, using the special powers delegated to him by the Christian Democratic government in Rome. There was a curfew that began at dusk and ended with dawn, citizens were immobilized in their homes and travelers without special passes were thrown into prison. The whole province was under an official reign of terror.

Don Croce watched with some trepidation as the tide turned against Guiliano.

CHAPTER
24

BEFORE THE coming of Luca's army, when Guiliano could enter Montelepre as he pleased, he had often seen Justina Ferra. Sometimes she had come to the Guiliano house on an errand or to receive the money Guiliano gave to her parents. Guiliano had never really noticed her growing into a beautiful young woman until one day he had seen her on the streets of Palermo with her parents. They had gone into the city to buy finery for the Festa not available in the small town of Montelepre. Guiliano and members of his band had gone to Palermo to buy supplies.

Guiliano had not seen her for perhaps six months, and she had grown taller and slimmer in that time. She was tall for a Sicilian woman, with long legs that tottered on newly bought high-heeled shoes. She was only sixteen years of age, but her face and form had flowered in the subtropical earth of Sicily and she was a mature woman physically. Her hair was pulled into a jet black crown studded with three gemlike combs, exposing a neck as long and golden as that of an Egyptian woman on a vase. Her eyes were enormous, questioning; her mouth sensuous, yet the only part of her face that betrayed her extreme youth. She wore a white dress with a slash of red ribbon running across the front.

She was such a picture of loveliness that Guiliano stared at her for a long time. He was sitting in an open café, his men scattered at the tables around him, when she walked by accompanied by her mother and father. They saw him. Justina's father kept his face stony and made no sign of recognition. The mother glanced quickly away. Only Justina stared at him as she went by. She was Sicilian enough not to greet him, but she stared directly into his eyes and he could see her mouth quivering to restrain a smile. In the sun-drenched street she was a pool of shimmering light, of the sensual Sicilian beauty that blooms at an early age. Since becoming an outlaw Guiliano had always distrusted love. To him it was an act of submission and held the seed for a fatal treachery, but in that moment he felt what he had never felt before—a suffusion in his body to kneel before another human being and willingly swear himself into an alien slavery. He did not identify this as love.

A month later, Guiliano found that his mind was obsessed with the memory of Justina Ferra standing in that pool of golden sunlight on the street in Palermo. He assumed it was merely sexual appetite, that he missed his passionate nights with La Venera. Then in his reveries he found himself not only dreaming of making love to Justina, but of spending time with her roaming around the mountains, showing her his caves, the narrow valleys filled with flowers, cooking meals for her over the open campfires. He still had his guitar in his mother's house and dreamed of playing for her. He would show her the poems he had written over the years, some of which had been published in the Sicilian newspapers. He even thought of sneaking into Montelepre and visiting her in her home, despite the two thousand soldiers of Colonel Luca's Special Force. At this time he came to his senses and knew something dangerous was going on inside him.

This was all foolishness. There were only two alternatives in his life. That he would be killed by the *carabinieri*, or that he would find sanctuary in America, and if he kept dreaming about this girl it would not be America. He had to get her out of his mind. If he seduced her or carried her off, her father would become his deadly enemy, and he had plenty of those already. He had once flogged Aspanu for seducing an innocent girl and over the years had executed three of his men for rape. This feeling he had for Justina was that he wanted to make her happy, to make her love and admire him and see him as he once saw himself. He wanted her eyes to be filled with love and trust.

But it was merely his tactical mind that explored his options. He had already decided on his course of action. He would marry the girl. In secret. Nobody except her family would know and of course Aspanu Pisciotta and a few trusted members of his band. Whenever it was safe to see her, he would have her escorted into the mountains so that they could spend a day or two together. It would be dangerous for her to be the wife of Turi Guiliano, but he could arrange to have her sent to America, and she would be waiting for him when he made his escape there. There was only one problem. What did Justina think of him?

■ ■ ■

CAESERO FERRA had been a secret member of Guiliano's band for the last five years, strictly as a gatherer of information, never in its operations. He and his wife had known Guiliano's parents and had been neighbors; they lived ten houses down the Via Bella from the Guiliano house. He was more educated than most of the people in Montelepre and was dissatisfied with farming. Then when Justina as a child had lost the money and Guiliano had replaced it and sent her home with the note that the family was under his protection, Caesero Ferra visited Maria Lombardo and offered his services. He gathered information in Palermo and Montelepre as to the movements of *carabinieri* patrols, the movements of rich merchants who were to be kidnapped by Guiliano's band, the identity of police informers. He received a share of the loot from these kidnappings and opened a small tavern in Montelepre, which also helped his secret activities.

When his son Silvio had returned from the war a Socialist

agitator, Caesero Ferra ordered him out of the house. Not because he disapproved of his son's beliefs, but because of the danger to the rest of the family. He had no illusions about democracy or the rulers in Rome. He had reminded Turi Guiliano of his promise to protect the Ferra family and Guiliano had done his best to protect Silvio. And after Silvio was murdered, it was Guiliano who promised him that the murder would be avenged.

Ferra had never blamed Guiliano. He knew that the massacre at Ginestra had profoundly disturbed Turi Guiliano, had caused him to grieve, that it still tormented him. He heard this from his wife who had listened for hours to Maria Lombardo talking about her son. How happy they had all been before that terrible day years ago when her son was shot down by the *carabinieri* and he had been forced against his better nature to kill in return. And of course every killing since then had been necessary, forced upon him by evil men. Maria Lombardo excused every killing, every crime, but she faltered when she spoke about the massacre at the Portella della Ginestra. Oh, the little children torn by machine-gun fire, the defenseless women killed. How could people think her son would do such a thing? Was he not the protector of the poor, the Champion of Sicily? Had he not given fortunes to help all the Sicilians in need of bread and homes? Her Turi could never have given the orders for such a massacre. So he had sworn to her on the statue of the black Madonna, and they had wept in each other's arms.

And so over the years Caesero had pursued the mystery of what had really happened at the Portella della Ginestra. Had Passatempo's machine-gunners made an honest mistake in the elevation of their fire? Had Passatempo, out of the sheer bloodthirstiness for which he was famous, slaughtered those people for his pleasure? Could the whole thing have been engineered to damage Guiliano? Was there perhaps even another band of men who had opened fire with their machine guns, men not under Guiliano's orders but perhaps sent by the Friends of the Friends or even by a branch of the Security Police? Caesero left nobody off his list of suspects except Turi Guiliano. For if Guiliano were guilty the whole world he lived in would collapse. He loved Guiliano as he had loved his son. He had seen him grow from a child to a man, and there had never been a moment when he had showed any meanness of spirit, any viciousness.

So Caesero Ferra kept his eyes and ears open. He bought drinks for other secret members of the band who had not been thrown into jail by Colonel Luca. He caught scraps of conversation among the Friends of the Friends who lived in town and occasionally came to his tavern to drink wine and play cards. On one night he heard them talking laughingly about "The Animal" and "The Devil" visiting with Don Croce, and how the great Don had turned those two feared men into whispering angels. Ferra pondered on this and with that unerring Sicilian paranoia made the connection. Passatempo and Stefan Andolini had at some time met with the Don. Passatempo was often called "The Brute" and *Fra Diavalo* was Andolini's bandit name. What were they doing holding a private conversation with Don Croce at his house in Villaba, which was far from the bandits' mountain base? He sent his teenaged son to the Guiliano house with an urgent message and two days later was given a rendezvous in the mountains to meet with Guiliano. He told Guiliano his story. The young man showed no emotion and only swore him to secrecy. Ferra heard no more. Now three months later he received another summons from Guiliano and expected to hear the rest of the story.

Guiliano and his band were deep in the mountains, out of range of Luca's army. Caesero Ferra traveled at night and was met by Aspanu Pisciotta at a rendezvous point to be led to the camp. They did not arrive until early morning and found a hot breakfast waiting for them. The meal was elaborate, spread out on a folding table with linen and silver. Turi Guiliano was dressed in a silk white shirt and tan moleskin trousers which were tucked into brown polished boots; his hair was freshly washed and combed. He had never looked so handsome.

Pisciotta was dismissed and Guiliano and Ferra sat down together. Guiliano seemed ill at ease. He said formally, "I want to
thank you for that information you brought me. It has been
pursued and now I know it is true. And it is very important. But
I have sent for you to speak about something else. Something
that I know will be a surprise and I hope that it will not offend
you."

Ferra was startled but he said politely, "You could never
offend me, I owe you too much."

At this Guiliano smiled, the frank open smile that Ferra remembered from the man's childhood.

"Listen to me carefully," Guiliano said. "Speaking to you is
my first step. And if you disapprove I will go no further. Disregard my position as the leader of our band; I am speaking to you
as the father of Justina. You know she is beautiful, you must
have had many young men of the town hanging around your
door. And I know you have guarded her virtue carefully. I must
tell you that this is the first time in my life I have had such
feelings. I want to marry your daughter. If you say no I will
never say another word. You will remain my friend and your
daughter will remain under my special protection as always. If
you say yes, then I will ask your daughter if the idea pleases
her. If she says no, that will be the end of the matter."

Caesero Ferra was so stunned by this speech that he could
only stutter, "Let me think, let me think." And for a long time
he was silent. When he began to speak it was with the utmost
respect. "I would rather have you for a husband to my daughter
than any man in the world. And I know my son Silvio, God rest
his soul, would agree with me." Again he stuttered when he
spoke. "I worry only about my daughter's safety. If Justina was
your wife, Colonel Luca would surely take any excuse to put
her under arrest. The Friends are now your enemies and might
do her some harm. And you must escape to America or die here
in the mountains. I would not want her to be a widow so young,
please forgive me for speaking so frankly. But it also compli-

cates life for you and that worries me most. A happy bridegroom is not so aware of traps, he is not wary of his enemies. A marriage could cause your death. I speak so frankly only because of my affection and respect for you. This is something that can be put aside for a better day when you can know your future in more detail and plan for it more intelligently." When he finished speaking he kept a wary eye on Guiliano to see if he had displeased him.

But he had only depressed him. And he recognized it as the disappointment of a young man in love. Which seemed to him so extraordinary that he said impulsively, "I am not saying no to you, Turi."

Guiliano sighed. "I've thought of all of those things. My plan is this. I would marry your daughter in secret. The Abbot Manfredi would perform the ceremony. We would be married here in the mountains. It would be too dangerous for me anyplace else. But I could arrange for you and your wife to accompany your daughter so that you could witness the marriage. She would stay with me for three days, and then I would send her back to your house. If your daughter becomes a widow she will have enough money to start a new life. So you need not fear for her future. I love your daughter and will cherish and protect her all of her life. I will provide for her future if the worst should happen. But still it's a risk to be married to a man like me, and as a prudent father you have every right to refuse to let her take that risk."

Caesero Ferra was immensely moved. The young man had spoken with such simplicity and directness. And with such wistful hope. But best of all he had been to the point. He had made provisions against the calamities of life and the future well-being of his daughter. Ferra rose from the table to embrace Guiliano. "You have my blessing," he said. "I will speak to Justina."

Before he left, Ferra said he was happy that the information he had given had proven useful. And he was astonished at the change in Guiliano's face. The eyes seemed to open wider, the beauty of the face seemed to harden into white marble.

"I will invite Stefan Andolini and Passatempo to my wedding," he said. "We can settle the matter then." It only occurred to Ferra later that this was a curious thing to do if the marriage was to be kept secret.

■ ■ ■

IN SICILY it was not uncommon for a girl to marry a man with whom she had never spent a moment alone. When the women sat outside their houses, those unwed had to sit always in profile, never staring full out into the street, lest they be called wanton. The young men going by would never get an opportunity to speak to them except at church, where young girls were protected by the statues of the Virgin Mary and their cold-eyed mothers. If a young man fell madly in love with the profile or the few words of respectful chatter, he had to put it in writing, in a well-composed letter declaring his intentions. This was a serious matter. Many times a professional writer was employed. The wrong tone might conceivably bring about a funeral rather than a marriage. And so Turi Guiliano's proposal through the father was not unusual, despite the fact that he had given Justina herself no sign of his interest.

Caesero Ferra was in no doubt about what Justina's answer would be. When she was a little girl she had ended her prayers with, "And save Turi Guiliano from the *carabinieri*." She was always anxious to run messages over to the mother, Maria Lombardo. And then when the news had come out about the tunnel that ran to La Venera's house, Justina had been wild with rage. At first her father and mother had thought it was rage at the arrest of the woman and Guiliano's parents, but then they realized that it was jealousy.

So Caesero Ferra could anticipate his daughter's answer; that was no surprise. But the way she received the news was a shock. She smiled wickedly at her father as if she had planned the seduction, as if she had known she could vanquish Guiliano.

■ ■ ■

DEEP IN the mountains was a small Norman castle, almost in ruins, that had not been occupied for twenty years. Guiliano decided to celebrate his wedding and honeymoon there. He ordered Aspanu Pisciotta to establish a perimeter of armed men so the couple would be guarded against any surprise attack. Abbot Manfredi left his monastery in a donkey cart and then was carried in a litter over the mountain trails by members of Guiliano's band. In the old castle he was delighted to find a private chapel, though all its valuable statues and woodwork had long since been stolen. But the bare stones were beautiful, as was the stone altar. The Abbot did not really approve of Guiliano getting married, and after they had embraced he said jokingly to Guiliano, "You should have heeded the old proverb, 'The man who plays alone never loses.' "

Guiliano laughed and said, "But I have to think of my own happiness." And then added one of the Abbot's most beloved peasant sayings, which he always used to excuse his moneymaking schemes: "Remember, Saint Joseph shaved his own beard before he shaved the Apostles." This put the Abbot into a better humor, and he had his casket of documents opened and handed Guiliano his marriage certificate. It was a beautiful document, with medieval calligraphy written in gold ink.

"The marriage will be recorded at the monastery," the Abbot said. "But have no fear, no one will know of it."

The bride and her parents had been brought in on donkeys the night before. They had stayed in rooms of the castle that had been cleaned by Guiliano's men and furnished with beds made of bamboo and straw. Guiliano felt a pang at not having his mother and father at the wedding, but they were under close observation by Colonel Luca's Special Force.

Aspanu Pisciotta, Stefan Andolini, Passatempo, Corporal Silvestro and Terranova were the only ones attending the wedding. Justina had changed from her traveling clothes into the white dress she had worn with such success in Palermo. She smiled at Guiliano, and he was stunned by the radiance of that smile. The

Abbot made short work of the ceremony, and then they went
out on the lawn of the castle where a table had been set with
wine and cold meat and bread. They all ate quickly and drank a
toast to the bride and groom. The trip back for the Abbot and
the Ferras would be long and dangerous. There was anxiety that
a patrol of *carabinieri* might wander into the area and the perimeter of armed bandit guards would have to engage them in battle.
The Abbot wanted to be on his way quickly, but Guiliano detained him.

"I want to thank you for what you have done today," Guiliano said. "And soon after my wedding day I want to perform an
act of mercy. But I need your help." They spoke quietly for a
few moments, and the Abbot nodded his head.

Justina embraced her parents; her mother wept and looked
imploringly at Guiliano. Then Justina whispered something in
her ear and the older woman laughed. They embraced again and
then the parents mounted their donkeys.

The bride and groom spent their nuptial night in the main
bedchamber of the castle. This room had been stripped bare but
Turi Guiliano had had a huge mattress brought in by donkey,
with silken sheets and a goose-down quilt and pillows bought
from the finest store in Palermo. There was a bathroom as huge
as the bedroom with marble tub and a vast washing sink. Of
course it had no running water and had to be supplied by buckets
which Guiliano himself hauled in from the sparkling stream that
ran beside the castle. He had also stocked it with toilet articles
and perfumes that Justina had never seen in her life.

Naked, she was shy at first, holding her hands down between
her legs. Her skin was golden. She was slim but with the full
breasts of a mature woman. When he kissed her, she averted
her head slightly so he touched only a corner of her mouth. He
was patient, not with a lover's skill but with the tactical sense
that had served him so well when he waged his guerrilla wars.
She had let down her long jet black hair so that it screened her
full breasts and he stroked her hair and talked about the first

time he had seen her as a woman that fateful day in Palermo. How beautiful she had been then. He recited from memory some of the poems he had written about her when he was alone in the mountains and dreamed about her beauty. She relaxed in the bed, the goose quilt over her body. Guiliano rested on top of the cover, but she averted her eyes.

Justina told him how she had fallen in love with him the day she had carried over a message from her brother and how crushed she had been when she realized he had not recognized her as the little girl whose money he had replaced years before. She told him how she had said prayers for him every night since she was eleven years old, that she had loved him since that day.

Turi Guiliano had an extraordinary feeling of happiness listening to her tell this. That she loved him, that she thought and dreamed of him while he was alone in the mountains. He kept stroking her hair and she caught his hand and held it, her own warm and dry. "Were you surprised when I asked your father to speak to you about marriage?" he asked her.

She smiled a sly, triumphant smile. "Not after you stared at me in Palermo," she said. "From that day I prepared myself for you."

He leaned over to kiss her full lips which were a dark winey red, and this time she did not avert her face. He was surprised by the sweetness of her mouth, the sweetness of her breath and the responsiveness of his own flesh. For the first time in his life he felt his body melting and falling away from him. He started to shiver, and Justina threw back the goose quilt so that he could come into the bed with her. She rolled over to her side so she could put her arms around him, so they could flow together, and the feel of her body was different from any other body he had ever touched. She closed her eyes.

Turi Guiliano kissed her mouth, her closed eyes and then her breasts, the skin so fragile that the heat of flesh almost burned his lips. He was stunned by the smell of her, so sweet, uninfected by the pain of life, so far removed from death. He ran his hand down over her thigh and the silkiness of her skin sent a thrill from his fingers to his groin to the top of his head where it almost gave him pain, at which he was so astonished that he laughed aloud. But then she put her hand between his legs, very lightly, and he almost literally lost his senses. He made love to her with a fierce yet gentle passion and she returned his caresses, slowly, tentatively and then after a time with equal passion. They made love for the rest of the night without speaking except for short exclamations of love, and when dawn broke, Justina fell into an exhausted sleep.

When she awoke near midday she found the huge marble bathtub filled with cool water, and buckets also filled next to the sink. Turi was nowhere to be seen. She was frightened for a moment at being alone; then she stepped into the tub and washed. When she got out she dried herself with a huge coarse brown towel and used one of the perfumes at the sink. When she had finally completed her toilette, she put on her traveling dress, a dark brown frock and a white button sweater. On her feet were sensible walking shoes.

Outside the May sun was hot, as usual in Sicily, but a mountain breeze cooled the air. There was a campfire by the trestle table, and Guiliano had breakfast ready for her—toasted slices of coarse bread, cold ham and some fruit. There were also mugs of milk poured from a metal container that had been wrapped in leaves.

There was no one else in sight so Justina ran into Turi's arms and kissed him passionately. Then she thanked him for making the breakfast but reproached him for not waking her up so that she could have prepared the meal. It was unheard of for a Sicilian male to do such a thing.

They ate in sunlight. Enclosing them, enclosing their enchantment, were the ruined castle walls, above them the remains of the Norman tower, its spire decorated with a mosaic of brightly colored stones. The entrance to the castle had handsome Norman portals, and through the broken stone they could see the altar arch of the chapel.

They stepped through the ruined walls of the castle grounds

and walked through an olive grove, a scattering of wild lemon trees. They waded through gardens of those flowers that grew so profusely all over Sicily—the asphodels of the Greek poets, the pink anemones, grape hyacinths, the scarlet Adonises that legend said were stained with the blood of the lover of Venus. Turi Guiliano put his arm around Justina; her hair and her body were drenched with the perfume these flowers gave. Deep in the olive grove, Justina boldly pulled him down onto the vast carpet of brilliantly colored flowers, and they made love. Above them a tiny cloud of yellow and black butterflies circled, then soared up into the infinitely azure sky.

On their third and last day they heard the sound of gunfire far off in the mountains. Justina was alarmed, but Guiliano reassured her. He was always careful throughout their three days together never to give cause for fear. He was never armed, there was not a weapon in sight; he had hidden his guns in the chapel. He never betrayed his wariness, and he had ordered his men to stay out of sight. But shortly after the gunfire Aspanu Pisciotta appeared with a brace of bloody rabbits over his shoulder. He threw them at Justina's feet and said, "Cook these for your husband, it's his favorite dish. And if you ruin them we have twenty more." He smiled at her and as she got busy skinning and cleaning the rabbits, he motioned to Guiliano. The two men went over to a fallen arch of the wall and sat down.

"Well, Turi," Pisciotta said, grinning, "was she worth us risking our lives for?"

Guiliano said quietly, "I'm a happy man. Now tell me about those twenty rabbits you've shot."

"One of Luca's patrols, but in strength," Pisciotta said. "We stopped them at the perimeter. Two armored cars. One of them ran into our minefield and burned as badly as your new wife will burn those rabbits. The other car fired its guns at the rocks and ran home to Montelepre. They will come back in the morning, of course, to find their comrades. In force. I suggest you leave here tonight."

"Justina's father is coming for her at dawn," Guiliano said. "Have you arranged our little meeting?"

"Yes," Pisciotta said.

"After my wife leaves—" Guiliano stuttered over the word "wife" and Pisciotta laughed. Guiliano smiled and continued, "—bring those men to me in the chapel and we will settle the matter." He paused for a moment and said, "Were you surprised when I told you the truth about Ginestra?"

"No," Pisciotta said.

"Will you stay for dinner?" Guiliano asked.

"On the last night of your honeymoon?" Pisciotta shook his head. "You know the proverb: Beware of the cookery of a new bride." The old proverb of course referred to the latent treachery of new friends as partners in crime. What Pisciotta was saying once again was that Guiliano should never have married.

Guiliano smiled. "All this can't last much longer—we have to prepare for a different life. Make sure the perimeter holds tomorrow until we have finished all of our business."

Pisciotta nodded. He glanced over to the campfire where Justina was cooking. "What a beautiful girl she is," he said. "And to think she grew up under our very noses and we never noticed her. But watch out, her father says she has a temper. Don't let her handle your guns."

Again this was sly Sicilian peasant vulgarity, but Guiliano seemed not to hear and Pisciotta swung himself over the garden wall to disappear through the olive groves.

Justina had gathered flowers and put them into an old vase she had found in the castle. These graced the table. She served the food she had cooked, rabbit with garlic and tomatoes, a wooden bowl of salad with olive oil and red wine vinegar. She seemed to Turi a little nervous, a little sad. Perhaps it was the gunfire, perhaps it was Aspanu Pisciotta appearing in their Garden of Eden with his saturnine face, black guns dangling from his body.

They sat opposite each other eating slowly. She wasn't a bad cook, Guiliano thought, and she was quick to supply him with bread, more meat and fill his wineglass; she had been well trained by her mother. He noticed with approval that she was a good eater—she wasn't sickly. She raised her eyes and saw him watching her. She grinned at him and said, "Is the food as good as your mother's?"

"Better," he said. "But never tell her that."

She was still looking at him like a cat. "And is it as good as La Venera's?"

Turi Guiliano had never had a love affair with a young girl. He was caught by surprise, but his tactical mind processed the question quickly. Next would come questions about his love-making with La Venera. He didn't want to hear such questions or answer them. He had not felt the love for the older woman that he felt for this young girl; still he felt a tenderness and respect for La Venera. She was a woman who had suffered tragedies and pain this young girl for all her charms had no knowledge of.

He smiled at Justina gravely. She had risen to clear the table but was waiting for his answer. Guiliano said, "La Venera was a great cook—it's not fair to judge you against her."

A dish went flying past his head and he began to laugh uncontrollably. He laughed with joy and delight at being part of such a domestic scene and because for the first time the mask of sweetness and docility was stripped from the young girl's face. But when she began sobbing he took her in his arms.

They stood there in that instant silvery twilight that falls so quickly in Sicily. He murmured into her ear that peaked so rosily from her jet black hair. "I was joking. You are the best cook in the world." But he buried his face in her neck so that she could not see his smile.

On their last night together, they talked more than made love. Justina asked him about La Venera and he told her that was the past and to be forgotten. She asked him how they would see each other in the future. He explained that he was arranging for

344

her to be sent to America and would join her there. But her father had already told her that; she was concerned only about how they would manage to see each other before she left for America. Guiliano saw that it never occurred to her that he might not escape, she was too young to imagine tragic endings.

Her father came in the early dawn. Justina clung to Turi Guiliano for one last moment and then was gone.

■ ■ ■

GUILIANO WENT to the chapel in the ruined castle and waited for Aspanu Pisciotta to bring him his chiefs. While he was waiting he armed himself with the guns he had hidden in the chapel.

In his conversation with Abbot Manfredi just before the wedding, Guiliano had told the old man about his suspicions that Stefan Andolini and Passatempo had had a meeting with Don Croce two days before the massacre at the Portella della Ginestra. He assured the Abbot he would not harm his son, but that it was essential he know the truth. The Abbot told him the whole story. As Turi had guessed, his son had confessed to him.

Don Croce had requested Stefan Andolini to bring Passatempo to him at Villaba for a secret meeting. Andolini had been ordered to wait outside the room where the two other men conferred. This had only been two days before the slaughter. After that May Day tragedy Stefan Andolini had confronted Passatempo, who had admitted that Don Croce had paid him a handsome sum of money to go against Guiliano's orders and have his machine guns fire into the crowd. Passatempo had threatened that if Andolini said anything about this to Guiliano he would swear that Andolini had been in the room with Don Croce when the bargain was struck. Andolini had been too afraid to tell anyone except his father, the Abbot Manfredi. Manfredi had counseled him to keep his mouth shut. The week after the massacre Guiliano had been in such a raging grief that he was sure to execute both men.

Again Guiliano assured the Abbot that he would not harm his

son. Guiliano instructed Pisciotta on what he was to do but said they would conclude the matter after Justina returned to Montelepre, after the honeymoon. He did not want to play the butcher before he played the groom.

He waited now in the chapel of the ruined Norman castle, its ceiling the blue Mediterranean sky. He leaned back against the remains of the altar, and that was how he received his chiefs when Aspanu Pisciotta led them in. The Corporal had been briefed by Pisciotta and stood where his gun could command Passatempo and Stefan Andolini. Those two men were led directly to face Guiliano before the altar. Terranova, who knew nothing, sat on one of the chapel stone benches. He had commanded the defense of the perimeter during the long night hours and he was exhausted. Guiliano had not told any of the others what he would do to Passatempo.

Guiliano knew that Passatempo was like a wild animal—he could sense changes in the atmosphere and the smell of danger as it came off other people. Guiliano was careful to behave exactly as he always had with Passatempo. He had always kept more of a distance between them than with the others. In fact he had assigned Passatempo and his band far away to control the area near Trapani, for Passatempo's savagery disgusted him. He used Passatempo to perform executions of informers and also to threaten stubborn "invited guests" until they paid their ransoms. Just the sight of Passatempo would usually frighten prisoners and shorten negotiations, but if that was not enough, Passatempo would tell them what he would do to them and their families if the ransom was not paid, and tell them with such relish that the "guests" would stop haggling to be released as quickly as possible.

Guiliano pointed his machine pistol at Passatempo and said, "Before we part we must all settle our debts. You disobeyed my orders, you took money from Don Croce to massacre the people at the Portella della Ginestra."

Terranova was looking at Guiliano with narrowed eyes wondering about his own safety, whether Guiliano was trying to find out who was guilty. Whether perhaps he too would be accused. He might have made a move to defend himself, but Pisciotta had also leveled his pistol at Passatempo.

Guiliano said to Terranova, "I know your band and you obeyed my orders. Passatempo did not. He endangered your life by doing so, since if I had not found out the truth, I would have had to execute both of you. But now we have to deal with him."

Stefan Andolini had not moved a muscle. Again he trusted to the fates. He had been faithful to Guiliano and, like those believers in God who cannot believe their God malignant, and commit all crimes in His honor, he had absolute faith he would not be harmed.

Passatempo also knew. With that deep animal instinct he sensed his death was at hand. Nothing could help him but his own ferocity, yet two guns were leveled at him. He could only play for time and make a last desperate attack. So he said, "Stefan Andolini gave me the money and the message—bring him to account," hoping that Andolini would make a move to protect himself and that under cover of that movement, an opportunity to attack would open.

Guiliano said to Passatempo, "Andolini has confessed his sins and his hand was never on the machine guns. Don Croce deceived him as he deceived me."

Passatempo said with brute bewilderment, "But I killed a hundred men and you never complained. And the Portella was almost two years ago. We have been together for seven years and that is the only time I disobeyed you. Don Croce gave me reason to believe that you would not be too sorry about what I did. That you were simply too soft to do the deed yourself. And what are a few people dead more or less after all the others we've killed? I've never been unfaithful to you personally."

At that moment Guiliano knew how hopeless it was to make this man understand the enormity of his deed. And yet, why should this offend him so? Over the years had he not himself ordered deeds almost as terrible? The execution of the barber, the crucifixion of the fraudulent priest, the kidnappings, the slaughter of *carabinieri*, the merciless killings of spies? If Passatempo was a brute, born and bred, then what was he, the Champion of Sicily? He felt his own reluctance to perform the execution. So Guiliano said, "I will give you time to make your peace with God. Kneel and say your prayers."

The other men had drifted away from Passatempo, leaving him in his own doomed circle of earth. He made as if to kneel and then his short squat form exploded toward Guiliano. Guiliano stepped forward to meet him and touched the trigger of his machine pistol. The bullets caught Passatempo in midair and yet his body hurtled forward and grazed Guiliano as he fell. Guiliano stepped away from him.

That afternoon Passatempo's body was found on a mountain road patrolled by the *carabinieri*. Pinned to it was a short note that read, SO DIE ALL WHO BETRAY GUILIANO.

BOOK
V

TURI GUILIANO AND MICHAEL CORLEONE

1950

25

MICHAEL WAS deep in sleep, then suddenly came awake. It was as if he had wrenched his body out of a pit. The bedroom was completely black; he had closed the wooden shutters to bar the pale lemon light of the moon. There was no sound, just an eerie stillness broken now by the racing of his heart. He could feel the presence of someone else in the room.

He turned over in the bed, and it seemed to him there was a lighter pool of blackness on the floor nearby. He reached over and turned on the bedside lamp. The pool became the severed head of the black Madonna. He thought it had fallen off the table and the sound had brought him awake. He relaxed and smiled with relief. At that moment he heard a small rustling sound at the door. He turned toward it, and in the shadows the dim orange light of the lamp did not quite reach, he could see the dark bony face of Aspanu Pisciotta.

He was sitting on the floor with his back against the door. The mustached mouth was spread in a triumphant grin, as if to say, so much for your guards, so much for the security of your sanctuary.

Michael looked at his wristwatch on the night table. It was three o'clock. "You keep strange hours—what were you waiting for?" he asked. He got out of bed and dressed quickly, then opened the shutters. The moonlight entered the room like a ghost, appearing and disappearing. "Why didn't you wake me up?" Michael said.

Pisciotta rolled to his feet like a snake raising its head on its body to strike. "I like to watch people sleep. Sometimes in their dreams they shout out their secrets."

"I never tell secrets," Michael said. "Not even in my dreams." He stepped out on the terrace and offered Pisciotta a cigarette. They smoked together. Michael could hear Pisciotta's chest rattle with suppressed coughs and indeed his face looked ghastly in the moonlight, the bones skeletal.

They were silent. Then Pisciotta said, "Did you ever get the Testament?"

"Yes," Michael said.

Pisciotta sighed. "Turi trusts me more than anyone on earth —he trusts me with his life. I am the only person who can find him now. But he did not trust me with the Testament. Do you have it?"

Michael hesitated for a moment. Pisciotta laughed. "You are like Turi," he said.

"The Testament is in America," Michael said. "It is safe with my father." He did not want Pisciotta to know it was on its way to Tunis simply because he did not want anyone to know.

Michael almost dreaded to ask the next question. There could be only one reason for Pisciotta to be visiting him so secretly. Only one reason he had risked evading the guards surrounding the villa; or had he been passed through? It could only be that finally Guiliano was ready to appear. "When is Guiliano coming?" he said.

"Tomorrow night," Pisciotta said. "But not here."

"Why not?" Michael asked. "This is safe ground."

Pisciotta laughed, "But I got in here, didn't I?"

Michael was irritated by this truth. He wondered again if Pisciotta had been passed in by the guards under the order of Don Domenic, or even brought here by him. "It's for Guiliano to decide," he said.

"No," Pisciotta said. "I must decide for him. You promised his family he will be safe. But Don Croce knows you are here, so does Inspector Velardi. Their spies are everywhere. What do you plan for Guiliano? A wedding, a birthday party? A funeral? What kind of foolishness do you tell us? Do you think we are all donkeys here in Sicily?" He said this in a dangerous tone.

"I'm not going to tell you my plan of escape," Michael said. "You can trust me or not as you choose. Tell me where you will deliver Guiliano and I will be there. Don't tell me and tomorrow night I will be safe in America, while you and Guiliano are still running for your lives."

Pisciotta laughed and said, "Spoken like a true Sicilian—you haven't wasted the years in this country." He sighed. "I can't believe it will finally be over," he said. "Almost seven years of fighting and running, of betrayals and killing. But we were the Kings of Montelepre, Turi and myself—there was glory enough for both of us. He was for the poor and I was for myself. I never believed at first, but in our second year as outlaws, he proved it to me and all of our band. Remember I am his second in command, his cousin, the man he trusts most. I wear the belt with the golden buckle as he does; he gave it to me. But I seduced the young daughter of a farmer in Partinico and made her pregnant. Her father went to Guiliano and told him the story. Do you know what Turi did? He tied me to a tree and beat me with a whip. Not in front of the farmer or any of our men. He would never expose me to such disrespect. It was our secret. But I knew if I disobeyed his orders again, he would kill me. That is our Turi." His hand shook as he brought it to his mouth. In the fading moonlight his tiny mustache gleamed like a thin sliver of black bone.

Michael thought, What a strange story. Why does he tell it to me?

They went back into the bedroom and Michael closed the shutters. Pisciotta picked up the severed head of the black Madonna off the floor and handed it to Michael. "I threw this on the floor to wake you," he said. "The Testament was inside, isn't that true?"

"Yes," Michael said.

Pisciotta's face sagged. "Maria Lombardo lied to me. I asked her if she had it. She said no. Then she gave it to you in front of my very eyes." He laughed bitterly. "I have been like a son to her." He paused for a moment and then said, "And she has been like a mother to me."

Pisciotta asked for another cigarette. There was still some wine left in the jug on the night table. Michael poured a glass for both of them, and Pisciotta drank it gratefully. "Thank you," he said. "Now we must get down to our business. I will turn over Guiliano to you outside the town of Castelvetrano. Ride in an open car so I can recognize you, and come directly on the road from Trapani. I will intercept you at a point of my own choosing. If there is danger, wear a cap and we will not appear. The time will be as soon as dawn breaks. Do you think you can manage that?"

"Yes," Michael said. "Everything is arranged. There is one thing I should tell you: Stefan Andolini did not keep his appointment with Professor Adonis yesterday. The Professor was very worried."

Pisciotta was startled for the first time. Then he shrugged. "The little man was always bad luck," he said. "Now we must say goodbye until tomorrow at dawn." He took Michael's hand in his own.

Michael said impulsively, "Come with us to America."

Pisciotta shook his head. "I have lived in Sicily all of my life and I have loved my life. And so I must die in Sicily if I must. But thank you."

Michael was strangely moved by these words. Even with his scant knowledge of Pisciotta, he sensed that this was a man who could never be transplanted from the earth and mountains of Sicily. He was too fierce, too bloodthirsty; his coloring, his voice were all of Sicily. He could never trust a strange land.

"I'll pass you through the gate," Michael said.

"No," Pisciotta said. "Our little meeting must remain a secret."

■ ■ ■

AFTER PISCIOTTA had left, Michael lay on his bed until dawn, unable to sleep. He would finally meet Turi Guiliano face to face; they would travel to America together. He wondered what kind of man he would find Guiliano to be. Would he be his legend? So much larger than life that he dominated this island and affected the course of a nation? He got up from the bed and opened the shutters. Dawn was finally breaking and he watched the sun move up in the sky and throw a golden highway across the sea, and riding on that broad beam of light he saw the motor launch speeding toward the dock. He rushed out of the villa and down to the beach to greet Peter Clemenza.

They had breakfast together, and Michael told him about Pisciotta's visit. Clemenza did not seem surprised that Pisciotta had penetrated the guarded villa.

They spent the rest of the morning making their plans for the meeting with Guiliano. There might be spies watching the villa for any extraordinary movement; a column of automobiles would surely attract attention. Also Michael would certainly be under close observation. True, the Sicilian Security Police under Inspector Velardi would not interfere, but who knew what treacheries might be afoot?

When they had finished their planning, they had lunch, and then Michael went to his room for an afternoon sleep. He wanted to be fresh for the long night. Peter Clemenza had too many details to attend to—giving orders to his men, arranging transport and briefing his brother, Don Domenic, upon his return home.

Michael closed the shutters in his bedroom and lay on the bed. His body was rigid; he could not sleep. Within the next twenty-four hours many terrible things could happen. He had a sense of foreboding. But then he weaved a dream of returning to his home on Long Island, his mother and father waiting for him at the door, his long exile at an end.

CHAPTER

26

IN THE seventh year of his banditry, Turi Guiliano knew that he must leave his mountain kingdom and flee to the America he had been conceived in, the America his parents had always told stories about when he was a child. The fabulous land where there was justice for the poor, where the government was not the lackey of the rich, where the penniless Sicilians rose to riches simply by good honest labor.

Persisting in his avowals of friendship, the Don had contacted Don Corleone in America to help rescue Guiliano and give him sanctuary there. Turi Guiliano understood quite well that Don Croce was also serving his own purposes, but Guiliano knew he had very few options. The power of his band was gone.

Now on this night he would start on his journey to meet with Aspanu Pisciotta; he would place himself in the hands of the American, Michael Corleone. He would leave these mountains now. These mountains that had given him sanctuary for seven years. He would leave his kingdom, his power, his family, and all his comrades. His armies had melted away; his mountains were being overrun; his protectors, the people of Sicily, were being crushed by Colonel Luca's Special Force. If he remained he would win some victories, but his final defeat would be certain. For now, he had no choice.

Turi Guiliano strapped on his *lupara*, took up his machine

pistol and started on the long journey toward Palermo. He was wearing a white sleeveless shirt, but over this was a leather jacket with large pockets that held clips of ammunition for his weapons. He paced himself. His watch said nine o'clock, and there were still traces of daylight in the sky despite the timid light of the moon. There was the danger of roving patrols of the Special Force to Repress Banditry, yet Guiliano walked without fear. Over the years he had earned a certain invisibility. All the people in this countryside threw their cloaks about him. If there were patrols they would inform him; if he was in danger they would protect him and hide him in their houses. If he were attacked, the shepherds and the farmers would reassemble under his solitary banner. He had been their champion; they would never betray him now.

■ ■ ■

IN THE months that followed his marriage, there were pitched battles between Colonel Luca's Special Force and segments of Guiliano's band. Colonel Luca had already taken credit for the killing of Passatempo, and the newspapers reported in huge headlines that one of Guiliano's most feared chiefs had been killed in a fierce gun battle with the heroic soldiers of the Special Force to Repress Banditry. Colonel Luca, of course, had suppressed the note left on the body, but Don Croce learned of it from Inspector Velardi. He knew then that Guiliano was fully aware of the treachery that had been done at the Portella della Ginestra.

Colonel Luca's five thousand–man army exerted an intense pressure on Guiliano. He could no longer dare to enter Palermo to buy supplies or sneak into Montelepre to visit his mother and Justina. Many of his men were being betrayed and killed. Some were emigrating on their own to Algeria or Tunisia. Others were disappearing into hiding places that cut them off from the activities of the band. The Mafia was now in active opposition to him, using its network to deliver Guiliano's men into the hands of the *carabinieri*.

And then finally one of the chiefs was brought down.

Terranova got unlucky, and it was his virtue that brought him misfortune. He had not the ferociousness of Passatempo, the malignant cunning of Pisciotta, the deadliness of *Fra Diavalo*. Nor the ascetic quality of Guiliano. He was intelligent but he was also of an affectionate temperament, and Guiliano had often used him to make friends with their kidnapping victims, to distribute money and goods to the poor. It was Terranova and his own band that plastered Palermo with posters in the dead of night to present Guiliano's propaganda. He did not often take part in the more bloody operations.

He was a man who required love and affection. A few years before, he had acquired a mistress in Palermo, a widow with three small children. She had never known he was a bandit; she thought he was a government official in Rome who took his holidays in Sicily. She was grateful for the money he gave her and the presents he brought for her children, but it had been made plain to her that they could never marry. And so she gave him the affection and care he needed. When he visited she cooked elaborate meals; she washed his clothes and made love with a grateful passion. Such a relationship could not remain a secret forever from the Friends of the Friends, and Don Croce stored the information away to be used at the proper time.

Justina had visited Guiliano a few times in the mountains, and Terranova had been her bodyguard on her voyages. Her beauty had stirred his feelings of longing, and though he knew it was not prudent, he decided to visit his mistress one last time. He wanted to give her a sum of money that would sustain her and her children in the years to come.

And so one night he sneaked into Palermo alone. He gave the widow the money and explained he might not be able to see her for a long time. She wept and protested and finally he told her who he really was. She was astonished. His usual demeanor was so mild, his nature was so gentle, and yet he was one of the famed Guiliano's great chiefs. She made love with a fiery passion that delighted him, and they spent a happy evening with the three children. Terranova had taught them to play cards, and when they won this time he paid them real money, which made them laugh with joy.

After the children were put to bed, Terranova and the widow continued their lovemaking until dawn. Then Terranova prepared to leave. At the door they embraced for the last time, and then Terranova walked quickly down the little street and into the main square before the cathedral. He felt a happy satiety of the body, and his mind was at peace. He was relaxed and off guard.

The morning air was blasted by the roar of motors. Three black cars sped toward him. Armed men appeared on every side of the square. Other armed men jumped out of the cars. One of the men shouted at him to surrender, to put up his hands.

Terranova took one last look at the cathedral, the statues of saints niched on its sides; he saw the blue and yellow balconies, the sun rising to light the azure sky. He knew that this was the last time he would see such wonders, that his seven years of luck were ended. There remained only one thing for him to do.

He took a great leap as if he would leap over death itself and hurl himself into a safe universe. As his body flew to one side and hit the ground, he drew his pistol and fired. One soldier reeled back and went down to one knee. Terranova tried to pull the trigger again, but by that time a hundred bullets converged on his body, blowing it to pieces, blowing the flesh off his bones. In one way he had been lucky—it had all happened so quickly that he did not have time to wonder if his mistress had betrayed him.

■ ■ ■

TERRANOVA'S DEATH brought a sense of doom to Guiliano. He had known that the reign of the band was finished. That they could no longer counterattack successfully, that they could no longer hide in the mountains. But he had always thought that he and his chiefs would make an escape, that they would not go down to death. Now he knew there was very little time left. There was one thing he had always wanted to do, and so he summoned Corporal Canio Silvestro.

"Our time is over," he said to Silvestro. "You once told me you had friends in England who would protect you. Now is the time for you to go. You have my permission."

Corporal Silvestro shook his head. "I can always leave when you are safe in America. You need me still. You know I will never betray you."

"I know that," Guiliano said. "And you know the affection I have always had for you. But you were never truly a bandit. You were always a soldier and a policeman. Your heart was always a lawful one. And so you can make a life for yourself when all this is over. The rest of us will find it difficult. We will be bandits forever."

Silvestro said, "I never thought of you as a bandit."

"Nor did I," Guiliano said. "And yet what have I done these seven years? I thought I was fighting for justice. I tried to help the poor. I hoped to free Sicily. I wanted to be a good man. But it was the wrong time and the wrong way. For now we must do what we can to save our lives. And so you must go to England. It will make me happy to know that you are safe." Then he embraced Silvestro. "You have been my true friend," he said, "and those are my orders."

■ ■ ■

AT DUSK, Turi Guiliano left his cave and moved on to the Cappuccini monastery just outside Palermo where he would await word from Aspanu Pisciotta. One of the monks there was a secret member of his band, and he was in charge of the catacombs of the monastery. In these catacombs were hundreds of mummified bodies.

For hundreds of years before World War I it had been the custom of the rich and noble families to pin to the walls of the monastery the costumes in which they wished to be buried.

When they died, after their funerals, their bodies were delivered to the monastery. There the monks were masters of the art of preserving bodies. They exposed the corpses to slow heat for six months, then dried the soft parts of the bodies. In the drying process the skin shriveled, the features contorted into all the grimaces of death, some of horror, some of risibility, all terrible to the viewer. Then the bodies were dressed in the costumes that had been left for them and placed in glass coffins. These coffins were placed in niches in the wall or strung from the ceiling by glass wires. Some of the bodies were seated on chairs, some stood against the wall. Some were propped into glass boxes like costumed dolls.

Guiliano lay down on a dank stone of the catacombs and used a coffin as his pillow. He studied all these Sicilians dead for hundreds of years. There was a knight of the Royal Court in a blue silk ruffled uniform, a helmet on his head, a sword cane in his hand. A courtier, foppish in the French style, with white wig and high-heeled boots. There was a Cardinal in his red robes, an archbishop in his miter. There were court beauties whose golden gowns looked now like spider webs strangling the mummified shrunken bodies as if they were flies. There was a young maiden in white gloves and white frilly nightdress enclosed in a glass box.

Guiliano slept badly the two nights he spent there. As who would not? he thought. These were the great men and women of Sicily for the three or four last centuries, and they thought they could escape the worms in this fashion. The pride and vanity of the rich, the darlings of fate. Much better to die in the road like La Venera's husband.

But what really kept Guiliano awake was a nagging worry. How had Don Croce escaped the attack on his life earlier that week? Guiliano knew that the operation had been perfectly planned. He had brooded on how to do it ever since he had learned the truth about the massacre at the Portella della Ginestra. The Don was so well guarded that a chink had to be found in his defenses. Guiliano had decided his best chance was when the Don felt secure in the heavily guarded Hotel Umberto of Palermo. The band had a spy in the hotel, one of the waiters. He gave the Don's schedule, the deployment of the guards. With this intelligence Guiliano was sure his attack would succeed.

He had mustered thirty men to rendezvous with him in Palermo. He had known of Michael Corleone's visit and lunch with the Don, and so he waited until late afternoon when the report reached him that Michael had left. Then twenty of his men had mounted a frontal assault on the hotel to draw guards off from the garden. A few moments later he and his remaining ten men had planted an explosive charge against the garden wall and blown a hole in it. Guiliano led the charge through the hole. There were only five guards left in the garden; Guiliano shot one and the other four fled. Guiliano rushed into the Don's suite but it was empty. And it had struck him as strange that it was unguarded. Meanwhile the other detachment of his band had forced their way through the defense barrier and joined up with him. They had searched the rooms and corridors along the way and found nothing. The Don's huge bulk made it impossible for him to move quickly, so only one conclusion could be drawn. The Don had departed from the hotel shortly after Michael left. And now it occurred to Guiliano for the first time that Don Croce had been warned about the attack.

It was too bad, Guiliano thought. It would have been a glorious last stroke, besides removing his most dangerous enemy. What ballads would have been sung if he had found Don Croce in that sunlit garden. But there would be another day. He would not stay forever in America.

On the third morning, the Cappuccini monk, his body and face almost as shrunken as the mummies in his charge, brought a message from Pisciotta. It read, "In the house of Charlemagne." Guiliano understood it immediately. Zu Peppino, the master carter of Castelvetrano, who had helped Guiliano in the hijacking of Don Croce's trucks and had been a secret ally of his band ever since, had three carts and six donkeys. All three of his carts had been painted with the legends of the great Emperor, and as boys, Turi and Aspanu had called his home the house of Charlemagne. The time of the meeting had already been set.

That night, his final night in Sicily, Guiliano made his way to Castelvetrano. Outside of Palermo he picked up some shepherds who were secret members of his band and used them as an armed escort. They made their way to Castelvetrano with such ease that a suspicion flickered in Guiliano's mind. The town looked too open. He dismissed his bodyguards, who slipped away into the night. Then he made his way to a little stone house outside of Castelvetrano whose courtyard held three painted carts, now all bearing the legends from his own life. This was the house of Zu Peppino.

Zu Peppino did not seem surprised to see him. He put down the brush with which he had been painting the slat of one of his carts. The he locked the door and said to Guiliano, "We have trouble. You attract the *carabinieri* like a dead mule attracts flies."

Guiliano felt a little shock of adrenaline. "Are they Luca's Special Force?" he asked.

"Yes," Zu Peppino said. "They are tucked out of sight, not in the streets patrolling. I spotted some of their vehicles on the road when I came back from work. And some carters tell me they saw other vehicles. We thought they were setting up traps for members of your band, but we never suspected it might be you. You never get this far south, so far away from your mountains."

Guiliano wondered how the *carabinieri* could have known about the rendezvous. Had they trailed Aspanu? Were Michael Corleone and his people indiscreet? Or was there an informer? In any case, he could not meet Pisciotta in Castelvetrano. But they had a fallback meeting place if one of them did not show up at the rendezvous here.

"Thanks for the warning," Guiliano said. "Keep an eye out for Pisciotta in town and tell him. And when you take your cart to Montelepre, pay my mother a visit and tell her I am safely in America."

Zu Peppino said, "Allow an old man to embrace you." And he kissed Guiliano on the cheek. "I never believed you could help Sicily, nobody can, nobody ever could, not even Garibaldi, not even that windbag *Il Duce*. Now if you like I can put my mules to a cart and carry you wherever you want to go."

Guiliano's rendezvous time with Pisciotta had been for midnight. It was now only ten. He had deliberately come in early to scout the ground. And he knew that the rendezvous with Michael Corleone was for dawn. The fallback meeting place was at least a two-hour fast walk from Castelvetrano. But it was better to walk than use Zu Peppino. He thanked the old man and slipped out into the night.

The fallback meeting place was the famous ancient Greek ruins called the Acropolis of Selinus. South of Castelvetrano, near Mazara del Vallo, the ruins stood on a desolate plain near the sea, ending where the sea cliffs began to rise. Selinus had been buried by an earthquake before Christ was born, but a row of marble columns and architraves still stood. Or rather had been raised by excavators. There was still the main thoroughfare, though now reduced to rubble by the skeletons of ancient buildings lining its way. There was a temple with its roof matted with vines and showing holes like a skull and stone columns exhausted and gray with centuries of age. The acropolis itself, the fortified center of ancient Greek cities, was, as usual, built on the highest ground, and so these ruins looked down on the stark countryside below.

The sirocco, a terrible desert wind, had been blowing all day. Now, at night, so close to the sea, it sent fog rolling through the ruins. Guiliano, weary of his long forced march, detoured around to the sea cliffs so he could look down and spy out the land.

It was a sight so beautiful that he forgot for a moment the danger he was in. The temple of Apollo had fallen in on itself in a twisted mass of columns. Other ruined temples gleamed in the moonlight—without walls, just columns, strands of roof and one fortress wall with what had been a barred window high up, now blackly empty, the moon shining through it. Lower down in what had been the city proper, below the acropolis, one column stood alone, surrounded by flat ruins, that in its thousands of years had never fallen. This was the famous "Il Fuso di la Vecchia," the Old Woman's Spindle. Sicilians were so used to the monuments of the Greeks scattered over the island that they treated them with affectionate contempt. It was only foreigners who made a fuss.

And the foreigners had raised the twelve great columns that stood before him now. Their grandeur was Herculean, but behind them was only the panorama of ruins. At the foot of those twelve columns, abreast like soldiers fronting their commander full face, was a platform of stone steps that seemed to have grown out of the ground. Guiliano sat down on the top step, his back resting against one of the columns. He reached under his coat and unhooked the machine pistol and the *lupara* and put them one stone step below him. Fog swirled through the ruins, but he knew he would hear anyone who approached over the rubble and that he could easily see any enemies before they could see him.

He leaned back against one of the columns, glad to be resting, his body sagging with fatigue. The July moon seemed to pass over the gray-white columns and rest against the cliffs that led to the sea. And across the sea was America. And in America was Justina and their child to be born. Soon he would be safe and the last seven years of his banditry would be a dream. For a moment he wondered what kind of a life that would be, if he could ever be happy not living in Sicily. He smiled. One day he would come back and surprise them all. He sighed with fatigue and unlaced his boots and slipped his feet out of them. He took off his socks and his feet welcomed the touch of cold stone. He reached into his pocket and took out the two prickly pears and their sweet night-cooled juice refreshed him. With one hand on the machine pistol resting beside him, he waited for Aspanu Pisciotta.

27

MICHAEL, PETER CLEMENZA and Don Domenic had an early supper together. If they were to make the dawn meeting hour, the operation to collect Guiliano would have to start at dusk. They went over the plan again and Domenic approved. He added one detail: Michael was not to be armed. If something went wrong and the *carabinieri* or Security Police arrested them, no charges could be brought against Michael, and he could leave Sicily no matter what happened.

They had a jug of wine and lemons in the garden and then it was time to go. Don Domenic kissed his brother goodbye. He turned to Michael and gave him a quick embrace. "My best wishes to your father," he said. "I pray for your future, I wish you well. And in the years to come, if you ever have need for my services, send me word."

The three of them walked down to the dock. Michael and Peter Clemenza boarded the motor launch which was already full of armed men. The boat pulled away, Don Domenic waving farewell from the dock. Michael and Peter Clemenza went down into the cabin where Clemenza went to sleep in one of the bunks. He had had a busy day and they would be at sea until nearly dawn the following morning.

They had changed their plans. The plane at Mazara del Vallo in which they had planned to fly to Africa would be used as a decoy; instead the escape to Africa would be by boat. Clemenza had argued for this, saying that he could control the road and guard the boat with his men, but he could not control the small airfield. There was too much ground area in the approaches and the plane was too fragile; it could become a deathtrap while still on the ground. Speed was not as important as deception, and the sea was easier to hide in than the sky. Also provisions could be made for transferring to another boat; you couldn't change planes.

Clemenza had been busy during the day dispatching some men and cars to an assembly point on the road to Castelvetrano; others to secure the town of Mazara del Vallo. He had sent them at intervals of an hour; he did not want spies observing the unusual movement of a convoy going through the villa gates. The cars went off in different directions to further confuse any observers. Meanwhile the motor launch was making its way around the southwestern point of Sicily to lie out over the horizon until the dawn started to break, when it would zoom into the port of Mazara del Vallo. Cars and men would be waiting for them. From there it would not be more than a half-hour drive to Castelvetrano despite the swing they would have to take north to meet the Trapani road that led to where Pisciotta would intercept them.

Michael lay down on one of the bunks. He could hear Clemenza snoring and was filled with amazed admiration that the man could actually sleep at such a time. Michael thought that in twenty-four hours he would be in Tunis and twelve hours after that he would be home with his family. After two years of exile he would have all the options of a free man, no longer on the run from the police, not subject to the rule of his protectors. He could do exactly what he wanted to do. But only if he got through the next thirty-six hours. As he fantasized about what he would do his first days in America, the gentle roll of the boat relaxed him and he fell into a dreamless sleep.

■ ■ ■

FRA DIAVALO was sleeping a far deeper sleep.

Stefan Andolini, on the morning of the day he was to pick up Professor Hector Adonis in Trapani, drove first to Palermo. He had an appointment with the Chief of the Sicilian Security Police, Inspector Velardi, one of their frequent meetings in which the Inspector briefed Andolini on Colonel Luca's operational plans for the day. Andolini would then transmit this information to Pisciotta who would carry it to Guiliano.

It was a beautiful morning; the fields alongside the road were carpeted with flowers. He was early for his appointment so he stopped by one of the roadside shrines for a cigarette and then knelt in front of the padlocked box that held the statue of Saint Rosalie. His prayer was simple and practical, a plea to the Saint to protect him from his enemies. On the coming Sunday he would confess his sins to Father Benjamino and take Communion. Now the radiant sun warmed his bare head; the flower-perfumed air was so heavy it washed his nostrils and palate clean of nicotine and he was enormously hungry. He promised himself a good breakfast in Palermo's finest restaurant after his meeting with Inspector Velardi.

■ ■ ■

INSPECTOR FREDERICO Velardi, head of the Security Police of Sicily, felt the virtuous triumph of a man who has waited patiently, believing always in a God who would finally bring order into his universe, and finally received his reward. For nearly a year, under the direct and secret orders of Minister Trezza, he had helped Guiliano escape the *carabinieri* and his own flying squads. He had met with the murderous Stefan Andolini, *Fra Diavalo*. For that year Inspector Velardi had, in effect, been a subordinate of Don Croce Malo.

Velardi was from the north of Italy, where people made something of themselves through education, a respect for the social contract, a belief in law and government. Velardi's service years in Sicily had instilled in him contempt and deep hatred for the

Sicilian people, high and low. The rich had no social conscience and kept down the poor by their criminal conspiracy with the Mafia. The Mafia, which pretended to protect the poor, hired themselves out to the rich to keep down those poor. The peasants were too proud, had such egos that they gloried in murder though they might spend the rest of their lives in prison.

But now things would be different. Inspector Velardi's hands had finally been untied and his flying squads could be unleashed. And people would see again the difference between his own Security Police and the clownish *carabinieri*.

To Velardi's astonishment Minister Trezza himself had given the order that all those people who had been given the red-bordered passes signed by the Minister, those all-powerful passes that enabled the users to pass through roadblocks, to carry arms, to be immune to routine arrests, were to be detained in solitary confinement. Those passes had to be gathered up. Especially those issued to Aspanu Pisciotta and Stefan Andolini.

Velardi prepared to go to work. Andolini was waiting in his anteroom for his briefing. He would get a surprise today. Velardi picked up the phone and summoned a captain and four police sergeants. He told them to be prepared for trouble. He himself was wearing a pistol in a belt holster, something he usually did not do in his office. Then he had Stefan Andolini brought in from the anteroom.

Stefan Andolini's red hair was neatly combed. He wore a black pin-striped suit, white shirt and dark tie. After all, a visit to the Chief of the Security Police was a formal occasion in which to show respect. He was not armed. He knew from experience that everyone was always searched when they entered the headquarters. He stood in front of Velardi's desk waiting for the usual permission to sit down. It was not given, so he remained standing and the first warning signal went off in his head.

"Let me see your special pass," Inspector Velardi said to him.

Andolini did not move. He was trying to fathom this strange

371

request. On principle he lied. "I don't have it with me," he said. "After all I was visiting a Friend." He put a special emphasis on the word "Friend."

This enraged Velardi. He moved around the desk and stood face to face with Andolini. "You were never a friend of mine. I obeyed orders when breaking bread with a swine like you. Now listen to me carefully. You are under arrest. You will be confined in my cells until further notice, and I must tell you that I have a *cassetta* down in the dungeons. But we'll have a quiet little talk here in my office tomorrow morning and spare you some pain, if you're clever."

The next morning Velardi received another phone call from Minister Trezza and a more explicit one from Don Croce. A few moments later Andolini was escorted from his cell to Velardi's office.

The night's solitude in his cell, thinking about his strange arrest, had convinced Andolini he was in mortal danger. When he entered, Velardi was striding up and down the room, his blue eyes flashing, obviously in a temper. Stefan Andolini was cold as ice. He observed everything—the Captain and four police sergeants at the alert, the pistol at Velardi's hip. He knew that the Inspector had always hated him, and he hated the Inspector no less. If he could talk Velardi into getting rid of the guards, he might at least kill him before he was killed himself. So he said, "I'll talk, but not with these other *sbirri* here." *Sbirri* was the vulgar and insulting idiom for the Security Police.

Velardi ordered the four policemen out of the room but gave the officer a signal to stay. He also gave him a signal to be ready to draw his gun. Then he turned his full attention to Stefan Andolini.

"I want any information on how I can put my hands on Guiliano," he said. "The last time you met with him and Pisciotta."

Stefan Andolini laughed, his murderous face twisted in a malevolent grimace. The skin grained with red beard seemed to blaze with violence.

No wonder they called him *Fra Diavalo,* Velardi thought. He was truly a dangerous man. He must have no inkling of what was coming.

Velardi said to him calmly, "Answer my question or I'll have you stretched out on the *cassetta.*"

Andolini said with contempt, "You traitorous bastard, I'm under the protection of Minister Trezza and Don Croce. When they have me released, I'll cut your *sbirri* heart out."

Velardi reached over and slapped Andolini's face twice, once with his palm and then backhand. He saw the blood well up on Andolini's mouth and the rage in his eyes. He deliberately turned his back to sit at his desk.

At that moment, anger blinding his instinct for survival, Stefan Andolini grabbed the pistol out of the Inspector's belt holster and tried to fire. In that same instant the police officer drew his own gun and fired four shots into Andolini's body. Andolini was hurled against the far wall and then lay on the floor. The white shirt was stained completely red and, Velardi thought, it matched his hair quite nicely. He reached down and took the pistol from Andolini's hand as other policemen rushed into the room. He complimented the Captain on his alertness, and then in full view of the officer he loaded his pistol with the bullets he had emptied out of it before the meeting. He did not want his Captain to get delusions of grandeur, that he had actually saved the life of a careless head of the Security Police.

Then he ordered his men to search the dead body. As he suspected the red-bordered security pass was in the sheaf of identification papers every Sicilian was required to carry. Velardi took the pass and put in into his safe. He would hand it over to Minister Trezza personally, and, with luck he would have Pisciotta's pass to go along with it.

■ ■ ■

ON DECK one of the men brought Michael and Clemenza small cups of hot espresso which they drank leaning against the rail.

The launch was slowly heading in to land, motor quiet, and they could see the lights on the dock, faint blue pinpoints.

Clemenza was walking around the deck, giving orders to the armed men and the pilot. Michael studied the blue lights which seemed to be running toward him. The boat was picking up speed, and it was as if that churning of the water swept away the darkness of the night. A chink of dawn opened in the sky, and Michael could see the dock and beaches of Mazara del Vallo; the colored umbrellas of café tables were a dusky rose beyond them.

When they docked there were three cars and six men waiting. Clemenza led Michael to the lead vehicle, an open and ancient touring car which held only a driver. Clemenza got into the front seat and Michael got into the back. Clemenza said to Michael, "If we get stopped by a *carabinieri* patrol, you duck down to the floor. We can't fool around here on the road, we just gotta blow them away and make our run."

The three wide-bodied touring cars were moving in the pale, early sunlight through a countryside almost unchanged since the birth of Christ. Ancient aqueducts and pipes spouted water over the fields. It was already warm and humid, and the air was filled with the smell of flowers beginning to rot in the heat of the Sicilian summer. They were passing through the Selinunte, the ruins of the ancient Greek city, and Michael could see from time to time the crumbling columns of marble temples scattered over Western Sicily by the Greek colonists more than two thousand years ago. These columns loomed eerily in the yellow light, their fragments of roof dripping blackly like rain against the blue sky. The rich black earth foamed up against walls of granite cliffs. There was not a house, not an animal, not a man to be seen. It was a landscape created by the slash of a giant sword.

Then they swung north to hit the Trapani–Castelvetrano road. And now Michael and Clemenza were more alert; it was along this road that Pisciotta would intercept them and bring them to Guiliano. Michael felt an intense excitement. The three touring cars went more slowly now. Clemenza had a machine pistol lying on the seat on his left side so he could bring it up quickly over the car door. His hands were positioned on it. The sun had climbed into its rightful dominance, and its rays were a hot gold. The cars kept slowly on; they were almost upon the town of Castelvetrano.

Clemenza ordered the driver to go even more slowly. He and Michael watched for any sign of Pisciotta. They were now on the outskirts of Castelvetrano, ascending a hilly road, and stopping so that they could look down the main street of the town lying below them. From their high vantage point Michael could see the road from Palermo clogged with vehicles—military vehicles; the streets were swarming with *carabinieri* in their black uniforms with white piping. There was the wail of many sirens that did not seem to scatter the crowds of people in the main street. Overhead two small planes were circling.

The driver cursed and stepped on the brake as he pulled the car to the side of the road. He turned to Clemenza and said, "Do you want me to go on?"

Michael felt a queasiness at the pit of his stomach. He said to Clemenza, "How many men do you have waiting for us in town?"

"Not enough," Clemenza said sourly. His face had an almost frightened look. "Mike, we have to get out of here. We have to get back to the boat."

"Wait," Michael said, now seeing the cart and donkey toiling slowly up the hill toward them. The driver was an old man with a straw hat pulled down tight around his head. The cart was painted with legends on the wheels, the shafts, and the sides. It halted alongside of them. The driver's face was wrinkled and showed no expression, and his arms, incongruously muscled, were bare to his shoulders, for he wore only a black vest over his wide canvas trousers. He came abreast of their car and said, "Don Clemenza, is that you?"

There was relief in Clemenza's voice. "Zu Peppino, what the

hell is going on there? Why didn't my men come out and warn
me?''

Zu Peppino's stony wrinkled face did not change expression.
"You can go back to America," he said. "They have massacred
Turi Guiliano."

■ ■ ■

MICHAEL FOUND himself strangely dizzy. Suddenly at that moment the light seemed to fall out of the sky. He thought of the
old mother and father, of Justina waiting in America, of Aspanu
Pisciotta and Stefan Andolini. Of Hector Adonis. For Turi Guiliano had been the starlight of their lives, and it was not possible
his light no longer existed.

"Are you sure it's him?" Clemenza asked harshly.

The old man shrugged. "It was one of Guiliano's old tricks,
to leave a corpse or dummy to entice the *carabinieri* so that he
could kill them. But it's been two hours now and nothing has
happened. The body is still lying in the courtyard where they
killed him. There are already newspapermen from Palermo here
with their cameras taking pictures of everybody, even my donkey. So believe what you like."

Michael was feeling ill but he managed to say, "We'll have to
go in and look. I have to make sure."

Clemenza said roughly, "Alive or dead, we can't help him
anymore. I'm taking you home, Mike."

"No," Michael said softly. "We have to go in. Maybe Pisciotta is waiting for us. Or Stefan Andolini. To tell us what to
do. Maybe it's not him, I can't believe it's him. He couldn't die,
not when he was this close to getting away. Not when his Testament is safe in America."

Clemenza sighed. He saw the look of suffering on Michael's
face. Perhaps it wasn't Guiliano; perhaps Pisciotta was waiting
to make a rendezvous. Perhaps even this was part of the plot to
distract attention from his escape if the authorities were close
on his heels.

Now the sun had fully risen. Clemenza ordered his men to park their cars and to follow him. Then he and Michael walked down the rest of the street which was crowded with people. They were gathered around the entrance to a side street that was filled with army cars and blocked by a cordon of *carabinieri*. On this side street was a row of separate houses split apart by court-yards. Clemenza and Michael stood at the rear of the crowd watching with the others. The *carabinieri* officer was admitting journalists and officials past the cordon of guards after examin-ing their credentials. Michael said to Clemenza, "Can you get us past that officer?"

Clemenza took Michael by the arm and led him out of the crowd.

In an hour they were in one of the small houses on a side street. This house too had a small courtyard and was only about twenty houses from where the crowd had gathered. Clemenza left Michael there with four men, and then he and two others went back into the town. They were gone for an hour and when Clemenza came back he was obviously badly shaken.

"It looks bad, Mike," he said. "They're bringing Guiliano's mother from Montelepre to identify the body. Colonel Luca is here, the Commander of the Special Force. And newspapermen from all over the world are flying in, even from the States. This town is going to be a madhouse. We gotta get outta here."

"Tomorrow," Michael said. "We'll run tomorrow. Now let's see if we can get past those guards. Did you do anything about that?"

"Not yet," Clemenza said.

"Well let's go out and see what we can do," Michael said.

Against Clemenza's protest, they went out into the street. The whole town seemed to be covered with *carabinieri*. There must be at least a thousand of them, Michael thought. And there were literally hundreds of photographers. The street was clogged with vans and automobiles and there was no way of getting near the courtyard. They saw a group of high-ranking officers going into

a restaurant, and the whisper went around that this was Colonel
Luca and his staff having a celebration lunch. Michael caught a
glimpse of the Colonel. He was a small wiry man with a sad
face, and because of the heat he had taken off his braided cap
and was wiping his partially bald head with a white handkerchief. A crowd of photographers was taking his picture and a
mob of journalists was asking him questions. He waved them
aside without answering and disappeared into the restaurant.

The town streets were so dense with people that Michael and
Clemenza could hardly move. Clemenza decided they should go
back to the house and wait for information. Late that afternoon
word was brought by one of his men that Maria Lombardo had
identified the body as that of her son.

They ate dinner in an open-air café. It had a blaring radio
giving news reports of Guiliano's death. The story was that the
police had surrounded a house in which they believed Guiliano
to be hiding. When he came out he was ordered to surrender.
He had immediately opened fire. Captain Perenze, Colonel Luca's chief of staff, was giving interviews on the radio to a panel
of journalists. He told how Guiliano had started to run and he,
Captain Perenze, had followed him and cornered him in the
courtyard. Guiliano had turned like a lion at bay, Captain Perenze said, and he, Perenze, had returned his fire and killed him.
Everybody in the restaurant was listening to the radio. Nobody
was eating. The waiters made no pretense of serving; they also
listened. Clemenza turned to Michael and said, "The whole
thing is fishy. We leave tonight."

But at that moment the street around the café filled with Security Police. An official car pulled up to the curb and out of it
stepped Inspector Velardi. He came up to their table and placed
his hand on Michael's shoulder. "You are under arrest," he
said. He fastened his icy blue eyes on Clemenza. "And for good
luck we'll take you with him. A word of advice. I have a hundred
men around this café. Don't make a fuss or you'll join Guiliano
in hell."

A police van had pulled up to the curb. Michael and Clemenza were swarmed over by Security Police, searched and then pushed roughly into the van. Some newspaper photographers eating in the café had jumped up with their cameras and were immediately clubbed back by the Security Police. Inspector Velardi watched all this with a grim satisfied smile.

■ ■ ■

THE NEXT day the father of Turi Guiliano spoke from the balcony of his home in Montelepre to the people in the street below. In the old tradition of Sicily, he declared a vendetta against the betrayers of his son. Specifically he declared a vendetta against the man who had killed his son. That man, he said, was not Captain Perenze, not a *carabiniere*. The man he named was Aspanu Pisciotta.

CHAPTER

28

ASPANU PISCIOTTA had felt the black worm of treachery growing in his heart for the past year.

Pisciotta had always been loyal. Since childhood he had accepted Guiliano's leadership without jealousy. And Guiliano had always proclaimed that Pisciotta was co-leader of the band, not one of the subchiefs like Passatempo, Terranova, Andolini and the Corporal. But Guiliano's personality was so overwhelming that the co-leadership became a myth; Guiliano commanded. Pisciotta accepted this without reservation.

Guiliano was braver than all the others. His tactics in guerrilla warfare were unmatched, his ability to inspire love in the people of Sicily unequaled since Garibaldi. He was idealistic and romantic, and he had the feral cunning so admired by Sicilians. But he had flaws that Pisciotta saw and tried to correct.

When Guiliano insisted on giving at least fifty percent of the band's loot to the poor, Pisciotta told him, "You can be rich or you can be loved. You think the people of Sicily will rise and follow your banner in a war against Rome. They never will. They will love you when they take your money, they will hide you when you need sanctuary, they will never betray you. But they don't have a revolution in them."

Pisciotta had opposed listening to the blandishments of Don Croce and the Christian Democratic party. He had opposed crushing the Communist and Socialist organizations in Sicily.

When Guiliano hoped for a pardon from the Christian Democrats, Pisciotta said, "They will never pardon you, and Don
Croce can never permit you to have any power. Our destiny is
to buy our way out of our banditry with money, or someday to
die as bandits. It's not a bad way to die, not for me anyway."
But Guiliano had not listened to him, and this finally aroused
Pisciotta's resentment and started the growth of that hidden
worm of treachery.

Guiliano had always been a believer, an innocent; Pisciotta
had always seen clearly. With the advent of Colonel Luca and
his Special Force, Pisciotta knew the end had come. They could
win a hundred victories, but a solitary defeat would mean their
death. As Roland and Oliver had quarreled in the legend
of Charlemagne, so Guiliano and Pisciotta had quarreled
and Guiliano had been too stubborn in his heroism. Pisciotta
had felt like Oliver, repeatedly begging Roland to blow his
horn.

Then when Guiliano fell in love with Justina and married her,
Pisciotta realized his and Guiliano's destinies were indeed separate. Guiliano would escape to America, have a wife and children. He, Pisciotta, would be a fugitive forever. He would never
have a long life; a bullet or his lung disease would finish him off.
That was his destiny. He could never live in America.

What worried Pisciotta most was that Guiliano, who had
found love and tenderness in a young girl, had become more
ferocious as a bandit. He killed *carabinieri* where previously he
had captured them. He had executed Passatempo while on his
honeymoon. He showed no mercy to anyone he suspected of
informing. Pisciotta was in terror that the man he had loved and
defended all these years might turn on him. He worried that if
Guiliano learned of some of the things he had recently done, he,
too, might be executed.

■ ■ ■

Don Croce had studied the relationship between Guiliano and
Pisciotta closely for the last three years. They were the sole

danger to his plans of empire. They were the only obstacles to his rule of Sicily. At first he had thought he could make Guiliano and his band the armed forces of the Friends of the Friends. He had sent Hector Adonis to sound Guiliano out. The proposition was clear. Turi Guiliano would be the great warrior, Don Croce the great statesman. But Guiliano would have to bend his knee, and this he refused to do. He had his own star to follow, to help the poor, to make Sicily a free country, to lift the yoke of Rome. This Don Croce could not comprehend.

But from 1943 to 1947, Guiliano's star was in ascendency. The Don still had to forge the Friends into one unified force. The Friends had not recovered from the terrible decimation of their ranks by Mussolini's Fascist government. So the Don gentled Guiliano's power by enticing him into an alliance with the Christian Democratic party. Meanwhile he built the Mafia empire anew and bided his time. His first stroke, the engineering of the massacre at the Portella della Ginestra, with the blame falling on Guiliano, had been a masterpiece, but he could not claim the credit his due. That stroke destroyed any chance that the government in Rome might pardon Guiliano and support his bid for power in Sicily. It also stained forever the hero's mantle Guiliano wore as the champion of the poor in Sicily. And when Guiliano executed the six Mafia chiefs the Don had no choice. The Friends of the Friends and Guiliano's band had to fight each other to the death.

So Don Croce had focused more intently on Pisciotta. Pisciotta was clever, but as young men are clever—that is, he did not give full weight to the hidden terror and evil in the hearts of the best of men. And Pisciotta too had a taste for the fruits and temptations of the world. Where Guiliano disdained money, Pisciotta loved the rewards money brought. Guiliano did not have a penny for his personal fortune though he had earned over a billion lire with his crimes. He distributed his share of the spoils to the poor and to help support his family.

But Don Croce had observed that Pisciotta wore the finest

tailored suits in Palermo and visited the most expensive prostitutes. Also that Pisciotta's family lived much better than Guiliano's. And Don Croce learned that Pisciotta had money stored in Palermo's banks under false names, and had taken other precautions that only a man interested in staying alive would make. Like false identity papers in three different names, a safe house prepared in Trapani. And Don Croce knew that all this was a secret held from Guiliano. So he awaited Pisciotta's visit, a visit requested by Pisciotta, who had known the Don's house was always open to him, with interest and pleasure. And also with prudence and foresight. He was surrounded by armed guards, and he had alerted Colonel Luca and Inspector Velardi to be ready for a conference if all went well. If it did not, if he had misjudged Pisciotta or if this was a triple-dyed treachery cooked up by Guiliano to have the Don killed, then it would be the grave for Aspanu Pisciotta.

■ ■ ■

PISCIOTTA ALLOWED himself to be disarmed before he was led into the presence of Don Croce. He had no fear, for he had just a few days before done the Don an enormous service; he had warned him of Guiliano's plan to attack the hotel.

The two men were alone. Don Croce's servants had prepared a table of food and wine, and Don Croce, an old-fashioned rustic host, filled Pisciotta's plate and glass.

"The good times are over," Don Croce said. "Now we must be very serious, you and I. The time has come to make the decision that will decide our lives. I hope you are ready to listen to what I have to say."

"I don't know what your trouble is," Pisciotta said to the Don. "But I know that I have to be very clever to save my skin."

"You don't wish to emigrate?" the Don asked. "You could go to America with Guiliano. The wine isn't as good and the olive oil is water and they have the electric chair, after all they are not as civilized as our government here. You couldn't do anything rash. But it's not a bad life there.''

Pisciotta laughed. "What would I do in America? I'll take my chances here. Once Guiliano is gone, they won't look so hard for me, and the mountains are deep.''

The Don said solicitously, "You still have troubles with your lungs? You still get your medicine?''

"Yes,'' Pisciotta said. "That isn't a problem. The chances are that my lungs will never get the chance to kill me.'' He grinned at Don Croce.

"Let's talk Sicilian together,'' the Don said gravely. "When we are children, when we are young, it is natural to love our friends, to be generous to them, to forgive their faults. Each day is fresh, we look forward to the future with pleasure and without fear. The world itself is not so dangerous; it is a happy time. But as we grow old and have to earn our bread, friendship does not endure so easily. We must always be on our guard. Our elders no longer look after us, we are no longer content with those simple pleasures of children. Pride grows in us—we wish to become great or powerful or rich, or simply to guard ourself against misfortune. I know how much you love Turi Guiliano, but now you must ask yourself, what is the price of this love? And after all these years does it still exist or is it just the memory that exists?'' He waited for Pisciotta to make an answer, but Pisciotta looked at him with a face stonier than the rocks on the Cammarata Mountains and as white. For Pisciotta's face had gone very pale.

Don Croce went on. "I cannot permit Guiliano to live or escape. If you remain faithful to him then you too are my enemy. Know this. With Guiliano gone, you cannot remain alive in Sicily without my protection.''

Pisciotta said, "Turi's Testament is safe with his friends in America. If you kill him that Testament will become public and the government will fall. A new government may force you to retire to your farm here in Villaba or even worse.''

The Don chuckled. Then roared with laughter. He said with contempt, "Have you read this famous Testament?"

"Yes," Pisciotta said, bewildered by the Don's reaction.

"I have not," the Don said. "But I have decided to act as if it does not exist."

Pisciotta said, "You ask me to betray Guiliano. What makes you think that is possible?"

Don Croce smiled. "You warned me about his attack on my hotel. That was an act of friendship?"

"I did that for Guiliano, not for you," Pisciotta said. "Turi is no longer rational. He plans to kill you. Once you are dead, then I know there is no longer hope for any of us. The Friends of the Friends will never rest until we are dead, Testament or no Testament. He could have been out of the country days ago but he lingers, hoping to get his revenge and your life. I came to this meeting to make an arrangement with you. Guiliano will leave this country within the next few days, he will end his vendetta with you. Let him go."

Don Croce leaned back from his plate of food on the table. He sipped his glass of wine. "You're being childish," he said. "We have come to the end of the history. Guiliano is too dangerous to remain alive. But I cannot kill him. I must live in Sicily—I cannot kill its greatest hero and do the things I must do. Too many people love Guiliano, too many of his followers will seek revenge for his death. It must be the *carabinieri* to do the job. That is how it must be arranged. And you are the only one who can lead Guiliano into such a trap." He paused for a moment and then said deliberately, "The end of your world has come. You can stay with it through its destruction or you can step out of that world and live in another."

Pisciotta said, "I could be under the protection of Christ, but I wouldn't live long if it was known that I betrayed Guiliano."

"You have only to tell me where you are meeting him again," Don Croce said. "No one else will know. I will arrange things with Colonel Luca and Inspector Velardi. They will take care of the rest." He paused a moment. "Guiliano has changed. He is no longer your childhood companion, no longer your best friend. He is a man who is looking after himself. As now you must do."

■ ■ ■

AND SO on the evening of July 5, as Pisciotta made his way to Castelvetrano, he had committed himself to Don Croce. He had told him where he would meet Guiliano, and he knew that the Don would tell Colonel Luca and Inspector Velardi. He had not told them that it would be at Zu Peppino's house, but only that it would be in the town of Castelvetrano itself. And he had warned them to be careful, that Guiliano had a sixth sense about traps.

But when Pisciotta arrived at Zu Peppino's house the old carter greeted him with an uncharacteristic coldness. Pisciotta wondered if the old man suspected him. He must have noticed the unusual activity of the *carabinieri* in the town and with that unerring Sicilian paranoia, put two and two together.

For a moment Pisciotta felt a thrilling pain of anguish. And then another agonizing thought. What if Guiliano's mother learned that it had been her beloved Aspanu who betrayed her son? What if one day she stood before him and spit in his face and called him traitor and murderer? They had wept in each other's arms and he had sworn to protect her son and he had given her a Judas kiss. For a moment he thought of killing the old man and thought too of killing himself.

Zu Peppino said, "If you're looking for Turi, he's been and gone." He took pity on Pisciotta; the man's face was white, he seemed to be gasping for air. "Do you want an anisette?"

Pisciotta shook his head and turned to leave. The old man said, "Be careful, the town is full of *carabinieri*."

Pisciotta felt a flash of terror. He had been a fool not to know that Guiliano would smell out the trap. And what if now Guiliano smelled out the betrayer?

Pisciotta ran out of the house, circled the town and then took the field paths that would lead him to the fallback meeting place, the Acropolis of Selinus in the ancient ghost town of Selinunte.

■ ■ ■

THE RUINS of the ancient Greek city glistened in the summer moonlight. Amidst them, Guiliano sat on the crumbling stone steps of the temple dreaming of America.

He felt an overwhelming melancholy. The old dreams had vanished. He had been so full of hope for his future and the future of Sicily; he had believed so fully in his immortality. So many people had loved him. Once he had been their blessing, and now, it seemed to Guiliano, he was their curse. Against all reason he felt deserted. But he still had Aspanu Pisciotta. And there would come a day when the two of them together would bring all those old loves and old dreams alive again. After all, it had been only the two of them in the beginning.

The moon disappeared and the ancient city vanished into darkness; now the ruins looked like skeletons sketched on the black canvas of night. Out of that blackness came the hiss of shifting small stones and earth, and Guiliano rolled his body back between the marble columns, his machine pistol ready. The moon sailed serenely out of the clouds, and he saw Aspanu Pisciotta standing in the wide ruined avenue that led down from the acropolis.

Pisciotta walked slowly down the rubbled path, his eyes searching, his voice whispering Turi's name. Guiliano, hidden behind the temple columns, waited until Pisciotta went past, then stepped out behind him. "Aspanu, I've won again," he said, playing their old childish game. He was surprised when Pisciotta whirled around in terror.

Guiliano sat down on the steps and put his gun aside. "Come and sit awhile," he said. "You must be tired, and this may be the last chance we can talk to each other alone."

Pisciotta said, "We can talk in Mazara del Vallo, we will be safer there."

Guiliano said to him, "We have plenty of time and you'll be

spitting blood again if you don't take a rest. Come on now, sit beside me." And Guiliano sat on the top stone step.

He saw Pisciotta unsling his gun and thought it was to lay it aside. He stood and reached out his hand to help Aspanu up the steps. And then he realized that his friend was leveling the gun at him. He froze, for the first time in seven years caught unaware.

Pisciotta's mind crumbled with all the terrors of what Guiliano would ask if they spoke. He would ask, "Aspanu, who is the Judas of our band? Aspanu, who warned Don Croce? Aspanu, who led the *carabinieri* to Castelvetrano? Aspanu, why did you meet with Don Croce?" And most of all, he was afraid that Guiliano would say, "Aspanu, you are my brother." It was that final terror that made Pisciotta pull the trigger.

The stream of bullets blew away Guiliano's hand and shattered his body. Pisciotta, horrified at his own action, waited for him to fall. Instead Guiliano came slowly down the steps, blood pouring from his wounds. Filled with superstitious dread, Pisciotta turned and fled, and he could see Guiliano running after him and then he saw Guiliano fall.

But Guiliano, dying, thought he was still running. The shattered neurons of his brain tangled and he thought he was running through the mountains with Aspanu seven years before, the fresh water flowing out of the ancient Roman cisterns, the smell of strange flowers intoxicating, running past the holy saints in their padlocked shrines, and he cried out, as on that night, "Aspanu, I believe," believing in his happy destiny, in the true love of his friend. Then the kindness of death delivered him of the knowledge of his betrayal and his final defeat. He died in his dream.

■ ■ ■

ASPANU PISCIOTTA fled. He ran through the fields and onto the road to Castelvetrano. There he used his special pass to contact Colonel Luca and Inspector Velardi. It was they who released the story that Guiliano had fallen into a trap and been killed by Captain Perenze.

■ ■ ■

MARIA LOMBARDO GUILIANO was up early that morning of July 5, 1950. She had been awakened by a knock on the door; her husband had gone down to answer it. He had returned to the bedroom and told her he had to go out and might be gone for the whole day. She had looked through the window and seen him get into Zu Peppino's donkey cart with its brightly painted legends on the panels and wheels. Had they news of Turi, had he made his escape to America or had something gone wrong? She felt the familiar anxiety building to terror that she had felt for the last seven years. It made her restless, and after she had cleaned the house and prepared vegetables for the day's meals, she opened the door and looked out into the street.

The Via Bella was swept clean of all her neighbors. There were no children playing. Many of the men were in prison on suspicion of being conspirators with the Guiliano band. The women were too frightened to let their children out into the street. Squads of *carabinieri* were at each end of the Via Bella. Soldiers with rifles slung over their shoulders patrolled up and down on foot. She saw other soldiers up on the roofs. Military jeeps were parked up against buildings. An armored car blocked the mouth of the Via Bella near the Bellampo Barracks. There were two thousand men of Colonel Luca's army occupying the town of Montelepre, and they had made the townspeople their enemies by molesting the women, frightening the children, physically abusing the men not thrown into prison. And all these soldiers were here to kill her son. But he had flown to America, he would be free, and when the time was ripe, she and her husband would join him there. They would live in freedom, without fear.

She went back into the house and found herself work to do. She went to the rear balcony and looked at the mountains.

Those mountains from which Guiliano had observed this house with his binoculars. She had always felt his presence; she did not feel it now. He was surely in America.

A loud pounding on the door froze her with terror. Slowly she went to open it. The first thing she saw was Hector Adonis, and he looked as she had never seen him look before. He was unshaven, his hair unruly, he wore no cravat. The shirt beneath his jacket was rumpled and the collar was smudged with dirt. But what she noticed most was that all dignity was gone from his face. It was crumpled with hopeless grief. His eyes were brimming with tears as he looked at her. She let out a muffled scream.

He came into the house and said, "Don't, Maria, I beg of you." A very young lieutenant of the *carabinieri* came in with him. Maria Lombardo looked past them into the street. There were three black cars parked in front of her house with *carabinieri* drivers. There was a cluster of armed men on each side of the door.

The Lieutenant was young and rosy cheeked. He took off his cap and put it under his arm. "You are Maria Lombardo Guiliano?" he asked formally. His accent was that of the north, of Tuscany.

Maria Lombardo said yes. Her voice was a croak of despair. There was no saliva in her mouth.

"I must ask you to accompany me to Castelvetrano," the officer said. "I have a car waiting. Your friend here will accompany us. If you approve, of course."

Maria Lombardo's eyes were open wide. She said in a firmer voice. "For what reason? I know nothing of Castelvetrano or anyone there."

The Lieutenant's voice was softer, hesitant. "There is a man there we wish you to identify. We believe he is your son."

"It is not my son, he never goes to Castelvetrano," Maria Lombardo said. "Is he dead?"

"Yes," the officer said.

Maria Lombardo let out a long wail and sank down to her knees. "My son never goes to Castelvetrano," she said. Hector Adonis came over to her and put his hand on her shoulder.

"You must go," he said. "Perhaps it is one of his tricks, he has done this before."

"No," she said. "I won't go. I won't go."

The Lieutenant said, "Is your husband at home? We can take him instead."

Maria Lombardo remembered Zu Peppino calling for her husband early that morning. She remembered the sense of foreboding when she had seen that painted donkey cart. "Wait," she said. She went into her bedroom and changed into a black dress and put a black shawl over her head. The Lieutenant opened the door for her. She went out into the street. There were armed soldiers everywhere. She looked down the Via Bella, to where it ended in the square. In the shimmering July sunlight she had a clear vision of Turi and Aspanu leading their donkey to be mated seven long years ago, on the day he was to become a murderer and an outlaw. She began to weep and the Lieutenant took her arm and helped her into one of the black cars that was waiting. Hector Adonis got in beside her. The car moved off through the silent groups of *carabinieri*, and she buried her face in the shoulder of Hector Adonis, not weeping now but in mortal terror of what she would see at the end of her journey.

■ ■ ■

THE BODY of Turi Guiliano lay in the courtyard for three hours. He seemed to be sleeping, his face down and turned to the left, one leg bent at the knee, his body sprawled. But the white shirt was almost scarlet. Near the mutilated arm was a machine pistol. Newspaper photographers and reporters from Palermo and Rome were already on the scene. A photographer for *Life* magazine was snapping pictures of Captain Perenze and the picture would appear with the caption that he was the slayer of the great Guiliano. Captain Perenze's face in the picture was good-natured and sad and also a little bewildered. He wore a cap on his head which made him look like an affable grocer rather than a police officer.

But it was the pictures of Turi Guiliano that filled the newspapers all over the world. On one outstretched hand was the emerald ring he had taken from the Duchess. Around his body was the belt with golden buckle with its engraved eagle and lion. A pool of blood lay beneath his body.

Before Maria Lombardo's arrival, the body was taken to the town mortuary and put on a huge oval marble slab. The mortuary was part of the cemetery, which was ringed with tall black cypresses. It was here that Maria Lombardo was brought and made to sit on a stone bench. They were waiting for Colonel and Captain to finish their victory lunch in the nearby Hotel Selinus. Maria Lombardo began to weep at the sight of all the journalists, the curious townspeople, the many *carabinieri* working to keep them under control. Hector Adonis tried to comfort her.

Finally they led her into the mortuary. Officials around the oval slab were asking questions. She raised her eyes and saw Turi's face.

He had never looked so young. He looked as he looked as a child after an exhausting day of play with his Aspanu. There was no mark on his face, only a smudge of powdery dirt where his forehead had lain in the courtyard. The reality sobered her, made her calm. She answered questions. "Yes," she said, "that is my son Turi, born of my body twenty-seven years ago. Yes I identify him." The officials were still talking to her, giving her papers to sign, but she did not hear or see them. She did not see or hear the crowd pressing around her, the journalists screaming, the photographers fighting with the *carabinieri* to take pictures.

She kissed his forehead, as white as the gray-veined marble, she kissed his blueing lips, the hand torn to pulp by bullets. Her mind dissolved in grief. "Oh my blood, my blood," she said, "what a terrible death you have died."

She lost consciousness then, and when the attending physician gave her a shot and she had been brought to her senses, she insisted on going to the courtyard where her son's body had been found. There she knelt and kissed the bloodstains on the ground.

When she was brought home to Montelepre she found her husband waiting for her. It was then she learned the murderer of her son was her beloved Aspanu.

CHAPTER

29

MICHAEL CORLEONE and Peter Clemenza were transported to the Palermo jail right after their arrest. From there they were taken to Inspector Velardi's office to be interrogated.

Velardi had six *carabinieri* officers, fully armed, with him. He greeted Michael and Clemenza with a cold courtesy and spoke to Clemenza first. "You are an American citizen," he said. "You have a passport that says you have come here to pay your brother a visit. Don Domenic Clemenza of Trapani. A very respectable man, they tell me. A man of respect." He said the traditional phrase with obvious sarcasm. "We find you with this Michael Corleone, and you are armed with lethal weapons in the town where Turi Guiliano has met his death just a few hours before. Would you care to make a statement?"

Clemenza said, "I was out hunting, we were looking for rabbits and foxes. Then we saw all the commotion in Castelvetrano when we stopped at a café for our morning coffee. So we went to see what had happened."

"In America do you shoot rabbits with a machine pistol?" Inspector Velardi asked. He turned to Michael Corleone. "We have met before, you and I, we know what you are here for. And your fat friend knows too. But things have changed since we had that charming lunch with Don Croce a few days ago. Guiliano is dead. You are an accomplice in a criminal conspiracy

394

to effect his escape. I am no longer required to treat scum like you as if you were human. Confessions are being prepared which I recommend you sign."

At this moment a *carabinieri* officer came into the room and whispered into Inspector Velardi's ear. Velardi said curtly, "Let him enter."

It was Don Croce, no better dressed than Michael remembered him from that famous lunch. His mahogany face was just as impassive. He waddled over to Michael and embraced him. He shook hands with Peter Clemenza. Then he turned and still standing stared Inspector Velardi full in the face without saying a word. A brute force emanated from that hulk of a man. Power radiated from his face and eyes. "These two men are my friends," he said. "What possible reason do you have to treat them with disrespect?" There was no anger in that voice, no emotion. It seemed merely to be a question demanding an answer with facts. It was also a voice that stated there was no fact that could justify their arrest.

Inspector Velardi shrugged. "They will appear before the magistrate and he will settle the matter."

Don Croce sat down in one of the armchairs next to Inspector Velardi's desk. He mopped his brow. He said in a quiet voice which again seemed to hold no threat, "Out of respect for our friendship, call Minister Trezza and ask his opinion on this matter. You will be rendering me a service."

Inspector Velardi shook his head. The blue eyes were no longer cold but blazing with hatred. "We were never friends," he said. "I acted under orders which are no longer binding now that Guiliano is dead. These two men will go before the magistrate. If it were within my power you would appear with them."

At that moment the phone on Inspector Velardi's desk rang. He ignored it waiting for Don Croce's answer. Don Croce said, "Answer your telephone, that will be Minister Trezza."

The Inspector slowly picked up the phone, his eyes watching Don Croce. He listened for a few minutes, then said, "Yes,

Your Excellency," and hung up the phone. He slumped down in his chair and said to Michael and Peter Clemenza, "You are free to go."

Don Croce rose to his feet and shepherded Michael and Clemenza out of the room with a shooing motion, as if they were chickens entrapped in a yard. Then he turned to Inspector Velardi. "I have treated you with every courtesy this past year though you are a foreigner in my Sicily. And yet here in front of friends and in front of your fellow officers you have shown disrespect to my person. But I'm not the man to hold a grudge. I hope in the near future we can have dinner together and renew our friendship with a clearer understanding."

Five days later in broad daylight Inspector Frederico Velardi was shot to death on the main boulevard of Palermo.

■ ■ ■

TWO DAYS later Michael was home. There was a family feast—his brother Fredo flew in from Vegas, there was Connie and her husband Carlo, there was Clemenza and his wife, Tom Hagen and his wife. They hugged and toasted Michael and commented on how well he looked. Nobody talked about his years of exile, nobody seemed to notice that the side of his face was caved in, nobody mentioned Sonny's death. It was a family homecoming party as if he had been away to college or on a long vacation. He was seated on his father's right. Finally he was safe.

The next morning he slept late, his first truly restful sleep since before he had fled the country. His mother had breakfast waiting and kissed him when he sat down at the table, an unusual sign of affection from her. She had done it only once before, when he had returned from the war.

When he finished eating he went to the library and found his father waiting for him. He was surprised that Tom Hagen was not there also and then realized that the Don wished to speak to him without any witnesses.

Don Corleone ceremoniously poured out two glasses of anisette and handed one to Michael. "To our partnership," the Don said.

Michael raised his glass. "Thank you," he said. "I have a lot to learn."

"Yes," Don Corleone said. "But we have plenty of time, and I'm here to teach you."

Michael said, "Don't you think we should clear up the Guiliano business first?"

The Don sat down heavily and wiped his mouth of the liqueur. "Yes," he said. "A sad business. I was hoping he would escape. His father and mother were my good friends."

Michael said, "I never really understood what the hell was happening. I never could get the sides right. You told me to trust Don Croce, but Guiliano hated him. I thought the Testament being held by you would keep them from killing Guiliano, but they killed him anyway. And now when we release the Testament to all the newspapers, they will have cut their own throats."

He saw his father looking at him coolly. "That is Sicily," the Don said. "There is always treachery within treachery."

Michael said, "Don Croce and the government must have given Pisciotta a deal."

"No doubt," Don Corleone said.

Michael was still puzzled. "Why did they do it? We have the Testament that proves the government was hand in glove with Guiliano. The Italian government will fall when the papers print what we give them. It doesn't make any sense at all."

The Don smiled slightly and said, "The Testament will remain hidden. We won't give it to them."

It took a full minute for Michael to grasp what his father had said and what it meant. Then, for the first time in his life, he was truly angry with his father. His face white, he said, "Does that mean we were working with Don Croce all the time? Does that mean I was betraying Guiliano instead of helping him? That I was lying to his parents? That you betrayed your friends and led

397

their son to his death? That you used me like a fool, a Judas goat? Pop, my God, Guiliano was a good man, a true hero to the poor people of Sicily. We must release the Testament."

His father let him speak then he rose from his chair and put his hands on Michael's shoulders. "Listen to me," he said. "Everything was prepared for Guiliano's escape. I made no bargain with Don Croce to betray Guiliano. The plane was waiting, Clemenza and his men were instructed to help you in every way. Don Croce did want Guiliano to escape, it was the easiest way. But Guiliano swore a vendetta against him and lingered hoping to fulfill it. He could have come to you within a few days, but he stayed away to make a final try. That is what undid him."

Michael walked away from his father and sat in one of the leather armchairs. "There's a reason why you're not making the Testament public," he said. "You made a deal."

"Yes," Don Corleone said. "You must remember that after you were injured by the bomb, I realized that I and my friends could no longer completely protect you in Sicily. You were exposed to more attempts. I had to be absolutely sure you came home safely. So I made a deal with Don Croce. He protected you and in return I promised that I would persuade Guiliano not to publish the Testament when he escaped to America."

With a sickening shock Michael recalled that he was the one who had told Pisciotta that the Testament was safe in America. In that moment he had sealed Guiliano's fate. Michael sighed. "We owe it to his mother and father," he said. "And to Justina. Is she all right?"

"Yes," said the Don. "She is being taken care of. It will take a few months for her to come to terms with what has happened." He paused for a moment. "She is a very clever girl, she'll do well here."

Michael said, "We betray his father and mother if we do not publish the Testament."

"No," Don Corleone said. "I've learned something over the years here in America. You have to be reasonable, negotiate.

What good would publishing the Testament do? Probably the Italian government would fall, but maybe it would not. Minister Trezza would be out of a job, but do you think they would punish him?''

Michael said angrily, "He is the representative of a government that conspired to murder its own people."

The Don shrugged. "So? But let me go on. Would publishing the Testament help Guiliano's mother and father or his friends? The government would go after them, put them in jail, persecute them in many ways. Far worse, Don Croce might put them in his bad books. Let them have peace in their old age. I'll make a deal with the government and Don Croce to protect them. And so my holding the Testament will be useful."

Michael said sardonically, "And useful to us if we should need it some day in Sicily."

"I can't help that," his father said with a twitch of a smile.

After a long silence Michael said quietly, "I don't know, it seems dishonorable. Guiliano was a true hero, he is already a legend. We should help his memory. Not let that memory go down in defeat."

For the first time the Don showed annoyance. He poured himself another glass of anisette and drank it down. He pointed a finger at his son. "You wanted to learn," he said. "Now listen to me. A man's first duty is to keep himself alive. Then comes what everyone calls honor. This dishonor, as you call it, I willingly take upon myself. I did it to save your life as you once took on dishonor to save mine. You would never have left Sicily alive without Don Croce's protection. So be it. Do you want to be a hero like Guiliano, a legend? And dead? I love him as the son of my dear friends, but I do not envy him his fame. You are alive and he is dead. Always remember that and live your life not to be a hero but to remain alive. With time, heroes seem a little foolish."

Michael sighed. "Guiliano had no choice," he said.

"We are more fortunate," the Don said.

■ ■ ■

IT WAS the first lesson Michael received from his father and the one he learned best. It was to color his future life, persuade him to make terrible decisions he could never have dreamed of making before. It changed his perception of honor and his awe of heroism. It helped him to survive, but it made him unhappy. For despite the fact that his father did not envy Guiliano, Michael did.

CHAPTER

30

THE DEATH of Guiliano crushed the spirit of the people of Sicily. He had been their champion, their shield against the rich and the nobility, the Friends of the Friends, the Christian Democratic government in Rome. With Guiliano gone, Don Croce Malo put the island of Sicily through his olive press and squeezed out an immense fortune from rich and poor alike. When the government tried to build dams to provide cheap water, Don Croce had heavy equipment for building dams blown up. After all, he controlled all the water wells in Sicily; dams supplying cheap water were not to his interest. With the postwar boom in building Don Croce's inside information and persuasive negotiation style procured the best building sites at a cheap price; he sold dear. He took under his personal protection all the businesses of Sicily. You could not sell an artichoke in Palermo's market stalls without paying Don Croce a few *centesimi;* the rich could not buy jewels for their wives or racing horses for their sons without taking out insurance with Don Croce. And with a firm hand he discouraged all the foolish hopes of peasants who wished to claim uncultivated land from the estate of Prince Ollorto, because of nonsensical laws passed by the Italian Parliament. Squeezed between Don Croce, the nobles and the government in Rome, the Sicilian people gave up hope.

In the two years after Guiliano's death, five hundred thousand

Sicilians, most of them young males, emigrated. They went to England and became gardeners, makers of ice cream, waiters in restaurants. They went to Germany and did heavy manual labor, to Switzerland to keep that country clean and build cuckoo clocks. They went to France as kitchen helpers and sweepers in garment houses. They went to Brazil to hack out clearings in the forest. Some went to the cold winters of Scandinavia. And of course there were the fortunate few recruited by Clemenza to serve in the Corleone Family in the United States. These were considered the luckiest of all. And so Sicily became a land of old men, young children and women who were widows by economic vendetta. The stone villages no longer supplied laborers for the rich estates, and the rich also suffered. Only Don Croce prospered.

Gaspare "Aspanu" Pisciotta had been tried for his crimes as a bandit and sentenced to a life term in the Ucciardone Prison. But it was understood by everyone that he would be given a pardon. His only worry was that he would be murdered while in prison. Still the amnesty did not come. He sent word to Don Croce that unless he was pardoned immediately, he would reveal all the contacts the band had with Trezza, how. the new Premier had conspired with Don Croce to murder his own citizens at the Portella della Ginestra.

On the morning after Minister Trezza's ascension to the premiership of Italy, Aspanu Pisciotta awoke at eight in the morning. He had a large cell, filled with plants and large screens of needlework he had taken up during his time in jail. The brilliant silk of the embroidery patterns seemed to quiet his mind, for now he often thought of his childhood with Turi Guiliano, of their love for each other.

Pisciotta prepared his morning coffee and drank it. He had a fear of being poisoned. So everything in that cup of coffee had been brought to him by his family. The prison food he first fed in tiny portions to the pet parrot he kept in a cage. And for emergencies he kept on one of his shelves, with the embroidery

needles and piles of fabric, a huge jar of olive oil. He hoped that
by pouring it down his throat, he would counter the effect of the
poison or cause himself to vomit it up. He did not fear any other
violence—he was too well guarded. Only visitors he approved
were allowed to his cell door; he was never permitted out of this
room. He waited patiently for the parrot to eat and digest his
food and then ate his own breakfast with good appetite.

■ ■ ■

HECTOR ADONIS left his Palermo apartment and used the tram
car to the Ucciardone Prison. The February sun was already hot
though it was early morning, and he regretted wearing his black
suit and tie. But he felt he must dress formally on such an occasion. He touched the important slip of paper in the breast pocket
of his jacket, securely pressed to the bottom.

As he rode through the city the ghost of Guiliano rode with
him. He remembered one morning watching a tram full of *carabinieri* blown up, one of Guiliano's retaliations for his parents
being put in this same prison. And he wondered again how the
gentle boy he had taught the classics could commit such a terrible act. Now, though the walls of the buildings he passed were
blank, he could still see in his imagination the bold red paint that
had inscribed LONG LIVE GUILIANO so often painted on them.
Well, his godson had not lived long. But what always troubled
Hector Adonis was that Guiliano had been murdered by his
lifelong and childhood friend. That was why he had been delighted to receive instructions to deliver the note in his jacket
pocket. The note had been sent by Don Croce with specific
instructions.

The tram stopped in front of the long brick building that was
the Ucciardone Prison. It was separated from the street by a
stone wall topped by barbed wire. Guards manned the gate, and
the perimeter of the wall was patrolled by heavily armed police.
Hector Adonis, all necessary documents in hand, was admitted,
taken in charge by a special guard, and escorted to the hospital

pharmacy. There he was greeted by the pharmacist, a man by the name of Cuto. Cuto wore an immaculate white smock over a business suit with a tie. He, too, had, by some subtle psychological process, decided to dress for the occasion. He greeted Hector Adonis cordially and they sat down to wait.

"Has Aspanu been taking his medicine regularly?" Hector Adonis asked. Pisciotta still had to take streptomycin for his tuberculosis.

"Oh, yes," Cuto said. "He is very careful about his health. He has even stopped smoking. It's something curious I've noticed about our prisoners. When they are free they abuse their health—they smoke to excess, they drink to drunkenness, they fornicate to exhaustion. They don't sleep enough or get enough exercise. Then when they have to spend the rest of their lives in prison, they do push-ups, they spurn tobacco, they watch their diet and are moderate in all things."

"Perhaps because they have less opportunity," Hector Adonis said.

"Oh, no, no," Cuto said. "You can have everything you want in Ucciardone. The guards are poor and the prisoners are rich, so it's reasonable that money should change hands. You can indulge every vice here."

Adonis looked around the pharmacy. There were shelves full of medicines and great oaken closets that held bandages and medical instruments, for the pharmacy served as a medical emergency room for the prisoners. There were even two neatly made-up beds in an alcove of the huge rooms.

"Do you have any trouble getting his medicine?" Adonis asked.

"No, we have a special requisition," Cuto said. "I delivered his new bottle this morning. With all those special seals that the Americans put on it for export. A very expensive medicine. I'm surprised that the authorities go to so much trouble to keep him alive."

The two men smiled at each other.

■ ■ ■

IN HIS cell Aspanu Pisciotta took the bottle of streptomycin and broke the elaborate seals. He measured out his dose and swallowed it. He was surprised at the bitterness of the taste for that one second he could think, then his body bent backward in a great arc and was thrown to the floor. He let out a scream that brought the guard running to the cell door. Pisciotta struggled to his feet, fighting off the agonizing pain that wracked his body. There was a terrible rawness in his throat and he staggered toward the jar of olive oil. His body arched again and he screamed to the guard, "I've been poisoned. Help me, help me." And then before he fell again there was a great furiousness that he had finally been outwitted by Don Croce.

■ ■ ■

THE GUARDS carrying Pisciotta rushed into the pharmacy shouting that the prisoner had been poisoned. Cuto made them lay Pisciotta on one of the beds in the alcove and examined him. Then he quickly prepared an emetic and poured it down Pisciotta's throat. To the guards he seemed to be doing everything to save Pisciotta. Only Hector Adonis knew that the emetic was a weak solution that would not help the dying man. Adonis moved to the side of the bed and took the slip of paper in his breast pocket, holding it concealed in the palm of his hand. With the pretense of helping the pharmacist, he slipped the paper inside Pisciotta's shirt. At the same time he looked down at Pisciotta's handsome face. It seemed to be contorted with grief, but Adonis knew it was the contraction of terrible pain. Part of the tiny mustache had been gnawed away in his agony. Hector Adonis at that moment said a prayer for his soul and felt a great sadness. He remembered when this man and his godson had walked arm in arm over the hills of Sicily reciting the poetry of Roland and Charlemagne.

MARIO PUZO

■ ■ ■

IT WAS almost six hours later that the note was found on the body, but that was still early enough for it to be included in the newspaper stories of Pisciotta's death and quoted all over Sicily. The piece of paper Hector Adonis had slipped inside Aspanu's shirt read SO DIE ALL WHO BETRAY GUILIANO.

CHAPTER

31

IN SICILY, if you have any money at all, you do not put your loved ones into the ground. That is too final a defeat, and the earth of Sicily has already been responsible for too many indignities. So the cemeteries are filled with little stone and marble mausoleums—square tiny buildings called *congregazioni*. Iron grill doors bar their entrances. Inside are tiers in which coffins are put and then that particular tier is sealed with cement. The other tiers are reserved for family use.

Hector Adonis chose a fine Sunday shortly after Pisciotta's death to visit the Montelepre Cemetery. Don Croce was to meet him there to pray at the grave of Turi Guiliano. And since they had business to discuss, what better place for the meeting of the minds without vanity, for forgiveness of past injuries, for discretion?

And what better place to congratulate a colleague for a job well done? It had been Don Croce's duty to eliminate Pisciotta, who was too eloquent and had too good a memory. He had chosen Hector Adonis to mastermind the job. The note left on the body was one of the Don's most subtle gestures. It satisfied Adonis, and a political murder was disguised as an act of romantic justice. In front of the cemetery gates, Hector Adonis watched as the chauffeur and bodyguards lifted Don Croce out of his car. The Don's girth had increased enormously in the last year, his body seeming to grow with the immense power he had accrued.

The two men passed through the gate together. Adonis looked up at the curved archway. On the wrought-iron frame the metal was twisted to spell out a message for complacent mourners. It read: WE HAVE BEEN LIKE YOU—AND YOU SHALL BE LIKE US.

Adonis smiled at the sardonic challenge. Guiliano would never be guilty of such cruelty, but it was exactly what Aspanu Pisciotta would shout from his grave.

Hector Adonis no longer felt the bitter hatred of Pisciotta that he had carried with him after Guiliano's death. He had taken his revenge. Now he thought of the two of them playing as children, becoming outlaws together.

Don Croce and Hector Adonis were deep in the sepulchral village of small stones and marble buildings. Don Croce and his bodyguards moved in a group, supporting each other on the rocky path; the driver carried a huge bouquet of flowers which he put on the gate of the *congregazione* that held Guiliano's body. Don Croce fussily rearranged the flowers, then peered at the small photograph of Guiliano pasted on the stone door. His bodyguards clung to the trunk of his body to keep him from falling.

Don Croce straightened up. "He was a brave lad," the Don said. "We all loved Turi Guiliano. But how could we live with him? He wanted to change the world, turn it upside down. He loved his fellow man and who killed more of them? He believed in God and kidnapped a Cardinal."

Hector Adonis studied the photograph. It had been taken when Guiliano was only seventeen, the height of beauty by the Mediterranean Sea. There was a sweetness in his face that made you love him, and you could never dream that he would order a thousand murders, send a thousand souls to hell.

Ah, Sicily, Sicily, he thought, you destroy your best and bring them to dust. Children more beautiful than the angels spring from your earth and turn into demons. The evil flourish in this soil like the bamboo and the prickly pear. And yet why was Don Croce here to lay flowers at Guiliano's grave?

"Ah," said the Don, "if only I had a son like Turi Guiliano. What an empire I could leave for him to rule. Who knows what glories he would win?"

Hector Adonis smiled. No doubt Don Croce was a great man, but he had no perception of history. Don Croce had a thousand sons who would carry on his rule, inherit his cunning, pillage Sicily, corrupt Rome. And he, Hector Adonis, Eminent Professor of History and Literature at Palermo University, was one of them.

Hector Adonis and Don Croce turned to leave. A long line of carts was waiting in front of the cemetery. Every inch of them was painted in bright colors with the legends of Turi Guiliano and Aspanu Pisciotta: the robbing of the Duchess, the great slaughter of the Mafia chiefs, the murder of Turi by Aspanu. And it seemed to Hector Adonis that he knew all things. That Don Croce would be forgotten despite his greatness, and that it was Turi Guiliano who would live on. That Guiliano's legend would grow, that some would believe he never died but still roamed the Cammarata Mountains and on some great day would reappear to lift Sicily out of its chains and misery. In thousands of stone- and dirt-filled villages, children yet unborn would pray for Guiliano's soul and resurrection.

And Aspanu Pisciotta with his subtle mind, who was to say he had not listened when Hector Adonis had recited the legends of Charlemagne and Roland and Oliver and so decided to go another way? By remaining faithful, Pisciotta would have been forgotten, Guiliano would fill the legend alone. But by committing his great crime, he would stand alongside his beloved Turi forever.

Pisciotta would be buried in this same cemetery. The two of them would gaze forever at their cherished mountains, those same mountains that held the skeleton of Hannibal's elephant, that once echoed with the great blasts of Roland's horn when he died fighting the Saracens. Turi Guiliano and Aspanu Pisciotta had died young, but they would live, if not forever, certainly longer than Don Croce or himself, Professor Hector Adonis.

The two men, one so huge, one so tiny, left the cemetery together. Terraced gardens girdled the sides of the surrounding mountains with green ribbons, great white rocks gleamed, a tiny red hawk of Sicily rode down toward them on a shaft of sunlight.

OMERTÀ

About the author

Mario Puzo was born in New York and, following military service in World War II, attended New York's New School for Social Research and Columbia University. His best-selling novel *The Godfather* was preceded by two critically acclaimed novels, *The Dark Arena* (1955) and *The Fortunate Pilgrim* (1965). In 1978, he published *Fools Die,* followed by *The Sicilian* (1984), *The Fourth K* (1991), and the second installment in his Mafia trilogy, *The Last Don* (1996), which became an international best-seller and the highest-rated TV miniseries of 1997. Mario Puzo also wrote many screenplays, including *Earthquake, Superman,* and all three *Godfather* movies, for which he received two Academy Awards. He died in July 1999 at his home in Long Island, New York, at the age of seventy-eight.

To
Evelyn Murphy

Omertà:

a Sicilian code of honor which forbids
informing about crimes thought to be the affairs
of the persons involved

World Book Dictionary

1967

IN THE STONE-FILLED VILLAGE of Castellammare del Golfo facing the dark Sicilian Mediterranean, a great Mafia Don lay dying. Vincenzo Zeno was a man of honor, who all his life had been loved for his fair and impartial judgment, his help to those in need, and his implacable punishment of those who dared to oppose his will.

Around him were three of his former followers, each of whom had gone on to achieve his own power and position: Raymonde Aprile from Sicily and New York, Octavius Bianco from Palermo, and Benito Craxxi from Chicago. Each owed him one last favor.

Don Zeno was the last of the true Mafia chiefs, having all his life observed the old traditions. He extracted a tariff on all business, but never on

1

drugs, prostitution, or other crime of any kind. And never did a poor man come to his house for money and go away empty-handed. He corrected the injustices of the law—the highest judge in Sicily could make his ruling, but if you had right on your side, Don Zeno would veto that judgment with his own force of will, and arms.

No philandering youth could leave the daughter of a poor peasant without Don Zeno persuading him into holy matrimony. No bank could foreclose on a helpless farmer without Don Zeno interfering to put things right. No young lad who hungered for a university education could be denied it for lack of money or qualification. If they were related to his *cosca,* his clan, their dreams were fulfilled. The laws from Rome could never justify the traditions of Sicily and had no authority; Don Zeno would overrule them, no matter what the cost.

But the Don was now in his eighties, and over the last few years his power had begun to wane. He'd had the weakness to marry a very beautiful young girl, who had produced a fine male child. She had died in childbirth, and the boy was now two years old. The old man, knowing that the end was near and that without him his *cosca* would be pulverized by the more powerful *coscas* of Corleone and Clericuzio, pondered the future of his son.

Now he thanked his three friends for the

courtesy and respect they had shown in traveling so many miles to hear his request. Then he told them that he wanted his young son, Astorre, to be taken to a place of safety and brought up under different circumstances but in the tradition of a man of honor, like himself.

"I can die with a clear conscience," he said, though his friends knew that in his lifetime he had decided the deaths of hundreds of men, "if I can see my son to safety. For in this two-year-old I see the heart and soul of a true Mafioso, a rare and almost extinct quality."

He told them he would choose one of these men to act as guardian to this unusual child, and with this responsibility would come great rewards.

"It is strange," Don Zeno said, staring through clouded eyes. "According to tradition, it is the first son who is the true Mafioso. But in my case it took until I reached my eightieth year before I could make my dream come true. I'm not a man of superstition, but if I were, I could believe this child grew from the soil of Sicily itself. His eyes are as green as olives that spring from my best trees. And he has the Sicilian sensibility—romantic, musical, happy. Yet if someone offends him, he doesn't forget, as young as he is. But he must be guided."

"And so what do you wish from us, Don Zeno?" Craxxi asked. "For I will gladly take this child of yours and raise him as my own."

Bianco stared at Craxxi almost resentfully. "I

know the boy from when he was first born. He is familiar to me. I will take him as my own."

Raymonde Aprile looked at Don Zeno but said nothing.

"And you, Raymonde?" Don Zeno asked.

Aprile said, "If it is me that you choose, your son will be my son."

The Don considered the three of them, all worthy men. He regarded Craxxi the most intelligent. Bianco was surely the most ambitious and forceful. Aprile was a more restrained man of virtue, a man closer to himself. But he was merciless.

Don Zeno, even while dying, understood that it was Raymonde Aprile who most needed the child. He would benefit most from the child's love, and he would make certain his son learned how to survive in their world of treachery.

Don Zeno was silent for a long moment. Finally he said, "Raymonde, you will be his father. And I can rest in peace."

The Don's funeral was worthy of an emperor. All the *cosca* chiefs in Sicily came to pay their respects, along with cabinet ministers from Rome, the owners of the great latifundia, and hundreds of subjects of his widespread *cosca*. Atop the black horse-drawn hearse, two-year-old Astorre Zeno, a fiery-eyed baby attired in a black frock and black pillbox hat, rode as majestically as a Roman emperor.

The cardinal of Palermo conducted the service and proclaimed memorably, "In sickness and in health, in unhappiness and despair, Don Zeno remained a true friend to all." He then intoned Don Zeno's last words: "I commend myself to God. He will forgive my sins, for I have tried every day to be just."

And so it was that Astorre Zeno was taken to America by Raymonde Aprile and made a part of his own household.

CHAPTER

1

WHEN THE STURZO TWINS, Franky and Stace,
pulled into Heskow's driveway, they saw four very
tall teenagers playing basketball on the small
house court. Franky and Stace got out of their big
Buick, and John Heskow came out to meet them.
He was a tall, pear-shaped man; his thin hair
neatly ringed the bare top of his skull, and his
small blue eyes twinkled. "Great timing," he said.
"There's someone I want you to meet."

The basketball game halted. Heskow said
proudly, "This is my son, Jocko." The tallest of the
teenagers stuck out his huge hand to Franky.

"Hey," Franky said. "How about giving us a
little game?"

Jocko looked at the two visitors. They were
about six feet tall and seemed in good shape. They

6

both wore Ralph Lauren polo shirts, one red and the other green, with khaki trousers and rubber-soled shoes. They were amiable-looking, handsome men, their craggy features set with a graceful confidence. They were obviously brothers, but Jocko could not know they were twins. He figured them to be in their early forties.

"Sure," Jocko said, with boyish good nature.

Stace grinned. "Great! We just drove three thousand miles and have to loosen up."

Jocko motioned to his companions, all well over six feet, and said, "I'll take them on my side against you three." Since he was the much better player, he thought this would give his father's friends a chance.

"Take it easy on them," John Heskow said to the kids. "They're just old guys futzing around."

It was midafternoon in December, and the air was chilly enough to spur the blood. The cold Long Island sunlight, pale yellow, glinted off the glass roofs and walls of Heskow's flower sheds, his front business.

Jocko's young buddies were mellow and played to accommodate the older men. But suddenly Franky and Stace were whizzing past them for layup shots. Jocko stood amazed at their speed; then they were refusing to shoot and passing him the ball. They never took an outside shot. It seemed a point of honor that they had to swing free for an easy layup.

7

The opposing team started to use their height to pass around the older men but astonishingly enough got few rebounds. Finally, one of the boys lost his temper and gave Franky a hard elbow in the face. Suddenly the boy was on the ground. Jocko, watching everything, didn't know exactly how it happened. But then Stace hit his brother in the head with the ball and said, "Come on. Play, you shithead." Franky helped the boy to his feet, patted him on the ass, and said, "Hey, I'm sorry." They played for about five minutes more, but by then the older men were obviously tuckered out and the kids ran circles around them. Finally, they quit.

Heskow brought sodas to them on the court, and the teenagers clustered around Franky, who had charisma and had shown pro skills on the court. Franky hugged the boy he had knocked down. Then, he flashed them a man-of-the-world grin, which set pleasantly on his angular face.

"Let me give you guys some advice from an old guy," he said. "Never dribble when you can pass. Never quit when you're twenty points down in the last quarter. And never go out with a woman who owns more than one cat."

The boys all laughed.

Franky and Stace shook hands with the kids and thanked them for the game, then followed Heskow inside the pretty green-trimmed house.

Jocko called after them, "Hey, you guys are good!"

Inside the house, John Heskow led the two brothers upstairs to their room. It had a very heavy door with a good lock, the brothers noticed as Heskow let them in and locked the door behind them.

The room was big, a suite really, with an attached bathroom. It had two single beds—Heskow knew the brothers liked to sleep in the same room. In a corner was a huge trunk banded with steel straps and a heavy metal padlock. Heskow used a key to unlock the trunk and then flung the lid open. Exposed to view were several handguns, automatic weapons, and munitions boxes, in an array of black geometric shapes.

"Will that do?" Heskow asked.

Franky said, "No silencers."

"You won't need silencers for this job."

"Good," Stace said. "I hate silencers. I can never hit anything with a silencer."

"OK," Heskow said. "You guys take a shower and settle in, and I'll get rid of the kids and cook supper. What did you think of my kid?"

"A very nice boy," Franky said.

"And how do you like the way he plays basketball?" Heskow said with a flush of pride that made him look even more like a ripened pear.

"Exceptional," Franky said.

"Stace, what do you think?" Heskow asked.

9

"Very exceptional," said Stace.

"He has a scholarship to Villanova," Heskow said. "NBA all the way."

When the twins came down to the living room a little while later, Heskow was waiting. He had prepared sautéed veal with mushrooms and a huge green salad. There was red wine on the table, which was set for three.

They sat down. They were old friends and knew each other's history. Heskow had been divorced for thirteen years. His ex-wife and Jocko lived a couple of miles west in Babylon. But Jocko spent a lot of time here, and Heskow had been a constant and doting father.

"You were supposed to arrive tomorrow morning," Heskow said. "I would have put the kid off if I knew you were coming today. By the time you phoned, I couldn't throw him and his friends out."

"That's OK," Franky said. "What the hell."

"You guys were good out there with the kids," Heskow said. "You ever wonder if you could have made it in the pros?"

"Nah," Stace said. "We're too short, only six feet. The eggplants were too big for us."

"Don't say things like that in front of the kid," Heskow said, horror-stricken. "He has to play with them."

"Oh, no," Stace said. "I would never do that."

Heskow relaxed and sipped his wine. He always liked working with the Sturzo brothers. They were both so genial—they never got nasty like most of the scum he had to deal with. They had an ease in the world that reflected the ease between them. They were secure, and it gave them a pleasant glow.

The three of them ate slowly, casually. Heskow refilled their plates direct from the frying pan.

"I always meant to ask," Franky said to Heskow. "Why did you change your name?"

"That was a long time ago," Heskow said. "I wasn't ashamed of being Italian. But you know, I look so fucking German. With blond hair and blue eyes and this nose. It looked really fishy, my having an Italian name."

The twins both laughed, an easy, understanding laugh. They knew he was full of shit, but they didn't mind.

When they finished their salad, Heskow served double espresso and a plate of Italian pastries. He offered cigars but they refused. They stuck to their Marlboros, which suited their creased western faces.

"Time to get down to business," Stace said. "This must be a big one, or why did we have to drive three thousand fucking miles? We could have flown."

"It wasn't so bad," Franky said. "I enjoyed it. We saw America, firsthand. We had a good time. The people in the small towns were great."

11

"Exceptional," Stace said. "But still, it was a long ride."

"I didn't want to leave any traces at the airports," Heskow said. "That's the first place they check. And there will be a lot of heat. You boys don't mind heat?"

"Mother's milk to me," Stace said. "Now, who the fuck is it?"

"Don Raymonde Aprile." Heskow nearly choked on his espresso saying it.

There was a long silence, and then for the first time Heskow caught the chill of death the twins could radiate.

Franky said quietly, "You made us drive three thousand miles to offer us this job?"

Stace smiled at Heskow and said, "John, it's been nice knowing you. Now just pay our kill fee and we'll be moving on." Both twins laughed at this little joke, but Heskow didn't get it.

One of Franky's friends in L.A., a freelance writer, had once explained to the twins that though a magazine might pay him expenses to do an article, they would not necessarily buy it. They would just pay a small percentage of the agreed-upon fee to kill the piece. The twins had adopted that practice. They charged just to listen to a proposition. In this case, because of the travel time and there were two of them involved, the kill fee was twenty thousand.

But it was Heskow's job to convince them to

take the assignment. "The Don has been retired for three years," he said. "All his old connections are in jail. He has no power anymore. The only one who could make trouble is Timmona Portella, and he won't. Your payoff is a million bucks, half when you're done and the other half in a year. But for that year, you have to lay low. Now everything is set up. All you guys have to be is the shooters."

"A million bucks," Stace said. "That's a lot of money."

"My client knows it's a big step to hit Don Aprile," Heskow said. "He wants the best help. Cool shooters and silent partners with mature heads. And you guys are simply the best."

Franky said, "And there are not many guys who would take the risk."

"Yeah," Stace said. "You have to live with it the rest of your life. Somebody coming after you, plus the cops, and the feds."

"I swear to you," Heskow said, "the NYPD won't go all out. The FBI will not take a hand."

"And the Don's old friends?" Stace asked.

"The dead have no friends." Heskow paused for a moment. "When the Don retired, he cut all ties. There's nothing to worry about."

Franky said to Stace, "Isn't it funny, in all our deals, they always tell us there's nothing to worry about?"

Stace laughed. "That's because they're not the shooters. John, you're an old friend. We trust you.

But what if you're wrong? Anybody can be wrong. What if the Don still has old friends? You know how he operates. No mercy. We get nailed, we don't just get killed. We'll spend a couple of hours in hell first. Plus our families are at stake under the Don's rule. That means your son. Can't play for the NBA in his grave. Maybe we should know who's paying for this."

Heskow leaned toward them, his light skin a scarlet red as if he were blushing. "I can't tell you that. You know that. I'm just the broker. And I've thought of all that other shit. You think I'm fucking stupid? Who doesn't know who the Don is? But he's defenseless. I have assurances of that from the top levels. The police will just go through the motions. The FBI can't afford to investigate. And the top Mafia heads won't interfere. It's foolproof."

"I never dreamed that Don Aprile would be one of my marks," Franky said. The deed appealed to his ego. To kill a man so dreaded and respected in his world.

"Franky, this is not a basketball game," Stace warned. "If we lose, we don't shake hands and walk off the court."

"Stace, its a million bucks," Franky said. "And John never steered us wrong. Let's go with it."

Stace felt their excitement building. What the hell. He and Franky could take care of themselves. After all, there was the million bucks. If the truth

14

were told, Stace was more mercenary than Franky, more business-oriented, and the million swung him.

"OK," Stace said, "we're in. But God have mercy on our souls if you're wrong." He had once been an altar boy.

"What about the Don being watched by the FBI?" Franky asked. "Do we have to worry about that?"

"No," Heskow said. "When all his old friends went to jail, the Don retired like a gentleman. The FBI appreciated that. They leave him alone. I guarantee it. Now let me lay it out."

It took him a half hour to explain the plan in detail.

Finally Stace said, "When?"

"Sunday morning," Heskow said. "You stay here for the first two days. Afterward the private jet flies you out of Newark."

"We have to have a very good driver," Stace said. "Exceptional."

"I'm driving," Heskow said, then added, almost apologetically, "It's a very big payday."

For the rest of the weekend, Heskow baby-sat for the Sturzo brothers, cooking their meals, running their errands. He was not a man easily impressed, but the Sturzos sometimes sent a chill to his heart. They were like adders, their heads constantly alert, yet they were congenial and even helped him tend to the flowers in his sheds.

The brothers played basketball one-on-one just before supper, and Heskow watched fascinated by how their bodies slithered around each other like snakes. Franky was faster and a deadly shooter. Stace was not as good but more clever. Franky could have made it to the NBA, Heskow thought. But this was not a basketball game. In a real crisis, it would have to be Stace. Stace would be the primary shooter.

THE GREAT 1990s FBI blitz of the Mafia families
in New York left only two survivors. Don
Raymonde Aprile, the greatest and most feared,
remained untouched. The other, Don Timmona
Portella, who was nearly his equal in power but a
far inferior man, escaped by what seemed to be
pure luck.

But the future was clear. With the 1970 RICO
laws so undemocratically framed, the zeal of
special FBI prosecuting teams, and the death of
the belief in *omertà* among the soldiers of the
American Mafia, Don Raymonde Aprile knew it
was time for him to retire gracefully from the
stage.

The Don had ruled his Family for thirty years
and was now a legend. Brought up in Sicily, he had

none of the false ideas or strutting arrogance of the American-born Mafia chiefs. He was, in fact, a throwback to the old Sicilians of the nineteenth century who ruled towns and villages with their personal charisma, their sense of honor, and their deadly and final judgment of any suspected enemy. He also proved to have the strategic genius of those old heroes.

Now, at sixty-two, he had his life in order. He had disposed of his enemies and accomplished his duties as a friend and a father. He could enjoy old age with a clear conscience, retire from the disharmonies of his world, and move into the more fitting role of gentleman banker and pillar of society.

His three children were safely ensconced in successful and honorable careers. His oldest son, Valerius, was now thirty-seven, married with children, and a colonel in the United States Army and lecturer at West Point. His career had been determined by his timidity as a child; the Don had secured a cadet appointment at West Point to rectify this defect in his character.

His second son, Marcantonio, at the early age of thirty-five, was, out of some mystery in the variation of his genes, a top executive at a national TV network. As a boy he had been moody and lived in a make-believe world and the Don thought he would be a failure in any serious enterprise. But now his name was often in the papers as some sort of creative visionary, which pleased the Don but did not convince him. After all, he was the boy's father. Who knew him better?

His daughter, Nicole, had been affectionately called Nikki as a young child but at the age of six demanded imperiously that she be called by her proper name. She was his favorite sparring partner. At the age of twenty-nine, she was a corporate lawyer, a feminist, and a pro bono advocate of those poor and desperate criminals who otherwise could not afford an adequate legal defense. She was especially good at saving murderers from the electric chair, husband killers from prison confinement, and repeat rapists from being given life terms. She was absolutely opposed to the death penalty, believed in the rehabilitation of any criminal, and was a severe critic of the economic structure of the United States. She believed a country as rich as America should not be so indifferent to the poor, no matter what their faults. Despite all this she was a very skilled and tough negotiator in corporate law, a striking and forceful woman. The Don agreed with her on nothing.

As for Astorre, he was part of the family, and closest to the Don as a titular nephew. But he seemed like a brother to the others because of his intense vitality and charm. From the age of three to sixteen he had been their intimate, the beloved youngest sibling—until his exile to Sicily eleven

years before. The Don had summoned him back
when he retired.

The Don planned his retirement carefully. He
distributed his empire to placate potential enemies
but also rendered tribute to loyal friends, knowing
that gratitude is the least lasting of virtues and that
gifts must always be replenished. He was especially
careful to pacify Timmona Portella. Portella was
dangerous because of his eccentricity and a
passionate murderousness that sometimes had no
relationship to necessity.

How Portella escaped the FBI blitz of the 1990s
was a mystery to everyone. For he was an
American-born don without subtlety, a man
incautious and intemperate, with an explosive
temper. He had a huge body with an enormous
paunch and dressed like a Palermo *picciotto,* a
young apprentice killer, all colors and silk. His
power was based in the distribution of illegal drugs.
He had never married and still at age fifty was a
careless womanizer. He only showed true affection
for his younger brother, Bruno, who seemed slightly
retarded but shared his older brother's brutality.

Don Aprile had never trusted Portella and
rarely did business with him. The man was
dangerous through his weakness, a man to be
neutralized. So now he summoned Timmona
Portella for a meeting.

Portella arrived with his brother, Bruno. Aprile met them with his usual quiet courtesy but came to the point quickly.

"My dear Timmona," he said. "I am retiring from all business affairs except my banks. Now you will be very much in the public eye and you must be careful. If you should ever need any advice, call on me. For I will not be completely without resources in my retirement."

Bruno, a small replica of his brother who was awed by the Don's reputation, smiled with pleasure at this respect for his older brother. But Timmona understood the Don far better. He knew that he was being warned.

He nodded respectfully to the Don. "You have always showed the best judgment of us all," he said. "And I respect what you are doing. Count on me as your friend."

"Very good, very good," the Don said. "Now, as a gift to you, I ask you to heed this warning. This FBI man, Cilke, is very devious. Do not trust him in any way. He is drunk with his success, and you will be his next target."

"But you and I have already escaped him," Timmona said. "Though he brought all our friends down. I don't fear him but I thank you."

They had a celebratory drink, and the Portella brothers left. In the car Bruno said, "What a great man."

"Yes," Timmona said. "He was a great man."

As for the Don, he was well satisfied. He had seen the alarm in Timmona's eyes and was assured there would no longer be any danger from him.

Don Aprile requested a private meeting with Kurt Cilke, the head of the FBI in New York City. Cilke, to the Don's own surprise, was a man he admired. He had sent most of the East Coast Mafia chiefs to jail and almost broken their power.

Don Raymonde Aprile had eluded him, for the Don knew the identity of Cilke's secret informer, the one who made his success possible. But the Don admired Cilke even more because the man always played fair, had never tried frame-ups or power-play harassments, had never given publicity pin marks on the Don's children. So the Don felt it was only fair to warn him.

The meeting was at the Don's country estate in Montauk. Cilke would have to come alone, a violation of the Bureau rules. The FBI director himself had given approval but insisted Cilke use a special recording device. This was an implant in his body, below his rib cage, which would not show on the outer walls of his torso; the device was not known to the public, and its manufacture was strictly controlled. Cilke realized that the real purpose of the wire was to record what he said to the Don.

They met on a golden October afternoon on the Don's verandah. Cilke had never been able to penetrate this house with a listening device, and a judge had barred constant physical surveillance. This day he was not searched in any way by the Don's men, which surprised him. Obviously Don Raymonde Aprile was not going to make him an illicit proposal.

As always, Cilke was amazed and even a little disturbed by the impression that the Don made on him. Despite knowing that the man had ordered a hundred murders, broken countless laws of society, Cilke could not hate him. And yet he believed such men evil, hated them for how they destroyed the fabric of civilization.

Don Aprile was clad in a dark suit, dark tie, and white shirt. His expression was grave and yet understanding, the lines in his face the gentle ones of a virtue-loving man. How could such a humane face belong to someone so merciless, Cilke wondered.

The Don did not offer to shake hands out of a sensibility not to embarrass Cilke. He gestured for his guest to be seated and bowed his head in greeting.

"I have decided to place myself and my family under your protection—that is, the protection of society," he said.

23

Cilke was astonished. What the hell did the old man mean?

"For the last twenty years you have made yourself my enemy. You have pursued me. But I was always grateful for your sense of fair play. You never tried to plant evidence or encourage perjury against me. You have put most of my friends in prison, and you tried very hard to do the same to me."

Cilke smiled. "I'm still trying," he said.

The Don nodded in appreciation. "I have rid myself of everything doubtful except a few banks, surely a respectable business. I have placed myself under the protection of your society. In return I will do my duty to that society. You can make it much easier if you do not pursue me. For there is no longer any need."

Cilke shrugged. "The Bureau decides. I've been after you for so long, why stop now? I might get lucky."

The Don's face became graver and even more tired. "I have something to exchange with you. Your enormous success of the past few years influenced my decision. But the thing is, I know your prize informant, I know who he is. And I have told no one."

Cilke hesitated for only seconds before he said impassively, "I have no such informant. And again, the Bureau decides, not me. So you've wasted my time."

24

"No, no," the Don said. "I'm not seeking an advantage, just an accommodation. Allow me, because of my age, to tell you what I have learned. Do not exercise power because it is easy to your hand. And do not get carried away with a certainty of victory when your intellect tells you there is even a hint of tragedy. Let me say I regard you now as a friend, not an enemy, and think to yourself what you have to gain or lose by refusing this offer."

"And if you are truly retired, then of what use is your friendship?" Cilke said, smiling.

"You will have my goodwill," the Don said. "That is worth something even from the smallest of men."

Later Cilke played the tape for Bill Boxton, his deputy, who asked, "What the hell was that all about?"

"That's the stuff you have to learn," Cilke told him. "He was telling me that he's not completely defenseless, that he was keeping an eye on me."

"What bullshit," Boxton said. "They can't touch a federal agent."

"That's true," Cilke said. "That's why I kept after him, retired or not. Still, I'm wary. We can't be absolutely sure . . ."

Having studied the history of the most prestigious

25

families in America, those robber barons who had ruthlessly built their fortunes while breaking the laws and ethics of human society, Don Aprile became, like them, a benefactor to all. Like them, he had his empire—he owned ten private banks in the world's largest cities. So he gave generously to build a hospital for the poor. And he contributed to the arts. He established a chair at Columbia University for the study of the Renaissance.

It was true that Yale and Harvard refused his twenty million dollars for a dormitory to be named for Christopher Columbus, who was at the time in disrepute in intellectual circles. Yale did offer to take the money and name the dorm after Sacco and Vanzetti, but the Don was not interested in Sacco and Vanzetti. He despised martyrs.

A lesser man would have felt insulted and nursed a grievance, but not Raymonde Aprile. Instead, he simply gave the money to the Catholic Church for daily masses to be sung for his wife, now twenty-five years in Heaven.

He donated a million dollars to the New York Police Benevolent Association and another million to a society for the protection of illegal immigrants. For the three years after his retirement, he showered his blessings on the world. His purse was open to any request except for one. He refused Nicole's pleas to contribute to the Campaign Against the Death Penalty—her crusade to stop capital punishment.

It is astonishing how three years of good deeds and generosity can almost wipe out a thirty-year reputation of merciless acts. But great men also buy their own goodwill, forgiveness of betraying friends and exercising lethal judgment. And the Don too had this universal weakness.

For Don Raymonde Aprile was a man who had lived by the strict rules of his own particular morality. His protocol had made him respected for over thirty years and generated the extraordinary fear that had been the base of his power. A chief tenet of that protocol was a complete lack of mercy.

This sprang not from innate cruelty, some psychopathic desire to inflict pain, but from an absolute conviction: that men always refused to obey. Even Lucifer, the angel, had defied God and had been flung from the heavens.

So an ambitious man struggling for power had no other recourse. Of course there were some persuasions, some concessions to another man's self-interest. That was only reasonable. But if all that failed, there was only the punishment of death. Never threats of other forms of punishment that might inspire retaliation. Simply a banishment from this earthly sphere, no more to be reckoned with.

Treachery was the greatest injury. The traitor's family would suffer, as would his circle of friends; his whole world would be destroyed. For there are

27

many brave, proud men willing to gamble their lives for their own gain, but they would think twice about risking their loved ones. And so in this way Don Aprile generated a vast amount of terror. He relied on his generosity in worldly goods to win their less necessary love.

But it must be said, he was as merciless to himself. Possessed of enormous power, he could not prevent the death of his young wife after she had given him three children. She died a slow and horrible death from cancer as he watched over her for six months. During that time he came to believe that she was being punished for all the mortal sins he had committed, and so it was that he decreed his own penance: he would never remarry. He would send his children away to be educated in the ways of lawful society, so they would not grow up in his world so full of hate and danger. He would help them find their way, but they would never be involved in his activities. With great sadness he resolved that he would never know the true essence of fatherhood.

So the Don arranged to have Nicole, Valerius, and Marcantonio sent to private boarding schools. He never let them into his personal life. They came home for the holidays, when he played the role of a caring but distant father, but they never became part of his world.

And yet despite everything and though they were aware of his reputation, his children loved him. They never talked about it among themselves. It was one of those family secrets that was not a secret.

No one could call the Don sentimental. He had very few personal friends, no pets, and he avoided holiday and social gatherings as much as possible. Only once, many years before, he had committed an act of compassion that astounded his colleagues in America.

Don Aprile, when he returned from Sicily with the infant, Astorre, found his beloved wife dying of cancer and his own three children desolate. Not wanting to keep the impressionable infant in such a circumstance for fear it would harm him in some way, the Don decided to place him in the care of one of his closest advisors, a man named Frank Viola, and his wife. This proved to be an unwise choice. At the time, Frank Viola had ambitions to succeed the Don.

But shortly after the Don's wife died, Astorre Viola, at the age of three, became a member of the Don's personal family when his "father" committed suicide in the trunk of his car, a curious circumstance, and his mother died of a brain hemorrhage. It was then that the Don had taken Astorre into his household and assumed the title of uncle.

When Astorre was old enough to begin asking about his parents, Don Raymonde told him that he had been orphaned. But Astorre was a curious and tenacious young boy, so the Don, to put an end to all his questions, told him that his parents had been peasants, unable to feed him, and had died, unknown, in a small Sicilian village. The Don knew this explanation didn't completely satisfy the boy, and he felt a twinge of guilt over deceiving him, but he knew it was important while the child was still young to keep his Mafia roots a secret— for Astorre's own safety and for the safety of the Aprile children.

Don Raymonde was a far-seeing man and knew that his success could not last forever—it was too treacherous a world. From the beginning he planned to switch sides, to join the safety of organized society. Not that he was truly conscious of his purpose, but great men have an instinct for what the future will demand. And in this case, truly, he acted out of compassion. For Astorre Viola, at the age of three, could have made no impression, could have given no hint of what he would later become as a man. Or how important a part he would play in the Family.

The Don understood that the glory of America was the emergence of great families, and that the best social class sprang from men who had at first committed great crimes against that society. It was such men who in the search for fortune had also built America and left evil deeds to crumble into forgotten dust. How else could it be done? Leave the Great Plains of America to those Indians who could not conceive of a three-story dwelling? Leave California to Mexicans who had no technical ability, no vision of great aqueducts to feed water to lands that would allow millions to enjoy a prosperous life? America had the genius to attract millions of laboring poor from all over the world, to entice them to the necessary hard work of building the railroads, the dams, and the sky-scratching buildings. Ah, the Statue of Liberty had been a stroke of promotional genius. And had it not turned out for the best? Certainly there had been tragedies, but that was part of life. Was not America the greatest cornucopia the world had ever known? Was not a measure of injustice a small price to pay? It has always been the case that an individual must sacrifice to further the advance of civilization and his particular society.

But there is another definition of a great man. Primarily that he does not accept that burden. In some way, criminal, immoral, or by sheer cunning, he will ride the crest of that wave of human progress without sacrifice.

Don Raymonde Aprile was such a man. He generated his own individual power by his intelligence and by his complete lack of mercy. He generated fear, he became a legend. But his children, when they were grown, never believed in the most atrocious stories.

31

2

2

2

There was the legend of the beginning of his rule as Family chief. The Don controlled a construction company run by a subordinate, Tommy Liotti, whom the Don had made rich at an early age with city building contracts. The man was handsome, witty, a thorough charmer, and the Don always enjoyed his company. He had only one fault: he drank to excess.

Tommy married the Don's wife's best friend, Liza, an old-fashioned handsome woman with a sharp tongue, who felt it her duty to curb her husband's obvious pleasure with himself. This led to some unfortunate incidents. He accepted her barbs well enough when he was sober, but when drunk he would slap her face hard enough to make her bite her tongue.

It was also unfortunate that the husband had a massive strength due to working hard and long on construction sites during his youth. Indeed, he always wore short-sleeved shirts to display his magnificent forearms and his great biceps.

Sadly, the incidents escalated over a period of two years. One night Tommy broke Liza's nose and knocked out a few teeth, which required expensive surgical repair. The woman did not dare ask Don Aprile's wife for protection, since such a request would probably make her a widow, and she still loved her husband.

It was not Don Aprile's desire to interfere in the domestic squabbles of his underlings. Such things could never be solved. If the husband had killed the wife, he would not have been concerned. But the beatings posed a danger to his business relationship. An enraged wife could make certain testimonies, give damaging information. For the husband kept large quantities of cash in his house for those incidental bribes so necessary to the fulfillment of city contracts.

So Don Aprile summoned the husband. With the utmost courtesy, he made it plain he interfered in the man's personal life only because it affected business. He advised the man to kill his wife outright or divorce her or never to ill-treat her further. The husband assured him it would never happen again. But the Don was mistrustful. He had noticed that certain gleam in the man's eyes, the gleam of free will. He considered this one of the great mysteries of life, that a man will do what he feels like doing with no regard to the cost. Great men have allied themselves with the angels at a terrible price to themselves. Evil men indulge their slightest whim for small satisfactions while accepting the fate of burning in hell.

And so it turned out with Tommy Liotti. It took nearly a year, and Liza's tongue grew sharper with her husband's indulgence. Despite the warning from the Don, despite his love for his children and his wife, Tommy beat her in the most violent fashion. She ended up in the hospital with broken ribs and a punctured lung.

Mario Puzo

With his wealth and political connections, Tommy bought one of the Don's corrupt judges with an enormous bribe. Then he talked his wife into coming back to him.

Don Aprile observed this with some anger and regretfully took charge of the affair. First, he attended to the practical aspects of the matter. He obtained a copy of the husband's will and learned that like a good family man, he had left all his worldly goods to his wife and children. She would be a rich widow. Then he sent out a special team with specific instructions. Within the week the judge received a long box wrapped in ribbons, and in it, like a pair of expensive long silk gloves, were the two massive forearms of the husband, one wearing on its wrist the expensive Rolex watch the Don had given him years before as a token of his esteem. The next day the rest of the body was found floating in the water around the Verrazano Bridge.

Another legend was chilling because of its ambiguity, like some childish ghost story. While the Don's three children were attending boarding school, an enterprising and talented journalist noted for his witty exposure of the frailties of famous people tracked them down and enticed them into what seemed like harmless verbal exchange. The writer had great fun with their innocence, their preppy clothes, their juvenile idealism about how to make a better world. The journalist

34

contrasted it with their father's reputation while admitting that Don Aprile had never actually been convicted of a crime.

The piece became famous, circulated in newsrooms throughout the country even before publication. It was the kind of success a writer dreams about. Everybody loved it.

The journalist was a nature lover, and every year he took his wife and two children to a cabin in upstate New York for hunting and fishing and living simply. They were there one long Thanksgiving weekend. On Saturday the cabin, ten miles from the nearest town, caught fire. There was no rescue for about two hours. By then the house had burned to smoking logs and the journalist and his family were merely charred and brittle sticks. There was an enormous outcry and a massive investigation, but no evidence of foul play could be found. The conclusion was that the family had been overcome by smoke before they could escape.

Then a curious thing happened. A few months after the tragedy, whispers and rumors began to circulate. Anonymous tips came in to the FBI, the police, the press. They all suggested that the fire was an act of vengeance by the infamous Don Aprile. The press, hot for a story, clamored for the case to be reopened. It was, but again there was no indictment. Yet, despite any proof, this became another legend of the Don's ferocity.

But that was the general public; the authorities

were satisfied, in this instance, that the Don was beyond reproach. Everybody knew journalists were exempt from any retaliation. You would have to kill thousands, so what was the point? The Don was too intelligent to take such a risk. Still, the legend never died. Some FBI teams even thought the Don himself had inspired the rumors to fulfill his legend. And so it grew.

But there was another side to the Don: his generosity. If you served him loyally, you became rich and had a formidable protector in times of travail. The rewards given by the Don were enormous but the punishments final. That was his legend.

After his meetings with Portella and Cilke, Don Aprile had details to tidy up. He set in motion the machinery to bring Astorre Viola back home after his eleven-year exile.

He needed Astorre, indeed had prepared him for this moment. Astorre was the Don's favorite, even above his own children. As a child Astorre was always a leader, precocious in his sociability. He loved the Don, and he did not fear him as his own children sometimes did. And though Valerius and Marcantonio were twenty and eighteen years old, when Astorre was ten, he established his independence from them. Indeed when Valerius, somewhat of a military martinet, tried to chastise him, he fought back. Marcantonio was much more affectionate to him and bought him his first banjo to encourage his singing. Astorre accepted this as the courtesy of one adult to another.

The only one Astorre took orders from was Nicole. And though she was two years older, she treated him as a suitor, as he demanded even as a small boy. She made him run her errands and listened soulfully to the Italian ballads he sang her. And she slapped his face when he tried to kiss her. For even as a small boy, Astorre was enraptured by feminine beauty.

And Nicole was beautiful. She had large dark eyes and a sensual smile; her face revealed every emotion she felt. She challenged anyone who tried to insinuate that as a female she was not as important as any man in her world. She hated the fact that she was not as physically strong as her brothers and Astorre, that she could not assert her will by force but only by her beauty. All this made her absolutely fearless, and she taunted them all, even her father, despite his dread reputation.

After his wife's death, when the children were still young, Don Aprile made it a practice to spend one summer month in Sicily. He loved the life in his native village, near the town of Montelepre, and he still owned property there, a house that had been the country retreat of a count, called Villa Grazia.

After a few years he hired a housekeeper, a Sicilian widow named Caterina. She was a very handsome woman, strong with a rich peasant beauty and a keen sense of how to run a property and command respect from the villagers. She became his mistress. All of this he kept secret from his family and friends, though now he was a man of forty and a king in his world.

Astorre Viola was only ten years old the first time he accompanied Don Raymonde Aprile to Sicily. The Don had been requested to mediate a great conflict between the Corleonesi *cosca* and the Clericuzio *cosca*. And it was also his pleasure to spend a quiet month of tranquillity at Villa Grazia.

Astorre, at ten, was affable—there was no other word. He was always cheerful, and his handsome round face with its olive skin radiated love. He continually sang in a sweet tenor voice. And when he was not singing, he offered lively conversation. Yet he had the fiery qualities of a born rebel, and he terrorized the other boys his age.

The Don brought him to Sicily because he was the best of company for a middle-aged man, which was a curious commentary on both, as well as a reflection on how the Don had brought up his own three children.

Once the Don settled his business affairs, he mediated the dispute and brought about temporary peace. Now he enjoyed his days reliving his childhood in his native village. He ate lemons, oranges, and olives from their briny barrels, and he took long walks with Astorre under the sullen deadly light of the Sicilian sun that reflected all the stone houses and countless rocks with a stunning heat. He told the small boy long-ago stories of the Robin Hoods of Sicily, their fights against the Moors, the French, the Spaniards, the pope himself. And tales of a local hero, the Great Don Zeno.

At night, together on the terrace of the Villa Grazia, they watched the azure sky of Sicily lit with a thousand shooting stars and the flashes of lightning hurling through the mountains just a short distance away. Astorre picked up the Sicilian dialect immediately and ate the black olives from the barrel as if they were bits of candy.

In just a few days Astorre established his leadership in a gang of young village boys. It was a wonder to the Don that he could do so, for Sicilian children were full of pride and feared no one. Many of these ten-year-old cherubs were already familiar with the *lupara,* the ever-present Sicilian shotgun.

Don Aprile, Astorre, and Caterina spent long summer nights eating and drinking al fresco in the luxuriant garden, the orange and lemon trees saturating the air with their citrus perfume. Sometimes old boyhood friends of the Don were invited to dinner and a game of cards. Astorre helped Caterina serve them drinks.

Caterina and the Don never showed public signs of affection, but all was understood in the village, so no man dared to present any gallantries to Caterina and all showed her all the respect the female head of the house was due. No time in his life was more pleasant to the Don.

It was just three days before the end of the visit that the unimaginable happened: the Don was kidnapped while walking the streets of the village.

In the neighboring province of Cinesi, one of the most remote and undeveloped in Sicily, the head of the village *cosca,* the local Mafioso, was a ferocious, fearless bandit by the name of Fissolini. Absolute in his local power, he really had no communication with the rest of the Mafia *coscas* on the island. He knew nothing of Don Aprile's enormous power, nor did he think it could penetrate his own remote and secure world. He decided to kidnap the Don and hold him for ransom. The only rule he knew he was breaking was that he was encroaching onto the territory of the neighboring *cosca,* but the American seemed a rich enough prize to warrant the risk.

The *cosca* is the basic unit of what is called the Mafia and is usually composed of blood relatives. Law-abiding citizens such as lawyers or doctors attach themselves to a *cosca* for protection of their interests. Each *cosca* is an organization in and of itself but may ally itself to a stronger and more powerful one. It is this interlinking that is commonly called the Mafia. But there is no overall chief or commander.

A *cosca* usually majors in a particular racket in its particular territory. There is the *cosca* that controls the price of water and prevents the central government from building dams to lower the price. In that way it destroys the government's monopoly. Another *cosca* will control the food and produce markets. The most powerful ones in Sicily at this time were the Clericuzio *cosca* of Palermo, which controlled the new construction in all of Sicily, and the Corleonesi *cosca* of Corleone, which controlled the politicians in Rome and engineered the transportation of drugs all over the world. Then there were the piddling *coscas* who demanded tribute from romantic youths to sing to the balconies of their beloveds. All *coscas* regulated crime. They would not tolerate lazy good-for-nothings burglarizing innocent citizens who paid their *cosca* dues. Those who stabbed for wallets or raped women were summarily punished by death. Also, there was no tolerance of adultery within the *coscas*. Both men and women were executed. That was understood.

Fissolini's *cosca* made a poor living. It controlled the sale of holy icons, was paid to protect a farmer's livestock, and organized the kidnapping of careless wealthy men.

41

And so it was that Don Aprile and little Astorre, strolling along the streets of their village, were picked up in two vintage American army trucks by the ignorant Fissolini and his band of men.

The ten men in peasant clothes were armed with rifles. They plucked Don Aprile off the ground and threw him into the first truck. Astorre, without hesitation, jumped into the open bed of the truck to stay with the Don. The bandits tried to throw him out, but he clung to the wooden posts. The trucks traveled an hour to the base of the mountains around Montelepre. Then everyone switched to horseback and donkey and climbed the rocky terraces toward the horizon. Throughout the trip, the boy observed everything with large green eyes but never spoke a word.

Near sunset, they reached a cave set deep in the mountains. There they were fed a supper of grilled lamb and homemade bread and wine. On the campsite was a huge statue of the Virgin Mary enclosed in a hand-carved dark wooden shrine. Fissolini was devout in spite of his ferocity. He also had a natural peasant courtesy and presented himself to the Don and the boy. There was no doubt he was chief of the band. He was short and built powerfully as a gorilla, and he carried a rifle and two guns on his body belt. His face was as stony as Sicily, but there was a merry twinkle in his eyes. He enjoyed life and its little jokes, especially that he held in his power a rich American worth his weight in gold. And yet there was no malice in him.

"Excellency," he said to the Don, "I don't want you to worry about this young lad. He will carry the ransom note to town tomorrow morning."

Astorre was eating lustily. He had never tasted anything so delicious as this grilled lamb. But he finally spoke up with cheerful bravery. "I'm staying with my Uncle Raymonde," he said.

Fissolini laughed. "Good food gives courage. To show my respect for His Excellency I prepared this meal myself. I used my mother's special spices."

"I'm staying with my uncle," Astorre said, and his voice rang out clear, defiant.

Don Aprile said to Fissolini sternly yet kindly, "It's been a wonderful night—the food, the mountain air, your company. I look forward to the fresh dew in the country. But then I advise you to bring me back to my village."

Fissolini bowed to him respectfully. "I know that you are rich. But are you that powerful? I am only going to ask for one hundred thousand dollars in American money."

"That insults me," the Don said. "You will injure my reputation. Double it. And another fifty for the boy. It will be paid. But then your life will be an eternal misery." He paused for a moment. "I'm astonished you could be so rash."

Fissolini sighed. "You must understand, Excellency, I am a poor man. Certainly I can take what I want in my province, but Sicily is such a cursed country that the rich are too poor to support men like myself. You must understand that you are the chance to make my fortune."

"Then you should have come to me to offer your services," the Don said. "I always have use for a talented man."

"You say that now because you are weak and helpless," Fissolini said. "The weak are always so generous. But I will follow your advice and ask double. Though I feel a little guilty about that. No human is worth so much. And I will let the boy go free. I have a weakness for children—I have four of my own whose mouths I must feed."

Don Aprile looked at Astorre. "Will you go?"

"No," Astorre said, lowering his head. "I want to be with you." He raised his eyes and looked at his uncle.

"Then let him stay," the Don said to the bandit.

Fissolini shook his head. "He goes back. I have a reputation to keep. I will not be known as a kidnapper of children. Because after all, Your Excellency, though I have the utmost respect, I will have to send you back piece by piece if they do not pay. But if they do, I give you the word of honor of Pietro Fissolini, not a hair of your mustache will be touched."

"The money will be paid," the Don said calmly. "And now let us make the best of things. Nephew, sing one of your songs for these gentlemen."

Astorre sang to the bandits, who were

enchanted and complimented him, ruffling his hair affectionately. Indeed it was a magical moment for all of them, the child's sweet voice filling the mountains with songs of love.

Blankets and sleeping bags were brought out of a nearby cave.

Fissolini said, "Your Excellency, what would you like for breakfast tomorrow? Some fish, fresh from the water perhaps? Then some spaghetti and veal for lunch? We are at your service."

"I thank you," the Don said. "A bit of cheese and fruit will be enough."

"Sleep well," Fissolini said. He was softened by the boy's look of unhappiness, and he patted Astorre on the head. "Tomorrow you will rest in your own bed."

Astorre closed his eyes to fall asleep immediately on the ground next to the Don. "Stay beside me," the Don said, as he reached his arms around the boy.

Astorre slept so soundly that the rising cinder-red sun was over his head when a clatter awoke him. He rose and saw that the hollow was filled with fifty armed men. Don Aprile, gentle, calm and dignified, was sitting on a great ledge of stone, sipping from a mug of coffee.

Don Aprile saw Astorre and beckoned to him. "Astorre, do you want some coffee?" He pointed a finger at the man before him. "This is my good friend, Bianco. He has rescued us."

Astorre saw a huge man who, though he was well encased in fat, wore a suit and tie, and seemed to be unarmed, was far more frightening than Fissolini. He had a curly head of white hair and large pink eyes, and he radiated power. But he seemed to blanket that power when he spoke with a soft, gravelly voice.

Octavius Bianco said, "Don Aprile, I must apologize for being so late and that you had to sleep like a peasant on the ground. But I came as soon as I got the news. I always knew Fissolini was a dunce, but I never expected him to do this."

There began the sound of hammering, and some men moved out of Astorre's vision. He saw two young boys, nailing together a cross. Then, lying on the far side of the hollow, he saw Fissolini and his ten bandits trussed on the ground and tethered to trees. They were encased by a web of wire and rope, their limbs entwined. They looked like a mound of flies on a lump of meat.

Bianco asked, "Don Aprile, which of these scum do you wish to judge first?"

"Fissolini," the Don said. "He is the leader."

Bianco dragged Fissolini before the Don; he was still tightly bound, like a mummy. Bianco and one of his soldiers lifted him and forced him to stand. Then Bianco said, "Fissolini, how could you be so stupid? Didn't you know the Don was under my protection or I would have kidnapped him myself? Did you think you were just borrowing a flask of oil? Some vinegar? Have I ever entered your province? But you were always headstrong, and I knew you would come to grief. Well, since like Jesus you must hang from the cross, make your apologies to Don Aprile and his little boy. And I will give you mercy and shoot you before we hammer in the nails."

"So," the Don said to Fissolini. "Explain your disrespect."

Fissolini stood upright and proud. "But the disrespect was not for your person, Excellency. I did not know how important and dear you were to my friends. That fool, Bianco, might have kept me fully informed. Excellency, I have made a mistake and I must pay." He stopped for a moment and then shouted angrily and scornfully at Bianco, "Stop those men from hammering those nails. I'm going deaf. And you can't scare me to death before you kill me!"

Fissolini paused again and said to the Don, "Punish me, but spare my men. They followed my orders. They have families. You will destroy an entire village if you kill them."

"They are responsible men," Don Aprile said sarcastically. "I would insult them if they did not share your fate."

At this moment Astorre, even in his child's mind, realized that they were talking life and death. He whispered, "Uncle, don't hurt him." The Don made no sign of having heard.

"Go on," he said to Fissolini.

Fissolini gave him a questioning look, at once proud and wary. "I will not beg for my life. But those ten men lying there are all in my blood family. If you kill them, you destroy their wives and their children. Three of them are my sons-in-law. They had absolute faith in me. They trusted my judgment. If you let them go, I would make them swear their undying loyalty to you before I die. And they will obey me. That is something, to have ten loyal friends. That is not nothing. I am told you are a great man, but you cannot be truly great if you do not show mercy. You shouldn't make a habit of it, of course, but just this once." He smiled at Astorre.

For Don Raymonde Aprile this was a familiar moment, and he was in no doubt as to his decision. He had always distrusted the power of gratitude, and he believed that no one could direct the influence of free will in any man, except by death. He regarded Fissolini impassively and shook his head. Bianco moved forward.

Astorre strode to his uncle and looked him square in the eyes. He had understood everything. He put out his hand to protect Fissolini.

"He didn't hurt us," Astorre said. "He just wanted our money."

The Don smiled and said, "And that's nothing?"

Astorre said, "But it was a good reason. He wanted the money to feed his family. And I like him. Please, Uncle."

The Don smiled at him and said, "Bravo." Then he remained silent for a long time, ignoring Astorre tugging at his hand. And for the first time in many years the Don felt the urge to show mercy.

Bianco's men had lit up small cigars, very strong, and the smoke wafted through the dawn air carried on the mountain breezes. One of the men came forward and from his hunting jacket took out a fresh cigar and offered it to the Don. With a child's clarity, Astorre understood this was not only a courtesy but a demonstration of respect. The Don took the cigar, and the man lit it for him within cupped hands.

The Don puffed his cigar slowly and deliberately, then said, "I will not insult you by showing you mercy. But I will offer you a business arrangement. I recognize you had no malice and you showed the utmost regard for my person and the boy. So this is the arrangement. You live. Your comrades live. But for the rest of your lives, you will be at my command."

Astorre felt an enormous relief, and he smiled at Fissolini. He watched Fissolini kneel to the ground and kiss the Don's hand. Astorre noticed that the surrounding armed men puffed furiously on their cigars, and even Bianco, grand as a mountain, trembled with pleasure.

Fissolini murmured, "Bless you, Your Excellency."

The Don put his cigar down on a nearby rock. "I accept your blessing, but you must understand. Bianco came to save me, and you are expected to do the same duty. I pay him a sum of money, and I will do the same for you every year. But one act of disloyalty and you and your world will be destroyed. You, your wife, your children, your nephews, your sons-in-law will cease to exist."

Fissolini rose from his knees. He embraced the Don and burst into tears.

And so it was that the Don and his nephew became most formally united. The Don loved the boy for persuading him to show mercy, and Astorre loved his uncle for giving him the lives of Fissolini and his ten men. It was a bond that lasted the rest of their lives.

The last night in Villa Grazia, Don Aprile had espresso in the garden and Astorre ate olives from their barrel. Astorre was very pensive, not his usual sociable self.

"Are you sorry to leave Sicily?" the Don asked.

"I wish I could live here," Astorre said. He put the pits of his olives in his pocket.

"Well, we will come every summer together," the Don said.

Astorre looked at him like a wise old friend, his youthful face troubled.

"Is Caterina your girlfriend?" he asked.

The Don laughed. "She is my good friend," he said.

Astorre thought about this. "Do my cousins know about her?"

"No, my children do not know." Again the Don was amused by the boy and wondered what would come next.

Astorre was very grave now. "Do my cousins know you have such powerful friends like Bianco who will do anything you tell them they must do?"

"No," the Don said.

"I won't tell them about anything," Astorre said. "Not even about the kidnapping."

The Don felt a surge of pride. *Omertà* had been bred into his genes.

Late that night, alone, Astorre went to the far corner of the garden and dug a hole with his bare hands. In that hole he put the olive pits he had secreted in his pocket. He looked up at the pale night blue of the Sicilian sky and dreamed of himself as an old man like his uncle, sitting in this garden on a similar night, watching his olive trees grow.

After that, everything was fate, the Don believed. He and Astorre made the yearly trip to Sicily until Astorre was sixteen. In the back of the Don's mind, a vision was forming, a vague outline of the boy's destiny.

Mario Puzo

It was his daughter who created the crisis that moved Astorre into that destiny. At the age of eighteen, two years older than Astorre, Nicole fell in love with him and with her fiery temperament did little to conceal the fact. She completely overwhelmed the susceptible boy. They became intimate with all the hot furiousness of youth.

The Don could not allow this, but he was a general who adjusted his tactics to the terrain. He never gave any hint he knew of the affair.

One night he called Astorre into his den and told him he would be sent to England for his schooling and to serve an apprenticeship in banking with a certain Mr. Pryor of London. He did not give any further reason, knowing the boy would realize he was being sent away to end the affair. But he had not reckoned with his daughter, who had listened outside the door. She came storming into the room, her passionate outrage making her even more beautiful.

"You're not sending him away," she screamed at her father. "We'll run away together."

The Don smiled at her and said placatingly, "You both have to finish school."

Nicole turned to Astorre, who was blushing with embarrassment. "Astorre, you won't go?" she said. "Will you?"

Astorre did not answer, and Nicole burst into tears.

It would be hard for any father not to be moved

52

by such a scene, but the Don was amused. His daughter was splendid, truly Mafioso in the old sense, a prize in any form. Despite that, for weeks afterward she refused to speak to her father and locked herself away in her room. But the Don did not fear she would be brokenhearted forever.

It amused him even more to see Astorre in the trap of all maturing adolescents. Certainly Astorre loved Nicole. And certainly her passion and her devotion made him feel like the most important person on earth. Any young man can be seduced by such attention. But just as certainly, the Don understood that Astorre wanted an excuse to be free of any encumbrance on his march to the glories of life. The Don smiled. The boy had all the right instincts, and it was time for his real schooling.

So now, three years after his retirement, Don Raymonde Aprile felt the security and satisfaction of a man who has made the right choices in life. Indeed the Don felt so secure that he began to develop a closer relationship with his children, finally enjoying the fruits of fatherhood—to some degree.

Because Valerius had spent most of the last twenty years in army foreign posts, he had never been close to his father. Now that he was stationed at West Point, the two men saw each other more often and began to speak more openly. Yet it was difficult.

With Marcantonio, it was different. The Don and his second son enjoyed some kind of rapport. Marcantonio explained his work in TV, his excitement over the dramatic process, his duty to his viewers, his desire to make the world a better place. The lives of such people were like fairy tales to the Don. He was fascinated by them.

Over family dinners, Marcantonio and his father could quarrel in a friendly way for the entertainment of the others. Once the Don told Marcantonio, "I have never seen people so good or so evil as your characters in those dramas."

Marcantonio said, "That is what our audience believes. We have to give it to them."

At one family gathering, Valerius had tried to explain the rationale for the war in the Persian Gulf, which in addition to protecting important economic interests and human rights had also been a ratings bonanza for Marcantonio's TV network. But to all of this the Don just shrugged. These conflicts were refinements in power that did not interest him.

"Tell me," he said to Valerius. "How do nations really win wars? What is the deciding factor?"

Valerius considered this. "There is the trained army, brilliant generals. There are the great battles, some lost, some won. When I worked in intelligence, and we analyzed everything, it comes

54

to this: the country that produces the most steel wins the war, simply that."

The Don nodded, finally satisfied.

His warmest and most intense relationship was with Nicole. He was proud of her accomplishments, her physical beauty, her passionate nature, and her intelligence. And, true, young as she was, just thirty-two, she was a powerful up-and-coming lawyer with good political connections, and she had no fear of anyone in a suit who represented entrenched power.

Here the Don had helped her secretly; her law firm was deeply indebted to him. But her brothers were wary of her for two reasons: she was unmarried and she did a great deal of pro bono work. Despite his admiration for her, the Don could never take Nicole seriously in the world. She was, after all, a woman. And one with troubling taste in men.

At family dinners the father and daughter argued constantly, like two great cats frolicking dangerously, occasionally drawing blood. They had one serious bone of contention, the only thing that could affect the Don's constant affability. Nicole believed in the sacredness of human life, that capital punishment was an abomination. She had organized and led the Campaign Against the Death Penalty.

"Why?" the Don asked.

And Nicole would become infuriated all over again. Because she believed capital punishment would eventually destroy humanity. That if killing was condoned under any circumstances, then it could be justified by another set of circumstances, another set of beliefs. Eventually, it would not serve evolution or civilization. And believing that brought her into constant conflict with her brother Valerius. After all, what else did the army do? The reasons didn't matter to her. Killing was killing and would set us all back to cannibalism or worse. At every opportunity, Nicole fought in courts all over the country to save condemned murderers. Although the Don considered this the sheerest nonsense, he nonetheless proposed a toast to her at a family dinner following her victory in a famous pro bono case. She had secured commutation of the death sentence of one of the decade's most notorious criminals, a man who had killed his best friend and sodomized the newly made widow. In his getaway, he had executed two gas station attendants while he robbed them. He had gone on to rape and murder a ten-year-old girl. His career was brought to a close only when he attempted to kill two policemen in their cruiser. Nicole had won the case on grounds of insanity, and on the assurance that he would live the rest of his life in an institution for the criminally insane without the hope of release.

The next family dinner was a celebration to honor Nicole for winning another case—this time her own. In a recent trial she had championed a difficult principle of law at great personal risk. And she had been brought before the Bar Association for unethical practice and had been acquitted. Now she was exuberant.

The Don, in a cheerful mood, showed an uncharacteristic interest in this case. He congratulated his daughter on the acquittal but was somewhat confused, or pretended to be, by the circumstances. Nicole had to explain it to him.

She had defended a man, thirty years of age, who had raped, sodomized, and killed a twelve-year-old girl, then secretly hidden her body so that it could not be found by the police. Circumstantial evidence against him had been strong, but without a *corpus,* the jury and judge would be reluctant to give him the death penalty. The parents of the victim were in anguish in their frustrated desire to find the body.

The murderer confided to Nicole, as his attorney, where the body was buried and authorized her to negotiate a deal—he would reveal the body's whereabouts in exchange for a life sentence rather than execution. However, when Nicole opened negotiations with the prosecutor, she was faced with a threat of prosecution herself if she did not immediately reveal the whereabouts of the body. She believed it mattered to society to protect the confidentiality between attorney and client. Therefore, she refused, and a prominent judge declared her in the right.

The prosecutor, after consulting with the parents of the victim, finally consented to the deal.

The murderer told them that he had dismembered the body, placed it in a box filled with ice, and buried it in a nearby marshland in New Jersey. And so the body was found and the murderer sentenced to life imprisonment. But then the Bar Association brought her up on charges of unethical negotiation. And today she had won her acquittal.

The Don toasted to all of his children and then asked Nicole, "And you behaved honorably in all this?"

Nicole lost her exuberance. "It was the principle of the thing. The government cannot be allowed to breach the lawyer/client privilege in any one situation, no matter how grave, or it is no longer sacrosanct."

"And you felt nothing for the victim's mother and father?" the Don asked.

"Of course I did," Nicole said, annoyed. "But how could I let this affect a basic principle of the law? I suffered for that, I really did; why wouldn't I? But unfortunately, in order to set precedents for future law sacrifices have to be made."

"And yet the Bar Association put you on trial," the Don said.

"To save face," Nicole said. "It was a political move. Ordinary people, unschooled in the complexities of the legal system, can't accept these principles of law, and there was an uproar. So my trial diffused everything. Some very prominent judge had to go public and explain that I had the right under the Constitution to refuse to give that information."

"Bravo," the Don said jovially. "The law is always full of surprises. But only to lawyers, of course."

Nicole knew he was making fun of her. She said sharply, "Without a body of law, no civilization can exist."

"That is true," the Don said as if to appease his daughter. "But it seems unfair that a man who commits a terrible crime escapes with his life."

"That's true," Nicole said. "But our system of law is based on plea bargaining. It is true that each criminal gets less punishment than he deserves. But in a way that's a good thing. Forgiveness heals. And in the long run, those who commit crimes against our society will be more easily rehabilitated."

So it was with a good-humored sarcasm that the Don proposed his toast. "But tell me," he said to Nicole. "Did you ever believe the man innocent by reason of his insanity? After all, he did exercise his free will."

Valerius looked at Nicole with cool, measuring eyes. He was a tall man, forty years of age with a bristly short mustache and hair already turning to steel gray. As an intelligence officer, he had himself

59

made decisions that overlooked human morality. He was interested in her reasoning.

Marcantonio understood his sister, that she aspired to a normal life partly out of shame for their father's life. He was more worried that she would say something rash, something that her father could never forgive her for.

As for Astorre, he was dazzled by Nicole—her flashing eyes, the incredible energy with which she responded to her father's goading. He remembered their lovemaking as teenagers and felt her still obvious affection for him. But now he was transformed, no longer what he was when they were lovers. That was understood. He wondered if her brothers knew about that long-ago affair. And he too worried that a quarrel would break the bonds of family, a family that he loved, that was his only refuge. He hoped Nicole would not go too far. But he had no sympathy for her views. His years in Sicily had taught him differently. But it amazed him that the two people he cared most about in the world could be so different. And it occurred to him that even if she were right, he could never side with Nicole against her father.

Nicole looked boldly into her father's eyes. "I don't believe he had free will," she said. "He was forced by the circumstances of his life—by his own distorted perceptions, his genetic heritage, his biochemistry, the ignorance of medicine—he was insane. So of course I believe it."

The Don pondered this for a moment. "Tell me," he said. "If he admitted to you all his excuses were false, would you still have tried to save his life?"

"Yes," Nicole said. "Each individual life is sacred. The state has no right to take it."

The Don smiled at her mockingly. "That's your Italian blood. Do you know that modern Italy has never had the death penalty? All those human lives saved." His sons and Astorre flinched at his sarcasm, but Nicole was unabashed.

She said to him sternly, "It is barbaric for the state under the mantle of justice to commit premeditated murder. I would think that you of all people would agree with that." It was a challenge, a reference to his reputation. Nicole laughed, then said more soberly, "We have an alternative. The criminal is locked away in an institution or a prison for life without hope of release or parole. Then he is no longer a danger to society."

The Don looked at her coolly. "One thing at a time," he said. "I do approve of the state taking a human life. And as for your lifetime without parole or release, that's a joke. Twenty years pass and supposedly new evidence is found, or rehabilitation is assumed and the criminal has made a new person of himself, so now spills the milk of human kindness. But no one cares for the dead. The man goes free. And that's not really important . . ."

Nicole frowned. "Dad, I didn't imply that the victim isn't important. But taking a life will not get the victim's life back. And the longer we condone killing, under any circumstances, the longer it will go on."

Here the Don paused and drank his wine as he looked around the table at his two sons and Astorre. "Let me tell you the reality," he said, and turned to his daughter. He spoke with an intensity rare for him. "You say human life is sacred? From what evidence? Where in history? The wars that have killed millions are endorsed by all governments and religions. The massacres of thousands of enemies in a political dispute, over economic interests, are recorded through time. How many times has the earning of money been placed above the sanctity of human life? And you yourself condone the taking of a human life when you get your client off."

Nicole's dark eyes flashed. "I have not condoned it," she said. "I have not excused it. I think it's barbaric. I have just refused to lay the ground for more of it!"

Now the Don spoke more quietly but more sincerely. "Above all this," he said, "the victim, your loved one, lies beneath the earth. He is forever banished from this world. We will never see his face, we will never hear his voice, we will never touch his flesh. He is in darkness, lost to us and our world."

They all listened silently as the Don took another sip of wine. "Now, my Nicole. Hear me. Your client, your murderer, is sentenced to life imprisonment. He will be behind bars or in an institution for the rest of his life. So you say. But each morning he will see the rising sun, he will taste hot food, he will hear music, the blood will run in his veins and interest him in the world. His loved ones can still embrace him. I understand he can even study books, learn carpentry to build a table and chairs. In short, he lives. And that is unjust."

Nicole was resolute. She did not flinch. "Dad, to domesticate animals, you don't let them eat raw meat. You don't let them get a taste of it or they want more. The more we kill, the easier it gets to kill. Can't you see that?" When he didn't answer her, she asked, "And how can you decide what's just or unjust? Where do you draw the line?" It had been meant as a defiance but was more of a plea to understand all her years of doubt in him.

They all expected an outburst of fury by the Don at her insolence, but suddenly he was in a good humor. "I have had my moments of weakness," he said, "but I never let a child judge his or her parents. Children are useless and live by our sufferance. And I consider myself beyond reproach as a father. I have raised three children who are pillars in society, talented, accomplished, and successful. And not completely powerless against fate. Can any of you reproach me?"

At this point Nicole lost her anger. "No," she said. "As a parent no one can reproach you. But you left something out. The oppressed are the ones who hang. The rich wind up escaping the final punishment."

The Don looked at Nicole with great seriousness. "Why, then, do you not fight to change the laws so that the rich hang with the poor? That is more intelligent."

Astorre murmured, smiling cheerfully, "There would be very few of us left." And that remark cut the tension.

"The greatest virtue of humanity is mercy," Nicole said. "An enlightened society does not execute a human being, and it refrains from punishment as much as common sense and justice allows."

It was only then that the Don lost his customary good humor. "Where did you get such ideas?" he asked. "They are self-indulgent and cowardly— more, they are blasphemous. Who is more merciless than God? He does not forgive, He does not ban punishment. There is a Heaven and there is a Hell by His decree. He does not banish grief and sorrow in His world. It is His Almighty duty to show no more than the necessary mercy. So who are you to dispense such marvelous grace? It's an arrogance. Do you think that if you are so saintly, you can create a better world? Remember, saints can only whisper prayers to God's ear and only when they have earned the right to do so by their own martyrdom. No. It is our duty to pursue our fellowman. Or what great sins he could be capable of committing. We would deliver our world to the devil."

This left Nicole speechless with anger and Valerius and Marcantonio smiling. Astorre bowed his head as if in prayer.

Finally Nicole said, "Daddy, you are just too outrageous as a moralist. And you certainly are no example to follow."

There was a long silence at the table as each one sat with memories of their strange relationship with the Don. Nicole never quite believing the stories she'd heard about her father and yet fearing they were true. Marcantonio remembering one of his colleagues at the network asking slyly, "How does your father treat you and the other kids?"

And Marcantonio, considering the question carefully, knowing the man was referring to his father's reputation, had said quite seriously, "My father is very cordial to us."

Valerius was thinking how much his father was like some generals he had served under. Men who got the job done without any moral scruples, without any doubts as to their duty. Arrows that sped to their mark with deadly swiftness and accuracy.

For Astorre it was different. The Don had always shown him affection and trust. But he was also the only one at the table who knew that the reputation of the Don was true. He was remembering three years before when he had returned from his years of exile. The Don had given him certain instructions.

The Don had told him, "A man my age can die from stubbing his toe on a door, or from a black mole on his back, or from a break in the beating of his heart. It is strange that a man does not realize his mortality every second of his life. No matter. He need not have enemies. But still one must plan. I have made you a majority heir to my banks; you will control them and share the income with my children. And for this reason: certain interests want to buy my banks, one headed by the consul general of Peru. The federal government continues to investigate me under the RICO laws so they can seize my banks. What a nice piece of business for them. They will find nothing. Now, my instructions to you are never sell the banks. They will be more profitable and powerful as time goes on. In time the past will be forgotten.

"If something unexpected happens, call Mr. Pryor, to assist you as controller. You know him well. He is extremely qualified, and he too profits from the banks. He owes me his loyalty. Also, I will introduce you to Benito Craxxi in Chicago. He is a man of infinite resources and also profits from the banks. He too is trustworthy. Meanwhile, I will give you a macaroni business simply to run and give you a good living. For all this I charge you with the safety and prosperity of my children. It is a harsh world, and I have brought them up as innocents."

Three years later, Astorre was pondering these words. Time had passed, and it seemed now that his services would not be needed. The Don's world could not be shattered.

But Nicole was not quite finished with her arguments. "What about the quality of mercy?" she said to her father. "You know, what Christians preach?"

The Don replied without hesitation. "Mercy is a vice, a pretension to powers we do not have. Those who give mercy commit an unpardonable offense to the victim. And that is not our duty here on earth."

"So you would not want mercy?" Nicole asked.

"Never," the Don said. "I do not seek it or desire it. If I must, I will accept the punishment for all my sins."

It was at this dinner that Colonel Valerius Aprile invited his family to attend the Confirmation of his twelve-year-old son, in New York City, two months hence. His wife had insisted on a big celebration at her family's old church. It was in the Don's newly transformed character to accept this invitation.

And so on a cold December Sunday noon, bright

with a lemon-colored light, the Aprile family went to Saint Patrick's on Fifth Avenue, where the brilliant sunshine etched the image of that great cathedral into the streets around it. Don Raymonde Aprile, Valerius and his wife, Marcantonio, anxious for a quick getaway, and Nicole, beautiful in black, watched the cardinal himself, red-hatted and sipping wine, give Communion and administer Heaven's admonitory ceremonial slap on the cheek.

It was a sweet and mysterious pleasure to see the boys on the brink of puberty, girls ripening into nubility in their white gowns with the red silk scarves draped around, marching down the aisles of the cathedral, stone angels and saints watching over them. Confirming that they would serve God for the rest of their lives. Nicole had tears in her eyes, though she didn't believe a word the cardinal was saying. She laughed to herself.

Out on the steps of the cathedral, the children shed their robes and showed off their hidden finery. The girls in frail cobwebby white lace dresses, the boys in their dark suits, glaring white shirts, and traditional red neckties knitted at their throats to ward off the Devil.

Don Aprile emerged from the church, Astorre on one side, Marcantonio on the other. The children milled around in a circle, Valerius and his wife proudly holding their son's gown as a photographer snapped their picture. Don Aprile began to descend the steps alone. He breathed in the air. It was a glorious day; he felt so alive and alert. And when his newly confirmed grandson came over to hug him, he patted his head affectionately and put a huge gold coin in the boy's palm—the traditional gift on a child's Confirmation day. Then with a generous hand he reached into his jacket pocket and pulled out a handful of smaller gold coins to give to the other boys and girls. He was gratified by their shouts of joy and indeed by being in the city itself, its tall gray stone buildings as sweet as the trees. He was quite alone, only Astorre a few paces behind. He looked down at the stone steps in front of him, then paused a moment as a huge black car pulled up as if to receive him.

In Brightwaters that Sunday morning Heskow got up early and went to get baked goods and the newspapers. He stored the stolen car in the garage, a huge black sedan packed with the guns and masks and boxes of ammunition. He checked the tires, the gas and oil, and the braking lights. Perfect. He went back into the house to wake up Franky and Stace, but of course they were already up and Stace had the coffee ready.

They ate breakfast in silence and read the Sunday papers. Franky checked the college basket-ball scores.

At ten o'clock Stace said to Heskow, "The car ready?" and Heskow said, "All set."

They got into the car and left, Franky sitting up front with Heskow, Stace in the back. The trip to the city would take an hour, so they would have an extra hour to kill. The important thing was to be on time.

In the car Franky checked the guns. Stace tried on one of the masks, little white shells attached to side strings, so that they could hang them around their necks until they had to put them on at the last moment.

They drove into the city listening to opera on the radio. Heskow was an excellent driver, conservative, steady-paced, no disturbing acceleration or deceleration. He always left a good space in front and back. Stace gave a little grunt of approval, which lifted part of the strain; they were tense but not jittery. They knew they had to be perfect. They couldn't miss the shot.

Heskow weaved slowly through the city; he seemed to catch every red light. Then he turned onto Fifth Avenue and waited half a block from the cathedral's great doors. The church bells began to ring, the sound clanging against the surrounding steel skyscrapers. Heskow started up the motor again. All three men watched the children swirling out into the streets. It worried them.

Stace murmured, "Franky, the head shot." Then they saw the Don come out, walk ahead of the men on either side of him, and begin to descend the steps. He seemed to look directly at them.

"Masks," Heskow said. He accelerated slightly, and Franky put his hand on the door handle. His left hand cradled the Uzi, ready to come out onto the sidewalk.

The car speeded up and stopped as the Don reached the last step. Stace jumped out of the backseat onto the street, the car between him and his target. In one quick move he rested his gun on the roof. He shot two-handed. He only fired twice.

The first bullet hit the Don square in the forehead. The second bullet tore out his throat. His blood spurted all over the sidewalk, showering yellow sunlight with pink drops.

At the same time Franky, on the sidewalk, fired a long burst of his Uzi over the heads of the crowd.

Then both men were back in the car and Heskow screeched down the avenue. Minutes later they were driving through the tunnel and then onto the little airport, where a private jet took them aboard.

At the sound of the first shot Valerius hurled his son and wife to the ground and covered them with his body. He actually saw nothing that happened. Neither did Nicole, who stared at her father with astonishment. Marcantonio looked down in disbelief. The reality was so different from the staged fiction of his TV dramas. The shot to the Don's forehead had split it apart like a melon so that you could see a slosh of brains and blood inside. The shot in the throat had hacked away the flesh in a jagged chunk so that he looked as if he had been hit with a meat cleaver. And there was an enormous amount of blood on the pavement around him. More blood than you could imagine in a human body. Marcantonio saw the two men with eggshell masks over their faces; he also saw the guns in their hands, but they seemed unreal. He could not have given any details about their clothing, their hair. He was paralyzed with shock. He could not even have said if they were black or white, naked or clothed. They could have been ten feet tall or two.

But Astorre had been alert as soon as the black sedan stopped. He saw Stace fire his gun and thought the left hand pulled the trigger. He saw Franky fire the Uzi, and that was definitely left-handed. He caught a fleeting glance at the driver, a round-headed man, obviously heavy. The two shooters moved with the grace of well-conditioned athletes. As Astorre dropped to the sidewalk, he reached out to pull the Don down with him, but he was a fraction of a second too late. And now he was covered with the Don's blood.

Then he saw the children move like a whirlwind of terror, a huge red dot at the center of it. They were screaming. He saw the Don splayed over the steps as if death had disjointed his skeleton itself. And he felt an enormous dread of what all this would do to his life and the lives of those dearest to him.

Nicole came to stand over the Don's body. Her knees folded against her will, and she kneeled next to him. Silently, she reached out to touch her father's bloody throat. And then she wept as if she would weep forever.

CHAPTER

3

THE ASSASSINATION of Don Raymonde Aprile was an astounding event to the members of his former world. Who would dare to risk killing such a man, and to what purpose? He had given away his empire; there was no realm to steal. Dead, he could no longer lavish his beneficent gifts or use his influence to help someone unfortunate with the law or fate.

Could it be some long-postponed revenge? Was there some hidden gain that would come to light? Of course, there might be a woman, but he had been a widower for close to thirty years and had never been seen with a woman; he was not regarded as an admirer of female beauty. The Don's children were above suspicion. Also, this was a professional hit, and they did not have the contacts.

So his killing was not only a mystery but almost sacrilegious. A man who had inspired so much fear, who had gone unharmed by the law and jackals alike while he ruled a vast criminal empire for over thirty years—how could he be brought so to death? And what an irony, when he had finally found the path of righteousness and placed himself under the protection of society, that he would live for only three short years.

What was even more strange was the lack of any longtime furor after the Don's death. The media soon deserted the story, the police were secretive, and the FBI shrugged it off as a local matter. It seemed as if all the fame and power of Don Aprile had been washed away in his mere three years of retirement.

The underground world showed no interest. There were no retaliatory murders—all the Don's friends and former loyal vassals seemed to have forgotten him. Even the Don's children seemed to have put the whole affair behind them and accepted their father's fate.

No one seemed to care—no one except Kurt Cilke.

Kurt Cilke, FBI agent in charge in New York, decided to take a hand in the case, though it was strictly a local homicide for the NYPD. He decided to interview the Aprile family.

75

A month after the Don's funeral, Cilke took his deputy agent, Bill Boxton, with him to call on Marcantonio Aprile. They had to be careful of Marcantonio. He was head of programming of a major TV network and had a lot of clout in Washington. A polite phone call arranged an appointment through his secretary.

Marcantonio received them in his plush office suite at the network's midtown headquarters. He greeted them graciously, offering them coffee, which they refused. He was a tall, handsome man with creamy olive skin, exquisitely dressed in a dark suit and an extraordinary pink-and-red tie manufactured by a designer whose ties were favored by TV anchors and hosts.

Cilke said, "We're helping out with the investigation of your father's death. Do you have knowledge of anyone who would bear him ill will?"

"I really wouldn't know," Marcantonio said, smiling. "My father kept us all at a distance, even his grandchildren. We grew up completely outside his circle of business." He gave them a small apologetic wave of his hand.

Cilke didn't like that gesture. "What do you think was the reason for that?" he asked.

"You gentlemen know his past history," Marcantonio said seriously. "He didn't want any of his children to be involved in his activities. We were sent away to school and to college to make our own place in the world. He never came to our homes for dinner. He came to our graduations; that was it. And of course, when we understood, we were grateful."

Cilke said, "You rose awfully fast to your position. Did he maybe help you out a little?"

For the first time Marcantonio was less than affable.

"Never. It's not unusual in my profession for young men to rise quickly. My father sent me to the best schools and gave me a generous living allowance. I used that money to develop dramatic properties, and I made the right choices."

"And your father was happy with that?" Cilke asked. He was watching the man closely, trying to read his every expression.

"I don't think he really understood what I was doing, but yes," Marcantonio said wryly.

"You know," Cilke said, "I chased your father for twenty years and could never catch him. He was a very smart man."

"Well, we never could either," Marcantonio said. "My brother, my sister, or me."

Cilke said, laughing as if at a joke, "And you have no feeling of Sicilian vengeance? Would you pursue anything of that kind?"

"Certainly not," Marcantonio said. "My father brought us up not to think that way. But I hope you catch his killer."

"How about his will?" Cilke asked. "He died a very rich man."

"You'll have to ask my sister, Nicole, about that," Marcantonio said. "She's the executor."

"But you do know what's in it?"

"Sure," Marcantonio said. His voice was steely.

Boxton broke in. "And you can't think of anyone at all who might wish to do him harm?"

"No," Marcantonio said. "If I had a name, I'd tell you."

"OK," Cilke said. "I'll leave you my card. Just in case."

Before Cilke went on to talk to the Don's two other children, he decided to pay a call on the city's chief of detectives. Since he wanted no official record, he invited Paul Di Benedetto to one of the fanciest Italian restaurants on the East Side. Di Benedetto loved the perks of the high life, as long as he didn't have to dent his wallet.

The two of them had often done business over the years, and Cilke always enjoyed his company. Now he was watching Paul sample everything.

"So," Di Benedetto said, "the feds don't often spring for such a fancy meal. What is it that you want?"

Cilke said, "That was a *great* meal. Right?"

Di Benedetto shrugged with heavy shoulders, like the roll of a wave. Then he smiled a little maliciously. For such a tough-looking guy, he had a great smile. It transformed his face into that of some beloved Disney character.

"Kurt," he said, "this place is full of shit. It's run by aliens from outer space. Sure, they make the food look Italian, they make it smell Italian, but it tastes like goo from Mars. These guys are aliens, I'm telling you."

Cilke laughed. "Hey, but the wine is good."

"It all tastes like medicine to me unless it's guinea red mixed with cream soda."

"You're a hard man to please," Cilke said.

"No," Di Benedetto said. "I'm easy to please. That's the whole problem."

Cilke sighed. "Two hundred bucks of government money shot to shit."

"Oh, no," Di Benedetto replied. "I appreciate the gesture. Now, what's up?"

Cilke ordered espresso for both of them. Then he said, "I'm investigating the Don Aprile killing. A case of yours, Paul. We kept tabs on him for years and nothing. He retires, lives straight. He has nothing anybody wants. So why the killing? A very dangerous thing for anybody to do."

"Very professional," Di Benedetto said. "A beautiful piece of work."

Cilke said, "So?"

"It doesn't make any sort of sense," Di Benedetto said. "You wiped out most of the Mafia bigwigs, a brilliant job too. My hat's off to you. Maybe you even forced this Don to retire. So the wiseguys that are left have no reason to knock him off."

"What about the string of banks he owns?" Cilke asked.

Di Benedetto waved his cigar. "That's your line of work. We just go after the riffraff."

"What about his family?" Cilke said. "Drugs, women chasing, anything?"

"Absolutely not," Di Benedetto said. "Up-standing citizens with big professional careers. The Don planned it that way. He wanted them to be absolutely straight." He paused now, and he was deadly serious. "It's not a grudge. He squared everything with everybody. It's not random. There has to be a reason. Somebody gains. That's what we're looking for."

"What about his will?" Cilke asked.

"His daughter files it tomorrow. I asked. She told me to wait."

"And you stood still for it?" Cilke asked.

"Sure," Di Benedetto said. "She's a top-notch lawyer, she has clout, and her law firm is a political force. Why the hell would I try to get tough with her? I just ate out of her hand."

"Maybe I can do better," Cilke said.

"I'm sure you can."

Kurt Cilke had known the assistant chief of detectives, Aspinella Washington, for over ten years. She was a six-foot-tall African-American with close-cropped hair and finely chiseled features. She was a terror to the police she commanded and the felons she apprehended. By design, she acted as offensively as possible, and she really wasn't too fond of Cilke or the FBI.

She received Cilke in her office by saying, "Kurt, are you here to make one of my black brethren wealthy again?"

Cilke laughed. "No, Aspinella," he said. "I'm here looking for information."

"Really," she said. "For free? After you cost the city five million dollars?"

She was wearing a safari jacket and tan trousers. Beneath her jacket he could see the holstered gun. On her right hand was a diamond ring that looked as if it could cut through facial tissue like a razor.

She still bore a grudge against Cilke because the FBI had proven a brutality case against her detectives and on the basis of civil rights the victim had won a huge judgment—and also sent two of her detectives to jail. The victim, who had gotten rich, had been a pimp and drug pusher whom Aspinella herself had once severely beaten. Although she had been appointed assistant chief as a political sop to the black vote, she functioned much more toughly on black felons than on whites.

"Stop beating innocent people," Cilke said, "and I'll stop."

"I never framed anyone who wasn't guilty," she said, grinning.

"I'm just checking in on the Don Aprile murder," Cilke said.

"What's it your business? It's a local gang hit. Or are you making that another fucking civil rights case?"

"Well, it could be related to currency or drugs," Cilke said.

"And how do you know that?" Aspinella asked.

"We have our informers."

Suddenly Aspinella was in one of her rages. "You fucking FBI guys come in for info and then you won't give me any? You guys are not even honest to good cops. You float around arresting white-collar pricks. You never get into the dirty work. You don't know what the hell that is. Get the fuck out of my office."

Cilke was pleased with the interviews. Their pattern was clear to him. Both Di Benedetto and Aspinella were going to go into the tank on the Don Aprile murder. They would not cooperate with the FBI. They would just go through the motions. In short, they had been bribed.

There was a reason for his beliefs. He knew that traffic in drugs could only survive if police officials were paid off, and he had word, not good in court, that Di Benedetto and Aspinella were on the drug lord's payroll.

*

Before Cilke interviewed the Don's daughter, he decided to take his chances with the older son, Valerius Aprile. For that he and Boxton had to drive up to West Point, where Valerius was a colonel in the United States Army and taught military tactics—whatever the hell that meant, Cilke thought.

Valerius received them in a spacious office that looked down upon the parade grounds where cadets were practicing marching drills. He was not as affable as his brother had been, though he was not discourteous. Cilke asked him if he knew his father's enemies.

"No," he said. "I've served out of the country for most of the last twenty years. I attended family celebrations when I could. My father was only concerned that I get promoted to general. He wanted to see me wearing that star. Even brigadier would have made him happy."

"He was a patriot, then?" Cilke asked.

"He loved this country," Valerius said curtly.

"He got you your appointment as a cadet?" Cilke pressed.

"I suppose so," Valerius said. "But he could never get me made a general. I guess he had no influence in the Pentagon, or at any rate I just wasn't good enough. But I love it anyway. I have my place."

"You're sure you can't give us a lead on any of your father's enemies?" Cilke asked.

"No, he didn't have any," Valerius said. "My father would have made a great general. When he retired he had everything covered. When he used power, it was always with preemptive force. He had the numbers and the materials."

"You don't seem to be that concerned that somebody murdered your father. No desire for vengeance?"

"No more than for a fellow officer fallen in battle," Valerius said. "I'm interested, of course. Nobody likes to see his father killed."

"Do you know anything about his will?"

"You'll have to ask my sister about that," Valerius said.

Late that afternoon Cilke and Boxton were in the office of Nicole Aprile, and here they received a completely different reception. Nicole's office could be reached only by going through three secretarial barriers and after passing what Cilke recognized as a personal security aide, who looked as though she could take both him and Boxton apart in two seconds. He could tell by the way she moved that she had trained her body to the strength of a male. Her muscles showed through her clothing. Her breasts were strapped down, and she wore a linen jacket over her sweater and black slacks.

Nicole's greeting was not warm, though she looked very attractive, dressed in a haute couture suit of deep violet. She wore huge gold hoop earrings, and her black hair was shiny and long. Her features were finely cut and stern but were betrayed by huge soft brown eyes.

"Gentlemen, I can give you twenty minutes," she said.

She was wearing a frilly blouse beneath the violet jacket, and its cuffs almost covered her hands as she extended one for Cilke's ID. She looked it over carefully and said, "Special agent in charge? That's pretty high up for a routine inquiry."

She spoke in a tone that was familiar to Cilke, one that he had always resented. It was the slightly scolding tone of the federal attorneys when they dealt with the investigative arm they oversaw.

"Your father was a very important man," Cilke said.

"Yes, until he retired and placed himself under the protection of the law," Nicole said bitterly.

"Which makes his killing even more mysterious," Cilke said. "We were hoping you might give us some idea about the people who might have a grudge against him."

"It's not so mysterious," Nicole said. "You know his life much better than I do. He had plenty of enemies. Including you."

"Even our worst critics would never accuse the FBI of a hit on the steps of a cathedral," Cilke said dryly. "And I wasn't his enemy. I was an enforcer of the law. After he retired he had no enemies. He bought them off." He paused for a moment. "I find it curious that neither you nor your brothers seem interested in finding out who the man was who murdered your father."

"Because we're not hypocrites," Nicole said. "My father was no saint. He played the game and paid the price." She paused. "And you're wrong about my not being interested. In fact I'm going to petition for my father's FBI file under the Freedom of Information Act. And I hope you don't cause any delay because then we will be enemies."

"That's your privilege," Cilke said. "But maybe you can help me by telling me the provisions of your father's will."

"I didn't draw up the will," Nicole said.

"But you are the executor, I hear. You must know the provisions by now."

"We're filing for probate tomorrow. It will be public record."

"Is there anything you can tell me now that may help?" Cilke asked.

"Just that I won't be taking early retirement."

"So why won't you tell me anything today?"

"Because I don't have to," Nicole said coolly.

"I knew your father pretty well," Cilke said. "He would have been reasonable."

For the first time Nicole looked at him with respect. "That's true," she said. "OK. My father gave away a lot of money before he died. All he left us was his banks. My brothers and I get forty-nine percent, and the other fifty-one percent goes to our cousin, Astorre Viola."

"Can you tell me anything about him?" Cilke asked.

"Astorre is younger than me. He was never in my father's business, and we all love him because he's such a charming nut. Of course, I don't love him as much now."

Cilke searched his memory. He could not recall a file on Astorre Viola. Yet there would have to be.

"Could you give me his address and phone number?" Cilke asked.

"Sure," Nicole said. "But you're wasting your time. Believe me."

"I have to clean up the details," Cilke said apologetically.

"And what gives the FBI an interest?" Nicole asked. "This is a local homicide."

Cilke said coolly, "The ten banks your father owned were international banks. There could be currency complications."

"Oh, really," Nicole said. "Then I better ask for his file right away. After all, I own part of those banks now." She gave him a suspicious glance. He knew he would have to keep an eye on her.

The next day Cilke and Boxton drove out to Westchester County to meet with Astorre Viola.

The wooded estate included a huge house and three barns. There were six horses in the meadow, which was enclosed by a waist-high split-rail fence and wrought-iron gates. Four cars and a van were parked in the lot in front of the house. Cilke memorized two of the license-plate numbers.

A woman of about seventy let them in and led them to a plush living room jammed with recording equipment. Four young men were reading sheet music on stands, and one was seated at the piano—a professional combo on sax, bass, guitar, and drums.

Astorre stood at the microphone opposite them singing in a hoarse voice. Even Cilke could tell that this was the kind of music that would find no audience.

Astorre stopped vocalizing and said to the visitors, "Can you wait just five minutes until we finish recording? Then my friends can pack up and you can have all the time you want."

"Sure," Cilke said.

"Bring them coffee," Astorre told the maid. Cilke was pleased. Astorre didn't just make a polite offer; he commanded it for them.

But Cilke and Boxton had to wait longer than five minutes. Astorre was recording an Italian folk song—while strumming a banjo—and he sang in a coarse dialect Cilke did not understand. It was enjoyable to listen to him, like hearing your own voice in the shower.

Finally they were alone and Astorre was wiping his face. "That wasn't so bad," he said, laughing. "Was it?"

Cilke found himself immediately liking the man. About thirty, he had a boyish vitality and did not seem to take himself seriously. He was tall and well built, with a boxer's grace. He had a dark-skinned beauty and the kind of irregular but sharp features you might see in fifteenth-century portraits. He did not seem vain, but around his neck he wore a collar of gold two inches wide, to which was attached an etched medallion of the Virgin Mary.

"It was great," Cilke said. "You're cutting a record for distribution?"

Astorre smiled, a wide, good-natured grin. "I wish. I'm not that good. But I love these songs, and I give them to friends as presents."

Cilke decided to get to work. "This is just routine," he said. "Do you know of anyone who would have wanted to harm your uncle?"

"No one at all," Astorre said, straight-faced. Cilke was tired of hearing this. Everyone had enemies, especially Raymonde Aprile.

"You inherit controlling interest in the banks," Cilke said. "Were you that close?"

"I really don't understand that," Astorre said. "I was one of his favorites when I was a kid. He set me up in my business and then sort of forgot about me."

"What kind of business?" Cilke asked.

"I import all the top-grade *macaroni* from Italy."

Cilke gave him a skeptical look. "Macaroni?"

Astorre smiled; he was used to this reaction. It was not a glamorous business. "You know how Lee Iacocca never says *automobiles,* he always says *cars*? Now, in my business, we never say *pasta* or *spaghetti,* we always say *macaroni.*"

"And now you'll be a banker?" Cilke said.

"I'll give it a whirl," Astorre said.

After they left, Cilke asked Bill Boxton, "What do you think?" He liked Boxton enormously. The man believed in the Bureau, as he did—that it was fair, that it was incorruptible and far superior to any other law-enforcement agency in its efficiency. These interviews were partly for his benefit.

"They all sound pretty straight to me," Boxton said. "But don't they always?"

Yes, they always did, Cilke thought. Then something struck him. The medallion hanging from Astorre's gold collar had never moved.

The last interview was the most important to Cilke. It was with Timmona Portella, the reigning Mafia boss in New York, the only one besides the Don who had escaped prosecution after Cilke's investigations.

Portella ran his enterprises from the huge penthouse apartment of a building he owned on the West Side. The rest of the building was occupied by subsidiary firms that he controlled. The security was as tight as Fort Knox, and Portella himself traveled by helicopter—the roof was equipped with a landing pad—to his estate in New Jersey. His feet rarely touched the pavement of New York.

Portella greeted Cilke and Boxton in his office with its overstuffed armchairs and bulletproof walls of glass that gave a wonderful view of the city skyline. He was a huge man, immaculately dressed in a dark suit and gleaming white shirt.

Cilke shook Portella's meaty hand and admired the dark tie hanging from his thick neck.

"Kurt, how can I help you?" Portella said in a high tenor voice that rang through the room. He ignored Bill Boxton.

"I'm just checking out the Aprile affair," Cilke said. "I thought you might have some information that could help me."

"What a shame, his death," Portella said. "Everybody loved Raymonde Aprile. It's a mystery to me who could have done this. In the last years of his life Aprile was such a good man. He became a saint, a real saint. He gave away his money like a Rockefeller. When God took him his soul was pure."

"God didn't take him," Cilke said dryly. "It was

91

an extremely professional hit. There has to be a motive." Portella's eye twitched, but he said nothing, so Cilke went on, "You were his colleague for many years. You must know something. What about this nephew of his who inherits the banks?"

"Don Aprile and I had some business together many years ago," Portella said. "But when Aprile retired he could just as easily have killed me. The fact that I'm alive proves we were not enemies. About his nephew I know nothing except that he is an artist. He sings at weddings, at little parties, even in some small nightclubs. One of those young men that old folks like myself are fond of. And he sells good macaroni from Italy. All my restaurants use it." He paused and sighed. "It is always a mystery when a great man is killed."

"You know your help will be appreciated," Cilke said.

"Of course," Portella said. "The FBI always plays fair. I know my help will be appreciated."

He gave Cilke and Boxton a warm smile, which showed square, almost perfect teeth.

On the way back to the office, Boxton said to Cilke, "I read that guy's file. He's big into porn and drugs, and he's a murderer. How come we could never get him?"

"He's not as bad as most of the others," Cilke said. "And we'll get him someday."

*

Kurt Cilke ordered an electronic surveillance on the homes of Nicole Aprile and Astorre Viola. A domesticated federal judge issued the necessary order. Not that Cilke was really suspicious—he just wanted to be certain. Nicole was born a troublemaker, and Astorre looked too good to be true. It was out of the question to bug Valerius, since his home was on the West Point grounds.

Cilke had learned that the horses in Astorre's meadow were his passion. That he brushed and groomed one stallion each morning before he took it out. Which was not so bad, except that he rode dressed in full English regalia, red coat and all, including a black suede hunting cap.

He found it hard to believe that Astorre was so helpless a target that three muggers in Central Park had taken a pass at him. He had escaped, it seemed—but the police report was foggy about what had happened to the muggers.

Two weeks later Cilke and Boxton were able to listen to the tapes he had planted in the house of Astorre Viola. The voices were those of Nicole, Marcantonio, Valerius, and Astorre. On tape they became human to Cilke; they had taken off their masks.

"Why did they have to kill him?" Nicole asked, her voice breaking with grief. There was none of the coldness she had shown to Cilke.

"There has to be a reason," Valerius said quietly. His voice was much gentler when talking to his family. "I never had any connection to the old man's business, so I'm not worried about myself. But what about you?"

Marcantonio spoke scornfully; obviously he did not like his brother. "Val, the old man got you an appointment to West Point because you were a wimp. He wanted to toughen you up. Then he helped in your intelligence work overseas. So you're in this. He loved the idea you could be a commander. General Aprile—he loved the sound of it. Who knows what strings he pulled." His voice sounded far more energetic, more passionate on tape than in person.

There was a long pause, and then Marcantonio said, "And of course he got me started. He bank-rolled my production company. The big talent agencies gave me a break on their stars. Listen, we were not in his life, but he was always in ours. Nicole, the old man saved you ten years of dues paying by getting you that job at the law firm. And Astorre, who do you think got your macaroni shelf space in the supermarkets?"

Suddenly Nicole was furious. "Dad may have helped me get through the door, but the only one responsible for my success in my career is me. I had to fight those sharks at the firm for everything I got. I'm the one who put in eighty-hour weeks reading the fine print." She paused, her voice cold now. She must have turned to Astorre then. "And what I want to know is why Dad put you in charge of the banks. What the hell do you have to do with anything?"

Astorre's voice sounded helpless with apology. "Nicole, I have no idea. I didn't ask for this. I have a business, and I love my singing and riding. Besides, there's a bright side for you. I have to do all the work, and the profits are divided equally among the four of us."

"But you have control and you're only a cousin," Nicole said. She added sarcastically, "He sure must have loved your singing."

Valerius said, "Are you going to try to run the banks yourself?"

Astorre's voice was filled with mock horror. "Oh, no, no, Nicole will give me a list of names, a CEO to do that."

Nicole sounded tearful with frustration. "I still don't understand why Dad didn't appoint me. Why?"

"Because he didn't want any one of his children to have leverage over the others," Marcantonio said.

Astorre said quietly, "Maybe it was to keep you all out of danger."

"How do you like that FBI guy coming on to us like he's our best friend?" Nicole said. "He hounded Dad for years. And now he thinks we're going to spill all our family secrets to him. What a creep."

Cilke felt a flush coming to his cheeks. He hadn't deserved that.

Valerius said, "He's doing his duty, and that's not an easy job. He must be a very intelligent man. He sent a lot of the old man's friends to jail. And for a long time."

"Traitors, informers," Nicole said scornfully. "And those RICO laws they enforce very selectively. They could send half of our political leaders to jail under those laws, and most of the Fortune Five Hundred."

"Nicole, you're a corporate lawyer," Marcantonio said. "Cut the crap."

Astorre said thoughtfully, "Where do the FBI agents get those snazzy suits? Is there a special 'Tailor to the FBI'?"

"It's the way they wear them," Marcantonio said. "That's the secret. But on TV we can never get a guy like Cilke right. Perfectly sincere, perfectly honest, honorable in every way. Yet you never trust him."

"Marc, forget your phony TV shows," Valerius said. "We are in a hostile situation, and there are two significant intelligence aspects. The why, then the who. Why was Dad killed? Then, who could it possibly be? Everyone says he had no enemies and nothing that anyone wanted."

"I have a petition to see Dad's file at the Bureau," Nicole said. "That may give us a clue."

"What for?" Marcantonio said. "We can't do

anything about it. Dad would want us to forget it. This should be left to the authorities."

Nicole sounded scornful. "So we don't give a crap who killed our father? How about you, Astorre? Do you feel like that too?"

Astorre's voice was soft, reasonable. "What can we do? I loved your father. I'm grateful he was so generous to me in his will. But let's wait and see what happens. Actually, I like Cilke. If there's anything to find, he'll find it. We all have good lives, so why twist them out of shape?" He paused and then said, "Look, I have to call one of my suppliers, so I have to go. But you can stay here and talk things out."

There was a long silence on the tape. Cilke couldn't help feeling goodwill toward Astorre and resentment against the others. Still, he was satisfied. These were not dangerous people; they would cause him no trouble.

"I love Astorre," Nicole's voice said now. "He was closer to our father than any of us. But he's such a flake. Marc, can he possibly go anywhere with that singing?"

Marcantonio laughed. "We see thousands of guys like him in our business. He's like a football star in a small high school. He's fun, but he hasn't really got the goods. But he's got a good business and he enjoys it, so what the hell?"

"He has control of multibillion-dollar banks—everything we have, and what really interests him

97

is singing and horseback riding," said Nicole.

Valerius said ruefully and with humor, "Sartorially splendid, but he has a lousy seat."

Nicole said, "How could Dad do that?"

"He made something very good out of that macaroni business," Valerius said.

"We have to protect Astorre," Nicole said. "He's too nice to run banks and too trusting to deal with Cilke."

At the end of the tape Cilke turned to Boxton. "What do you think?" he asked.

"Oh, like Astorre, I think you're a splendid fellow," Boxton said.

Cilke laughed. "No, I mean, are these people possible suspects in the murder?"

"No," Boxton said. "First, they are his kids, and second, they don't have the expertise."

"They are smart though," Cilke said. "They ask the right question. Why?"

"Well, it's not our question," Boxton said. "This is local, not federal. Or do you have a connection?"

"International banks," Cilke said. "But no sense wasting any more of the Bureau's money; cancel all the phone taps."

Kurt Cilke liked dogs because they could not conspire. They could not hide hostility, and they were not cunning. They did not lie awake at night planning to rob and murder other dogs. Treachery was beyond their scope. He had two German shepherds to help guard his home, and he walked with them through the nearby woods at night with complete harmony and trust.

When he went home that night, he was satisfied. There was no danger in the situation, not from the Don's family. There would be no bloody vendetta.

Cilke lived in New Jersey with a wife he truly loved and a ten-year-old daughter he adored. His house was wrapped up with a tight security-alarm system plus the two dogs. The government paid. His wife had refused training to use a gun, and he relied on remaining anonymous. His neighbors thought he was a lawyer (which he was), as did his daughter. Cilke always kept his gun and bullets locked up with his Bureau ID when he was at home.

He never took his car to the railroad station for his commute to the city. Petty thieves might steal the car radio. When he arrived back in New Jersey, he called his wife on his cell phone and she came to pick him up. It was a five-minute ride home.

Tonight Georgette gave him a cheerful kiss on the mouth, a warm touch of flesh. His daughter, Vanessa, so boundlessly alive, bowled into him for a hug. The two dogs frolicked around him but were restrained. They all fitted easily into the big Buick.

It was this part of his life that Cilke treasured.

With his family he felt secure, at peace. His wife loved him, he knew that. She admired his character, that he did his work without malice or trickery, with a sense of justice to his fellowman no matter how depraved. He valued her intelligence and trusted her enough to talk to her about his work. But of course he could not tell her everything. And she was busy with her own work, writing about famous women in history, teaching ethics at a local college, fighting for her social causes.

Now Cilke watched his wife as she prepared dinner. Her beauty always enchanted him. He watched Vanessa setting the table, imitating her mother, even trying to walk with that graceful balletlike movement. Georgette did not believe in having household help of any kind, and she had raised her daughter to be self-reliant. At the age of six, Vanessa was already making her own bed, cleaning her room, and helping her mother cook. As always, Cilke wondered why his wife loved him, felt blessed that she did.

Later, after they put Vanessa to bed (Cilke checked the bell she could ring if she needed them), they went into their own bedroom. And as always, Cilke felt the thrill of almost religious fervor when his wife undressed. Then her huge gray eyes, so intelligent, became smoky with love. And afterward, falling into sleep, she held his hand to guide them through her dreams.

Cilke had met her when he was investigating radical college organizations suspected of minor terrorist acts. She was a political activist who taught history at a small New Jersey college. His investigation showed she was simply a liberal and had no connection with a radical extremist group. And so Cilke wrote in his report.

But when he interviewed her as part of the investigation, he had been struck by her absolute lack of prejudice or hostility toward him as an FBI agent. In fact, she seemed curious about his work, how he felt about it, and oddly enough he answered her frankly: simply that he was one of the guardians of a society that could not exist without some regulation. He added half-jokingly that he was the shield between people like her and those who would devour her for their own agenda.

The courtship was short. They married quickly, really so that their common sense would not interfere with their love, for they both recognized they were opposites in almost every way. He shared none of her beliefs; when it came to the world he lived in, she was an innocent. She definitely shared none of his reverence for the Bureau. But she listened to his complaints, how he resented the character assassination of the Bureau saint, J. Edgar Hoover. "They paint him as a closet homosexual and reactionary bigot. What he really was was a dedicated man who simply did not develop a liberal conscience." He told her,

"Writers deride the FBI as the Gestapo or KGB. But we have never resorted to torture, and we have never framed anybody—unlike the NYPD, for instance. We have never planted false evidence. The kids in college would lose their freedom if it wasn't for us. The right wing would destroy them, they are so dumb politically."

She smiled at his passion, was touched by it.

"Don't expect me to change," she told him, smiling. "If what you say is true, we have no quarrel."

"I don't expect you to change," Cilke said. "And if the FBI affects our relationship, I'll just get another job." He didn't have to tell her what a sacrifice that would be for him.

But how many people can say that they are perfectly happy, that they have one human being they can absolutely trust? He took such comfort in his guardianship and faithfulness to her spirit and her body. She could sense his alertness every second of the day for her safety and survival.

Cilke missed her terribly when he was away on training courses. He never was tempted by other women because he never wanted to be a conspirator against her. He cherished his return to her, to her trusting smile, her welcoming body, as she waited for him in the bedroom, naked, vulnerable, pardoning him for his work, a benediction to his life.

But his happiness was haunted by the secrets he

had to keep from her, the serious complications of his job, his knowledge of a world that festered with the pus of evil men and women, the stains of humanity that spilled over into his own brain. Without her, it was simply not worth living in the world.

At one time, early, still shaky with fear of happiness, he had done the one thing he was truly ashamed of. He had bugged his own home to record his wife's every word, then listened in the basement to the tapes. He had listened to every inflection. And she had passed the test; she was never malicious, never petty or traitorous. He had done that for a year.

That she loved him despite his imperfections, his feral cunning, his need to hunt down fellow human beings seemed to Cilke a miracle. But he was always afraid that she would discover his true nature and then abhor him. And so in his work, he also became as fastidious as possible and acquired his reputation for fairness.

Georgette never doubted him. She had proved that one night when they were dinner guests at the director's house, along with twenty other guests, a semiofficial affair and a signal honor.

At one point during the evening the director managed to secure a moment alone with Cilke and his wife. He said to Georgette, "I understand you are involved in many liberal causes. I respect your right to do so, of course. But perhaps you don't

103

truly comprehend that your actions could damage Kurt's career in the Bureau?"

Georgette smiled at the director and said gravely, "I do know that, and that would be the Bureau's mistake and misfortune. Of course, if it became too much of a problem, my husband would resign."

The director turned to Cilke, a look of surprise on his face. "Is that true?" he asked. "Would you resign?"

Cilke didn't hesitate. "Yes, it's true. I'll turn in the papers tomorrow if you like."

The director laughed. "Oh, no," he said. "We don't come by men like you often." Then he gave Georgette his steely aristocratic eye. "Uxuriousness may be the last refuge of the honest man," he said.

They all laughed at the laborious witticism to show their goodwill.

CHAPTER

4

FOR FIVE MONTHS after the Don's death, Astorre
was busy conferring with some of the Don's old
retired colleagues, taking measures to protect the
Don's children from harm and investigating the
circumstances of his murder. Most of all he had to
find a reason for such a daring and outrageous act.
Who would give the order to kill the great Don
Aprile? He knew he had to be very careful.

Astorre had his first meeting with Benito Craxxi
in Chicago.

Craxxi had retired from all illegal operations ten
years before the Don. He was the man who had
been the great *consigliere* of the National Mafia
Commission itself and had an intimate knowledge
of all Family structures in the United States. He
had been the first to spot the decay in the power of

the great Families, foreseeing their decline. And so he had prudently retired to play the stock market, where he was pleasantly surprised that he could steal as much money with no risk of legal punishment whatsoever. The Don had given Craxxi's name to Astorre as one of the men he must consult, if necessary.

Craxxi, at seventy, lived with two bodyguards, a chauffeur, and a young Italian woman who served as cook and housekeeper and was rumored to be his sexual companion. He was in perfect health, for he had lived a life of moderation; he ate prudently and drank only occasionally. For breakfast a bowl of fruit and cheese; for lunch an omelet or vegetable soup; mostly beans and escarole; for dinner a simple cutlet of beef or lamb and a great salad of onions, tomatoes, and lettuce. He smoked only one cigar a day, directly after dinner with his coffee and anisette. He spent his money generously and wisely. He was also careful to whom he gave advice. For a man who gives the wrong counsel is as hated as any enemy.

But with Astorre, he was generous, for Craxxi was one of the many men who was greatly in the debt of Don Aprile. It was the Don who had protected Craxxi when he retired, always a dangerous move in the business.

It was a breakfast meeting. There were bowls of fruit—glossy yellow pears, russet apples, a bowl of strawberries almost as large as lemons, white grapes, and dark red cherries. A huge crag of cheese was laid out on a wooden board like a sliver of gold-crated rock. The housekeeper served them coffee and anisette and disappeared.

"So, my young man," Craxxi said. "You are the guardian Don Aprile has chosen."

"Yes," Astorre said.

"I know he trained you for this task," Craxxi said. "My old friend always looked ahead. We consulted on it. I know you are qualified. The question remains, do you have the will?"

Astorre's smile was engaging, his countenance open. "The Don saved my life and gave me everything I have," he said. "I am what he made me. And I vowed I would protect the family. If Nicole isn't made a partner in the law firm, if Marcantonio's TV network fails, if something happens to Valerius, they still have the banks. I've had a happy life. I regret the reason I have the task. But I gave the Don my word, and I must keep it. If not, what can I believe in the rest of my life?"

There were moments of his childhood that flashed through his mind, moments of great joy for which he felt gratitude. Scenes of himself as a boy in Sicily with his uncle, walking through the vast mountainous terrain, listening to the Don's stories. He dreamed then of a different time, when justice was served, loyalty valued, and great deeds accomplished by kind and powerful men. And at that moment he missed both the Don and Sicily.

"Good," Craxxi said, interrupting Astorre's reverie and bringing him back to the present. "You were at the scene. Describe everything to me."

Astorre did so.

"And you are certain that both shooters were left-handed?" Craxxi asked.

"At least one, and probably the other," Astorre said.

Craxxi nodded slowly and seemed lost in thought. After what seemed long moments, he looked directly at Astorre and said, "I think I know who the shooters were. But not to be hasty. It is more important to know who hired them and why. You must be very careful. Now, I have thought very much of this matter. The most probable suspect is Timmona Portella. But for what reasons and to please who? Now, Timmona was always rash. But the killing of Don Aprile had to be a very risky enterprise. Even Timmona feared the Don, retirement or not.

"Now, here is my thought about the shooters. They are brothers who live in Los Angeles, and they are the most highly qualified men in the country. They never talk. Few people even know they are twins. And they are both left-handed. They have courage, and they are born fighters. The danger would appeal to them, and the reward must have been great. Also, they must have had some reassurances—that the authorities would not

108

pursue the case with conviction. I find it strange that there was no official police or federal surveillance of the Confirmation at the cathedral. After all, Don Aprile was still an FBI target even after he retired.

"Now, understand, everything I've said is theory. You will have to investigate and confirm. And then, if I am correct, you must strike with all your might."

"One thing more," Astorre said. "Are the Don's children in danger?"

Craxxi shrugged. He was carefully peeling the skin off a golden pear. "I don't know," he said. "But don't be too proud to ask them to help. You yourself are undoubtedly in some peril. Now, I have a final suggestion for you. Bring your Mr. Pryor from London to run your banks. He is a supremely qualified man in every way."

"And Bianco in Sicily?" Astorre asked.

"Leave him there," Craxxi said. "When you are further along, we will meet again."

Craxxi poured anisette into Astorre's coffee. Astorre sighed. "It seems strange," he said. "I never dreamed I would have to act for the Don, the great Don Aprile."

"Ah, well," Craxxi said. "Life is cruel and hard for the young."

For twenty years Valerius had lived in the military-intelligence world, not a fictional world like his brother's. He seemed to anticipate everything Astorre said and reacted without any surprise.

"I need your help," Astorre said. "You may have to break some of your strict rules of conduct."

Valerius said dryly, "Finally you're showing your true colors. I wondered how long it would take."

"I don't know what that means," Astorre said, somewhat surprised. "I think your father's death was a conspiracy that involved the NYPD and the FBI. You may think I'm fantasizing, but that's what I hear."

"It's not impossible," Valerius said. "But I don't have access to secret documents in my job here."

"But you must have friends," Astorre said. "In the intelligence agencies. You can ask them certain questions."

"I don't have to ask questions," Valerius said, smiling. "They gossip like magpies. That 'need to know' is all bullshit. Have you any idea what you're after?"

"Any information about the killers of your father," Astorre said.

Valerius leaned back in his chair, puffing on a cigar, his only vice. "Don't bullshit me, Astorre," he said. "Let me tell you something. I did an analysis. It could be a gangland act of retaliation or revenge. And I thought about you being in control of the banks. The old man always had a plan. I figure it like this. The Don made you his point man for the family. What follows from that? That you are trained, that you were his agent in place to be activated only at a crucial moment in time. There is an eleven-year gap in your life, and your cover is too good to be true—an amateur singer, a sporting horseman? And the gold collar you always wear is suspicious." He stopped, took a deep breath, and said, "How's that for analysis?"

"Very good," Astorre said. "I hope you kept it to yourself."

"Certainly," Valerius said. "But then it follows that you are a dangerous man. And that therefore there is an extreme action you will take. But some advice: your cover is thin; it will be blown before much longer. As for my help, I live a very good life and I'm opposed to everything I think you are. So for now my answer is no. I won't help. If things change, I'll get in touch."

A woman came out to guide Astorre into Nicole's office. Nicole gave him a hug and a kiss. She was still fond of him; their teen romance had left no bitter scars.

"I have to speak to you in private," Astorre said.

Nicole turned to her bodyguard. "Helene, can you leave us alone? I'm safe with him."

Helene gave Astorre a long look. She was impressing herself on his consciousness, and she

Mario Puzo

succeeded. Like Cilke, Astorre noted her extreme confidence—the kind of confidence shown by a card player with an ace in the hole or a person holding a concealed weapon. He looked to see where it could be hidden. The tight trousers and jacket molded her impressive physique—no gun there. Then he noted the slit in her trouser leg. She was wearing an ankle holster, which wasn't really that smart. He smiled at her as she left, exerting his charm. She looked back at him blankly.

"Who recruited her?" Astorre asked.

"My father," Nicole said. "It worked out very well. It's amazing how she can handle muggers and mashers."

"I'll bet," Astorre said. "Did you manage to get the old man's file from the FBI?"

"Yes," Nicole said. "And it's the most horrible list of allegations I've ever read. I simply don't believe it, and they could never prove any of it."

Astorre knew that the Don would want him to deny the truth. "Will you let me have the file for a couple of days?" he asked.

Nicole gave her blank-faced lawyer stare. "I don't think you should see it right now. I want to write an analysis of it, underline what's important, then give it to you. Actually, there's nothing that will help you. Maybe you and my brothers shouldn't see it."

Astorre looked at her thoughtfully, then smiled. "That bad?"

112

"Let me study it," Nicole said. "The FBI are such shits."

"Whatever you say is OK with me. Just remember, this is a dangerous business. Look after yourself."

"I will," Nicole said. "I have Helene."

"And I'm here if you need me." Astorre placed his hand on Nicole's arm to reassure her, and for a moment she looked at him with such longing he felt uncomfortable. "Just call."

Nicole smiled. "I will. But I'm OK. I am." In fact, she was really looking forward to her evening with an incredibly charming and attractive diplomat.

In his elaborate office suite lined with six TV screens, Marcantonio Aprile was having a meeting with the head of the most powerful advertising agency in New York. Richard Harrison was a tall, aristocratic-looking man, perfectly dressed, with the appearance of a former model but the intensity of a paratrooper.

On Harrison's lap was a small case of videotapes. With absolute assurance, without asking permission, he went to a TV set and inserted one of the tapes.

"Watch this," he said. "It's not one of my clients, but I think it's just astounding."

The videotape played a commercial for American pizza, and the pitchman was Mikhail

Gorbachev, the former president of the Soviet Union. Gorbachev sold with quiet dignity, never saying a word, just feeding his grandchildren pizza while the crowd voiced its admiration.

Marcantonio smiled at Harrison. "A victory for the free world," he said. "So what?"

"The former leader of the Soviet Republic, and now he's clowning around doing a commercial for an American pizza company. Isn't that astonishing? And I hear they only paid him half a million."

"OK," Marcantonio said. "But why?"

"Why does anyone do anything so humiliating?" Harrison said. "He needs the money desperately."

And suddenly Marcantonio thought of his father. The Don would feel such contempt for a man who had ruled a great country and did not provide financial security for his family. Don Aprile would think him the most foolish of men.

"A nice lesson in history and human psychology," Marcantonio said. "But again, so what?"

Harrison tapped his box of videos. "I have more, and I anticipate some resistance. These are a little more touchy. You and I have done business for a long time. I want to make sure you let these commercials run on your network. The rest will necessarily follow."

"I can't imagine," Marcantonio said.

Harrison inserted another tape and explained. "We have purchased the rights to use deceased celebrities in our commercials. It is such a waste that the famous dead cease to have a function in our society. We want to change that and restore them to their former glory."

The tape began to play. There was a succession of shots of Mother Teresa ministering to the poor and sick of Calcutta, her nun's habit draping over the dying. Another shot of her receiving the Nobel Peace Prize, her homely face shining, her saintly humility so moving. Then a shot of her ladling out soup from a huge pot to the poor in the streets. All of these are black and white.

Suddenly the picture blazes with color. A richly dressed man comes to a pot with an empty bowl. He says to a beautiful young woman, "Can I have some soup? I hear it's wonderful." The young woman gives him a radiant smile and ladles some soup into his bowl. He drinks, looking as if he's in ecstasy.

Then the screen dissolves to a supermarket and a whole shelf of soup cans labeled "Calcutta." A voice-over proclaims, "Calcutta Soup, a life giver to rich and poor alike. Everyone can afford the twenty varieties of delicious soup. Original recipes by Mother Teresa."

"I think that's done in pretty good taste," Harrison said.

Marcantonio raised his eyebrows.

Harrison inserted another video. A brilliant shot of Princess Diana in her wedding dress filled the screen, followed by shots of her in Buckingham

Palace. Then dancing with Prince Charles, surrounded by her royal entourage, all in frenetic
motion.

A voice-over intones, "Every princess deserves a
prince. But this princess had a secret." A young
model holds up an elegant crystal bottle of
perfume, the product label clear. The voice-over
continues, "With one small spray of Princess
perfume, you too can capture your prince—and
never have to worry about vaginal odor."

Marcantonio pressed a button on his desk and
the screen went black.

Harrison said, "Wait, I have more."

Marcantonio shook his head. "Richard, you are
amazingly inventive—and insensitive. Those
commercials will never play on my network."

Harrison protested, "But some of the proceeds
go to charity—and they are in good taste. I hoped
you would lead the way. We're good friends, after
all."

"So we are," Marcantonio said. "But still, the
answer is no."

Harrison shook his head and slowly put his
videos back in the box.

Marcantonio, smiling, asked, "By the way, how
did the Gorbachev spot do?"

Harrison shrugged. "Lousy. The poor son of a
bitch couldn't even sell *pizza.*"

*

Marcantonio cleared up other work and prepared for his evening duties. Tonight he had to attend the Emmys. His network had three big tables for its executives and stars and several nominations. His date was Matilda Johnson, an established newscaster.

His office had a bedroom suite with a bathroom and shower attached and a closet full of clothes. He often stayed there overnight when he had to work late.

At the ceremony he was mentioned by some of his winners as being important to their success. This was always pleasant. But while he was clapping and kissing cheeks, he thought of all the awards celebrations and dinners he had to attend during the year: the Oscars, the People's Choice Awards, the AFI tributes, and other special awards to aging stars, producers, and directors. He felt like a teacher awarding homework stars to elementary school children who would run home to show their mothers. And then he felt a momentary shame for his malice—these people deserved their honors, needed the approval as much as they needed the money.

After the ceremony he amused himself by watching actors with slight credentials trying to impress their personalities on people like himself who had clout, and an editor of a successful magazine being courted by some freelance writers—he noted the wariness on her face, the careful and cold cordiality, as if she were Penelope waiting for a more famous suitor.

Then there were the anchors, the heavyweights, men and women of intelligence, charisma, and talent who had the exquisite dilemma of wooing stars they wanted for interviews while discouraging those not yet quite important enough.

The star actors were sparkling with hope and desire. They were already successful enough to make the jump from TV to the movie screens, never to return—or so they thought.

Finally Marcantonio was exhausted; the continual grinning with enthusiasm, the cheery voice he must use to losers, the note of exuberance with his winners all wore him out. Matilda whispered to him, "Are you coming to my place tonight, a little later?"

"I'm tired," Marcantonio said. "Tough day, tough night."

"That's OK," she said with sympathy. They both had tight schedules. "I'll be in town for a week."

They were good friends because they didn't have to take advantage of each other. Matilda was secure. She didn't need a mentor or a patron. And Marcantonio never took part in negotiations with news talent; that was a job for the chief of Business Affairs. The lives they led could not possibly result in marriage. Matilda traveled extensively; he worked fifteen hours a day. But they were buddies who sometimes spent the night together. They made love, gossiped about the business, and appeared together at some social functions. And it was understood that theirs was a secondary relationship. The few times Matilda fell in love with some new man, their nights were cut out. Marcantonio never fell in love, so this was not a problem for him.

Tonight he suffered a certain fatigue with the world he lived in. So he was almost delighted to find Astorre waiting for him in the lobby of his apartment building.

"Hey, great to see you," Marcantonio said. "Where have you been?"

"Busy," Astorre said. "Can I come up and have a drink?"

"Sure," Marcantonio said. "But why the cloak and dagger? Why didn't you call? You could have been hanging out in this lobby for hours; I was supposed to go to a party."

"No problem," Astorre said. He'd had his cousin under surveillance all evening.

In the apartment Marcantonio fixed them both drinks.

Astorre seemed a little embarrassed. "You can initiate projects at your network, right?"

"I do it all the time," Marcantonio said.

"I have one for you," Astorre said. "It has to do with your father being killed."

"No," Marcantonio said. It was his famous *no*

119

in the industry that barred all further discussion. But it didn't seem to intimidate Astorre.

"Don't say no to me like that," Astorre said. "I'm not selling you something. This concerns the safety of your brother and sister. And you." Then he gave a huge grin. "And me."

"Tell me," Marcantonio said. He saw his cousin in an astonishing new light. Could that happy-go-lucky kid have something in him after all?

"I want you to do a documentary on the FBI," Astorre said. "Specifically how Kurt Cilke managed to destroy most of the Mafia Families. There would be a huge audience for that, right?"

Marcantonio nodded. "What's your purpose?"

"I just can't get any data on Cilke," Astorre told him. "It would be too dangerous to try. But if you're doing a documentary, no government agency will dare to step on your toes. You can find out where he lives, his history, how he operates, and where he stands in the power structure of the Bureau. I need all that info."

"The FBI and Cilke would never cooperate," Marcantonio said. "That would make a show difficult." He paused. "It's not like the old days when Hoover was director. These new guys play their cards very close."

"You can do it," Astorre said. "I need you to do it. You have an army of producers and investigative reporters. I have to know all about him. Everything. Because I think he may be part of

120

a conspiracy against your father and our family."

"That's a really crazy theory," Marcantonio said.

"Sure," Astorre said. "Maybe it's not true. But I know it was no simple gangland killing. And that Cilke does a funny kind of inquiry. Almost like he's smoothing over tracks, not uncovering them."

"So I help you get the information. Then what can you do?"

Astorre spread his hands and smiled. "What can I do, Marc? I just want to know. Maybe I can make a deal to get the family off the hook. And I just have to look at the documentation. I won't make a copy of it. You won't be compromised."

Marcantonio stared at him. His mind was making the adjustment to the pleasant, charming face of Astorre. He said thoughtfully, "Astorre, I'm curious about you. The old man left you in control. Why? You're a macaroni importer. I always thought of you as a charming eccentric with your scarlet riding jacket and your little music group. But the old man would never trust the man you seem to be."

"I don't sing anymore," Astorre said, smiling. "I don't ride much either. The Don always had a good eye; he had faith in me. You should have the same." He paused for a moment and then said with utmost sincerity, "He picked me so that his children wouldn't have to take the heat. He chose

121

me and taught me. He loved me but I was expendable. It's that simple."

"You have the ability to fight back?" Marcantonio said.

"Oh, yes," Astorre said, and he leaned back and smiled at his cousin. It was a deliberately sinister smile that a TV actor would give to show that he was evil, but it was done with such mocking high spirits that Marcantonio laughed.

He said, "That's all I have to do? I won't be involved further?"

"You're not qualified to go further," Astorre said.

"Can I think it over for a few days?"

"No," Astorre said. "If you say no, it will be me against them."

Marcantonio nodded. "I like you, Astorre, but I can't do it. It's just too much risk."

The meeting with Kurt Cilke in Nicole's office proved a surprise for Astorre. Cilke brought Bill Boxton and insisted that Nicole be present. He was also very direct.

"I have information that Timmona Portella is trying to establish a billion-dollar fund in your banks. Is that true?"

"That's private information," Nicole said. "Why should we tell you?"

"I know he made the same offer he made your

father," Cilke said. "And your father refused."

"Why should all this interest the FBI?" Nicole asked in her "go fuck yourself" voice.

Cilke refused to be irritated. "We think he is laundering drug money," he said to Astorre. "We want you to cooperate with him so we can monitor his operation. We want you to appoint some of our federal accountants to positions in your bank." He opened his briefcase. "I have some papers for you to sign, which will protect both of us."

Nicole took the papers out of his hand and read the two pages very quickly.

"Don't sign," she warned Astorre. "The bank's customers have a right to privacy. If they want to investigate Portella, they should get a warrant."

Astorre took the papers and read them. He smiled at Cilke. "I trust you," he said. He signed the papers and handed them to Cilke.

"What's the quid pro quo?" Nicole asked. "What do we get for cooperating?"

"Performing your duty as good citizens," Cilke said. "A letter of commendation from the president, and the stopping of an audit of all your banks that could cause you a lot of trouble if you're not absolutely clean."

"How about a little information on my uncle's murder?" Astorre said.

"Sure," Cilke said. "Shoot."

"Why was there no police surveillance at the

Confirmation service?" Astorre asked.

"That was the decision of the chief of detectives, Paul Di Benedetto," Cilke said. "And also his right hand. A woman named Aspinella Washington."

"And how come there were no FBI observers?" Astorre asked.

"I'm afraid that was my decision," Cilke said. "I didn't feel there was any need."

Astorre shook his head. "I don't think I can go through with your proposition. I need a few weeks to think it over."

"You've already signed the papers," Cilke said. "This information is now classified. You can be prosecuted if you reveal this conversation."

"Why would I do that?" Astorre asked. "I just don't want to be in the banking business with the FBI or Portella."

"Think it over," Cilke said.

When the two FBI men left, Nicole turned on Astorre with fury. "How dare you veto my decision and sign those papers! That was just stupid."

Astorre was glaring at her; it was the first time she had ever seen any trace of anger in him. "He feels secure with that piece of paper I signed," Astorre said. "And that's what I want him to feel."

CHAPTER

5

MARRIANO RUBIO was a man with a finger in a dozen pies, all of which had fillings of pure gold. He held the post of consul general for Peru, though he spent much of his time in New York. He also was international representative of big-business interests for many South American countries and for Communist China. He was a close personal friend of Inzio Tulippa, the leader of the primary drug cartel in Colombia.

Rubio was as fortunate in his personal life as he was in business. A forty-five-year-old bachelor, he was a respectable womanizer. He kept only one mistress at a time, all suitable and generously supported when they were replaced by a younger beauty. He was handsome, an interesting conversationalist, a marvelous dancer. He had a truly great wine cellar and an excellent three-star chef.

But like many fortunate men, Rubio believed in pushing fate. He enjoyed pitting his wits against dangerous men. He needed risk to flavor the exotic dish that was his life. He was involved in the illegal shipping of technology to China; he established a line of communication on the highest levels for the drug barons; and he was the bagman who paid off American scientists to emigrate to South America. He even had dealings with Timmona Portella, who was as eccentrically dangerous as Inzio Tulippa.

Like all high-risk gamblers, Rubio prided himself on an ace in the hole. He was safe from all legal peril because of his diplomatic immunity, but he knew there were other dangers, and in those areas he was careful.

His income was enormous, and he spent lavishly. There was such power in being able to buy anything he wanted in the world, including the love of women. He enjoyed supporting his ex-mistresses, who remained valued friends. He was a generous employer and intelligently treasured the goodwill of people dependent on him.

Now, in his New York apartment, which was very fortunately part of the Peruvian consulate, Rubio dressed for his dinner date with Nicole Aprile. The engagement was, as usual with him, part business and part pleasure. He had met Nicole at a Washington dinner given by one of her prestigious corporate clients. At first sight he had been intrigued by her not-quite-regular beauty, the sharp, determined face with intelligent eyes and mouth, her small, voluptuous body, but also by her being the daughter of the great Mafia chief Don Raymonde Aprile.

Rubio had charmed her, but not out of her senses, and he was proud of her for that. He admired romantic intelligence in a woman. He would have to win her respect with deeds, not words. Which he had immediately set about doing by asking her to represent one of his clients in a particularly rich deal. He had learned that she did a great deal of pro bono work to abolish the death penalty and had even defended some notorious convicted murderers to put off their executions. To him she was the ideal modern woman—beautiful, with a highly professional career, and com-passionate in the bargain. Barring some sort of sexual dysfunction, she would make a most agreeable companion for a year or so.

All this was before the death of Don Aprile.

Now the main purpose of his courtship was to learn if Nicole and her two brothers would put their banks at the disposal of Portella and Tulippa. Otherwise there would be no point in killing Astorre Viola.

Inzio Tulippa had waited long enough. More than

nine months after the killing of Raymonde Aprile, he still had no arrangement with the inheritors of the Don's banks. A great deal of money had been spent; he had given millions to Timmona Portella to bribe the FBI and the police in New York, and to procure the services of the Sturzo brothers, and yet he was no further in his plans.

Tulippa was not the vulgar impersonation of a high-powered drug dealer. He came from a reputable and wealthy family and had even played polo for his native land of Argentina. He now lived in Costa Rica, and he had a diplomatic Costa Rican passport, which gave him immunity from prosecution in any foreign land. He handled the relations with the drug cartels in Colombia, with the growers in Turkey, refineries in Italy. He made arrangements for transport, the necessary bribing of officials from the highest rank to the lowest. He planned the smuggling of huge loads into the United States. He was also the man who lured American nuclear scientists to Latin American countries and supplied the money for their research. In all ways he was a prudent, capable executive, and he had amassed an enormous fortune.

But he was a revolutionary. He furiously defended the selling of drugs. Drugs were the salvation of the human spirit, the refuge of those damned to despair by poverty and mental illness. They were the salve for the lovesick, for the lost souls in our spiritually deprived world. After all, if you no longer believed in God, society, your own worth, what were you supposed to do? Kill yourself? Drugs kept people alive in a realm of dreams and hope. All that was needed was a little moderation. After all, did drugs kill as many people as alcohol and cigarettes, as poverty and despair? No. On moral grounds, Tulippa was secure.

Inzio Tulippa had a nickname all over the world. He was known as "the Vaccinator." Foreign industrialists and investors with enormous holdings in South America—whether oil fields, car manufacturing plants, or crops – necessarily had to send top executives there. There were many from the United States. Their biggest problem was the kidnapping of their executives on foreign soil, for which they had to pay ransoms in the millions of dollars.

Inzio Tulippa headed a company that insured these executives against kidnapping, and every year he visited the United States to negotiate contracts with these corporations. He did this not only for money but because he needed some of the industrial and scientific resources of these companies. In short, he performed a vaccinating service. This was important to him.

But he had a more dangerous eccentricity. He viewed the international persecution of the illegal drug industry as a holy war against himself, and he

129

was determined to protect his empire. So he had ridiculous ambitions. He wanted to possess a nuclear capability as a lever in case disaster ever struck. Not that he would use it except as a last resort, but it would be an effective bargaining weapon. It was a desire that would seem ridiculous to everyone except the New York FBI agent in charge, Kurt Cilke.

At one point in his career, Kurt Cilke had been sent to an FBI antiterrorist school. His selection for the six-month course had been a mark of his high standing with the director. During that time he had access (complete or not, he didn't know) to the most highly classified memoranda and case scenarios on the possible use of nuclear weapons by terrorists from small countries. The files detailed which countries had weapons. To public knowledge there was Russia, France, and England, possibly India and Pakistan. It was assumed that Israel had nuclear capability. Kurt read with fascination scenarios detailing how Israel would use nuclear weapons if an Arab bloc were at the point of overwhelming it.

For the United States there were two solutions to the problem. The first was that if Israel were so attacked, the United States would side with Israel before it had to use nuclear weapons. Or, at the crucial point, if Israel could not be saved, the

United States would have to wipe out Israel's nuclear capability.

England and France were not seen as problems; they could never risk nuclear war. India had no ambitions, and Pakistan could be wiped out immediately. China would not dare; it did not have the industrial capacity short-term.

The most immediate danger was from small countries like Iraq, Iran, and Libya, where leaders were reckless, or so the scenarios claimed. The solution here was almost unanimous. Those countries would be bombed to extinction with nuclear weapons.

The greatest short-term danger was that terrorist organizations secretly financed and supported by a foreign power would smuggle a nuclear weapon into the United States and explode it in a large city. Probably Washington, D.C., or New York. This was inevitable. The proposed solution was the formation of task forces to use counterintelligence and then the utmost punitive measures against these terrorists and whoever backed them. It would require special laws that would abridge the rights of American citizens. The scenarios acknowledged the impossibility of these laws until somebody finally succeeded at blowing up a good portion of an American metropolis. Then the laws would pass easily. But until then, as one scenario airily remarked, "It was the luck of the draw."

There were only a few scenarios depicting criminal use of nuclear devices. This was almost absolutely discounted on the grounds that the technical capacity, the procurement of material, and the broad scope of people involved would inevitably lead to informers. One solution to this was that the Supreme Court would condone a death warrant without any judicial process on any such criminal mastermind. But this was fantasy, Kurt Cilke thought. Mere speculation. The country would have to wait until something happened.

But now, years later, Cilke realized it was happening. Inzio Tulippa wanted his own little nuclear bomb. He lured American scientists to South America and built them labs and supplied money for their research. And it was Tulippa who wanted access to Don Aprile's banks to establish a billion-dollar war chest for the purchase of equipment and material—so Cilke had determined in his own investigation. What was he to do now?

He would discuss it soon with the director on his next trip to FBI headquarters in Washington. But he doubted they would be able to solve the problem. And a man like Inzio Tulippa would never give up.

Inzio Tulippa arrived in the United States to meet with Timmona Portella and to pursue the acquisition of Don Aprile's banks. At the same time, the head of the Corleonesi *cosca* of Sicily, Michael Grazziella, arrived in New York to work out with Tulippa and Portella the details on the distribution of illegal drugs all over the world. Their arrivals were very different.

Tulippa arrived in New York on his private jet, which also carried fifty of his followers and bodyguards. These men wore a certain uniform: white suits, blue shirts, and pink ties, with floppy yellow Panama hats on their heads. They could have been members of some South American rhumba band. Tulippa and his entourage all carried Costa Rican passports; Tulippa, of course, had Costa Rican diplomatic immunity.

Tulippa and his men moved into a small private hotel owned by the consul general in the name of the Peruvian consulate. And Tulippa did not slink around like some shady drug dealer. He was, after all, the Vaccinator, and the representatives of the large American corporations vied to make his stay a pleasant one. He attended the openings of Broadway shows, the Lincoln Center ballet, the Metropolitan Opera, and concerts given by famous South American artists. He even appeared on talk shows in his role as president of the South American Confederation of Farm Workers and used the forums to defend the use of illegal drugs. One of these interviews—with Charlie Rose on PBS—became notorious.

Tulippa claimed it was a disgraceful form of colonialism that the United States fought against the use of cocaine, heroin, and marijuana all over the world. The South American workers depended on the drug crops to keep themselves alive. Who could blame a man whose poverty entered his dreams to purchase a few hours of relief by using drugs? It was an inhumane judgment. And what about tobacco and alcohol? They did much more damage.

At this, fifty followers in the studio, Panama hats in laps, applauded vigorously. When Charlie Rose asked about the damage drugs wreaked, Tulippa was especially sincere. His organization was pouring huge sums of money into research to modify drugs so that they would not be harmful; in short, they would be prescription drugs. The programs would be run by reputable doctors rather than pawns of the American Medical Association, who were so unreasonably antinarcotics and lived in dread of the United States Drug Enforcement Agency. No, narcotics could be the next great blessing for humanity. The fifty yellow Panama hats went flying into the air.

Meanwhile, the Corleonesi *cosca* chief, Michael Grazziella, made an altogether different entry into the United States. He slipped in unobtrusively, with only two bodyguards. He was a thin and scrawny man with a faunlike head and a knife scar across his mouth. He walked with a cane, for a bullet had shattered his leg when he was a young Palermo *picciotto*. He had a reputation for diabolical cunning—and it was said that he had planned the murder of the two greatest anti-Mafia magistrates in Sicily.

Grazziella stayed at Portella's estate as his guest. He had no qualms about his own safety, for Portella's entire drug-dealing business depended on him.

The conference had been arranged to plan a strategy to control the Aprile banks. This was of the utmost importance in order to launder the billions of dollars of black-market money from drugs and also to acquire power in the financial world of New York. And for Inzio Tulippa, it was crucial not only to launder his drug money but to finance his nuclear arsenal. It would also make his role as the Vaccinator safer.

They all met at the Peruvian consulate, which was security-proof in addition to supplying the cloak of diplomatic immunity. The consul general, Marriano Rubio, was a generous host. Since he received a cut of all their revenues and he would head their legitimate interests in the States, he was full of goodwill.

Gathered around the small oval table, they made an interesting scene.

Grazziella looked like an undertaker in his black shiny suit, white shirt, and thin black tie, for he was still in mourning for his mother, who had died six months before. He spoke in a low, doleful voice with a thick accent, but he was clearly understood. He seemed such a shy, polite man to have been responsible for the death of a hundred Sicilian law-enforcement officials.

Timmona Portella, the only one of the four whose native tongue was English, spoke in a loud bellow, as if all the others were deaf. His attire too seemed to shout: he wore a gray suit and lime shirt with a shiny blue silk tie. The perfectly tailored jacket would have hidden his huge belly if it was not unbuttoned to show blue suspenders.

Inzio Tulippa looked classically South American, with a white, loose-draped silk shirt and scarlet handkerchief around his neck. He carried his yellow Panama hat in his hand reverently. He spoke a lilting accented English, and his voice had the charm of a nightingale. But today he had a forbidding frown on his sharp Indian face; he was a man not pleased with the world.

Marriano Rubio was the only man who seemed pleased. His affability charmed them all. His voice was well bred in the English style, and he was dressed in a style he called *"en pantoufle"*: pajamas of green silk and a bathrobe of a darker forest green. He wore soft brown slippers lined with white wool fur. After all, it was his building and he could relax.

Tulippa opened the discussion, speaking

directly to Portella with a deadly politeness. "Timmona, my friend," he said, "I paid handsomely to get the Don out of the way, and we still do not own the banks. This after waiting almost a year."

The consul general spoke in his lubricating, calming way. "My dear Inzio," he said. "I tried to buy the banks. Portella tried to buy the banks. But we have an obstacle we did not foresee. This Astorre Viola, the Don's nephew. He has been left in control, and he refuses to sell."

"So?" Inzio said. "Why is he still alive?"

Portella laughed, a huge bellow. "Because he is not so easy to kill," he said. "I put a four-man surveillance team on his house, and they disappeared. Now I don't know where the hell he is, and he has a cloud of bodyguards whenever he moves."

"Nobody is that hard to kill," Tulippa said, the charming lilt of his voice delivering the words like a lyric to a popular song.

Grazziella spoke for the first time. "We knew Astorre back in Sicily, years ago. He is a very lucky man, but then, he is also extremely Qualified. We shot him in Sicily and thought him dead. If we strike again, we must be sure. He is a dangerous man."

Tulippa said to Portella, "You claim you have an FBI man on the payroll? Use him, for the sake of God."

137

"He's not that bent," Portella said. "The FBI is classier than the NYPD. They would never do a straight-out hit job."

"OK," Tulippa said. "So we snatch one of the Don's kids and use them to bargain with Astorre. Marriano, you know his daughter." He winked. "You can set her up."

Rubio did not warm to this proposal. He puffed on his thin after-breakfast cigar and then said stormily, without courtesy, "No." He paused. "I'm fond of the girl. I won't put her through anything like that. I veto any of you doing so."

At this the other men raised their eyebrows. The consul general was inferior to them in actual power. He saw their reaction and smiled at them, again becoming his affable self.

"I know I have this weakness. I fall in love. But indulge me. I'm on strong and correct political ground. Inzio, I know kidnapping is your métier, but it doesn't really work in America. Especially a woman. Now, if you take one of the brothers and make a quick deal with Astorre, you have a chance."

"Not Valerius," Portella said. "He is army intelligence and has CIA friends. We don't want to bring down that load of shit."

"Then it will have to be Marcantonio," the consul general said. "I can do a deal with Astorre."

"Make a bigger offer for the banks," Grazziella said softly. "Avoid violence. Believe me, I've been through this kind of thing. I've used guns instead of money, and it's always cost me more."

They looked at him with astonishment. Grazziella had a fearsome reputation for violence.

"Michael," the consul general said, "you're talking about billions of dollars. And Astorre still won't sell."

Grazziella shrugged. "If we must take action, so be it. But be very careful. If you can get him out in the open during negotiations, then we can get rid of him."

Tulippa gave them all a huge grin. "That's what I like to hear. And Marriano," he said, "don't keep falling in love. That is a very dangerous vice."

Marriano Rubio finally persuaded Nicole and her brothers to sit down with his syndicate and discuss the sale of the banks. Of course, Astorre Viola also had to be present, though Nicole could not guarantee this.

Before the meeting Astorre briefed Nicole and her brothers on what to say and exactly how to behave. They understood his strategy: that the syndicate was to think he alone was their opponent.

This meeting was held in a conference room of the Peruvian consulate. There were no caterers, but a buffet had been prepared and Rubio himself poured their wine. Due to scheduling differences, the meeting took place at ten in the evening.

Rubio made the introductions and led the meeting. He handed Nicole a folder. "This is the proposition in detail. But to put it very briefly, we offer fifty percent over the market price. Though we will have complete control, the Aprile interest will receive ten percent of our profits over the next twenty years. You can all be rich and enjoy your leisure without the terrible strains that such a business life entails."

They waited while Nicole glanced briefly through the papers. Finally she looked up and said, "This is impressive, but tell me why such a generous offer?"

Rubio smiled at her fondly. "Synergy," he said. "All business now is synergy; as with computers and aviation, books and publishing, music and drugs, sports and TV. All synergy. With the Aprile banks, we will have a synergy in international finance, we will control the building of cities, the election of governments. This syndicate is global and we need your banks, so our offer is generous."

Nicole spoke to the other members of the syndicate. "And you gentlemen are all equal partners?"

Tulippa was quite taken with Nicole's dark good looks and stern speech, so he was at his most charming when he answered. "We are legally equal in this purchase, but let me assure you I consider it an honor to be in association with the Aprile name. No one admired your father more."

Valerius, stone-faced, spoke out coolly, directly

to Tulippa. "Don't misunderstand me, I want to sell. But I prefer an outright sale without the percentage. On a personal level, I want to be completely out of this thing."

"But you are willing to sell?" Tulippa asked.

"Certainly," Valerius said. "I want to wash my hands of it."

Portella started to speak, but Rubio cut him off.

"Marcantonio," he said, "how do you feel about our offer? Does it appeal to you?"

Marcantonio said in a resigned voice, "I'm with Val. Let's make the deal without the percentages. Then we can all say good-bye and good luck."

"Fine, we can make the deal that way," Rubio said.

Nicole said coolly, "But then of course you have to increase the premium. Can you handle that?"

Tulippa said, "No problem," and gave her a dazzling smile.

Grazziella, his face concerned, his voice polite, asked, "And what about our dear friend Astorre Viola? Does he agree?"

Astorre gave an embarrassed laugh. "You know I've come to like the banking business. And Don Aprile made me promise I would never sell. I hate to go against my whole family here, but I have to say no. And I control a majority of voting stock."

"But the Don's children have an interest," the consul general said. "They could sue in a court of law."

141

Mario Puzo

Astorre laughed aloud.

Nicole said tightly, "We would never do that."

Valerius smiled sourly, and Marcantonio seemed to find the idea hilarious.

Portella muttered, "The hell with this," and started to rise to leave.

Astorre said in a voice of conciliation, "Be patient. I may get bored with being a banker. In a few months we can meet again."

"Certainly," Rubio said. "But we may not be able to hold the financial package together for that long. You may get a lower price."

There was no shaking of hands when they parted.

After the Apriles left with Astorre, Michael Grazziella said to his colleagues, "He is just buying time. He will never sell."

Tulippa sighed. "Such a simpatico man. We could become good friends. Maybe I should invite him to my plantation in Costa Rica. I could show him the best time of his life."

The others laughed. Portella said coarsely, "He's not going on a honeymoon with you, Inzio. I have to take care of him up here."

"With better success than before, I hope," Tulippa said.

"I underestimated him," Portella said. "How could I tell? A guy who sings at weddings? I did the job on the Don right. No complaints there."

The consul general, his handsome face beaming in appreciation, said, "A magnificent job, Timmona. We have every confidence in you. But this new job should be done as soon as possible."

When they left the meeting, the Aprile family and Astorre went for a late supper to the Partinico restaurant, which had private dining rooms and was owned by an old friend of the Don's.

"I think you all did very well," Astorre told them. "You convinced them you were against me."

"We are against you," Val said.

"Why do we have to play this game?" Nicole said. "I really don't like it."

"These guys may be involved in your father's death," Astorre said. "I don't want them to think they can get anyplace by hurting any of you."

"And you're confident you can handle anything they throw at you," Marcantonio said.

"No, no," Astorre protested. "But I can go into hiding without ruining my life. Hell, I'll go to the Dakotas and they'll never find me." His smile was so broad and convincing that he would have fooled anyone but the children of Don Aprile. "Now," he said. "Let me know if they contact any of you directly."

"I've gotten a lot of calls from Detective Di Benedetto," Valerius said.

Astorre was surprised. "What the hell is he calling you for?"

Valerius smiled at him. "When I was in field intelligence, we got what was labeled 'What do you know' calls. Somebody wanted to give you information or help in some deal. What they really wanted was information on how your investigation was doing. So Di Benedetto calls me as a courtesy to keep me up to date on his case. Then he pumps me for info on you, Astorre. He has a great interest in you."

"That's very flattering," Astorre said with a grin. "He must have heard me sing someplace."

"No chance," Marcantonio said dryly. "Di Benedetto has been calling me too. He says he has an idea for a cop series. There's always room for another cop show on TV, so I've been encouraging him. But the stuff he's sent me is just bullshit. He's not serious. He just wants to keep track of us."

"Good," Astorre said.

"Astorre, you want them to target you instead of us?" Nicole said. "Isn't that too dangerous? That Grazziella guy gives me the creeps."

"Oh, I know about him," Astorre said. "He's a very reasonable man. And your consul general is a true diplomat; he can control Tulippa. The only one I have to worry about right now is Portella. The guy is just dumb enough to start real trouble."

144

He said all this as though it were just an everyday business dispute.

"But how long does this go on?" Nicole asked.

"Give me another few months," Astorre told her. "I promise that we will all be in agreement by then."

Valerius gave him a disdainful look. "Astorre, you were always an optimist. If you were an intelligence officer under my command, I'd transfer you to the infantry just to wake you up."

It was not a happy dinner. Nicole kept studying Astorre as if she were trying to learn some secret. Valerius obviously had no confidence in Astorre, and Marcantonio was reserved. Finally Astorre raised a glass of wine and said cheerfully, "You are a gloomy crew, but I don't care. This is going to be a lot of fun. Here's to your father."

"The great Don Aprile," Nicole said sourly.

Astorre smiled at her and said, "Yes, to the great Don."

Astorre always rode in the late afternoon. It relaxed him, gave him a good appetite for dinner. If he was courting a woman, he always made her ride with him. If the woman couldn't ride, he gave her lessons. And if she didn't like horses, he would cease to pursue her.

He had built a special riding trail on his estate that led through the forest. He enjoyed the chattering of the birds, the rustle of small animals, the occasional sighting of a deer. But most of all he enjoyed dressing up for riding. The bright red jacket, the brown riding boots, the whip in his hand that he never used. The black suede hunting cap. He smiled at himself in the mirror, fancying himself an English lord of the manor.

He went down to the stables, where he kept six horses, and was pleased to see that the trainer, Aldo Monza, had already fitted out one of his stallions. He mounted and slowly cantered onto the forest trail. Picking up speed, he rode through a tattered canopy of red and gold leaves that made a lace curtain against the sinking sun. Only slender sheaves of gold lit the trail. The horse's hooves kicked up the smell of decaying leaves. He saw the fragrant pile of wheaty manure and spurred his horse past it, then rode onto a split in the trail, which gave him a different route to circle home. The gold on the trail disappeared.

He reined in the horse. At that moment two men appeared before him. They were dressed in the floppy clothes of farm laborers. But they wore masks, and metal gleamed silver in their hands. Astorre spurred his horse and put his head down along its flank. The forest filled with light and the sound of exploding bullets. The men were very close, and Astorre felt the bullets hit him in the side and back. The horse panicked into a wild gallop as Astorre concentrated on keeping his seat. He galloped on down the trail, and then two other men appeared. They were not masked or armed. He lost consciousness and slid off the horse and into their arms.

Within an hour Kurt Cilke received a report from the surveillance team that had rescued Astorre Viola. What really surprised him was that Astorre, beneath all his foppish dress, wore a bulletproof vest that covered his torso the length of his red riding jacket. And not just your ordinary Kevlar, but one specially handmade. Now, what the hell was a guy like Astorre doing wearing armor? A macaroni importer, a club singer, a flaky horse rider. Sure, the impact of the bullets had stunned him, but they had not penetrated. Astorre was already out of the hospital.

Cilke started writing a memo to have Astorre's life investigated from childhood on. The man might be the key to everything. But he was sure of one thing: he knew who had attempted to murder Astorre Viola.

Astorre met with his cousins at Valerius's home. He told them of the attack, how he had been shot. "I've asked you for help," he said. "And you refused and I understood. But now I think you should reconsider. There is some sort of a threat to

all of you. I think it could be solved by selling off
the banks. That would be a win-win situation.
Everybody gets what they want. Or we can go for
a win-lose situation. We keep the banks and fight
off and destroy our enemies, whoever they are.
Then there is the lose-lose situation, which we
must be careful not to fall into. That we fight our
enemies and win but the government gets us
anyway."

"That's an easy choice," Valerius said. "Just sell
the banks. The win-win."

Marcantonio said, "We're not Sicilians; we
don't want to throw everything away for the sake
of vengeance."

"We sell the banks and we're throwing away our
future," Nicole said calmly. "Marc, someday you'd
like your own network. Val, with big political
donations you could become an ambassador or a
secretary of defense. Astorre, you could sing with
the Rolling Stones." She smiled at him. "OK, that's
a little far-fetched," she said, changing her tone.
"Forget the jokes. Is killing our father nothing to
us? Do we reward them for murder? I think we
should help Astorre as much as we can."

"Do you know what you're saying?" Valerius
said.

"Yes," Nicole said quietly.

Astorre said to them gently, "Your father
taught me that you can't let other men impose
their will on you or life's not worth living. Val,

that's what war is, right?"

"War is a lose-lose decision," Nicole said sharply.

Valerius showed his irritation. "No matter what the liberals say, war is a win-lose situation. You are much better off to win a war. Losing is an unthinkable horror."

"Your father had a past," Astorre said. "That past now has to be reckoned with by all of us. So now I ask you for your help again. Remember, I am under your father's orders, and my job is to protect the family, which means holding on to the banks."

Valerius said, "I'll have some information for you within a month."

Astorre said, "Marc?"

Marcantonio said, "I'll get to work on that program right away. Let's say two months, three."

Astorre looked at Nicole. "Nicole, have you completed the analysis of the FBI file on your father?"

"No, not yet." She seemed upset. "Shouldn't we get Cilke's help on this?"

Astorre smiled. "Cilke is one of my suspects," he said. "When I have all the information we can decide what to do."

In a month Valerius came through with some information—unexpected, unwelcome. Through his CIA contacts, he had learned the truth about Inzio Tulippa. He had contacts in Sicily, Turkey, India, Pakistan, Colombia, and other Latin American countries. He even had a relationship with the Corleonesi in Sicily and was more than their equal.

According to Valerius, it was Tulippa who was financing certain nuclear-research labs in South America. Tulippa who was desperately trying to set up a huge fund in America to buy equipment and material. Who, in his dreams of grandeur, wanted to possess an awful weapon of defense against the authorities if worse ever came to worst. It therefore followed that Timmona Portella was a front for Tulippa. This was happy news for Astorre. This was another player in the game, another front on which to have to fight.

"Is what Tulippa plans possible?" Astorre asked.

"He certainly thinks it is," Valerius said. "And he has the protection of government officials, where he's located the labs."

"Thanks, Val," Astorre said, patting his cousin on the shoulder affectionately.

"Sure," Valerius said. "But that's all the help you get from me."

It took six weeks for Marcantonio to research the network profile on Kurt Cilke. He gave Astorre a huge file of information; Astorre kept it for twenty-four hours and returned it.

It was only Nicole who worried him. She'd lent him a copy of the FBI file on Don Aprile, but there was a whole section that was completely blacked out. When he questioned her about this she said, "That's how I received it."

Astorre had studied the document carefully. The blacked-out section seemed to be about the period of time when he was only two years old. "That's OK," he told Nicole, "It's too long ago to be important."

Now Astorre could no longer be put off. He had enough information to begin his war.

Nicole had been dazzled by Marriano Rubio and his courtship. She had never really recovered from Astorre's betrayal of her when she was a young girl, when he had elected to obey her father. Though she had had some prudent short affairs with powerful men, she knew that men would always conspire against women.

But Rubio seemed an exception. He never got angry with her when her schedule interfered with their plans to be together. He understood her career came first. And he never indulged in that ridiculous, insulting emotion of many men who thought their jealousy was proof of true love.

It helped that he was generous in his gifts; it

was even more important that she found him interesting and enjoyed listening to him talk about literature and the theater. But his greatest virtue was that he was an enthusiastic lover, expert in bed, and aside from that did not take up too much of her time.

One evening Rubio took Nicole to dinner at Le Cirque with some of his friends: a world-famous South American novelist who charmed Nicole with his sly wit and extravagant ghost stories; a renowned opera singer who at every dish hummed an aria of delight and ate as though he were going to the electric chair; and a conservative columnist, the reigning oracle on world affairs for *The New York Times* who took great pride in being hated by liberals and conservatives alike.

After dinner Rubio took Nicole home to his opulent apartment in the Peruvian consulate. There he made love to her passionately, both physically and with whispered words. Afterward, he lifted her naked from his bed and danced with her while reciting poetry in Spanish. Nicole had a wonderful time. Especially when they were quiet and he poured them champagne and said sincerely, "I do love you." His magnificent nose and brow shone with truthfulness. How brazen men were. Nicole felt a quiet satisfaction that she had betrayed him. Her father would have been proud of her. She had acted in a truly Mafioso fashion.

As head of the New York FBI office, Kurt Cilke had far more important cases than the murder of Don Raymonde Aprile. One was the broad investigation of six giant corporations who conspired illegally to ship banned machinery, including computer technology, to Red China. Another was the conspiracy of the major tobacco companies perjuring themselves before a congressional investigating committee. The third was the emigration of middle-level scientists to South American countries such as Brazil, Peru, and Colombia. The director wanted to be briefed on these cases.

On the flight down to Washington, Boxton said, "We have the tobacco guys nailed; we have the China shipments nailed—internal documents, informers saving their asses. The only thing we don't have is those scientists. But I guess you become a deputy director after this. They can't deny your record."

"That's up to the director," Cilke said. He knew why the scientists were down in South America, but he didn't correct Boxton.

In the Hoover Building, Boxton was barred from the meeting.

*

It was eleven months after the killing of Don Aprile. Cilke had prepared all his notes. The Aprile case was dead, but he had better news on even more important cases. And this time there was a real chance that he would be offered one of the key deputy director jobs in the Bureau. He had made his mark with good work, and he had put in his time.

The director was a tall, elegant man whose ancestors came to America on the *Mayflower*. He was extremely wealthy in his own right and had entered politics as a public duty. And he had laid down strict rules at the beginning of his tenure. "No hanky-panky," he said good-humoredly in his Yankee twang. "By the book. No loopholes in the Bill of Rights. An FBI agent is always courteous, always fair. He is always correct in his private life." Any bit of scandal—wife beating, drunkenness, too close a relationship with a local police official, any third-degree antics—and you were out on your ass even if your uncle was a senator. These had been the rules for the last ten years. Also, if you got too much press, even good, you were on your way to surveillance of igloos in Alaska.

The director invited Cilke to sit down in an extremely uncomfortable chair on the other side of his massive oak desk.

"Agent Cilke," he said, "I called you down for several reasons. Number one: I have placed in your personal file a special commendation for your work against the Mafia in New York. Due to you we have broken their backs. I congratulate you." He leaned over to shake Cilke's hand. "We don't make it public now because the Bureau takes credit for its individual achievements. And also, it might place you in some danger."

"Only from some crazy," Cilke said. "The criminal organizations understand they cannot harm an agent."

"You're implying that the Bureau carries out personal vendettas," the director said.

"Oh, no," Cilke said. "It's just that we would pay more attention."

The director let that pass. There were boundaries. Virtue always had to tread a very thin line. "It's not fair to keep you on the hook," the director said. "I've decided not to appoint you one of my deputies here in Washington. Not at the present time. For these reasons. You are enormously street-smart, and there is still work to be done in the field. The Mafia, for lack of a better word, is still operational. Number two: Officially you have an informant whose name you refuse to divulge even to the top supervising personnel of the Bureau. Unofficially, you have told us. That is classified AFLAX. So you're OK, unofficially. Third: Your relationship with a certain New York chief of detectives is too personal."

The director and Cilke had other items on their

meeting agenda. "And how is our operation *'Omertà'*?" the director asked. "We must be very careful that we have legal clearance on all our operations."

"Of course," Cilke said, straight-faced. The director knew damn well that corners would have to be cut. "We've had a few obstacles. Raymonde Aprile refused to cooperate with us. But of course that obstacle no longer exists."

"Mr. Aprile was very conveniently killed," the director said sardonically. "I won't insult you by asking if you had any prior knowledge. Your friend Portella, perhaps?"

"We don't know," Cilke said. "Italians never go to authorities. We just have to look for dead bodies turning up. Now, I approached Astorre Viola as we discussed. He signed the confidentiality papers but refused to cooperate. He won't do business with Portella, and he won't sell the banks."

"So what do we do now?" the director asked. "You know how important this is. If we can indict the banker under RICO, we can get the banks for the government. And that ten billion would go to fight crime. It would be an enormous coup for the Bureau. And then we can put an end to your association with Portella. He's outlived his usefulness. Kurt, we are in a very delicate situation. Only my deputies and myself know of your cooperation with Portella. That you receive payments from him, that he thinks of you as his confederate. Your life could be in danger."

"He wouldn't dare harm a federal agent," Cilke said. "He's crazy, but he's not that crazy."

"Well, Portella has to go down in this operation," the director said. "What are your plans?"

"This guy Astorre Viola is not the innocent everyone says he is," Cilke said. "I'm having his past checked out. Meanwhile, I'm going to ask Aprile's children to override him. But I worry, can we make RICO stick all the way back ten years for something they do now?"

"That's the job of our attorney general," the director said. "We just have to get our foot in the door, and then a thousand lawyers will go all the way back. We're bound to come up with something the courts can uphold."

"About my secret Cayman account that Portella puts money into," Cilke said. "I think you should draw some out so that he thinks I'm spending it."

"I'll arrange that," the director said. "I must say, your Timmona Portella is not frugal."

"He really believes I sold out," Cilke said, smiling.

"Be careful," the director said. "Don't give them the grounds that would make you a true confederate, an accomplice to a crime."

"I understand," Cilke said. And thought, easier said than done.

"And don't take unnecessary risks," the director said. "Remember, drug people in South America and Sicily are linked with Portella, and they are reckless fellows."

"Shall I keep you advised day by day orally or in writing?" Cilke asked.

"Neither," the director said. "I have absolute confidence in your integrity. And besides, I don't want to have to lie to some congressional committee. To become one of my deputies, you will have to clear these things up." He waited expectantly.

Cilke never dared even to think his real thoughts in the presence of the director, as if the man could read his mind. But still, the rebellion flashed. Who the fuck did the director think he was, the American Civil Liberties Union? With his memos to emphasize that the Mafia was not Italian, Muslims were not terrorists, that blacks were not the criminal class. Who the fuck did he think committed the street crimes?

But Cilke said quietly, "Sir, if you want my resignation, I've built up enough time for an early retirement."

"No," the director said. "Answer my question. Can you clean up your relationships?"

"I have given the names of all the informants to the Bureau," Cilke said. "As for cutting corners, that's a matter of interpretation. As for being friends with the local police force, that's PR for the Bureau."

"Your results speak for your work," the director said. "Let's try another year. Let's go on." He paused for a long moment and sighed. Then he asked almost impatiently, "Have we got enough on the tobacco-company executives for perjury in your judgment?"

"Easily," Cilke said, and wondered why the director even asked. He had all the files.

"But it could be their personal beliefs," the director said. "We have polls that show that half the American people agree with them."

"That's not relevant to the case," Cilke said. "The people in the poll did not commit perjury in their testimony to Congress. We have tapes and internal documents that prove the tobacco executives knowingly lied. They conspired."

"You're right," the director said with a sigh. "But the attorney general has made a deal. No criminal indictments, no prison time. They will pay fines of hundreds of billions of dollars. So close that investigation. It's out of our hands."

"Fine, sir," Cilke said. "I can always use the extra manpower on other things."

"Good for you," the director said. "I'll make you even happier. On that shipping of illegal technology to China, that's very serious business."

"There's no option," Cilke said. "Those companies deliberately broke a federal law for financial gain and breached the security of the United States. The heads of those companies conspired."

159

"We do have the goods on them," the director said, "but you know conspiracy is a catchall. Everybody conspires. But that's another case you can close and save the manpower."

Cilke said incredulously, "Sir, are you saying a deal has been made on that?"

The director leaned back in his chair and frowned at Cilke's implied insolence, but he made allowances. "Cilke, you are the best field man in the Bureau. But you have no political sense. Now listen to me, and never forget this: you cannot send six billionaires to prison. Not in a democracy."

"And that's it?" Cilke asked.

"The financial sanctions will be very heavy," the director said. "Now, on to other things, one very confidential. We're going to exchange a federal prisoner for one of our informers who is being held hostage in Colombia, a very valuable asset in our war on the drug trade. This is a case you're familiar with." He referred to a case four years ago in which a drug dealer took five hostages, a woman and four children. He killed them and also killed a Bureau agent. He was given life without parole. "I remember that you were adamant on the death penalty," the director said. "Now we are going to let him go, and I know you won't be too happy. Remember, all this is secret, but the papers will probably dig it up and there will be an enormous fuss. You and your office will never comment. Is that understood?"

Cilke said, "We can't let anyone kill our agents and get away with it."

"That attitude is not acceptable in a federal officer," the director said.

Cilke tried not to show his outrage. "Then all our agents will be endangered," Cilke said. "That's how it is on the streets. The agent was killed trying to save the hostages. It was a cold-blooded execution. Setting the killer free is an insult to the life of that agent."

"There can be no vendetta mentality in the Bureau," the director said. "Otherwise we're no better than they are. Now, what do you have about those scientists who've emigrated?"

At that moment Cilke realized he could no longer trust the director. "Nothing new," he lied. He had decided from now on he would not be part of the agency's political compromises. He would play a lone hand.

"Well, now you have a lot of manpower, so work on it," the director said. "And after you nail Timmona Portella, I'd like to bring you up here as one of my deputies."

"Thank you," Cilke said. "But I've decided after I clear up Portella, I'm taking my retirement.'

The director gave a deep sigh. "Reconsider it. I know how all this deal making must distress you. But remember this: the Bureau is not only responsible for protecting society against law-breakers, but we must also take only the actions that, in the long run, benefit our society as a whole."

"I remember that from school," Cilke said. "The end justifies the means."

The director shrugged. "Sometimes. Anyway, reconsider your retirement. I'm putting a letter of recommendation in your file. Whether you stay or go, you will receive a medal from the president of the United States."

"Thank you, sir," Cilke said. The director shook his hand and escorted him to the door. But he had one final question. "What happened to that Aprile case? It's been months and it seems nothing has been done."

"It's NYPD, not ours," Cilke said. "Of course, I looked into it. So far no motive. No clues. I would think there's no chance of it being solved."

That night Cilke had dinner with Bill Boxton.

"Good news," Cilke told him. "The tobacco and the China machine cases are closed. The attorney general is going after financial sanctions, not criminal. That frees a lot of manpower."

"No shit," Boxton said. "I always thought the director was straight. A square shooter. Will he resign?"

"There are square shooters and there are square shooters with little nicks on the edges," Cilke said.

"Anything else?" Boxton asked.

"When I bring Portella down, I get to be the director's deputy. Guaranteed. But by then I'll be retired."

"Yeah," Boxton said. "Put in a word for me for that job."

"No chance. The director knows you use four-letter words." He laughed.

"Shit," Boxton said, in mock disappointment. "Or is it *fuck*?"

The next night Cilke walked home from the railroad station. Georgette and Vanessa were in Florida visiting Georgette's mother for a week, and he hated taking a taxi. He was surprised not to hear the dogs barking when he walked up the driveway. He called out for them but nothing happened. They must have wandered off into the neighborhood or the nearby woods.

He missed his family, especially at mealtimes. He had eaten dinner alone or with other agents in too many cities all over America, always alert to any kind of danger. He prepared a simple meal for himself as his wife had taught him to do—a vegetable, a green salad, and a small steak. No coffee, but a brandy in a small thimble of a glass. Then he went upstairs to shower and call his wife before reading himself to sleep. He loved books, and he was always made unhappy when the FBI was portrayed as heavy villains in detective novels. What the hell did they know?

When he opened the bedroom door he could smell the blood instantly and his whole brain fell into a chaotic jumble; all the hidden fears of his life came rushing in on him.

The two German shepherds lay on his bed. Their brown white fur was mottled red, their legs tied together, their muzzles wrapped in gauze. Their hearts had been cut out and rested on their flanks.

With great effort, his mind came together. Instinctively, he called his wife to make sure she was OK. He told her nothing. Then he called the FBI duty officer for a special forensic team and a cleanup squad. They would have to get rid of all the bedclothes, the mattress, the rug. He did not notify the local authorities.

Six hours later the FBI teams had left and he wrote a report to the director. He poured himself a regular-sized glass of brandy and tried to analyze the situation.

For a moment he considered lying to Georgette, concocting a story about the dogs running away. But there were the missing rug and bedsheets to be explained. And besides, it wouldn't be fair to her. She had a choice to make. More than anything, she would never forgive him if he lied. He would have to tell her the truth.

*

164

The next day Cilke flew first to Washington to confer with the director and then down to Florida, where his wife and daughter were vacationing with his in-laws.

There, after having lunch with them, he took Georgette for a walk along the beach. As they watched the glimmering blue water he told her about the dogs being killed, that it was an old Sicilian Mafia warning used to intimidate.

"According to the papers you got rid of the Mafia in this country," Georgette said musingly.

"More or less," Cilke said. "We have a few of the drug organizations left, and I'm pretty sure who did this."

"Our poor dogs," Georgette said. "How can people be so cruel? Have you talked to the director?"

Cilke felt a surge of irritation that she was so concerned about the dogs. "The director gave me three options," he said. "That I resign from the Bureau and relocate. I refused that option. The second was that I relocate my family under Bureau protection until this case is over. The third is that you remain in the house as if nothing has happened. We would have a twenty-four-hour security team guarding us. A woman agent would live in the house with you, and you and Vanessa will be accompanied by two bodyguards wherever you go. There will be security posts set up around the house with the latest alarm equipment. What do you think? In six months this will all be over."

"You think it's a bluff," Georgette said.

"Yes. They don't dare harm a federal agent or his family. It would be suicide for them."

Georgette gazed out at the calm blue water of the bay. Her hand clasped his more tightly.

"I'll stay," she said. "I'd miss you too much, and I know you won't leave this case. How can you be certain you'll finish in six months?"

"I'm certain," Cilke said.

Georgette shook her head. 'I don't like you being so certain. Please don't do anything awful. And I want one promise. When this case is over, you'll retire from the Bureau. Start your own law practice or teach. I can't live this way the rest of my life." She was in deadly earnest.

The phrase that stuck in Cilke's head was that she would miss him too much. And as he so often did, he wondered how a woman like her could possibly love a man like him. But he had always known that someday she would make this demand. He sighed and said, "I promise."

They continued their walk along the beach and then sat in a little green park that protected them against the sun. A cool breeze from the bay ruffled his wife's hair, making her look very young and happy. Cilke knew he could never break his promise to her. And he was even proud of her cunning in extracting his promise at the exact proper moment, when she risked her life to stay on

166

his side. After all, who would want to be loved by an unintelligent woman? At the same time agent Cilke knew his wife would be horrified, humiliated by what he was thinking. Her cunning was probably innocent. Who was he to judge it? She had never judged him, never suspected his own not-so-innocent cunning.

FRANKY AND STACE STURZO owned a huge sporting-goods store in L.A. and a house in Santa Monica that was only five minutes from the Malibu beach. Both of them had been married once, but their marriages didn't take, so now they lived together.

They never told any of their friends they were twins, and it was not even obvious they were brothers except that they had the same easygoing confidence and extraordinary athletic suppleness. Franky was the more charming and temperamental. Stace was the more levelheaded, just a little stolid, but they were both noted for their amiability.

They belonged to one of the large classy gyms that dotted L.A., a gym filled with digital body-building machines and wide-screen wall TVs to watch while working out. It had a basketball court, a swimming pool, and even a boxing ring. Its staff of trainers were good-looking, sculptured men and pretty, well-toned women. The brothers used the gym to work out and also to meet women who trained there. It was a great hunting ground for men like them, surrounded by hopeful actresses trying to keep their bodies beautiful and bored, neglected wives of high-powered movie people.

But mostly Franky and Stace enjoyed pickup basketball games. Good players came to the gym —sometimes even a reserve on the L.A. Lakers. Franky and Stace had played against him and felt they had held their own. It brought back fond memories of when they had been high school all-stars. But they had no illusions that in a real game they would have been so fortunate. They had played all out, and the Laker guy had just been having a good time.

In the gym's health-food restaurant, they struck up friendships with the female trainers and gym members and even sometimes a celebrity. They always had a good time, but it was a small part of their lives. Franky coached the local grade-school basketball team, a job he took very seriously. He always hoped to discover a superstar in the making, and he radiated a stern amiability that made the kids love him. He had a favorite coaching tactic. "OK," he would say. "You're twenty points down, it's the last quarter. You come out and score the first ten points. Now you got them where you want them—you can win. It's just nerve and confidence. You can always win. You're ten points down, then five, then you're even. And you've got them!"

Of course, it never worked. The kids were not developed enough physically or tough enough mentally. They were just kids. But Franky knew the really talented ones would never forget the lesson and that it would help them later on.

Stace concentrated on running the store, and he made the final decision on which hit jobs they would take. There had to be minimum risk and maximum price. Stace believed in percentages all the way and also had a gloomy temperament. What the brothers had going for them was that they rarely disagreed on anything. They had the same tastes and they were almost always evenly matched in physical skills. They sometimes sparred against each other in the boxing ring or played each other one-on-one on the basketball court.

They were now forty-three years old and their lives suited them, but they often talked about getting married again and having families. Franky kept a mistress in San Francisco, and Stace had a girlfriend in Vegas, a showgirl. Both women had shown no inclination for marriage, and the brothers felt they were just treading water, hoping for someone to show up.

Since they were so genial, they made friends easily and had a busy social life. Still, they spent the year after killing the Don with some apprehension. A man like the Don could not be killed without some danger.

Around November, Stace made the necessary call to Heskow about picking up the second five hundred grand of the payment. The phone call was brief and seemingly ambiguous.

"Hi," Stace said. "We're coming in about a month from now. Everything OK?"

Heskow seemed glad to hear from him. "Everything's perfect," he said. "Everything's ready. Could you be more specific on time? I don't want you coming when I'm out of town somewhere."

Stace laughed and said casually, "We'll find you. OK? Figure a month." Then he hung up.

The money pickup in a deal like this always had an element of danger. Sometimes people hated to pay up for something already done. That happened in every business. Then sometimes people had delusions of grandeur. They thought they were as good as the professionals. The danger was minimal with Heskow—he had always been a reliable broker. But the Don's case was special, as was the money. So they didn't want Heskow to have a fix on their plans.

The brothers had taken up tennis the past year,

171

but it was the one sport that defeated them. They were so athletically gifted that they could not accept this defeat, though it was explained to them that tennis was a sport where you had to acquire the strokes early in life by instruction, that it really depended on certain mechanics, like learning a language. So they had made arrangements to stay for three weeks at a tennis ranch in Scottsdale, Arizona, for an introductory course. From there they would travel to New York to meet Heskow. Of course during these weeks at the tennis ranch they could pass some of their evenings in Vegas, which was less than an hour from Scottsdale by plane.

The tennis ranch was superluxurious. Franky and Stace were given a two-bedroom adobe cottage with air conditioning, an Indian-motif dining room, a balconied living room, and a small kitchen. They had a superb view of the mountains. There was a built-in bar, a big refrigerator, and a huge TV.

But the three weeks started off on a sour note. One of the instructors gave Franky a hard time. Franky was easily the best in the group of beginners, and he was especially proud of his serve, which was completely unorthodox and wild. But the instructor, a man named Leslie, seemed particularly irritated by it.

One morning Franky hit the ball to his opponent, who couldn't come near it, and he said

172

proudly to Leslie, "That's an ace, right?"

"No," Leslie said coldly. "That's a foot fault. Your toe went over the serving line. Try again, with a proper serve. The one you have will more often be out than in."

Franky hit another serve, fast and accurate. "Ace, right?" he said.

"That is a foot fault," Leslie said slowly. "And that serve is a bullshit serve. Just get the ball in. You're a very decent player for a hacker. Play the point."

Franky was annoyed but controlled himself. "Match me up with somebody who's not a hacker," he said. "Let's see how I do." He paused. "How about you?"

Leslie looked at him with disgust. "I don't play matches with hackers," he said. He pointed to a young woman in her late twenties or early thirties. "Rosie?" he said, "Give Mr. Sturzo a one-set match."

The girl had just come to the court. She had beautiful tanned legs coming out of white shorts, and she wore a pink shirt with the tennis-ranch logo. She had a mischievous pretty face, and her hair was pulled back in a ponytail.

"You have to give me a handicap," Frank said disarmingly. "You look too good. Are you an instructor?"

"No," Rosie said. "I'm just here to get some serving lessons. Leslie is a champ trainer for that."

"Give him a handicap," Leslie said. "He's way below you in the levels."

Franky said quickly, "How about two games in each four-game set?" He would bargain down to less.

Rosie gave him a quick, infectious smile. "No," she said, "that won't do you any good. What you should ask for is two points in each game. Then you would have a chance. And if we get to deuce, I have to win by four instead of two."

Franky shook her hand. "Let's go," he said. They were standing close together, and he could smell the sweetness of her body. She whispered, "Do you want me to throw the match?"

Franky was thrilled. "No," he said. "You can't beat me with that handicap."

They played with Leslie watching, and he didn't call the foot faults. Franky won the first two games, but after that Rosie rolled over him. Her ground strokes were perfect, and she had no trouble at all with his serve. She was always standing where Franky had to hit the ball, and though several times he got to deuce, she put him away 6–2.

"Hey, you're very good for a hacker," Rosie said. "But you didn't start playing until you were over twenty, right?"

"Right." Franky was beginning to hate the word *hacker*.

"You have to learn the strokes and serve when you're a kid," she said.

"Is that right?" Franky teased. "But I'll beat you before we leave here."

Rosie grinned. She had a wide, generous mouth for such a small face. "Sure," she said. "If you have the best day of your life and I have my worst." Franky laughed.

Stace came up and introduced himself. Then he said, "Why don't you have dinner with us tonight? Franky won't invite you because you beat him, but he'll come."

"Ah, that's not true," Rosie said. "He was just about to ask me. Is eight o'clock okay?"

"Great," Stace said. He slapped Franky with his racquet.

"I'll be there," Franky said.

They had dinner at the ranch restaurant, a huge vaulting room with glass walls that let in the desert and mountains. Rosie proved to be a find, as Franky told Stace later. She flirted with both of them, she talked all the sports and knew her stuff, past and present—the great championship games, the great players, the great individual moments. And she was a good listener; she drew them out. Franky even told her about coaching the kids and how his store provided them with the best equipment, and Rosie said warmly, "Hey, that's great, that's just great." Then they told her they had been high school basketball all-stars in their youth.

Rosie also had a good appetite, which they approved of in a woman. She ate slowly and daintily, and she had a trick of lowering her head and tilting it to the side with an almost mock shyness when she talked about herself. She was studying for a Ph.D. in psychology at New York University. She came from a moderately wealthy family, and she had already toured Europe. She had been a tennis star in high school. But she said all this with a self-deprecating air that charmed them, and she kept touching their hands to maintain contact with them as she spoke.

"I still don't know what to do when I graduate," she said. "With all my book knowledge, I can never figure people out in real life. Like you two guys. You tell me your history, you are two charming bastards, but I have no idea what makes you tick."

"Don't worry about that," Stace said. "What you see is what you get."

"Don't ask me," Franky said to her. "Right now my whole life is centered on how to beat you at tennis."

After dinner the two brothers walked Rosie down the red clay path to her cottage. She gave them each a quick kiss on the cheek, and they were left alone in the desert air. The last image they took with them was Rosie's pert face gleaming in the moonlight.

"I think she's exceptional," Stace said.

"Better than that," Franky said.

*

For the rest of Rosie's two weeks at the ranch, she became their buddy. In late afternoons after tennis they went golfing together. She was good, but not as good as the brothers. They could really whack the ball far out and had nerves of steel on the putting green. A middle-aged guy at the tennis ranch came with them to the golf course to make up a foursome and insisted on being partnered with Rosie and playing for ten dollars a hole, and though he was good, he lost. Then he tried to join them for dinner that night at the tennis ranch. Rosie rebuffed him, to the delight of the twins. "I'm trying to get one of these guys to propose to me," she said.

It was Stace who got Rosie into bed by the end of the first week. Franky had gone down to Vegas for the evening to gamble and to give Stace a clear shot. When he returned at midnight, Stace wasn't in the room. The next morning when he appeared Franky asked him, "How was she?"

"Exceptional," Stace said.

"You mind if I take a shot?" Franky asked.

This was unusual. They had never shared a woman; it was one area where their tastes differed. Stace thought it over. Rosie fitted in perfectly with both of them. But the three couldn't keep hanging out together if Stace was getting Rosie and Franky was not. Unless Franky brought another girl into the combo—and that would spoil it.

"It's OK," Stace said.

So the next night Stace went down to Vegas and Franky took his shot with Rosie. Rosie made no trouble at all, and she was delightful in bed—no fancy tricks, just good-hearted fun and games. She didn't seem uncomfortable about it at all.

But the next day when the three of them had breakfast, Franky and Stace didn't know quite how to act. They were a little too formal and polite. Deferential. Their perfect harmony was gone. Rosie polished off her eggs and bacon and toast and then leaned back and said with amusement, "Am I going to have trouble with you two guys? I thought we were buddies."

Stace said sincerely, "It's just that we're both crazy about you, and we don't know exactly how to handle this."

Rosie said, laughing, "I'll handle it. I like you both a lot. We're having a good time. We're not getting married, and after we leave the tennis ranch, we'll probably never see each other again. I'll go back to New York, and you guys will go back to L.A. So let's not spoil it now unless one of you is the jealous type. Then we can just cut out the sex part."

The twins were suddenly at ease with her. "Fat chance," Stace said.

Franky said, "We're not jealous, and I'm going to beat you at tennis one time before we leave here."

"You haven't got the strokes," Rosie said

firmly, but she reached out and clasped both their hands.

"Let's settle it today," Franky said.

Rosie tilted her head shyly. "I'll give you three points a game," she said. "And if you lose, you won't give me any more of that macho crap."

Stace said, "I'll put a hundred bucks on Rosie."

Franky smiled wolfishly at both of them. There was no way he would let himself lose to Rosie with a three-point handicap. He said to Stace, "Make that bet five."

Rosie had a mischievous smile on her face. "And if I win, Stace gets tonight with me."

Both brothers laughed aloud. It gave them pleasure that Rosie was not that perfect, that she had a touch of malice in her.

Out on the tennis court, nothing could save Franky—not his whirlwind serve, not his acrobatic returns or the three-point spot. Rosie had a top spin she had never used before that completely baffled Franky. She zipped him 6–0. When the set was over, Rosie gave Franky a kiss on the cheek and whispered, "I'll make it up to you tomorrow night." As promised, she slept with Stace after the three of them had dinner. This alternated for the rest of the week.

The twins drove Rosie to the airport the day she left. "Remember, if you ever get to New York, give me a ring," she said. They had already given her an open invitation to stay with them anytime she

179

came to L.A. Then she surprised them. She held out two small gift-wrapped boxes. "Presents," she said, and smiled happily. The twins opened the boxes, and each found a Navajo ring with a blue stone. "To remember me by."

Later, when the brothers went shopping in town, they saw the rings on sale for three hundred bucks.

"She could have bought us a tie each or one of those funny cowboy belts for fifty bucks," Franky said. They were extraordinarily pleased.

They had another week to spend at the ranch, but they spent little of it playing tennis. They golfed and flew to Vegas in the evenings. But they made it a rule not to spend the night there. That's how you could lose big—take a shellacking in the early-morning hours when your energy was down and your judgment was impaired.

Over dinner they talked about Rosie. Neither would say a disloyal word about her, though in their hearts they held her in lower esteem because she had fucked both of them.

"She really enjoyed it," Franky said. "She never got mean or moody after."

"Yeah," Stace said. "She was exceptional. I think we found the perfect broad."

"But they always change," Franky said.

"Do we call her when we get to New York?" Stace asked.

"I will," Franky said.

*

A week after they left Scottsdale they registered at the Sherry-Netherland in Manhattan. The next morning they rented a car and drove out to John Heskow's house on Long Island. When they pulled into the driveway, they saw Heskow sweeping his basketball court clean of a thin skin of snow. He raised his hand in welcome. Then he motioned them to pull into the garage attached to the house. His own car was parked outside. Franky jumped out of the car before Stace pulled in, to shake Heskow's hand but really to put him in close range if anything happened.

Heskow unlocked the door and ushered them inside.

"It's all ready," he said. He led them upstairs to the huge trunk in the bedroom and unlocked it. Inside were stacks of money rubber-banded into six-inch bundles, along with a folded leather bag, almost as big as a suitcase. Stace threw the bundles onto the bed. Then the brothers rifled through each stack to make sure they were all hundreds and that there were no counterfeits. They only counted the bills in one stack and multiplied it by one hundred. Then they loaded the money into the leather bag. When they were finished, they looked up at Heskow. He was smiling. "Have a cup of coffee before you go," he said. "Take a leak or whatever."

"Thanks," Stace said. "Is there anything we should know? Any fuss?"

"None at all," Heskow said. "Everything's perfect. Just don't be too flashy with the dough."

"It's for our old age," Franky said, and the brothers laughed.

"What about all his friends?" Stace asked.

"The dead have no friends," Heskow said.

"What about his kids?" Franky asked. "They didn't make any noise?"

"They were brought up straight," Heskow said. "They're not Sicilians. They are very successful professionals. They believe in the law. And they're lucky they're not suspects."

The twins laughed and Heskow smiled. It was a good joke.

"Well, I'm just amazed," Stace said. "Such a big man and so little fuss."

"Well, it's been a year now and not a peep," Heskow said.

The brothers finished their coffee and shook hands with Heskow. "Keep well," Heskow said. "I may be calling you again."

"You do that," Franky said.

Back in the city the brothers dumped the money into a joint security safe deposit box. Actually, two. They didn't even dip any casual spending money. Then they went back to the hotel and called Rosie.

She was surprised and delighted to hear from

them so soon. Her voice was eager as she urged them to come to her apartment at once. She would show them New York, her treat. So that evening they arrived at her apartment and she served them drinks before they all left for dinner and the theater.

Rosie took them to Le Cirque, which she told them was the finest restaurant in New York. The food was great, and even though it was not on the menu, at Franky's request they cooked him up a plate of spaghetti that was the best he'd ever tasted. The twins could not get over the fact that a fancy restaurant could serve the food they liked so much. They also noted that the maître d' treated Rosie in a very special way, and that impressed them. They had their usual great time, Rosie urging them to tell their stories. She looked especially beautiful. It was the first time they had seen her dressed formally.

Over coffee, the brothers gave Rosie their present. They had bought it at Tiffany's that afternoon and had it wrapped in a maroon velvet box. It had cost five grand, a simple gold chain with a diamond-encrusted locket of white platinum.

"From me and Stace," Franky said. "We chipped in."

Rosie was stunned. Her eyes became watery and gleaming. She put the chain over her head so that the locket rested between her breasts. Then she leaned over and kissed both of them. It was a simple sweet kiss on the lips that tasted of honey.

The brothers had once told Rosie they had never gone to a Broadway musical, so the next night she was taking them to see *Les Misérables*. She promised them they would really love it. And they did, but with a few reservations. Later, in her apartment, Franky said, "I don't believe he didn't kill the cop Javert when he had the chance."

"It's a musical," Stace said. "Musicals don't make sense even in the movies. It's not their job."

But Rosie disputed this. "It shows Jean Valjean has become a really good man," she said. "It's about redemption. A man who sins and steals and then reconciles with society."

This irritated even Stace. "Wait a minute," he said. "The guy started off a thief. Once a thief, always a thief. Right, Franky?"

Now Rosie took fire. "What would you two guys know about a man like Valjean?" And that broke the brothers up. Rosie smiled her good-humored smile. "Which of you is staying tonight?" she asked.

She waited for the answer and finally said, "I don't do threesomes. You have to take turns."

"Who do you want to stay?" Franky asked.

"Don't start that," Rosie warned. "Or we'll have a beautiful relationship like in the movies. No screwing. And I'd hate that," she said, smiling to take the edge off. "I love you both."

"I'll go home tonight," Franky said. He wanted her to know she didn't have power over him.

Rosie kissed Franky good night and accompanied him to the door. She whispered, "I'll be special tomorrow night."

They had six days to spend together. Rosie had to work on her dissertation during the day, but she was available in the evenings.

One night the twins took her to a Knicks game at the Garden when the Lakers were in town, and they were delighted that she appreciated all the fine points of the game. Afterward they went to a fancy deli and Rosie told them that the next day, the day before Christmas Eve, she had to leave town for the week. The brothers had assumed she would spend Christmas with her family. But now they noticed that for the first time since they had known her, she looked a little depressed.

"No, I'm spending Christmas alone in a house my family owns Upstate. I wanted to duck all that phony Christmas stuff, to just study and sort out my life."

"So just cancel and spend Christmas with us," Franky said. "We'll change our flight back to L.A."

"I can't," Rosie said. "I have to study, and that's the best place."

"All alone?" Stace asked.

Rosie ducked her head. "I'm such a dope," she said.

"Why don't we go up with you for just a few days?" Franky asked. "We'll leave the day after Christmas."

"Yeah," Stace said, "we could use some peace and quiet."

Rosie's face was glowing. "Would you really?" she said happily. "That's so great. We could go skiing on Christmas. There's a resort just thirty minutes from the house. And I'll cook a Christmas dinner." She paused for a moment and then said unconvincingly, "But promise you'll leave after Christmas; I really have to work."

"We have to get back to L.A.," Stace said. "We have a business to run."

"God, I love you guys," Rosie said.

Stace said casually, "Franky and me were talking. You know we've never been to Europe, and we thought when you're finished with school this summer, we could all go together. You be our guide. Top of the line in everything. Just a couple of weeks. We could have a great time if you were with us."

"Yeah," Franky said. "We can't go alone." They all laughed.

"That is just a wonderful idea," Rosie said. "I'll show you London and Paris and Rome. And you will absolutely adore Venice. You may never leave.

But hell, summer is a long time away, you guys. I know you, you'll be chasing other women by then."

"We want you," Franky said almost angrily.

"I'll be ready when I get the call," Rosie said.

On the morning of December 23 Rosie pulled up to their hotel to pick up the twins. She was driving a huge Cadillac whose trunk held her big suitcases and a few gayly wrapped presents and still had room for their more modest ones.

Stace took the backseat and let Franky ride up front with Rosie. The radio was playing, and none of them talked for about an hour. That was what was great about Rosie.

While waiting for Rosie to pick them up, the brothers had had a conversation over breakfast. Stace could see Franky was uneasy with him, which was rare between the twins.

"Spit it out," Stace said.

"Don't take this wrong," Franky said. "I'm not jealous or anything. But could you lay off Rosie while we're up there?"

"Sure," Stace said. "I'll tell her I caught the clap in Vegas."

Franky grinned and said, "You don't have to go that far. I'd just like to try having her for myself. Otherwise, I'll lay off and you can have her."

"You're a jerk," Stace said. "You'll ruin

everything. Look, we didn't muscle her, we didn't con her. This is what she wants to do. And I think it's great for us."

"I'd just like to try it by myself," Franky said again. "Just for a little while."

"Sure," Stace said. "I'm the older brother, I have to watch out for you." It was their favorite joke, and indeed it always did seem Stace was a few years older than Franky instead of ten minutes.

"But you know she'll be wise to you in two seconds," Stace said. "Rosie is smart. She'll know you're in love with her."

Franky looked at his brother with astonishment. "I'm in love with her?" he said. "Is that it? Jesus fucking Christ." And they both laughed.

Now the car was out of the city and rolling through the farmland of Westchester County. Franky broke the silence. "I never saw so much snow in my life," he said. "How the hell can people live here?"

"Because it's cheap," Rosie said.

Stace asked, "How much longer?"

"About an hour and a half," Rosie said. "You guys need to stop?"

"No," Franky said, "let's get there."

"Unless you have to stop," Stace said to Rosie. Rosie shook her head. She looked very determined, hands tight on the wheel, peering intently at the slow-falling snowflakes.

About an hour later they went through a small town, and Rosie said, "Just another fifteen minutes."

The car went up a steep incline, and on top of a small hill was a house, gray as an elephant, surrounded by snow-covered fields, the snow absolutely pure white and unmarked, no footprints, no car tracks.

Rosie pulled to a stop at the front-porch entrance, and they got out. She loaded them down with suitcases and the Christmas boxes. "Go on in," she said. "The door is open. We don't lock up out here."

Franky and Stace crunched up the steps of the porch and opened the door. They were in a huge living room decorated with animal heads on the walls, and there was a huge fire in a hearth as big as a cave.

Outside suddenly, they could hear the roar of the Cadillac's motor, and at that moment six men appeared from the two entryways of the house. They were holding guns, and the leader, a huge man with a great mustache, said in a slightly accented voice, "Don't move. Don't drop the packages." Then the guns were pressed against their bodies.

Stace understood at once, but Franky was worried about Rosie. It took him about thirty seconds to put it together—the roar of the engine and Rosie not being there. Then with the worst feeling he had ever had in his life, he realized the truth. Rosie was bait.

CHAPTER

7

ON THE NIGHT before Christmas Eve Astorre attended a party given by Nicole at her apartment. She had invited professional colleagues and members of her pro bono groups, including her favorite, the Campaign Against the Death Penalty.

Astorre liked parties. He loved to chat with people he would never see again and who were so different from him. Sometimes he met interesting women with whom he had brief affairs. And he always hoped to fall in love; he missed it. Tonight Nicole had reminded him of their teenage romance, not coy or flirting but with good humor.

"You broke my heart when you obeyed my father and went to Europe," she said.

"Sure," Astorre said. "But that didn't stop you from meeting other guys."

For some reason Nicole was very fond of him tonight. She held his hand in an intimate schoolgirl way, she kissed him on the lips, she clung to him as if she knew that he was about to escape her once again.

This confused him because all his old tenderness was aroused, but he understood starting up again with Nicole would be a terrible mistake at this junction of his life. Not with the decisions he had to make. Finally she led him to a group of people and introduced him.

Tonight there was a live band, and Nicole asked Astorre to sing in his now gravelly but warm lilting voice, which he always loved doing. They sang an old Italian love ballad together.

When he serenaded Nicole, she clung to him and looked into his eyes searching for something in his soul. Then, with a final sorrowful kiss, she let him go.

Afterward Nicole had a surprise for him. She led him to a guest, a quietly beautiful woman with wide intelligent gray eyes. "Astorre," she said, "this is Georgette Cilke, who chairs the Campaign Against the Death Penalty. We often work together."

Georgette shook his hand and complimented him on his singing. "You remind me of a young Sinatra," she said.

Astorre was delighted. "Thank you," he said. "He's my hero. I know his entire catalogue of songs by heart."

"My husband is a big fan, too," Georgette said. "I like his music, but I don't like the way he treats people."

Astorre sighed, knowing he was on the losing end of an argument, but one he had to make anyway as a certified soldier to the cause. "Yes, but we must separate the artist from the man."

Georgette was amused by the gallantry of Astorre's defense. "Must we?" she asked with a playful twinkle in her eyes. "I don't think we should ever condone that kind of insensitivity and loutish behavior, to say nothing of the violence."

Astorre could see Georgette wasn't going to give in on this point, so all he did was begin to sing a few bars of one of the Chairman's most famous love songs. He looked deeply into her gray eyes, swaying to the music, and he saw her beginning to smile.

"OK, OK," she said. "I'll admit the songs are good. But I'm still not ready to let him off the hook."

She touched him gently on the shoulder before drifting away. Astorre spent the rest of the party observing her. She was a woman who did nothing to enhance her beauty but had a natural grace and a gentle kindness that took away any threat that beauty makes. And Astorre, like everybody in the room, fell a little bit in love with her. Yet she seemed genuinely unaware of the effect she had on people. She had not an ounce of the flirt in her.

By this time Astorre had read Marcantonio's documentary notes on Cilke, a stubborn ferret on the trail of human flaws, coldly efficient in his work. And he also had read that his wife truly loved him. There was the mystery.

Halfway through the party, Nicole came up to him and whispered that Aldo Monza was in the reception room.

"I'm sorry, Nicole," Astorre said. "I have to go."

"OK," Nicole said. "I was hoping you'd get to know Georgette better. She is absolutely the brightest and best woman I've ever met."

"Well, she is beautiful," Astorre said, and he thought to himself how foolish he still was about women—already he was building such fantasy on one meeting.

When Astorre went into the reception room, he found Aldo Monza sitting uncomfortably in one of Nicole's fragile but beautiful antique chairs. Monza rose and whispered to him, "We have the twins. They await your pleasure."

Astorre felt his heart sink. Now it would begin. Now he would be tested, again. "How long will it take to drive up there?" he asked.

"Three hours at least. We have a blizzard."

Astorre looked at his watch. It was ten-thirty P.M. "Let's get started," he said.

When they left the building the air was white with snow and the parked cars were half buried in

194

drifts. Monza had a huge dark Buick waiting.

Monza drove, Astorre beside him. It was very cold, and Monza turned on the heater. Gradually the car turned into an oven smelling of tobacco and wine.

"Sleep," Monza said to Astorre. "We have a long ride ahead of us, and a night of labor."

Astorre let his body relax and his mind slip into dreams. Snow blurred the road. He remembered the burning heat of Sicily and the eleven years during which the Don had prepared him for this final duty. And he knew how inevitable was his fate.

Astorre Viola was sixteen years old when Don Aprile ordered him to study in London. Astorre was not surprised. The Don had sent all his children to private schools and made them grow up in college; it was not only because he believed in education but to keep them isolated from his own business and way of life.

In London Astorre stayed with a prosperous couple who had emigrated many years before from Sicily and who seemed to have a very comfortable life in England. They were middle-aged and childless, and they had changed their name from Priola to Pryor. They looked extremely English, their skins bleached by English weather, their dress and movement serenely un-Sicilian. Mr. Pryor went off to work wearing a bowler hat and carrying a furled umbrella; Mrs. Pryor dressed in the flowered dresses and swooping bonnets of dowdy English matrons.

In the privacy of their home they reverted to their origins. Mr. Pryor wore patched baggy pants and collarless black shirts, while Mrs. Pryor dressed in a very loose black dress and cooked in the old Italian style. He called her Marizza and she called him Zu.

Mr. Pryor worked as the chief executive of a private bank that was a subsidiary of a huge Palermo bank. He treated Astorre as a favorite nephew yet kept his distance. Mrs. Pryor indulged him with food and affection as if he were a grandson.

Mr. Pryor gave Astorre a car and a handsome living allowance. Schooling had already been arranged at a small obscure college just outside London that specialized in business and banking but also had a good reputation in the arts. Astorre enrolled in the required curriculum, but his real interest was in his acting and singing classes. He filled his schedule with electives in music and history. It was during this stay in London that he fell in love with the imagery of fox hunting—not the killing and the chase but the pageantry—the red coats, the brown dogs, the black horses.

In one of his acting classes Astorre met a girl his own age, Rosie Conner. She was extremely pretty, with that air of innocence that can be devastating to young men and provocative to older ones. She was also talented and played some of the leading roles in the plays staged by the class. Astorre, on the other hand, was relegated to smaller parts. He was handsome enough, but something in his personality prevented him from sharing himself with an audience. Rosie had no such problem. It was as if she were inviting every audience to seduce her.

They took vocal classes together too, and Rosie admired Astorre's singing. It was evident the teacher did not share her admiration; in fact, he advised Astorre to drop his music courses. He did not really have more than a pleasant voice, but even worse, he had no musical comprehension.

After only two weeks Astorre and Rosie became lovers. This was more by her initiation than by his, though by this time he was madly in love with her—as madly in love as any sixteen-year-old can be. He almost completely forgot Nicole. Rosie seemed more amused than passionate. But she was so vibrantly alive, she adored him when she was with him; she was ardent in bed and always generous in every way. A week after they became lovers, she bought him an expensive present: a red hunting jacket with a black suede hunting cap and fine leather whip. She presented them as something of a joke.

As young lovers do, they told each other their

life stories. Rosie told him her parents owned a huge ranch in South Dakota and that she had spent her childhood in a dreary Plains town. She finally escaped by insisting she wanted to study drama in England. But her childhood had not been a total loss. She had learned to ride, hunt, and ski, and in high school she had been a star in the drama club as well as on the tennis court.

Astorre poured his heart out to her. He told her how he longed to be a singer, how he loved the English way of life with its old medieval structures, its royal pageantry, its polo matches and fox hunts. But he never told her about his uncle, Don Raymonde Aprile, and his childhood visits to Sicily.

She made him dress in his hunting garb and then undressed him. "You are so handsome," she said. "Maybe you were an English lord in a past life."

This was the only part of her that made Astorre uncomfortable. She truly believed in reincarnation. But then she made love to him and he forgot everything else. It seemed that he had never been so happy, except in Sicily.

But at the end of one year, Mr. Pryor took him into his den to give him some bad news. Mr. Pryor was wearing pantaloons and a peasant knit jacket, his head covered with a checkered, billed cap whose shadow hid his eyes.

He said to Astorre, "We have enjoyed your stay with us. My wife loves your singing. But now regretfully we must say our good-byes. Don Raymonde has sent orders for you to go to Sicily to live with his good friend Bianco. There is some business you must learn there. He wants you to grow up a Sicilian. You know what that means."

Astorre was shocked by the news but never questioned that he must obey. And though he yearned to be in Sicily again, he could not bear the thought of never seeing Rosie again. He said to Mr. Pryor, "If I visit London once a month, can I stay with you?"

"I would be insulted if you did not," Mr. Pryor said. "But for what reason?"

Astorre explained about Rosie, professed his love for her.

"Ah," Mr. Pryor said, sighing with pleasure. "How fortunate you are to be parted from the woman you love. True ecstasy. And that poor girl, how she will suffer. But go, don't worry. Leave me her name and address so I can look after her."

Astorre and Rosie had a tearful farewell. He swore he would fly back to London each month to be with her. She swore she would never look at another man. It was a delicious separation. Astorre would worry about her. Her appearance, her cheerful manner, her smile always invited seduction. The very qualities he loved her for were always a danger. He had seen it many times, as lovers always do, believing that all the men in the world must desire the woman he loved, that they too must be attracted to her beauty, her wit and high spirits.

Astorre was on the plane to Palermo the very next day. He was met by Bianco, but a drastically changed Bianco. The huge man now wore a tailored silk suit and white broad-brimmed hat. He dressed to fit his status, for now Bianco's *cosca* ruled most of the construction business in war-ravaged Palermo. It was a rich living but far more complicated than in the old days. Now he had to pay off all the city and ministry officials from Rome and defend his territory from rival *coscas* like the powerful Corleonesi.

Octavius Bianco embraced Astorre and recalled the long-ago kidnapping and then told him of Don Raymonde's instruction. Astorre was to be trained to be Bianco's bodyguard and pupil in business deals. This would take at least five years, but at the end of that time, Astorre would be a true Sicilian and so worthy of his uncle's trust. He had a head start: because of his childhood visits he could speak the Sicilian dialect like a native.

Bianco lived in an enormous villa just outside Palermo, staffed with servants and a platoon of guards around the clock. Because of his wealth and power he was now connected intimately with the high society of Palermo. During the day Astorre was trained in shooting and explosives and instruction with the rope. In the evenings Bianco took him to meet friends in their homes and in the coffee bars. Sometimes they attended society dances, where Bianco was the darling of the rich conservative widows and Astorre sang gentle love songs to their daughters.

What amazed Astorre the most was the open bribery of high-placed officials from Rome.

One Sunday the national minister of reconstruction came to visit and cheerfully, without any trace of shame, took a suitcase full of cash, thanking Bianco effusively. He explained almost apologetically that half of it had to go to the prime minister of Italy himself. Later, when Astorre and Bianco were back home, Astorre asked if that was possible.

Bianco shrugged. "Not half, but I would hope some. It's an honor to give His Excellency a little pocket money."

During the following year Astorre visited Rosie in London, flying in for just one day and night at a time. These were nights of bliss for him.

Also, that year he had his baptism of fire. A truce had been arranged between Bianco and the Corleonesi *cosca*. A leader of the Corleonesi was a man named Tosci Limona. A small man with a terrible cough, Limona had a striking hawklike profile and deep-socketed eyes. Even Bianco voiced some fear of him.

The meeting between the two leaders was to take place on neutral ground and in the attendance of one of the highest-ranking magistrates in Sicily.

This judge, called "the Lion of Palermo," took great pride in his absolute corruption. He reduced the sentences of Mafia members convicted of murder, and he refused to allow prosecutions to go forward. He made no secret of his friendship with the Corleonesi *cosca* and that of Bianco. He had a great estate ten miles from Palermo, and it was here that the meeting was to take place in order to insure that no violence would be done.

The two leaders were permitted to bring four bodyguards each. They also shared the Lion's fee for arranging the meeting and presiding over it and of course, the rent of his home.

With his huge mane of white hair almost obscuring his face, the Lion was the picture of respectable jurisprudence.

Astorre commanded Bianco's group of bodyguards, and he was impressed by the affection shown between the two men. Limona and Bianco showered each other with embraces, kissing cheeks and clasping hands stoutly. They laughed and whispered intimately over the elaborate dinner the Lion presented to them.

So he was surprised when, once the party was over and he and Bianco were alone, Bianco said to him, "We have to be very careful. That bastard Limona is going to kill us all."

And Bianco proved to be right.

A week later an inspector of police on Bianco's payroll was murdered as he left the home of his mistress. Two weeks after that one of the society swells of Palermo, a partner in Bianco's construction business, was killed by a squad of masked men invading his house and riddling him with bullets.

Bianco responded by increasing the number of his bodyguards and taking special pains to secure the vehicles he traveled in. The Corleonesi were known for their skill with explosives. Bianco also stuck very close to his villa.

But there came a day when he had to go into Palermo to pay off two high-ranking city officials and decided to dine in his favorite restaurant there. He chose a Mercedes and a top driver guard. Astorre sat in the backseat with him. A car preceded him and a car followed, both with two armed men in addition to the drivers.

They were driving along a broad boulevard when suddenly a motorcycle with two riders zoomed out of a side street. The passenger had a Kalashnikov rifle and pumped bullets toward the car. But Astorre had already shoved Bianco to the floor and then returned fire as the cyclists zoomed away. The motorcycle went down another side street and vanished.

Three weeks later, under cover of night, five men were captured and brought to Bianco's villa, where they were tied up and hidden in the cellar. "They are Corleonesi," Bianco said to Astorre. "Come down the cellar with me."

The men were bound in Bianco's old peasant style, their limbs interlocked. Armed guards stood over them. Bianco took one of the guard's rifles and without saying a word shot all five men in the back of the head.

"Throw them in the streets of Palermo," he commanded. Then he turned to Astorre. "After you decide to kill a man, never speak to him. It makes things embarrassing for both of you."

"Were they the cyclists?" Astorre asked.

"No," Bianco said. "But they will serve."

And it did. From then on peace reigned between the Palermo *cosca* and the Corleonesi.

Astorre had not been back to London to see Rosie for almost two months. Early one morning he received a call from her. He had given her his number, to be used only in an emergency.

"Astorre," she said in a very calm voice. "Can you fly back right away? I'm in terrible trouble."

"Tell me what it is," Astorre said.

"I can't, over the phone," Rosie said. "But if you really love me, you'll come."

When Astorre asked Bianco's permission to leave, Bianco said, "Bring money." And he gave him a huge bundle of English pounds.

When Astorre arrived at Rosie's apartment, she let

him in quickly and then carefully locked the door. Her face was dead white, and she was huddled in a bulky bathrobe he had never seen before. She gave him a quick grateful kiss. "You're going to be angry with me," she said sadly.

In that moment Astorre thought she was pregnant, and he said quickly, "Darling, I can never be angry at you."

She held him tightly. "You've been gone over a year, you know. I tried so hard to be faithful. But that's a long time."

Suddenly Astorre's mind was clear, icy. Here again was betrayal. But there was something more. Why had she wanted him to come so quickly? "OK," he said, "why am I here?"

"You have to help me," Rosie said, and led him into the bedroom.

There was something in the bed. Astorre threw back the sheet to find a middle-aged man lying on his back, completely naked, yet with a dignified look. This was partly due to the small silver goatee or perhaps more to the delicate carvings of his face. His body was spare and thin, with a great mat of fur across his chest; oddest of all, he wore gold-rimmed spectacles over his open eyes. Though his head was large for his body, he was a handsome man. He was about as dead a man as Astorre had ever seen, despite the fact that there were no wounds. The spectacles were crooked, and Astorre reached to straighten them.

Rosie whispered, "We were making love and he went into this horrible spasm. He must have had a heart attack."

"When did this happen?" Astorre asked. He was in minor shock.

"Last night," Rosie said.

"Why didn't you just call the emergency medical team?" Astorre said. "It's not your fault."

"He's married and maybe it is my fault. We used amyl nitrate. He had trouble climaxing." She said it without any embarrassment.

Astorre was genuinely astonished by her self-possession. Looking at the corpse, he had the strange feeling that he should dress the man and remove his spectacles. He was too old to be naked, at least fifty—it didn't seem right. He said to Rosie without malice but with the incredulity of the young, "What did you see in this guy?"

"He was my history professor," Rosie said. "Really very sweet, very kind. It was a spur-of-the-moment thing. This was only the second time. I was so lonely." She paused for a moment and then, looking directly into his eyes, said, "You've got to help me."

"Does anyone know he was seeing you?" Astorre asked.

"No."

"I still think we should call the police."

"No," Rosie said. "If you're afraid, I'll take care of it myself."

"Get dressed," Astorre said with a stern look. He pulled the sheet back over the dead man.

An hour later they were at Mr. Pryor's house; he answered the door himself. Without a word, he took them to the den and listened to their story. He was very sympathetic to Rosie and patted her hand in consolation, at which point Rosie burst into tears. Mr. Pryor took off his cap and actually clucked with sympathy.

"Give me the keys to your apartment," he said to Rosie. "Stay the night here. Tomorrow you can return to your home and everything will be in order. Your friend will have disappeared. You will then stay here a week before you go back to America."

Mr. Pryor showed them to their bedroom as if he assumed that nothing had happened to spoil their love affair. And then he took leave of them to take care of business.

Astorre always remembered that night. He lay on the bed with Rosie, comforting her, wiping her tears. "It was only the second time," she whispered to him. "It didn't mean anything, and we were such close friends. I missed you. I admired him for his mind, and then one night it just happened. He couldn't climax, and I hate to say this about him, but he couldn't even keep an erection. So he asked to use the nitrate."

She seemed so vulnerable, so hurt, so broken by her tragedy that all Astorre could do was comfort

CHAPTER

8

DURING THOSE YEARS in Sicily, Astorre was trained
to be a Qualified Man. He even led a squad of six
of Bianco's *cosca* men into Corleone itself to
execute their premier bombardier, a man who had
blown up an Italian Army general and two of the
most able anti-Mafia magistrates in Sicily. It was a
daring raid that established his reputation in the
upper levels of the Palermo *cosca* led by Bianco.

Astorre also led an active social life and
frequented the cafés and nightclubs of Palermo—
mostly to meet beautiful women. Palermo was full
of the young Mafia *picciotti,* or foot soldiers, of
different *coscas,* all insistent on their manhood, all
careful to cut a fine figure with their tailored suits,
their manicured nails, and hair sleeked back like
skin. All looking to make their mark—to be feared

and to be loved. The youngest of them were in their teens, sporting finely groomed mustaches, their lips red as coral. They never gave an inch to another male, and Astorre avoided them. They were reckless, killing even those of high rank in their world and thus ensuring their own almost immediate death. For the killing of a fellow Mafia member was like the seduction of his wife, punished by murder. To assuage their pride, Astorre always showed these *picciotti* an amiable deference. And he was popular with them. It helped that he fell half in love with a club dancer called Buji and so avoided their ill will in matters of the heart.

Astorre spent several years as Bianco's right-hand man against the Corleonesi *cosca.* Periodically he received instructions from Don Aprile, who no longer made his annual visit to Sicily.

The great bone of contention between the Corleonesi and Bianco's *cosca* was a matter of long-term strategy. The Corleonesi *cosca* had decided on a reign of terror against the authorities. They assassinated investigating magistrates and blew up generals sent to suppress the Mafia in Sicily. Bianco believed that this was harmful in the long run despite some immediate benefits. But his objections led to his own friends being killed. Bianco retaliated, and the carnage became so pervasive that both sides again sought a truce.

During his years in Sicily, Astorre made one close friend. Nello Sparra was five years older than Astorre and played with a band in a Palermo nightclub where the hostesses were very pretty and some did duty as high-class prostitutes.

Nello did not lack for money—he seemed to have various sources of income. He dressed beautifully in the Palermo Mafioso style. He was always high-spirited and ready for adventure, and the girls in the club loved him because he gave them small presents on their birthday and holidays. And also because they suspected he was one of the secret owners of the club, which was a nice safe place to work thanks to the strict protection of the Palermo *cosca* that controlled all the entertainment in the province. The girls were only too glad to accompany Nello and Astorre on private parties and excursions into the countryside.

Buji was a tall, striking, and voluptuous brunette who danced at Nello Sparra's nightclub. She was famous for her temper and her independence in taking lovers. She never encouraged a *picciotto:* the men who courted her had to have money and power. She had a reputation for being mercenary in a frank and open way that was considered Mafioso. She required expensive gifts, but her beauty and ardor made the rich men of Palermo eager to satisfy her needs.

Over the years Buji and Astorre established a liaison on the hazardous brink of true love. Astorre was Buji's favorite, though she did not hesitate to abandon him for an especially remunerative weekend with a rich Palermo businessman. When she first did this Astorre tried to reproach her, but she overwhelmed him with her common sense.

"I'm twenty-one years old," she said. "My beauty is my capital. When I'm thirty I can be a housewife with a bunch of kids or be independently wealthy with my own little shop. Sure, we have good times, but you will return to America, where I have no wish to go—and where you have no wish to take me. Let's just enjoy ourselves as free human beings. And despite everything, you will get the best of me before I get tired of you. So stop this nonsense. I have my own living to make." Then she added slyly, "And besides, you have too dangerous a trade for me to count on you."

Nello owned an enormous villa outside Palermo, on the seashore. With ten bedrooms, it easily accommodated their parties. On the grounds was a swimming pool shaped like the island of Sicily and two clay tennis courts, which were rarely used.

On weekends the villa would fill up with Nello's

extended family, who came to visit from the countryside. The children who did not swim were penned into the tennis courts with their toys and old racquets to play with the small yellow tennis balls, which they kicked around like soccer balls until they were strewn on the clay like small yellow birds.

Astorre was included in this family life and accepted as a darling nephew. Nello became like a brother to him. At night Nello even invited him up to the club bandstand and they sang Italian love ballads to the audience, which cheered them enthusiastically and to the delight of the hostesses.

The Lion of Palermo, that eminently corruptible judge, again offered his house and his presence for a meeting between Bianco and Limona. Again, they were each allowed to bring four bodyguards. Bianco was even willing to give up a small piece of his Palermo construction empire to secure peace.

Astorre was taking no chances. He and his three guards were heavily armed for the meeting.

Limona and his entourage were waiting at the magistrate's home when Bianco, Astorre, and the guards arrived. A multi-course dinner had been prepared. None of the bodyguards sat down to the meal, only the magistrate—his full white mane tied out of the way with a pink ribbon—and Bianco and Limona. Limona ate very little but was extremely amiable and receptive to Bianco's expressions of affection. He promised that there would be no more assassination of officials, especially the ones in Bianco's pocket.

At the end of the dinner, as they prepared to go into the living room for a final discussion, the Lion excused himself and said he would be back in five minutes. He did so with a deprecatory smile that made them understand he was answering a call of nature.

Limona opened another bottle of wine and filled Bianco's glass. Astorre went to a window and glanced down into the huge driveway. A lone car was waiting, and as he watched, the great white head of the Lion of Palermo appeared in the driveway. The magistrate got into the car, which quickly sped away.

Astorre did not hesitate one moment. His mind instantly pieced things together. His gun was in his hand without his even thinking. Limona and Bianco had their arms entwined, drinking from their glasses. Astorre stepped close to them, brought up his gun, and fired into Limona's face. The bullet hit the glass first before entering Limona's mouth, and shards of glass flew like diamonds over the table. Astorre immediately turned his gun on Limona's four bodyguards and started firing. His own men had their guns out shooting. The bodies fell to the floor.

Bianco looked at him dumbfounded.

Astorre said, "The Lion has left the villa," and Bianco immediately understood that it had been a trap.

"You must be careful," Bianco told Astorre, gesturing at Limona's corpse. "His friends will be after you."

It is possible for a headstrong man to be loyal, but it is not so easy for him to keep himself out of trouble. And so it proved with Pietro Fissolini. Following Don Raymonde's rare show of mercy toward him, Fissolini never betrayed the Don, but he betrayed his own family. He seduced the wife of his nephew Aldo Monza. And this was many years after his promise to the Don, when he was sixty years old.

This was extraordinarily foolhardy. When Fissolini seduced his nephew's wife, he destroyed his leadership of the *cosca*. Because in the Mafia's separate clusters, to maintain power, one must put family above all. What made the situation even more dangerous was that the wife was the niece of Bianco. Bianco would not tolerate any vengeance on his niece by the husband. The husband inevitably had to kill Fissolini, his favorite uncle and the leader of the *cosca*. Two provinces would engage in bloody strife, and it would decimate the countryside. Astorre sent word to the Don asking for his instructions.

The reply came: "You saved him once; you must decide again."

Aldo Monza was one of the most valued members of the *cosca* and the extended family. He had been one of the men spared death by the Don years earlier. So when Astorre summoned him to the Don's village, he came willingly. Astorre barred Bianco from the conference with assurances that he would protect the daughter.

Monza was tall for a Sicilian, nearly six feet. He was magnificently built, his body molded by hard labor since he was a child. But his eyes were cavernous and his face barely covered with flesh pulled so tight his head looked like a skull. It made him seem particularly unattractive and dangerous—and, in some sense, tragic. Monza was the most intelligent and most educated of Fissolini's *cosca.* He had studied in Palermo to be a veterinarian, and he always carried his professional bag. He had a natural sympathy for animals and was always much in demand. Yet he was as fiercely dedicated to the Sicilian code of honor as any peasant. Next to Fissolini, he was the most powerful man in the *cosca.*

Astorre had made his decision. "I am not here to plead for Fissolini's life. I understand that your *cosca* has agreed to your vengeance. I understand your grief. But I am here to plead for the mother of your children."

Monza stared at him. "She was a traitor, to me

and my children. I cannot let her live."

"Listen to me," Astorre said. "No one will seek vengeance for Fissolini. But the woman is Bianco's niece. He will seek vengeance for her death. His *cosca* is stronger than yours. It will be a bloody war. Think of your children."

Monza gave a contemptuous wave of his hand. "Who knows even if they are mine? She is a whore." He paused. "And she will die a whore's death." His face became illumined with death. He was beyond rage. He was willing to destroy the world.

Astorre tried to imagine the man's life in his village, his wife lost, his dignity betrayed by his uncle and his wife.

"Listen very carefully," Astorre said. "Years ago Don Aprile spared your life. Now he asks this favor. Take your revenge on Fissolini as we know you must. But spare your wife, and Bianco will arrange to have her and the children go to relatives in Brazil. As for you personally, I make this offer with approval from the Don. Come with me as my personal assistant, my friend. You will live a rich and interesting life. And you will be spared the shame of living in your village. You will also be safe from the vengeance of Fissolini's friends."

It pleased Astorre that Aldo Monza made no gesture of anger or surprise. For five minutes he remained silent, thinking carefully. Then Monza said, "Will you continue payment to my family *cosca*? My brother will lead them."

217

"Certainly," Astorre said. "They are valuable to us."

"Then after I kill Fissolini, I will come with you. Neither you nor Bianco can interfere in any way. My wife does not go to Brazil until she sees the dead body of my uncle."

"Agreed," Astorre said. And remembering Fissolini's joyful, jolly face and roguish smile, he felt a pang of regret. "When will it happen?"

"On Sunday," Monza said. "I will be with you on Monday. And may God burn Sicily and my wife in a thousand eternal hells."

"I will go with you back to your village," Astorre said. "I will take your wife under my protection. I'm afraid you may be carried away."

Monza shrugged. "I cannot let my fate be decided by what a woman puts in her vagina."

The Fissolini *cosca* met early that Sunday morning. The nephews and sons-in-law had to decide whether or not to kill Fissolini's younger brother also, to avoid his vengeance. Certainly, the brother must have known of the seduction and, by not speaking, condoned it. Astorre did not take any part in that discussion. He simply made clear that the wife and children could not be harmed. But his blood chilled at the ferocity of these men over what seemed to him not so grave an offense. He realized now how merciful the Don had been with him.

He understood it was not only a sexual matter. When a wife betrays her husband with a lover, she lets a possible Trojan horse into the political structure of the *cosca*. She can leak secrets and weaken defenses; she gives her lover power over her husband's Family. She is a spy in a war. Love is no excuse for such treachery.

So the *cosca* assembled Sunday morning for breakfast in the home of Aldo Monza, and then the women went to mass with the children. Three men of the *cosca* took Fissolini's brother out to the fields—and to his death. The others listened to Fissolini hold court with the rest of his *cosca* gathered around him. Only Aldo Monza didn't laugh at his jokes. Astorre, as an honored guest, sat next to Fissolini.

"Aldo," Fissolini said to his nephew with a raffish smile, "you've become as sour as you look."

Monza stared back at his uncle. "I can't be as cheerful as you, Uncle. After all, I'm not sharing your wife, am I?"

At the same time, three men of the *cosca* grabbed Fissolini and held him to his chair. Monza went into the kitchen and came back with his bag of veterinary tools. "Uncle," he said, "I am teaching what you have forgotten."

Astorre turned his head away.

*

In the bright Sunday-morning sunlight, on the dirt road leading to the famous Church of the Blessed Virgin Mary, a huge white horse cantered slowly. On that horse was Fissolini. He was fastened to the saddle with wire, and his back was supported by a huge wooden crucifix. He almost looked alive. But on his head, like a crown of thorns, was a nest of twigs filled with green grass to form a mound, and mounted on that nest were his penis and testicles. From them, running down his forehead were tiny spiders of blood.

Aldo Monza and his beautiful young wife watched from the steps of the church. She started to cross herself, but Monza struck down her arm and held her head straight to see. Then he shoved her out into the road to follow the corpse.

Astorre followed her and guided her to his car to take her to Palermo and safety.

Monza made a move toward him and the woman, his face masked with hate. Astorre gazed at him quietly and raised a warning finger. Monza let them go.

Six months after the killing of Limona, Nello invited Astorre for a weekend at his villa. They would play tennis and bathe in the sea. They would feast on the fantastic local fish, and they would have the company of two of the prettiest hostesses at the club, Buji and Stella. And the villa would be clear of relatives, who would be attending a huge family wedding in the countryside.

It was beautiful Sicilian weather, with that particular shadow to the sunlight that kept the heat from being unbearable and made the sky a startling canopy overhead. Astorre and Nello played tennis with the girls, who had never seen a racquet before but hit out lustily and sent balls flying over the fence. Finally Nello suggested they go for a walk on the beach and a swim.

The four bodyguards were enjoying themselves in the shade of the verandah, the servants bringing them drinks and food. But this did not relax their vigilance. For one thing, they enjoyed watching the lithe bodies of the two women in their bathing suits, speculating about which of them was better in bed, and all agreeing on Buji, whose vivacious speech and laughter gave evidence of a higher potential for arousal. Now they prepared for the walk on the beach in good humor, even rolling up their trouser legs.

But Astorre motioned for them. "We'll stay in sight," he told them. "Enjoy your drinks."

The four of them strolled down the beach just out of reach of the surf, Astorre and Nello in front and the two women behind them. When the women had gone fifty yards, they began to strip off their bathing suits. Buji took down her shoulder straps to show her breasts and cupped them to hold the sun.

They all jumped into the surf, which was mild and rippling. Nello was a first-class swimmer, and he dove underwater and came up between Stella's legs so that when he stood she was on his shoulders. He shouted to Astorre, "Come on out!!" and Astorre waded to where he could swim, Buji holding on to him from behind. He pushed her underwater, sinking with her below the surface, but instead of being frightened, Buji tugged at his shorts to uncover his behind.

Submerged, he felt a throbbing in his ears. At the same time he saw Buji's exposed white breasts suspended in the green water below the sea and her laughing face close to his. Then the throbbing in his ears came to a roar, and he surfaced, Buji clinging to his bare hips.

The first thing he saw was a speedboat roaring toward him, its motor a thunderstorm churning up air and water. Nello and Stella were on the beach. How did they get there so fast? Far off, he could see his bodyguards, trousers rolled, starting to run toward the sea from the villa. He pushed Buji underwater and away from him and tried to wade to the beach. But he was too late. The speedboat was very close, and he saw a man with a rifle aiming carefully. The noise of the shots was muffled by the roar of the motor.

The first bullet spun Astorre around so that he was a broad target to the gunman. His body seemed to jump out of the water, then collapsed below the surface. He could hear the boat receding, and then he felt Buji tugging at him, dragging him, and trying to lift him onto the beach.

When the bodyguards arrived they found Astorre facedown in the surf, a bullet in his throat, Buji weeping at his side.

It took Astorre four months to recover from his wounds. Bianco had him hidden in a small private hospital in Palermo where he could be guarded and given the best treatment. Bianco visited him every day, and Buji came on her days off from the club.

It was near the end of his stay that Buji brought him a two-inch-wide gold neckband from the center of which hung a gold disk etched with an image of the Virgin Mary. She put it around his neck like a collar and positioned the medallion over his wound. It had been treated with adhesive that made it stick to the skin. The disk was no bigger than a silver dollar, but it covered the wound and looked like an adornment. Still, there was nothing effeminate about it.

"That does the job," Buji said affectionately. "I couldn't bear looking at it." She kissed him gently.

"You just wash off the adhesive once a day," Bianco said.

"I'll get my throat slit by somebody who wants gold," Astorre said wryly. "Is this really necessary?"

"Yes," Bianco said. "A man of respect cannot flaunt an injury inflicted by an enemy. Also, Buji is right. Nobody can bear the sight of it."

The only thing that registered with Astorre was that Bianco had called him a man of respect. Octavius Bianco, that ultimate Mafioso, had done him the honor. He was surprised and flattered.

After Buji left—for a weekend with the wealthiest wine merchant in Palermo—Bianco held a mirror up for Astorre. The band of gold was handsomely made. The Madonna, Astorre thought; she was all over Sicily, in roadside shrines, in cars and houses, on children's toys.

He said to Bianco, "Why is it the Madonna Sicilians worship, instead of the Christ?"

Bianco shrugged. "Jesus was, after all, a man, and so cannot be fully trusted. Anyway, forget all that. It's done. Before you go back to America, you will spend a year with Mr. Pryor in London to learn about the banking business. Your uncle's orders. There is another thing. Nello must be killed."

Astorre had gone over the whole affair many times in his mind and knew Nello was guilty. But what was the reason? They had been good friends for such a long time, and it had been a genuine friendship. But then there had come the killing of the Corleonesi. Nello must be related in some way to the Corleonesi *cosca* and he had no choice.

And there was the fact that Nello had never

224

tried to visit him in the hospital. In fact, Nello had disappeared from Palermo. He played at the club no more. Still, Astorre hoped he might be wrong.

"Are you sure it was Nello?" Astorre said. "He was my dearest friend."

"Who else could they use?" Bianco said. "Your most bitter enemy? Of course, your friend. In any case you will have to punish him yourself as a man of respect. So get well."

On Bianco's next visit Astorre said to him, "We have no proof against Nello. Let the matter rest, and make your peace with the Corleonesi. Let the word go out that I died of my wounds."

At first Bianco argued furiously, but then he accepted the wisdom of Astorre's advice and thought him a clever man. He could make peace with the Corleonesi, and the score would be even. As for Nello, he was just a pawn and not worth killing. Until another day.

It took a week for arrangements to be made. Astorre would return to the United States through London, to be briefed by Mr. Pryor. Bianco told Astorre that Aldo Monza would be sent to America directly to stay with Don Aprile and would be waiting for him in New York.

Astorre spent a year with Mr. Pryor in London. It was an enlightening experience.

In Mr. Pryor's den, over a jug of wine with

lemon, it was explained that there were extraordinary plans for him. That his stay in Sicily had been part of a specific plan by the Don to prepare him for a certain important role.

Astorre asked him about Rosie. He had never forgotten her—her grace, her pure joy in living, her generosity in all things, including lovemaking. He missed her.

Mr. Pryor raised his eyebrows. "That Mafioso girl," he said. "I knew you would not forget her."

"Do you know where she is?" Astorre asked.

"Certainly," Pryor said. "In New York."

Astorre said hesitantly, "I've been thinking about her. After all, I was gone a long time and she was young. What happened was very natural. I was hoping to see her again."

"Of course," Mr. Pryor said. "Why would you not? After dinner I will give you all the information you need."

So late that night in Mr. Pryor's den, Astorre got the full story on Rosie. Mr. Pryor played tapes of Rosie's phone conversations that revealed her meetings with men in her flat. These tapes made clear that Rosie had sexual liaisons with them, that they gave her expensive gifts and money. It was a shock for Astorre to hear her voice, using tones that he had thought were meant only for him—the clear laugh, the witty, affectionate quips. She was extremely charming and never coarse or vulgar. She made herself sound like a high school girl going on a prom date. Her innocence was a work of genius.

Mr. Pryor was wearing his cap low over his eyes, but he was watching Astorre.

Astorre said, "She's very good, isn't she?"

"A natural," Mr. Pryor said.

"Were these tapes made when I was going with her?" Astorre asked.

Mr. Pryor made a deprecating gesture. "It was my duty to protect you. Yes."

"And you never said anything?" Astorre said.

"You were really madly in love," Mr. Pryor said. "Why should I spoil your pleasure? She was not greedy, she treated you well. I was young myself once, and believe me, in love the truth is of no importance. And despite everything, she is a marvelous girl."

"A high-class call girl," Astorre said, almost bitterly.

"Not really," Mr. Pryor said. "She had to live by her wits. She ran away from home when she was fourteen, but she was highly intelligent and wanted an education. She also wanted to live a happy life. All perfectly natural. She could make men happy, a rare talent. It was fair that they should pay a price."

Astorre laughed. "You are an enlightened Sicilian. But what about spending twenty-four hours with the dead body of a lover?"

Mr. Pryor laughed with delight. "But that is the best part of her. Truly Mafioso. She has a warm heart but a cold mind. What a combination. Magnificent. But then, you must always be wary of her. Such a person is always dangerous."

"And the amyl nitrate?" Astorre asked.

"Of that she is innocent. Her affair with the professor had been going on before she met you, and he insisted on the drug. No, what we have here is a girl who straightforwardly thinks of her own happiness to the exclusion of everything else. She has no social inhibitions. My advice to you is stay in touch. You may want to make some professional use of her."

"I agree," Astorre said. He was surprised that he felt no anger toward Rosie. That her charm was all she needed to be forgiven. He would let it go, he told Mr. Pryor.

"Good," Mr. Pryor said. "After a year here, you will go to Don Aprile."

"And what will happen to Bianco?" Astorre asked.

Mr. Pryor shook his head and sighed. "Bianco must yield. The Corleonesi *cosca* is too strong. They will not pursue you. The Don made the peace. The truth is that Bianco's success has made him too civilized."

Astorre kept track of Rosie. Partly out of caution, partly out of fond remembrance of the great love of his life. He knew that she had returned to school and was working toward her Ph.D. in psychology at New York University and that she lived in a secure apartment building nearby where she had finally become more professional with older and richer men.

She was very clever. She ran three liaisons at a time and apportioned her rewards among expensive gifts of money, jewelry, and vacations to the spas of the rich—where she made further contacts. No one could call her a professional call girl, since she never asked for anything, but she never refused a gift.

That these men fell in love with her was a foregone conclusion. But she never accepted their offers of marriage. She insisted that they were friends who loved each other, that marriage was not suitable for her or them. Most of the men accepted this decision with grateful relief. She was not a gold digger; she did not press for money and showed no evidence of greed. All she wanted was to live in a luxurious style, free of encumbrance. But she did have an instinct to squirrel money away for a rainy day. She had five different bank accounts and two safety deposit boxes.

It was a few months after the Don's death that Astorre decided to see Rosie again. He was certain that was only to get her help in his plans. He told himself that he knew her secrets and she could not dazzle him again. And she was in his debt and he knew her fatal secret.

Mario Puzo

He knew also that in a certain sense she was amoral. That she put herself and her pleasure in an exalted realm, an almost religious belief. She believed with all her heart that she had a right to be happy and that this took precedence over everything else.

But more than anything, he wanted to see her again. Like many men, the passage of time had lessened her betrayals and heightened her charms. Now her sins seemed more a youthful carelessness, not some proof that she did not love him. He remembered her breasts, how they blotched with pink when she made love; the way she ducked her head in shyness; her infectious high spirits; her gentle good humor. The way she walked so effortlessly with her stiltlike legs and the incredible heat of her mouth on his lips. Despite all this, Astorre convinced himself that this visit was strictly business. He had a job for her to do.

Rosie was about to enter her apartment building when he stopped in front of her, smiled, and said hello. She was carrying books in her right arm and she dropped them on the pavement. Her face blushed with pleasure; her eyes sparkled. She threw her arms around him and kissed him on the mouth.

"I knew I'd see you again," she said. "I knew you'd forgive me." Then she pulled him into the building and led him up one flight of stairs to her apartment.

There she poured them drinks, wine for her, brandy for him. She sat next to him on the sofa. The room was luxuriously furnished, and he knew where the money came from.

"Why did you wait so long?" Rosie asked. As she spoke, she was removing the rings from her fingers, detaching her earrings, tugging at the lobes. She slipped off the three bracelets from her left arm, all gold and diamonds.

"I was busy," Astorre said. "And it took me a long time to find you."

Rosie gave him an affectionate, tender look. "Do you still sing? Do you still ride in that ridiculous red outfit?" She kissed him again, and Astorre felt a warmth in his brain, a hopeless response.

"No," he said. "Rosie, we can't go back."

Rosie pulled him to his feet. "It was the happiest time of my life," she said. Then they were in the bedroom, and in seconds they were naked.

Rosie took a bottle of perfume from her night table and sprayed first herself, then him. "No time for a bath," she said, laughing. And then they were in bed together and he saw the pink blotches grow slowly over her breasts.

For Astorre it was a disembodied experience. He enjoyed the sex but he could not enjoy Rosie. A vision arose in his mind of her keeping vigilance over the dead professor's body for a night and a day. Had he been alive, could he have been helped to live? What had Rosie done alone with death and the professor?

Lying on her back, Rosie reached out to touch his cheek. She ducked her head down and murmured softly, "That old black magic doesn't work anymore." She had been toying with the gold medallion on his neck, saw the ugly purple wound, and kissed it.

Astorre said, "It was fine."

Rosie sat up, her naked torso and breasts hanging over him. "You can't forgive me for the professor, that I let him die and stayed with him. Isn't that right?"

Astorre didn't answer. He would never tell her what he knew about her now. That she had never changed.

Rosie got out of bed and started to dress. He did the same.

"You're a much more terrible person," Rosie said. "The adopted nephew of Don Aprile. And your friend in London who helped clean up my mess. He did a very professional job for an English banker, but not when you know he immigrated from Italy. It wasn't hard to figure out."

They were in the living room, and she made them another drink. She looked earnestly into his eyes. "I know what you are. And I don't mind, I really don't. We're really soul mates. Isn't that perfect?"

Astorre laughed. "The last thing I want to find is

a soul mate," he said. "But I did come to see you on business."

Rosie was impassive now. All the charm was gone from her face. She began to slip her rings back onto her fingers. "My price for a quickie is five hundred dollars," she said. "I can take a check." She smiled at him mischievously—it was a joke. He knew she only took gifts on holidays and birthdays, and those were far more substantial. In fact, the apartment they were in had been a birthday gift from an admirer.

"No, seriously," said Astorre. And then he told her about the Sturzo brothers and what he wanted her to do. And he put the closer on it. "I'll give you twenty thousand now for expenses," he said, "and another hundred thousand when you're done."

Rosie looked at him very thoughtfully. "And what happens afterward?" she asked.

"You don't have to worry," Astorre said.

"I see," Rosie said. "And what if I say no?"

Astorre shrugged. He didn't want to think about that. "Nothing," he said.

"You won't turn me in to the English authorities?" she said.

"I could never do that to you," Astorre said, and she could not doubt the sincerity in his voice.

Rosie sighed. "OK." And then he saw her eyes sparkle. She grinned at him. "Another adventure," she said.

*

Now, riding out through Westchester, Astorre was awakened from his memories by Aldo Monza pressing his leg. "A half hour to go," Monza said. "You have to prepare yourself for the Sturzo brothers."

Astorre stared out the car window at the fresh snowflakes falling. They were in a countryside barren but for large, bare trees, whose sparkling branches stuck out like magicians' wands. The blanket of luminescent snow made the covered stones seem like bright stars. At that moment Astorre felt a cold desolation in his heart. After this night, his world would change, he would change, and in some way his true life would begin.

Astorre reached the safe house at three in the morning in a landscape ghostly white, snow in huge drifts.

Inside, the Sturzo twins were handcuffed, their feet shackled and special restraining jackets fitted onto their bodies. They were lying on the floor of one bedroom, guarded by two armed men.

Astorre regarded them with sympathy. "It's a compliment," he told them. "We appreciate how dangerous you are."

The two brothers were completely different in their attitudes. Stace seemed calm, resigned, but Franky glared at them with hatred that transfigured his face from its usual amiable look into a gargoyle.

Astorre sat on the bed. "I guess you guys have figured it out," he said.

Stace said quietly, "Rosie was bait. She was very good, right, Franky?"

"Exceptional," Franky said. He was trying to keep his voice from ranging hysterically high.

"That's because she really liked you guys," Astorre said. "She was crazy about you, especially Franky. It was tough for her. Very tough."

Franky said contemptuously, "Then why did she do it?"

"Because I gave her a lot of money," Astorre said. "Really a lot of money. You know how that is, Franky."

"No, I don't," Franky said.

"I figure it took a big price for two smart guys like you to take the contract on the Don," Astorre said. "A million? Two million?"

Stace said, "You have it all wrong. We had no part in that. We're not that stupid."

Astorre said, "I know you're the shooters. You have a rep for having big balls. And I checked you out. Now, what I want from you is the name of the broker."

"You're wrong," Stace said. "There is no way you can put that on us. And who the hell are you, anyway?"

"I'm the Don's nephew," Astorre said. "His

sweeper-upper. And I've been checking you two guys out for nearly six months. At the time of the shooting, you weren't in L.A. You didn't show for over a week. Franky, you missed two games coaching the kids. Stace, you never dropped in to see how the store went. You never even called. So just tell me where you were."

"I was in Vegas gambling," Franky said. "And we could talk better if you took off some of these restraints. We're not fucking Houdinis."

Astorre gave him a sympathetic smile. "In a bit," he said. "Stace, how about you?"

"I was up with my girlfriend in Tahoe," Stace said. "But who the hell can remember?"

Astorre said, "Maybe I'll have better luck talking to you separately."

He left them and went down to the kitchen, where Monza had coffee waiting for him. He told Monza to put the brothers into different bedrooms and keep two guards with each man at all times. Aldo was working with a six-man team.

"Are you sure you have the right fellows?" Monza said.

"I think so," Astorre said. "If not them, it's just their bad luck. I hate to ask you, Aldo, but you may have to help them talk."

"Well, they don't always talk," Monza said. "It's hard to believe, but people are willful. And these two look very hard to me."

"I just hate to go that low," Astorre said.

He waited an hour before going up to the room where Franky was. Night had fallen, but reflected in the lamplight outside he could see snowflakes swirling slowly down. He found Franky on the floor in full restraints.

"It's very simple," Astorre said to him. "Give us the name of the broker, and you may get out of here alive."

Franky looked at him with hatred. "I'll never fucking tell you anything, you asshole. You got the wrong guys. And I'll remember your face and I'll remember Rosie."

"That's absolutely the wrong thing to say," Astorre told him.

"Were you fucking her, too?" Franky said. "You're a pimp?"

Astorre understood. Franky would never forgive the betrayal by Rosie. What a frivolous response to a serious situation.

"I think you're being stupid," Astorre said. "And you guys have a rep for being smart."

"I don't give a flying fuck what you think," Franky said. "You can't do anything if you have no proof."

"Really? So I'm wasting my time with you," Astorre said. "I'll go talk with Stace."

Astorre went down to the kitchen for more coffee before he went up to Stace. He pondered the fact that Franky could look so confident and speak so brashly while under such strict constraints. Well, he would have to do better with Stace. He found the man propped up uncomfortably in bed.

"Take his jacket off," Astorre said. "But check his cuffs and shackles."

"I figured it out," Stace said to him calmly. "You know we have a stash. I can arrange for you to pick it up and end this nonsense."

"I just had a talk with Franky," Astorre said. "I was disappointed in him. You and your brother are supposed to be very smart guys. Now you talk to me about money, and you know this is about you hitting the Don."

"You have it wrong," Stace said.

Astorre said gently, "I know you weren't in San Francisco, and I know Franky wasn't in Vegas. You are the only two freelancers who had the balls to take the job. And the shooters were lefties like you and Franky. So all I want to know is, who was your broker?"

"Why should I tell you?" Stace said. "I know the story is over. You guys didn't wear masks, you exposed Rosie, so you are not going to let us out of here alive. No matter what you promise."

Astorre sighed. "I won't try to con you. That's about it. But you have one thing you can bargain for. Easy or hard. I have a very Qualified Man with me, and I'm going to put him to work on Franky." As he said this, Astorre felt a queasiness in his stomach. He remembered Aldo Monza working on Fissolini.

"You're wasting your time," Stace said. "Franky won't talk."

"Maybe not," Astorre said. "But he'll be taken apart piece by piece, and each piece will be brought to you to check. I figure you to talk to save him from that. But why even start down that road? And Stace, why would you want to protect that broker? He was supposed to cover you, and he didn't."

Stace didn't answer. Then he said, "Why don't you let Franky go?"

Astorre said, "You know better than that."

"How do you know I won't lie to you?" Stace said.

"Why the hell should you?" Astorre said. "What do you gain? Stace, you can keep Franky from going through something really terrible. You have to see it clear."

"We were just the shooters, doing a job," Stace said. "The guy higher is the one you want. Why can't you just let us go?"

Astorre was patient. "Stace, you and your brother took the job of killing a great man. Big price, big ego thing. Come on. It boosted you. You guys took your shot and lost, and now you have to pay or else the whole world is on a tilt. It has to be. Now, all you have is the choice, easy or hard. In an hour from now you can be looking at a very important piece of Franky on that table. Believe me, I don't want to do that, I really don't."

Stace said, "How do I know you're not full of shit?"

Astorre said, "Think, Stace. Think how I set you up with Rosie. A lot of time and patience. Think, I got you to this place and have eight armed men. A lot of expenses and a lot of trouble. And just before Christmas Eve. I'm a very serious fellow, Stace, you can see that. I'll give you an hour to think it over. I promise if you talk, Franky will never know it's coming."

Astorre went down to the kitchen again. Monza was waiting for him.

"So?" Monza said.

"I don't know," Astorre said. "But I have to be at Nicole's Christmas Eve party tomorrow, so we have to end this tonight."

"It won't take me over an hour," Monza said. "He'll either talk or be dead."

Astorre relaxed by the roaring fire for a short time and then went upstairs again to see Stace. The man looked weary and resigned. He had thought it over. He knew Franky would never talk—Franky thought there was still hope. Stace believed Astorre had put all the cards on the table. And now Stace comprehended the fears of all the men he had killed, their last despairing and fruitless hopes

240

for some fate to save them. Against all probabilities. And he didn't want Franky to die like that, piece by piece. He studied Astorre's face. It was stern, implacable despite his youth. He had the gravity of a high judge.

The heavily falling snow was coating the windowpanes like white fur. Franky, in his room, was daydreaming about being in Europe with Rosie, the snow coating the Paris boulevards, falling into the canals of Venice. The snow like magic. Rome like magic.

Stace lay on his bed worrying about Franky. They had taken the shot and lost. And it was the end of the story. But he could help Franky think they were only twenty points down.

"I'm OK with it now," Stace said. "Make sure Franky doesn't know what's happening, OK?"

"I promise," Astorre said. "But I'll know if you're lying."

"No," Stace said. "What's the point? The broker is a guy named Heskow, and he lives in a town called Brightwaters, just past Babylon. He's divorced, lives alone, and has a sixteen-year-old humongous kid who's a terrific basketball player. Heskow's hired us for some jobs over the years. We go back to when we were kids. The price was a million, but still me and Franky were leery about taking it. Too big a hit. We took it because he said we didn't have to worry about the FBI and we didn't have to worry about the police. That it was a great big fix. He also told us that the Don no longer had any juice connections. But he was obviously wrong on that. You're here. It was just too big a payday to turn down."

"That's a lot of info to give a guy you think is full of shit," Astorre said.

"I want to convince you I'm telling the truth," Stace said. "I figured it out. The story is over. I don't want Franky to know it."

"Don't worry," Astorre said. "I believe you."

He left the room and went down to the kitchen to give Monza his instructions. He wanted their IDs, licenses, credit cards, et cetera. He kept his word to Stace: Franky was to be shot in the back of the head without any warning. And Stace was also to be executed without pain.

Astorre left to drive back to New York. The snow had turned to rain, and it rinsed the countryside of snow.

It was rare that Monza disregarded an order, but as the executioner he felt he had the right to protect himself and his men. There would be no guns. He would use rope.

First he took four guards to help him strangle Stace. The man didn't even try to resist. But with Franky it was different. For twenty minutes he tried to twist away from the rope. For a terrible twenty minutes Franky Sturzo knew he was being murdered.

Then the two bodies were wrapped in blankets and carried through the heavy glades as the rain changed back into snow. They were deposited in the forest behind the house. A hole in a very dense thicket was the hiding place, and they would not be discovered until spring, if ever. By that time the bodies would be so destroyed by nature that, Monza hoped, the cause of death could not be determined.

But it was not only for this practical reason that Monza had disobeyed his chief. For like Don Aprile, he felt deeply that mercy could only come from God. He despised the idea of any kind of mercy for men who hired themselves out as killers of other men. It was presumptuous for one man to forgive another. That was the duty of God. For men to pretend such mercy was an idle pride and a lack of respect. He did not desire any such mercy for himself.

CHAPTER
9

KURT CILKE BELIEVED in the law, those rules man invented to live a peaceful life. He had always tried to avoid those compromises that undermine a fair society, and he fought without mercy against the enemies of the state. After twenty years of the struggle, he had lost a great deal of his faith.

Only his wife lived up to his expectations. The politicians were liars, the rich merciless in their greed for power, the poor vicious. And then there were the born con men, the swindlers, the brutes and murderers. The enforcers of the law were only slightly better, but he had believed with all his heart that the Bureau was the best of all.

Over the past year he'd had a recurring dream. In it he was a boy of twelve, and he had to take a crucial school exam that would last all day. When he left the house his mother was in tears, and in his dream he understood why. If he did not pass the exam, he would never see her again.

In the dream he understood murder had become so rampant that laws had been set up with the help of the psychiatric community to develop a protocol of mental-health tests that could predict which twelve-year-olds would grow up to become murderers. Those who failed the test simply vanished. For medical science had proved that murderers killed for the pleasure of killing. That political crimes, rebellion, terrorism, jealousy, and stealing were simply the surface excuses. So it was only necessary to weed out these genetic murderers at an early age.

The dream jumped to his return home after the exam, and his mother hugged and kissed him. His uncles and cousins had prepared a huge celebration. Then he was alone in his bedroom shaking with fear. For he knew there had been a mistake. He should never have passed the exam, and now he would grow up to be a murderer.

The dream had occurred twice, and he did not mention it to his wife because he knew what the dream meant, or thought he did.

Cilke's relationship with Timmona Portella was now over six years old. It had begun when Portella murdered an underling in a blind rage. Cilke had immediately seen the possibilities. He had made arrangements for Portella to be an informant on the Mafia in return for nonprosecution of the murder. The director had approved the plan, and the rest was history. With Portella's help, Cilke had crushed the New York Mafia but had had to turn a blind eye to Portella's operations, including his supervision of the drug trade.

But Cilke, with approval from the director, had plans to bring Portella down again. Portella was determined to acquire the use of the Aprile banks to launder the drug money. But Don Aprile had proved obstinate. At one fateful meeting Portella had asked Cilke, "Will the FBI be surveilling Don Aprile when he attends his grandson's Confirmation?" Cilke understood immediately, but he hesitated before he answered. Then he said slowly, "I guarantee that they will not be. But what about the NYPD?"

"That's taken care of," Portella said.

And Cilke knew he would be an accomplice to murder. But didn't the Don deserve it? He had been a ruthless criminal most of his life. He had retired with enormous wealth, untouched by the law. And look at the gain. Portella would walk right into his trap by acquiring the Aprile banks. And of course, there was always Inzio in the background, with his dreams of his own nuclear arsenal. Cilke knew that with luck he could wrap it all up and the government could get ten billion dollars' worth of Aprile banks under RICO, for there was no doubt that the Don's heirs would sell the banks, make a deal with Portella's secret emissaries. And ten or eleven billion dollars would be a powerful weapon against crime itself.

But Georgette would despise him, so she must never know. After all, she lived in a different world.

But now he had to meet with Portella again. There was the matter of his butchered German shepherds and who was behind it. He would start with Portella.

Timmona Portella was that rarity in Italian men of achievement: a bachelor in his fifties. But he was by no means celibate. Every Friday he spent most of the night with a beautiful woman from one of the escort services controlled by his underlings. The instructions were that the girl be young, not too long in the game, that she be beautiful and delicately featured. That she be jolly and upbeat but not a wise-ass. And that no kinkiness be proposed. Timmona was a straight-from-the-shoulder sex guy. He had his little quirks, but they were harmlessly avuncular. One of them being that the girls had to have a plain Anglo-Saxon name like Jane or Susan; he could cope with something like Tiffany or even Merle, but nothing with any ethnicity. Rarely did he have the same woman twice.

These assignations were always held in a

relatively small East Side hotel owned by one of his companies, where he had the use of an entire floor, consisting of two interlocking suites. One had a fully stocked kitchen, for Portella was a gifted amateur chef, oddly enough of Northern Italian cuisine, though his parents had been born in Sicily. And he loved to cook.

Tonight the girl was brought to his suite by the owner of the escort service, who stayed for a drink and then disappeared. Then Portella whipped up supper for two while they chatted and got acquainted. Her name was Janet. Portella cooked with quick efficiency. Tonight he made his specialty: veal Milanese, spaghetti in a sauce with Gruyere cheese, tiny roasted eggplants on the side, and a salad of greens with tomatoes. Dessert was an assortment of pastries from a famous French patisserie in the neighborhood.

He served Janet with a courtliness that belied his exterior; he was a large, hairy man with a huge head and coarse skin, but he always ate in shirt, tie, and jacket. Over dinner, he asked Janet questions about her life with concern unexpected in so brutal a man. He delighted to hear her tales of misfortune, how she had been betrayed by her father, brothers, lovers, and the powerful men who led her into a sinful life through economic pressures and unwanted pregnancies so she could save her poverty-stricken family. He was amazed at the varieties of dishonorable behavior displayed by his fellow men and marveled at his own goodness with women. For he was extremely generous with them, not only by giving them huge sums of money.

After dinner he took the wine into the sitting room and showed Janet six boxes of jewelry: a gold watch, a ruby ring, diamond earrings, a jade necklace, a jeweled armband, and a perfect string of pearls. He told her she could choose one as a gift. They were all worth a few thousand dollars—the girls would usually have them appraised.

Years ago one of his crews had hijacked a jewelry truck, and he had warehoused the contents rather than have them fenced. So the gifts cost him nothing.

While Janet considered what she wanted, and finally chose the watch, he drew her a bath, carefully testing the temperature of the water and providing her with his favorite perfumes and powders. It was only then, after she had relaxed, that they retired to bed and had good normal sex, as any happily married couple would do.

If he was particularly amorous, he might keep a girl until four or five in the morning, but he never went to sleep while she was in his suite. This night he dismissed Janet early.

He did it all for his health. He knew that he had a wild temper that could get him into trouble. These weekly sex trysts calmed him down. Women in general had a quieting effect on him, and he proved the efficacy of his strategy by going to his doctor every Saturday and hearing with satisfaction that his blood pressure had returned to normal. When he told this to his doctor, the man had only murmured, "Very interesting." Portella was very disappointed in him.

There was another advantage to this arrangement. Portella's bodyguards were isolated in front of the suite. But the back door led to the adjoining suite with its entrance into a separate hallway, and it was there that Portella had meetings he did not want his closest advisors to know about. For it is a very dangerous business for a Mafia chief to meet in private with an FBI special agent. He would be suspected as an informer, and Cilke might be suspected by the Bureau of being a bribe taker.

It was Portella who supplied the phone numbers to be tapped, named the weaklings who would cave under pressure, pointed to clues to racket murders, and explained how certain rackets worked. And it was Portella who did some dirty jobs that the FBI could not legally do.

Over the years they had developed a code for arranging meetings. Cilke had a key to the suite door in the opposite hallway so he could enter without being detected by Portella's bodyguards and wait in the minor suite. Portella would get rid of his girl, and their meeting would begin. On this particular night, Portella was waiting for Cilke.

Cilke was always a little nervous at these

meetings. He knew that not even Portella would dare harm an FBI agent, but the man had a temperament that verged on insanity. Cilke was armed, but to hide the identity of his informant he couldn't bring bodyguards.

Portella had a wineglass in his hand, and his first words of greeting were "What the fuck's wrong now?" But he was smiling genially and gave Cilke a half hug. Portella's massive belly was hidden in an elegant Chinese robe over white pajamas.

Cilke refused a drink, sat on the sofa, and said calmly, "A few weeks ago, I went home after work and found my two dogs with their hearts cut out. I thought you might have a clue." He watched Portella closely.

Portella's surprise seemed genuine. He had been sitting in an armchair and seemed galvanized out of his seat. His face filled with rage. Cilke was not impressed; in his experience the guilty could react with the purest innocence. He said, "If you're trying to warn me off something, why not tell me directly?"

At this Portella said almost tearfully, "Kurt, you come here armed; I felt your gun. I am not armed. You could kill me and claim I resisted arrest. I trust you. I've deposited over a million dollars in your Cayman Island account. We're partners. Why would I pull such an old Sicilian trick? Somebody is trying to split us up. You have to see that."

"Who?" Cilke said.

Portella was thoughtful. "It can only be that Astorre kid. He has delusions of grandeur because he got away from me once. Check him out and meanwhile, I'll put a contract on him."

Finally Cilke was convinced. "OK," he said, "but I think we have to be very careful. Don't underestimate this guy."

"Don't worry," Portella said. "Hey, did you eat? I have some veal and spaghetti, a salad and some good wine."

Cilke laughed. "I believe you. But I have no time for dinner."

The truth was he did not want to break bread with a man he would soon be sending to prison.

Astorre now had enough information to draw up a battle plan. He was convinced that the FBI had a hand in the Don's death. And that Cilke was in charge of the operation. He now knew who the broker was. He knew that Timmona Portella had put out the contract. And yet there remained some mysteries. The ambassador, through Nicole, had offered to buy the banks with foreign investors. Cilke had offered him a deal to betray Portella into a criminal situation. These were disturbing and dangerous variations. He decided to consult with Craxxi in Chicago and to bring Mr. Pryor with him.

Astorre had already requested that Mr. Pryor come to America to run the Aprile banks. Mr. Pryor had accepted the offer, and it was extraordinary how quickly he changed from English gentleman to American high-powered executive. He wore a homburg instead of the bowler; he discarded his furled umbrella and carried a folded newspaper, and he arrived with his wife and two nephews. His wife changed from English matron to a sleeker style of dress, quite in fashion. His two nephews were Sicilians who spoke perfect English and had degrees in accounting. Both were devoted hunters and kept their hunting gear in the trunk of a limousine, which one of the nephews drove. In fact, both of them served as Mr. Pryor's bodyguards.

The Pryors settled into an Upper West Side townhouse protected by security patrols from a private agency. Nicole, who had opposed the appointment, was soon charmed by Mr. Pryor, especially when he told her they were distant cousins. There was no doubt that Mr. Pryor had a certain fatherly charm with women; even Rosie had adored him. And there was no doubt he could run the banks—even Nicole was impressed by his knowledge of international banking. Just by trading currencies he had increased the profit margins. And Astorre knew that Mr. Pryor had been an intimate of Don Aprile. Indeed, it had been Pryor who had persuaded the Don to acquire the banks with an interlock run by Mr. Pryor in England and Italy. Mr. Pryor had described their relationship.

"I told your uncle," Mr. Pryor said, "that banks can acquire more wealth with less risk than the business he was in. Those old-time enterprises are passé; the government is too strong and they are too focused on our people. It was time to get out. Banks are the gateway to make money if you have the experience, personnel, and political contacts. Without boasting, I can say I have the goodwill of the politicians of Italy with money. Everybody gets rich, and nobody gets hurt or winds up in jail. I could be a university professor teaching people how to get rich without breaking the law and resorting to violence. You just have to make certain the correct laws are passed. After all, education is the key to a higher civilization."

Mr. Pryor was being playful, yet he was somewhat in earnest. Astorre felt a deep rapport with him and gave him his absolute trust. Don Craxxi and Mr. Pryor were men he could rely on. Not only from friendship: both of them earned a fortune from the ten banks the Don owned.

When Astorre and Mr. Pryor arrived at Don Craxxi's home in Chicago, Astorre was surprised to see Pryor and Craxxi embrace each other with great warmth. They obviously knew each other.

Craxxi provided a meal of fruit and cheese and chatted with Mr. Pryor while they ate. Astorre listened with intense curiosity; he loved to hear old men tell stories. Craxxi and Mr. Pryor agreed that the old ways of doing business had been fraught with peril. "Everybody had high blood pressure, everybody had heart problems," Craxxi said. "It was a terrible way to live. And the new element have no sense of honor. It's good to see them being wiped out."

"Ah," Mr. Pryor said. "But we all had to start somewhere. Look at us now."

All this talk made Astorre hesitate to bring up the business at hand. What the hell did these two old guys think they were doing now? Mr. Pryor chuckled at Astorre's look. "Don't worry, we are not yet saints, we two. And this situation challenges our own interests. So tell us what you need. We are ready to do business."

"I need your advice, nothing operational," Astorre said. "That's my job."

Craxxi said, "If it is solely for vengeance, I would advise you to go back to your singing. But I recognize, as I hope you do, that it is a matter of protecting your family from danger."

"Both," said Astorre. "Either reason would be sufficient. But my uncle had me trained for just this situation. I can't fail him."

"Good," Mr. Pryor said. "But recognize this fact: what you are doing is in your nature. Be careful about the risks you take. Don't be carried away."

Don Craxxi asked mildly, "How can I help you?"

"You were right about the Sturzo brothers," Astorre said. "They confessed to the hit, and they told me the broker was John Heskow, a man I've never heard of. So now I have to go after him."

"And the Sturzo brothers?" Craxxi asked.

"They are out of the picture."

The two old men were silent. Then Craxxi said, "Heskow I know. He has been a broker for twenty years. There are wild rumors about how he brokered some political assassinations, but I don't believe them. Now, whatever tactics you used to make the Sturzo brothers talk won't work with Heskow. He is a great negotiator, and he will recognize that he has to bargain his way out of death. He will know you must have information only he can give you."

"He has a son he adores," Astorre said. "A basketball player, and he is Heskow's life."

"That is an old card and he will trump it," Mr. Pryor said, "by withholding information that is crucial and giving you information that is not crucial. You have to understand Heskow. He has bargained with death all his life. Find another approach."

"There are a lot of things I want to know before I can go any further," Astorre said. "Who was behind the killing, and most of all, why? Now, here's my thought. It must be the banks. Somebody needs the banks."

"Heskow might know some of that," Craxxi said.

"It bothers me," Astorre said, "that there was no police or FBI surveillance at the cathedral for the Confirmation. And the Sturzo brothers told me that they had been guaranteed there would be no surveillance. Can I believe that the police and the FBI had prior knowledge of the hit? Is that possible?"

"It is," Don Craxxi said. "And in that case you must be very careful. Especially with Heskow."

Mr. Pryor said coolly, "Astorre, your primary goal is to save the banks and protect Don Aprile's children. Vengeance is a minor goal that can be abandoned."

"I don't know," Astorre said, noncommittal now. "I'll have to think about that." He gave both men a sincere smile. "But we'll see how it works out."

The two old men did not believe him for a moment. In their lifetimes they had known and recognized young fellows like Astorre. They saw him as a throwback to the great Mafia leaders of the early days, men they had not become themselves because of a certain lack of charisma and will possessed only by the great ones: the men of respect who had dominated provinces, defied the rules of the state, and emerged triumphant. They recognized in Astorre that will, that charm, that single-mindedness that he himself was not aware of. Even his foolishness, his singing, his riding of horses were weaknesses that did not harm his destiny. They were merely youthful joys and showed his good heart.

Astorre told them about the consul general, Marriano Rubio, and about Inzio Tulippa trying to buy the banks. About Cilke trying to use him to trap Portella. The two old men listened carefully.

"Send them to me the next time," Mr. Pryor said. "From my information Rubio is the financial manager of the world drug trade."

"I won't sell," Astorre said. "The Don instructed me."

"Of course," Craxxi said. "They are the future and can be your protection." He paused and then went on. "Let me tell you a little story. Before I retired I had an associate, a very straight businessman, a credit to society. He invited me to lunch at his office building, in his private dining room. Afterward he took me on a tour and showed me these enormous rooms that held a thousand computer cubicles manned by young men and women.

"He said to me, 'That room earns me a billion dollars a year. There are nearly three hundred million people in this country, and we are devoted to making them buy our products. We plan special lotteries, prizes, and bonuses, we make extravagant promises, all legally defined to make them spend their money for all our companies. And you know what is crucial? We must have banks who will supply these three hundred million people credit to spend money they don't have.' Banks are the name of the game, you must have banks on your side."

"That's true," Mr. Pryor said. "And both sides profit. Though interest rates are high, those debts spur people on, make them achieve more."

Astorre laughed. "I'm glad that keeping the banks is smart. But it doesn't matter. The Don told me not to sell. That's enough for me. And that they killed him makes a difference."

Craxxi said to Astorre very firmly, "You cannot do harm to that man Cilke. The government is now too strong to take such ultimate action against. But I agree he is a danger of some kind. You must be clever."

"Your next step is Heskow," Pryor said. "He is crucial, but again you have to be careful. Remember, you can call on Don Craxxi for help and I myself have resources. We are not fully retired. And we have an interest in the banks—not to mention our affection for Don Aprile, rest in peace."

"OK," Astorre said. "After I see Heskow, we can meet again."

*

Astorre was acutely aware of his dangerous position. He knew that his successes were small, despite his punishment of the assassins. They were only a thread pulled out of the mystery of Don Aprile's murder. But he relied on the infallible paranoia drilled into him during his years of training in Sicily's endless treacheries. He had to be especially careful now. Heskow seemed like an easy target, but he could also be booby-trapped.

One thing surprised him. He had thought himself happy in his life as a small businessman and amateur singer, but now he felt an elation that he had never experienced before. A feeling that he was back in a world in which he belonged. And that he had a mission. To protect the children of Don Aprile, to avenge the death of a man he had loved. He simply had to crack the will of the enemy. Aldo Monza had brought back ten good men from his village in Sicily. At Astorre's instructions he had insured the livelihood of their families for life, no matter what happened to them.

"Do not count on the gratitude of deeds done for people in the past," he remembered the Don lecturing him. "You must make them grateful for things you will do for them in the future." The banks were the future for the Aprile family, Astorre, and his growing army of men. It was a future worth fighting for, no matter the cost.

Don Craxxi had supplied him with another six men he absolutely vouched for. And Astorre had turned his home into a fortress with these men and the latest security detection devices. He had also set up a safe house to disappear to, if the authorities wanted to grab him for whatever reason.

He did not use close bodyguards. Instead, he relied on his own quickness and used his guards as advance scouts on the routes he would take.

He would let Heskow sit for a time. Astorre wondered about Cilke's reputation as an honorable man, as even Don Aprile had so described him.

"There are honorable men who spend all their lives preparing for a supreme act of treachery," Pryor had said to him. But despite all this, Astorre felt confident. All he would have to do was to stay alive as the puzzle pieces fit together.

The real test would come from men like Heskow, Portella, Tulippa, and Cilke. He would personally have to get his hands bloody once again.

It took a month for Astorre to figure out exactly how to handle John Heskow. The man would be formidable, tricky, easy to kill but difficult to extract information from. Using his son as leverage was too dangerous—it would force Heskow to plot against him while pretending to cooperate. He decided that he would not let Heskow know that the Sturzo brothers had told him Heskow was the driver on the hit. That might scare him too much.

Meanwhile, he amassed the necessary information on Heskow's daily habits. It seemed he was a temperate man whose primary love was growing flowers and selling them wholesale to florists and even personally from a roadside stand in the Hamptons. His only indulgence was attending the basketball games of his son's team, and he followed Villanova's basketball schedule religiously.

One Saturday night in January Heskow was going to the Villanova-Temple game at Madison Square Garden in New York. When he left his house he buttoned it up with his sophisticated alarm system. He was always careful in the everyday details of life, always confident that he had made provisions for every possible accident. And it was that confidence Astorre wanted to shatter at the very beginning of their interview.

John Heskow drove into the city and had a solitary dinner at a Chinese restaurant near the Garden. He always ate Chinese when he went out because it was the one thing he could not cook better at home. He liked the silver covers over each dish as if it contained some delightful surprise. He liked Chinese people. They minded their own business, didn't make small talk or show obsequious familiarity. And never, ever, had he found a mistake in his bill, which he always checked carefully because he ordered numerous dishes.

Tonight he went all out. He was particularly fond of Peking duck and crayfish and Cantonese lobster sauce. There was a special white fried rice and of course a few fried dumplings and spicy spareribs. He finished off with green-tea ice cream, an acquired taste, but one that showed he was a gourmet of Eastern food.

When he arrived at the Garden, the arena was only half full, though Temple had a high-ranked team. Heskow took his choice seat, provided by his son, near the floor and middle of the court. This made him proud of Jocko.

The game was not exciting. Temple crushed Villanova, but Jocko was the high scorer in the game. Afterward Heskow went back to the locker room.

His son greeted him with a hug. "Hey, Dad, I'm glad you came. You want to come out and eat with us?"

Heskow was enormously gratified. His son was a true gentleman. Of course these kids didn't want an old geezer like him around on their night out in the city. They wanted to get drunk, have some laughs, and maybe get laid.

"Thanks," Heskow said. "I already had dinner, and I have a long drive home. You played great tonight. I'm proud of you. Now go out and have a good time." He gave his son a farewell kiss and wondered how he had gotten so lucky. Well, his son had a good mother, though she'd been a lousy wife.

It took Heskow only an hour to drive home to Brightwaters—the Long Island parkways were almost deserted at this hour. He was tired when he got there, but before going into the house he checked the flower sheds to make sure the temperature and moisture were OK.

In the moonlight reflected through the glass roof of the shed, the flowers had a wild, nightmarish beauty, the red almost black, the whites a ghostly vaporish halo. He loved looking at them, especially just before he went to sleep.

He walked the gravel driveway to his house and unlocked the door. Once inside he quickly pushed the numbers on the panel that would keep the alarm from going off, then went into the living room.

His heart took a giant leap. Two men stood waiting for him; he recognized Astorre. He knew enough about death to recognize it at a glance. These were the messengers.

But he reacted with the perfect defense mechanism. "How the fuck did you two guys get in here, and what the hell do you want?"

"Don't panic," Astorre said. He introduced himself, adding that he was the nephew of the deceased Don Aprile.

Heskow made himself get calm. He had been in tight spots before, and after the first rush of adrenaline, he had always been OK. He sat down on the sofa so that his hand was on the wooden armrest and reached for his hidden gun. "So what do you want?"

Astorre had an amused smile on his face, which irritated Heskow, who had meant to wait for the right moment. Now he flipped open the armrest and reached for the gun. The hollow was empty.

At that moment three cars appeared in the driveway, headlights flashing into the room. Two more men entered the house.

Astorre said pleasantly, "I didn't underestimate you, John. We searched the house. We found the gun in the coffeepot, another taped underneath your bed, another in that fake letterbox, and the one in the bathroom taped behind the bowl. Did we miss any?"

Heskow didn't answer. His heart had started pounding again. He could feel it in his throat.

"What the hell are you growing in those flower sheds?" Astorre asked, laughing. "Diamonds, hemp, coke, what? I thought you'd never come in. By the way, that's a lot of firepower for someone who grows azaleas."

"Stop jerking me around," Heskow said quietly.

Astorre sat down in the chair opposite Heskow and then tossed two wallets—Gucci, one gold, one brown—on the coffee table between them. "Take a look," he said.

Heskow reached over and opened them. The first thing he saw was the Sturzo brothers' driving licenses with their laminated photos. The bile in his throat was so sour he almost vomited.

"They gave you up," Astorre said. "That you were the broker on Don Aprile's hit. They also said you guaranteed there would be no NYPD or FBI surveillance at the church ceremony."

Heskow processed everything that had happened. They hadn't just killed him, though the Sturzo brothers were certainly dead. He felt one tiny pang of disappointment for that betrayal. But Astorre didn't seem to know he had been the driver. There was a negotiation here, the most important of his life.

Heskow shrugged. "I don't know what you're talking about."

Aldo Monza had been listening alertly, keeping a close eye on Heskow. Now he went into the kitchen and came back with two cups of black coffee, handing one to Astorre and one to Heskow. He said, "Hey, you got Italian coffee—great." Heskow gave him a contemptuous look.

Astorre drank his coffee and then said to Heskow, slowly, deliberately, "I hear you're a very intelligent man, that that's the only reason you're not dead. So listen to me and really think. I'm Don Aprile's cleanup man. I have all the resources he had before he retired. You knew him, you know what that means. You would never have dared to be the broker if he wasn't retired. Right?"

Heskow didn't say anything. Just kept watching Astorre, trying to judge him.

"The Sturzos are dead," Astorre continued. "You can join them. But I have a proposition, and you have to be very alert here. In the next thirty minutes you will have to convince me you're on my side, that you will act as my agent. If you don't, you will be buried beneath your flowers in the shed. Now let me tell you better news. I will never involve your son in this affair. I don't do that, and besides, such action would make you my enemy and ready to betray me. But you must realize that I am the one who keeps your son alive. My enemies want me dead. If they succeed, my friends will not spare your son. His fate rests on mine."

"So what do you want?" Heskow asked.

"I need information," Astorre said. "So you talk. If I'm satisfied, we have a deal. If I'm not, you're dead. So your immediate problem is staying alive tonight. Begin."

Heskow did not speak for at least five minutes. First he evaluated Astorre—such a nice-looking guy, not brutal or terrorizing. But the Sturzo brothers were dead. Then the breaking through the security of his house and the finding of the guns. Most ominous was Astorre waiting for him to reach for the nonexistent gun. So this was not a bluff, and certainly not a bluff he could call. Finally Heskow drank his coffee and made his decision, with reservations.

"I have to go with you," he said to Astorre. "I have to trust you to do the right thing. The man who hired me to broker the deal and gave me the money is Timmona Portella. The NYPD non-surveillance I bought. I was Timmona's bagman and gave the NYPD chief of detectives, Di Benedetto, fifty grand and his deputy, Aspinella Washington, twenty-five. As for the FBI guarantee, Portella gave it to me. I insisted on credentials, and he told me he had this guy, Cilke, New York Bureau chief, in his pocket. It was Cilke who gave the OK for the hit on the Don."

"You worked for Portella before?"

"Oh, yeah," Heskow said. "He runs the drugs in New York, so he has a lot of hits for me. None in the league of the Don. I never did get the connection. That's it."

"Good," Astorre said. His face was sincere. "Now I want you to be careful. For your own good. Is there anything more you can tell me?"

And suddenly Heskow knew he was seconds from death. That he had not done the job of convincing Astorre. He trusted his instincts. He gave Astorre a weak smile. "One more thing," he added, very slowly. "I have a contract with Portella right now. On you. I'm going to pay the two detectives a half million to knock you off.

They come to arrest you, you resist arrest, and they shoot you."

Astorre seemed a little bemused. "Why so complicated and expensive?" he said. "Why not hire a straight hit man?"

Heskow shook his head. "They put you higher than that. And after the Don, a straight hit would draw too much attention. You being his nephew. The media would go wild. This way there's cover."

"Have you paid them yet?" Astorre asked.

"No," Heskow said. "We have to meet."

"OK," Astorre said. "Set up the meeting out of traffic. Let me know the details beforehand. One thing. After the meeting, don't leave with them."

"Oh, shit," Heskow said. "Is that how it is? There will be enormous heat."

Astorre leaned back in his chair. "That's how it is," he said. He got up out of the chair and gave Heskow a half hug of friendship. "Remember," he said, "we have to keep each other alive."

"Can I hold out some of the money?" Heskow asked.

Astorre laughed. "No. That's the beauty of it. How do the cops explain the half million they have on them?"

"Just twenty," Heskow said.

"OK," Astorre said good-naturedly. "But no more. Just a little sweetener."

*

Now it was imperative for Astorre to have another meeting with Don Craxxi and Mr. Pryor for their advice on the wide operational plan he had to execute.

But circumstances had changed. Mr. Pryor insisted on bringing his two nephews to Chicago to act as bodyguards. And when they arrived in the Chicago suburb they found that Don Craxxi's modest estate had been turned into a fortress. The driveway leading to the house was blocked by little green huts manned by very tough-looking young men. A communications van was parked in the orchard. And there were three young men who answered doorbells and phones and checked visitors' IDs.

Mr. Pryor's nephews, Erice and Roberto, were lean and athletic, expert in firearms, and they clearly adored their uncle. They also seemed to know Astorre's history in Sicily and treated him with enormous respect, performing the smallest personal services for him. They carried his luggage to the plane. They poured his wine at dinner, brushing him off with their napkins; they paid his tips and opened doors, making it plain they regarded him as a great man. Astorre good-humoredly tried to put them at ease, but they would never descend to familiarity.

The men guarding Don Craxxi were not so polite. They were courteous but rigid, steady men in their fifties, completely focused on their job.

And they were all armed.

That evening when Don Craxxi, Mr. Pryor, and Astorre had finished dinner and were eating fruit for their dessert, Astorre said to the Don, "Why all the security?"

"Just a precaution," his host answered calmly. "I've heard some disturbing news. An old enemy of mine, Inzio Tulippa, has arrived in America. He is a very intemperate man and very greedy, so it is always best to be prepared. He comes to meet with our Timmona Portella. They whack up their drug profits and whack out their enemies. It is best to be ready. But now, what is on your mind, my dear Astorre?"

Astorre told them both the information he had learned and how he had turned Heskow. He told them about Portella and Cilke and the two detectives.

"Now I have to go operational," he said. "I need an explosives guy and at least ten more good men. I know you two can supply them, that you can call on the Don's old friends." He carefully skinned the greenish yellow pear he was eating. "You understand how dangerous this will be and do not want to be too closely involved."

"Nonsense," Mr. Pryor said impatiently. "We owe our destiny to Don Aprile. Of course we will help. But remember, this is not vengeance. It is self-defense. So you cannot harm Cilke. The federal government will make our lives too hard."

"But that man must be neutralized," Don Craxxi said. "He will always be a danger. However, consider this. Sell the banks and everybody will be happy."

"Everybody except me and my cousins," Astorre said.

"It is something to consider," Mr. Pryor said. "I'm willing to sacrifice my share in the banks with Don Craxxi, though I know it will grow to be an enormous fortune. But certainly there is something to be said for a peaceful life."

"I'm not selling the banks," Astorre said. "They killed my uncle and they have to pay the price, not achieve their purpose. And I can't live in a world where my place is granted by their mercy. The Don taught me that."

Astorre was surprised that Don Craxxi and Mr. Pryor looked relieved by his decision. They tried to hide little smiles. He realized that these two old men, powerful as they were, held him in respect, saw in him what they themselves could never acquire.

Craxxi said, "We know our duty to Don Aprile, may he rest in peace. And we know our duty to you. But one note of prudence: if you are too rash, and something happens to you, we will be forced to sell the banks."

"Yes," Mr. Pryor said. "Be prudent."

Astorre laughed. "Don't worry. If I go down, there will be nobody left."

They ate their pears and peaches. Don Craxxi seemed to be lost in thought. Then he said, "Tulippa is the top drug man in the world. Portella is his American partner. They must want the banks to launder the drug money."

"Then how does Cilke fit in?" Astorre asked.

"I don't know," Craxxi said. "But still, you cannot attack Cilke."

"That would be a disaster," Mr. Pryor said.

"I'll remember that," Astorre said.

But if Cilke was guilty, what could he do?

Detective Aspinella Washington made sure her eight-year-old daughter ate a good supper, did her homework, and said her prayers before putting her to bed. She adored the girl and had banished her father from her life a long time ago. The baby-sitter, the teenage daughter of a uniformed cop, arrived at 8:00 P.M. Aspinella instructed her on the child's medications and said she would be back before midnight.

Soon the lobby buzzer rang and Aspinella ran down the stairs and out into the street. She never used the elevator. Paul Di Benedetto was waiting in his unmarked tan Chevrolet. She hopped in and strapped on her seat belt. He was a lousy night driver.

Di Benedetto was smoking a long cigar, so Aspinella opened her window. "It's about an

hour's ride," he said. "We have to think it over."
He knew it was a big step for both of them. It was
one thing to take bribes and drug money; it was
another to perform a hit.

"What's to think over?" Aspinella asked. "We
get a half mil to knock off a guy who should be on
death row. You know what I can do with a quarter
mil?"

"No," Di Benedetto said. "But I know what I
can do. Buy a super condo in Miami when I retire.
Remember, we're going to have to live with this."

"Taking drug payoffs is already over the line,"
Aspinella said. "Fuck 'em all."

"Yeah," Di Benedetto said. "Let's just make
sure that this guy Heskow has the money tonight,
that he's not just jerking us off."

"He's always been reliable," Aspinella said.
"He's my Santa Claus. And if he doesn't have a big
sack to give us, he'll be a dead Santa."

Di Benedetto laughed. "That's my girl. You
been keeping track of this Astorre guy so we can
get rid of him right away?"

"Yeah. I've had him under surveillance. I know
just the spot to pick him up—his macaroni
warehouse. Most nights he works late."

"You got the throwaway to plant on him?" Di
Benedetto asked.

"Of course," Aspinella said. "I wouldn't give
shit to a shield if he didn't carry a throwaway."

They drove in silence for ten minutes. Then Di

Benedetto said in a deliberately calm, emotionless voice, "Who's going to be the shooter?"

Aspinella gave him an amused look. "Paul," she said, "you've been behind the desk for the last ten years. You've seen more tomato sauce than blood. I'll shoot." She could see that he looked relieved. Men—they were fucking useless.

They fell silent again as both were lost in thought about what had brought them to this point in their lives. Di Benedetto had joined the force as a young man, over thirty years ago. His corruption had been gradual but inevitable. He had started out with delusions of grandeur—he would be respected and admired for risking his life to protect others. But the years wore this away. At first it was the little bribes from the street vendors and small shops. Then testifying falsely to get a guy to beat a felony rap. It seemed a small step to accepting money from high-ranking drug dealers. Then finally from Heskow, who, it was clear, acted for Timmona Portella, the biggest Mafia chief left in New York.

Of course, there was always a good excuse. The mind can sell itself anything. He saw the higher-ranking officers getting rich on drug-bribe money, and the lower ranks were even more corrupt. And after all, he had three kids to send to college. But most of all it was the ingratitude of the people he protected. Civil-liberty groups protesting police brutality if you slapped a black mugger around.

The news media shitting on the police department every chance they got. Citizens suing cops. Cops getting fired after years of service, deprived of their pensions, even going to jail. He himself had once been brought up for discipline on the charge that he singled out black criminals, and he knew he wasn't racially prejudiced. Was it his fault that most criminals in New York were black? What were you supposed to do—give them a license to steal, as affirmative action? He had promoted black cops. He had been Aspinella's mentor in the department, giving her the promotion she'd earned by terrorizing the same black criminals. And you couldn't accuse her of racism. In a nutshell, society crapped on the cops who protected them. Unless of course they got killed in the line of duty. Then came the tide of bullshit. The final truth? It didn't pay to be an honest cop. And yet—and yet, he had never thought it would come to murder. But after all, he was invulnerable; there was no risk; there was a hell of a lot of money; and the victim was a killer. Still . . .

Aspinella too was wondering how her life had come to such a pass. God knows she had fought the criminal underworld with a passion and relentlessness that had made her a New York legend. Certainly, she had taken bribes, suborned felony. She had only started late in the game when Di Benedetto had persuaded her to take drug money. He had been her mentor for years and for a few months her lover—not bad, just a clumsy bear who used sex as part of a hibernational impulse.

But her corruption had really started her first day on the job after being promoted to detective. In the station-house rec room an overbearing white cop named Gangee had jollied her in a good-natured way. "Hey, Aspinella," he said, "with your pussy and my muscle, we'll wipe out crime in the civilized world." The cops, including some blacks, laughed.

Aspinella looked at him coldly and said, "You'll never be my partner. A man who insults a woman is a small-dick coward."

Gangee tried to keep it on a friendly basis. "My small dick can stop up your pussy anytime you want to try. I want to change my luck anyhow."

Aspinella turned her cold face to him. "Black is better than yellow," she said. "Go whack off, you dumb piece of shit."

The room seemed frozen with surprise. Now she had Gangee blushing red. Such virulent contempt was not permitted without a fight. He started toward her, his huge body clearing space.

Aspinella was dressed for duty. She drew her gun, not pointing it. "Try and I'll blow your balls off," she said, and in that room there was no doubt in anyone's mind that she would pull the trigger. Gangee halted and shook his head with disgust.

The incident, of course, was reported. It was a

serious offense on Aspinella's part. But Di Benedetto was shrewd enough to know that a departmental trial would be a political disaster for the NYPD. He quashed the whole thing and was so impressed by Aspinella that he put her on his personal staff and became her mentor.

What had affected Aspinella more than anything else was that there had been at least four black cops in the room and not one of them had defended her. Indeed, they had laughed at the white cop's jokes. Gender loyalty was stronger than racial loyalty.

Her career, after that, established her as the best cop in the division. She was ruthless with drug dealers, muggers, armed robbers. She showed them no mercy, black or white. She shot them, she beat them, she humiliated them. Charges were made against her but could never be substantiated, and her record for valor spoke for her. But the charges aroused her rage against society itself. How did they dare question her when she protected them from the worst scum in the city? Di Benedetto backed her all the way.

There had been one tricky situation when she shot dead two teenage muggers as they tried to rob her on a brightly lit Harlem street right outside her apartment. One boy punched her in the face, and the other grabbed her purse. Aspinella drew her gun and the boys froze. Quite deliberately, she shot them both. Not only for the punch in the face, but to send a message not to try mugging in her neighborhood. Civil-liberties groups organized a protest, but the department ruled that she had used justifiable force. She knew she had been guilty on that one.

It was Di Benedetto who talked her into taking her first bribe on a very important drug deal. He spoke like a loving uncle. "Aspinella," he said, "a cop today doesn't worry much about bullets. That's part of the deal. He has to worry about the civil-liberties groups, the citizens and the criminals who sue for damages. The political bosses in the department, who will put you in jail to get votes. Especially somebody like you. You're a natural victim, so are you going to wind up like those other poor dopes in the street who get raped, robbed, murdered? Or are you going to protect yourself? Get in on this. You'll get more protection from the wheels in the department who are already bought. In five or six years you can retire with a bundle. And you won't have to worry about going to jail for messing up some mugger's hair."

So she had given way. And little by little she enjoyed socking the bribe money into disguised bank accounts. Not that she let up on the criminals.

But this stuff was different. This was a conspiracy to commit murder, and yes, this Astorre was a Mafia big shot who would be a pleasure to take out. In a funny way, she would be doing her job. But the final argument was that it had so little risk and such a big payoff. A quarter mil.

Di Benedetto drove off the Southern State Parkway and a few minutes later rolled into the parking lot of a small two-story mall. All of the dozen or so shops were closed, even the pizza joint, which displayed a bright red neon sign in its window. They got out of the car. "That's the first time I've seen a pizza joint closed so early," Di Benedetto said. It was only 10:00 P.M.

He led Aspinella to a side door of the pizza joint. It was unlocked. They climbed up a dozen stairs to a landing. There was a suite of two rooms to the left and a room to the right. He made a motion, and Aspinella checked the suite on the left while he stood guard. Then they went to the room on the right. Heskow was waiting for them.

He was sitting at the end of a long wooden table with four rickety wooden chairs around it. On the table was a duffel bag the size of a punching bag, and it seemed to be stuffed full. Heskow shook Di Benedetto's hand and nodded to Aspinella. She thought she had never seen a white man looking so white. His face and even his neck were drained of color.

The room had only a dim bulb and no windows. They sat around the table, Di Benedetto reached out and patted the bag. "It's all there?" he asked.

"Sure is," Heskow said shakily. Well, a man carrying $500,000 in a duffel bag had a right to be nervous, Aspinella thought. But still, she scanned the room to see if it was wired.

"Let's have a peek," Di Benedetto said.

Heskow untied the cord around the neck of the duffel bag and half dumped it out. About twenty packets of bills bound by rubber bands tumbled onto the table. Most of the packages were hundreds, no fifties, and two packets were twenties.

Di Benedetto sighed. "Fucking twenties," he said. "OK, put them back."

Heskow stuffed the packets back into the bag and retied the cord. "My client requests that it be as quick as possible," he said.

"Inside two weeks," Di Benedetto said.

"Good," Heskow said.

Aspinella lifted the duffel bag onto her shoulder. It wasn't that heavy, she thought. A half mil wasn't that heavy.

She saw Di Benedetto shake hands with Heskow and felt a wary impatience. She wanted to get the hell out of there. She started down the stairs, the bag balanced on her shoulder, held with one hand, her other hand free to draw her gun. She heard Di Benedetto following her.

Then they were out in the cool night. They were both dripping with sweat.

"Put the bag in the trunk," Di Benedetto said. He got into the driver's seat and lit up a cigar. Aspinella came around and got in.

"Where do we go to split it up?" Di Benedetto asked.

"Not my place. I have a baby-sitter."

"Not mine," Di Benedetto said. "I have a wife at home. How about we rent a motel room?"

Aspinella grimaced, and Di Benedetto said smilingly, "My office. We'll lock the door." They both laughed. "Check the trunk just one more time. Make sure it's locked tight."

Aspinella didn't argue. She got out, opened the trunk, and pulled out the duffel bag. At that moment Paul turned on the ignition.

The explosion sent a shower of glass over the mall. It was raining glass. The car itself seemed to float in the air and came down in a hail of metal that destroyed Paul Di Benedetto's body. Aspinella Washington was blown almost ten feet away, an arm and leg broken, but it was the pain from her torn-out eye that rendered her unconscious.

Heskow, exiting in the rear of the pizza shop, felt the air press his body against the building. Then he jumped into his car and twenty minutes later was in his home in Brightwaters. He made himself a quick drink and checked the two packets of hundred-dollar bills he had taken out of the duffel bag. Forty grand—a nice little bonus. He'd give his kid a couple of grand for spending money. No, a grand. And sock the rest away.

He watched the late TV news that reported the

explosion as a breaking story. One detective killed, the other badly hurt. And at the scene, a duffel bag with a huge amount of money. The TV anchor didn't say how much.

When Aspinella Washington regained consciousness in the hospital two days later, she was not surprised to be closely questioned about the money and why it was just forty grand shy of a half million. She denied she had any knowledge of the money. They questioned her about what a chief of detectives and an assistant chief were doing out together. She refused to answer on the grounds that it was a personal matter. But she was angry that they questioned her so relentlessly when she was obviously in such grave condition. The department didn't give a shit about her. They did not honor her record of achievement. But it ended okay. The department didn't pursue her and set it up so that the investigation of the money came to nothing.

It took another week of convalescence for Aspinella to figure things out. They had been set up. And the only guy who could have set them up was Heskow. And the fact that there was forty grand missing from the payoff meant the greedy pig couldn't resist grafting his own people. Well, she would get better, she thought, and then she would meet with Heskow once again.

ASTORRE WAS now very careful of his movements. Not only to avoid a hit but also not to allow himself to be arrested for any reason. He kept close to his heavily guarded home with its five-man round-the-clock security teams. He had sensors planted in the woods and grounds around the house and infrared lights for night surveillance. When he ventured out, it was with six bodyguards in three two-man teams. He sometimes traveled alone, counting on stealth and surprise and a confidence in his own powers if he should meet only one or two assassins. The blowing up of the two detectives had been necessary, but it generated a lot of heat. And when Aspinella Washington recovered she would figure out it was Heskow who had betrayed her. And if Heskow spilled, she would come after Astorre himself.

But by now he knew the enormity of his problem. He knew all the men guilty of the Don's death and the serious problems before him. There was Kurt Cilke, essentially untouchable; Timmona Portella, who ordered the murder; as well as Inzio Tulippa, Grazziella, and the consul general of Peru. The only ones he had succeeded in punishing were the Sturzo brothers, and they had been mere pawns.

All the information had come from John Heskow, Mr. Pryor, Don Craxxi, and Octavius Bianco in Sicily. If possible, he had to get all his enemies in one place at the same time. To pick them off singly would surely be impossible. And Mr. Pryor and Craxxi had already warned him he could not touch Cilke.

And then there was the consul general of Peru, Marriano Rubio, Nicole's companion. What was the extent of her loyalty to him? What had she blotted out in the Don's FBI file that she did not want Astorre to see? What was she hiding from him?

In his spare moments, Astorre dreamed of the women he had loved. First there had been Nicole, so young and so willful, her small, delicate body so passionate that she had forced him into loving her. And now how changed she was, her passion absorbed by politics and her career.

He remembered Buji in Sicily, not exactly a call

girl, but very close and yet with an impulsive goodness that could easily turn into rage. He remembered her gorgeous bed, in the soft Sicilian nights, when they swam and ate olives out of oil-filled barrels. Most fondly of all he remembered that she never lied; she was completely frank about her life, her other men. And her loyalty when he had been shot, how she had dragged him out of the sea, the blood from his throat staining her body. Then her gift of the golden collar with its pendant to hide the ugly wound.

Then he thought of Rosie, his treacherous Rosie, so sweet, so beautiful, so sentimental, who always claimed she truly loved him while betraying him. Yet she could always make him feel happy when he was with her. He had wanted to break down his feeling for her by using her against the Sturzo brothers, and he had been surprised that she relished the role, an adjustment to her make-believe life.

And then flitting through his mind like some ghost came the vision of Cilke's wife, Georgette. What stupidity. He had spent one evening watching her, listening to her talk nonsense he didn't believe, about the pricelessness of every human soul. Yet he could not forget her. How the hell had she married a guy like Kurt Cilke?

On some nights Astorre drove to Rosie's neighborhood and called her on his car phone. She was always free, which surprised him, but she explained that she was too busy studying to go out. Which suited him perfectly, since he was too cautious to eat in a restaurant or take her to a movie. Instead he stopped at Zabar's on the East Side and brought in delicacies that made Rosie smile with delight. Meanwhile Monza waited in the car outside.

Rosie would lay out the food and open a bottle of wine. As they ate she put her legs in his lap in a comradely way, and her face glowed with happiness at being with him. She seemed to welcome his every word with a pleased smile. That was her gift, and Astorre knew that she was that way with all her men. But it didn't matter.

And then when they went to bed she was passionate but also very sweet and clinging. She touched his face all over and kissed him and said, "We're really soul mates." And those words would send a chill through Astorre. He didn't want her to be a soul mate with a man like himself. He yearned for classic virtue at these times, yet he couldn't stop himself from seeing her.

He'd stay for five or six hours. At three in the morning he would leave. Sometimes when she was asleep he would gaze down at her and see in the relaxation of her facial muscles a sad vulnerability and struggle, as if the demons she held in her innermost soul were fighting to get free.

One night he left early from a visit with Rosie.

When he got into the waiting car, Monza told him there was an urgent message to call a Mr. Juice. This was a code name that he and Heskow used, so he immediately picked up the car phone.

Heskow's voice was urgent. "I can't talk on the wire. We have to meet right away."

"Where?" Astorre said.

"I'll be standing right outside Madison Square Garden," Heskow said. "Pick me up on the fly. In one hour."

When Astorre drove by the Garden, he saw Heskow standing on the sidewalk. Monza had his gun in his lap when he stopped the car in front of Heskow. Astorre pulled open the door, and Heskow hopped into the front seat with them. The cold left watery streaks on his cheeks. He said to Astorre, "You have big trouble."

Astorre now felt a cold chill. "The kids?" he asked.

Heskow nodded. "Portella snatched your cousin Marcantonio and has him stashed someplace. I don't know where. Tomorrow he invites you to a meeting. He wants to trade something for his hostage. But if you're careless, he has a four-man hit team to focus on you. He's using his own men. He tried to give me the job, but I turned him down."

They were in a dark street. "Thanks," Astorre said. "Where can I let you off?"

"Right here. My car is just a block away."

Astorre understood. Heskow was anxious about

288

being seen with him.

"One other thing," Heskow said. "You know about Portella's suite at his private hotel? His brother, Bruno, is using it tonight with some broad. And no bodyguards."

"Thanks again," Astorre said. He opened the door of the car, and Heskow disappeared into the darkness.

Marcantonio Aprile was having his last meeting of the day, and he wanted to keep it short. It was now seven in the evening, and he had a dinner engagement at nine.

The meeting was with his favorite producer and best friend in the movie business, a man named Steve Brody, who never went over budget, had great instincts for dramatic stories, and often introduced Marcantonio to up-and-coming young actresses who needed a little help in their careers.

But this evening they were on opposite sides of the fence. Brody had come with one of the most powerful agents in the business, a man named Matt Glazier, who had a vehement loyalty to his clients. He was there pleading the case of a novelist whose latest book he had turned into an epic, eight-hour TV serial drama. Now Glazier wanted to sell the novelist's three previous books.

"Marcantonio," Glazier said, "the other three books are great but didn't sell. You know how publishers are—they couldn't sell a jar of caviar for a nickel. Brody here is ready to produce them. Now you've made a shitload of money on his last book, so be generous and let's make a deal."

"I don't see it," Marcantonio said. "These are old books we're talking about. They were never best-sellers. And now they're out of print."

"That doesn't matter," Glazier said with the eager confidence of all agents. "As soon as we make the deal, the publishers will reprint them."

Marcantonio had heard this argument many times before. True, the publishers would reprint, but actually this was not much help to the TV presentation. The TV broadcast would help the publishers of the book more. It was essentially a bullshit argument.

"All that aside," Marcantonio said, "I've read the books. They have nothing for us. They're too literary. It's the language that makes them work, not incident. I enjoyed them. I'm not saying they can't work, I'm just saying it's not worth the risk and the extraordinary effort."

"Don't bullshit me," Glazier said. "You read a reader's report. You're the head of programming—you don't have time to read."

Marcantonio laughed. "You're wrong. I love to read and I love those books. But they are not good TV." His voice was warm and friendly. "I'm sorry, but for us it's a pass. But keep us in mind. We'd love to work with you."

After the two had gone, Marcantonio showered in his executive-suite bathroom and changed his clothes for his dinner date. He said good night to his secretary, who always stayed until he left, and took the elevator to the lobby of the building.

His date was at the Four Seasons, just a few blocks away, and he would walk. Unlike most top executives, he did not keep a car and driver exclusively for himself but just called one when necessary. He prided himself on his economy and knew he had learned it from his father, who had a strong prejudice against wasting money on foolishness.

When he stepped out onto the street, he felt a cold wind and shivered. A black limo pulled up, and the chauffeur got out of the car and opened the door for him to enter. Had his secretary ordered the car for him? The driver was tall, a sturdy man whose cap stood oddly on his head, a size too small. He bowed and said, "Mr. Aprile?"

"Yes," Marcantonio said. "I won't need you tonight."

"Yes, you do," the chauffeur said with a cheerful smile. "Get into the car or get shot."

Suddenly Marcantonio was aware of three men at his back. He hesitated. The chauffeur said, "Don't worry, a friend just wants to have a little chat with you."

Marcantonio got into the backseat of the limo, and the three men crowded in beside him.

They drove a block or two, and then one of the men gave Marcantonio a pair of dark glasses and told him to put them on. Marcantonio did so— and seemed to go blind. The glasses were so dark they screened out all light. He thought that clever and made a mental note to use this in a story. It was a hopeful sign. If they did not want him to see where he was going, that meant they were not planning to kill him. And yet it all seemed as unreal as one of his TV dramas. Until he suddenly thought about his father. That he was finally in his father's world, which he had never completely believed in.

After about an hour, the car came to a stop and he was helped out by two of the guards. He could feel a brick path under his feet, and then he was led up four steps and into a house. Up more stairs to a room, the door closing behind him. Only then were the glasses removed. He was in a small bed-chamber whose windows were heavily curtained. One of the guards sat in a chair beside the bed.

"Lie down and take a little snooze," the guard said to him. "You have a tough day ahead." Marcantonio looked at his watch. It was almost midnight.

Just after four in the morning, with the skyscrapers ghosts in darkness, Astorre and Aldo Monza were let off in front of the Lyceum Hotel; the driver waiting in front. Monza jangled his ring of keys as they ran up the three flights of stairs and then to the door of Portella's suite.

Monza used his keys to open the door to the suite, and they entered the living room. They saw the table littered with cartons of Chinese takeout food, empty glasses, and bottles of wine and whiskey. There was a huge whipped-cream cake, half-eaten, with a crushed-out cigarette adorning the top like a birthday candle. They went to the bedroom, and Astorre flicked on the light from the wall switch. There, lying on the bed, clad only in shorts, was Bruno Portella.

The air was filled with a heavy perfume, but Bruno was alone in the bed. He was not a pretty sight. His face, heavy and slack, glistened with night sweat, and the stale smell of seafood came from his mouth. His huge chest made him appear bearish, and indeed he wore a look of teddy bear sweetness, Astorre thought. At the foot of the bed was an open bottle of red wine, which created its own island of raw fragrance. It seemed a shame to wake him, and Astorre did it gently by tapping on his forehead.

Bruno opened one eye, then the other. He didn't seem frightened or even astonished. "What the hell are you doing here?" His voice was husky with sleep.

"Bruno, there's nothing to worry about," Astorre said gently. "Where's the girl?"

Mario Puzo

Bruno sat up. He laughed. "She had to go home early to get her kid off to school. I already fucked her three times, so I let her go." He said this proudly, because of both his virility and his understanding of a working girl's problems. He casually reached out a hand to the bedside table. Astorre gently grabbed it, and Monza opened the drawer and took out a gun.

"Listen, Bruno," Astorre said soothingly. "Nothing bad is going to happen. I know your brother doesn't confide in you, but he snatched my cousin Marc last night. So now I have to trade you to get him back. Your brother loves you, Bruno; he'll make the trade. You believe that, don't you?"

"Sure," Bruno said. He looked relieved.

"Just don't do anything foolish. Now, get dressed."

When Bruno finished dressing, he seemed to have trouble tying his shoelaces. "What's the matter?" Astorre asked.

"This is the first time I wore these shoes," Bruno said. "Usually I wear slip-ons."

"You don't know how to tie shoelaces?" Astorre asked.

"These are the first shoes I've had with laces."

Astorre laughed. "Jesus Christ. OK, I'll tie them." And he let Bruno put his foot in his lap.

When he was finished, Astorre handed Bruno the bedside phone. "Call your brother," he said.

"At five in the morning?" Bruno said.

"Timmona will kill me."

Astorre realized that it wasn't sleep that dulled Bruno's brain; he was genuinely dim-witted.

"Just tell him I've got you," Astorre said. "Then I'll talk to him."

Bruno took the phone and said in a plaintive voice, "Timmona, you got me in a lot of trouble, that's why I'm calling you this early."

Astorre could hear a roar over the phone, and then Bruno said hurriedly, "Astorre Viola has me and he wants to talk to you." He quickly passed the phone to Astorre.

Astorre said, "Timmona, sorry to wake you up. But I had to snatch Bruno because you have my cousin."

Portella's voice came over the phone in another angry roar. "I don't know anything about that. Now, what the hell do you want?"

Bruno could hear and he shouted, "You got me into this, you prick! Now get me out."

Astorre said calmly, "Timmona, make this swap and we can talk about the deal you want. I know you think I've been bullheaded, but when we meet I'll tell you the reason and you'll know I've been doing you a favor."

Portella's voice was quiet now. "OK," he said. "How do we set up this meeting?"

"I'll meet you at the Paladin restaurant at noon," Astorre said. "I have a private room there. I'll bring Bruno with me, and you bring Marc. You can bring bodyguards if you're leery, but we don't want a bloodbath in a public place. We talk things over and make the exchange."

There was a long pause, and then Portella said, "I'll be there, but don't try anything funny."

"Don't worry," Astorre said cheerfully. "After this meeting we'll be buddies."

Astorre and Monza put Bruno between them, Astorre linking arms with Bruno in a friendly way. They took him down the stairs to the street. There were an additional two cars with Astorre's men waiting. "Take Bruno with you in one of the cars," Astorre told Monza. "Have him at the Paladin at noon. I'll meet you there."

"What the hell do I do with him until then?" Monza asked. "That's hours from now."

"Take him for breakfast," Astorre said. "He likes to eat. That should take up a couple of hours. Then take him for a walk in Central Park. Go to the zoo. I'll take one of the cars and a driver. If he tries to run away, don't kill him. Just catch him."

"You'll be on your own," Monza said. "Is that smart?"

"I'll be OK." In the car Astorre used his cell phone to call Nicole's private number. It was now nearly six in the morning, and light transfixed the city into long thin lines of stone.

Nicole's voice was sleepy when she answered. Astorre remembered it had been like that when she was a young girl and his lover. "Nicole, wake up," he said. "You know who this is?"

The question obviously irritated her. "Of course, I know who it is. Who else would call at this hour?"

"Listen carefully," Astorre said. "No questions. That document you're holding for me, the one I signed for Cilke, remember you told me not to sign?"

"Yes," Nicole said curtly, "of course I remember."

"Do you have it at home or in your office safe?" Astorre asked.

"In my office, of course," Nicole said.

"OK," Astorre said. "I'll be at your house in thirty minutes. I'll ring your bell. Be ready and come down. Bring all your keys. We're going to your office."

When Astorre rang Nicole's bell, she came down immediately dressed in a blue leather coat and carrying a large purse. She kissed him on the cheek but didn't dare say a word until they were in the car and she had to give instructions to the driver. Then she continued her silence until they were in her office suite.

"Now, tell me why you want that document," she said.

"You don't have to know," Astorre said.

He saw she was angry with the answer, but she

went to the office safe that was part of the desk and produced a file folder.

"Don't close the safe," Astorre said. "I want the tape you made of our meeting with Cilke."

Nicole handed him the folder. "You have a right to these documents," she said. "But you have no right to any tape, even if it existed."

"Long ago you told me you taped every meeting in your office, Nicole," Astorre said. "And I watched you at the meeting. You were a little too satisfied with yourself."

Nicole laughed with scornful affection. "You've changed," she said. "You were never one of those assholes who thought they could read other people's minds."

Astorre gave her a rueful grin and said apologetically, "I thought you still liked me. That's why I never asked what you deleted in your father's file before you showed it to me."

"I deleted nothing," Nicole said coolly. "And I don't give the tape until you tell me what this is all about."

Astorre was silent, then he said, "OK, you're a big girl now." He laughed when he saw how angry she was, her eyes flashing, her lips curled with contempt. It reminded him of how she looked when she confronted him and her father long ago.

"Well, you always wanted to play with the big boys," Astorre said. "And you certainly do that.

As a lawyer, you've scared almost as many people as your father."

"He wasn't as bad as the press and the FBI painted him," Nicole said angrily.

"OK," Astorre said soothingly. "Marc was kidnapped last night by Timmona Portella. Not to worry though. I went out and got his brother Bruno. Now we can bargain."

"You committed a kidnapping?" Nicole said incredulously.

"So did they," Astorre said. "They really want us to sell them the banks."

Nicole almost shrieked, "Then give them the fucking banks!"

"You don't understand," Astorre said. "We give them nothing. We have Bruno. They hurt Marc, I hurt Bruno."

Nicole was looking at him with horror in her eyes. Astorre stared at her calmly, and one hand went up to finger the gold collar around his neck. "Yeah," he said, "I'd have to kill him."

Nicole's firm face broke up into creases of sorrow. "Not you, Astorre, not you too."

"So now you know," Astorre said. "I'm not the man to sell the banks after they killed your father and my uncle. But I need the tape and the document to make the deal go through and get Marc back without bloodshed."

"Just sell them the banks," Nicole whispered to him. "We'll be rich. What does it matter?"

"It matters to me," Astorre said. "It mattered to the Don."

Silently Nicole reached into the safe and took out a small packet, which she placed on top of the folder.

"Play it for me now," Astorre said.

Nicole reached into her desk for a small cassette player. She inserted the tape, and they listened to Cilke reveal his plan to entrap Portella. Then Astorre pocketed everything and said, "I'll have it all back to you later today, and Marc too. Don't worry. Nothing will happen. And if it does, it will be worse for them than for us."

A little after noon Astorre, Aldo Monza, and Bruno Portella were seated in a private dining room at the Paladin restaurant in the East Sixties.

Bruno seemed not at all worried about being a hostage. He chatted cheerfully with Astorre. "You know, I lived all my life in New York and I never knew Central Park had a zoo. More people should know that and go see it."

"So you had a good time," Astorre said in a good-humored voice, thinking that if things went badly, Bruno would at least have a pleasant memory before death. The door of the dining room swung open, and the owner of the restaurant appeared behind him with Timmona Portella and Marcantonio. Portella's broad figure with its well-cut suit almost masked Marcantonio behind him. Bruno rushed into Timmona's arms and kissed him on both cheeks, and Astorre was astonished to see the look of love and satisfaction on Timmona's face.

"What a brother," Bruno exclaimed loudly "What a brother."

In contrast, Astorre and Marcantonio shook hands, then Astorre gave a half hug and said, "Everything is OK, Marc."

Marcantonio turned away from him and sat down. His legs had gone weak partly with relief at his safety and partly because of Astorre's appearance. The young boy who loved to sing, the intense yet joyous youth so carefree and loving, now appeared in his true form as the Angel of Death. The power of his presence dominated Portella in his fear and bluster.

Astorre sat down next to Marcantonio and patted his knee. He was smiling his affable smile as though this were just a friendly lunch. "Are you OK?" he asked.

Marcantonio looked directly into his eyes. He had never before noticed how clear and merciless they were. He looked at Bruno, the man who would have paid for his life. The man was babbling to his brother, something about the Central Park zoo.

Astorre said to Portella, "We have things to discuss."

"OK," Portella said. "Bruno, get the fuck out of here. There's a car waiting outside. I'll talk to you when I get home."

Monza came into the dining room. "Take Marcantonio to his house," Astorre said to him. "Marc, wait for me there."

Portella and Astorre now sat alone across from each other at the table. Portella opened a bottle of wine and filled his glass. He didn't offer a glass to Astorre.

Astorre reached into his pocket, pulled out a brown envelope, and emptied its contents onto the table. There was the confidential document he had signed for Cilke, the one in which he was asked to betray Portella.

Then there was the small cassette player with the tape in it.

Portella looked at the document with the FBI logo and read it. He tossed it aside. "That could be a forgery," he said. "And why would you be so dumb to sign it?"

In answer Astorre flipped the switch on the cassette player, and Cilke's voice could be heard asking Astorre to cooperate to trap Portella. Portella listened and tried to control the surprise and rage he felt, but his face had flushed a deep red and his lips moved in unspoken curses. Astorre clicked off the tape.

"I know you worked with Cilke over the last six years," Astorre said. "You helped him wipe out the New York Families. And I know you got immunity from Cilke for that. But now he's after you. Those guys who wear badges are never satisfied. They want it all. You thought he was your friend. You broke *omertà* for him. You made him famous, and now he wants to send you to jail. He doesn't need you anymore. He's going to come after you as soon as you buy the banks. That's why I couldn't make the deal. I would never break *omertà*."

Portella was very quiet and then seemed to come to a decision. "If I solve the Cilke problem, what deal would you make for the banks?"

Astorre put everything back into his attaché case. "Outright sale," he said. "Except for me—I keep a five percent piece."

Portella seemed to have recovered from his shock. "OK," he said. "We can work it out after the problem is solved."

They shook hands on it, and Portella left first. Astorre realized he was very hungry and ordered a thick red steak for lunch. One problem solved, he thought.

At midnight Portella met with Marriano Rubio, Inzio Tulippa, and Michael Grazziella, at the Peruvian consulate.

Rubio had been a superb host to Tulippa and Grazziella. He had accompanied them to the theater, the opera, and the ballet, and he had supplied discreet beautiful young women who had achieved some fame in the arts and music. Tulippa and Grazziella were having a wonderful visit and were reluctant to return to their natural environments, which were much less stimulating. They were subordinate kings being wooed by an overruling emperor who did everything to please them.

This night the consul general exceeded himself in his hospitality. The conference table was laden with exotic dishes, fruits, cheeses, and huge bonbons of chocolate; beside every chair stood a bottle of champagne in an ice bucket. Small elegant pastries rested on delicate ladders of spun sugar. A huge coffee urn steamed, and boxes of Havana cigars, maduros, light brown, and green were strewn carelessly over the table.

He opened the proceedings by saying to Portella, "Now, what is so important that we had to cancel our engagements for this meeting?" Despite his exquisite courtesy there was a slight condescension in his voice that infuriated Portella. And he knew that he would be lessened in their eyes when they learned of Cilke's duplicity. He told them the whole story.

Tulippa was eating a bonbon when he said, "You mean you had his cousin Marcantonio Aprile, and you made a deal to get your brother released without consulting us." His voice was full of contempt.

"I could not let my brother die," Portella said. "And besides, if I hadn't made the deal, we would have fallen into Cilke's trap."

"True," Tulippa said. "But it was not your decision to make."

"Yeah," Portella said. "Then who—"

"All of us!" Tulippa barked. "We are your partners."

Portella looked at him and wondered what kept him from killing the greasy son of a bitch. But then remembered the fifty Panama hats flying in the air.

The consul general seemed to have read his mind. He said soothingly, "We all come from different cultures and have different values. We must accommodate ourselves to each other. Timmona is an American, a sentimentalist."

"His brother is a dumb piece of shit," Tulippa said.

Rubio shook his finger at Tulippa. "Inzio, stop making trouble for the fun of it. We all have a right to decide our personal affairs."

Grazziella smiled a thin amused smile. "This is true. You, Inzio, have never confided to us your secret laboratories. Your desire to own your own personal weapons. And such a foolish notion. Do you think the government will put up with such a threat? They will change all the laws that now protect us and permit us to thrive."

Tulippa laughed. He was enjoying this meeting. "I am a patriot," he said. "I want South America to be in a position to defend itself from countries like Israel and India and Iraq."

Rubio smiled at him benignly. "I never knew you were a nationalist."

Portella was unamused. "I have a big problem here. I thought Cilke was my friend. I invested a lot of money in him. And now he is coming after me and all of you."

Grazziella spoke directly and strongly. "We must abandon the whole project. We must live with less." He was no longer the amiable man they had known. "We must find another solution. Forget Kurt Cilke and Astorre Viola. They are too dangerous as enemies. We must not pursue a course that could destroy us all."

"That won't solve my problem," Portella said. "Cilke will keep coming after me."

Tulippa also dropped his mask of affability. He said to Grazziella, "That you should advocate such a peaceful solution is against everything we know about you. You killed police and magistrates in Sicily. You assassinated the governor and his wife. You and your Corleonesi *cosca* killed the army general who was sent out to destroy your organization. Yet now you say, abandon a project that will earn us billions of dollars. And desert our friend Portella."

"I'm going to get rid of Cilke," Portella said.

"No matter what you say."

"That is a very dangerous course of action," the consul general said. "The FBI will declare a vendetta. They will use all their resources to track down his killer."

"I agree with Timmona," Tulippa said. "The FBI operates under legal constraints and can be handled. I will supply an assault team, and hours after the operation they will be on the airplane to South America."

Portella said, "I know it's dangerous, but it's the only thing to do."

"I agree," Tulippa said. "For billions of dollars one must take risks. Or what are we in business for?"

Rubio said to Inzio, "You and I are at minimal risk because we have diplomatic status. Michael, you return to Sicily for the time being. Timmona, you will be the one who must bear the brunt of what follows."

"If worse comes to worst," Tulippa said, "I can hide you in South America."

Portella spread his hands in the air in a helpless gesture. "I have a choice," he said. "But I want your support. Michael, do you agree?"

Grazziella's face was impassive. "Yes, I agree," he said. "But I would worry more about Astorre Viola than Kurt Cilke."

WHEN ASTORRE RECEIVED the urgent coded message that Heskow wanted a meeting, he took his precautions. There was always the danger that Heskow might turn against him. So instead of answering the message, he suddenly appeared at Heskow's home in Brightwaters at midnight. He took Aldo Monza with him and an extra car with four more men. He also wore a bulletproof vest. He called Heskow when he was in the driveway so that he would open the door.

Heskow did not seem surprised. He prepared coffee and served Astorre and himself. Then he smiled at Astorre and said, "I have good news and bad news. Which one first?"

"Just tell it," Astorre said.

"The bad news is that I have to leave the country

for good, and that's because of the good news. And I want to ask you to keep your promise. That nothing will happen to my boy even if I can't work for you anymore."

"You have that promise," Astorre said. "Now, why do you have to leave the country?"

Heskow shook his head in a comical act of sorrow. He said, "Because that dumb prick Portella is going over the top. He is going to knock off Cilke, the FBI guy. And he wants me to be operational chief of the crew."

"So just refuse," Astorre said.

"I can't," Heskow said. "The hit is ordered by his whole syndicate, and if I refuse, I go down the drain and maybe my son does too. So I'll organize the hit, but I won't be in the hit party. I'll be gone. And then when Cilke goes down the FBI will pour a hundred men into the city to solve it. I told them that, but they don't give a shit. Cilke double-crossed them or something. They think they can smear him enough so that it won't be such a big deal."

Astorre tried not to show his satisfaction. It had worked out. Cilke would be dead with no danger to himself. And with a little luck the FBI would get rid of Portella.

He said to Heskow, "You want to leave me an address?"

Heskow smiled at him almost scornfully with distrust. "I don't think so," he said. Not that I don't trust you. But I can always get in touch with you."

"Well, thanks for letting me know," Astorre said, "but who really made this decision?"

"Timmona Portella," Heskow said. "But Inzio Tulippa and the consul general signed off on it. That Corleonesi guy, Grazziella, washed his hands of it. He's distancing himself from the operation. I think he's leaving for Sicily. Which is funny because he's killed practically everybody there.

"They don't really understand how America works, and Portella is just dumb. He says he thought he and Cilke were really friends."

"And you are going to lead the hit team," Astorre said. "That's not so smart either."

"No, I told you when they hit the house I'll be long gone."

"The house?" Astorre said, and at that moment he felt dread over what he was about to hear.

"Yeah," Heskow said. "A massive assault team flies back to South America and disappears."

"Very professional," Astorre said. "When does this all happen?"

"Night after tomorrow. All you have to do is stand aside and they solve all your problems. That's the good news."

"So it is," Astorre said. He kept his face expressionless, but in his mind was the vision of Georgette Cilke, her beauty and goodness.

"I thought you should know about it so that

you'll have a good alibi," Heskow said. "So you owe me one, and take care of my kid."

"Damn right," Astorre said. "Don't worry about him."

He shook hands with Heskow before he left. "I think you're being very smart leaving the country. All hell will break loose."

"Yeah," Heskow said.

For a moment Astorre wondered what he would do about Heskow. The man, after all, had driven the hit car in the killing of the Don. He had to pay for that despite all his help. But Astorre had suffered a certain loss of energy when he learned that Cilke's wife and child were to be killed with him. Let him go, he thought. He might be useful later. Then it would be time to kill him. And he looked at Heskow's smiling face and smiled back.

"You're a very clever man," he said to Heskow.

Heskow's face turned pink with pleasure. "I know," he said. "That's how I stay alive."

The next day, at 11:00 A.M., Astorre arrived at FBI headquarters accompanied by Nicole Aprile, who had arranged an appointment.

He had spent a long night pondering his course of action. He had planned all this to have Portella kill Cilke. But he knew that he could not let Georgette or her daughter be killed. He also knew that Don Aprile would never have interfered with

311

fate in this matter. But then he remembered a story about the Don that gave him pause.

One night, when Astorre was twelve years old and in Sicily with the Don on his annual visit, they were served dinner by Caterina in the garden pavilion. Astorre, with his peculiar innocence, said to them abruptly, "How did you two get to know each other? Did you grow up together as children?" The Don and Caterina exchanged a glance and then laughed at the serious intensity of his interest.

The Don had placed his fingers on his lips and whispered mockingly, "*Omertà*. It's a secret."

Caterina rapped Astorre's hand with the wooden mixing spoon. "That's none of your business, you little devil," she said. "And besides, it's nothing I'm proud of."

Don Aprile gazed upon Astorre with fondness. "Why should he not know? He's a Sicilian to the bone. Tell him."

"No," Caterina said. "But you can tell him if you like."

After dinner Don Aprile lit his cigar, filled his glass with anisette, and told Astorre the story.

"Ten years ago the most important man in the town was a certain Father Sigusmundo, a very dangerous man and yet good-humored. When I visited Sicily he often came to my house and played cards with my friends. At that time I had a different housekeeper."

But Father Sigusmundo was not irreligious. He

was a devout and hardworking priest. He scolded
people into going to mass and even at one time
engaged in fisticuffs with an exasperating atheist.
He was most famous for giving last rites to victims
of the Mafia as they lay dying; he shrived their
souls and cleansed them for their voyage to
Heaven. He was revered for this, but it happened
too often and some people began to whisper,
saying the reason he was always so handy was
because he was one of the executioners—that he
was betraying the secrets of the confessional box
for his own ends.

Caterina's husband at that time was a strong
anti-Mafia policeman. He had even pursued a case
of murder after he had been warned off by the
provincial Mafia chief, an unheard-of act of
defiance at that time. A week after that threat,
Caterina's husband was ambushed and lay dying
in a back alley of Palermo. And it so happened
that Father Sigusmundo appeared to give him last
rites. The crime was never solved.

Caterina, the grief-stricken widow, spent a year
in mourning and devotion to the church. Then one
Saturday she went to confession with Father
Sigusmundo. When the priest came out of the
confessional, in full sight of everyone, she stabbed
him through the heart with her husband's dagger.

The police threw her in jail, but that was the
least of it. The Mafia chief pronounced a death
sentence upon her.

Astorre stared wide-eyed at Caterina. "Did you really do that, Aunt Caterina?"

Caterina looked at him with amusement. He was filled with curiosity and not a bit of fear. "But you must understand why. Not because he killed my husband. Men are always killing each other here in Sicily. But Father Sigusmundo was a false priest, an unshriven murderer. He could not give last rites with legitimacy. Why would God listen? So my husband was not only murdered but denied his entrance to Heaven and descended into Hell. Well, men don't know where to stop. There are things you can't do. That's why I killed the priest."

"Then how come you're here?" Astorre asked.

"Because Don Aprile took an interest in the whole affair," Caterina said. "So naturally everything was settled."

The Don said gravely to Astorre, "I had a certain standing in the town, a respect. The authorities were easily satisfied, and the church did not want the public attention of a corrupt priest. The Mafia chief was not so sensitive and refused to cancel his death sentence. He was found in the cemetery where Caterina's husband was buried, with his throat cut, and his *cosca* was destroyed and made powerless. By that time I had grown fond of Caterina, and I made her chief of this household. And for the last nine years my summer months in Sicily have been the sweetest of my life."

To Astorre this was all magic. He ate a handful

of olives and spit out the pits. "Caterina's your girlfriend?" he asked.

"Of course," Caterina said. "You're a twelve-year-old boy, you can understand. I live under his protection as if I were his wife, and I perform all my wifely duties."

Don Aprile seemed a little embarrassed, the only time Astorre had seen him so. Astorre said, "But why don't you marry?"

Caterina said, "I could never leave Sicily. I live like a queen here, and your uncle is generous. Here I have my friends, my family, my sisters and brothers and cousins. And your uncle could not live in Sicily. So we do the best we can."

Astorre said to Don Aprile, "Uncle, you can marry Caterina and live here. I'll live with you. I never want to leave Sicily." At this they both laughed.

"Listen to me," the Don said. "It took a great deal of work to put a stop to the vendetta against her. If we married, plots and mischief would be born. They can accept the fact that she is my mistress but not my wife. So with this arrangement we are both happy and both free. Also, I do not want a wife who refuses to accept my decisions, and when she refuses to leave Sicily I am not a husband."

"And it would be an *infamita,*" Caterina said. Her head drooped slightly, and then she turned her eyes to the black Sicilian sky and began to weep.

315

Astorre was bewildered. It made no sense to him as a child. "Really, but why? Why?" he said.

Don Aprile sighed. He puffed on his cigar and took a sip of anisette. "You must understand," the Don said. "Father Sigusmundo was my brother."

Astorre remembered now that their explanation hadn't convinced him. With the willfulness of a romantic child he had believed that two people who loved each other were permitted any license in the world. Only now he understood the terrible decision his uncle and aunt had made. That if he married Caterina, all the Don's blood relatives would become his enemies. Not that they did not know that Father Sigusmundo was a villain. But he was a brother and that excused all his sins. And a man like the Don could not marry his brother's murderer. Caterina could not ask such a sacrifice. And then what if Caterina believed that the Don had somehow been implicated in her husband's murder? What a leap of faith for both of them, and perhaps, what a betrayal of everything they believed in.

But this was America, not Sicily. During the long night Astorre had made up his mind. In the morning he had called Nicole.

316

"I'm going to pick you up for breakfast," he had said. "Then you and I are going to visit Cilke at FBI headquarters."

Nicole had said, "This has to be serious, right?"

"Yeah. I'll tell you over breakfast."

"Do you have an appointment with him?" Nicole had asked.

"No, that's your job."

An hour later the cousins were having breakfast together at a posh hotel with widely separated tables for privacy because it was an early-hour meeting place for the power brokers of the city.

Nicole believed in a hearty breakfast to fuel her twelve-hour working day. Astorre settled for orange juice and coffee, which with a basket of breakfast rolls cost him twenty dollars. "What crooks," he said to Nicole with a grin.

Nicole was impatient with this. "You're paying for the atmosphere," she said. "The imported linen, the crockery. What the hell is wrong now?"

"I'm going to do my civic duty," Astorre said. "I have information from an unimpeachable source that Kurt Cilke and his family will be killed tomorrow night. I want to warn him. I want to get credit for warning him. He'll want to know my source, and I can't tell him."

Nicole pushed away her plate and leaned back. "Who the hell is that stupid?" she said to Astorre. "Christ, I hope you're not involved."

"Why do you think that?" Astorre asked.

317

"I don't know," Nicole said. "The thought just came. Why not let him know anonymously?"

"I want to get credit for my good deeds. I get the feeling nobody loves me these days." He smiled.

"I love you," Nicole said, leaning toward him. "OK, here's our story. As we came into the hotel a strange man stopped us and whispered the information in your ear. He was wearing a gray striped suit, a white shirt, and a black tie. He was average height, dark-skinned, could be Italian or Hispanic. After that we can vary. I'll be witness to your story, and he knows he can't screw around with me."

Astorre laughed. His laughter was always disarming; it had the unfettered glee of a child. "So he's more afraid of you than he is of me," he said.

Nicole smiled. "And I know the director of the FBI. He's a political animal, he has to be. I'll call Cilke and tell him to expect us." She took her phone out of her purse and made the call.

"Mr. Cilke," she said into the phone, "this is Nicole Aprile. I'm with my cousin Astorre Viola, and he has important information he wants to give you."

After a pause she said, "That's too late. We'll be there within the hour." She hung up before Cilke could say anything.

An hour later Astorre and Nicole were ushered into Cilke's office. It was a large corner office with Polaroid bulletproof windows that could not be seen out of, so there was no view.

Cilke, standing behind a huge desk, was waiting for them. There were three black leather chairs facing his desk. Behind it, oddly enough, was a schoolroom blackboard. In one of the chairs sat Bill Boxton, who did not offer to shake hands.

"Are you going to tape this?" Nicole asked.

"Of course," Cilke said.

Boxton said reassuringly, "Hell, we tape everything, even our coffee-and-doughnut orders. We also tape anybody we think we may have to put in jail."

"You're a pretty fucking funny guy," Nicole said, deadpan. "On the best day of your life you couldn't put me in jail. Think another way. My client Astorre Viola is meeting you voluntarily to give you an important piece of information. I'm here to protect him from any abuse after he does so."

Kurt Cilke was not quite so charming as he had been in their previous meetings. He waved them into chairs and took his seat behind the desk. "OK," he said. "Let's have it."

Astorre felt the man's hostility, as if being on his own turf didn't require his usual businesslike friendliness. How would he react? He looked directly into Cilke's eyes and said, "I received information that there will be a heavily armed assault on your home tomorrow night. Late. The purpose is to kill you for some reason."

Cilke did not respond. He was frozen in his chair, but Boxton sprang up and stood behind Astorre. To Cilke he said, "Kurt, keep calm."

Cilke rose. His entire body seemed to blow up with rage. "This is an old Mafia trick," he said. "He sets up the operation and then sabotages it. And he thinks I'll be grateful. Now, how the hell did you get such information?"

Astorre told him the story he and Nicole had prepared. Cilke turned to Nicole and asked, "You witnessed this incident?"

"Yes," Nicole said, "but I didn't hear what the man said."

Cilke said to Astorre, "You are under arrest now."

"For what?" Nicole said.

"For threatening a federal officer," Cilke said.

"I think you better call your director," Nicole said.

"It's my decision to make," Cilke told her.

Nicole looked at her watch.

Cilke said softly, "Under executive order of the president, I'm authorized to hold you and your client for forty-eight hours without legal counsel, as a threat to national security."

Astorre was startled. In his wide-eyed, childish way, he said, "Is that really true? You can do that?" He was really impressed by such power. He turned back to Nicole and said cheerfully, "Hey, this is getting more and more like Sicily."

"If you take that step, the FBI will be in court for the next ten years and you'll be history," Nicole said to Cilke. "You have time to get your family out and ambush the attackers. They won't know they've been informed on. If you capture any, you can question them. We won't talk. Or warn them."

Cilke seemed to consider this. He said to Astorre with contempt, "At least I respected your uncle. He would never have talked."

Astorre gave an embarrassed smile. "Those were the old days and that was the old country, and besides, you're not so different, with your secret executive orders." He wondered what Cilke would say if he told him the real reason. That he had saved the man simply because he had spent an evening in the presence of his wife and had romantically and uselessly fallen in love with his idea of her.

"I don't believe your bullshit story, but we'll go into that if there is really an assault tomorrow night. If anything happens, then I lock you up, and maybe you, too, counselor. But why did you tell me?"

Astorre smiled. "Because I like you," he said.

"Get the hell out of here," Cilke said. He turned to Boxton. "Get the commander of the special tactical force in here, and tell my secretary to set up a call to the director."

They were kept another two hours to be interrogated by Cilke's staff. Meanwhile, Cilke in his office talked to the director in Washington over the scramble phone.

"Do not arrest them under any circumstances," the director told him. "Everything would come out in the media, and we'd be a joke. And don't fool with Nicole Aprile unless you have the goods on her. Keep everything top secret, and we'll see what happens tomorrow night. Guards at your house have been alerted, and your family is already being moved out as we speak. Now put Bill on the phone. He'll run the ambush operation."

"Sir, that should be my job," Cilke protested.

"You'll help with the planning," the director said, "but under no circumstance will you take part in the tactical operation. The Bureau operates under very strict rules of engagement to avoid unnecessary violence. You would be suspect if things go bad. You understand me?"

"Yes, sir." Cilke understood perfectly.

CHAPTER

12

AFTER A MONTH in the hospital Aspinella Washington was released but still had to heal sufficiently for the insertion of an artificial eye. A splendid physical specimen, her body seemed to assemble itself around her injuries. True, her left foot dragged a little, and her eye socket looked hideous. But she wore a square green eye patch instead of black, and the dark green accentuated the beauty of her mocha skin. She reported back to work wearing a costume of black trousers, a green pullover shirt and a green leather coat. When she looked at herself in the mirror she thought herself a striking figure.

Though she was on medical leave she would sometimes go into the Detective Bureau headquarters and help in interrogations. Her injury gave her a sense of liberation—she felt like she could do anything, and she stretched her power.

On her first interrogation there were two suspects, an unusual pair in that one was white and one was black. The white suspect, about thirty, was immediately frightened of her. But the black partner was delighted by the tall beautiful woman with the green eye patch and the cold level stare. This was one cool sister.

"Holy shit," he cried out, his face happy. It was his first bust, he had no criminal record, and he really didn't know he was in serious trouble. He and his partner had broken into a home, tied up the husband and wife, and then looted the house. They had been laid low by an informant. The black kid was still wearing the house owner's Rolex watch. He said cheerily to Aspinella, without malice, indeed in a voice of admiration, "Hey, Captain Kidd, you gonna make us walk the plank?"

The other detectives in the room smirked at this foolishness. But Aspinella didn't respond. The kid was in handcuffs and couldn't ward off her blow. Snakelike, her truncheon crashed against his face, breaking his nose and splitting his cheekbone. He didn't go down; his knees sagged, and he gave her a reproachful look. His face was a mess of blood. Then his legs folded and he toppled to the ground. For the next ten minutes Aspinella beat him unmercifully. As if from a fresh spring, blood started to flow from the boy's ears.

"Jesus," one of the detectives said, "how the hell do we question him now?"

"I didn't want to talk to him," Aspinella said. "I want to talk to *this* guy." She pointed her truncheon to the white suspect. "Zeke, right? I want to talk to you, Zeke." She took him roughly by the shoulder and threw him into a chair facing her desk. He stared at her, terrified. She realized her eye patch had slipped to one side and that Zeke was staring into that empty orb. She reached up and adjusted the patch to cover her milky socket.

"Zeke," she said, "I want you to listen very carefully. I want to save time here. I want to know how you got this kid into this. How you got into this. Understand? Are you going to cooperate?"

Zeke had turned very pale. He didn't hesitate. "Yes, ma'am," he said. "I'll tell you everything."

"OK," Aspinella said to another detective. "Get that kid into the medical ward and send down the video people to take Zeke's confession of his own free will."

Once the monitors were set up, Aspinella said to Zeke, "Who fenced your goods? Who gave you information about your target? Give me the exact details of the robbery. Your partner is obviously a nice kid. He has no record and he's not that smart. That's why I took it easy on him. Now, you, Zeke, have a very distinguished record, so I figure you're the Fagin that got him into this. So start rehearsing for the video."

When Aspinella left the station house she drove her car over the Southern State Parkway to Brightwaters, Long Island.

Oddly enough, she found driving with one eye was more pleasurable than not. The landscape was more interesting because it was focused, like some futuristic painting that dissolved into dreams around the edges. It was as if half the world, the globe itself, had been bisected and the half she could see claimed more attention.

Finally she was driving through Brightwaters and passing John Heskow's house. She could see his car in the driveway and a man carrying a huge azalea plant from the flower shed to the house. Then another man came out of the shed carrying a box filled with yellow flowers. This was interesting, she thought. They were emptying the flower shed.

While in the hospital she had done research on John Heskow. She had gone through the New York State car-registration records and found his address. Then she checked all the criminal databases and found that John Heskow was really Louis Ricci; the bastard was Italian, though he looked like a German pudding. But his criminal record was clear. He had been arrested several times for extortion and assault but never convicted. The flower shed could not generate the amount of money to support his style of living.

She had done all this because she had figured out that the only one who could have put the finger on her and Di Benedetto was Heskow. The only thing that puzzled her was that he had given them the money. That money found had the Internal Affairs Bureau on her ass, but she had soon gotten rid of their unenthusiastic inquiries, since they were happy to have the money for themselves. Now she was preparing to get rid of Heskow.

Twenty-four hours before the scheduled assault on Cilke, Heskow drove to Kennedy airport for his flight to Mexico City, where he would disappear from the civilized world with fake passports he had prepared years ago.

Details had been settled. The flower sheds had been emptied; his ex-wife would take care of selling the house and put the proceeds in the bank for their son's college expenses. Heskow had told her he would be away for two years. He told his son the same story, over dinner at Shun Lee's.

It was early evening when he got to the airport. He checked two suitcases, all he needed, except for the one hundred thousand dollars in one-hundred-dollar bills taped around his body in small pouches. He was wallpapered with money for immediate expenses, and he had a secret account in the Caymans, holding nearly five million dollars. Thank God, because he certainly could not apply for Social Security. He was proud that he had lived a prudent life and had not squandered his bankroll on gambling, women, or other foolishness.

Heskow checked in for his flight and boarding pass. Now he only carried a briefcase with his false ID and passports. He had left his car at permanent parking; his ex-wife would pick it up and hold it for him.

His was at least an hour early for his flight. He felt a little uneasy being unarmed, but he had to pass the detectors to get on the flight, and he would be able to get plenty of weaponry from his contacts in Mexico City.

To pass the time he bought some magazines in the bookshop and then went to the terminal cafeteria. He loaded up a tray with dessert and coffee and sat down at one of the small tables. He looked through the magazines and ate his dessert, a false strawberry tart covered with fake whipped cream. Suddenly he was aware that someone was sitting down at his table. He looked up and saw Detective Aspinella Washington. Like everyone, he was entranced by the square, dark green eye patch. It gave him a flutter of panic. She looked much more beautiful than he remembered.

"Hi, John," she said. "You never did come to visit me in the hospital."

He was so flustered he took her seriously. "You know I couldn't do that, Detective. But I was sorry to hear about your misfortune."

Aspinella gave him a huge smile. "I was kidding, John. But I did want to have a little chat with you before your flight."

"Sure," Heskow said. He expected he would have to pay off, and he had ten grand in the briefcase ready for just such surprises. "I'm glad to see you looking so well. I was worried about you."

"No shit," Aspinella said, her one eye glittering like a hawk's. "Too bad about Paul. We were good friends, you know, besides his being my boss."

"That was a shame," Heskow said. He even gave a little cluck, which made Aspinella smile.

"I don't have to show you my badge," Aspinella said. "Right?" She paused. "I want you to come with me to a little interrogation room we have here in the terminal. Give me some good interesting answers, and you can catch your flight."

"OK," Heskow said. He rose to his feet clutching his briefcase.

"And no funny business or I'll shoot you dead. Funny thing, I'm a better shot with just one eye." She rose and took his arm and led him to a stairway up to the mezzanine, which held the administrative offices of the airlines. She led him down a long hallway and unlocked an office door. Heskow was surprised not only by the largeness of the room but by the banks of TV monitors on the

329

walls, at least twenty screens, monitored by two men who sat in soft armchairs and studied them as they ate sandwiches and drank coffee. One of the men stood up and said, "Hey, Aspinella, what's up?"

"I'm going to have a private chat with this guy in the interrogation room. Lock us in."

"Sure" the man said. "You want one of us in there with you?"

"Nah. It's just a friendly chat."

"Oh, one of your famous friendly chats," the man said, and laughed. He looked at Heskow closely. "I saw you on the screens down in the terminal. Strawberry tart, right?" He led them to a door in the back of the room and unlocked it. After Heskow and Aspinella entered the interrogation room he locked the door behind them.

Heskow was reassured now that there were other people involved. The interrogation chamber was disarming, with a couch, a desk and three comfortable-looking chairs. In one corner was a water cooler with paper cups. The pink walls were decorated with photographs and paintings of flying machines.

Aspinella made Heskow sit in a chair facing the desk, on which she sat and looked down at him.

"Can we get on with it? Heskow asked. "I cannot afford to miss that flight."

Aspinella didn't answer. She reached out and

took Heskow's briefcase from his lap. Heskow twitched. She opened it and leafed through the contents, including the stacks of one-hundred-dollar bills. She studied one of the false passports, then put everything back in the briefcase and returned it to him.

"You're a very clever man," she said. "You knew it was time to run. Who told you I was after you?"

"Why would you be after me?" Heskow asked. He was more confident now that she had given him back his briefcase.

Aspinella lifted her eye patch so that he could see the wretched crater. But Heskow did not flinch; he had seen much worse in his day.

"You cost me that eye," she said. "Only you could have informed and set Paul and me up."

Heskow spoke with the utmost sincerity, which had been one of his best weapons in his profession. "You're wrong, absolutely wrong. If I did that, I would have kept the money—you can see that. Look, I really have to catch that flight." He unbuttoned his shirt and tore a piece of tape. Two packets of money appeared on the table. "That's yours, and the money in the briefcase. That's thirty grand."

"Gee," Aspinella said. "Thirty grand. That's a lot of money for just one eye. OK. But you have to tell me the name of the guy who paid you to set us up."

Heskow made up his mind. His one chance was to get on that flight. He knew she wasn't bluffing. He had dealt with too many homicidal maniacs in his line of work to misjudge her.

"Listen, believe me," he said. "I never dreamed this guy would knock off two high-ranking cops. I just made a deal with Astorre Viola so he could hide out. I never dreamed he would do such a thing."

"Good," Aspinella said. "Now, who paid you for the hit on him?"

"Paul knew," Heskow said. "Didn't he tell you? Timmona Portella."

At that Aspinella felt a surge of rage. Her fat partner had not only been a lousy fuck but a lying bastard as well.

"Stand up," she said to Heskow. Suddenly a gun appeared in her hand.

Heskow was terrified. He had seen that look before, only he had not been the victim. For one moment he thought of his hidden five million dollars that would die with him, unclaimed, and the five million dollars seemed a living creature. What a tragedy. "No," he cried out, and huddled his body further into the chair. Aspinella grabbed his hair with her free hand and pulled him to his feet. She held the gun away from his neck and fired. Heskow seemed to fly out of her grasp and crashed to the floor. She knelt by his body. Half his throat had been blown away. Then she took her throwaway gun from its ankle holster, placed it in Heskow's hand, and stood up. She could hear the door being unlocked, and then the two screen men rushed in with guns drawn.

"I had to shoot him," she said. "He tried to bribe me and then he pulled a gun. Call the terminal medical van and I'll call homicide myself. Don't touch anything, and don't let me out of your sight."

The next night Portella launched his attack. Cilke's wife and daughter had already been spirited away to a restricted heavily guarded FBI station in California. Cilke, at the director's orders, was at FBI headquarters in New York with his full staff on duty. Bill Boxton had been given the overall command of the special task force and would spring the trap at Cilke's house. The rules of engagement were strict, however. The Bureau didn't want a bloodbath that would cause complaint from liberal groups. The FBI team would not fire unless it was fired upon. Every effort would be made to give the attackers a chance to surrender.

As an assistant planning officer, Kurt Cilke met with Boxton and the special task forces commander, a comparatively young man of thirty-five whose face was set in the rigid lines of command. But his skin was gray and he had a regrettable dimple in his chin. His name was Sestak and his accent was pure Harvard. They met in Cilke's office.

"I expect you to be in constant communication with me during the operation," Cilke said. "The rules of engagement will be strictly observed."

"Don't worry," Boxton said. "We have a hundred men with firepower that exceeds theirs. They will surrender."

Sestak said in a soft voice, "I have another hundred men to establish a perimeter. We let them in but we don't let them out."

"Good," Cilke said. "When you capture them you will ship them to our New York interrogation center. I'm not permitted to take part in the interrogation, but I want information as soon as possible."

"What if something goes wrong and they wind up dead?" Sestak asked.

"Then there will be an internal investigation and the director will be very unhappy. Now, here's the reality: they will be arrested for conspiracy to commit murder, and they will get out on bail. Then they will vanish into South America. So we have only a few days to interrogate them."

Boxton looked at Cilke with a little smile. Sestak said to Cilke in his cultured tone, "I think that would make you terribly unhappy."

"Sure, it bothers me," Cilke said. "But the director has to worry about political complications. Conspiracy charges are always tricky."

"I see," Sestak said. "So your hands are tied."

"That's right," Cilke said.

Boxton said quietly, "It's a damn shame, they can attempt the murder of a federal officer and get off."

Sestak was looking at them both with an amused smile. His gray skin took on a reddish tinge. "You're preaching to the choir," he said. "Anyway, these operations always go wrong. Guys with guns always think they can't be shot. Very funny thing about human nature."

That night Boxton accompanied Sestak to the operational area around Cilke's home in New Jersey. Lights had been left on in the house to make it look like someone was home. Also there were three cars parked in the driveway to give the impression that the house guards were inside. The cars were booby-trapped so that if they were started, they would blow up. Otherwise Boxton could see nothing.

"Where the hell are your hundred men?" Boxton asked Sestak.

Sestak gave him a huge grin. "Pretty good, huh? They're all around here, and even you can't see them. They already have lines of fire. When the attackers come in, the road will be sealed behind them. We'll have a basket full of rats."

Boxton remained at Sestak's side at a command

post fifty yards from the house. With them was a communications team of four men who wore camouflage to match the patch of woods they used as cover. Sestak and his team were armed with rifles, but Boxton only had his handgun.

"I don't want you in the fighting," Sestak told Boxton. "Besides, that weapon you carry is useless here."

"Why not?" Boxton said. "I've been waiting my whole career to shoot the bad guys."

Sestak laughed. "Not today. My team is protected by executive order from any legal inquiries or prosecution. You're not."

"But I'm in command," Boxton said.

"Not when we become operational," Sestak told him coolly. "Then I'm in sole command. I make all the decisions. Even the director can't supersede me."

They waited together in the darkness. Boxton looked at his watch. It was ten minutes to midnight. One of the communications team whispered to Sestak, "Five cars filled with men are on approach to the house. The road behind them has been sealed. Estimated time of arrival is five minutes."

Sestak was wearing infrared goggles that gave him night vision. "OK," he said. "Send the word. Don't fire unless fired upon or at my order."

They waited. Suddenly five cars raced to the driveway and men spilled out. One of them immediately threw a firebomb into Cilke's house, breaking a pane of glass and sending a thin blaze of red fire inside the room.

Then suddenly the whole area was flooded with bright searchlights that froze the group of twenty attackers. At the same time a helicopter whirred overhead with glaring lights. Loudspeakers roared a message into the night. "This is the FBI. Throw away your weapons and lie on the ground."

Dazzled by the light and the helicopters, the trapped men froze. Boxton saw with relief that they had lost all will to resist.

So he was surprised when Sestak brought up his rifle and fired into the group of attackers. Immediately the attack group started firing back. And then Boxton was deafened by the roar of gunfire that swept the driveway and mowed down the attackers. One of the booby-trapped cars exploded. It was as if a hurricane of lead had completely devastated the driveway. Glass shattered and poured down a silver rain. The other cars sank to the ground so riddled with bullets that their outsides had no color. The driveway seemed to spout a spring of blood that flowed and eddied around the cars. The twenty attackers were blood-soaked bundles of rags looking like sacks of laundry to be picked up.

Boxton was in shock. "You fired before they could surrender," he said to Sestak accusingly. "That will be my report."

"I differ." Sestak grinned at him. "Once they

firebombed the house, that was attempted murder. I couldn't risk my men. That will be my report. Also that they fired first."

"Well, it won't be mine," Boxton said.

"No kidding," Sestak said. "You think the director wants your report? You'll be on his shit list. Forever."

"He'll want your ass because you disobeyed orders," Boxton said. "We'll go down in flames together."

"Good," Sestak said. "But I'm the tactical commander. I can't be overruled. Once I'm called in, that's it. I don't want criminals to think they can attack a federal officer. That's the reality, and you and the director can go fuck yourselves."

"Twenty dead men," Boxton said.

"And good riddance to them," Sestak said. "You and Cilke wanted me to blast them, but you didn't have the balls to come right out with it."

Boxton suddenly knew this was true.

Kurt Cilke prepared for another meeting with the director in Washington. He had his notes with an outline of what he would say and a report on all the circumstances of the attack on his home.

As always, Bill Boxton would accompany him, but this time it was at the express wish of the director.

Cilke and Boxton were in the director's office

with its row of TV monitors showing reports of activities of the local FBI office. The director, always courteous, shook hands with both men and invited them to sit down, though he gave Boxton a cold, fishy look. Two of his deputies were in attendance.

"Gentlemen," he said, addressing the whole group. "We have to clean up this mess. We cannot allow such an outrageous act to go without answering it with all our resources. Cilke, do you want to stay on the job or take retirement?"

"I stay," Cilke said.

The director turned to Boxton, and his lean aristocratic face was stern. "You were in charge. How is it that all the attackers were killed and we have no one to interrogate? Who gave the order to fire? You? And on what grounds?"

Boxton sat up in his chair stiffly. "Sir," he said, "the attackers threw a bomb in the house and opened fire. There was no choice."

The director sighed. One of his deputies gave a grunt of scorn.

"Captain Sestak is one of our beauties," the director said. "Did he try, at least, for one prisoner?"

"Sir, it was over in two minutes," Boxton said. "Sestak is a very efficient tactician in the field."

"Well, there hasn't been any fuss by the media or the public," the director said. "But I must say I consider it a bloodbath."

"Yes, it was," volunteered one of the deputies.

"Well, it can't be helped," the director said. "Cilke, have you come up with an operational plan?"

Cilke had felt a surge of anger at their criticism, but he answered calmly. "I want a hundred men assigned to my office. I want you to request a full audit of the Aprile banks. I am going into deep background on everyone involved in this business."

The director said, "You don't feel any debt to this Astorre Viola for saving you and your family?"

"No," Cilke said. "You have to know these people. First they get you into trouble, then they help you out."

The director said, "Remember, one of our primary interests is to appropriate the Aprile banks. Not only because we benefit but because those banks are destined to be a center for laundering drug money. And through them we get Portella and Tulippa. We have to look at this as global. Astorre Viola refuses to sell the banks, and the syndicate is trying to eliminate him. So far they've failed. We have learned that the two hired killers who shot the Don have disappeared. Two detectives in the NYPD were blown up."

"Astorre is cunning and elusive, and he isn't involved in any rackets," Cilke told them, "so we can't really put something on him. Now, the syndicate may succeed in getting rid of him, and the children will sell the banks to them. Then I'm sure in a couple of years they will step over the line."

It was not unusual for government law enforcement to play a long game, especially with the drug people. But to do so they had to permit crimes to be committed.

"We've played it long before," the director said. "But that doesn't mean you give Portella carte blanche."

"Of course," Cilke said. He knew that everyone was speaking for the record.

"I'll give fifty men," the director said. "And I'll request a full audit of the banks just to shake things up."

One of the deputies said, "We have audited them before and never found anything."

"There's always a chance," Cilke said. "Astorre is no banker, and he could have made mistakes."

"Yes," the director said. "One little slip is all the attorney general needs."

Back in New York Cilke met with Boxton and Sestak to plan his campaign. "We're getting fifty more men to investigate the attack on my home," he told them. "We have to be very careful. I want everything you can get on Astorre Viola. I want to go into the blowing up of the detectives. I want all the dope on the disappearance of the Sturzo brothers and all the information we can get on the syndicate. Zero in on Astorre and also Detective Washington. She has a reputation for bribe taking and brutality, and the story she gives of getting blown up and all that money at the scene is very fishy."

"What about this guy Tulippa?" Boxton asked. "He can leave the country anytime."

"Tulippa is touring the country giving speeches for drug legalization and also collecting his blackmail payment from big companies."

"Can't we nail him on that?" Sestak asked.

"No, Sestak," Cilke said. "He has an insurance company and sells them insurance. We might be able to make a case, but the business people oppose it. They've solved the safety problem of their personnel in South America. And Portella has no place to go."

Sestak grinned at him coldly. "What are the rules of engagement here?"

Cilke said smoothly, "The director ordered no more massacres, but protect yourself. Especially against Astorre."

"In other words, we can leave Astorre for dead," Sestak said.

Cilke seemed lost in thought for a moment. "If necessary," he replied.

*

It was only a week later that the federal auditors swarmed over the Aprile bank records and Cilke came personally to see Mr. Pryor in his office.

Cilke shook his hand and then said genially, "I always like to meet personally with people I may have to send to prison. Now, can you help us in any way and get off the train before it's too late?"

Mr. Pryor looked at the young man with a benevolent concern. "Really?" he said. "You are completely on the wrong track, I assure you. I run these banks impeccably according to national and international law."

"Well, I just wanted you to know that I'm tracking down your background and everyone else's," Cilke said. "And I hope you are all clean. Especially the Sturzo brothers."

Mr. Pryor smiled at him. "We are immaculate."

After Cilke left, Mr. Pryor leaned back in his chair. The situation was becoming alarming. What if they tracked down Rosie? He sighed. What a shame. He would have to do something about her.

When Cilke notified Nicole that he wanted her and Astorre in his office the next day, he still did not have a true understanding of Astorre's character, nor did he wish to. He just felt the contempt he had for anyone who broke the law. He did not understand the resolve of a true Mafioso.

Astorre believed in the old tradition. His

343

followers loved him not only because of his charisma but because he valued honor above all.

A true Mafioso was strong enough in his will to avenge any insult to his person or his *cosca.* He could never submit to the will of another person or government agency. And in this lay his power. His own will was paramount; justice was what he decreed justice must be. His saving of Cilke and his family was a flaw in his character. Still, he went with Nicole to Cilke's office vaguely expecting some thanks, a relaxation of Cilke's hostility.

It was evident that careful arrangements had been made to receive them. Two security men searched Astorre and Nicole before they entered Cilke's office. Cilke himself stood behind his desk and glared at them. Without any sign of friendliness he gestured them to sit down. One of the guards locked them all in and waited outside the door.

"Is this being recorded?" Nicole asked.

"Yes," Cilke said. "Audio and video. I don't want any misunderstanding about this meeting." He paused for a moment. "I want you to understand that nothing has changed. I consider you a piece of scum I won't allow to live in this country. I don't buy this Don bullshit. I don't buy your story about the informant. I think you engineered this with him and then betrayed your conspirator to gain more lenient treatment from me. I despise such trickery."

Astorre was astonished that Cilke had penetrated so near to the truth. He looked at him with new respect. And yet his feelings were hurt. The man had no gratitude, no respect for a man who had saved him and his family. He smiled at the contradictions within himself.

"You think it's funny, one of your Mafia jokes," Cilke said. "I'll wipe that smile off your face in two seconds."

He turned to Nicole. "First, the Bureau demands that you tell us the true circumstances of how you got this information. Not that phony story your cousin gave. I'm surprised at you, counselor. I'm thinking of charging you as coconspirator."

Nicole said coolly, "You can try, but I suggest you take it to your director first."

"Who told you about the attack on my house?" Cilke asked. "We want the true informant."

Astorre shrugged. "Take it or leave it," he said.

"Neither," Cilke said coldly. "Let's get this straight. You are just another dirtbag. Another murderer. I know you blew up Di Benedetto and Washington. We're looking into the disappearance of the two Sturzo brothers in L.A. You killed three of Portella's hoods, and you took part in a kidnapping. We're going to get you in the long run. And then you'll be just another piece of shit."

For the first time Astorre seemed to lose some of his composure, and his mask of affability slipped.

He caught Nicole watching him with a sort of terrified pity. And so he permitted some of his anger to escape.

"I don't expect favors from you," he said to Cilke. "You don't even know what honor means. I saved the lives of your wife and daughter. They could be lying underground if it wasn't for me. Now you invite me here to abuse me. Your wife and daughter are alive because of me. Show me respect for that at least."

Cilke stared at him. "I'll show you nothing," he said, and he felt a terrible anger at being in Astorre's debt.

Astorre rose from his seat to walk out of the room, but a security guard pushed him down.

"I'm going to make your life miserable," Cilke said.

Astorre shrugged. "Do what you like. But let me tell you this. I know you helped put Don Aprile on the spot. Just because you and the Bureau want to get hold of the banks."

At this the two security men moved toward him, but Cilke waved them off. "I know you can stop the attacks on my family," he said. "I'm telling you now that I make it your responsibility."

From the other side of the room, Bill Boxton looked at Astorre and drawled, "Are you threatening a federal officer?"

Nicole broke in. "Of course not, he is just asking for his help."

Cilke now seemed more cool. "All this for your beloved Don. Well, obviously you haven't read the file I gave to Nicole. Your beloved Don was the man who killed your father when you were only three years old."

Astorre flinched and glanced at Nicole. "Is that the part you tried to erase?"

Nicole nodded. "I didn't think that part was true, and if it was, I didn't think you should know. It could only hurt you."

Astorre felt the room begin to spin, but he kept his composure. "It doesn't make any difference," he said.

Nicole said to Cilke, "Now that everything is clear, can we go?"

Cilke had an overpowering build, and as he came out from behind the desk he gave Astorre a playful slap on the head. Which surprised Cilke as much as Astorre, for he had never done such a thing before. It was a blow to show his contempt, which masked true hatred. He realized that he could never forget Astorre saving his family. As for Astorre, he looked steadily into Cilke's face. He understood exactly how Cilke felt.

Nicole and Astorre went back to Nicole's apartment, and Nicole tried to show her sympathy for Astorre in his humiliation, but this angered him even more. Nicole prepared a light lunch and then

347

persuaded him to lie down on her bed for a nap. In the middle of his nap, he was conscious that Nicole was on the bed beside him, hugging him. He pushed her away.

"You heard what Cilke said about me," he said. "You want to get mixed up in my life?"

"I don't believe him or his reports," Nicole said. "Astorre, I really do think I still love you."

"We can't go back to when we were kids," Astorre said gently. "I'm not the same person, and neither are you. You're just wishing we were kids again."

They lay in each other's arms. Then Astorre said sleepily, "Do you think it's true what they say about the Don killing my father?"

The next day Astorre flew out to Chicago with Mr. Pryor and consulted with Benito Craxxi. He brought them up to date and then asked, "Is it true that Don Aprile killed my father?"

Craxxi ignored the question and asked Astorre, "Did you have anything to do with inspiring the attack on Cilke's family?"

"No," Astorre lied. He lied to them because he did not want anyone to know the depth of his cunning. And he knew that they would have disapproved.

"And yet you saved them," Don Craxxi said. "Why?"

Again Astorre had to lie. He could not let his allies know he was capable of such sentimentality, that he could not bear to see Cilke's wife and daughter killed.

"You did well," Craxxi said.

Astorre said, "You haven't answered my question."

"Because it is complicated," Craxxi said. "You were the newborn son of a great Mafia chief in Sicily, eighty years old, and head of a very powerful *cosca.* Your mother was very young when she died in childbirth. The old Don was in extremis, and he summoned myself, Don Aprile, and Bianco to his bedside. The whole of his *cosca* would tumble at his death, and he was worried about your future. He made us promise to look after you and chose Don Aprile to take you to America. There, because his wife was dying and he wanted to save you any more suffering, he placed you with the Viola family, which was a mistake, because your foster father turned out to be a traitor and had to be executed. Don Aprile took you into his home as soon as his trouble had passed. The Don had a macabre sense of humor, and so he arranged to have the death labeled suicide in the trunk of a car. Then, as you grew older, you showed all the traits of your real father, the great Don Zeno. And so Don Aprile made the decision that you would be the defender of his family. So he sent you to Sicily to be trained."

Astorre was not really surprised. Somewhere in his memory was a picture of a very old man and a ride on a funeral hearse.

"Yes," Astorre said slowly, "and I am trained. I know how to take the offensive. Still, Portella and Tulippa are well protected. And I have to worry about Grazziella. The only one I could kill is the consul general, Marriano Rubio. Meanwhile, I have Cilke hounding me. I don't even know where to start."

"You must never never strike at Cilke," Don Craxxi said.

"Yes," Mr. Pryor said. "That would be disastrous."

Astorre smiled at them reassuringly. "Agreed," he said.

"There is some good news," Craxxi told him. "Grazziella, in Corleone, has requested Bianco in Palermo to arrange a meeting with you. Bianco will send you word to come within a month. He may be your key."

Tulippa, Portella, and Rubio met in the conference room of the Peruvian consulate. In Sicily, Michael Grazziella expressed his profoundest regret that he was unable to attend.

Inzio opened the meeting without his usual South American charm. He was impatient. "We must solve the question: do we get the banks or

350

not? I've invested millions of dollars, and I am very disappointed in the results."

"Astorre is like a ghost," Portella said. "We can't get at him. He won't take more money. We have to kill him. Then the others will sell."

Inzio turned to Rubio. "You're sure your little love will agree?"

"I will persuade her," Rubio said.

"And the two brothers?" Inzio asked.

"They have no interest in vendetta," Rubio said. "Nicole has assured me."

"There is only one way," Portella said. "Kidnap Nicole and then lure Astorre out to rescue her."

Rubio protested, "Why not one of the brothers?"

"Because now Marcantonio is heavily guarded," Portella said. "And we can't fuck around with Valerius because army intelligence will come down on us, and they are a vicious bunch."

Tulippa turned to Rubio. "I will not hear any more of that bullshit from you. Why should we risk billions of dollars to go easy on your girlfriend?"

"It's just that we tried that trick before," Rubio said. "And remember, she has her bodyguard." He was being very careful. It would be disastrous for Tulippa to be angry with him.

"The bodyguard is no problem," Portella said.

"Well, I'll go along with you as long as Nicole doesn't get hurt," Rubio said.

special attention. But he had arranged for a limo for the night.

After the ball, the limo took her to the front of her apartment. Helene got out before her. But before they could enter her building, four men surrounded them. Helene bent down to her ankle holster, but she was too late. One of the men fired a bullet into her head, forcing her crown of flowers to bloom into blood.

At that moment another group of men came out of the shadows. Three of the attackers fled, and Astorre, who had discreetly followed Nicole to the ball, had her behind his back. The shooter of Helene had been disarmed.

"Get her out of here," Astorre said to one of the men. He held the gun on the killer and demanded, "OK, who sent you?"

The killer seemed unafraid. "Fuck you," he said.

Nicole saw Astorre's face go cold just before he fired a bullet into the man's chest. He strode closer and grabbed the man by the hair as he fell, then fired another bullet into his head. At that moment she saw what her father must have been. She vomited over Helene's body. Astorre turned to her with a regretful smile on his lips. Nicole could not look at him.

Astorre brought her up into her apartment. He instructed her on what to tell the police, that she had fainted as soon as Helene was shot and had seen nothing. When he left, she called the police.

The next day, after arranging an around-the-clock bodyguard for Nicole, Astorre flew to Sicily to meet with Grazziella and Bianco in Palermo. He followed his usual route, flying first down to Mexico and there boarding a private jet to Palermo, so there would be no record of his journey.

In Palermo he was met by Octavius Bianco, now so well groomed and elegant in the Palermo style that it was hard to remember him as a bearded and ferocious bandit. Bianco was delighted to see Astorre and embraced him with affection. They were driven out to Bianco's villa at the seashore.

"So you're in trouble in America," Bianco said in the villa's courtyard, which was decorated with statues of the old Roman Empire. "But I have some good news for you." Then he digressed to ask, "Your wound. Does it give you trouble?"

Astorre touched the gold chain. "No," he said. "It just ruined my singing voice. Now I'm a croaker instead of a tenor."

"Better a baritone than a soprano," Bianco said, laughing. "Italy has many tenors anyway. One less won't hurt. You are a true Mafioso, and that's what we need."

Astorre smiled and began to think of that day so

long ago when he went swimming. Now, instead of the sharp sting of betrayal, he only remembered how he felt when he woke up. He touched the amulet at his throat and said, "What's the good news?"

"I have made peace with the Corleonesi and Grazziella," Bianco said. "He was never involved in the killing of Don Aprile. He came into the syndicate afterward. But now he feels dissatisfied with Portella and Tulippa. He thinks they are too rash and bunglers besides. He disapproved of the attempt on the federal agent. And he also has enormous respect for you. He knows you from your service with me. He sees you as a remarkably hard man to kill. Now he wants to drop any previous vendettas with you and help you."

Astorre felt relief. His task would be easier if he did not have to worry about Grazziella.

"Tomorrow, meet us here at the villa," Bianco said.

"He trusts you that much?" Astorre asked.

"He must," Bianco said. "Because without me here in Palermo, he cannot rule Sicily. And we are more civilized today than when you were here last."

The next afternoon Michael Grazziella arrived at the villa, and Astorre noted he was dressed in the ultrarespectable mode of a Roman politician—

dark suit, white shirt, and dark tie. He was accompanied by two bodyguards dressed in a similar fashion. Grazziella was a small man, courteous, with a very soft voice—you would not have guessed he was responsible for the murders of high ranking anti-Mafia magistrates. He gripped Astorre's hand and said, "I have come here to help you as a token of my deep esteem for our friend Bianco. Please forget the past. We must begin again."

"Thank you," Astorre said. "It is my honor."

Grazziella motioned to the guards, and they walked out onto the beach.

"So Michael," Bianco said. "How can you help?"

Grazziella said, "Portella and Tulippa are too reckless for my taste. And Marriano Rubio is too dishonest. Whereas I find you a clever man and a qualified man. Also, Nello is my nephew, and I learned you spared him, no small thing. So there are my motives."

Astorre nodded. Beyond Grazziella, he saw the black-green waves of the Sicilian sea and glinting off them, the dull deadly rays of the Sicilian sun. He had a sudden feeling of nostalgia, and a pang because he knew he had to leave. All this was familiar to him as America could never be. He longed for the streets of Palermo, the sound of Italian voices, his own tongue in a language more natural to him than English. He returned his attention to Grazziella. "So what can you tell me?"

"The syndicate wants me to meet with them in America," Grazziella said. "I can inform you as to the whereabouts and the security. If you take drastic action, I can then give you refuge in Sicily, and if they try to extradite you, I have friends in Rome who can stop the process."

"You have that kind of power?" Astorre asked.

"Certainly," Grazziella said with a little shrug. "How could we exist otherwise? But you must not be too rash."

Astorre knew he was referring to Cilke. He smiled at Grazziella. "I would never do anything rash."

Grazziella smiled politely and said, "Your enemies are my enemies, and I pledge myself to your cause."

"I assume you will not be at the meeting," Astorre said.

Grazziella smiled at him again. "At the last moment I will be detained: I will not be present."

"And when will this be?" Astorre asked.

"Within a month," Grazziella said.

After Grazziella left, Astorre said to Bianco, "Really, tell me, why is he doing this?"

Bianco smiled at him in appreciation. "How easily you understand Sicily. All the reasons that he gave were valid. But there is a primary motive he did not mention." He hesitated. "Tulippa and Portella have been cheating him out of his correct share of the drug money, and he would soon have to go to war over that in any case. He could never tolerate that. He thinks highly of you, and it would be perfect if you wiped out his enemies and became his ally. He's a very clever man, Grazziella."

That evening Astorre walked along the beach and thought about what he should do. Finally the end of the war was coming.

Mr. Pryor had no worries about controlling the Aprile banks and defending them against the authorities. But when the FBI flooded New York following the assassination attempt on Cilke, he became a little concerned about what they would dig up. Especially after Cilke's visit.

In his early youth Mr. Pryor had been one of the prized assassins of the Palermo Mafia. But he had seen the light and gone into banking, where his natural charm, intelligence, and criminal connections ensured his success. In essence, he became a Mafia banker to the world. He was soon an expert in currency-rate storms and the stashing of black money. He also had a talent for buying legitimate businesses at good prices. Eventually he had emigrated to England because the fairness of the English system could better protect his wealth than the bribery in Italy.

However, his long arm still stretched out to
Palermo and the United States. And he was the
prime banker for Bianco's *cosca* in their control
of construction in Sicily. He also was the link
between the Aprile banks and Europe.

Now, with all the police activity, he was
reminded of a possible danger point: Rosie. She
could link Astorre to the Sturzo brothers. Also,
Mr. Pryor knew Astorre had a weak spot and still
took some comfort in Rosie's charms. This did not
make him respect Astorre any less; this weakness
in men had existed since the beginning of recorded
time. And Rosie was such a Mafioso girl. Who
could resist her? But as much as he admired the
girl, he did not think it wise to have her around.

So he decided to take a part in this affair as he
had once done in London. He knew he would not
win Astorre's approval for such an act—he knew
Astorre's character and did not underestimate his
dangerousness. But Astorre was always a reasonable man. Pryor would persuade him after the fact,
and Astorre would recognize the sagacity behind
the deed.

But it had to be done. So Mr. Pryor called Rosie
one evening. She was delighted to hear from him,
especially when he assured her he had good news.
When he hung up the phone he let out a sigh of
regret.

He took his two nephews with him as drivers
and bodyguards. He left one in the car outside the

building and took the other up with him to Rosie's apartment.

Rosie greeted them by running into Mr. Pryor's arms, startling his nephew, who made a motion inside his jacket.

She had made coffee and served a dish of pastries that she said were specially imported from Naples. They tasted nothing like it to Mr. Pryor, who considered himself to be an expert in such matters.

"Ah, you're such a sweet girl," Mr. Pryor said. To his nephew he said, "Here, try one." But the nephew had retreated into a corner of the room and sat in a chair to watch this little comedy his uncle was playing.

Rosie thumped Mr. Pryor's homburg lying beside him and said mischievously, "I like your English bowler better. You didn't look so stuck-up then."

"Ah," Mr. Pryor said with great good humor, "when one changes one's country, one must always change one's hat. And, my dear Rosie, I'm here to ask you a great favor."

He caught her slight hesitation before she clapped her hands in glee. "Oh, you know I will," she said. "I owe you so much." Mr. Pryor was softened by her sweetness, but what had to be done had to be done.

"Rosie," he said, "I want you to arrange your affairs so that tomorrow you can leave for Sicily, but just for a short time. Astorre is waiting for you there, and you must deliver some papers to him from me, in the strictest confidence. He misses you and wants to show you Sicily."

Rosie blushed. "He really wants to see me?"

"Of course," Mr. Pryor said.

The truth was that Astorre was on his way home from Sicily and would be in New York the following night. Rosie and Astorre would cross paths over the Atlantic Ocean in their separate planes.

Rosie now became businesslike as a form of coyness. "I can't get away so quickly," she said. "I'd need to get reservations, go to the bank, and a lot of other little things."

"Don't think me presumptuous," Mr. Pryor said. "But I've arranged everything."

He took a long white envelope from inside his jacket. "This is your plane ticket," he said. "First-class. And also ten thousand American dollars to do some last-minute shopping and for travel expenses. My nephew, sitting there dazzled in the corner, will pick you up in his limousine tomorrow morning. In Palermo you will be met by Astorre or one of his friends."

"I have to be back after a week," Rosie said. "I have to take some tests for my doctorate."

"Don't concern yourself," Mr. Pryor said. "You will not have to worry about missing your tests. I promise. Have I ever failed you?" His voice was sweetly avuncular. But he was thinking, what a pity that Rosie would never see America again.

They drank coffee and ate the pastries. The nephew again refused refreshments though Rosie begged him prettily. Their chat was interrupted when the phone rang. Rosie picked it up. "Oh, Astorre," she said. "Are you calling from Sicily? Mr. Pryor told me. He's sitting right here having coffee."

Mr. Pryor continued to sip his coffee calmly, but his nephew rose from his chair and then sat down again when Mr. Pryor gave him a commanding look.

Rosie was silent and looked questioningly at Mr. Pryor, who nodded at her reassuringly.

"Yes, he was arranging for me to meet you in Sicily for a week," Rosie said. She paused to listen. "Yes, of course I'm disappointed. I'm sorry you had to come back unexpectedly. So you want to talk to him? No? OK, I'll tell him." She hung up the phone.

"What a shame," she said to Mr. Pryor. "He had to come back early. But he wants you to wait here for him. He said about half an hour."

Mr. Pryor reached for another pastry. "Certainly," he said.

"He'll explain everything when he gets here," Rosie said. "More coffee?"

Mr. Pryor nodded, then sighed. "You would have had such a wonderful time in Sicily. Too bad." He imagined her burial in a Sicilian cemetery, how sad that would have been.

"Go down and wait in the car," he told his nephew.

The young man rose reluctantly, and Mr. Pryor made a shooing motion. Rosie let him out of the apartment. Then he gave Rosie his most concerned smile and asked, "Have you been happy these last years?"

Astorre had arrived a day early and been picked up by Aldo Monza at the small airport in New Jersey. He had, of course, traveled by private jet under a false passport. It was only on impulse that he had called Rosie, out of a desire to see her and spend a relaxing night with her. When Rosie told him that Mr. Pryor was in her apartment, his senses raced with the signals of danger. As for her trip to Sicily, he understood Mr. Pryor's plans immediately. He tried to control his anger. Mr. Pryor had wanted to do the right thing according to his experience. But it was too big a price to pay for safety.

When Rosie opened the door, she flew into his arms. Mr. Pryor rose from his chair, and Astorre went to him and embraced him. Mr. Pryor concealed his surprise—Astorre was not usually so affectionate.

Then, to Mr. Pryor's astonishment, Astorre said

363

to Rosie, "Go to Sicily tomorrow as we planned and I'll join you there in a few days. We'll have a great time."

"Great," Rosie said. "I've never been to Sicily."

Astorre said to Mr. Pryor, "Thanks for arranging everything."

Then he turned to Rosie again. "I can't stay," he said. "I'll see you in Sicily. Tonight I have some important business to do with Mr. Pryor. So start getting ready for your trip. And don't bring too many clothes; we can go shopping in Palermo."

"OK," Rosie said. She kissed Mr. Pryor on the cheek and gave Astorre a long embrace and a lingering kiss. Then she opened the door to let them out.

When the two men were out in the street, Astorre told Mr. Pryor, "Come with me to my car. Tell your nephews to go home—you won't need them tonight."

It was only then that Mr. Pryor felt a little nervous. "I was doing it for your own good," he said to Astorre.

In the backseat of Astorre's car, Monza driving, Astorre turned to Mr. Pryor. "Nobody appreciates you more than I do," he said. "But am I the chief or am I not?"

"Without question," Mr. Pryor said.

"It was a problem I have been meaning to address," Astorre said. "I recognize the danger and I'm glad you made me act. But I need her. We can take some risks. So here are my instructions. In Sicily, supply her with a luxurious house with servants. She can enroll at Palermo University. She will have a very generous allowance, and Bianco will introduce her to the best of Sicilian society. We will make her happy there, and Bianco can control any problem that may arise. I know you don't approve of my affection for her, but that's something I can't help. I count on her faults to help her be happy in Palermo. She has a weakness for money and pleasure, but who doesn't? So now I hold you responsible for her safety. No accidents."

"I'm very fond of the girl myself, as you know," Mr. Pryor said. "A truly Mafioso girl. Are you going back to Sicily?"

"No," Astorre said. "We have more important business."

CHAPTER
13

ONCE NICOLE gave the waiter her order, she focused intently on Marriano Rubio. She must deliver two important messages on this day, and she wanted to be certain she got both of them right.

Rubio had chosen the restaurant, a classy French bistro where waiters hovered nervously with tall varnished pepper mills and long straw baskets of crusty fresh bread. Rubio disliked the food, but he knew the maître d', so he was assured a good table in a quiet corner. He brought his women there often.

"You're quieter than usual tonight," he said, reaching across the table for her hand. Nicole felt a shiver run through her body. She realized that she hated him for having that power over her, and she pulled her hand away. "Are you all right?" he asked.

"It's been a difficult day," she said.

"Ah," he said with a sigh, "the price of working with snakes." Rubio had no regard for Nicole's law firm. "Why do you put up with them? Why don't you let me take care of you instead?"

Nicole wondered how many other women had fallen for his line and then thrown away their careers to be with him.

"Don't tempt me," she said flirtatiously.

This surprised Rubio, who knew Nicole was devoted to her career. But this was what he had hoped. "Let me take care of you," he repeated. "Besides, how many more corporations can you sue?"

One of the waiters opened a cold bottle of white wine, offered Rubio the cork to smell, and poured a small amount into an elegant crystal wineglass. Rubio tasted it and nodded. Then he turned his attention back to Nicole.

"I'd quit right now," she said, "but there are some pro bono cases I want to see through." She sipped her wine. "Lately, I've been thinking a lot about banking."

Rubio's eyes narrowed. "Well," he said, "lucky for you that banks run in the family."

"Yes," Nicole agreed, "but unfortunately my father didn't believe women were capable of running a business. So I have to stand by and watch my crazy cousin screw things up." She raised her head to look at him when she added, "By the way, Astorre thinks you're out to get him."

Rubio tried to look amused. "Really? And how would I accomplish this?"

"Oh, I don't know," Nicole said, annoyed. "Remember, this is a guy who sells macaroni for a living. He's got flour on the brain. He says you want to use the bank for money laundering and who knows what else. He even tried to convince me that you were trying to kidnap me." Nicole knew she had to be careful here. "But I can't believe that. I think Astorre is behind everything that's been happening. He knows that my brothers and I want to control the bank, so he's trying to make us paranoid. But we're tired of listening to him."

Rubio studied Nicole's face. He was proud of his ability to separate truth from fiction. In his years as a diplomat, he had been lied to by some of the most respected statesmen in the world. And now, as he looked deeply into Nicole's eyes, he determined she was telling him the absolute truth.

"Just how tired are you?" he asked.

"We're all exhausted," Nicole said.

Several waiters appeared and fussed over them for long minutes in order to deliver their main course. When the waiters had finally retreated, Nicole leaned toward Rubio and whispered,

"Most nights my cousin works late at his warehouse."

"What are you suggesting?" Rubio asked.

Nicole lifted her knife and began to slice her main course, dark medallions of duck swimming in a light shimmery orange sauce. "I'm not suggesting anything," she said. "But what is the controlling shareholder of an international bank doing spending all his time at a macaroni warehouse? If I had control, I'd be at the banks constantly, and I'd make sure my partners were getting a better return on their investment." With that, Nicole tasted her duck. She smiled at Rubio. "Delicious," she said.

Along with all her other qualities, Georgette Cilke was a very organized woman. Each Tuesday afternoon she volunteered exactly two hours of her time at the national headquarters of the Campaign Against the Death Penalty, where she helped answer the phone and reviewed pleas from lawyers of prisoners on death row. So Nicole knew exactly where to deliver her second important message of the day.

When Georgette saw Nicole walk into the office, her face brightened. She rose to embrace her friend. "Thank goodness," she said. "Today has been dreadful. I'm glad you're here. I can use the moral support."

"I don't know how much help I'm going to be," Nicole said. "I've got something troubling that I have to discuss with you."

In the years they had worked together, Nicole had never confided in Georgette before, though they maintained a warm professional relationship. Georgette never discussed her husband's work with anyone. And Nicole never saw the point in talking about her lovers with married women, who always thought they had to offer advice on how to get a man to the altar, which was not what she wanted. Nicole preferred talking about the raw sex, but she noticed that this made most married women uncomfortable. Maybe, Nicole thought, they didn't like hearing about what they were missing.

Georgette asked Nicole whether she wanted to talk in private, and when Nicole nodded, they found a small empty office down the hall.

"I've never discussed this with anyone," Nicole began. "But you must know that my father was Raymonde Aprile—the one known as Don Aprile. Have you heard of him?"

Georgette stood up and said, "I don't think I should be having this conversation with you—"

"Please sit down," Nicole interrupted. "You need to hear this."

Georgette looked uncomfortable but did as Nicole asked. In truth, she had always been curious about Nicole's family but knew she couldn't bring it up. Like many others, Georgette assumed Nicole, through her pro bono work, was trying to make up for the sins of her father. How frightening childhood must have been for Nicole, growing up in the shadow of criminals. And how embarrassing. Georgette thought of their own daughter, who was embarrassed to be seen with either of her parents in public. She wondered how Nicole had survived those years.

Nicole knew Georgette would never betray her husband in any way, but she also knew Georgette was a compassionate woman with an open mind. Someone who spent her free time as an advocate for convicted murderers. Now Nicole looked at her with a steady gaze and said, "My father was killed by men who have a close relationship with your husband. And my brothers and I have proof that your husband accepted bribes from these men."

Georgette's first reaction was shock, then disbelief. She said nothing. But it was only seconds before she felt the first clear flush of anger. "How dare you," she whispered. She looked Nicole squarely in eyes. "My husband would rather die than break the law."

Nicole was surprised by the intensity of Georgette's response. She could see now that Georgette truly believed in her husband. Nicole continued: "Your husband is not the man he seems to be. And I know how you feel. I just read my father's FBI file, but as much as I love him, I know he kept secrets from me. Just as Kurt is keeping secrets from you."

Then Nicole told Georgette about the million dollars Portella had wired into Cilke's bank account and about Portella's dealings with drug kingpins and hit men, who could only do their work with the tacit blessing of her husband. "I don't expect you to believe me," Nicole said. "All I hope is that you'll ask your husband whether I'm telling you the truth. If he's the man you say he is, he won't lie."

Georgette betrayed no hint of the turmoil she was feeling. "Why are you telling me this?"

"Because," Nicole said, "your husband has a vendetta against my family. He's going to allow his associates to murder my cousin Astorre and take over control of our family's banking business. It's going to happen tomorrow night at my cousin's macaroni warehouse."

At the mention of macaroni, Georgette laughed and said, "I don't believe you." Then she got up to leave. "I'm sorry, Nicole," she said. "I know you're upset, but we have nothing more to say to each other."

That night, in the sparsely decorated bedroom of the furnished ranch house where his family had been moved, Cilke faced his nightmare. He and his wife had finished dinner and were sitting across from each other, both of them reading. Suddenly, Georgette put down her book and said, "I need to talk to you about Nicole Aprile."

In all their years together, Georgette had never asked her husband to discuss his work. She didn't want the responsibility of keeping federal secrets. And she knew this was a part of his life Cilke needed to keep to himself. Sometimes, lying in bed next to him at night, she would wonder how he did his job—the tactics he used to get information, the pressure he must have to put on suspects. But in her mind she always pictured him as the ultimate federal agent, in his neatly pressed suit, with his thumbed-over copy of the Constitution tucked into his back pocket. In her heart she was smart enough to know this was a fantasy. Her husband was a determined man. He would go far to defeat his enemies. But this was a reality she never chose to examine.

Cilke had been reading a mystery novel—the third book in a series about a serial killer who raises his son to become a priest. When Georgette asked her question, he immediately closed the book. "I'm listening," he said.

"Nicole said some things today—about you and the investigation you're conducting," Georgette said. "I know you don't like to talk about your work, but she made some strong accusations."

Cilke felt the rage rising within him, until he was

in a blind fury. First they had killed his dogs. Then they had destroyed his home. And now they had tarnished his purest relationship. Finally, when his heart stopped racing, he asked Georgette in the calmest voice he could manage to tell him exactly what had happened.

Georgette repeated her entire conversation with Nicole and watched her husband's expression carefully as he absorbed the information. His face betrayed no hint of surprise or outrage. When she was finished, Cilke said, "Thank you, sweetheart. I'm sure it was very difficult for you to tell me. And I'm sorry you had to do it." Then he rose from his chair and walked toward the front door.

"Where are you going?" Georgette asked.

"I need some air," Cilke said. "I need to think."

"Kurt, honey?" Georgette's voice was questioning; she needed reassurance.

Cilke had sworn he would never lie to his wife. If she insisted on the truth, he would have to tell her and suffer the consequences. He was hoping she would understand and decide it was better to pretend these secrets did not exist.

"Is there anything you can tell me?" she asked.

He shook his head. "No," he said. "I would do anything for you. You know that, don't you?"

"Yes. But I need to know. For us and for our daughter."

Cilke saw there was no escape. He realized she would never look at him the same way again if he told her the truth. At that moment, he wanted to crush Astorre Viola's skull. He thought of what he could possibly say to his wife: I only accepted the bribes the FBI wanted me to? We overlooked the small crimes in order to focus on the big ones? We broke some laws to enforce more important ones? He knew these answers would only infuriate her, and he loved and respected her too much to do such a thing.

Cilke left the house without saying a word. When he returned, his wife pretended to be asleep. He made up his mind then. The following night he would confront Astorre Viola and reclaim his own vision of justice.

Aspinella Washington did not hate all men, but she was repeatedly surprised by just how many of them turned her off. They were all so . . . useless.

After she had taken care of Heskow, she was briefly interrogated by two officers in airport security, who were either too dumb or too intimidated to challenge her version of events. When the cops found $100,000 taped to Heskow's body, they figured his motive was obvious. They decided it was appropriate to reward themselves with a service fee for cleaning up the mess she'd made before the ambulance arrived. They also gave Aspinella a clump of blood-stained bills, which she added to the $30,000 Heskow had already given her.

She had only two uses for the money. She locked all but $3,000 in her safety deposit box. She had left instructions with her mother that if anything ever happened to her, all of the money in the box— over $300,000 in payoffs—should be put in a trust for her daughter. With the remaining $3,000, she took a cab to Fifth Avenue and Fifty-third Street, where she entered the fanciest leather-goods store in the city and took an elevator to a private suite on the third floor.

A woman wearing designer glasses and a navy pinstripe suit took her payment and escorted her down the hall, where she bathed in a tub filled with fragrant oils imported from China. She soaked herself for about twenty minutes and listened to a CD of Gregorian chants while she waited for Rudolfo, a licensed sexual-massage therapist.

Rudolfo received $3,000 for a two-hour session, which, he was delighted to point out to his very satisfied customers, was more than even the most famous lawyers received per hour. "The difference," he said with a Bavarian accent and a sly grin, "is that they just fuck you over. I fuck you over the moon."

Aspinella had heard about Rudolfo during an undercover vice investigation she conducted in the city's elite hotels. One concierge was worried that he might be asked to testify, so in exchange for not being summoned, he gave her the tip about Rudolfo. Aspinella thought about making the bust, but once she met Rudolfo and experienced one of his massages, she felt it would be an even bigger crime to deny women the pleasure of his extraordinary talents.

After several minutes he knocked on the door and asked, "May I come in?"

"I'm counting on it, baby," she said.

He walked in and looked her over. "Great eye patch," he said.

During her first session, Aspinella had been surprised when Rudolfo entered the room naked, but he had said, "Why bother getting dressed just to get undressed?" He was an extraordinary specimen, tall and taut, with a tattoo of a tiger on his right biceps and a silken mat of blond hair on his chest. She particularly liked the chest hair, which separated Rudolfo from those magazine models who'd been plucked, shaved, and greased so carefully you couldn't tell whether they were male or female.

"How have you been?" he asked.

"You don't wanna hear about it," Aspinella said. "All you need to know is that I need some sexual healing."

Rudolfo began with her back, pressing deep, honing in on all her knots. Then he gently kneaded her neck before turning her over and lightly massaging her breasts and stomach. By the time he began to caress between her legs, she was already moist and breathing hard.

"Why can't other men do this to me?" Aspinella said with a sigh of ecstasy.

Rudolfo was about to begin the premium part of the service, his tongue massage, which he did expertly and with remarkable stamina. But he was struck by her question, which he had heard many times. It always amazed him. It seemed to him that the city was exploding with sexually under-nourished women.

"It's a mystery to me, why other men can't do it," he said. "What do you think?"

She hated to interrupt her sexual reverie, but she could tell Rudolfo needed pillow talk before the grand finale. "Men are weak," she said. "We're the ones who make all the important decisions. When to get married. When to have kids. We rein them in and hold them accountable for the things they do."

Rudolfo smiled politely. "But what does that have to do with sex?"

Aspinella wanted him to get back to work. "I don't know," she said. "It's just a theory."

Rudolfo began to massage her again—slowly, steadily, rhythymically. He never seemed to tire. And each time he brought her to great heights of pleasure, she imagined the terrible depths of pain to which she would bring Astorre Viola and his gang of thugs the following night.

The Viola Macaroni Company was located in a

large brick warehouse on the Lower East Side of Manhattan. More than one hundred people worked there, unloading giant burlap bags of imported Italian macaroni onto a conveyor belt, which then automatically sorted and boxed it.

A year before, inspired by a magazine article he'd read about how small businesses were improving their operations, Astorre had hired a consultant straight out of Harvard Business School to recommend changes. The young man told Astorre to double his prices, change the brand name of his macaroni to Uncle Vito's Homemade Pasta, and fire half of his employees, who could be replaced by temporary help at half the price. At that suggestion Astorre fired the consultant.

Astorre's office was on the main floor, which was roughly the size of a football field, lined with shiny stainless steel machines on both sides. The back of the warehouse opened to a loading dock. Video cameras had been placed outside the entrances and inside the factory, so he could keep track of visitors and monitor production from his office. Normally, the warehouse closed down at 6:00 P.M., but on this night Astorre had retained five of his most qualified employees and Aldo Monza. He was waiting.

The night before, when Astorre had told Nicole his plan at her apartment, she was adamantly opposed to it. She shook her head violently. "First of all, it won't work. And second, I don't want to be an accessory to murder."

"They killed your assistant and they tried to kidnap you," Astorre said quietly. "We're all in danger, unless I take action." Nicole thought of Helene, and then she remembered her many dinner-table arguments with her father, who would certainly have sought vengeance. Her father would have said that she owed this to the memory of her friend, and he would have reminded her that it was reasonable and necessary to take precautions to protect the family.

"Why don't we go to the authorities?" she asked.

Astorre's response was curt: "It's too late for that."

Now Astorre sat in his office, live bait. Thanks to Grazziella, he knew that Portella and Tulippa were in the city for a meeting of the syndicate. He couldn't be sure that Nicole's leak to Rubio would force them to pay a visit, but he hoped they might try one last attempt at persuading him to turn over the banks before resorting to violence. He assumed they would check him for weapons, so he didn't arm himself, except for a stiletto, which he stored in a special pocket sewn into his shirtsleeve.

Astorre was carefully watching his video monitor when he saw a half dozen men enter the back of the building from the loading dock. He had given his own men instructions to hide and not to attack until he gave them the signal.

He studied the screen and recognized Portella and Tulippa among the six. Then, as they faded off the monitor, he heard the sound of footsteps approaching his office. If they had already decided to kill him, Monza and his crew were at the ready and would be able to save him.

But then Portella called out to him.

He didn't answer.

Within seconds Portella and Tulippa paused at the door.

"Come in," Astorre said with a warm smile. He stood to shake their hands. "What a surprise. I hardly ever get visitors at this hour. Is there something I can do for you?"

"Yeah," Portella cracked. "We're having a big dinner and we ran out of macaroni."

Astorre waved his hands magnanimously and said, "My macaroni, your macaroni."

"How about your banks?" Tulippa asked ominously.

Astorre was ready for this. "It's time we talked seriously. It's time we did business. But first I'd like to give you a tour of the plant. I'm very proud of it."

Tulippa and Portella exchanged a confused look. They were wary. "OK, but let's keep it short," Tulippa said, wondering how such a clown had been able to survive this long.

Astorre led them to the floor. The four men who

had accompanied them were standing nearby. Astorre greeted them warmly, shaking hands with each of them and complimenting them on their dress.

Astorre's own men were watching him carefully, waiting for his command to strike. Monza had stationed three shooters on a mezzanine overlooking the floor, hidden from view. The others had fanned out to opposite sides of the warehouse.

Long minutes passed as Astorre showed his guests through the warehouse. Then Portella finally said, "It's clear that this is really where your heart is. Why don't you let us run the banks? We will make you one more offer and cut you in for a percentage."

Astorre was about to give his men the signal to shoot. But suddenly he heard a rattle of gunshots and saw three of his men fall twenty feet from the mezzanine and land facedown on the concrete floor in front of him. He scanned the warehouse, looking for Monza, as he quickly slipped behind a huge packaging machine.

From there he saw a black woman with a green eye patch sprint toward them and grab Portella by the neck. She jabbed him in his protruding belly with her assault rifle, then she pulled out a revolver and threw the rifle to the ground.

"OK," Aspinella Washington said. "Everybody drop your weapons. Now." When no one moved, she did not hesitate. She grabbed Portella by the neck, turned him around, and fired two bullets into his stomach. As he doubled over, she slammed her revolver down on his head and kicked him in the teeth.

Then she grabbed Tulippa and said, "You're next unless everybody does what I say. This is an eye for an eye, you bastard."

Portella knew that without help, he would only live for a few more minutes. His vision was already beginning to fade. He was sprawled across the floor, breathing heavily, his florid shirt soaked with blood. His mouth was numb. "Do what she says," he groaned weakly.

Portella's men obeyed.

He had always heard that being shot in the stomach was the most painful way to die. Now he knew why. Every time he took a deep breath, he felt like he had been stabbed in the heart. He lost control of his bladder, his urine making a dark stain on his new blue trousers. He tried to focus his eyes on the shooter, a muscular black woman he didn't recognize. He tried to utter the words "Who are you?" but he couldn't find the breath. His final thought was an oddly sentimental one: he wondered who would tell his brother Bruno that he was dead.

It took Astorre only a moment to figure out what had happened. He had never before seen Detective Aspinella Washington, except in newspaper photos and on TV news shows. But he knew if she had discovered him, she must have gotten to Heskow first. And Heskow must certainly be dead. Astorre did not mourn for the slippery bagman. Heskow had the great flaw of being a man who would say or do anything to stay alive. It was good that he was now in the ground with his flowers.

Tulippa had no idea why this angry bitch was holding a gun to his neck. He had trusted Portella to handle the security and given his own loyal bodyguards the night off. A stupid mistake. America is such a strange country, he thought to himself. You never know where the next violence is coming from.

As Aspinella dug the nozzle of the gun deep into his skin, Tulippa made a promise to himself that if he escaped and could return to South America, he would speed up production of his nuclear arsenal. He would personally do everything he could to blow up as much of this America as possible, especially Washington, D.C., an arrogant capital of lazy bullies in armchairs, and New York City, where they seemed to breed crazy people like this one-eyed bitch.

"All right," Aspinella said to Tulippa. "You offered us half a mil to take care of this guy." She pointed to Astorre. "It would be my pleasure to accept the job, but since my accident I've had to double my fee. With only one eye, I have to concentrate twice as hard."

*

Kurt Cilke had been staking out the warehouse throughout the day. Sitting in his blue Chevy with nothing but a pack of gum and a copy of *Newsweek,* he waited for Astorre to make his move.

He had come alone, not wanting to involve any other federal agents in what he believed might be the end of his career. When he saw Portella and Tulippa enter the building, he felt the bile rising in his stomach. And he realized what a clever foe Astorre was. If, as Cilke suspected, Portella and Tulippa attacked Astorre, Cilke would have a legal duty to protect him. Astorre would be free and would clear his name without breaking his silence. And Cilke would blow years of hard work.

But when Cilke saw Aspinella Washington storm into the building toting an assault rifle, he felt something different—cold fear. He had heard about Aspinella's role in the airport shooting. It sounded suspicious to him. Just didn't add up.

He checked the ammunition in his revolver and felt a distant hope that he would be able to count on her for help. Before leaving the car, Cilke decided it was time to inform the Bureau. On his cell phone, he dialed Boxton.

"I'm outside Astorre Viola's warehouse," Cilke told him. Then he heard the sound of rapid gunfire. "I'm going in now, and if things go wrong, I want you to tell the director I was acting on my own. Are you recording this call?"

Boxton paused, not sure whether Cilke would appreciate being taped. But ever since Cilke had become a target, all of his calls were being monitored. "Yes," he said.

"Good," Cilke responded. "For the record, neither you nor anyone else within the FBI is responsible for what I'm going to do now. I am entering a hostile situation involving three reputed organized-crime figures and one renegade New York City cop who is heavily armed."

Boxton interrupted Cilke. "Kurt, wait for backup."

"There isn't time," Cilke said. "And besides, this is my mess. I'll clean it up." He thought of leaving a message for Georgette, but he decided that would be too morbid and self-indulgent. Better to let his actions speak for themselves. He hung up the phone without saying anything more. As he left the car, he noticed he was illegally parked.

The first thing Cilke saw when he entered the warehouse was Washington's gun digging into Tulippa's neck. Everyone in the room was silent. No one moved.

"I am a federal officer," Cilke announced, waving his gun upward. "Lay all your weapons down."

Aspinella turned to Cilke and spoke with derision: "I know who the fuck you are. This is my bust. Go collar some accountants or stockbrokers or whatever the hell it is you suits spend your pansy-ass time on. This is an NYPD matter."

"Detective," Cilke said calmly, "drop your weapon now. If you don't, I will use force if necessary. I have reason to believe you are part of a racketeering conspiracy."

Aspinella had not counted on this. From the look in Cilke's eyes and the steadiness of his voice, she knew he would not back down. But she was not about to give in, not as long as she had a gun in her hand. Cilke probably hadn't fired on anyone in years, she thought. "You think I'm part of a conspiracy?" she yelled. "Well, I think *you're* part of a conspiracy. I think you've been taking bribes from this piece of shit for years." She jabbed Tulippa again with the gun. "Isn't that right, *señor*?"

At first Tulippa didn't say anything, but when Aspinella kneed him in the groin, he folded and nodded.

"How much?" Aspinella asked him.

"Over a million dollars," Tulippa gasped.

Cilke controlled his fury and said, "Each dollar they wired into my account was monitored by the FBI. This is a federal investigation, Detective Washington." He took a deep breath, counting down, before he told her, "This is my final warning. Put down your weapon or I'll fire."

Astorre coolly watched them. Aldo Monza was standing unnoticed behind another of the machines. Astorre saw a twitch in Aspinella's face.

Then, as if it were happening in slow motion, he saw her slip behind Tulippa and fire at Cilke. But as soon as she fired, Tulippa broke free and dove to the ground, pushing her off balance.

Cilke had been hit in the chest. But he fired once at Aspinella and saw her stagger backward, blood spurting from below her right shoulder. Neither had been shooting to kill. They were following their training to the very end, aiming for the widest part of the body. But as Aspinella felt the searing pain of the bullet and saw its damage, she knew it was time to forget procedure. She took aim between Cilke's eyes. She fired four times. Each bullet hit its mark until Cilke's nose was a flattened pulp of cartilage and she could see chunks of his brain splattered on what was left of his forehead.

Tulippa saw that Aspinella was wounded and reeling. He tackled her and elbowed her in the face, knocking her out cold. But before he had a chance to grab her gun, Astorre came out from behind the machine and kicked it across the room. Then he stood over Tulippa and gallantly offered his hand.

Tulippa accepted it and Astorre pulled him up. Meanwhile, Monza and the surviving members of his team rounded up the rest of Portella's men and tied them to steel support beams of the warehouse. No one touched Cilke and Portella.

"So," Astorre said, "I believe we have some business to finish."

Tulippa was puzzled. Astorre was a mass of

contradictions—a friendly adversary, a singing assassin. Could such a wild card ever be trusted?

Astorre walked to the center of the warehouse and signaled Tulippa to follow. When he reached an open space, he stopped and faced the South American. "You killed my uncle and you tried to steal our banks. I should not even waste my breath on you." Then Astorre pulled out the stiletto, its silver blade flashing, and showed it to Tulippa. "I should just slice your throat and be done with it. But you are weak, and there is no honor in butchering a defenseless old man. So I'll give you a fighting chance."

With those words and an almost imperceptible nod toward Monza, Astorre raised both of his hands, as if in surrender, dropped his knife, and took several steps back. Tulippa was older and bulkier than Astorre, but he had carved rivers of blood in his lifetime. He was an extremely qualified man with a knife. Still, he was no match for Astorre.

Tulippa picked up the stiletto and began to move toward Astorre. "You are a stupid and reckless man," he said. "I was ready to accept you as a partner." He lunged at Astorre several times, but Astorre was quicker and evaded him. When Tulippa stopped momentarily to catch his breath, Astorre removed the gold medallion from his neck and threw it to the ground, exposing the purple scar in his throat. "I want this to be the last thing you see before you die."

Tulippa was transfixed by the wound, a shade of purple he had never seen. And before he knew it, Astorre kicked the stiletto out of his hand and with rapid precision kneed Tulippa in the back, put him in a headlock, and snapped his neck. Everyone heard the crack.

Without pausing to look at his victim, Astorre picked up his medallion, placed it back on his throat, and left the building.

Five minutes later a squadron of FBI cars arrived at the Viola Macaroni Company. Aspinella Washington, still alive, was taken to the intensive care unit of the hospital.

When the FBI officers had completed their study of the silent videotape recorded by the cameras Monza had run, they determined that Astorre, who had raised his hands and dropped his knife, had acted in self-defense.

NICOLE SLAMMED down the phone and yelled to her secretary, "I am sick of hearing about how weak the damn Eurodollar is. See if you can track down Mr. Pryor. He's probably on the ninth hole of some golf course."

Two years had passed, and Nicole had taken over as head of the Aprile banks. When Mr. Pryor was ready to retire, he had insisted she was the best person for the job. She was a skilled corporate fighter who wouldn't fold under pressure from bank regulators and demanding customers.

Today Nicole was frantically trying to clear her desk. Later that night she and her brothers would fly to Sicily for a family celebration with Astorre. But before she could go, she had to deal with Aspinella Washington, who was waiting to hear whether Nicole would represent her in an appeal to avoid the death penalty. The thought of it filled her with dread, and not just because she had a full-time job.

At first, when Nicole had offered to run the banks, Astorre had hesitated, remembering the Don's final wishes. But Mr. Pryor convinced him that Nicole was her father's daughter. Whenever a big loan was due, the bank could count on her to deploy a potent combination of sweet talk and veiled intimidation. She knew how to get results.

Nicole's intercom buzzed, and Mr. Pryor greeted her in his courtly manner: "What can I do for you, my dear?"

"We're getting killed on these exchange rates," she said. "What do you think of moving more heavily into Deutsche Marks?"

"I think that's an excellent idea," Mr. Pryor said.

"You know," Nicole said, "all of this currency trading is about as logical as going to Vegas and playing baccarat all day."

Mr. Pryor laughed. "That may be true, but baccarat losses aren't guaranteed by the Federal Reserve."

When Nicole hung up, she sat for a moment and reflected on the bank's progress. Since taking over, she had acquired six more banks in booming countries and doubled corporate profits. But she was even more pleased that the bank was providing larger loans to new businesses in developing parts of the world.

She smiled to herself as she remembered her first day.

As soon as her new stationery had arrived, Nicole had drafted a letter to Peru's finance minister demanding repayment of all of the government's overdue loans. As she expected, this produced an economic crisis in the country, resulting in political turmoil and a change of government. The new party demanded the resignation of Peru's consul general to the United Nations, Marriano Rubio.

In the months that followed, Nicole was delighted to read that Rubio had declared personal bankruptcy. He was also involved in fighting a series of complicated lawsuits with Peruvian investors who had bankrolled one of his many ventures—a failed theme park. Rubio had vowed it would become "the Latino Disneyland," but all he had been able to attract was a Ferris wheel and a Taco Bell.

The case, which the tabloids dubbed the Macaroni Massacre, had become an international incident. As soon as Aspinella Washington recovered from the wound inflicted by Cilke's gunshot—a punctured lung—she had made a series of pronouncements to the media. While awaiting her trial, she portrayed herself as a martyr on the scale of Joan of Arc. She sued the FBI for attempted murder, slander, and violation of her civil rights. She also sued the New York Police Department for back pay she was owed while under suspension.

Despite her protestations, it had taken the jury only three hours of deliberation to convict her. When the guilty verdict was announced, Aspinella fired her attorneys and petitioned the Campaign Against the Death Penalty for representation. Demonstrating further flair for publicity, she demanded that Nicole Aprile take her case. From her cell on death row, Aspinella told the press, "Her cousin got me into this, so now she can get me out."

At first Nicole refused to meet with Aspinella, saying that any good lawyer would rescue herself from such an obvious conflict of interest. But then Aspinella accused Nicole of racism, and Nicole— not wanting bad blood with minority lenders— agreed to see her.

The day of their meeting, Nicole had to wait twenty minutes while Aspinella greeted a small congress of foreign dignitaries. They hailed Aspinella as a brave warrior against America's barbaric penal code. Finally Aspinella gave Nicole the signal to approach the glass window. She had taken to wearing a yellow eye patch stitched with the word FREEDOM.

Nicole launched into all of her reasons for wanting to turn down the case and concluded by pointing out that she had represented Astorre in his testimony against her.

Aspinella listened carefully, twirling her new dreadlocks. "I hear you," she said, "but there's a lot you don't know. Astorre was right: I am guilty of the crimes I've been convicted of, and I will spend the rest of my life atoning for them. But please, help me live long enough to begin to make whatever amends I can."

At first Nicole figured this was just another one of Aspinella's ploys to gain sympathy, but there was something in her voice that moved Nicole. She still believed that no human being had the right to condemn another to death. She still believed in redemption. She felt Aspinella deserved a defense, just as every death row inmate did. She just wished she didn't have to handle this one.

Before Nicole could make a final decision, she knew there was one person she had to face.

After the funeral, at which Cilke had received a hero's burial, Georgette had requested a meeting with the director. An FBI escort picked her up from the airport and took her to Bureau head-quarters.

When she entered the director's office, he wrapped her in a hug and promised that the

Bureau would do everything necessary to help her
and her daughter cope with their loss.

"Thank you," Georgette said. "But that's not
why I came. I need to know why my husband was
killed."

The director paused quite a while before
speaking. He knew she had heard rumors. And
those rumors could pose a threat to the Bureau's
image. He needed to reassure her. Finally, he said,
"I'm embarrassed to admit that we even needed to
mount an investigation. Your husband was a
paragon of what an FBI man should be. He was
devoted to his work, and he followed every law to
the letter. I know he never would have done anything to compromise the Bureau or his family."

"Then why did he go to that warehouse alone?"
Georgette asked. "And what was his relationship
with Portella?"

The director followed the talking points he had
practiced with his staff prior to the meeting. "Your
husband was a great investigator. He had earned
the freedom and respect to follow his own leads.
We don't believe he ever took a bribe or crossed
the line with Portella or anyone else. His results
speak volumes. He's the man who broke up the
Mafia."

As she left his office, Georgette realized that
she didn't believe him. She knew that in order to
find any peace, she would have to believe the
truth she felt in her heart: that her husband,

despite his zeal, was as good a man as she would ever know.

After the murder of her husband, Georgette Cilke continued to volunteer at the New York headquarters of the Campaign Against the Death Penalty, but Nicole had not seen her since their fateful conversation. Because of her responsibilities at the bank, Nicole had said she was too busy for the Campaign. The truth was, she could not bear to face Georgette.

Even so, when Nicole walked through the door, Georgette greeted her with a warm embrace. "I've missed you," she said.

"I'm sorry I haven't been in touch," Nicole responded. "I tried to write you a condolence letter, but I couldn't find the words."

Georgette nodded and said, "I understand."

"No," Nicole said, her throat tightening, "you don't understand. I deserve some of the blame for what happened to your husband. If I hadn't spoken to you that afternoon—"

"It still would have happened," Georgette cut in. "If it hadn't been your cousin, it would have been someone else. Something like this was bound to happen sooner or later. Kurt knew it and so did I." Georgette hesitated only a moment before she added, "The important thing now is that we remember his goodness. So let's not talk any more about the past. I'm sure we all have regrets."

Nicole wished it were that easy. She took a deep breath. "There's more. Aspinella Washington wants me to represent her."

Though Georgette tried to hide it, Nicole saw her flinch at the mention of Aspinella's name. Georgette was not a religious woman, but at this moment she was certain God was testing her powers of conviction. "OK," she said, biting her lip.

"OK?" Nicole asked, surprised. She had hoped Georgette would object, forbid it, and that Nicole would be able to refuse Aspinella out of loyalty to her friend. Nicole could hear her father telling her, "There would be honor in such loyalty."

"Yes," Georgette said, closing her eyes. "You should defend her."

Nicole was amazed. "I don't have to do this. Everyone will understand."

"That would be hypocritical," Georgette said. "A life is sacred or it isn't. We can't adjust what we believe just because it causes us pain."

Georgette became silent and extended her hand to Nicole to say good-bye. There was no hug this time.

After replaying that conversation in her mind all day, Nicole finally phoned Aspinella and, with reluctance, accepted the case. In one hour Nicole would be leaving for Sicily.

*

The following week Georgette sent a note to the coordinator of the Campaign Against the Death Penalty. She wrote that she and her daughter were moving to another city to start a new life and that she wished everyone well. She did not leave a forwarding address.

Astorre had kept his vow to Don Aprile, to save the banks and ensure the well-being of his family. In his own mind he was now free of any obligations.

The week after he had been cleared of all wrongdoing in the warehouse murders, he met with Don Craxxi and Octavius Bianco in his warehouse office and told them about his desire to return to Sicily. He explained that he felt a longing for the land itself, that it had insinuated itself into his dreams for many years. He had many happy memories of his childhood at Villa Grazia, the country retreat of Don Aprile, and he had always hoped to return. It was a simpler life but a richer one in many ways.

It was then that Bianco told him, "You do not have to return to Villa Grazia. There is a vast property that belongs to you in Sicily. The entire village of Castellammare del Golfo."

Astorre was puzzled. "How can that be?"

Benito Craxxi told him of the day the great Mafia chief, Don Zeno, had called his three friends to his bedside as he lay dying. "You are the young boy of his heart and soul," he said. "And now you are his only surviving heir. The village has been bequeathed to you by your natural father. It is your birthright.

"When Don Aprile took you to America, Don Zeno left provisions for all those in his village, until the day you would come to claim it. We provided protection for the village after your father's death, according to his wishes. When the farmers suffered a bad season, we offered the means to purchase fruits and grains to plant—a helping hand."

"Why didn't you tell me before?" Astorre asked.

"Don Aprile swore us to secrecy," Bianco said. "Your father wanted your safety and Don Aprile wanted you as part of his family. He also needed you to protect his children. In truth, you had two fathers. You are blessed."

Astorre landed in Sicily on a beautiful sun-filled day. Two of Michael Grazziella's bodyguards met him at the airport and escorted him to a dark blue Mercedes.

As they drove through Palermo, Astorre marveled at the beauty of the city: marble columns and ornate carvings of mythic figures made some buildings Greek temples, others Spanish cathedrals with saints and angels carved deep into the gray stone. The descent into Castellammare del Golfo took over two hours on a rocky, single-lane road. To Astorre as always, the most striking thing about Sicily was the beauty of the countryside, with its breathtaking view of the Mediterranean Sea.

The village, in a deep valley surrounded by mountains, was a labyrinth of cobblestone, lined with small, two-story stucco houses. Astorre noticed several people peeking through the cracks of the painted white shutters pulled shut against the scorching midday sun.

He was greeted by the mayor of the village, a short man in peasant clothes who introduced himself as Leo DiMarco and bowed with respect. "Il Padrone," he said. "Welcome."

Astorre, uncomfortable, smiled and asked in Sicilian, "Would you please take me through the village?"

They passed a few old men playing cards on wooden benches. On the far side of the piazza was a stately Catholic church. And it was into this church, Saint Sebastian's, that the mayor first took Astorre, who had not said a formal prayer since the murder of Don Aprile. Astorre knelt, head bowed, to be blessed by Father Del Vecchio, the village priest.

Afterward, Mayor DiMarco led Astorre to the small house in which he would stay. Along the way, Astorre noticed several *carabinieri,* or Italian National Police, leaning against the houses, with rifles at the ready. "Once night falls, it is safer to stay in the village," the mayor explained. "But during the days, it is a joy to be in the fields."

For the next few days Astorre took long walks through the countryside, fresh with the scent of the orange and lemon orchards. His primary purpose was to meet the villagers and explore the ancient stone-carved houses built like Roman villas. He wanted to find one he could make his home.

By the third day he knew he would be happy there. The usual wary and solemn villagers greeted him in the street, and as he sat in the café in the piazza, the old men and children teased him playfully.

There were only two more things he must do.

The following morning Astorre asked the mayor to show him the way to the village cemetery.

"For what purpose?" DiMarco asked.

"To pay my respects to my father and my mother," Astorre replied.

DiMarco nodded and quickly grabbed a large wrought-iron key from the office wall.

"How well did you know my father?" Astorre asked him.

DiMarco quickly made the sign of the cross on his chest. "Who did not know Don Zeno? It is to him we owe our lives. He saved our children with expensive medicines from Palermo. He protected our village from looters and bandits."

"But what was he like as a man?" Astorre asked.

DiMarco shrugged. "There are few people left who knew him in that way, and even fewer who will speak to you about him. He has become a legend. So who would wish to know the real man?"

I would, Astorre thought.

They walked through the countryside and then climbed a steep hill, with DiMarco stopping occasionally to catch his breath. Finally, Astorre saw the cemetery. But instead of gravestones, there were rows of small stone buildings. Mausoleums, all surrounded by a high, cast-iron fence, which was locked at a gate. The sign above read: WITHIN THESE GATES, ALL ARE INNOCENT.

The mayor unlocked the gate and led Astorre to his father's gray marble mausoleum, marked by the epitaph VINCENZO ZENO: A GOOD AND GENEROUS MAN. Astorre entered the building and on the altar studied the picture of his father. It was the first time he'd seen a picture of him, and he was struck by how familiar his face looked.

DiMarco then took Astorre to another small building, several rows away. This stone was white marble, the only hint of color a light blue raiment of the Virgin Mary carved into the arch of the entrance. Astorre walked in and examined the picture. The girl was not more than twenty-two years old, but her wide green eyes and radiant smile warmed him.

Outside, he said to DiMarco, "When I was a

boy, I used to dream of a woman like her, but I thought she was an angel."

DiMarco nodded. "She was a beautiful girl. I remember her from church. And you're right. She sang like an angel."

Astorre rode bareback across the countryside, only stopping long enough to eat the fresh goat-milk cheese and crusty bread that one of the village women had packed.

Finally, he reached Corleone. He could no longer put off seeing Michael Grazziella. He owed the man at least that courtesy.

He was tan from all his time in the fields, and Grazziella greeted him with open arms and a crushing bear hug. "The Sicilian sun has been good to you," he said.

Astorre struck the proper note of gratitude: "Thank you for everything. Especially your support."

Grazziella walked with him toward his villa. "And what brings you to Corleone?"

"I think you know why I'm here," Astorre replied.

Grazziella smiled. "A strong young man like yourself? Of course! And I will take you to her right away. She is a joy to behold, this Rose of yours. And she has brought pleasure to everyone she has met."

Knowing of Rosie's sexual appetite, Astorre wondered for just a moment if Grazziella was trying to tell him something. But he quickly caught himself. Grazziella was far too proper to say such a thing, and too Sicilian to allow such impropriety to occur under his watchful eye.

Her villa was only minutes away. When they reached it, Grazziella called out, "Rose, my dear, you have a visitor."

She was wearing a simple blue sundress with her blonde hair tied back at the neck. Without her makeup, she looked younger and more innocent than he remembered.

She stopped when she saw him, surprised. But then she cried out, "Astorre!" She ran to him, kissed him, and began talking excitedly. "I've already learned to speak the Sicilian dialect fluently. And I've learned some famous recipes, too. Do you like spinach gnocchi?"

He took her to Castellammare del Golfo and spent the next week showing her around his village and the countryside. Each day they swam, talked for hours, and made love to each other with the comfort that only comes with time.

Astorre watched Rosie carefully to see if she was getting bored with him or restless with the simple life. But she seemed truly at peace. He wondered if, after all they'd been through together, he could ever really trust her. And then he wondered whether it was smart to love any woman so much that you would trust her completely. He and Rosie both had secrets to protect—things he did not wish to remember or share. But Rosie knew him and still loved him. She would keep his secrets, and he would keep hers.

There was only one thing that still troubled him. Rosie had a weakness for money and fancy gifts. Astorre wondered if she would ever be satisfied with what any one man could offer her. He needed to know.

On their last day together in Corleone, Astorre and Rosie rode their horses through the hills, flying over the countryside until dusk. Then they stopped in a vineyard, where they picked grapes and fed each other.

"I can't believe I've stayed so long," Rosie said as they rested together in the grass.

Astorre's green eyes glistened intensely. "Do you think you could stay a little longer?"

Rosie looked surprised. "What did you have in mind?"

Astorre got down on one knee and extended his hand. "Maybe fifty or sixty years," he said with a sincere smile. In his palm was a simple bronze ring.

"Will you marry me?" he asked.

Astorre looked for some sign of hesitation in Rosie's eyes, some mild disappointment with the quality of the ring, but her response was immediate. She threw her arms around his neck and showered him with kisses. Then they fell to the ground and rolled together in the hills.

One month later, Astorre and Rosie were married in one of his citrus groves. Father Del Vecchio performed the ceremony. Everyone from both villages attended. The hill was carpeted with purple wisteria, and the smell of lemons and oranges perfumed the air. Astorre was dressed in a white peasant suit, and Rosie wore a pink gown of silk.

There was a pig on a spit roasting over red coals and warm ripe tomatoes from the fields. There were hot loaves of bread and freshly made cheese. Homemade wine ran like a river.

When the ceremony was over and they had exchanged vows, Astorre serenaded his bride with his favorite ballads. There was so much drinking and dancing that the festivities lasted until sunrise.

The following morning, when Rosie awakened, she saw Astorre readying their horses. "Ride with me?" he asked.

They journeyed all day until Astorre found what he was looking for—Villa Grazia. "My uncle's secret paradise. I spent my happiest times here as a child."

He walked behind the house to the garden, with

407

Rosie following. And finally they came upon his olive tree, the one that had grown from the pit he planted as a young boy. The tree was as tall as he was now, and the trunk was quite thick. He took a sharp blade from his pocket and grabbed one of the branches. Then he cut it from the tree.

"We will plant this in our garden. So when we have a child, he will have happy memories too."

One year later, Astorre and Rosie celebrated the birth of their son, Raymonde Zeno. And when it came time to baptize him, they invited Astorre's family to join them at the Church of Saint Sebastian.

After Father Del Vecchio had finished, Valerius, as the eldest of the Aprile children, lifted a glass of wine and made a toast. "May you all thrive and live joyfully. And may your son grow up with the passion of Sicily and the romance of America beating in his heart."

Marcantonio lifted his glass and added, "And if he ever wants to be on a sitcom, you know who to call."

Now that the Aprile banks were so profitable, Marcantonio had established a twenty-million-dollar line of credit to develop his own dramatic properties. He and Valerius were working together on a project based on their father's FBI files. Nicole thought it was a terrible idea, but they all agreed that the Don would have appreciated the idea of receiving large sums of money for dramatizing the legend of his crimes.

"*Alleged* crimes," Nicole added.

Astorre wondered why anyone still cared. The old Mafia was dead. The great Dons had accomplished their goals and blended gracefully into society, as the best criminals always do. The few pretenders who remained were a disappointing assortment of dim, second-class felons and impotent thugs. Why would anyone want to bother with the rackets when it was much easier to steal millions by starting your own company and selling shares to the public?

"Hey Astorre, do you think you could be our special consultant on the movie?" Marcantonio asked. "We want to make sure it's as authentic as possible."

"Sure," Astorre said, smiling. "I'll have my agent get back to you."

Later that night, in bed, Rosie turned to Astorre. "Do you think you'll ever want to go back?"

"Where?" Astorre asked. "To New York? To America?"

"You know," Rosie said hesitantly. "To your old life."

"This is where I belong, with you, here."

"Good," Rosie said. "But what about the baby? Shouldn't he have the chance to experience everything America has to offer?"

Astorre pictured Raymonde, running through the hills of the country, eating olives from barrels, hearing tales of the great dons and the Sicily of old. He looked forward to telling his son those stories. And yet he knew that those myths would not be enough.

One day his son would go to America, a land of vengeance, mercy, and magnificent possibility.

ACKNOWLEDGMENTS

Very special thanks to Carol Gino; my literary agents, Candida Donadio and Neil Olson; my attorneys, Bert Fields and Arthur Altman; my editor at Random House, Jonathan Karp; and my children and grandchildren.

ABOUT THE TYPE

This book was set in Times Roman, designed by Stanley Morison specifically for *The Times* of London. The typeface was introduced in the newspaper in 1932. Times Roman had its greatest success in the United States as a book and commercial typeface, rather than one used in newspapers.